The Complete McAUSLAN

The Complete McAUSLAN

George MacDonald Fraser

SKYHORSE PUBLISHING

Skyhorse Publishing books may be purchased in bulk at special discounts for sales promotion, corporate gifts, fund-raising, or educational purposes. Special editions can also be created to specifications. For details, contact the Special Sales Department, Skyhorse Publishing, 307 West 36th Street, 11th Floor, New York, NY 10018 or info@skyhorsepublishing.com.

Visit our website at www.skyhorsepublishing.com.

10 9 8 7 6 5 4 3 2 1

Library of Congress Cataloging-in-Publication Data

Fraser, George MacDonald, 1925-2008.
The complete McAuslan / George McDonald Fraser.
p. cm.
Includes bibliographical references and index.
ISBN 978-1-60239-656-2 (alk. paper)
1. Soldiers--Fiction. 2. Scots--Fiction. I. Title.
PR6056.R287C66 2009
823'.914--dc22

2009024304

Printed in the United States of America

THE GENERAL DANCED AT DAWN

FOR MY FATHER

Monsoon Selection Board

Our coal-bunker is old, and it stands beneath an ivy hedge, so that when I go to it in wet weather, I catch the combined smells of damp earth and decaying vegetation. And I can close my eyes and be thousands of miles away, up to my middle in a monsoon ditch in India, with my face pressed against the tall slats of a bamboo fence, and Martin-Duggan standing on my shoulders, swearing at me while the rain pelts down and soaks us. And all around there is mud, and mud, and more mud, until I quit dreaming and come back to the mundane business of getting a shovelful of coal for the sitting-room fire.

It is fifty years and more since I was in India. My battalion was down on the Sittang Bend, trying to stop the remnants of the Japanese Army escaping eastwards out of Burma – why we had to do this no one really understood, because the consensus of opinion was that the sooner Jap escaped the better, and good luck to him. Anyway, the war was nearly over, and one lance-corporal more or less on the battalion strength didn't make much difference, so they sent me out of the line to see if a War Office Selection Board would adjudge me fit to be commissioned.

I flew out and presented myself to the board, bush-hat on head, beard on chin, kukri on hip, all in sweaty jungle green and as tough as a buttered muffin. Frankly, I had few hopes of being passed. I had been to a board once before, back in England, and had fallen foul of a psychiatrist, a mean-looking little man who bit his nails and asked me if I had an adventurous spirit. (War Office Selection Boards were always asking questions like that.)

Of course, I told him I was as adventurous as all get-out, and he helped himself to another piece of nail and said cunningly:

'Then why don't you sign on to sail on a Norwegian whaler?'

This, in the middle of the war, mark you, to a conscript. So, thinking he was being funny, I replied with equal cunning that I didn't speak Norwegian, ha-ha. He just loved that; anyway, I didn't pass.

So I flew out of Burma without illusions. This particular board had a tough reputation; last time, the rumour went, they had passed only three candidates out of thirty. I looked round at my fellow applicants, most of whom had at least three stripes and seemed to be full of confidence, initiative, leadership, and flannel – qualities that Selection Boards lap up like gravy – and decided that whoever was successful this time it wasn't going to be me. There were two other Fourteenth Army infantrymen, Martin-Duggan and Hayhurst, and the three of us, being rabble, naturally drifted together.

I should explain about Selection Boards. They lasted about three days, during which time the candidates were put through a series of written and practical tests, and the Board officers just watched and made notes. Then there were interviews and discussions, and all the time you were being assessed and graded, and at the finish you were told whether you were in or out. If in, you went to an Officer Cadet Training Unit where they trained you for six months and then gave you your commission; if out, back to your unit.

But the thing that was universally agreed was that there was no known way of ensuring success before a Selection Board. There were no standard right answers to their questions, because their methods were all supposed to be deeply psychological. The general view throughout the Army was that they weren't fit to select bus conductors, let alone officers, but that is by the way.

One of the most unpleasant features of a Selection Board was that you were on test literally all the time. At meal times, for instance, there was an examining officer at each table of about six candidates, so we all drank our soup with exaggerated care, offered each other the salt with ponderous politeness, and talked on a plane so lofty that by comparison a conversation in the Athenaeum Club would have sounded like an argument in a gin-mill. And all the time our examiner, a smooth, beady gentleman, kept an eye on us and weighed us up while pretending to be a boon companion.

It wasn't too easy for him, for at our second meal I displayed such zeal in offering him a bottle of sauce that I put it in his lap. I saw my chances fading from that moment, and by the time we fell in outside for our first practical test my nerves were in rags.

It was one of those idiotic problems where six of you are given a log, representing a big gun-barrel, and have to get it across a river with the aid of a few ropes and poles. No one is put in command; you just have to co-operate, and the examiners hover around to see who displays most initiative, leadership, ingenuity, and what-have-you. The result is that everyone starts in at once telling the rest what to do. I had been there before, so I let them argue and tried to impress the Board by being practical. I cleverly tied a rope round the log, and barked a sharp command to Martin-Duggan and Hayhurst. They tugged on the rope and the whole damned thing went into the river. At this there was a deadly silence broken only by the audible scribbling of the examiners, and then the three of us sheepishly climbed down the bank to begin salvage operations.

This set the tone of our whole performance in the tests. Given a bell tent to erect we reduced it to a wreck of cord and canvas inside three minutes; ordered to carry from Point A to Point B an ammunition box which was too heavy for one man and which yet did not provide purchase for two, we dropped it in a ditch and upbraided each other in sulphurous terms, every word of which the examiners recorded carefully. Asked to swing across a small ravine on a rope, we betrayed symptoms of physical fear, and Hayhurst fell and hurt his ankle. Taking all in all, we showed ourselves lacking in initiative, deficient in moral fibre, prone to recrimination, and generally un-officer-like.

So it went on. We were interviewed by the psychiatrist, who asked Hayhurst whether he smoked. Hayhurst said no – he had actually given it up a few days before – and then noticed that the psychiatrist's eyes were fixed on his right index finger, which was still stained yellow with nicotine. My own interview was, I like to think, slightly less of a triumph from the psychiatrist's point of view. He asked me if I had an adventurous spirit, and I quickly said yes, so much so that my only regret about being in the Army was that it prevented me from signing on to sail on a Norwegian whaler.

If, at this point, he had said: 'Oh, do you speak Norwegian, then?' he would have had me over a barrel. But instead he fell back on the Selection Board classic, which is: 'Why do you want to be an officer?'

The honest answer, of course, is to say, like Israel Hands, 'Because I want their pickles and wines and that,' and to add that you are sick of being shoved around like low-life, and want to lord it over your fellow-man for a change. But honest answer never won fair psychiatrist yet, so I assumed my thoughtful, stuffed look, and said earnestly that I simply wanted to serve the army in my most useful capacity, and I felt, honestly, sir, that I could do the job. The pay was a lot better, too, but I kept that thought to myself.

He pursed up and nodded, and then said: 'I see you want to be commissioned in the – Highlanders. They're a pretty tough bunch, you know. Think you can handle a platoon of them?'

I gave him my straight-between-the-eyes look which, coupled with my twisted smile, tells people that I'm a lobo wolf from

Kelvinside and it's my night to howl. Just for good measure I added a confident, grating laugh, and he asked with sudden concern if I was going to be sick. I quickly reassured him, but he kept eyeing me askance and presently he dismissed me. As I went out he was scribbling like crazy.

Then there were written tests, in one of which we had to record our instant reactions to various words flashed on a blackboard. With me there was not one reaction in each case, but three. The first was just a mental numbness, the second was the reaction which I imagined the examiners would regard as normal, and the third (which naturally was what I finished up writing down) was the reaction which I was sure would be regarded as abnormal to a degree. Some people are like this: they are compelled to touch naked electric wiring and throw themselves down from heights. Some perverse streak makes them seek out the wrong answers.

Thus, given the word 'board', I knew perfectly well that the safe answer would be 'plank' (unless you chose to think that 'board' meant 'Selection Board', in which case you would write down 'justice', 'mercy', or 'wisdom'). But with the death wish in full control I had to write down 'stiff'.

Similarly, reason told me to react to 'cloud', 'father', and 'sex' by writing down 'rain', 'W. G. Grace', and 'birds and bees'. So of course I put down 'cuckoo', 'Captain Hook', and 'Grable'. To make matters worse I then scored 'Grable' out in a panic and wrote 'Freud', and then changed my mind again, scoring out 'Freud' and substituting 'Lamour'. Heavy breathing at my elbow at this point attracted my attention, and there was one of the examiners, peeking at my paper with his eyes bugging. By this time I was falling behind in my reactions, and was in such a frenzied state that when they eventually flashed 'Freud' on the board I think my response was 'Father Grable'. That must have made them think.

They then showed us pictures, and we had to write a story

about each one. The first picture showed a wretch with an expression of petrified horror on his face, clinging to a rope. Well, that was fairly obviously a candidate escaping from a Selection Board and discovering that his flight was being observed by a team of examiners taking copious notes. Then there was a picture of a character with a face straight out of Edgar Allan Poe, being apprehended by a policeman. (Easy: the miscreant was the former principal of a Selection Board, cashiered for drunkenness and embezzlement, and forced to beg his bread in the gutter, being arrested for vagrancy by a copper who turned out to be a failed candidate.)

But the one that put years on all the many hundreds of candidates who must have regarded it with uninspired misery was of an angelic little boy sitting staring soulfully at a violin. There are men all over the world today who will remember that picture when Rembrandt's Night Watch is forgotten. As art it was probably execrable, and as a mental stimulant it was the original lead balloon. Just the sight of that smug, curly-headed little Bubbles filled you with a sense of gloom. One Indian candidate was so affected by it that he began to weep; Hayhurst, after much mental anguish, produced the idea that it was one of Fagin's apprentices gloating over his first haul; my own thought was that the picture represented the infant Stradivarius coming to the conclusion that given a well-organised sweat-shop there was probably money in it.

Only Martin-Duggan dealt with the thing at length; the picture stirred something in his poetic Irish soul. The little boy, he recorded for the benefit of the examiners, was undoubtedly the son of a famous concert violinist. His daddy had been called up to the forces during the war, and the little boy was left at home, gazing sadly at the violin which his father would have no opportunity of playing until the war was over. The little boy was terribly upset about this, the thought of his father's wonderful music being silenced; he felt sure his daddy would pine away through being deprived of his violin-playing. Let the little boy take heart, said Martin-Duggan; he needn't worry, because if his daddy played his cards right he would get himself promoted to the post of quarter-master, and then he would be able to fiddle as much as he liked.

Martin-Duggan was terribly pleased with this effort; the poor sap didn't seem to understand that in military circles a joke is only as funny as the rank of its author is exalted, and Martin-Duggan's rank couldn't have been lower.

Of course, by the time the written tests were over, the three of us were quite certain that we were done for. Our showing had probably been about as bad as it could be, we thought, and our approach to the final ordeal of the Selection Board, on the third afternoon, was casual, not to say resigned. This was a trip over the assault course – a military obstacle race in which you tear across country, climb walls, swing on ropes, crawl through tunnels, and jump off ramps. The climax is usually something pretty horrid, and in this case it consisted of a monsoon ditch four feet deep in water, at the end of which was a huge bamboo fence up which you had to climb in three-man teams, helping each other and showing initiative, intelligence, cheerfulness, and other officer-like qualities, if possible.

We were the last three over, and as we waded up the ditch, encouraging each other with military cries, the rain was lashing down something awful. There was a covered shelter overlooking the ditch, and it was crammed with examiners – all writing away as they observed the floundering candidates – as well as the top brass of the board. All the other candidates had successfully scaled the fence, and were standing dripping with mud and water, waiting to see how we came on.

Our performance, viewed from the bank, must have been something to see. I stood up to my waist in water against the fence, and Martin-Duggan climbed on my shoulders, and Hayhurst climbed on his, and I collapsed, and we all went under. We did this about five or six times, and the gallery hooted with mirth. Martin-Duggan, who was a proud sensitive soul, got mad, and swore at me and kicked me, and Hayhurst made a tremendous effort and got on to the top of the fence. He pulled Martin-Duggan up, and the pair of them tried to pull me up, too, but I wasn't having any. I was rooted up to my middle in the sludge, and there I was going to stay, although I made it look as though I was trying like hell to get up.

They tugged and strained and swore, and eventually Martin-Duggan slipped and came down with a monumental splash, and Hayhurst climbed down as well. The spectators by this time were in hysterics, and when we had made three or four more futile efforts – during which I never emerged from the water once – the officer commanding the board leaned forward and said:

'Don't you chaps think you'd better call it a day?'

I don't know what Martin-Duggan, a mud-soaked spectre, was going to reply, but I beat him to it. Some heaven-sent inspiration struck me, because I said, in the most soapy, sycophantic, Eric-or-Little-by-Little voice I have ever used in my life:

'Thank you, sir, we'd prefer to finish the course.'

It must have sounded impressive, for the C.O. stood back, almost humbly, and motioned us to continue. So we did, floundering on with tremendous zeal and getting nowhere, until we were almost too weary to stand and so mud-spattered that we were hardly recognisable as human beings. And the C.O., bless him, leaned forward again, and I'll swear there was a catch in his voice as he said:

'Right, that's enough. Well tried. And even if you didn't finish it, there's one thing I'd like to say. I admire guts.' And all the examiners, writing for dear life, made muted murmurs of assent.

What they and the C.O. didn't know was that my trousers had come off while we were still wading up the ditch, and that was why I had never budged out of the water and why we had never got up the fence. A good deal I had endured, but I was not going to appear soaked and in my shirt-tail before all the board and candidates, not for anything. And as we waded back down the ditch and out of sight round the bend, I told Martin-Duggan and Hayhurst so.

And we passed, I suppose because we showed grit, determination, endurance, and all the rest of it. Although with Selection Boards you never could tell. Only the three of us know that what got us through was the loss of my pants, and military history has been made out of stranger things than that.

Silence in the Ranks

The life of the very young officer is full of surprises, and perhaps the most shaking is the moment when he comes face to face with his men for the first time. His new sergeant stamps to a halt in front of him, salutes, and barks: 'Platoon-presnready-frinspeckshun-sah!', and as he clears his throat and regards the thirty still figures, each looking to its front with frozen intensity, the young subaltern realises that this is it, at last; this is what he is drawing his meagre pay for.

In later years he may command armies or govern great territories, but he will never feel again the same power-drunk humility of the moment when he takes over his platoon. It is elating and terrifying – mostly terrifying. These thirty men are his responsibility, to look after, to supervise, to lead (whatever that means). Of course, they will do what he tells them – or he hopes they will, anyway. Suppose they don't? Suppose that ugly one in the front rank suddenly says 'No, I will not slope arms for you, or shave in the morning, or die for king and country'? The subaltern feels panic stealing over him, until he remembers that at his elbow there is a sergeant, who is wise in dealing with these matters, and he feels better.

There are young officers, of course, who seem to regard themselves as born to the job, and who cruise through their first platoon inspection with nonchalant interest, conversing airily with the sergeant as they go; possibly Hannibal and Napoleon were like that. But I doubt it. A man would have to be curiously insensitive not to realise that for the first time in his life thirty total strangers are regarding him with interest and suspicion and anxiety, wondering if he is a soft mark or a complete pig, or worse still, some kind of nut. When he realises this he feels like telling them that he is, really, all right and on their side, but of course he can't. If he did, they would know for certain he was some kind of nut. They will just have to find out about each other gradually, and it can be a trying process.

I have only a hazy impression of inspecting my platoon for the first time. They were drawn up in the sunlight with their backs to the white barrack wall, against which an Arab tea-vendor was squatting, waiting for the ten-minute break. But all I can remember is the brown young faces staring earnestly to their front, with here and there a trickle of sweat or a limb shaking with the strain of standing still. I remember telling one that he was smartly turned-out, and he gave a controlled shudder, like a galvanised frog, and licked his lips nervously. I asked another whether he had volunteered for this particular regiment, and he stammered: 'Nossir, I wanted to go intae the coal-mines.'

Perhaps I was over-sensitive because I had been more than two years in the ranks myself, and had stood sweating while pinkish young men with one painfully new pip on their shoulders had looked at me. I remembered what I had thought about them, and how we had discussed them afterwards. We had noted their peculiarities, and now I wondered what mine were – what foibles and mannerisms were being observed and docketed, and what they would say about me later.

I don't know what I expected from that first inspection – a rapturous welcome, three cheers, or an outbreak of mutiny – but what I got was nothing at all. It was a bit damping; they didn't seem to react to me one way or the other. Maybe I should have made a speech, or at least said a few introductory words, but all that I could think of was Charles Laughton's address to the crew of the *Bounty*, which ran: 'You don't know wood from canvas, and you evidently don't want to learn. Well, I'll teach you.' It wouldn't have gone over.

So eventually I watched them fall out, and turn from wooden images into noisy, raucous young men crowding round the tea-man, abusing him happily in Glasgow-Arabic. One or two glanced in my direction, briefly, but that was all. I walked back to the company office, suddenly lonely.

The trouble was, of course, that in the exultation of being commissioned at the end of a hectic training in India, and the excitement of journeying through the Middle East and seeing the wonderful sights, and arriving in this new battalion which was to be home, I had overlooked the fact that all these things were secondary. What it all added up to was those thirty people and me; that was why the king had made me 'his trusty and well-beloved friend'. I wondered, not for the first time, if I was fit for it.

It had seemed to go well on the day of my arrival. The very sound of Scottish voices again, the air of friendly informality which you find in Highland regiments, the sound of pipe music, had all been reassuring. My initial discomfort – I had arrived with two other second-lieutenants, and while they had been correctly dressed in khaki drill I had still been wearing the jungle green of the Far East, which obviously no one in the battalion had seen before – had quickly blown over. The mess was friendly, a mixture of local Scots accents and Sandhurst drawls, and my first apprehensions on meeting the Colonel had been unfounded. He was tall and bald and moustached, with a face like a vulture and a handkerchief tucked in his cuff, and he shook hands as though he was really glad to see me.

Next morning in his office, before despatching me to a company, he gave me sound advice, much of which passed me by although I remembered it later.

'You've been in the ranks. Good. That' – and he pointed to my Burma ribbon – 'will be a help. Your Jocks will know you've been around, so you may be spared some of the more elementary try-ons. I'm sending you to D Company – my old company, by the way.' He puffed at his pipe thoughtfully. 'Good company. Their march is 'The Black Bear', which is dam' difficult to march to, actually, but good fun. There's a bit where the Jocks always stamp, one-two, and give a great yell. However, that's by the way. What I want to tell you is: get to know their names; that's essential, of course. After a bit you'll get to know the nicknames, too, probably, including your own. But once you know their names and faces, you'll be all right.'

He hummed on a bit, and I nodded obediently and then took myself across to D Company office, where the company commander, a tall, blond-moustached Old Etonian named Bennet-Bruce, fell on me with enthusiasm. Plainly D Company, and indeed the entire battalion, had just been waiting a couple of centuries for this moment; Bennet-Bruce was blessed above all other company commanders in that he had got the new subaltern.

'Splendid. Absolutely super. First-class.' He pumped me by the hand and shouted for the company clerk. 'Cormack, could you find another cup for Mr MacNeill? This is Cormack, invaluable chap, has some illicit agreement with the Naafi manager about tea and excellent pink cakes. Mr MacNeill, who has joined our company. You do take sugar? First-class, good show.'

I had been in the army quite long enough not to mistake Bennet-Bruce for just a genial, care-free head-case, or to think that because he prattled inconsequentially he was therefore soft. I'd seen these caricature types before, and nine times out of ten there was a pretty hard man underneath. This one had the Medaille Militaire, I noticed, and the French don't hand that out for nothing.

However, he was making me at home, and presently he

wafted me round the company offices and barrack-rooms on a wave of running commentary.

'Company stores here, presided over by Quartermaster Cameron, otherwise known as Blind Sixty. Biggest rogue in the army, of course, but a first-class man. First-class. Magazine over there – that's Private Macpherson, by the way, who refuses to wear socks. Why won't you wear socks, Macpherson?'

'Ma feet hurt, sir.'

'Well, so do mine, occasionally. Still, you know best. Over yonder, now, trying to hide at the far end of the corridor, that's McAuslan, the dirtiest soldier in the world. In your platoon, by the way. Don't know what to do with McAuslan. Cremation's probably the answer. Nothing else seems to work. Morning, Patterson, what did the M. O. say?'

'Gave me some gentian violent, sir, tae rub on.'

'Marvellous stuff,' said Bennet-Bruce, with enthusiasm. 'Never travel without it myself. Now, let's see, Ten platoon room over there, Eleven in there, and Twelve round there. Yours is Twelve. Good bunch. Good sergeant, chap called Telfer. Very steady. Meet him in a minute. No, Rafferty, not like that. Give it here.'

We were at a barrack-room door, and a dark, wiry soldier at the first bed was cleaning his rifle, hauling the pull-through along the barrel. 'Not like that,' said Bennet-Bruce. 'Pull it straight out, not at an angle, or you'll wear away the muzzle and your bullets will fly off squint, missing the enemy, who will seize the opportunity to unseam you, from nave to chaps.' He tugged at the pull-through. 'What the hell have you got on the end of this, the battalion colours?'

'Piece of four-by-two, sir,' said Rafferty. 'An' a bit o' wire gauze.'

'Who authorised the gauze?'

'Eh, Ah got it fae the store,' said Rafferty uneasily.

'Take it back,' said Bennet-Bruce, 'and never, never use

it without the armourer's permission. You know that, don't you? Next time you'll be in company office. Carry on. I really do despair, sometimes. Morning, Gray. Morning, Soutar. Now, let's see.' He stopped at the company notice-board. '"Team to play A Company". Good God, you've got me on the right wing, Corporal Stevenson. That means that Forbes here will bully and upbraid me through the entire game. I don't really think we're the best thing since Matthews and Carter, do you, Forbes?'

'Just stay on yer wing,' said the saturnine Forbes. 'Ah'll pit the ba' in front of you.'

'Well, I rely on you,' said Bennet-Bruce, passing on. 'That chap Forbes is a marvellous footballer,' he went on to me. 'Signed by Hearts, I understand. You play football? Good show. Of course, that's the great game. The battalion team are district champions, really super team they are, too. Morning, Duff . . .'

And so on. Bennet-Bruce was at home. Finally, he introduced me to Sergeant Telfer, a sturdy, solid-looking man in his mid-thirties who said very little, and left us to get acquainted. This consisted of going over the nominal roll, meeting the corporals, and making polite remarks on my part; obviously if I didn't make the running we would have long silences. However, it seemed to be going well enough for a start.

Next day came that first inspection, and after that the routine drills and exercises, and learning people's names, and getting into the company routine. I worked rather cautiously, by the book, tried a joke or two without response, and told myself it was early days yet. They were a better platoon than I had expected; they were aged round about twenty, a year younger than I was, they were good on drill, did a fifteen-mile route march in five hours without any sign of distress, and on the rifle range were really impressive. But they were not what could be called forthcoming; off parade they were cheery enough with each other, but within my orbit they fell quiet, stolid and watchful.

As I say, I don't know what I expected, but I began to feel depressed. There was something missing; they did what they were told smartly – well, fairly smartly; they took no liberties that I noticed. But if they didn't dislike me they certainly didn't seem to like me either. Perhaps it was my fault; they were happy enough with Bennet-Bruce and any other company officers who came into contact with them. I envied Macmillan, the subaltern of Ten platoon, who had been in the battalion about six months and abused his platoon good-naturedly one minute and tore strips off them the next; they seemed to get on with him. I wondered if I was the Tiberius type ('let them hate me so long as they fear me'), and concluded I wasn't; it seemed more likely that the Selection Board who took me out of the ranks had just been wrong.

In the mess things went fairly well until one evening I knocked a pint glass accidentally off the arm of a chair, and a liverish major blasted my clumsiness and observed that there were only about half a dozen of those glasses left. I apologised, red-faced but faintly angry; we looked at each other with mutual dislike, and the trivial incident stuck in my mind. Other things were prickling vaguely, too; my service dress wasn't a good fit, and I knew it. I suspected (wrongly) that this gave rise to covert amusement and once this tiny seed had taken root I was half-way to seeing myself as a laughing-stock.

This can be a dreadful thing to the young, and not only the young. In no time at all I was positive that my platoon found me faintly ridiculous; occasionally I caught what I thought was a glint of amusement in an eye on parade, or heard a stifled laugh. I would tell myself I just imagined these things, but then the doubts would return.

One morning there was a platoon rifle inspection, and I must have been on the down-swing, because I went on it half-conscious of a resolve to put somebody on a charge for something. This, of course, was a deplorable attitude. I had never charged anyone yet, and I may have felt that I ought to, pour encourager the platoon in general. Anyway, when I came to a rifle in the middle rank that seemed to have dirt in the grooves of the barrel, I nailed its owner.

He was a nondescript man called Leishman, rather older than the others, a quiet enough character. He seemed genuinely shocked when I told him his rifle was dirty, and then I turned to Sergeant Telfer and said, 'Put him on a charge.' (Six months later I would have said, 'Leishman, did you shave this morning?' And he, dumbfounded, knowing his chin was immaculate, would have said, 'Yes, sir. I did, sir.' And I would have said, 'Of course you did, and it's all gone down the barrel of your gun. Clean the thing.' And that would have been that.)

I went off parade feeling vaguely discontented, and ten minutes later, in the company office, Cormack the clerk observed that I had shaken Leishman, no mistake. He said it deadpan, and added that Leishman was presently in the armoury, cleaning his rifle. Puzzled, for I wondered why Cormack should be telling me this, I went off to the armoury.

Sure enough, there was Leishman, pulling the cleaning-cloth through his rifle, and crying. He was literally weeping. I was shocked.

'What's the matter?' I said, for this was a new one to me.

He snuffled a bit, and wiped his nose, and then it came out. He had been five years in the army, his discharge was coming up in a few weeks, he had never been on a charge in his life before. He was going to have his clean sheet marred almost on the eve of getting out.

'Well, for God's sake,' I said, relieved more than anything else. 'Look, don't get into a state. It's all right, we'll scrub the charge.' I was quite glad to, because I felt a warning would have done. 'I'm certainly not going to spoil your record,' I said.

He mumped some more, and pulled his rifle through again.

'Let's have a look at it,' I said. I looked down the barrel, and it still wasn't all that good, but what would you? He was obviously badly upset, but he muttered something about thanks, which just made me uncomfortable. I suppose only born leaders don't find authority embarrassing.

'Forget it,' I said. 'Give it another few pulls-through, and keep your eye on it until your ticket comes through. Okay?'

I left him to it, and about ten minutes later I was passing the door of Twelve platoon barrack-room, and heard somebody laughing inside. I just glanced as I went by, and stopped short. It was Leishman, sitting on his bunk at the far end, laughing with a bunch of his mates.

I moved on a few steps. All right, he had made a quick recovery. He was relieved. There was nothing in that. But he had seemed really upset in the armoury, shaken, as Cormack said. Now he was roaring his head off – the quality of the laughter somehow caught the edge of my nerves. I stood undecided, and then wheeled round and shouted:

'Sergeant Telfer!'

He came out of his room. 'Yessir?'

'Sergeant Telfer,' I said, 'stop that man laughing.'

He gaped at me. 'Laughing, sir?'

'Yes, laughing. Tell him to stop it – now.'

'But . . .' he looked bewildered. 'But . . . he's just laughin', sir . . .'

'I know he's just laughing. He's braying his bloody head off. Tell him to stop it.'

'Right, sir.' He obviously thought the sun had got me, but he strode into the barrack-room. Abruptly, Leishman's laughter stopped, then there was what might have been a smothered chuckle, then silence.

Feeling suicidal, I went back to my billet. Obviously Leishman had thought I was a mug; I should have let the charge stick. Let someone get away with it, even a good soldier, and you have taken some of his virtue away. On the other hand, maybe he had been laughing about something else entirely; in that case, I had been an idiot to give Sergeant Telfer that ridiculous order. Either way, I looked a fool. And my service dress didn't fit. To hell with it, I would see the Adjutant tomorrow and ask for a posting.

I didn't, of course. That night in the mess the liverish major, of all people, asked me to partner him in a ludo doubles against the Adjutant and the M.O. (In stations where diversion is limited games like ludo tend to get elevated above their usual status.) In spite of the M.O.'s constant gamesmanship, directed against my partner's internal condition, we won by one counter in a grandstand finish, and thereafter it was a happy evening. We finished with a sing-song – 'Massacre of Macpherson' and 'The Lum Hat Wantin' the Croon', and other musical gems – and the result was that I went to bed thinking that the world could be worse, after all.

In the morning when I inspected my platoon, Sergeant Telfer did not roll on the ground, helpless with laughter, at the sight of me. If anything, the platoon was smarter and faster than usual; I inspected the rifles, and Leishman's was gleaming as though he had used Brasso on the barrel, which he quite probably had. I said nothing; there was no hint that the incident of yesterday had ever happened.

On the other hand, there was still no sign of the happy officer-man relationship by which the manual sets such store. We were still at a distance with each other, and so it continued. It didn't matter whether I criticised or praised, the reception was as wary as ever.

Remembering the C.O.'s advice, I had reached the stage where I knew every man by name, and had picked up a few nicknames as well. Brown, a clueless, lanky Glaswegian, was Daft Bob; Forbes, the villainous-looking footballer, was Heinie (after Heinrich Himmler, it transpired); my own batman, McGilvray, was Chick; and Leishman was Soapy. But others I had not yet identified – Pudden, and Jeep, and Darkie, and Hi-Hi; one heard the names shouted along the company corridors and floating through the barrack-room doors – 'Jeep's away for ile* the day', which signified that the mysterious Jeep was hors de combat, physically or spiritually; 'Darkie's got a rare hatchet on', meaning that Darkie was in a bad temper; 'yon Heinie's a wee brammer', which was the highest sort of compliment, and so on. It was interesting stuff, but it was still rather like studying the sounds of a strange species; I couldn't claim to be with it.

My own batman, McGilvray, reflected the situation. He was a good worker, and my kit was always in excellent condition, but whereas with his mates he was a cheery, rather waggish soul, with me he was as solemn as a Free Kirk elder. He was a round, tousled lad with a happy pug face and a stream of 'Glasgow patter' which dried up at the door of my room and thereafter became a series of monosyllabic grunts.

Well, I thought, this is the way it's going to be, and it could be worse. If I couldn't like them, yet, I could at least respect them, for they were a good platoon; when Bennet-Bruce held his full-dress monthly inspection for the Colonel, the great man was pleased to say that Twelve platoon's kit layout was the best in the battalion. It should have been; they had worked hard enough. Having been, for a time at least, in the Indian Army, I had my own ideas about how kit should be laid out; I had taken aside Fletcher, the platoon dandy, and shown him how I thought it should be presented for inspection – if you black the soles of your boots, for example, they look better, and a little square of red and white four-by-two cloth under an oil-bottle and pull-through is smarter than nothing at all. Fletcher had watched me stonily as I went over his kit, but afterwards he had supervised the whole room in laying out their stuff on the same pattern. Our one problem had been

* ile = oil (castor oil).

what to do with Private McAuslan, the dirtiest soldier in the world; I solved that by sending him into town for the day as guard on the company truck, which had nothing in it anyway. His kit was placed in an out-of-the-way cupboard, his associates affecting to be disgusted by the mere sight of it, and securely locked up.

Anyway, the Colonel limped through, inspecting and approving, and when he had gone and the quiet, involuntary sigh had sounded through the big, white-washed room, I said, 'Nice show, sons'. But none of them made any comment, so I left them to it.

About two days later, which was shortly before Christmas, I fell from grace in the mess. There was a mess meeting called, and I forgot about it, and went into town to play snooker at the officers' club. As a result I got a nasty dig next day from the Adjutant, and was told that I was orderly officer for the whole of next week; normally you do orderly officer only a day at a time.

This was a nuisance, since the orderly officer has to stay in barracks, but the worst of it was that I would miss the great Hogmanay party on New Year's Eve. To Highlanders, of course, Christmas is a pagan festival which they are perfectly prepared to enjoy as long as no one sees them doing it, but Hogmanay is the night of the year. Then they sing and drink and eat and drink and reminisce and drink, and the New Year comes in in a tartan, whisky-flavoured haze. The regimental police shut up shop, haggis is prepared in quantity, black bun is baked, the padre preaches a sermon reminding everyone that New Year is a time for rededication ('ye can say that again,. meenister,' murmurs a voice at the back), and the sergeants extend their annual invitation to the officers.

This is the great event. The Colonel forms the officers up as a platoon, and marches them to the sergeants' mess, where they are greeted with the singing of 'We are Fred Karno's Army', or some other appropriate air, and the festivities go on until well into the next morning. The point was that the sergeants' mess was outside barracks, so as orderly officer I would be unable to attend.

Not that I minded, particularly, but it would be a very silent, sober night in barracks all by myself, and even if you are not a convivial type, when you are in a Scottish regiment you feel very much out of it if you are on your own on Hogmanay. Anyway, there it was; I mounted my guards and inspected my cookhouses during that week, and on December 31 I had had about enough of it. The battalion was on holiday; the Jocks were preparing to invade the town en masse ('there'll be a rerr terr in the toon the night', I heard McGilvray remarking to one of the other batmen), and promptly at seven o'clock the Colonel marched off the officers, every one dressed in his best, for the sergeants' mess.

After they had gone, I strolled across the empty parade ground in the dusk, and mooched around the deserted company offices. I decided that the worst bit of it was that every Jock in the battalion knew that the new subaltern was on defaulters, and therefore an object of pity and derision. Having thought this, I promptly rebuked myself for self-pity, and whistled all the way back to my quarters.

I heard Last Post at ten o'clock, watched the first casualty of the night being helped into the cells, saw that the guard were reasonably sober, and returned to my room. There was nothing to do now until about 4 a.m., when I would inspect the picquets, so I climbed into my pyjamas and into bed, setting my alarm clock on the side table. I smoked a little, and read a little, and dozed a little, and from time to time very distant sounds of revelry drifted through the African night. The town would be swinging on its hinges, no doubt.

It must have been about midnight that I heard feet on the gravel outside, and a muttering of voices in the dark. There was a clinking noise which indicated merry-makers, but they were surprisingly quiet considering the occasion. The footsteps came into the building, and up the corridor, and there was a knock on my door.

I switched on the light and opened up. There were five of them, dressed in the best tartans they had put on for Hogmanay. There was McGilvray, my batman, Daft Bob Brown, Fletcher of the wooden countenance, Forbes, and Leishman. Brown carried a paper bag which obviously contained bottles, and Forbes had a carton of beer under his arm. For a moment we looked at each other.

'Well,' I said at last. 'Hullo.'

Then we looked at each other some more, in silence, while I wondered what this was in aid of, and then I searched for something further to say – the situation was fairly unusual. Finally I said,

'Won't you come in?'

They filed in, Daft Bob almost dropping the bottles and being rebuked in hideous terms by Fletcher. I closed the door, and said wouldn't they sit down, and Leishman and Daft Bob sat on my room-mate's empty bed, Fletcher placed himself on the only chair, and Forbes and McGilvray sat on the floor. They looked sidelong at each other.

'Well,' I said. 'This is nice.'

There was a pause, and then Fletcher said,

'Uh-huh'.

I thought furiously for something to say. 'Er, I thought you were going into the town, McGilvray?'

He looked sheepish. 'Ach, the toon. Naethin' doin'. Deid quiet.'

'Wisnae bad, though, at the Blue Heaven,' said Daft Bob. 'Some no' bad jiggin'.' (Dancing, that is.)

'Ach, jiggin',' said Fletcher contemptuously. 'Nae talent in this toon.'

'I'm sorry,' I said, conscious that in these unusual circumstances I was nevertheless the host. 'I don't have anything . . .'

'. . . in the hoose,' said Leishman unexpectedly, and we laughed.

'No' tae worry,' said Fletcher. He slapped Daft Bob sharply on the knee. 'C'mon, you. Gie the man a drink.'

'Comin' up,' said Daft Bob, and produced a bottle of beer from his bag. He held it out to me.

'In the name o' the wee man,' said Fletcher. 'Where the hell were you brought up? Gie 'im a glass, ya mug.'

Daft Bob said, 'Ach!' and rummaged for tumblers, McGilvray came to his assistance, and Fletcher abused them both, striking them sharply about the knees and wrists. Finally we were all provided for, and Fletcher said,

'Aye, weel, here's tae us.'

'Wha's like us?' said McGilvray.

'Dam' few,' said Forbes.

'And they're a' deid,' I said, completing the ritual.

'Aw-haw-hey,' said Daft Bob and we drank.

Conversationally, I asked: 'What brought you over this way?'

They grinned at each other, and Forbes whistled the bugle call 'You can be a defaulter as long as you like as long as you answer your na-a-a-me'. They all chuckled and shook their heads.

I understood. In my own way, I was on defaulters.

'Fill them up, ye creature ye,' said Fletcher to Daft Bob, and this time Daft Bob, producing more glasses from his bag, gave us whisky as well. It occurred to me that the penalty for an officer drinking in his own billet with enlisted men was probably death, or the equivalent, but frankly, if Montgomery himself had appeared in the doorway I couldn't have cared less.

'They're fair gaun it up at the sergeants' mess,' said Forbes. 'Ah heard the Adjutant singing "Roll me over".'

'Sair heids the morn,' said McGilvray primly.

'The Jeep'll be away for ile again,' said Leishman.

'The Jeep?' I said.

'Captain Bennet-Bruce,' said Fletcher. 'Your mate.'

'Oh,' I said.

'Stoap cuddlin' that bottle tae yerself as if it wis Wee Willie, the collier's dyin' child,' said Fletcher to Daft Bob.

'Ye'd think you'd paid for it,' said Daft Bob, indignantly. 'Honest, sir, d'ye hear him? Ah hate him. I do.'

They snarled at each other, happily, and the quiet Forbes shook his head at me as over wayward children. We refilled the glasses, and I handed round cigarettes, and a few minutes later we were refilling them again, and Leishman, tapping his foot on the floor, was starting to hum gently. McGilvray, after an anxious glance at me, took it up, and they sang 'The Muckin' o' Geordie's Byre' – for Leishman was an Aberdonian, and skilled in that strange tongue.

'That's a right teuchter song,' said Fletcher, and gave tongue:

As I gaed doon tae Wilson Toon
Ah met wee Geordie Scobie,
Says he tae me 'Could ye gang a hauf?'
Says I, 'Man, that's my hobby.'

We came in quietly on the chorus, which is 'We're no awa' to bide awa', we'll aye come back and see ye,' which Scottish soldiers invariably sing after the first two or three drinks, and which the remnants of the regiment had sung as they waited for the end at St Valery. Then we refilled them again, and while Fletcher and Daft Bob wrangled over the distribution, Forbes asked me with casual unconcern how I was liking the battalion. I said I liked it very well, and we talked of this and that, of platoon business and how the Rangers were doing, and the Glasgow police force and the North African weather. And after a few more drinks, in strict sobriety, Fletcher said:

'We'll have tae be gettin' along.'

'Not a bit of it,' I said. 'It's not late.'

'Aye, weel,' said Fletcher, 'mebbe it's no'.'

'Aw-haw-hey,' said Daft Bob.

So another half hour passed, and I wondered how I would find out the answers to the questions which could not be asked. Probably I wouldn't, but it didn't matter, anyway. Next day, on parade, Fletcher would be looking to his front as stonily as ever, Leishman would have given several extra minutes' attention to his rifle, I would be addressing Daft Bob severely, and all would be as it had been – except that for some reason they had thought it worth while to come and see me on Hogmanay. Some things you don't ponder over; you are just glad they happened.

'You gaunae sit boozin' a' night?' Fletcher snapped at Daft Bob. 'Sup, sup, sup, takin' it in like a sponge, I'm ashamed o' ye.'

'Ah'll no' be rollin' in your gutter, Fletcher,' said Daft Bob. 'So ye neednae worry. It's no' me Mr MacNeill'll be peggin' in the mornin' for no' bein' able tae staun up on parade.'

'Peg the baith o' ye,' said Forbes. 'Ye're aye greetin' at each other.'

'Sharrup,' said Fletcher. 'C'mon, get the bottles packed up. Let the man get tae his bed.'

Daft Bob and McGilvray collected the empties, while Fletcher bossed them, and they all straightened their bonnets, and looked at each other again.

'Aye, weel,' said Forbes.

'Well,' I said, and stopped. Some things are impossible to put into words. 'Well,' I said again. 'It was great to see you. Thank you for coming.'

'Ye'll be seein' us again,' said Fletcher.

'Aw-haw-hey,' said Daft Bob.

'Every mornin', numbered aff by the right, eh, Heinie?' said McGilvray.

'That's the way,' said Forbes.

'Tallest on the right, shortest on the left.'

'Clean, bright, and slightly oiled.'

'We're the wee boys.'

'Gi' the ba' tae the man wi' glasses.'

'Here's tae us, wha's like us?'

'Aw-haw-hey.'

'Ye gaunae staun' there a' night, then?' demanded Fletcher.

'Ah'm gaun. Ah'm gaun,' said Daft Bob. 'Night, sir. Guid New Year.' They jostled out, saying good-night and a good New Year, and exchanging their incredible slogans.

'Good night,' I said. 'Thanks again. Good night, Fletcher. Good night, Forbes. Good night, Daf –, er, Brown. Good night.'

They clattered off up the corridor, and I closed the door. The room was full of cigarette smoke and bar-room smell, the ash-trays were overflowing, and there was a quarter-full bottle of whisky still on the sidetable, forgotten in the packing. I sat on the edge of my bed feeling about twenty feet tall.

Their feet sounded on the gravel, and I heard Daft Bob muttering, and being rebuked, as usual, by Fletcher.

'Sharrup, ye animal.'

'Ah'll no' sharrup. Ah'll better go back an' get it; it was near half-full.'

'Ach, Chick'll get it in the mornin'.'

There was a doubt-laden pause, and then Daft Bob: 'D'ye think it'll be there in the mornin'?'

'Ach, for the love o' the wee wheel!' exclaimed Fletcher. 'Are ye worried aboot yer wee bottle? Yer ain, wee totty bottle? Ye boozy bum, ye! D'ye think Darkie's gaun tae lie there a' night sookin' at yer miserable bottle? C'mon, let's get tae wir kips.'

The sound of their footsteps faded away, and I climbed back into bed. In addition to everything else, I had found out who Darkie was.

Play Up, Play Up, and Get Tore In

The native Highlanders, the Englishmen, and the Lowlanders played football on Saturday afternoons and talked about it on Saturday evenings, but the Glaswegians, men apart in this as in most things, played, slept, ate, drank, and lived it seven days a week. Some soldiering they did because even a peace-time battalion in North Africa makes occasional calls on its personnel, but that was incidental; they were just waiting for the five minutes when they could fall out crying: 'Haw, Wully, sees a ba'.'

From the moment when the drums beat 'Johnnie Cope' at sunrise until it became too dark to see in the evening, the steady thump-thump of a boot on a ball could be heard somewhere in the barracks. It was tolerated because there was no alternative; even the parade ground was not sacred from the small shuffling figures of the Glasgow men, their bonnets pulled down over their eyes, kicking, trapping, swerving and passing, and occasionally intoning, like ugly little high priests, their ritual cries of 'Way-ull' and 'Aw-haw-hey'. The simile is apt, for it was almost a religious exercise, to be interrupted only if the Colonel happened to stroll by. Then they would wait, relaxed, one of them with the ball underfoot, until the majestic figure had gone past, flicking his brow in acknowledgment, and at the soft signal, 'Right, Wully,' the ball would be off again.

I used to watch them wheeling like gulls, absorbed in their wonderful fitba'. They weren't in Africa or the Army any longer; in imagination they were running on the green turf of Ibrox or Paradise, hearing instead of bugle calls the rumble and roar of a hundred thousand voices; this was their common daydream, to play (according to religion) either for Celtic or Rangers. All except Daft Bob Brown, the battalion idiot; in his fantasy he was playing for Partick Thistle.

They were frighteningly skilful. As sports officer I was expected actually to play the game, and I have shameful recollections still of a company practice match in which I was pitted against a tiny, wizened creature who in happier days had played wing half for Bridgeton Waverley. What a monkey he made out of me. He was quicksilver with a glottal stop, nipping past, round, and away from me, trailing the ball tantalisingly close and magnetising it away again. The only reason he didn't run between my legs was that he didn't think of it. It could have been bad for discipline, but it wasn't. When he was making me look the biggest clown since Grock I wasn't his platoon commander any more; I was just an opponent to beat.

With all this talent to choose from – the battalion was seventy-five per cent Glasgow men – it followed that the regimental team was something special. In later years more than half of them went on to play for professional teams, and one was capped for Scotland, but never in their careers did they have the opportunity for perfecting their skill that they had in that battalion. They were young and as fit as a recent war had made them; they practised together constantly in a Mediterranean climate; they had no worries; they loved their game. At their peak, when they were murdering the opposition from Tobruk to the Algerian border, they were a team that could have given most club sides in the world a little trouble, if nothing more.

The Colonel didn't speak their language, but his attitude to them was more than one of paternal affection for his soldiers. He respected their peculiar talent, and would sit in the stand at games crying 'Play up!' and 'Oh, dear, McIlhatton!' When they won, as they invariably did, he would beam and patronise the other colonels, and when they brought home the Command Cup he was almost as proud as he was of the Battle Honours.

In his pride he became ambitious. 'Look, young Dand,' he said. 'Any reason why they shouldn't go on tour? You know, round the Med., play the garrison teams, eh? I mean, they'd win, wouldn't they?'

I said they ought to be far too strong for most regimental sides.

'Good, good,' he said, full of the spirit that made British sportsmanship what it is. 'Wallop the lot of them, excellent. Right, I'll organise it.'

When the Colonel organised something, it was organised; within a couple of weeks I was on my way to the docks armed with warrants and a suitcase full of cash, and in the back of the truck were the battalion team, plus reserves, all beautiful in their best tartans, sitting with their arms folded and their bonnets, as usual, over their faces.

When I lined them up on the quayside, preparatory to boarding one of H.M. coastal craft, I was struck again by their lack of size. They were extremely neat men, as Glaswegians usually are, quick, nervous, and deft as monkeys, but they were undoubtedly small. A century of life – of living, at any rate – in the hell's kitchen of industrial Glasgow, has cut the stature and mighty physique of the Scotch-Irish people pitifully; Glasgow is full of little men today, but at least they are stouter and sleeker than my team was. They were the children of the hungry 'thirties, hard-eyed and wiry; only one of them was near my size, a fair, dreamy youth called McGlinchy, one of the reserves. He was a useless, beautiful player, a Stanley Matthews for five minutes of each game, and for the rest of the time an indolent passenger who strolled about the left wing, humming to himself. Thus he was normally in the second eleven ('He's got fitba',' the corporal who captained the first team would say, 'but whit the hell, he's no' a' there; he's wandered.')

The other odd man out in the party was Private McAuslan, the dirtiest soldier in the world, who acted as linesman and baggage-master, God help us. The Colonel had wanted to keep him behind, and send someone more fit for human inspection, but the team had protested violently. They were just men, and McAuslan was their linesman, foul as he was. In fairness I had backed them up, and now I was regretting it, for McAuslan is not the kind of ornament that you want to advertise your team in Mediterranean capitals. He stood there with the baggage, grimy and dishevelled, showing a tasteful strip of grey vest between kilt and tunic, and with his hosetops wrinkling towards his ankles.

'All right, children,' I said, 'get aboard,' and as they chattered up the gangplank I went to look for the man in charge. I found him in a passageway below decks, leaning with his forehead against a pipe, singing 'The Ash Grove' and fuming of gin. I addressed him, and he looked at me. Possibly the sight of a man in Highland dress was too much for him, what with the heat, for he put his hands over his eyes and said, 'Oh dear, oh dear,' but I convinced him that I was real, and he came to quite briskly. We got off to a fine start with the following memorable exchange.

Me: Excuse me, can you tell me when this boat starts?

He: It's not a boat, it's a ship.

Me: Oh, sorry. Well, have you any idea when it starts?

He: If I hadn't, I wouldn't be the bloody captain, would I?

Now that we were chatting like old friends, I introduced myself. He was a Welshman, stocky and middle-aged, with the bland, open face of a cherub and a heart as black as Satan's waistcoat. His name was Samuels, and he was not pleased to see me, but he offered me gin, muttering about the indignity of having his fine vessel used as a floating hotel for a lot of blasted pongos, and Scotch pongos at that. I excused myself, went to see that my Highlanders were comfortably installed – I found them ranged solemnly on a platform in the engine room, looking at the engines – and having shepherded them to their quarters and prevented McAuslan falling over the side, I went to my cabin. There I counted the money – it was a month's pay for the party – and before I had finished the ship began to vibrate and we were away, like Hannibal, to invade the North.

I am no judge of naval behaviour, but looking back I should say that if the much-maligned William Bligh had been half as offensive as Lieutenant Samuels the *Bounty* would never have got the length of Land's End, let alone Tahiti. At the first meal in the ward-room – which consisted for him of gin and chocolate biscuits – he snarled at his officers, bullied the stewards, and cross-examined me with a hackle-raising mixture of contempt and curiosity. We were going to the Grand Island, he knew; and what did we think we were going to do there? Play football, was it? Was that all pongos had to do? And who were we going to play, then?

Keeping my temper I told him we had several matches arranged against Service and civilian teams on the island, and he chose to make light of our chances. He had seen my team come aboard; they were midgets, and anyway who had they ever beaten?

At this one of his officers said he had seen us play, and we were good, very good. Samuels glared at him, but later he became thoughtful, applying himself to his gin, and when the meal ended he was still sitting there, brooding darkly. His officers looked nervous; they seemed to know the signs.

Next morning the African coast was still in view. I was surprised enough to ask Samuels about this, and he laughed and looked at me slantendicular.

'We're not goin' straight to the Island, Jocko,' he explained. 'Got to look in at Derna first, to pick up supplies. Don't worry, it won't take long.' He seemed oddly excited, but distinctly pleased with himself.

I didn't mind, and when Samuels suggested that we take the opportunity to go ashore at Derna so that my boys could have a practice kick-about, I was all for it. He went further; having vanished mysteriously into the town to conclude his official business, he returned to say that he was in a position to fix up a practice match against the local garrison side – 'thought your boys might like a try-out against some easy opposition, like; some not bad footballers yere, give you a game, anyway.'

Since we had several hours before we sailed it seemed not a bad idea; I consulted with the corporal-captain, and we told Samuels to go ahead. And then things started happening.

First of all, Samuels suggested we change into football kit on the ship. There was nothing odd about that, but when we went to the baggage room the team's fine yellow jerseys with the little tartan badge were missing; it transpired that through some inexplicable mix-up they were now in the ship's laundry, being washed. Not to worry, said Samuels, we'll lend you some blue shirts, which he did.

He took personal charge of our party when we went ashore – I was playing myself, as it was an unimportant game, and I wanted to rest our left-half, who had been slightly seasick. We played on a mud-baked pitch near the harbour, and coasted to a very gentle 7–0 win. Afterwards the garrison team invited us for drinks and supper, but Samuels interrupted my acceptance to say we hadn't time; we had to catch the tide, or the wind, or something, and we were bundled into the truck and hurried back to the harbour. But one remark the garrison captain let fall in parting, and it puzzled me.

'It's odd,' he said, 'to find so many Scotsmen in one ship's crew.'

I mentioned this to Samuels, back on board, and he sniggered wickedly.

'Well, now, natural enuff,' he said. 'He thought you was all in the ship's company.'

A horrid suspicion was forming in my mind as I asked him to explain.

'Well, see now,' he said, 'I 'ad an idea. When I went ashore first, I looks in on the garrison an' starts talkin' football. "Got a pretty fair team yere, 'aven't you?" I says. "District champions," says they. "Couldn't beat my ship's company," I says – cuttin' a long story short, you understand. "Couldn't what?" says they. "You want to bet?" says I.' He sat back, beaming wickedly at me. "So I got on a little bet.'

I gaped at the man. 'You mean you passed off my team, under false pretences . . . You little shark! You could get the jail for this.'

'Grow up, boyo,' said Samuels. 'Lissen, it's a gold mine. I was just tryin' it out before lettin' you in. Look, we can't go wrong. We can clean up the whole coast, an' then you can do your tour on the Island. Who knows your Jocks aren't my matelots? And they'll bite every time; what's a mingy little coaster, they'll say, it can't have no football team.' He cackled and drank gin. 'Oh, boy! They don't know we've got the next best thing to the Arsenal on board!'

'Right,' I said. 'Give me the money you won.' He stared at me. 'It's going back to the garrison,' I explained.

'You gone nuts, boyo?'

'No, I haven't. Certainly not nuts enough to let you get away with using my boys, my regiment, dammit, to feather your little nest. Come on, cough up.'

But he wouldn't, and the longer we argued the less it seemed I could do anything about it. To expose the swindle would be as embarrassing for me and my team as for Samuels. So in the end I had to drop it, and got some satisfaction from telling him that it was his first and last killing as far as we were concerned. He cursed a bit, for he had planned the most plunderous operation seen in the Med. since the Barbary corsairs, but later he brightened up.

'I'll still win a packet on you on the Island,' he said. 'You're good, Jocko. Them boys of yours are the sweetest thing this side of Ninian Park. Football is an art, is it? But you're missin' a great opportunity. I thought Scotsmen were sharp, too.'

That disposed of, it was a pleasant enough voyage, marred only by two fights between McAuslan on the one hand and members of the crew, who had criticised his unsanitary appearance, on the other. I straightened them out, upbraided McAuslan, and instructed him how to behave.

'You're a guest, you horrible article,' I said. 'Be nice to the sailors; they are your friends. Fraternise with them; they were on our side in the war, you know? And for that matter, when we get to the Island, I shall expect a higher standard than ever from all of you. Be a credit to the regiment, and keep moderately sober after the games. Above all, don't fight. Cut out the Garscube Road stuff or I'll blitz you.'

Just how my simple, manly words affected them you could see from the glazed look in their eyes, and I led them down the gangplank at Grand Island feeling just a mite apprehensive. They were good enough boys, but as wild as the next, and it was more than usually important that they keep out of trouble because the Military Governor, who had been instrumental in fixing the tour, was formerly of a Highland regiment, and would expect us not only to win our games but to win golden opinions for deportment.

He was there to meet us, with aides and minions, a stately man of much charm who shook hands with the lads and then departed in a Rolls, having assured me that he was going to be at every game. Then the Press descended on us, I was interviewed about our chances, and we were all lined up and photographed.

The result, as seen in the evening paper, was mixed. The team were standing there in their kilts, frowning suspiciously, with me at one end grinning inanely. At the other end crouched an anthropoid figure, dressed apparently in old sacking; at first I thought an Arab mendicant had strayed into the picture, but closer inspection identified it as McAuslan showing, as one of the team remarked, his good side.

Incidentally, it seemed from the paper's comments that we were not highly rated. The hint seemed to be that we were being given a big build-up simply because we were from the Governor's old brigade, but that when the garrison teams – and I knew they were good teams – got at us, we would be pretty easy meat. This suited me, and it obviously didn't worry the team. They were near enough professional to know that games aren't won in newspaper columns.

We trained for two days and had our first game against the German prisoners-of-war. They were men still waiting to be repatriated, ex-Africa Korps, big and tough, and they had played together since they went into the bag in '42. Some of our team wore the Africa Star, and you could feel the tension higher than usual in the dressing-room beforehand. The corporal, dapper and wiry, stamped his boots on the concrete, bounced the ball, and said, 'Awright fellas, let's get stuck intae these Huns,' and out they trotted.

(I should say at this point that this final exhortation varied only according to our opponents. Years later, when he led a famous league side out to play Celtic, this same corporal, having said his Hail-Mary and fingered his crucifix, instructed his team, 'Awright fellas, let's get stuck intae these Papes.' There is a lesson in team spirit there, if you think about it.)

The Germans were good, but not good enough. They were clever for their size, but our boys kept the ball down and the game close, and ran them into a sweat before half-time. We should have won by about four clear goals, but the breaks didn't come, and we had to be content with 2–0. Personally I was exhausted: I had had to sit beside the Governor, who had played Rugby, but if I had tried to explain the finer points he wouldn't have heard them anyway. He worked himself into a state of nervous frenzy, wrenching his handkerchief in his fingers, and giving antique yelps of 'Off your side!' and 'We claim foul' which contrasted oddly with the raucous support of our reserve players, whose repertoire was more varied and included 'Dig a hole for 'im!' 'Sink 'im!' and the inevitable 'Get tore intae these people!' At the end the Germans cried 'Hoch! Hoch!' and we gave three cheers, and both sides came off hating each other.

Present in body and also in raw spirit was Lieutenant Samuels, who accosted me after the game with many a wink and leer. It seemed he had cleaned up again.

'An' I'll tell you, boyo, I'll do even better. The Artillery beat the Germans easy, so they figure to be favourites against you. But I seen your boys playin' at half-steam today. We'll murder 'em.' He nudged me. 'Want me to get a little bet on for you, hey? Money for old rope, man.'

Knowing him, I seemed to understand Sir Henry Morgan and Lloyd George better than I had ever done.

So the tour progressed, and the Island sat up a little straighter with each game. We came away strongly against the Engineers, 6–0, beat the top civilian team 3–0, and on one of those dreadful off-days just scraped home against the Armoured Corps, 1–0. It was scored by McGlinchy, playing his first game and playing abysmally. Then late on he ambled on to a loose ball on the edge of the penalty circle, tossed the hair out of his eyes, flicked the ball from left foot to right to left without letting it touch the ground, and suddenly unleashed the most unholy piledriver you ever saw. It hit the underside of the bar from 25 yards out and glanced into the net with the goalkeeper standing still, and you could almost hear McGlinchy sigh as he trotted back absently to his wing, scratching his ear.

'Wandered!' said the corporal bitterly afterwards. 'Away wi' the fairies! He does that, and for the rest o' the game he micht as well be in his bed. He's a genius, sir, but no' near often enough. Ye jist daurnae risk 'im again.'

I agreed with him. So far we hadn't lost a goal, and although I had no illusions about preserving that record, I was beginning to hope that we would get through the tour unbeaten. The Governor, whose excitement was increasing with every game, was heard to express the opinion that we were the sharpest thing in the whole Middle East; either he was getting pot-valiant or hysterical, I wasn't sure which, but he went about bragging at dinners until his commanders got sick of him and us.

But the public liked us, and so did the Press, and when we took the Artillery to the cleaners, 3–2, in one of the fastest and most frantic games I have ever seen, amateur or pro., they were turning crowds away from the stadium. The Governor was like an antelope full of adrenalin, eating his handkerchief and shivering about in his seat, crying, 'Oh, my goodness gracious me!' and 'Ah, hah, he has, he hasn't, oh my God!' and flopping back, exhausted. I was too busy to steady him; I was watching (it dawned on me) a really fine football team. They moved like a machine out there, my wiry, tireless wee keelies, and it wasn't just their speed, their trickiness, or their accuracy; it was their cool, impregnable assurance. What gets into a man, who is nervous when a sergeant barks at him, but who, when he is put out in front of 20,000 shouting spectators, and asked to juggle an elusive leather ball, reacts with all the poise and certainty of an acrobat on a high wire?

I didn't need to tell them they were good. They knew it, and perhaps some of them knew it too well. Following the Artillery game, two of them got picked up by the M.P.s, fighting drunk and out of bounds, and I had to pull out all the stops to save their necks. I dropped them from the next game (which we won narrowly, 4–3), and then came our final match, and we won it 4–0, and that was it. I relaxed, the Governor took to his bed for a couple of days, wheezing like a deflating balloon, Lieutenant Samuels danced on the bar at the Officers' Club ('Jocko, boy, you're luv-ley, an' all your little Scotch Pongoes are luv-ley, hoots mon, an' I've won a dirty, great, big, luv-ley packet. You know what? I 'ad all the ship's funds as well as my own money on 'em for the Artillery game') and my team took it easy at last. That is to say that during the day they punted the ball about on the practice pitch, crying 'Way-ull' and 'Aw-haw-hey,' and at night they sat in the bars, drinking beer and eyeing the talent, and keeping their bonnets over their eyes.

With the pressure off they drank more and ate more, and I was not surprised when, a few days before we were due to leave the Island, two of them came down with one of those bugs which inhabit melons in foreign parts and give you gyppy tummy, or as they call it in India, Delhi Belly. They were packed off to bed and I read the others a lecture on the perils of overindulgence. It was good, strong stuff, and so influenced me personally that I declined to join Lieutenant Samuels in the celebratory dinner which he tried to press on me at the Officers' Club that night.

I regarded him with distaste. 'Why aren't you out sinking submarines or something?'

'This is peace-time, boyo,' said he. 'Anyway, we're gettin' a refit; we'll be yere for weeks. I can stand it, I'm tellin' you.' I doubted whether he could; the gin was obviously lapping against his palate and his complexion was like a desert sunrise. He insisted loudly on buying me a drink at least, and I was finishing it and trying not to listen to his gloating account of how he would spend the filthy amount of money he had won, when I was called to the 'phone.

It was the Governor, excited but brisk. 'MacNeill,' he said, 'How's your team?'

Wondering, I said they were fine.

'Excellent, capital. I think I can arrange another game for them, farewell appearance, y'know. That all right with you?'

I was about to mention the two men in hospital, and that we wouldn't be at full strength, but after all, we were here to play, not to make excuses. So I said, 'Splendid, any time', and before I could ask about our opponents and the where and when, he had said he would ring me later and hung up.

Samuels, now fully lit, was delighted. 'It never rains but it pours,' he exclaimed gleefully. 'Send it down, David. Let's see, put a packet on your boys – who they playin'? doesn't matter – collect on that, crikeee, Jocko, what a killin'! I'll plank the bet first thing . . . trouble is, they're gettin' to know me. Ne'mind, I'll get my clerk to put it on, he can go in mufti.' He crowed and rubbed his hands. 'Luv-ley little pongoes; best cargo I ever had!'

It seemed to me he was taking a lot for granted; after all, our opponents might be somebody really good. But we'd beaten the best in the Island, so he probably couldn't go wrong.

So I thought, until I heard from the Governor's aide late that night. 'Two-thirty, at the Stadium,' he said. 'Full uniform for you, of course, and *do* see, old man, that your Jocks are respectable. Can't you get them to wear their hats on the *tops* of their heads? They tend rather to look like coalmen.'

'Sure, sure. Who are we playing?'

'Mmh? Oh, the other lot? The Fleet.'

For a moment I didn't follow. He explained.

'The Fleet. The Navy. *You* know, chaps in ships with blue trousers.' He began to sing 'Heart of Oak'.

'But . . . but . . . but,' I said. 'That's like playing the Army. I mean, there are thousands of them. They'll be all-professional . . . they'll murder us . . . they . . .'

'That's what the Admiral thought,' said the aide, 'but our Chief wouldn't see it. Got rather excited actually; they're still arguing in there; can't you hear 'em? Amazing,' he went on, 'how the Chief's manner changes when he gets worked up about a thing like this; he sounds positively Scotch. What's a sumph, by the way?'

I wasn't listening any longer. I was sweating. It wasn't panic, or the fear of defeat. After all, we had done well, and no one could expect us to hold the Navy; we would just have to put on a good show. I was just concentrating on details – get the boys to bed quickly, two men in hospital, choose the team, balance it as well as possible. I ran over the reserves: Beattie, Forbes, McGlinchy, myself . . . Lord, the Fleet! And I had 14 to choose from. Well, barring miracles, we would lose. The Governor would be in mourning; that was his hard luck, if he didn't know better than to pit us against a side that would be half First Division pros, and possibly even an internationalist. Suddenly I felt elated. Suppose . . . oh, well, we'd give them something to remember us by.

I simply told the boys at bed-time who they were playing, and they digested it, and the corporal said:

'Aw-haw-hey. Think they're any good, sir?'

'Not as good as we are.'

'We're the wee boys,' said the corporal, and the wee boys cried 'Way-ull,' mocking themselves. They were pleased at the thought of another game, that was all. I doubt if their reaction would have been different if their opponents had been Moscow Dynamo or the Eye Infirmary.

The corporal and I pored over the team all morning; the one doubtful spot was left wing, and after much heart-searching we fixed on McGlinchy, but the corporal didn't like it. He at least knew what we were up against 'an' we cannae afford a passenger. If Ah thought he'd wake up mebbe half the match, O.K., but no' kiddin', sir, yon yin's no' a' there.'

'He's all we've got,' I said. 'Beattie's a half-back, and I'm just not good enough. It's got to be McGlinchy.'

'Aye, weel,' said the corporal, 'that's so. But by half-time I'll bet we're wishin' we'd picked . . . McAuslan, even.'

In the unlikely event that we had been daft enough to do just that, we would have been disappointed. For when we embussed for the stadium McAuslan was mysteriously absent. We waited and swore, but he didn't appear, so Beattie was detailed to run the touchline, and off we went. With any luck McAuslan had fallen in the harbour.

The dressing-room was hot and sunny under the stand as we sat around waiting. The boys chewed gum and McGlinchy played 'wee heidies' against the wall – nodding a ball against the partition like a boxer hitting a punch-ball. ('Close-mooth, tanner-ba' merchant,' muttered the corporal.) Outside we could hear the growing rumble of the crowd, and then there was the peep of a whistle and the referee's step in the passage, and the boys shifted and said, 'Way-ull, way-ull,' and boots stamped and shorts were hitched, and outside a brass band was thumping out 'Heart of Oak' and a great thunder of voices was rolling up as the Fleet came out, and the corporal sniffed and said:

'Awright, fellas, let's get stuck intae these matlows,' and I was left alone in the dressing-room.

I went out by the street door and was walking along to the grandstand entrance when I came face to face with Samuels in the crowd that was still pouring into the ground. It was a shock: I hadn't given him a thought since last night. Before I could say anything, he slapped me on the back, addressed me as Old Jocko, and said I was luv-ley.

'Goin' up to watch the slaughter?' he shouted. He was well ginned up. 'The massacre of the innocents, hey?'

'I like that,' I said. 'You've won enough off them; you could at least show some sympathy.'

'Who for?' he guffawed. 'The other lot?'

A horrible cold hand suddenly laid itself on the base of my spine.

'The other lot,' I said. 'You know who we're playing?'

'Been on the ship all mornin', checkin' stores,' he said, shaking his head. 'Who's the unfortunate party?'

'Tell me,' I said carefully. 'Have you put a bet on?'

'Have I, boyo? The lot, you bet. The sub-cheese. The bundle.'

I looked at my watch. It was two minutes to kick-off.

'Phone the bookie,' I said. 'Get it off. No matter what, cancel that bet.'

He didn't seem to be receiving me. 'The whole lot,' he said. 'Boyo, I cleaned out the safe. I shot the works. I'm tellin' . . .'

'Shut up, you Welsh oaf,' I shouted. 'Don't you understand? We're playing the Fleet, the Navy, all the great horrible battleships and aircraft carriers, millions of talented sailors. They will eat us alive. Your bet, if you let it ride, will go down the nick. Get it off.'

In all the world there is no sight so poignant as that of the confident mug when he feels the first sharp bite of the hook and realises it is going to sink inexorably home. His face went from sweating red to dry grey, and he seemed to crumple.

'You're drunk, boyo,' he croaked.

'I'm drunk? Look who's talking. Look, Taffy, you'll have to cancel . . .' And just then what he had said came home to me. 'You say you cleaned out the safe? The ship's safe? But you've got two weeks of my Jocks' pay in there . . . Oh, brother.' I just stared at him. This was death, court-martial, ruin, and disaster. He was cooked. Unless the bet was scrubbed.

'It's no use,' he said. 'I cannot do it.' Odd, I thought, he says cannot, not can't. 'I didn't place it myself, see? The clerk did. Peterson. I gave him half a dozen addresses. I dunno where he is, now.'

The crowd was moving in, the last of it. There was nothing to be done. The band had stopped. I left him standing there, like a busted flush, and climbed the stairs to the stand. Poor Samuels, I thought. Idiot, mad Samuels. Of all the . . .

The roar hit me in the face as I came out into the stand. I sat at the back of the main box; down front the Governor was starting work on his first handkerchief of the game, and beside him was a massive, grizzled hero in blue, with gold lace up to his armpits. That would be the Admiral. Their henchmen were about them, full of well-bred enthusiasm; the stadium was jammed, and every second man seemed to be a sailor. Our support was confined to a handful of khaki down below the box: our own reserves and a few associates.

'Flee-eet!' rolled across the brown, iron-hard pitch, and I saw the concentration of yellow shirts down near one goal: the Navy were attacking, powerful dark-blue figures with red stockings. They smacked the ball about with that tough assurance that is the mark of the professional; I saw the corporal slide in to tackle, and red stockings deftly side-stepped and swept the ball past him. The roar mounted, there was a surge in our goal-mouth, and then the ball was trickling past into the crowd. I felt slightly sick.

'Get tore intae these people!' came from in front of the box, to be drowned in the Navy roar. Yes, I thought, get tore in. It's your pay and Samuels' reputation you're playing for. Then I thought, no, the heck with that, it's just for yourselves, that's all.

And they played. The hard ground and the light ball were on our side, for we were ball-players first and last; on grass the Navy would have been just too strong. They didn't rush things; they passed with deliberation and looked for their men, unlike our team, who were used to fast, short passing controlled by some sort of telepathy. If we played at their pace we were done for, so we didn't. The doll-like yellow figures moved and ran as though they were at practice, easy and confident.

We scored in the sixth minute, a zig-zag of passes down the middle that left Campbell, the centre, clear of the defence, and he lofted the ball over the Navy goal-keeper's head as he came out. There was a shocked roar from the crowd, a neigh of triumph from the Governor, a perceptible empurpling of the Admiral's neck, and an exulting 'Aw-haw-hey!' from below the box.

Two minutes later Campbell had the ball in the net again, but was ruled offside. Then he headed against the cross-bar, and we forced three corners in a row. But you could feel it slackening; the Fleet were as steady as ever, and presently they came away, swinging long passes through the open spaces, using their extra length of leg, keeping the ball up where their height counted. They *were* good; in their way they were a better team. In their way. And for a moment, as they broke through on the left and centred and their inside right chose his spot in the net and banged in the equaliser, they were imposing that way.

There was worse to come. The Fleet went ahead with a penalty, when the corporal, in a momentary lapse into close-mouth warfare, obeyed our supporters' behest to 'Ca' the feet fae 'im,' and brought down a Navy forward close to goal. It was a critical point: when we kicked off again the Navy, one goal up, came storming through. Their centre got away and side-footed the ball past the advancing goalkeeper. It was rolling home, but the corporal came from nowhere and stopped it on the line. And then he did the ridiculous, unspeakable thing. I can still see him, the stocky yellow figure with his foot on top of the ball, watching three blue jerseys tearing down on him; alone, in his own goal. Bobby Moore himself would have belted it away for touch and been thankful. But not our boy. He shifted his hips, beat the first Navy forward on a sixpence, showed the ball to the other two, feinted amidst agonised yells of 'Get rid of it!' stepped over a scything foot, looked about him, and patted the ball into the hands of the goalkeeper, who was so stricken with anxiety that he nearly dropped it.

It was perhaps the cheekiest piece of ball-juggling that I've ever seen; it shook the Fleet momentarily for it seemed to indicate a careless contempt. It said, more clearly than words could have done, that there was no sense of panic in this defence. The Admiral roared with laughter, and I hoped again.

We scored again, just before the interval, a goal against the run of play headed in from a long, free kick, and the teams came off and the Marine band marched up and down playing 'Iolanthe'. I stayed where I was, listening to the Governor chattering Good game, good game, my goodness, and the Admiral's bass rumble, and staring out at the sunlight on the great crowd lining the saucer of the arena. There was no point in my going down to the dressing-room; we were doing well, and nothing I could say could make it better.

The second half began disastrously. A high ball went into our goal-mouth, the centre-half and the Fleet centre went up for it; the sailor came down on his feet and our man on his back. He lay still, and my heart turned over. I watched them lifting him, crowding around, but his head hung forward, and presently they took him behind the goal. 'Dirty, dirty!' came the cry from down front, drowned in the answering roar of 'Wheel 'im off!' from the Navy. The referee bounced the ball to restart the game, and as the injured man was supported towards the dressing-room I was bounding down the stairs.

He was slightly concussed, the doctor said; he wanted to go back on, but the doctor said it was out of the question. I watched while they bandaged his head, and told him – what I honestly felt – that it didn't matter a damn about the game. His face took on that look of whining rage that the Glaswegian wears in times of stress, and he said, 'We had them bate. We'd've sorted them this half.'

Maybe we would, I thought; with ten men it was certain that we wouldn't now. The doctor broke in to say that he ought to go to bed, and as they took him away I went back to the stand. Dimly I had been aware of the distant roar swelling and dying;

when I climbed into my seat we were kicking off again. We were down 4–2.

The Fleet were out for blood now. Even the Admiral was joining in the roar, and the Governor was just sitting eating his hankie. Ten men don't look very different on the field from eleven; for a time they may even play above themselves, but they don't win. They never deserve to lose, but they lose.

Oddly enough, we held our own now, and with the tension gone I began to take in details. McGlinchy was playing like an elderly horse; he hadn't seen much of the ball in the first half, and now he was using it as if it was a landmine, shying away from it, stumbling, and generally living up to the corporal's expectations. His inside man, little Forbes, was obviously cursing himself hoarse. The crowd enjoyed it.

'Windy!' roared the Fleet.

'Ah, you sharrap! Get back on the front o' the Players packet!'

'Turn blue, pongoes!'

'Play up,' cried the Governor. 'Come along, come along.'

The Admiral said something to him, and they both laughed, and I watched the handkerchief being twisted. There were about fifteen minutes left.

Then it happened, and you can read about it in the files of the Island's leading daily paper.

McGlinchy got the ball and lost it; it came back to him and he fell over it and it went into touch. The Navy threw in, the ball ran to McGlinchy again, and for once he beat his man and was moving down the wing when a sailor whipped the heels from him. The crowd roared, McGlinchy got up hopping painfully, the Governor exclaimed, 'Oh, I say,' and little Forbes went scurrying in, fists clenched, to avenge the foul. Oh no, I said, please God, don't let Forbes hit him, not out there with everyone looking. Please don't, Forbes. But the referee was in between, shaking his finger, Forbes was hustled away by his mates, and the referee gave a free kick – against McGlinchy.

It was taken amid much hubbub, and I watched McGlinchy, standing looking puzzled, too surprised to protest, and then his head lifted, and the ball was running towards him. He stopped it, turned, swerved past the half-back, and was away. He could run when he wanted; he swerved infield, then out again towards the flag. The back went sliding in and McGlinchy side-stepped him and came in along the by-line, teasing that he was going to cross the ball, but holding it, like Matthews in his good years.

'Get rid of it!' cried an unhappy voice, but he held it, sand-dancing, looking up, and then he made a dart towards the near post, with the back straining at his heels, and he passed across and back when he couldn't have been more than three yards out, and Forbes had the empty goal in front of him.

The net shook, and the Admiral pounded his fist amidst the uproar, and the Governor made strange sounds, and I could see the corporal slapping McGlinchy's back and unbraiding him for holding on so long, and I thought regretfully that that had been McGlinchy's one brilliant flash. He was trotting back thoughtfully to his wing, with the applause dying down. It was 4–3 for the Navy and perhaps twelve minutes to go.

Then he did it again. Or very nearly. He went down the touch-line and then cut square across the field, beating two men on the way. He had an opening towards goal, with the Fleet defence floundering, but being McGlinchy he back-heeled the ball to nobody and it was cleared. I saw the corporal beating his breast, the Governor tore his handkerchief across, the Admiral bellowed jovially – and McGlinchy got the second chance he didn't deserve. The back's clearance hit a Fleet man and ran loose. McGlinchy, still in midfield, fastened on and this time went straight ahead, turned out to the left as the centre-half closed in, and centred hard and high. Duff, the right-winger, met it at the post with his head, and I realised that I was making ridiculous noises of triumph and delight. It was 4–4, the Fleet defence were gesturing at each other, and the little knot of yellow shirts was hurrying back towards the centre circle, embracing as they ran.

Then the Navy showed how good they were. They attacked, and for the first and only time in my experience of them I saw my team panicked. They had snatched a possible draw from certain defeat, and they were scared stiff of slipping back. They were wild; they fouled twice, once perilously close to the 18-yard line, and I could see, although I couldn't hear, the corporal barking at them, swearing horribly, no doubt, steadying them. He was wise, that corporal; whenever he got the ball he looked for McGlinchy. He sensed, like me, that he was in the presence of a phenomenon; it couldn't last, but he knew to use it while it was there. 'Feed him, feed him, he's bewitched,' I found myself saying, and McGlinchy went off down the wing, fair hair flying – I made a note to make him get it cut – and was tackled and the ball ran out.

He clapped his hands for it, trapped it as it was thrown in, back-heeled it through an opponent's legs, and ran on to it. He stopped, on the edge of the centre circle, foot on the ball, looking round. And for a split second the sound died. Then:

'Coom to 'im, man!' in a great Yorkshire voice.

'Get rid o' it, mac! See the winger.'

The roar swelled up, and he swerved away, dummied past a half-back, reached the penalty circle, slid heaven knows how between two defenders, almost lost the ball, scratched for it, pushed it forward, feinted to shoot, swerved again, and now he was on the penalty spot, with the blue jerseys converging, and little Forbes screaming for the ball, unmarked, and Campbell on the other side of him beating his hands. But he went on, the Admiral covered his face, the Governor rose to his feet cramming his handkerchief into his mouth, McGlinchy had one sailor at his elbow and another lunging desperately in front of him; he checked and side-stepped, looked at Forbes, shoved the ball under the tackler's leg, went after it, and just for a split second was clear, with every sailor except Lord Nelson thundering in on him, the goalkeeper diving at his feet, and then the blue flood swept down on him.

'Get rid o' it!'

'Kill him!' bawled the Admiral, decency forgotten.

'Get tore in!' cried the Governor.

He went down in a heap of navy jerseys, and a sudden bellow went up from behind the goal. I couldn't see why, and then I saw why. The ball was lying, rolling just a little, a foot over the goal-line. It came to rest in the net, just inside the post.

At such times, when all around is bedlam, the man of mark is distinguished by his nonchalance and detachment. Calmly I took out my cigarette case, selected a cigarette, struck a match, set fire to my sporran, roared aloud, dropped cigarettes, case, and matches, and scrambled on my knees along the floor of the box trying to beat the flames out. By the time I had succeeded the box was full of smoke and a most disgusting stench, one of the Admiral's aides was looking round muttering that expressions of triumph were all very well, but the line should be drawn somewhere, and the Fleet were kicking off in a last attempt to retrieve the game.

They didn't make it, but it was a near thing. There was one appeal for a penalty when the corporal seemed to handle – if I'd been the referee I believe I'd have given it – but the claim was disallowed, and then the long whistle blew. We had won, 5–4, and I found myself face to face with a red-faced petty officer who was exclaiming, 'By, you were lucky! I say, you were lucky! By!'

I made deprecating noises and shot downstairs. They were trooping into the dressing-room, chattering indignantly – it was their curious way not to be exultant over what had gone right, but aggrieved over what had gone wrong. I gathered that at least two of the Fleet should have been ordered off, that the referee had been ignorant of the offside law, that we should have had a penalty when . . . and so on. Never mind, I said, we won, it had all come out all right. Oh, aye, but . . .

The Governor looked in, beaming congratulation, and there was a lot of noise and far too many people in the dressing-room. The team were pulling off their jerseys and trying to escape to the showers; clothes were falling on the floor and bare feet were being stepped on; the Governor was saying to Forbes, Well done, well played indeed, and Forbes was saying See yon big, dirty, ignorant full-back, and at last the door was shut and we were alone with the smell of sweat and embrocation and steam and happy weariness.

'Well done, kids,' I said, and the corporal said, 'No' sae bad,' and rumpled McGlinchy's hair, and everyone laughed. Through in the showers someone began to make mouth-music to the tune of 'The Black Bear', and at the appropriate moment the feet stamped in unison and the towel-clad figures shuffled, clapping and humming.

'Not too loud,' I said. 'Don't let the Navy hear.'

I went over to McGlinchy, who was drying his hair and whistling. I wanted to ask: What gets into you? Why don't you play like that all the time? But I didn't. I knew I wouldn't ever find out.

For no reason I suddenly thought of Samuels, and realised that he was off the hook. Resentment quickly followed relief: he was not only in the clear, he had probably made a small fortune. How lucky, how undeservedly lucky can you get, I thought bitterly: but for McGlinchy's inexplicable brilliance Samuels would now be facing the certainty of court-martial and dismissal, possibly even prison. As it was he was riding high.

Or so I thought until that evening, when I was summoned to the local bastille at the request of the Provost-Marshal, to identify a soldier, one McAuslan, who had been arrested during the afternoon. It appeared that he and an anonymous sailor had been making a tour of all the bars in town, and the sailor had eventually passed out in the street. McAuslan's primitive efforts to minister to him had excited attention, and the pair of them had been hauled off by the redcaps.

They brought him out of his cell, looking abominable but apparently sober. I demanded to know what he thought he had been doing.

Well, it was like this, he and his friend the sailor had gone for a wee hauf, and then they had had anither, and . . .

'He'll be singing "I belong to Glasgow" in a minute,' observed the redcap corporal. 'Stand to attention, you thing, you.'

'Who was the sailor?' I asked, puzzled, for I remembered McAuslan's antipathy to the ship's crew.

'Wan o' the boys off the ship. Fella Peterson. He was gaun tae the toon, an' Ah offered tae staun' 'im a drink. Ye remember,' he went on earnestly, 'ye told me tae fraternise. Well, we fraternised, an' he got fu'. Awfy quick, he got fu',' McAuslan went on, and it was plain to see that his companion's incapacity offended him. 'He drank the drink Ah bought 'im, and it made 'im fleein', and then he was buyin' drink himself' at an awfy rate . . .'

'That was the thing, sir,' explained the redcap. 'This sailor had more money than you've ever seen; he looked like he'd robbed a bank. That was really why we pulled them in, sir, for protection. Weedy little chap, the sailor, but he had hundreds of pounds worth of lire on him.'

Suddenly a great light dawned. Peterson was the name of Samuels' clerk, who had been going to place his bets for him, and McAuslan had obviously encountered him beforehand, and full of good fellowship had bought him liquor, and Peterson, the weedy little chap, must have been unused to strong waters, and had forgotten responsibility and duty and his captain's orders, and had proceeded to go on an almighty toot. So it seemed obvious that whatever custom the bookies had attracted that day, Samuels' had not been part of it. His money (and the ship's funds and my jocks' pay) was safely in the military police office safe, less what McAuslan and Peterson had expended with crying 'Bring in!' Samuels could make that up himself, and serve him right. Also, he could have fun explaining to the M.P.s just how one of his sailors came to be rolling about town with all that cash on his person.

'McAuslan,' I said, 'in your own way you're a great man. Tell me,' I asked the redcap, 'are you going to charge him?'

'Well,' said the redcap, 'he wasn't what you'd call incapably stinking, just happy. It was the sailor who was paralytic. He still is. So . . .'

'Thank you,' I said. 'Look, McAuslan, you're a lucky man. You shouldn't go about getting little sailors stotius . . .'

'I was jist fraternisin', honest . . .'

'Right. You can fraternise some more. What I want you to do is go over to the ship, look out Lieutenant Samuels, and tell him, in your own well-chosen words, what happened today. Tell him the money's in the M.P. safe. And then you might offer to buy him a drink; he'll probably need one. And McAuslan, if he tries to hit you, you're not to clock him one, understand? Remember, be fraternal and polite; he's your superior officer and you wouldn't want to hurt his feelings.'

We took our leave of the civil redcaps, and I watched McAuslan striding purposefully towards the harbour, bonnet down over his eyes, to break the glad news to Samuels. It was growing dusk, and all in all, it had been quite a day.

I saw McGlinchy many years after, from the top of a Glasgow bus. Although his fair hair was fading and receding, and his face looked middle-aged and tired, there was no mistaking the loose-jointed, untidy walk. He was carrying a string bag, and he looked of no account at all in his stained raincoat and old shoes. And then the bus took me past. I wondered if he remembered those few minutes out in the sunlight. Perhaps not; he wasn't the kind who would think twice about it. But I remember McGlinchy when . . .

Wee Wullie

The duties of a regimental orderly officer cover pretty well everything from inspecting the little iced cakes in the canteen to examining the prisoners in the guardroom cells to ensure that they are still breathing. In our battalion, the cells were seldom occupied; the discipline imposed on our volatile mixture of Aberdonians and Glaswegians was intelligent rather than tough, and more often than not trouble was dealt with before it got the length of a charge sheet.

So when I walked into the guardroom for a late night look round and saw one of the cell doors closed and padlocked, and a noise issuing from behind it like the honking of a drowsy seal, I asked McGarry, the provost sergeant, who his guest for the night might be.

'It's yon animal, Wee Wullie,' he said. 'Sharrap, ye Glasgow heathen! He's gey fu' sir, an' half-killed a redcap in the toon. They had to bring him here in a truck wi' his hands tied and a man sittin' on his heid. And afore I could get him in there I had to restrain him, mysel'.'

I realised that McGarry had a swelling bruise on one cheek and that his usually immaculate khaki shirt was crumpled; he was a big man, with forearms like a blacksmith, and the skin on his knuckles was broken. I was glad it wasn't me he had had to restrain.

'He's sleepin' like a bairn noo, though,' he added, and he said it almost affectionately.

I looked through the grill of the cell. Wee Wullie was lying on the plank, snoring like an organ. Between his massively booted feet at one end, and the bonnet on his grizzled head at the other, there was about six and a half feet of muscular development that would have done credit to a mountain gorilla. One of his puttees was gone, his shirt was in rags, and there was a tear in his kilt; his face, which at the best of times was rugged, looked as though it had been freshly trampled on. On the palm of one outstretched hand still lay a trophy of his evening's entertainment – a Military Police cap badge. In that enormous brown paw it looked about as big as a sixpence.

'You did well to get him inside,' I told McGarry.

'Ach, he's no' bad tae manage when he's puggled,' said the provost. 'A big, coorse loon, but the booze slows him doon.'

I had some idea of what McGarry called 'no' bad tae manage'. I recalled Hogmanay, when Wee Wullie had returned from some slight jollification in the Arab quarter having whetted his appetite for battle on the local hostelries, and erupted through the main gate intent on slaughter. It had been at that moment of the day which, for a soldier, is memorable above all others; the hour when the Last Post is sounded, and everything else is still while the notes float sadly away into the velvet dark; the guard stand stiffly to attention by the main gate with the orderly officer behind, and the guardroom lanterns light up the odd little ceremony that has hardly changed in essentials since the Crimea. It is the end of the Army's day, peaceful and rather beautiful.

Into this idyll had surged Wee Wullie, staggering drunk and bawling for McGarry to come out and fight. For a moment his voice had almost drowned the bugle, and then (because he was Wee Wullie with 30 years' service behind him) he had slowly come to attention and waited, swaying like an oak in a storm, until the call was ended. As the last note died away he hurled aside his bonnet, reeled to the foot of the guardroom steps, and roared:

'Coom oot, McGarry! Ah'm claimin' ye! Ye've had it, ye big Hielan' stirk! Ye neep! Ye teuchter, ye!'

McGarry came slowly out of the guardroom, nipping his cigarette, and calmly regarded the Neanderthal figure waiting for him. It looked only a matter of time before Wee Wullie started drumming on his chest and pulling down twigs to eat, but McGarry simply said,

'Aye, Wullie, ye're here again. Ye comin' quiet, boy?'

Wullie's reply was an inarticulate bellow and a furious fist-swinging charge, and five minutes later McGarry was kneeling over his prostrate form, patting his battered face, and summoning the guard to carry the body inside. They heaved the stricken giant up, and he came to himself just as they were manhandling him into the cooler. His bloodshot eyes rolled horribly and settled on McGarry, and he let out a great cry of baffled rage.

'Let me at 'im! Ah want at 'im!' He struggled furiously, and the four men of the guard clung to his limbs and wrestled him into the cell.

'Wheesht, Wullie,' said McGarry, locking the door. 'Just you lie doon like a good lad. Ye'll never learn; ye cannie fight McGarry when ye're fu'. Now just wheesht, or I'll come in tae ye.'

'You!' yelled Wullie through the bars. 'Oh, see you! Your mither's a Tory!'

McGarry laughed and left him to batter at the door until he was tired. It had become almost a ritual with the two of them, which would be concluded when Wullie had sobered up and told McGarry he was sorry. It was Wullie's enduring problem that he liked McGarry, and would fight with him only when inflamed by drink; yet drunk, he could not hope to beat him as he would have done sober.

I thought of these things as I looked into the cell at Wee Wullie asleep. On that wild Hogmanay I should, of course, have used my authority to reprimand and restrain him, and so prevented the unseemly brawl with the provost sergeant, but you don't reprimand a rogue elephant or a snapped wire hawser, either of which would be as open to sweet reason as Wee Wullie with a bucket in him. The fact that he would have been overwhelmed by remorse afterwards for plastering me all over the guardroom wall would not really have been much consolation to either of us. So I had remained tactfully in the background while Sergeant McGarry had fulfilled his regimental duty of preserving order and repressing turbulence.

And now it had happened again, for the umpteenth time, but this time it was bad. From what McGarry had told me, Wee Wullie had laid violent hands on a military policeman, which meant that he might well be court-martialled – which, inevitably, for a man with a record like his, would mean a long stretch in the glasshouse at Cairo.

'He'll no' get away wi' it this time, poor loon,' said McGarry. 'It'll be outwith the battalion, ye see. Aye, auld Wullie, he'll be the forgotten man of Heliopolis nick if the redcaps get their way.' He added, apparently irrelevantly, 'For a' the Colonel can say.'

I left the guardroom and walked across the starlit parade ground through the grove of tamarisks to the white-walled subalterns' quarters, wondering if this was really the finish of Wee Wullie. If it was, well, the obvious thing to do would be to thank God we were rid of a knave, an even bigger battalion pest than the famous Private McAuslan, the dirtiest soldier in the world, an Ishmael, a menace, a horrible man. At the same time . . .

All that was really wrong with Wee Wullie was his predilection for strong drink and violent trouble. He was drunk the first time I ever saw him, on a desert convoy passing under Marble Arch, that towering monument to Mussolini's vanity which bestrides the road on the Libyan border. I had noticed this huge man, first for his very size, secondly for his resemblance to the late William Bendix, and lastly for his condition, which was scandalous. He was patently tight, but still at the good-humoured stage, and was being helped aboard a truck by half a dozen well-wishers. They dropped him several times, and he lay in the sand roaring. I was a green subaltern, but just experienced enough to know when not to intervene, so I left them to it, and eventually they got him over the tailboard. (It is astonishing just how often an officer's duty seems to consist of looking the other way, or maybe I was just a bad officer.)

In the battalion itself he was a curious mixture. As far as the small change of soldiering went, Wullie was reasonably efficient. His kit at inspections was faultless, his knowledge and deportment exact, so far as they went, which was just far enough for competence. In his early days he had been as high as sergeant before being busted (I once asked the Adjutant when this had been, and he said, 'God knows, about the first Afghan War, I should think'), but in later years the authorities had despaired of promoting him to any rank consistent with his length of service. Occasionally they would make him a lance-corporal, just for variety, and then Wullie would pick a fight with the American Marines, or tip a truck over, or fall in alcoholic stupor into a river and have to be rescued, and off would come his stripe again. He had actual service chevrons literally as long as his arm, but badges of rank and good conduct he had none.

Yet he enjoyed a curiously privileged position. In drill, for example, it was understood that there were three ways of doing things: the right way, the wrong way, and Wee Wullie's way. His movements were that much slower, more ponderous, than anyone else's; when he saluted, his hand did not come up in a flashing arc, but jerked up so far, and then travelled slowly to his right eyebrow. On parade, there was some incongruity in the sight of a platoon of wee Gleska keelies and great-chested

Aberdonians (who run to no spectacular height, as a rule) with Gargantua in their midst, his rifle like a popgun in his huge fist, and himself going through the motions with tremendous intensity, half a second behind everyone else. There was almost a challenge in the way he performed, as though he was conscious of being different, and yet there was about him a great dignity. Even the Regimental Sergeant Major recognised it, and excused much.

This was when he was sober and passive. Even then he was withdrawn and monosyllabic; only when he was slightly inebriated could he be described as sociable. Beyond that he was just outrageous, a dangerous, wickedly powerful ruffian whom only the redoubtable McGarry could manage single-handed.

Yet there was in the battalion a curiously protective instinct towards him. It seemed to emanate from the Colonel, who had ordered that Wullie was never to be brought before him for disciplinary action except when it was unavoidable. Thus his crimes and misdemeanours were usually dealt with at company level, and he got off fairly lightly. When the Colonel did have to deal with him he would consign Wullie to the cells and afterwards try to find him a quiet niche where he would be out of trouble, invariably without success. When he was made medical orderly he got at the M.O.'s medicinal brandy and wrecked the place; he lost the job of padre's batman through his unceasing profanity; attached to the motor transport section he got tremendously high and put a three-ton truck through a brick wall ('I always said that particular experiment was sheer lunacy,' said the Adjutant. 'I mean, a truck was all he needed, wasn't it?'). An attempt was even made to get him into the band, and the little pipe-sergeant was scandalised. 'He has no sense of time, colonel sir,' he protested. 'Forbye, look at the size of his feet, and think of that clumph-clumph-clumphing on the great ceremonial parades.'

In the end he was made the M.O.'s gardener, and he seemed

to take to it. He did not do any actual gardening himself, but he could address the Arab gardeners in their own language, and got all the plants neatly arranged in columns of threes, dressed by the right, and in order of what he considered their seniority. For in his quiet moments there was a strong military sense in Wullie, as there should have been after 30 years in uniform. This was brought home to me in the only conversation of any duration I ever had with him, one day when I was orderly officer and was inspecting the whitewashed stones which Wullie's Arabs were arranging in the headquarters plot. For some reason I mentioned to Wullie that I was not intending to stay in the Army when my number came up, and he said, with his direct, intent stare, 'Then ye're a fool, sir.' Only Wullie could have called an officer a fool, in a way which carried no disrespect, and only Wullie would have added 'sir' to the rebuke.

And on another occasion he did me a great service. It was shortly after his Hogmanay escapade, and I was again orderly officer and was supervising the closing of the wet canteen. The joint was jumping and I hammered with my walking-stick on the bar and shouted, 'Last drinks. Time, gentlemen, please,' which was always good for a laugh. Most of them drank and went, but there was one bunch, East End Glaswegians with their bonnets pulled down over their eyes, who stayed at their table. Each man had about three pints in front of him; they had been stocking up.

'Come on,' I said. 'Get it down you.'

There were a few covert grins, and someone muttered about being entitled to finish their drinks – which strictly speaking they were. But there was no question they were trying it on: on the other hand, how does a subaltern move men who don't want to be moved? I know, personality. Try it some time along the Springfield Road.

'You've got two minutes,' I said, and went to supervise the closing of the bar shutters. Two minutes later I looked across; they were still there, having a laugh and taking their time.

I hesitated; this was one of those moments when you can look very silly, or lose your reputation, or both. At that moment Wee Wullie, who had been finishing his pint in a corner, walked past and stopped to adjust his bonnet near me.

'Tak' wan o' them by the scruff o' the neck and heave 'im oot,' he said, staring at me, and then went out of the canteen.

It was astonishing advice. About the most awful crime an officer can commit is to lay hands on an other rank. Suppose one of them belted me? It could be one hell of a mess, and a scandal. Then one of them laughed again, loudly, and I strode across to the table, took the nearest man (the smallest one, incidentally) by the collar, and hauled him bodily to the door. He was too surprised to do anything; he was off balance all the way until I dropped him just outside the doorway.

He was coming up, spitting oaths and murder, when Wee Wullie said out of the shadows at one side of the door:

'Jist you stay down, boy, or ye'll stay down for the night.'

I went into the canteen again. The rest were standing, staring. 'Out,' I said, like Burt Lancaster in the movies, and they went, leaving their pints. When I left the canteen Wee Wullie had disappeared.

And now he was probably going to disappear for keeps, I thought that night after seeing him in the cell. How long would he get for assaulting a redcap? Two years? How old was he, and how would he last out two years on the hill, or the wells, or whatever diversions they were using now in the glasshouse? Of course, he was as strong as an ox. And what had McGarry meant, 'For a' the Colonel can say'?

What the Colonel did say emerged a few days later when the Adjutant, entering like Rumour painted full of tongues, recounted what had taken place at Battalion H.Q. when the town Provost Marshal had called. The P.M. had observed that the time had come when Wee Wullie could finally get his come-uppance, and had spoken of general courts-martial and long terms of detention. The Colonel had said, uh-huh, indeed, and suggested that so much was hardly necessary: it could be dealt with inside the battalion. By no means, said the P.M., Wee Wullie had been an offence to the public weal too long; he was glasshouse-ripe; a turbulent, ungodly person whom he, the P.M., was going to see sent where he wouldn't hear the dogs bark. The Colonel then asked, quietly, if the P.M., as a special favour to him, would leave the matter entirely in the Colonel's hands.

Taken aback the P.M. protested at length, and whenever he paused for breath the Colonel would raise his great bald hawk head and gently repeat his request. This endured for about twenty minutes, after which the P.M. gave way under protest – under strong protest – and stumped off muttering about protecting pariahs and giving Capone a pound out of the poor box. He was an angry and bewildered man.

'So the matter need not go to the General Officer Commanding,' concluded the Adjutant mysteriously. 'This time.' Pressed for details, he explained, in a tone that suggested he didn't quite believe it himself, that the Colonel had been ready, if the P.M. had been obdurate, to go to the G.O.C. on Wee Wullie's behalf.

'All the way, mark you,' said the Adjutant. 'For that big idiot. Of course, if the G.O.C. happens to have been your fag at Rugby, I dare say it makes it easier, but I still don't understand it.'

Nor did anyone else. Generals were big stuff, and Wullie was only one extremely bad hat of a private. The Colonel called him several other names as well, when the case came up at orderly room, and gave him 28 days, which was as much as he could award him without sending him to the military prison.

So Wullie did his time in the battalion cells, expressing repentance while he cleaned out the ablutions, and exactly twenty-four hours after his release he was back inside for drunkenness, insubordination, and assault, in that he, in the cookhouse, did wilfully overturn a cauldron of soup and, on being reprimanded by the cook-sergeant, did strike the cook-sergeant with his fist . . .

And so on. 'I don't know,' said the Adjutant in despair. 'Short of shooting him, what *can* you do with him? What *can* you do?'

He asked the question at dinner, in the Colonel's absence. It was not a mess night, and we were eating our spam informally. Most of the senior officers were out in their married quarters; only the second-in-command, a grizzled major who was also a bachelor, represented the old brigade. He sat chewing his cheroot absently while the Adjutant went on to say that it couldn't last for ever; the Colonel's curious – and misguided – protection of Wee Wullie would have to stop eventually. And when it did, Wee Wullie would be away, permanently.

The second-in-command took out his cheroot and inspected it. 'Well, it won't stop, I can tell you that,' he said.

The Adjutant demanded to know why, and the second-in-command explained.

'Wee Wullie may get his deserts one of these days; it's a matter of luck. But I do know that it will be over the Colonel's dead body. You expressed surprise that the Colonel would go to the G.O.C.; I'm perfectly certain he would go farther than that if he had to.'

'For heaven's sake, why? What's so special about Wee Wullie?'

'Well, he and the Colonel have served together a long time. Since the first war, in fact. Same battalion, war and peace, for most of the time – joined almost the same day, I believe. Wounded together at Passchendaele, that sort of thing.'

'We all know that,' said the Adjutant impatiently. 'But even so, granted the Colonel feels responsible, I'd have said Wee

Wullie has overstepped the mark too far and too often. He's a dead loss.'

'Well,' said the second-in-command, 'that's as may be.' He sat for a moment rolling a new cheroot in his fingers. 'But there are things you don't know.' He lit the cheroot and took a big breath. Everyone was listening and watching. 'You know,' said the second-in-command, 'that after the battalion came out of France in 'forty, it was sent to the Far East. Well, Wullie didn't go with it. He was doing time in Sowerby Bridge glasshouse, for the usual offences – drunkenness, assault on a superior, and so on. When he came out the battalion had gone into the bag after Singapore, so Wullie was posted to one of our Terrier battalions in North Africa – it was Tom Crawford's, in fact. I don't suppose Tom was particularly happy to see the regiment's Public Enemy Number One, but he had other things to think about. It was the time when the desert war was going to and fro like ping-pong – first Rommel on top, then us – and his battalion had taken a pretty fair hammering, one way and another.

'Anyway, when Rommel made his big breakthrough, and looked like going all the way to Shepheard's Hotel, Tom's chaps were being pushed back with the rest. There was some messy fighting, and in it they picked up a prisoner – a warrant officer in the German equivalent of the service corps. They learned from him about the existence of one of those petrol dumps that Rommel had put down on an earlier push – you know the sort of thing, we did it, too. When you're on the run you bury all the fuel you can, and when you come back that way, there it is. How they got this chap to spill the beans I don't know, but he did.

'Well, Tom saw at once that if they could scupper this buried dump it might be a telling blow to the Jerry advance, so he went after it. One of his company commanders, fellow called MacLennan, took off with a truck, a couple of Sappers, the German prisoner as a guide, a driver – and Wee Wullie. They took him along because he was big and rough, and just the chap to keep an eye on the Hun. And off they went into the blue to blow the dump sky-high.

'It was away out of the main run, down to the southward, and it was going to be a near thing for them to get there before Rommel's crowd, so they went hell for leather. They didn't make it. Somewhere along the way the truck went over a land-mine, the driver was killed, and MacLennan's knee-cap was smashed. The Sappers and Wullie and the Hun were just shaken, but the truck was a complete write-off. And there they were, miles behind their own retreating brigade, stranded in the middle of God knows where, and no way of getting home but walking.'

The second-in-command's cheroot had gone out. He chewed it out of the side of his mouth, staring at the table-cloth.

'You know what the desert's like. If you haven't got transport, you die. Unless someone finds you. And MacLennan knew the only people who might find them were the Germans, and that was a thin chance at best. If they'd made it to the dump it would have been different. As it was, they would have to shift for themselves – with about two days' water and upwards of forty miles to go before they had even a reasonable chance of being picked up.

'MacLennan couldn't go, of course, with his leg smashed. He got them to make him comfortable in the lee of the wrecked truck, kept one water bottle himself, and ordered the four of them to clear out. One of the Sappers wanted to stay with him, but MacLennan knew there was no point to it. Barring miracles, he was done for. He just laid down the law to them, told them to head north, and wished them luck. We Wullie never said anything, apparently – not that that was unusual, since he was sober.

'MacLennan watched them set off, into that hellish burning waste, and then settled down to die. He supposed his water might last him through the next day, and decided that whatever happened, he wouldn't shoot himself. Cool boy, that one. He's at Staff College now, I believe. But it didn't come to that; his miracle happened. Up north, although he didn't know it, Rommel was just coming to a halt near Alamein, and by sheer chance on the second day one of our long-range group patrols came on him just as he was drinking the last of his water.'

The second-in-command paused to relight his cheroot, and I noticed the Adjutant's hand stray towards his glass, and stop half-way.

'Well, they took MacLennan in,' said the second-in-command, 'and of course he got them on the hunt right away for the other four. It took them some time. They found one body about twenty miles north of where MacLennan had been, and another a little farther on. And when they were on the point of giving up, they found Wee Wullie. He was walking north, or rather, he was staggering north, and he was carrying the fourth chap in a fireman's lift.

'He was in a fearful state. His face was black, his tongue and mouth were horribly dried up, all his gear was gone, of course, and he must have been on the very edge of collapse. He couldn't see, he couldn't hear, he couldn't speak – but he could march. God knows how long he'd been without water, or how long he'd been carrying the other fellow; he was so done that when they found him they had to stop him, physically, in his tracks, because they couldn't make him understand. One of them said afterwards' – the second-in-command hesitated and drew on his cheroot – 'that he believed Wee Wullie would just have gone on for ever.'

Knowing Wee Wullie, I could have believed it too. After a moment the Adjutant said: 'That was pretty good. Didn't he – well, he hasn't any decorations, has he? You'd have thought, seeing he saved a comrade's life –'

'It wasn't a comrade,' said the second-in-command. 'He

was carrying the German. And it didn't save his life. He died soon after.'

'Even so,' said the Adjutant. 'It was pretty bloody heroic.'

'I'd say so,' said the second-in-command. 'But Wee Wullie's his own worst enemy. When he was taken back to base and the hospital, he made a splendid recovery. Managed to get hold of drink, somehow, terrified the nursing staff, climbed out on the roof and sang "The Ball of Kirriemuir" at the top of his voice – all seventy-odd verses, they tell me. They tried to drag him in, and he broke a military policeman's jaw. Then he fell off the roof and got concussion. It isn't easy to hang gongs on a man like that. Although I dare say if it had been, say, MacLennan that he'd been carrying, and not the German, that might have made a difference.'

'Well,' said the Adjutant, 'it would have made our Colonel's attitude . . . well, easier to understand.'

'Maybe that's the point,' said the second-in-command. 'Wee Wullie tried to save an enemy. The German to him was really a nuisance – a dead loss. But he was prepared to risk his own life for him, to go all the way. I don't know. Anyway,' he added, looking as near embarrassment as was possible for him, 'that may explain some of the things you haven't understood about him. Why, as far as the Colonel is concerned, he can set fire to the barracks and murder half the redcaps in the garrison, but the Colonel will still be bound to go all along the line for him. So will I, if it means the G.O.C., and the High Command, the whole lot. And so will the battalion. It's an odd situation. Oh, perhaps Wullie understands it and plays on it. So what? I know the Provost Marshal's right: he's a drunken, dangerous, disgraceful, useless ruffian. But whenever I see him at his worst, I can't help thinking of him going through that desert, marching, and not falling. Just marching. Now, where's the ludo set? There isn't a subaltern can live with me on the board tonight.'

* * *

I have my own view of Wee Wullie, which is naturally coloured by my own experience of him. When I finally left the battalion, he was still there, pottering about the M.O.'s garden and fighting with the guard; they were still protecting him, rightly or wrongly. What is worth protecting? Anyway, his story is as I saw it, and as the second-in-command told it to me. Only the times have changed.

The General Danced at Dawn

Friday night was always dancing night. On the six other evenings of the week the officers' mess was informal, and we had supper in various states of uniform, mufti and undress, throwing bits of bread across the table and invading the kitchen for second helpings of caramel pudding. The veranda was always open, and the soft, dark night of North Africa hung around pleasantly beyond the screens.

Afterwards in the ante-room we played cards, or ludo, or occasional games of touch rugby, or just talked the kind of nonsense that subalterns talk, and whichever of these things we did our seniors either joined in or ignored completely; I have seen a game of touch rugby in progress, with the chairs and tables pushed back against the wall, and a heaving mass of Young Scotland wrestling for a 'ball' made of a sock stuffed with rags, while less than a yard away the Adjutant, two company commanders, and the M.O. were sitting round a card table holding an inquest on five spades doubled. There was great toleration.

Friday night was different. On that evening we dressed in our best tartans and walked over to the mess in two's and three's as soon as the solitary piper, who had been playing outside the mess for about twenty minutes, broke into the slow, plaintive 'Battle of the Somme' – or, as it is known colloquially, 'See's the key, or I'll roar up yer lobby'.

In the mess we would have a drink in the ante-room, the captains and the majors sniffing at their Talisker and Glengrant, and the rest of us having beer or orange juice – I have known messes where subalterns felt they had to drink hard stuff for fear of being thought cissies, but in a Highland mess nobody presses anybody. For one thing, no senior officer with a whisky throat wants to see his single malt being wasted on some pink and eager one-pipper.

Presently the Colonel would knock his pipe out and limp into the dining-room, and we would follow in to sit round the huge white table. I never saw a table like it, and never expect to; Lord Mayor's banquets, college dinners, and American conventions at 100 dollars a plate may surpass it in spectacular grandeur, but when you sat down at this table you were conscious of sitting at a dinner that had lasted for centuries.

The table was a mass of silver: the horse's-hoof snuff-box that was a relic of the few minutes at Waterloo when the regiment broke Napoleon's cavalry, and Wellington himself took off his hat and said, 'Thank you, gentlemen'; the set of spoons from some forgotten Indian palace with strange gods carved on the handles; the great bowl, magnificently engraved, presented by an American infantry regiment in Normandy, and the little quaich that had been found in the dust at Magersfontein; loot that had come from Vienna, Moscow, Berlin, Rome, the Taku Forts, and God knows where, some direct and some via French, Prussian, Polish, Spanish, and other regiments from half the countries on earth – stolen, presented, captured, bought, won, given, taken, and acquired by accident. It was priceless, and as you sat and contemplated it you could almost feel the shades elbowing you round the table.

At any rate, it enabled us to get through the tinned tomato soup, rissoles and jam tart, which seemed barely adequate to such a splendid setting, or to the sonorous grace which the padre had said beforehand ('I say, padre, can you say it in Gaelic?' 'Away, a' he talks is Glesca.' 'Whessht for the minister'). And when it was done and the youth who was vice-president had said, 'The King, passed the port in the wrong direction, giggled, upset his glass, and been sorrowfully rebuked from the table head, we lit up and waited for the piper. The voices, English of Sandhurst and Scottish of Kelvinside, Perthshire, and Peterhead, died away, and the pipe-major strode in and let us have it.

A twenty-minute pibroch is no small thing at a range of four feet. Some liked it, some affected to like it, and some buried their heads in their hands and endured it. But in everyone the harsh, keening siren-sound at least provoked thought. I can see them still, the faces round the table; the sad padre, tapping slowly to 'The Battle of the Spoiled Dyke'; the junior subaltern, with his mouth slightly open, watching the tobacco smoke wreathing in low clouds over the white cloth; the signals officer, tapping his thumb-nail against his teeth and shifting restlessly as he wondered if he would get away in time to meet that Ensa singer at the club; the Colonel, chin on fist like a great bald eagle with his pipe clamped between his teeth and his eyes two generations away; the men, the boys, the dreamer's eyes and the boozer's melancholy, all silent while the music enveloped them.

When it was over, and we had thumped the table, and the pipe-major had downed his whisky with a Gaelic toast, we would troop out again, and the Colonel would grin and rub tobacco between his palms, and say:

'Right, gentlemen, shall we dance?'

This was part of the weekly ritual. We would take off our tunics, and the pipers would make preparatory whines, and the Colonel would perch on a table, swinging his game leg which the Japanese had broken for him on the railway, and would say:

'Now, gentlemen, as you know there is Highland dancing as performed when ladies are present, and there is Highland dancing. We will have Highland dancing. In Valetta in '21 I saw a Strip the Willow performed in eighty-nine seconds, and an Eightsome reel in two minutes twenty-two seconds. These are our targets. All right, pipey.'

We lined up and went at it. You probably know both the dances referred to, but until you have seen Highland subalterns and captains giving them the treatment you just don't appreciate them. Strip the Willow at speed is lethal; there is much swinging round, and when fifteen stone of heughing humanity is whirled at you at close range you have to be wide awake to sidestep, scoop him in, and hurl him back again. I have gone up the line many times, and it is like being bounced from wall to wall of a long corridor with heavy weights attached to your arms. You just have to relax and concentrate on keeping upright.

Occasionally there would be an accident, as when the padre, his Hebridean paganism surging up through his Calvinstic crust, swung into the M.O., and the latter, his constitution undermined by drink and peering through microscopes, mistimed him and received him heavily amidships. The padre simply cried: 'The sword of the Lord and of Gideon!' and danced on, but the M.O. had to be carried to the rear and his place taken by the second-in-command, who was six feet four and a danger in traffic.

The Eightsome was even faster, but not so hazardous, and when it was over we would have a breather while the Adjutant, a lanky Englishman who was transformed by pipe music to a kind of Fred Astaire, danced a 'ragged trousers' and the cooks and mess waiters came through to watch and join in the gradually mounting rumble of stamping and applause. He was the clumsiest creature in everyday walking and moving, but out there, with his fair hair falling over his face and his shirt hanging open, he was like thistledown on the air; he could have left Nijinsky frozen against the cushion.

The pipe-sergeant loved him, and the pipe-sergeant had

skipped nimbly off with prizes uncounted at gatherings and games all over Scotland. He was a tiny, india-rubber man, one of your technically perfect dancers who had performed before crowned heads, viceroys, ambassadors, 'and all sorts of wog presidents and the like of that'. It was to mollify him that the Colonel would encourage the Adjutant to perform, for the pipe-sergeant disliked 'wild' dancing of the Strip the Willow variety, and while we were on the floor he would stand with his mouth primly pursed and his glengarry pulled down, glancing occasionally at the Colonel and sniffing.

'What's up, pipe-sarnt,' the Colonel would say, 'too slow for you?'

'Slow?' the pipe-sergeant would say. 'Fine you know, sir, it's not too slow for me. It's a godless stramash is what it is, and shouldn't be allowed. Look at the unfortunate Mr Cameron, the condition of him; he doesn't know whether it's Tuesday or breakfast.'

'They love it; anyway, you don't want them dancing like a bunch of old women.'

'No, not like old women, but chust like proper Highlandmen. There is a form, and a time, and a one-two-three, and a one-two-three, and thank God it's done and here's the lovely Adjutant.'

'Well, don't worry,' said the Colonel, clapping him on the shoulder. 'You get 'em twice a week in the mornings to show them how it ought to be done.'

This was so. On Tuesdays and Thursdays batmen would rouse officers with malicious satisfaction at 5.30, and we would stumble down, bleary and unshaven, to the M.T. sheds, where the pipe-sergeant would be waiting, skipping in the cold to put us through our session of practice dancing. He was in his element, bounding about in his laced pumps, squeaking at us while the piper played and we galumphed through our eightsomes and foursomes. Unlovely we were, but the pipe-sergeant was lost in the music and the mists of time, emerging from time to time to rebuke, encourage and commend.

'Ah, the fine sound,' he would cry, pirouetting among us. 'And a one, two, three, and a one, two, three. And there we are, Captain MacAlpine, going grand, going capital! One, two, three and oh, observe the fine feet of Captain MacAlpine! He springs like a startled ewe, he does! And a one, two, three, Mr Elphinstone-Hamilton, and a pas-de-bas, and, yes, Mr Cameron, once again. But now a one, two, three, four, Mr Cameron, and a one, two, three, four, and the rocking-step. Come to me, Mr Cameron, like a full-rigged ship. But, oh, dear God, the horns of the deer! Boldly, proudly, that's the style of the masterful Mr Cameron; his caber feidh is wonderful, it is fit to frighten Napoleon.'

He and Ninette de Valois would have got on a fair treat. The Colonel would sometimes loaf down, with his greatcoat over his pyjamas, and lean on his cromach, smoking and smiling quietly. And the pipe-sergeant, carried away, would skip all the harder and direct his running commentary at his audience of one.

'And a one, two, three, good morning to you, sir, see the fine dancing, and especially of Captain MacAlpine! One, two, three, and a wee bit more, Mr Cameron, see the fine horns of the deer, colonel sir, how he knacks his thoos, God bless him. Ah, yes, that is it, Mr Elphinstone-Hamilton, a most proper appearance, is it not, Colonel?'

'I used to think,' the Colonel would say later, 'that the pipe-sergeant must drink steadily from three a.m. to get into that elevated condition. Now I know better. The man's bewitched.'

So we danced, and it was just part of garrison life, until the word came of one of our periodic inspections, which meant that a general would descend from Cairo and storm through us, and report to G.H.Q. on our condition, and the Colonel, Adjutant, Regimental Sergeant Major and so on would either receive respective rockets or pats on the back. Especially the Colonel. And this inspection was rather more than ordinarily important to the old boy, because in two months he and the battalion would be going home, and soon after that he would be retiring. He should by rights have retired long before, but the war had kept him on, and he had stayed to the last possible minute. After all it was his life: he had gone with this battalion to France in '14 and hardly left it since; now he was going for good, and word went round that his last inspection on active service must be something for him to remember in his old age, when he could look back on a battalion so perfect that the inspecting general had not been able to find so much as a speck of whitewash out of place. So we hoped.

Now, it chanced that, possibly in deference to the Colonel, the Very Senior Officer who made this inspection was also very Highland. The pipe-sergeant rubbed his hands at the news. 'There will be dancing,' he said, with the air of the Creator establishing land and sea. 'General MacCrimmon will be enchanted; he was in the Argylls, where they dance a wee bit. Of course, being an Argyll he is chust a kind of Campbell, but it will have to be right dancing for him, I can assure you, one, two, three, and no lascivious jiving.'

Bursting with zeal, he worked our junior officers' dancing class harder than ever, leaping and exhorting until he had us exhausted; meanwhile, the whole barracks was humming with increased activity as we prepared for inspection. Arab sweepers brushed the parade ground with hand brushes to free it of dust, whitewash squads were everywhere with their buckets and stained overalls; every weapon in the place, from dirks and revolvers to the three-inch mortars, was stripped and oiled and cleaned three times over; the cookhouses, transport sheds, and even the little church, were meticulously gone over; Private McAuslan, the dirtiest soldier in the world, was sent on leave, squads roamed the barrack grounds continually, picking up paper, twigs, leaves, stones, and anything that might offend military symmetry; the Colonel snapped and twisted his handkerchief and broke his favourite pipe; sergeants became hoarse and fretful, corporals fearful, and the quartermasters and company clerks moved uneasily in the dark places of their stores, sweating in the knowledge of duty ill-done and judgment at hand. But, finally, we were ready; in other words we were clean. We were so tired that we couldn't have withstood an attack by the Tiller Girls, but we were clean.

The day came, and disaster struck immediately. The sentry at the main gate turned out the guard at the approach of the General's car, and dropped his rifle in presenting arms. That was fairly trivial, but the General commented on it as he stepped out to be welcomed by the Colonel, and that put everyone's nerves on edge; matters were not improved by the obvious fact that he was pleased to have found a fault so early, and was intent on finding more.

He didn't have far to look. He was a big, beefy man, turned out in a yellowing balmoral and an ancient, but beautifully cut kilt, and his aide was seven feet of sideways invisibility in one of the Guards regiments. The General announced that he would begin with the men's canteen ('men's welfare comes first with me; should come first with every officer'), and in the panic that ensued on this unexpected move the canteen staff upset a swill-tub in the middle of the floor five seconds before he arrived; it had been a fine swill-tub, specially prepared to show that we had such things, and he shouldn't have seen it until it had been placed at a proper distance from the premises.

The General looked at the mess, said 'Mmh,' and asked to see the medical room ('always assuming it isn't rife with bubonic plague'); it wasn't, as it happened, but the M.O.'s terrier had chosen that morning to give birth to puppies, beating the Adjutant to it by a short head. Thereafter a fire broke out in the cookhouse, a bren-gun carrier broke down, an empty cigarette packet was found in 'B' company's garden, and Private McAuslan came back off leave. He was tastefully dressed in shirt and boots, but no kilt, and entered the main gate in the company of three military policemen who had foolishly rescued him from a canal into which he had fallen. The General noted his progress to the guardroom with interest; McAuslan was alternately singing the Twenty-third Psalm and threatening to write to his Member of Parliament.

So it went on; anything that could go wrong, seemed to go wrong, and by dinner-time that night the General was wearing a sour and satisfied expression, his aide was silently contemptuous, the battalion was boiling with frustration and resentment, and the Colonel was looking old and ill. Only once did he show a flash of spirit, and that was when the junior subaltern passed the port the wrong way again, and the General sighed, and the Colonel caught the subaltern's eye and said loudly and clearly: 'Don't worry, Ian; it doesn't matter a damn.'

That finally froze the evening over, so to speak, and when we were all back in the ante-room and the senior major remarked that the pipe-sergeant was all set for the dancing to begin, the Colonel barely nodded, and the General lit a cigar and sat back with the air of one who was only mildly interested to see how big a hash we could make of this too.

Oddly enough, we didn't. We danced very well, with the pipe-sergeant fidgeting on the outskirts, hoarsely whispering, 'One, two, three,' and afterwards he and the Adjutant and two of the best subalterns danced a foursome that would have swept the decks at Braemar. It was good stuff, really good, and the General must have known it, but he seemed rather irritated than pleased. He kept moving in his seat, frowning, and when we had danced an eightsome he finally turned to the Colonel.

'Yes, it's all right,' he said. 'But, you know, I never cared much for the set stuff. Did you never dance a sixteensome?'

The Colonel said he had heard of such a thing, but had not, personally, danced it.

'Quite simple,' said the General, rising. 'Now, then. Eight more officers on the floor. I think I remember it, although it's years now . . .'

He did remember; a sixteensome is complicated, but its execution gives you the satisfaction that you get from any complex manoeuvre; we danced it twice, the General calling the changes and clapping (his aide was studying the ceiling with the air of an archbishop at a cannibal feast), and when it was over the General actually smiled and called for a large whisky. He then summoned the pipe-sergeant, who was looking disapproving.

'Pipe-sergeant, tell you what,' said the General. 'I have been told that back in the 'nineties the First Black Watch sergeants danced a thirty-twosome. Always doubted it, but suppose it's possible. What do you think? Yes, another whisky, please.'

The pipe-sergeant, flattered but slightly outraged, gave his opinion. All things were possible; right, said the General, wiping his mouth, we would try it.

The convolutions of an eightsome are fairly simple; those of a sixteensome are difficult, but a thirty-twosome is just murder. When you have thirty-two people weaving and circling it is necessary that each one should move precisely right, and that takes organisation. The General was an organiser; his tunic came off after half an hour, and his voice hoarsely thundered the time and the changes. The mess shook to the crash of feet and the skirling of the pipes, and at last the thirty-twosome rumbled, successfully, to its ponderous close.

'Dam' good! Dam' good!' exclaimed the General, flushed and applauding. 'Well danced, gen'men. Good show, pipe-sarn't! Thanks, Tom, don't mind if I do. Dam' fine dancing. Thirty-twosome, eh? That'll show the Black Watch!'

He seemed to sway a little as he put down his glass. It was midnight, but he was plainly waking up.

'Thirty-twosome, by Jove! Wouldn't have thought it possible.' A thought seemed to strike him. 'I say, pipe-sarn't, I wonder . . . d'you suppose that's as far as we can go? I mean is there any reason . . . ?'

He talked, and the pipe-sergeant's eyes bulged. He shook his head, the General persisted, and five minutes later we were all outside on the lawn and trucks were being sent for so that their headlights could provide illumination, and sixty-four of us were being thrust into our positions, and the General was shouting orders through cupped hands from the verandah.

'Taking the time from me! Right, pipers? It's p'fickly simple. S'easy. One, two, an' off we go!'

It was a nightmare, it really was. I had avoided being in the sixty-four; from where I was standing it looked like a crowd scene from 'The Ten Commandments', with the General playing Cecil de Mille. Officers, mess-waiters, batmen, swung into the dance as the pipes shrilled, setting to partners, circling forwards and back, forming an enormous ring, and heughing like things demented. The General bounded about the verandah, shouting; the pipe-sergeant hurtled through the sets, pulling, directing, exhorting; those of us watching clapped and stamped as the mammoth dance surged on, filling the night with its sound and fury.

It took, I am told, one hour and thirteen minutes by the Adjutant's watch, and by the time it was over the Fusiliers from the adjoining barracks were roused and lined along the wall, assorted Arabs had come to gaze on the wonders of civilisation, and the military police mobile patrol was also on hand. But the General was tireless; I have a vague memory of him standing on the tailboard of a truck, addressing the assembled mob; I actually got close enough to hear him exhorting the pipe-sergeant in tones of enthusiasm and entreaty:

'Pipe-sarn't! Pipey! May I call you Pipey? . . . never been done . . . three figures . . . think of it . . . hunner'n-twenty-eightsome . . . never another chance . . . try it . . . rope in the Fusiliers . . . massed pipers . . . regimental history . . . please, Pipey, for me . . .'

Some say that it actually happened, that a one hundred and twenty-eightsome reel was danced on the parade ground that night, General Sir Roderick MacCrimmon, K.C.B., D.S.O., and bar, presiding; that it was danced by Highlanders, Fusiliers, Arabs, military police, and three German prisoners of war; that it was danced to a conclusion, all figures. It may well have been; all I remember is a heaving, rushing crowd, like a mixture of Latin Carnival and Scarlett's uphill charge at Balaclava, surging ponderously to the sound of the pipes; but I distinctly recall one set in which the General, the pipe-sergeant, and what looked like a genuine Senussi in a burnous, swept by roaring, 'One, two, three,' and I know, too, that at one point I personally was part of a swinging human chain in which my immediate partners were the Fusiliers' cook-sergeant and an Italian café proprietor from down the road. My memory tells me that it rose to a tremendous crescendo just as the first light of dawn stole over Africa, and then all faded away, silently, in the tartan-strewn morning.

No one remembers the General leaving later in the day, although the Colonel said he believed he was there, and that the General cried with emotion. It may have been so, for the inspection report later congratulated the battalion, and highly commended the pipe-sergeant on the standard of the officers' dancing. Which was a mixed pleasure to the pipe-sergeant, since the night's proceedings had been an offence to his orthodox soul.

'Mind you,' he would say, 'General MacCrimmon had a fine agility at the pas-de-bas, and a decent sense of the time. Och, aye, he wass not bad, not bad . . . for a Campbell.'

Night Run to Palestine

I had two grandmothers, one Presbyterian, the other pagan. Each told me stories, in her own way. The pagan, an incredibly old, bright-eyed creature from the Far West, peopled the world with kelpies and pixies and giants, or fair cold princesses and their sea-rover lovers; these were the tales her people had brought in the long ships centuries ago. And sometimes she would tell of our more immediate mainland ancestors, of the Red Fox and Robin Roy Macgregor and the caterans of the Highlands and the dirty tricks they played each other. But always her stories were full of passion and fighting and magic and cunning stratagems, and above all, laughter. Watching her old, wrinkled face, so eager, and the play of her ancient thin hands, it was easy to believe that her own grandmother had known a woman who had seen the men coming back from the '45, thrusting their broadswords into the thatch for another time, and stamping while the tears ran down their faces. Afterwards she would give me a penny or a potato scone, which she baked with great skill.

My other grandmother had only one story, the point of which eludes me still. She was a Glencoe MacDonald, strong and of few words, worshipping a stern God on whom she kept a close eye to see that he didn't get up to anything the Presbytery wouldn't have approved of, like granting salvation to Catholics and Wee Frees. She frightened me, for she was hard and forbidding and insisted that we walk miles to church on Sundays. On these walks I was naturally forbidden to take my ball; on weekdays I could dribble it along beside her, and on one occasion she even condescended to kick it, watching it with a cold eye to see that it rolled straight. It did. And it was on that occasion that she told me the story; the sight of a distant train puffing along the hillside had brought it to mind.

It appears that on the West Highland railway near Tyndrum there was a steep hill. A train of cattle in open trucks was steaming up it, when a coupling broke and the trucks began to run back downhill. In the rear truck was the elderly guard and a young assistant, and the guard, as the train gathered speed, cried to the young man:

'When you see me shump, you shump too. Better to be killed on the bank than smochtered among the cattle.'

They had both jumped, and the young man broke his ankle and the old guard smashed his watch, and the train thundered on to the bottom of the hill and glided gradually to a stop in perfect safety.

At this point my grandmother paused, and I waited for the punchline. She stood gazing out across the glen with that stony look that she would fasten on the minister if he looked like letting up in his sermon after a mere forty minutes; her mind was away somewhere else.

'And that,' she said impressively at last, 'is what happened on the West Highland railway.'

I thought it was a pretty feeble story then, and it doesn't look much better in retrospect, although I have a feeling she saw a point to it which she didn't explain. But both the story and that grim old lady who told it come back to me every time I smell engine smoke or hear a whistle wail. I have remembered it on the long haul across the prairies, where the horizon stretches out for ever; on the sweaty Punjab Mail, jam-packed inside with white-robed Orientals, with more on the roof and in the windows and doorways and fat babus clinging for dear life a yard above the tracks; in the damp, blacked-out, blue-lit corridors of war-time trains clanking on and halting interminably;

in football specials carrying the raucous, boozed-up supporters to Wembley; in a huge German train rattling across France with its solemn script notices, like ancient texts, telling you that pots were to be found under the seats, by order; in little trains at country halts, where beyond the misted windows you could see the glare of the porters' lamps and hear the sudden bang of a carriage door and the lonely call of 'Symington!' or 'Tebay!'

Most of all I remembered it on the Cairo–Jerusalem run in 1946 or '47, when the Stern Gang and the Irgun were at large, and the windows were sometimes boarded because the glass had been shot out, and lines were being blown up, and the illegal immigrant ships were coming in through the blockade, and a new nation was being uncomfortably born in a welter of hatred and confusion and total misunderstanding on all sides. Ben Hecht was having a holiday in his heart every time a British soldier died, and British soldiers were having a holiday in theirs at the prospect of getting away from a country they detested, in which some kind of illusion was shattered for them because the names of Bible stories had turned out to be places where machine-pistols rattled and grenades came in through windows. In the U.N. there was much talk and seeking of viable solutions and exploration of channels, and in the Palestine clubs young subalterns danced with their guns pushed round out of the way but still handy.

It was my gun that had got me into trouble. I had been on a course up at Acre – one of those courses where you walk miles across stony hills and look at maps, and a Guards officer instructor says, 'Now this is the picture . . .' – and I was staying one night in Cairo before flying on to the battalion, which was living away along the North African coast, blancoing itself and playing football hundreds of miles from the shooting. Being me, I set off for the airport in the morning without my pistol, which was in the transit camp armoury, and so I missed my plane.

You simply could not travel in those days without your gun; not that it was dangerous where I was going. It was just The Law. So I turned back for it, and the Movements Officer had a fit. Missing a plane was practically a capital charge. Apart from that, I couldn't get another for several days, so they looked for something unpleasant for me to do while I was waiting.

'You can be O.C. train to Jerusalem tonight,' said the Movements Officer, with sadistic satisfaction. 'Report to Victoria Station at twenty-two hundred hours, don't be late, and this time take your blasted gun with you.'

So I had a bath, played snooker against myself all afternoon, and in the neon-lit Cairo evenfall rolled up to Victoria, clutching my little pistol in a damp palm. I fought my way through a press of enormous dragomans – huge, ugly people with brass badges who offer to carry your kit, and when you agree they whistle up some tiny assistant who shoulders your trunks and staggers off like an ant under a haystack. The dragoman doesn't carry anything; he just clears a way, roaring, and demands an exorbitant fee.

The Movements Office gave me a great sheaf of documents, a few instructions on how to command a troop train, reminded me that we left at ten sharp, and waved me away. The place looked like a stock market during a boom, everyone was running and shouting and chalking on boards; I got out to the bar, where sundry wellwishers cheered me up with anecdotes about the Jerusalem run.

'Tell me they're blowing one train in three,' said an American Air Corps major.

'Doing it dam' neatly, too,' said a captain in the Lincolns. ''Course, most of 'em are British or American-trained. On our side a year or two ago.'

A quarter-master from the South Lancs said the terrorists' equipment and stores were of the finest: Jerry landmines, piles o' flamin' gun-cotton, and more electrical gear than the G.P.O.

'Schmeiser machine-pistols,' said the American cheerfully. 'Telescopic sights. Draw a bead on your ear at six hundred yards with those crossed wires – then, bam! You've had it. Who's having another?'

'Trouble is, you can't tell friend from foe,' said the Lincoln. 'No uniforms, dam' nasty. Thanks, Tex, don't mind if I do. Well, thank God they don't get me past Gaza again; nice low demob. group, my number'll be up in a month or two. Cheers.'

I said I had better be getting along to my train, and they looked at me reflectively, and I picked up my balmoral, dropped my papers, scrabbled them up, and went out in search of Troop Train 42, Jerusalem via Zagazig, Gaza and Tel Aviv, officer commanding Lt MacNeill, D., and the best of luck to him.

The platform was jammed all along its narrow length; my cargo looked like the United Nations. There were Arab Legion in their red-checked head-cloths, leaning on their rifles and saying nothing to anybody, A.T.S. giggling in little groups and going into peals of laughter at the attempts of one of them to make an Egyptian tea-seller understand that she didn't take milk; service wives and families on the seats, the women wearing that glassy look of worn-out boredom and the children scattering about and bumping and shrieking; a platoon of long bronzed Australians, bush-hatted and talking through their noses; worried-looking majors and red-faced, phlegmatic corporals; at least one brigadier, red-tabbed, trying to look as though he was thinking of something important and was unaware of the children who were playing tig round him; unidentified semi-military civilians of the kind you get round bases – correspondents, civil servants, welfare and entertainment organisers; dragomans sweeping majestically ahead of their porters and barking strange Arabic words. Hurrying among them, swearing pathetically, was a fat little man with R.T.O. on his sleeve and enormous khaki shorts on his withers;

he seized on me and shouted above the noise of people and escaping steam.

'Stone me! You MacNeill? What a blasted mess! You've got the short straw, you have. Fourteen service families, Gawd knows how many kids, but they're all in the manifest. A.T.S. an' all. I said we shouldn't have it, ought to be eighty per cent troops on any troop train, but you might as well talk to the wind that dried your first shirt.' He shoved another sheaf of papers at me. 'You can cope, anyway. Just don't let any of 'em off before Jerusalem, that's all. There's at least two deserters under escort, but they're in the van, handcuffed. It's the civvies you've got to watch for; they don't like taking orders. If any of 'em get uppity, threaten to shoot 'em, or better still threaten to drop 'em off in a nice stretch of desert – there's plenty. Damn my skin, I'm misting up again!' He removed his spectacles from his pug nose, wiped them on a service hankie, and replaced them; he was running sweat down his plump red cheeks. 'Now then, there's a padre who's worried about the A.T.S., God knows why, but he knows his own mind best, I dare say; keep an eye on the Aussies, but you know about them. And don't let the wog who's driving stop except at stations – that's important. If he tries, don't threaten to shoot *him*, just tell him he'll lose his pension. An' remember, you're the boss; to hell with ranks, they don't count on a train. You're the skipper, got it?'

The loudspeaker boomed overhead.

'Attention, please, attention. Will Captain Tanner please go to platform seven, plat-form sev-en. Captain Tanner, please.'

'All right, all right,' said the little man, savagely. 'I can only be one place at a time, can't I? Where was I? Oh, yes, you've a second-in-command, over there.' He pointed to a figure, standing alone near the engine. 'One of your crowd,' he added, looking at my tartan shoulder-flash. 'Seems all right. Sergeant Black!' he shouted, and the figure came over to us.

He was about middle height, with the big spreading chest

and shoulders you often see in Highland regiments; his chin was blue and his profile was like a Red Indian's under the tilted bonnet with its red hackle. He was neat, professional, and as hard as a gangster, and he had the M.M. in front of the Africa and Italy ribbons. A pair of stony eyes looked me over, but he didn't say anything.

'The run takes about seven hours,' went on the R.T.O. He stopped and shuffled his papers. He was thinking. 'If you hit trouble,' he said at last, 'you use your initiative. Sorry it's not much help, but there you are. You've got some signallers, and the telegraph line's never far away. You'll be O.K. as far as Gaza anyway; after that there's more chance of . . . well, anyway, it's not likely there'll be any bother.'

The loudspeaker crackled again for Captain Tanner.

'Oh, shut up!' he snapped. 'Honest, it's the only blasted name they know. Well, look, you're off in about ten minutes. Better start getting 'em aboard. I'll get a bleat for you on the tannoy. Best of luck.' He hurried off, and then turned back. 'Oh, one other thing; there's a captain's wife with a baby and she thinks it's getting German measles. I wouldn't know.'

He bustled off into the crowd, and as he disappeared I felt suddenly lonely and nervous. One train, two hundred people – a good third of them women and children – seemed a lot of responsibility, especially going into a country on fire with civil strife and harried by armed terrorist gangs. Two deserters, a worried padre, and possible German measles. Oh, well, first things first. How does one start clearing a crowded platform into a train?

'Sergeant Black,' I said, 'have you made this trip before?'

'No, sir.'

'Oh. I see. Well, start getting them aboard, will you?'

God bless the British sergeant. He flicked his bonnet with his hand, swung round, and thundered, 'All aboard for Jerusalem,' as though he had been a stationmaster all his life. The tannoy boomed into sound overhead and there was a general move towards the train. Sergeant Black moved in among the crowd, pointing and instructing – he seemed to know, by some God-given instinct, what to do – and I went to look at the engine.

I'm no authority, but it looked pretty rickety, and the genial Arab driver seemed to be in the grip of some powerful intoxicating drug. He had a huge laugh and a glassy eye, spoke no English, and fiddled with his controls in a reckless, unnerving way. I thought of asking him if he knew the way to Jerusalem, but it would have sounded silly, so I climbed into the front carriage, dumped my hand baggage on a seat in the compartment marked 'O.C. Train, Private' (with the added legend 'Kilroy was here – he hated it') and set off down the corridor to tour the train.

It was like the lower gun-deck of the Fighting Temeraire at Trafalgar, a great heaving mass of bodies trying to sort themselves out. There were no Pullman cars, and the congestion in the carriage doorways was brutal. I worked my way through to the guard's van, and found Sergeant Black eyeing the two deserters, tow-headed ruffians handcuffed to a staple on the wall.

'Let them loose,' he was saying to the M.P. escort.

'I'm responsible . . .' the M.P. began, and Black looked at him. There was one of those pregnant silences while I examined the instructions on the fire extinguisher, and then the M.P. muttered some defiance and unlocked the handcuffs. Sergeant Black lit a cigarette and tapped the butt of his Luger.

'See, you two,' he said. 'Run for it, and I'll blow yer — — — — heids aff.' He caught sight of me and nodded. 'Awright this end, sir.'

'So I see,' I said and beckoned him out in the corridor. 'You think it's safe to loose those two?'

'Well, it's like this. If there's trouble, it's no' right they should be tied up.'

'You mean if we hit the Stern Gang?'

'Aye.'

I thought about this, but not for long. There would certainly be other, more important decisions to make on the journey, and there was no point in worrying myself at this stage about the security of two deserters who were hardly likely to take off into the desert anyway. So I allotted Sergeant Black the rear half of the train, struggled back to my place at the front, checked my notorious pistol to see that it was loaded, satisfied myself that everyone was off the platform, and settled down with *The Launching of Roger Brook*, which was the current favourite with the discerning literati, although closely challenged by two other recent productions, *Animal Farm* and *Forever Amber*. The train suddenly heaved and clanked, and we were off.

The Cairo–Jerusalem run is one of the oldest and most well-worn routes in the world. By train in those days you went due north towards the Nile delta and then swung east through Zagazig to Ismailia on the Canal. Then north along the Canal again to El Kantara, 'the Bridge' by which Mary and Joseph travelled and before them Abraham. Then you are running east again along the coast, with the great waste of the Sinai on your right and the Mediterranean on your left. This was the way the world walked in the beginnings of recorded time, Roman, Arab, Assyrian, Greek; if you could talk to everyone who used this road you could write the history of the human race. Everyone was here, except the Children of Israel who made it the hard way, farther south. And now they were trying to make it again, from a different direction, over the sea from Europe and elsewhere – still the hard way, they being Jews.

The tracks stick to the coast as far as the Palestine border, where the names become familiar, echoing childhood memories of Sunday school and the Old Testament – Rafa and Gaza and Askalon away to the left, where the daughters of the uncircumcised were getting ready to cheer for Goliath; and then the line curves slowly away from the coast to Lydda, and doubles almost back on itself for the last lap south and east into Jerusalem.

At various points along the route Samson had destroyed the temple, Philip had begun preaching the gospel, Herod had been born, the Lord smote the thousand thousand Ethiopians, Peter cured in the name of Jesus, Solomon dreamed of being wise, and Uzziah broke down the walls of Jabneh. And Lt MacNeill, D., was following in their footsteps with Troop Train 42, which just shows that you can always go one better.

We had just rattled through Zagazig and Roger Brook was squaring up to the finest swordsman in France when there was a knock at my door and there stood a tall, thin man with a big Adam's apple knocking on his dog collar, wearing the purple-edged pips of the Royal Army Chaplain's Department. He peered at me through massive horn-rims and said:

'There are A.T.S. travelling on this train.'

I admitted it; and he sucked in his breath.

'There are also officers of the Royal Air Force.'

His voice was husky, and you could see that, to his mind, Troop Train 42 was a potential White Slave Special. In his experience, R.A.F. types and A.T.S. were an explosive formula.

'I shouldn't worry, padre,' I said, 'I'm sure . . .'

'But I must worry,' he said indignantly. 'After all, if we were not in this train, it would be time for Lights Out. These young girls would be asleep. The young men . . .' he paused; he wasn't so sure about the young men. 'I think that, as O.C. train, you should ensure that a curfew of compartments is observed after eleven o'clock,' he finished up.

'I doubt if there's any regulation . . .'

'You could enforce it. You have the authority.'

That was true enough: an O.C. train, however junior in rank, is like the captain of a ship; obviously he exercises tact where big brass is concerned, but when the chips are down he is the man. But authority cuts two ways. Now that I'd been reminded of it, I resented having a young sky-pilot (he was ribbonless and under 30), telling me my job. I got formal.

'A curfew would be impractical,' I said. 'But I shall be patrolling the train from time to time, as will my sergeant.

You could see he was wondering about that, too. He looked at me doubtfully and muttered something about spiritual duty and promiscuity. Plainly he was a nut. After shifting from one foot to the other for a moment, he bade me good night unhappily, and lurched off down the corridor, colliding with a fresh-faced young flight-lieutenant who was coming the other way. The R.A.F. type was full of bonhomie, duty-free in the Service.

'Hiya, Padre,' said he. 'Playing at home this weather, eh?'

'I beg your pardon?'

'Well, this is your territory, isn't it?' said the youth. 'Y'know, bound for the Holy Land. Genesis, Exodus, Leviticus, Jezebel,' he waved expansively, 'Goliath of Gath, Sodom and Gomorrah and Gomorrah and Gomorrah creeps in this petty pace from day to day . . .

I went inside quickly and closed the door. Something told me the padre was going to have a worrying trip.

He wasn't the only one, although it was past El Kantara that the next interruption came. I had taken a trip along the train, and seen that everyone was reasonably installed for the night, conferred with Sergeant Black, and come back to my compartment. Roger Brook had pinked the villain long ago, and was now rifling the Marquis's closet for the secret plans, when the knock came.

It was a small A.T.S., blonde and snub-nosed, wearing two stripes. She saluted smartly and squeaked at me.

'Please, sir, could something be done about our carriage window? It's broken and boarded up, and Helen is in a draught.

Actually, we all are, sir; it's very cold. But Helen feels it most.'

A young officer appealed to by A.T.S. is a sorry sight. He becomes tremendously paternal and dignified, as only a 21-year-old can. Elderly staff officers look like babbling lads beside him. He frowns thoughtfully, and his voice drops at least two octaves. I was no exception.

'Very good, corporal,' I said, sounding like Valentine Dyall with a heavy cold. 'Show me the way, please.'

She bounced off, with me following. Her billet was two coaches behind, and as we entered the second one I glanced into a compartment and found the padre staring at me with a mistrustful eye. Quis custodiet, by gum, he was thinking, so to assure him that all was well I gave him a big smile and the O.K. sign, thumb and forefinger together, other fingers raised. A second after I did it, I realised that it was open to misunderstanding, but it was too late then.

There were seven other A.T.S. in the compartment, shivering, with the wind whistling through the boarded window. They emitted cries, and while the corporal told them it was O.K. now, because the O.C. train would fix it in person, I ploughed through their piles of kitbags, shoes, parcels, and general clutter to the window. There was a big crack in the boarding, but it looked as though it could be forced to quite easily.

'Can you manage, sir?' they cried. 'Will it shut?' 'I'm freezing.' 'Help him, Muriel.'

I heaved at the board and the whole damned thing came loose and vanished into the Palestine night. A tremendous blast of cold night air came in through the empty window. They shrieked.

'Oh, he's broken it!'

'Oh, it's perishing!'

'These Highlanders,' said a soulful-looking A.T.S. with an insubordinate sniff, 'don't know their own strength.'

'Take it easy,' I said, nonplussed, to coin a phrase. 'Er, corporal, I think they'd better all move into the corridor . . .'

'Into the corridor!' 'We can't stay there all night.' 'We're entitled to a compartment' – even in the A.T.S. they had barrack-room lawyers, yet.

'. . . into the corridor until I get you fixed in other compartments,' I said. 'You can't stay here.'

'Too right we can't.' 'Huh, join the A.T.S. and freeze to death.' 'Some people.' Mutters of mutiny and discontent while they gathered up their belongings.

I trampled out, told the corporal to keep them together, and, if possible to keep them quiet, and headed up the train. There was a compartment, I remembered, with only two officers in it. I knocked on its door, and a pouchy eye looked out at me.

'Well, what is it?' He was a half-colonel, balding and with a liverish look. I explained the situation.

'I thought you might not object if, say, four of the girls came in here, sir. It's one of the few compartments that isn't full.' Looking past him, I could see the other man, a major, stretched out on a seat.

'What? Bring A.T.S. in here?'

'Yes, sir, four of them. I can get the other four placed elsewhere.'

'This is a first-class compartment,' he snapped. 'A.T.S. other ranks travel third.'

'Yes, I know, but their compartment hasn't got a window . . .'

'Then I suggest you find them one that has.'

'I'm afraid there isn't one; they're all full.'

'That is your business. And I would point out that you have no right to suggest that they move in here.'

'Why not, for Pete's sake? Look,' I said, trying to sound reasonable, 'they have to go somewhere . . .'

'Don't address me in that way,' he barked. 'What's your name?'

'MacNeill.'

'MacNeill what?'

He had me there. 'MacNeill, sir.'

He gave me a nasty look. 'Well, MacNeill, I suggest that you study the regulations governing the movement of troop trains. Also the limitations of authority of damned young whipper-snappers who are put in charge of them, but are not, strange as it may seem, empowered to address their superiors in an insolent manner, or request them to vacate their compartments in favour of A.T.S.'

'I didn't ask you to vacate your compartment, sir,' I said, my voice shaking just a little, as it always does when I'm in that curious state half-way between backing down shamefaced and belting somebody. 'I merely asked, since they *are* women . . .'

'Don't dam' well argue,' said the man lying on the seat, speaking for the first time.

'No,' said the pouchy half-colonel. 'Don't argue, if you know what's good for you.' And he shut the door.

I stood there, hesitating. The choice was clear. I could fling open the door and give him a piece of my mind, taking the consequences, or I could creep off towards my own compartment. Eventually I compromised, creeping away and giving him a piece of my mind as I did so, in a reckless whisper. Not that it helped: the A.T.S. were still homeless and had to be fitted in somewhere.

I needn't have worried. When I got back to the corridor where I had left them it was empty, but shrieks of female laughter led me to the primitive restaurant car, where they had found refuge with a mixed company of R.A.F. and our gallant Australian cousins. From the way these two branches of the service were looking at one another it was obvious that the A.T.S. were safer than they would have been in a convent; jealousy would see to that. Both sides were making heavy running, one big lean Aussie explaining to three of the

A.T.S. what a didgery-doo was, and offering them sips from his hip-flask, while my Biblical flight-lieutenant was leading the remainder in the singing of 'Bless''em all', the revised version. I just hoped the padre was a sound sleeper.

Thereafter things were fairly uneventful for about an hour. A fight broke out in one compartment because somebody snored; the soulful-looking A.T.S. girl was sick – as a result, she insisted, of what the Australian had given her from his hip-flask; she hinted darkly that he had wanted to drug her, which seemed unlikely – a kitbag mysteriously fell from a window and the owner was only just prevented from pulling the communication cord, and one of the Arab Legion got locked in the lavatory. These things I observed on my hourly tour of the train; the Arab Legionnaire's predicament I came on after pushing through a small group of well-wishers singing 'Oh, dear, what can the matter be?' I scattered them, and watched with interest while Sergeant Black painstakingly shouted orders through the locked door. It did no good; the entrapped one alternately bawled dreadful Arabic words and beat the panelling, and sent out a keening wail which was probably a lament that T. E. Lawrence hadn't minded his own business in the first place. Finally Black lost his temper and upbraided the man in purest Perthshire, at which the door flew open and the occupant, his face suffused, emerged with his rifle at the trail – why he had it with him he alone knew.

I congratulated Black and strolled back towards my compartment, speculating on whether there was an affinity between Arabic and the Crieff dialect, or whether the Arab had finally found how the bolt worked. I was pondering this in the corridor and listening to the rumbling ring of the wheels and looking through the window at the scrubstudded desert, black and silver in the moonshine, when the compartment door nearest me opened and a dishevelled young captain emerged, clutching a bundle. Beyond him a young woman was sitting with another bundle over her knees; both bundles were wailing plaintively and the compartment, which was otherwise unoccupied, was littered with clothes, towels, small clothes, utensils, and all the paraphernalia that an ignorant young bachelor associates with children.

'Yes, dear, I'll try,' the man was saying. 'There, there, Petey-Petey, all right, all right.'

'And it *must* be sterilised,' called the young woman, agitated. 'They must have some boiling water, somewhere. Yes, yes, Angie dear, mummy's going to fix it as soon as she possibly can . . . *Do* hurry, dear, please!'

'Yes, darling, I *am* hurrying, as fast as I can. What shall I do with Petey?'

'Not on that seat!' cried the mother. 'He'll roll off!'

'Oh, God!' said the man, wild-eyed. He saw me. 'Have you any idea where there's boiling water?'

Some questions are best answered with a helpless gape.

'Please, Charles, hurry! Oh, no, Angela, did you have to?'

'She hasn't!' said the man, aghast.

'Oh, she has. Again. And I've only got a few clean ones left. Oh, Charles, do go for that water. It's past feeding-time. Oh, Angela.'

'Right, dear. What shall I . . . ?' He wheeled on me. 'Look, can you hold Petey for a moment? I shan't be an instant.'

'Why, er . . .'

'Good man.' Harassed, he very gently passed the tiny bundle to me. It was stirring manfully, and letting out a noise that my toilet-locked Arab would have envied. 'Got him? Just like that: marvellous. I'm going, darling; this gentleman . . .'

'What? Oh, Angela, you little horror! Oh, really, I never knew babies could be so foul!'

'I'm leaving Petey with this . . . this officer,' cried the man. 'With Mr, er . . .'

'MacNeill.'

'Mr MacNeill. How d'ye do? My name's Garnett. This is my wife . . .'

'How do you do?' I said, clutching Petey tenderly.

'Charles! Please!'

'Yes, dear.' He grabbed a feeding-bottle and fled. Two seconds later he was back. 'Darling, where will I get the water?'

'Oh, darling, how do I know? The engine, or someplace. The train runs on boiling water, doesn't it?'

'Oh, yes,' he said, and fled again.

I sat down opposite Mrs Garnett. Angela, disrobed, was lying across her knees squealing blue murder, while her mother, frantically sorting among the litter on the seat, cried endearments and shocking threats in turn. I turned Petey as though he were made of eggshells; I like babies, and the feel of his tiny, squirming body was somehow delightful. So was the tiny red face, all screwed up and raging as it was, eyes tight shut, minute toothless gums showing, and little legs kicking under his dress. My delight was temporary; I became aware that all was not well with Petey.

'Er,' I said. 'Er, I think Petey has . . .'

She seemed to see me for the first time. Normally she would have been a pretty, dark-haired young woman; now, clutching a nappy in one hand, and trying to steady her young with the other, her hair disordered and her manner disturbed, she looked like a gypsy wench preparing to attack a gamekeeper.

'Of course he has,' she snarled. 'They always do it together. I had to have twins! Oh, Angela, please lie still. Still, dearest! Mummy's trying to get you all comfy, you little monster! There, darling, Mummy has some nice, cool cream for iddums.' She was trying to tuck the nappy under Angela's midriff, and making rough work of it.

'But,' I said. 'What . . . I mean . . .' Petey was getting noxious. He suddenly changed gear in his screaming, taking up a new, intense note.

'Oh, dear, Petey-Petey!' She was distraught for her other young now. 'Just a minute, precious! Lie still, Angela, dearest, blast you! Well, don't just sit holding him! Do something!' She spared a hand to hurl nappies across. 'Change him, can't you?'

Ask me that question today, and rusty as I am with lack of practice, you will see an efficient response. I know the drill: newspaper on the floor, up with the dress, child face down and lightly gripped with the left hand; rubber pants down to knee-level with two swift pulls either side, pins out and thrust into the upholstery convenient to hand, nappy drawn down cleanly as child is slightly raised with left hand to permit front of nappy to come away; pause and gulp, drop nappy on to paper and fold paper over it with foot, mop the patient, anoint with cream to accompaniment of some rhythmic chant, whip clean nappy on and, with encouraging cries, pin one side, up and under, pin the other, make sure child has not been transfixed in process, up with rubber pants, and congratulations. Thirty seconds if you're lucky.

Today, yes, but this was many years ago, and all I knew of baby care was prodding them in the navel and saying 'Grrrtsh'. Changing nappies was outside my experience, and the way little Petey was delivering I wanted it to stay outside. Yet the British soldier is meant to be capable of anything. Could Wellington have changed a nappy? Or Marlborough? Doubtful. Or Slim? Yes, I decided, Slim could have changed a nappy, and almost certainly had. So for the honour of XIVth Army I began painfully and messily to strip Master Petey's abominable lower reaches, and in my innocence I sang him a lullaby at the same time – the old Gaelic one that goes 'Hovan, hovan gorriago' and relates how the fairies stole away a baby from a careless mother. Mrs Garnett said that was all right with her, and what would they charge for twins?

So we worked away, myself the brutal soldier humming

and coo-cooing, and the gentle mother opposite rebuking her daughter in terms that would have made a Marine corporal join the Free Kirk. And I was just pausing before the apparently impossible task of slipping a nappy on to the tiny creature, and marvelling at the very littleness of the squirming atom, with its perfect little fingers and their minia are nails, and pondering the wonder that he would probably grow into a great, hairy-chested ruffian full of sin and impudence, when the lights went out.

Mrs Garnett shrieked; I just clamped my hands as gently as I could on Petey and held on. My first thought, naturally enough, was of terrorists, until I realised that we were still a good way from the border, and the train was still rattling on. I assured her that everything was all right, and that Petey was in great shape – he wasn't, actually; he was at it again, spoiling all my good work – and presently the man Garnett came lumbering up the corridor, calling for directions and announcing that there was no hot water to be had, and what had happened to the lights.

It seemed to me I should be doing something about it, as O.C. train, so in the darkness I negotiated with him for the return of his infant, whom he accepted with exclamations of fatherly affection, changing to disgust, but by that time I was off roaring for Sergeant Black. I found him in the guard's van, with a candle and a fusebox; he and an Arab in dungarees – who he was, heaven knows – were wrestling in the dark with wires, and presently the lights blinked on again.

'Just a fuse,' he said. 'No panic.'

'Is that right?' I said. 'You try grappling with an independent baby in the dark. Which reminds me, there's a woman back there wants boiling water.'

'In the name of God,' said Sergeant Black. 'Is she havin' a wean?'

'Don't say that, even in jest,' I said. 'It's about all that hasn't happened on this bloody train so far. She wants to sterilise a feeding-bottle. How about it?'

He said he would see what he could do, pulled down his bonnet, and set off up the train. Within a quarter of an hour there was boiling water, feeding-bottles were being sterilised, and Mrs Garnett was being rapturously thankful. The sergeant had realised that although the restaurant car was without actual cooking appliances, there was at least a place where a fire could be lit.

After that there was peace until we reached the border. Black and I stood together at an open window near the front of the train, looking out over the desert and wondering about it. Up ahead was Gaza, where we were due for a stop; after that there was the Holy Land, where the Stern Gang and the Irgun operated. I said that probably we wouldn't see any trouble; Black scratched his blue chin and said, 'Aye'. It was getting cold. I went back to my compartment and tried to get some sleep.

We drew into Gaza not long after, and everyone got off for tea or coffee at the platform canteen, except Black and the prisoners. We crowded the platform and I was halfway through my second cup and discussing child psychology with Captain Garnett when I suddenly realised that the crowd wasn't as thick as it had been five minutes before. But I didn't think they had got back on the train; where, then, were they going? Troops moving by train were confined to the platform at all halts; anywhere else was out of bounds. Oh, God, I thought, they're deserting.

They weren't, in fact. They were playing the Gaza Game, which was a feature of Middle Eastern travel in those days. It worked like this. At Gaza, you changed your Egyptian pounds for the Military Administration Lire (mals) used in Palestine. The exchange rate was, say, 100 mals per £E1 at the currency control post on Gaza station. But if you knew the Game, you were aware that in a back street a few hundred yards from the station there dwelt Ahmed el Bakbook of the Thousand Fingers, otherwise Ahmed the Chatterer, who would give 120 mals per £E1. So you went to him, changed your £E to mals, hastened to the control office, changed your mals back to £E, raced off to Ahmed again, did another change, and so on until you had to board the train, showing a handsome profit. How the economies of Egypt and Palestine stood it I wouldn't know, nor yet how Ahmed made a living at it. But that was how it worked, as I discovered when I was investigating the sudden exodus from the platform, and was accosted by the pouchy lieutenant-colonel who claimed to have detected several soldiers sneaking out of the station. Oh, he knew what they were up to, all right, he said, and what was I doing, as O.C. train, to stop it? I was keen enough on finding A.T.S. girls billets to which they were not entitled, but I appeared to be unable to control the troops under my command. Well, well, and so on.

Personally, I couldn't have cared less if the troops had changed the entire monetary reserves of Egypt into roubles, at any rate of exchange, but technically he was right, which was why I found myself a few moments later pounding down a dirty back alley in Gaza, damning the day I joined the Army. In a dirty shop, easily identified by the khaki figures furtively sneaking in and out, I confronted a revolting Arab. He was sitting at a big plain table, piled with notes and silver, with an oil lamp swinging overhead and a thug in a burnous at his elbow.

He gave me a huge smile, all yellow fangs and beard, and said, 'How much, lieutenant?'

'You,' I said, 'are conducting an illegal traffic in currency.'

'Granted,' he replied. 'What do you require?'

'Dammit,' I said. 'Stop it.'

He looked hurt. 'Is not possible,' he said. 'I fill a need. That is all.'

'You'll be filling a cell in Acre jail when the military police get wise to you,' I said.

'Everyone gets out of Acre jail, you know?' he said cheerfully. 'And you do not suggest I work in defiance of the military police? They do not trouble me.'

He was just full of confidence, a little amused, a little surprised. I wondered if I was hearing right.

'Come on, old boy, get a move on,' said a voice behind. One of the R.A.F. types was standing there with his wallet out. 'Time presses, and all that. And you did jump the queue, you know.'

I gave up. Ahmed dealt courteously with the R.A.F. type, and then asked me almost apologetically how much I wanted to change. I answered him coldly, and he shrugged and dealt with the next customer. Then he asked me again, remarked that it must be getting near train time, and pointed out that since I had already infringed the regulations myself by leaving the station, I might as well take advantage of his unrivalled service.

He was right, of course, this good old man. I shovelled across my £E, accepted his mals, declined his invitation to join him in a draught of Macropoulos's Fine Old Highland Dew Scotch Whisky – 'a wee-doch-and-dorus', as he called it – and fled back to the station. I had no time to make another transaction, but I looked in at the currency office to see how trade was going, and asked the Royal Army Pay Corps sergeant if he was not worried about six months on the Hill at Heliopolis for knowingly assisting the traffic in black market exchange.

'Don't make me laugh,' he said. 'I'm buyin' a pub on the Great West Road when I get my ticket.'

My lieutenant-colonel was still on the platform. He had watched several score military personnel leave the station, he said, and I had done nothing that he could see to stop them. Would I explain? His manner was offensive.

I asked him what he, as an officer, had done about it himself, he went pale and told me not to be impertinent, and after a few more exchanges I said rudely that I was not responsible to him for how I conducted the affairs of Troop Train 42, and he assured me that he would see that disciplinary action was taken against me. I got on the train again shaking slightly with anger and, I admit it, apprehension, and ran slap into the padre, who was all upset about the A.T.S. still.

I needed him. Perhaps I was overwrought, but I told him rather brusquely to stop bringing me unnecessary complaints, to mind his own business, to go back to his compartment, and generally to get off my neck. He was indignant, and shocked, he said. I advised him again to go back to his compartment, and he said stiffly that he supposed he must take my orders, but he would certainly make a report . . .

'All right, padre,' I said. 'Do that. But for the present just remember that to obey is better than sacrifice, and hearkening than the fat of rams. O.K.?'

He said something about the Devil and Scripture, and I went back to my compartment pretty depressed. It seemed suddenly that I had loused things up fairly substantially: two rockets were on the way, I had failed to control the troops efficiently at Gaza, I hadn't covered myself with glory in accommodating the A.T.S., I couldn't even change a nappy. What was I good for? I lay down and fell asleep.

Your real hero can sleep through an elephant stampede, but wakes at the sound of a cat's footfall. I can sleep through both. But the shriek of ancient brakes as a train grinds violently to a halt wakes me. I came upright off the seat like a bleary panther, groping for my gun, knowing that something was wrong and trying to think straight in a second. We shouldn't be stopping before Jerusalem; one glance through the window showed only a low, scrubby embankment in moon-shadow. As the wheels screamed to a halt I dived into the corridor, ears cocked for the first shot. We were still on the rails, but my mind was painting vivid pictures of a blocked line and an embankment stiff with sharpshooters.

I went through the door to the platform behind the tender; in the cabin I could see the driver, peering ahead over the side of his cab.

'What the hell is it?' I shouted.

He shouted back in Arabic, and pointed ahead.

Someone was running from the back of the train. As I dropped from the platform to the ground he passed through the shaft of light between two coaches and I recognised Black's balmoral. He had his Luger out.

He slowed down beside me, and we went cautiously up past the engine, with the little wisps of steam curling up round us. The driver had his spotlight on, and the long shaft lit up the line, a tunnel of light between the embankment walls. But there was nothing to see; the embankment itself was dead still. I was turning to ask the driver what was up when he gave an excited little yelp behind us. Far down the track, on the edge of the spotlight beam, a red light winked and died. Then it winked again, and died.

A hoarse voice said: 'Get two men with rifles to the top of the bank, either side. Keep everyone else on the train. Then come back here.'

It had almost finished speaking before I realised it was my own voice. Black faded away, and a moment or two later was back.

'They're posted,' he said.

I wiped my sweaty hand on my shirt and took a fresh grip of the revolver which I ought to have remembered back in Cairo, so that some other mug could have been here, playing cops and robbers with Bert Stern or whoever it was. 'Let's go,' I said, just like Alan Ladd if he was a soprano. My hoarse voice had deserted me.

We walked up the line, our feet thumping on the sleepers,

the spotlight behind us throwing our shadows far ahead, huge grotesques on the sand. The line 'The dust of the desert is sodden red' came into my head, but I hadn't had time even to think the uncomfortable thought about it when he just materialised in front of us on the track, so suddenly that I was within an ace of letting fly at him. I know I gasped aloud in surprise; Black dropped on one knee, his Luger up.

'Hold it!' It was my hoarse voice again, sounding loud and nasty. And with the fatal gift of cliché that one invariably displays in such moments, I added, 'Don't move or I'll drill you!'

He was a young man, in blue dungarees, hatchet-faced, Jewish rather than Arab. His hands were up; they were empty.

'Pliz,' he said. 'Friend. Pliz, friend.'

'Cover him,' I said to Black, which was dam' silly, since he wasn't liable to be doing anything else. Keeping out of line, I went closer to him.

'Who are you?'

'Pliz,' he said again. He was one of these good-looking, black-curled Jews; his mouth hung open a bit. 'Pliz, line brok'.' And he pointed ahead up the track.

I left Black with him, collected the driver and his mate, and went off up the track. Sure enough, after a little search we found a fish-plate unscrewed and an iron stake driven between the rail ends – enough to put us off the track for sure. I didn't quite realise what that signified until the driver broke into a spate of Arabic, gesturing round him. I looked, and saw we were out of the cutting; now the ground fell away from the track on both sides, a rock-strewn slide that we would have crashed down.

While the driver and his mate banged out the stake and got to work on the fishplate, I went back to where Black had the young Jew in the lee of the engine. There was a small crowd round them, contrary to my orders, but one of them – an Arab Legion officer – was talking to him in Hebrew, and getting results.

'What's he say?' I asked.

'Oh, God, he's a dope,' said the officer. 'He found the rail broken, I think, and heard the train coming. So he stopped us.'

'He found the rail broken? In the middle of the bloody night? What was he doing here?'

'He doesn't seem to know.' He directed a stream of Hebrew at the youth and got one back, rather slower. The voice was thick, soft.

'Don't believe a word of it,' a voice was beginning, but I said, 'Shut up,' and asked the officer to translate.

'He was looking for a goat. He lives in a village somewhere round here.' It sounded vaguely biblical; what was the story again . . . the parable of the shepherd . . .

'What about the red light?' It was Sergeant Black.

Questioned, the youth pulled from his pocket a lighter and a piece of red cellophane.

'For God's sake,' I said.

'He's probably a bloody terrorist,' said someone.

'Don't be a fool,' I said. 'Would he warn us if he was?'

'How dare you call me a fool?' I realised it was my old friend the pouchy half-colonel. 'Who the –'

'Button your lip,' I said, and I thought he would burst. 'Who authorised you to leave the train? Sergeant Black, I thought I gave orders?'

'You did, sir.' Just that.

'Then get these people back on the train – now.'

'Now, look here, you.' The half-colonel was mottling. 'I'll attend to you in due course, I promise you. Sergeant, I'm the senior officer: take this man' – he indicated the Jew – 'and confine him in the guard's van. It's my opinion he's a terrorist . . .'

'Oh, for heavens' sake,' I said.

'. . . and we'll find out when we get to Jerusalem. And

you,' he said to me, 'will answer for your infernal impudence.'

It would have been a great exit line, if Sergeant Black had done anything except just stand there. He just waited a moment, staring at the ground, and then looked at me.

'O.C. train, sir?' he said.

I didn't catch on for a moment. Then I said, 'Carry on, sergeant. Take him aboard. Get the others aboard, too – except those who want to stand around all night shooting off their mouths in a soldier-like manner.' What had I got to lose?

I went up the track, to where the driver was gabbling away and yanking fiercely on a huge spanner. He gave me a great grin and a torrent of Arabic, from which I gathered he was coming on fine.

I went back to the train: Sergeant Black was whistling in the sentries from the banks; everyone was aboard. Presently the driver and his mate appeared, chattering triumphantly, and as I climbed aboard the engine crunched into life and we lumbered up track. The whole incident had occupied about ten minutes.

In the guard's van Black and the Arab Legion captain and my half-colonel were round the prisoner – that's what he was, no question. The captain interrogated him some more, and the half-colonel announced there was no doubt about it, the damned Yid was a terrorist. To the captain's observation that he was an odd terrorist, warning trains instead of wrecking them, he paid no heed.

'I hold you responsible, sergeant,' he told Black. 'He must be handed over to the military police in Jerusalem for questioning, and, I imagine, subsequent trial and sentence. You will . . .'

'You won't hold my sergeant responsible,' I said. 'I'll do that. I'm still in command of this train.'

For a moment I thought he was going to hit me, but unfortunately he didn't. He just bottled his apoplexy and marched out, and the captain went with him, leaving me and Black and the Jew. The two deserters, I supposed, were farther up the train. We were rattling along at full clip now; Black reckoned we were maybe two hours out of Jerusalem. I gave him a cigarette, and nodded him over to the window.

'Well?' I said. 'What d'you make of him?'

He took off his bonnet and shook his cropped head.

'He's no terrorist, for certain,' I said. 'Well, ask yourself, is he?'

'I wouldnae know. He looks the part.'

'Oh, come off it, sergeant. He warned us.'

'Aye.' He dragged on the cigarette. 'What was he doin' there, in the middle of the night?'

'Looking for a goat.'

'In dungarees stinkin' o' petrol. Aye, well. And makin' signals wi' a lighter an' cellophane. Yon's a right commando trick for a farmer. That yin's been a sodger, you bet. Probably wi' us, in Syria, in the war.'

'But he doesn't speak English.'

'He lets on he disnae.' He smiled. 'And if you're lookin' for goats, ye don't go crawling aboot on yer belly keekin' at fish-plates, do ye?'

'You think he knew, before, about the broken rail?'

'I'm damned sure of it, sir. Yon was a nice, professional job. He knew aboot it, but why he tellt us . . . search me.'

I looked over at the Jew. He was sitting with his head in his hands.

'He told us, anyway,' I said. 'Whether he's a terrorist or not, or knows terrorists, doesn't much matter.'

'It'll matter tae the military police in Jerusalem. Maybe they've got tabs on him.'

'But, dammit, if he is a Stern Gangster, why the hell would he stop the train?'

Black ground out his cigarette and looked me in the face.

'Maybe he's just soft-hearted. Maybe he doesnae want tae kill folk after all.'

'Who are you kidding? You believe that?'

'Look, sir, how the hell dae I know? Maybe he's a bloody Boy Scout daein' his good deed. Maybe he's no' a' there.'

'Yes,' I said. 'Maybe.' It was difficult to see any rational explanation. 'Anyway, all we have to do is see that he gets to Jerusalem. Then he's off our backs.'

'That's right.'

I hesitated about telling Black to keep a close eye on him, and decided it was superfluous. Then I went back up the train, full of care, noticing vaguely that the two deserters were in a group playing rummy, and that the blinds were down on the padre's compartment. Captain and Mrs Garnett had their door open, and were talking animatedly; in the background one of the twins was whimpering quietly.

'But, darling,' he was saying. 'German measles isn't serious. In fact, it's a good thing if they get it when they're little.'

'Who says?'

'Oh, medical people. It's serious if you get it when you're older, if you're a girl and you're pregnant. I read that in *Reader's Digest*.'

'Well, who's to say it's true? Anyway, I'm worried about Angie now, not . . . not twenty years hence. She may never get married, anyway, poor little beetle.'

'But it may not be German measles, anyway, darling. It may be nappy rash or something . . .'

Everybody had their troubles, including the formerly incarcerated Arab legionnaire, who was now trying to get *into* the lavatory, and wrestling with the door handle. The young pilot officer was lending a hand, and saying, 'Tell you what, Abdul, let's try saying "Open Sesame" . . .'

All was well with the A.T.S., the Australians, and the airmen; the excitement caused by our halt had quieted down, and I closed my compartment door hoping nothing more would happen before we got to Jerusalem. How much trouble could the pouchy half-colonel make, I wondered. The hell with him, I had been within my rights. Was the young Jew a terrorist, and if he was, why had he stopped the train? And so on, and I must have been dozing, for I remember being just conscious of the fact that the rhythm of the wheels had changed, and we were slowing, apparently to take a slight incline, and I was turning over on the seat, when the shot sounded.

It was a light-calibre pistol, by the sharp, high crack. As I erupted into the corridor it came again, and then again, from the back of the train. An A.T.S. shrieked, and there were oaths and exclamations, and I burst into the guard's van to find Sergeant Black at the window, his Luger in his hand, and the smell of burned cordite in the air. The train was picking up speed again at the top of the incline. The Jew was gone.

'What the hell . . .' I was beginning, and stopped. 'Are you all right?'

He was standing oddly still, looking out at the desert going by. Then he holstered his gun, and turned towards me.

'Aye, I'm fine. I'm afraid he got away.'

'The Jew? What happened?'

'He jumped for it. When we slowed down to take the hill. Went out o' that windae like a hot rivet, and doon the bank. I took a crack at him, two or three shots . . .'

'Did you hit him?'

'Not a chance.' He said it definitely. 'It's no use shootin' in this light.'

There were people surging at my back, and I wheeled round on them.

'Get back to your carriages, all of you! There's nothing to get alarmed about.'

'But the shooting . . .' 'What the hell . . .'

'There's nothing to it,' I said. 'A prisoner jumped the train, and the sergeant took a pot at him. He got away. Now, go back to your compartments and forget it. We'll be in Jerusalem shortly.'

Through the confusion came Old Inevitable himself, the pouchy half-colonel, demanding to know what had happened. I told him, while the others faded down the corridor, and he wheeled to the drawling major, who was at his elbow, and bawled:

'Stop the train!'

'Now, take it easy,' I said. 'There's no point in stopping; he's over the hills and far away by now, and he's a lot less important than the safety of this train. We're not stopping until we get to Jerusalem.'

'I'll decide that!' he snapped, and he had an ugly, triumphant look as he said it. 'You've lost the prisoner, in spite of my instructions, and this train is being stopped . . .'

'Not while I command it.'

'You don't! You're a complete bloody flop! I'm taking over. John, pull that communication . . .'

It must have been pure chance, but when the major turned uncertainly to touch the communication cord, Sergeant Black was right in his way. There was one of those pregnant silences, and I jumped into it.

'Now look, sir,' I said to the half-colonel. 'You're forgetting a few things. One, I *am* O.C. train, and anyone who tries to alter that answers to a general court-martial. Two, I intend to report you to the G.O.C. for your wilful hampering of my conduct of this train, and your deliberate disobedience of orders from properly constituted authority.'

'Damn you!' he shouted, going purple.

'You left the train when we halted, in flat defiance of my instructions. Three, sir, I've had about my bellyful of you, sir, and if you do not, at once, return to your compartment, I'm going to put you under close arrest. Sir.'

He stood glaring and heaving. 'Right,' he said, at last. He was probably wondering whether he should try, physically, to take over. He decided against it. 'Right,' he said again, and he had his voice under control. 'Major Dawlish, you have overheard what has been said here? Sergeant, you are a witness . . .'

'Aye, sir,' said Black. 'I am that.'

'What do you mean?' snapped the half-colonel, catching Black's tone. 'Let me tell you, Sergeant, you're in a pretty mess yourself. A prisoner in your . . .'

'Not a prisoner,' I said. 'A man who had warned us about the railway line and was being carried on to Jerusalem, possibly for interrogation.

He looked from me to Black and back again. 'I don't know what all this is about,' he said, 'but there's something dam' fishy here. You,' he said to me viciously, 'are going to get broken for this, and you, Sergeant, are going to have a great deal of explaining to do.' He wheeled on his buddy. 'Come along, John.' And they stumped off down the corridor.

When they had gone I lit a cigarette. I was shaking. I gave another one to Black, and he lit up, too, and I sat down on a box and rested my head on my hand.

'Look,' I said. 'I don't understand it either. But there is something dam' fishy, isn't there? How the hell did he get away?'

'I told ye, sir. He jumped.'

'Oh, yes, I know. But look, Sergeant, let's not fool around. Between ourselves, I'm not Wild Bill Bloody Hickock, but he couldn't have broken from me, so I'm damned sure he couldn't break from you. People as experienced as you, I mean, you carry a Luger, you know?'

He said, poker-faced, 'I must have dozed off.'

I just looked at him. 'You're a liar,' I said. 'You never dozed off in your life – except when you wanted to.'

His head came up at that, and he sat with smoke trickling

up from his tight mouth into his nostrils. But he didn't say anything.

'What are we going to tell them in Jerusalem?' I said.

'Just what I told you, sir. He was a gey fast mover.'

'You could get busted,' I said. 'Me, too. Oh, it'll be well down my crime-sheet, after tonight. I've done everything already. But it could be sticky down at your end too.'

He smiled. 'My number's up in the next couple of months. I've got a clean sheet. I'm no' worried about being busted.'

He seemed quite confident of that. He looked so damned composed, and satisfied somehow, that I wondered if perhaps the exigencies of the journey had unhinged me a little.

'Sergeant Black,' I said. 'Look here. The man was a terrorist – you think so, anyway. Well, why on earth . . .'

'Yes, sir?'

'Never mind,' I said wearily. 'The hell with it.'

I knew what he was going to come back to. Terrorist or not, he had saved the train, and everyone on it, me and the pouchy half-colonel and Angie and Petey and the A.T.S. and lavatory-locked legionnaire. Why, God alone knew. Maybe he hadn't meant to, or something. But I knew Black and I were speculating the same way, and giving him the benefit of the doubt, and thinking of what would have happened if he *had* been a terrorist, and there had been tabs on him in Jerusalem.

'The hell with it,' I said again. 'Sergeant, I'm out of fags. You got one?'

It was while I was lighting up and looking out at the desert with the ghostly shimmer that is the Mediterranean dawn beginning to touch its dark edges, that for no reason at all I remembered Granny's story about the cattle-train at Tyndrum. I suppose it was the association of ideas: people jumping from trains. I told Sergeant Black about it, and we discussed grannies and railways and related subjects, while the train rattled on towards Jerusalem.

Just before we began to run into the suburbs, the white buildings perched on the dun hillsides, Sergeant Black changed the topic of conversation.

'I wouldn't worry too much about yon half-colonel,' he said.

'I'm not worried,' I said. 'You couldn't call it worry. I've just got mental paralysis about him.'

'He might think twice about pushing charges against you,' said Black. 'Mind you, he stepped over the mark himsel'. He wouldnae come well out of a court-martial. And ye were quite patient wi' him, all things considered.' He grinned. 'Your granny wouldnae have been as patient.'

'Huh. Wonder what my granny would have said if she had been wheeled before the brigadier?'

'Your granny would have *been* the brigadier,' he said. 'We're here, sir.'

Jerusalem station was an even bigger chaos than Cairo had been; there were redcaps everywhere, and armed Palestine Police, and tannoys blaring, and people milling about the platforms. Troop Train 42 disgorged its occupants: I didn't see the half-colonel go, but I saw the Arab Legion forming up to be inspected, and Captain Garnett and his wife, laden with heaps of small clothes and handbags from which bottles and rolls of cotton wool protruded, carrying Angie and Petey in a double basket; and the A.T.S. giggling and walking arm-in-arm with the Aussies and the R.A.F. types, and the padre with loads of kit, bargaining with a cross-eyed thug wearing a porter's badge. Sergeant Black strode through the train, seeing everyone was off; then he snapped me a salute and said:

'Permission to fall out, sir?'

'Carry on, Sergeant,' I said.

He stamped his feet and hoisted his kit-bag on to his shoulder. I watched him disappear into the crowd, the red hackle on his bonnet bobbing above the sea of heads.

I went to the R.T.O.'s office, and sank into a chair.

'Thank God that's over,' I said. 'Where do I go from here? And I hope it's bed.'

The R.T.O. was a grizzled citizen with troubles. 'You MacNeill?' he said. 'Troop Train 42?'

'That's me,' I said, and thought, here it comes. Pouchy had probably done his stuff already, and I would be requested to report to the nearest transit camp and wait under open arrest until they were ready to nail me for – let's see – insubordination, permitting a prisoner to escape, countenancing illegal trafficking in currency, threatening a superior, conduct unbecoming an officer in that I had upbraided a clergyman, and no doubt a few other assorted offences that I had overlooked. One way and another I seemed to have worked my way through a good deal of the prohibitions of the Army Act: about the only one I could think of that I hadn't committed was 'unnatural conduct of a cruel kind, in that he threw a cat against a wall'. Not that that was much consolation.

'MacNeill,' muttered the R.T.O., heaving his papers about. 'Yerss, here it is. Got your train documents?' I gave them to him. 'Right,' he said. 'Get hold of this lot.' And he shoved another pile at me. 'Troop Train 51, leaves oh-eight-thirty for Cairo. You'll just have time to get some breakfast.'

'You're kidding,' I said.

'Don't you believe it, boy,' he said. 'Corporal Clark! Put these on the wire, will you? And see if there's any word on 44, from Damascus. Dear God,' he rubbed his face. 'Well, what are you waiting for?'

'You can't put me on another train,' I said. 'I mean, they'll be wanting me for court-martial or something.' And I gave him a very brief break-down.

'For God's sake,' he said. 'You were cheeky to a half-colonel! Well, you insubordinate thing, you. It'll have to keep, that's all. You weren't the only one who was getting uppish last night, you know. Some people gunned up a convoy near Nazareth, and apart from killing half a dozen of us they did for a United Nations bigwig as well. So there's activity today, d'you see? Among other things, there aren't enough perishing subalterns to put in charge of troop trains. Now, get the hell out of here, and get on that train!'

I got, and made my way to the buffet, slightly elated at the idea of making good my escape on the 8.30. Not that it would do any good in the long run; the Army always catches up, and the half-colonel was the vindictive sort who would have me hung up if it took him six months. In the meantime I wasn't going to see much of the famous old city of Jerusalem; eating my scrambled eggs I wondered idly if some Roman centurion had once arrived here after a long trek by camel train, only to be told that he was taking the next caravan out because everyone was all steamed up and busy over the arrest of a preaching carpenter who had been causing trouble. It seemed very likely. If you ever get on the fringe of great events, which have a place in history, you can be sure history will soon lose it as far as you are concerned.

I got the 8.30, and there was hardly a civilian on it; just troops who behaved themselves admirably except at Gaza, where there was the usual race in the direction of Ahmed's back street banking and trust corporation; I just pretended it wasn't happening; you can't fight international liquidity. And then it was Cairo again, just sixteen hours since I had left it, and I dropped my papers with the R.T.O., touched my revolver butt for the hundred and seventeenth time to make sure I still had it, and went back to the transit camp, tired and dirty. I went to sleep wondering where the escaping Jew had got to by this time, and why Sergeant Black had let him go. It occurred to me that the Jew might have had a pretty rough time in Jerusalem, what with everyone's nerves even more on edge with the Nazareth business. Anyway, I wasn't sorry he had got away; all's well that ends well; I slept like a log.

All hadn't ended well, of course; two mornings later a court of inquiry was convened in an empty barrack-room at the transit camp, to examine the backsliding and evil behaviour of Lieutenant MacNeill, D., and report thereon. It consisted of a ravaged-looking wing-commander as president, an artillery major, a clerk, about a dozen witnesses, and me, walking between with the gyves (metaphorically) upon my wrists. The redcap at the door tried to keep me out because I didn't have some pass or other, but on finding that I was the star attraction he ushered me to a lonely chair out front, and everyone glared at me.

They strip a man's soul bare, those courts of inquiry. With deft, merciless questioning they had found out in the first half hour not only who I was, but my rank and number; an officer from the transit camp deponed that I had been resident there for several days; yet another certified that I had been due out on such-and-such a flight; an airport official confirmed that this was true, and then they played their mastercard. The pilot of the aircraft (this is sober truth) produced an affidavit from his co-pilot (who was unable to attend because of prickly heat) that I had not, to anyone's knowledge, boarded the plane, and that my seat had been given to Captain Abraham Phillipowski of the Polish Engineers, attached to No. 117 Field Battery, Ismailia.

They were briefly sidetracked because the president plainly didn't believe there was such a person as Captain Abraham Phillipowski, but once this had been established to their satisfaction the mills of military justice ground on, and another officer from the transit camp described graphically my return after missing the plane, and my despatch to Jerusalem.

The president wanted to know why I had been sent to Jerusalem; witness replied that they had wanted to keep me employed pending a court of inquiry into why I had missed my plane; the president said, pending this court, you mean; witness said yes, and the president said it seemed bloody silly to him sending a man to Jerusalem in between. Witness said huffily it was no concern of his, the president said not to panic, old boy, he had only been making a comment, and witness said all very well, but he didn't want it appearing in the record that he had been responsible for sending people to Jerusalem when he hadn't.

The president suggested to the clerk that any such exchange be deleted from the record (which was assuming the proportions of the Greater London telephone directory, the way the clerk was performing with his shorthand), and I unfortunately coughed at that moment, which was taken as a protest. A judicial huddle ensued, and the president emerged, casting doubtful glances at me, to ask if I had anything to say.

'I forgot my gun,' I said.

He seemed disappointed. 'He forgot his gun,' he repeated to the clerk.

'I heard,' said the clerk.

'All right, all right!' cried the president. 'Keep your hair on.' He looked at me. 'Anything else?'

'Should there be?' I asked. It seemed to me that they hadn't really started yet, but I wasn't volunteering information about events on the train, which seemed to me to dwarf such trivia as my missing my plane in the first place.

'Dunno,' said the president. He turned to the clerk. 'How do we stand, old boy?'

'He forgot his gun, he missed the plane,' said the clerk bitterly. 'That's what we're here to establish. What more do you want?'

'Search me,' said the president. 'You did miss the plane, didn't you?' he asked me.

'That's irregular,' bawled the clerk. 'At least, I think it is. You're asking him to convict himself.'

'Rot,' said the president. 'He hasn't been charged, has he? Anyway, old boy, you're mixing it up with wives not being able to testify against their husbands.'

'I need a drink,' said the clerk.

'Good show,' said the president. 'Let's adjourn, and then you can type all this muck out and we'll all sign it. Any objections, objection overruled. Smashing.'

The proceedings of that court occupied about forty-five minutes, and heaven knows how many sheets of foolscap, but it did establish what it had set out to do – that I had negligently failed to take a seat on an aircraft. It was all carefully forwarded to my unit, marked attention Commanding Officer, and he blew his stack, mildly, and gave me three days' orderly officer for irresponsible idiocy – not so much for missing the aircraft as for causing him to waste time reading the report. But of Black, and the escaping Jew, and threats, and insubordination, and currency offences there was never a word.

And, as my grandmother would have said, that is what happened on the Cairo–Jerusalem railway.

The Whisky and the Music

The ignorant or unwary, if asked whether they would rather be the guests of an officers' mess or a sergeants', would probably choose the officers'. They might be motivated by snobbery, but probably also by the notion that the standards of cuisine, comfort, and general atmosphere would be higher. They would be dead wrong.

You will get a bit of the old haut monde from the officers in most units, although in a Highland regiment the native savagery has a tendency to show through. I remember the occasion when two Guards officers, guests of our mess, were having a delicate Sunday morning breakfast and discussing Mayfair and the Season with the Adjutant, himself an exquisite, when there entered the motor transport officer, one Elliot, a hard man from the Borders. Elliot surveyed the table and then roared:

'Naethin' but toast again, bigod! You,' he shouted at the Adjutant, 'ye bloody auld vulture, you, ye've been gobblin' my plain bread!' And he wrenched the Adjutant's shirt-front out of his kilt, slapped him resoundingly on the solar plexus, and ruffled his hair. This was Elliot's way of saying good morning, but it upset the Guards. They just looked at each other silently, like two Jack Bennys, and then got slowly to their feet and went out, looking rather pale.

That would never happen in a sergeants' mess. Sergeants are too responsible. They tend to be young-middle-aged soldiers, with a sense of form and dignity; among officers there is always the clash of youth and age, but with sergeants you have a disciplined, united front. And whereas the provisioning and amenities of an officers' mess are usually in the hands of a president who has had the job forced on him and isn't much good at it, your sergeants look after their creature comforts with an expertise born of long service in hard times. Wherever you are, whoever goes short, it won't be the sergeants; they've been at the game too long.

Hogmanay apart, officers never saw inside our sergeants' mess ('living like pigs as we do,' said the Colonel, 'it would make us jealous,') so when Sergeant Cuddy of the signals section invited me in for a drink I accepted like a shot. We had been out in the desert on an exercise, and Cuddy and I had spent long hours on top of a sand-hill with a wireless set, watching the company toiling over the sun-baked plain below, popping off blanks at each other. Cuddy was a very quiet old soldier with silver hair; his first experience of signals had been with flags and pigeons on the Western Front in the old war, and I managed to get him to talk about it a little. It emerged that he had heard of, although he had not known, my great-uncle, who had been a sergeant with the battalion at the turn of the century.

'There'll be a picture of him in the mess,' said Cuddy. And then, after a long pause, he added: 'Perhaps ye'd care to come in and see it, when we go back to barracks?'

'Will it be all right?' I asked, for regimental protocol is sometimes a tricky thing.

'My guest,' said Cuddy, so I thanked him, and when we had packed up the exercise that afternoon I accompanied him up the broad steps of the whitewashed building just outside the barracks where the sergeants dwelt in fortified seclusion.

In the ante-room there was only the pipe-sergeant, perched in state at one end of the bar, and keeping a bright eye on the mess waiters to see that they kept their thumbs out of the glasses.

'Guest. Mr MacNeill,' announced Cuddy, and the pipey hopped off his stool and took over.

'Come away ben, Mr MacNeill,' he cried. 'Isn't this the pleasure? You'll take a little of the creature? Of course, of course. Barman, where are you? Stand to your kit.'

I surveyed the various brands of 'the creature' on view behind the bar, and decided that the Colonel was right. You would never have seen the like in an officers' mess. There was the Talisker and Laphroaig and Islay Mist and Glenfiddich and Smith's Ten-year-old – every Scotch whisky under the sun. How they managed it, in those arid post-war years, I didn't like to think.

I'm not a whisky man, but asking for a beer would have been unthinkable; I eventually selected an Antiquary, and the pipe-sergeant raised his brows and pursed his lips approvingly.

'An Edinburgh whisky,' he observed judicially. 'Very light, very smooth. I'm a Grouse man, myself.' He watched jealously as the barman poured out the very pale Antiquary and gave me my water in a separate glass (if you want to be a really snob whisky drinker, that is the way you take it, in alternate sips, a right 'professional Highlander' trick). Then we drank, the three of us, and the pipe-sergeant discoursed on whisky in general – the single malts and the blends, and 'the Irish heresies', and strange American concoctions of which he affected to have heard, called 'Burboon'.

Sergeant Cuddy eventually interrupted to say that I had come to view the group photographs lining the mess walls, to see my great-uncle, and the pipe-sergeant exclaimed in admiration.

'And he was in the regiment? God save us, isn't that the thing?' He bounded from his stool and skipped over to the row of pictures, some of them new and grainy-grey, others deepening into yellow obscurity. 'About when would that be, sir? The 'nineties? In India? Well, well, let's see. There's the '02, but that was in Malta, whatever they were doing there. Let's see

– Ross, Chalmers, Robertson, McGregor – all the teuchters, and look at the state of them, with their bellies hanging over their sporrans. I'd like to put *them* through a foursome, wouldn't I just.' He went along the row, Cuddy and I following, calling out names and bestowing comments.

'South Africa, and all in khaki aprons. My, Cuddy, observe the whiskers. Hamilton, Fraser, Yellowlees, O'Toole – and what was he doing there, d'ye suppose? A right fugitive from the Devil's Own, see the bog-Irish face of him. Murray, Johnstone –'

'I mind Johnstone, in my time,' said Cuddy. 'Killed at Passchendaele.'

'– Scott, Allison – that'll be Gutsy Allison's father, Cuddy. Ye mind Gutsy.' The pipe-sergeant was searching out new treasures. 'Save us, see there.' He pointed to a picture of the 'twenties. 'Behold the splendour there, Mr MacNeill.' I looked at a face in the back rank, vaguely familiar, grim and tight-lipped. 'He's filled out since then,' said the pipe-sergeant. 'Seventeen stone of him now, if there's an ounce. That's our present Regimental Sergeant-Major. Anderson, McColl, Brand, Hutcheson –'

'Hutcheson got the jail,' said Cuddy. 'He played the fiddle for his recreation, and went poaching with snares made from violin strings. An awfy man.'

They chattered on, or at least the pipey chattered, and I made polite murmurs, and at last they ran my great-uncle to earth, reclining at the end of a front row and showing his noble profile in the Victorian manner. Showing as much of it, anyway, as was visible through his mountainous beard: he gave the impression of one peering through a quickset hedge.

'Fine, fine whiskers they had,' cried the pipe-sergeant admiringly. 'You don't get that today. Devil the razor there must have been among them, the wee nappy-wallahs of India must have done a poor, poor trade at the shaving, I'm thinking. He's a fine figure, your respected great-uncle, Mr MacNeill, a fine figure. Ye have the same look, the same keek under the brows, has he not, Cuddy? See there,' and he pointed to the minute portion of my ancestor that showed through the hair, 'isn't that the very spit? Did ye know him, sir?'

'No,' I said. 'I didn't. He died in South Africa, of fever, I think.'

'Tut, tut,' said the pipe-sergeant. 'Isn't that just damnable? No proper medical provisions then, eh, Cuddy?'

I was studying the picture – 'Peshawar, 1897', it was labelled – and thinking how complete a stranger one's closest relative can be, when a voice at my elbow said formally:

'Good evening, sir,' and I turned to find the impressive figure of the R.S.M. beside me. He nodded in his patriarchal style – even without his bonnet and pace-stick he was still a tremendous presence – and even deigned to examine great-uncle's likeness.

'If he had lived I would have known him,' he said. 'I knew many of the others, during my boy service. You have a glass there, Mr MacNeill? Capital. Your good health.'

The mess was beginning to fill up now, and as we chatted under the pictures one or two others joined us – old Blind Sixty, my company quarter-master, and young Sergeant McGaw, who had been organiser of a Clydeside Communist Party in civilian life. 'How's Joe Stalin these days?' demanded the pipe-sergeant, and McGaw's sallow face twitched into a grin and he winked at me as he said, 'No' ready tae enrol you, onyway, ye capitalist lackey.'

They gagged with each other, and presently I finished my drink and straightened my sporran and said I should be getting along . . .

'Have you shown Mr MacNeill his forebear's other portrait?' demanded the R.S.M., and the pipey, at a loss for once, said he didn't know there was one. At which the R.S.M. moved majestically over to the other wall, and tapped a fading print with a finger like a banana. 'Same date, you see,' he said, ''97. This is the battalion band. Now, then . . . there, Pipe-Sergeant MacNeill.' And there, sure enough, was the ancestor, with his pipes under his arm, covered in hair and dignity.

The pipe-sergeant squeaked with delight. 'Isn't that the glory! He wass a pipe-sergeant, *the* pipe-sergeant, like myself! And hasn't he the presence for it? You can see he is just bursting with the good music! My, Mr MacNeill, what pride for you, to have a great-uncle that wass a pipe-sergeant. You have no music yourself, though? Ach, well. You'll have a suggestion more of the Antiquary before ye go? Ye will. And yourself, Major? Cuddy? McGaw?'

While they were stoking them up, the R.S.M. drew my attention to the band picture again, to another figure in the ranks behind my great-uncle. It was of a slim, dark young piper with a black moustache but no beard. Then he traced down to the names underneath and stopped at one. 'That's him,' he said. 'Just a few months, I would say, before his name went round the world.' And I read, 'Piper Findlater, G.'

'Is that *the* Findlater?' I asked.

'The very same,' said the R.S.M.

I knew the name from childhood, of course, and I suppose there was a time when, as the R.S.M. said, it went round the world. There was the little jingle that went to our regimental march, which the children used to sing at play:

> Piper Findlater, Piper Findlater,
> Piped 'The Cock o' the North',
> He piped it so loud
> That he gathered a crowd
> And he won the Victoria Cross.

There are, as Sapper pointed out, 'good V.C.s' and ordinary

V.C.s – so far as winning the V.C. can ever be called ordinary. Among the 'good V.C.s' were people like little Jack Cornwell, who stayed with his gun at Jutland, and Lance-Corporal Michael O'Leary, who took on crowds of Germans singlehanded. But I imagine if it were possible to take a poll of the most famous V.C.s over the past century Piper George Findlater would be challenging for the top spot. I don't say that because he was from a Highland regiment, but simply because what he did on an Afghan hillside one afternoon caught the public imagination, as it deserved to, more than such things commonly do.

'Well,' I said. 'My great-uncle was in distinguished company.'

'Who's that?' said the pipey, returning with the glasses. 'Oh, Findlater, is it? A fair piper, they tell me – quite apart from being heroical, you understand. I mind him fine – not during his service, of course, but in retirement.'

'I kent him weel,' said Old Sixty. 'He was a guid piper, for a' I could tell.'

'A modest man,' said the R.S.M.

'He had a' the guts he needed, at that,' said McGaw.

'I remember the picture of him, in a book at home,' I said. 'You know, at Dargai, when he won the V.C. And then it came out in a series that was given away with a comic-paper.'

'Aye,' said the pipe-sergeant, on a triumphant note, and everyone looked at him. 'Everybody kens the story, right enough. But ye don't ken it all, no indeed, let me tell you. There wass more of importance to Findlater's winning the cross than just the superfeecial facts. Oh, aye.'

'He's at it again,' said Old Sixty. 'If you were as good at your trade as ye are at bletherin', ye'd have been King's Piper lang syne.'

'I'd be most interested to hear any unrelated facts about Piper Findlater, Pipe-sergeant,' said the R.S.M., fixing him with his eye. 'I thought I was fully conversant wi' the story.'

'Oh, yes, yes,' said the pipey. 'But there is a matter closely concerned with regimental tradition which I had from Findlater himself, and it's not generally known. Oh, aye. I could tell ye.' And he wagged his head wisely.

'C'mon then,' said McGaw. 'Let's hear your lies.'

'It's no lie, let me tell you, you poor ignorant Russian lapdog,' said the pipey. 'Just you stick to your balalaikeys, and leave music to them that understands it.' He perched himself on the arm of a chair, glass in hand, and held forth.

'You know how the Ghurkas wass pushed back by the Afghans from the Dargai Heights? And how our regiment wass sent in and came under torrents of fire from the wogs, who were snug as foxes in their positions on the crest? Well, and then the pipers wass out in front – as usual – and Findlater was shot through first one ankle and then through the other, and fell among the rocks in front of the Afghan positions. And he pulled himself up, and crawled to his pipes, and him pourin' bleed, and got himself up on a rock wi' the shots pingin' away round him, and played the regimental march so that the boys took heart and carried the crest.'

'Right enough,' said Old Sixty. 'How they didn't shoot him full of holes. God alone knows. He was only twenty yards from the Afghan sangars, and in full view. But he never minded; he said after that he was wild at the thought of his regiment being stopped by a bunch o' niggers.'

Sergeant McGaw stirred uncomfortably. 'I don't like that. He shouldn't have called them niggers.'

'Neither he should, and you're right for once,' said the pipey. He sipped neatly at his glass. 'They wass not niggers; they wass wogs. Any roads, they carried him oot, and Queen Victoria pinned the V.C. on him and said: "You're a canny loon, Geordie", and he said, "You're a canny queen, wifie", and –'

The R.S.M. snorted. 'He did nothing of the sort, Pipe-sergeant.'

'Well, not in so many words, maybe,' conceded the pipey. 'But here's what none of you knows. The papers wass full of it, how he had played the regimental march under witherin' fire, and "Cock o' the North" was being sounded up the length and breadth of the land, in music halls, and by brass bands, and by street fiddlers, and everybody. The kids wass singing it. And Findlater, when his legs wass mended, suddenly took thought, and said to his pal, the corporal piper, "Ye know, I'm no' certain, but I doubt it wass the regimental march I played at all. I think it was 'Haughs o' Cromdale'."

'The corporal piper considered this, and cast his mind back to the battle, and said Findlater was right. It wasnae "Cock o' the North" at all, but he didnae think it was "Haughs o' Cromdale" either; by his recollection it was "The Black Bear".

'They argued awa', and got naewhere. So they called on the Company Sergeant-Major, who confessed he couldnae tell one from t'ither, but thought it might have been "Bonnie Dundee".

'Finally, it got to the Colonel's ears, and he wass dismayed. Here wass the fame of Piper Findlater ringin' through the land, and everyone talking about how he had played "Cock o' the North" in the face of the enemy, and the man himself wasnae sure what he had played at all. There wass consternation throughout the battalion. "A fine thing this," says the Colonel. "If this gets out we'll be the laughin'-stock o' the Army. Determine at once what tune he played, and let's have no more damned nonsense."

'But they couldn't do it. Every man who had been within earshot on the Dargai slope, as soon as you asked him, had a different notion of what the tune was, but how could they be sure, with the bullets flying and them grappling with their bayonets against the Khyber knives? You have to have a very appreciative ear for music to pay much heed to it at a time like that. One thing they decided: there was general agreement that whatever he played, it wasn't "Lovat's Lament".'

'Lovat's Lament' is a dirge; played with feeling it can make Handel's Largo sound like the Beatles.

The pipe-sergeant beamed at us. 'Well, there it was. No one was certain at all. So the Colonel did the only thing there was to do. He sent for the Regimental Sergeant-Major. "Major," says he, "what did Piper Findlater play on the Dargai Heights?"

'The R.S.M. never blinked. "'Cock o' the North', sir," says he. "Ye're sure?" says the Colonel. "Positive," says the R.S.M. "Thank God for that," says the Colonel. And it was only later that it occurred to him that the R.S.M. had not been within half a mile of Findlater during the battle, and couldn't know at all. But "Cock o' the North" the R.S.M. had said, and "Cock o' the North" it has been ever since, and always will be.'

Sergeant McGaw made impatient noises. 'What the hell did it matter, anyway? They took the heights, and he won his V.C. It would have been just the same if he had been playin' "Roll out the Barrel".'

The pipe-sergeant swelled up at once. 'You know nothing, McGaw. You have neither soul nor experience. Isn't it important that regimental history should be right, and that people shouldn't have their confidence disturbed? Suppose it was to transpire at this point that Nelson at Trafalgar had said nothing about England expecting, but had remarked instead that he was about due for leave, and once the battle was over it was him for a crafty forty-eight-hour pass?'

'Not the same thing at a',' said McGaw.

'You're descending to the trivial,' said the R.S.M.

'The country would degenerate at once!' cried the pipe-sergeant, and at this point I finally made my excuses, thanked them for their hospitality, and left them in the throes of philosophic debate.

Back in our own mess, I mentioned to the Colonel that I

had been entertained by the sergeants, and had heard of the Findlater controversy. He smiled and said:

'Oh, yes, that one. It comes up now and then, not so often now, because of course the survivors are thinning out.' He sighed. 'He was a great old fellow, you know, Findlater. I used to see him going about. Indeed, touching on the pipe-sergeant's story, I even asked him once what he did play at Dargai.'

'What did he say?'

'Wasn't quite sure. Of course, he was an old man then. He had an idea it might have been "The Barren Rocks of Aden". Or possibly "The 79th's Farewell to Gibraltar". I had my own theory at one time, I forget why, that it must have been "The Burning Sands of Egypt".'

I digested this. 'So it's never been settled, then?'

'Settled? Of course it has. He played "Cock o' the North". Everyone knows that.'

'Yes, sir, but how do they know?'

The Colonel looked at me as at a rather dim-witted child. 'The R.S.M. said so.'

'Of course,' I said. 'Foolish of me. I was forgetting.'

Guard at the Castle

It is one of the little ironies of Army life that mounting guard is usually more of an ordeal than actually standing guard. And frequently the amount of anguish involved in mounting is in inverse proportion to the importance of the object to be guarded. For example, as a young soldier I have been turned out in the middle of the night in jungle country, unwashed, half-dressed, with a bully-beef sandwich in one hand and a rifle in the other, to provide an impromptu bodyguard for the great Slim himself; this was accomplished at ten seconds' notice, without ceremonial. On the other hand, I have spent hours perfecting my brass and blanco to stand sentry on a bank in Rangoon which had no roof, no windows, and had been gutted by the Japanese anyway.

This merely proves that Satan finds mischief for idle hands, and there are few hands idler than those of military authority outside the firing line.

Edinburgh Castle, from the guards' point of view, is in a class by itself. It is tremendously important, in a traditional rather than a strategic sense; if someone broke into it and pinched Mons Meg the actual well-being of the country would not be affected, but the blow to national prestige would be tremendous. The papers would be full of it. Consequently, providing a guard for the Castle involves – or used to – more frantic preparation, ceremonial, organisation, and general nervous tension than the filming of *Ben Hur*. It is rather like a combination of putting on a Paris fashion display and planning a commando raid, and the fact that its object is to provide a skeleton guard which couldn't stop a marauding party of intelligent Brownies is, in the military view, beside the point.

It was a few months after our battalion had come home from the Middle East to be stationed near Edinburgh. It was one of those summers just after the war when there was gaiety and eagerness in the air, and the dark years were just behind and everyone was enjoying themselves. Princes Street was all sunshine and uniforms and pretty dresses, the American Fleet was in the Forth, royalty was coming to town, God was in his heaven, and I was once again the battalion orderly officer. It was a restful job, wandering round barracks drinking cups of tea in the cookhouse, chivvying the Jocks out of the canteen at closing time, casting a critical eye at the guards and picquets, and generally taking life easy – until some genius in the High Command woke up one morning with the brilliant idea that during the royal visit, with distinguished American naval dignitaries also being on hand, it would be nice to have a Highland regiment on guard at the Castle. That meant us, and us meant me.

The turmoil that broke out from our orderly room was indescribable. The Colonel, that kindly, vulture-faced man who had looked Japanese guards in the face on the Moulmein Railway and said, 'No', now became visibly agitated for the first time in living memory; he took me aside, addressed me as 'Young Dand', twisted his moustache, and spoke rapidly and incoherently about the importance of putting on a good show. The Adjutant got on the other side of me and rattled instructions into my ear, impressing the necessity of perfect organisation, split-second timing, immaculate appearance, and perfect co-ordination. He gave me to understand that the slightest slip would mean the ruin of the regimental reputation and my own personal destruction, and exhorted me to keep calm.

Like every young officer in dire need, I went straight to the Regimental Sergeant-Major, who drew up his enormous bulk an inch higher at the thought of exhibiting his perfections before royalty, soothed my hysterics, and suggested that we go through the drill. As he reminded me, it was perfectly simple; we had done it together scores of times without a hitch. All we needed was an intelligent guard consisting of sergeant, corporal, and five good men, and we could take our pick of my company.

We went through the drill. What happens at guard-mounting is this: the orderly officer and R.S.M. wait at one end of the parade ground, just in front of the object to be guarded – in our case the Castle gateway. The guard march on at the other end of the parade ground, and the R.S.M. brings them to a halt roughly in its middle. He then invites the orderly officer to inspect them, and the pair of them march the fifty or so yards to the guard, look them over, and march back again. The R.S.M. roars out more orders, the guard present their rifles for inspection, officer and R.S.M. march forward again, look at the rifles, march back, and the R.S.M. marches the guard into the Castle, the orderly officer standing off to one side and taking the salute. There is a pause of a couple of minutes, in which the officer has the parade ground to himself, then the old guard is marched out, briefly inspected, and marched off. The officer retires, and that is that. Easy; in our case the only difference was that a vast crowd, including royalty and a fearsome array of home and foreign brass, would be watching.

We summoned the Company Sergeant-Major, a hard-bitten Aberdonian, and he produced the list of men who were due for guard.

'You've got McAuslan down here,' I said.

'He's due,' said the C.S.M.

'He's overdue,' I said. 'I'd sooner go on guard with Laurel and Hardy.'

McAuslan, as I have explained, was one of those soldiers. He was short, pimply, revoltingly dirty, incredibly unseemly, and dense to a degree. Not that he didn't try; he was pathetically eager to please, but it was no good. His stupidity and uncleanliness were a sort of gift, and combined with his handlessness made him a military disaster. He had been twice forcibly washed by his comrades, and had never been off defaulters until it was discovered that punishment was wasted on him. The thought of having him on the Castle guard, out there in the sunlight, with royalty watching . . .

'No,' I said. 'Lose him. Forget him. Get anyone you like, get one of the cooks, but not McAuslan.'

The C.S.M. said he would see to it, and for two days my platoon barrack-room went at it as never before. The sergeant, corporal and five men were scrubbed, polished, drilled, examined, pleaded with, threatened, cajoled, and watched over like newborn chicks. I took them through the drill until they could have done it in their sleep; the best belts, tartans, cap badges, pouches, and small packs were borrowed from the ends of the battalion and worked on by the whole platoon; their boots were boned and polished till they gleamed like black diamonds; their rifles and bayonets were oiled and polished till they glittered; even their puttees were ironed, and when they stood up on the morning of the great day in the barrack-room, in all their glory, they were a lovely sight to see.

The R.S.M. and the C.S.M. and I buzzed round them, peering and pulling and encouraging them; the Colonel looked in, hummed, approved, got in the way, and was tactfully rebuked by the R.S.M.; he fidgeted for a while, clicking his lighter and chewing his cigarette, and then said, 'All right, young Dand; good luck, lads, must be off,' and shot out – poor soul, he was going to be next to royalty, suffering agonies.

Then we waited. A truck was to take us to the Castle in about half an hour; I still had to get dressed, but my kit was all in order, with my batman standing guard on it, and for the moment we had the barracks almost to ourselves. The rest of the battalion were out on an exercise which was going on at Redford, and we sat in silence, smoking and watching the sweat on the backs of our hands.

There was a clatter of boots in the corridor, the door opened, and I looked up to see McAuslan in the doorway. Amazingly he was dressed as for guard-mounting – that is, all his equipment was there, but in its usual state of rank disorder. You wouldn't have let him guard a coal-bunker.

'In Goad's name!' said the C.S.M. 'Whit are you on?'

'Guard, sir,' said McAuslan. His bonnet was squint, and there was an oil-stain on his shirt. He had perhaps washed his face three days ago.

'Guard?' echoed the R.S.M. 'Not you, my lad. You were taken off the rota days ago. Don't you look at the notice-board?'

'Ah cannae read,' said McAuslan.

'Aye, weel, ye can hear,' said the C.S.M. 'And ye're not on guard, nor likely tae be. Ye know why? Ye're dirty, ye're idle, an' – an' ye're a positive disgrace. Now, oot o' this and report to the quartermaster for fatigues.'

McAuslan, pimply and unkempt, wiped his nose and looked unhappy. For a minute I couldn't think why; not one man in that guard but would have gladly slipped out of it if he could; they were sitting quaking, and here was this tartan Caliban looking miserable at news that would have delighted any of them.

'All right, McAuslan,' I said. 'Carry on to the quartermaster.' And for some reason I found myself adding: 'Sorry.'

He went, and the truck rumbled up outside. I was just stubbing out my cigarette and preparing to go to my quarters to dress when it happened. I still see it in nightmares.

One of the guards, a stocky, dapper Glaswegian named Grant, had stretched himself and strolled to the door. What he put his foot on I don't know, but one moment he was standing, and then he was falling, and some evil spirit had caused a drum of yellow paint, used for marking kit-bags, to be in a corner by the door, and one moment there was a beautiful soldier and the next there was a swearing creature whose kilt and left arm and left leg were a different colour. His comrades leaped back squealing like debs at Ascot.

We gazed at him appalled. Plainly he was beyond repair, there was no one else to take his place, we could not go on a man short – or so it seemed to me then, with military procedure drilled into my mind. I still had to dress, fool that I was to have left it so late, we had about five minutes – and royalty and the rest of them would be waiting. This was desperate. Where to find another man?

The R.S.M. was looking at me. I looked from him to the C.S.M. We all had the same thought.

'My God!' I said.

'We cannae take him,' said the C.S.M.

'We must,' said the R.S.M., and lifted up his voice. 'McAuslan!'

Two minutes later I was in my quarters, wrenching on my dress uniform, tearing at the kilt buckles, my batman blaspheming as he adjusted my sporran and buckled on my Sam Browne. Then I was running, the truck was at the door, I had a horrid vision of a pallid ragamuffin sitting opposite the R.S.M. in the back, being told the intricacies of guard drill – guard drill, to McAuslan, the man who thought slope arms was something to do with the Nazi salute.

I don't remember the drive through Edinburgh, mercifully; and to this day even my memories of Edinburgh Castle itself are hazy. I remember being there in the sunlight, before the gateway, and the murmur of a brightly coloured holiday crowd, and the little group of green-tartaned figures coming on at the other end, with McAuslan shachling in the middle of the rear rank, managing to swing his left arm in time with his left leg. (Try that, sometime; only McAuslan can do it.)

Then they halted, rigid in the heat haze, and the thunder of the R.S.M.'s voice broke the silence, and behind me I heard the mutter of the C.S.M. – 'Goad, look at 'im. No two pun' of him hingin' straight.' I knew who he meant.

Then the R.S.M., huge and magnificent, was saluting in front of me, and my own voice was barking (surprisingly strong) and I came awake again, and paced across the vast distance to the guard.

They were doing well. They were all red in the face, and when you got near you could see them trembling, but they were standing up straight; they were with it. As I moved slowly along the front row I heard my own voice again, softly this time.

'Easy does it, now, easy. You're doing fine. Nothing to worry about. You're looking good, McFarlane, you're looking very good. Head up a wee bit, Nichol, that's it. You're a good-looking guard.' And behind me the R.S.M. whispering: 'Next order is port arms. Take it steady.'

Now the second rank, and I was opposite McAuslan. The R.S.M. and C.S.M. had done their best, but I was thankful the spectators were a hundred yards away. His face was grimy, his boots were dull, his shirt and kilt appeared to have been slept in. When I got behind him I noticed his bayonet: there was a ring of rust between blade and sheath.

'Easy, MacAuslan,' I said, and, God forgive me; 'You're looking fine.'

We marched back, the R.S.M. and I, gave them port arms, and marched forward again. I made a pretence of looking at the rifles, which were held up for inspection, but no more than a glance, until we came to the second row. As I passed McAuslan – his rifle looked as though it had been at the bottom of the Monkland Canal for a month – I heard the R.S.M. make a noise. If you think there is no such thing as a yelp and whisper combined, there is.

I looked, and nearly passed out. At port arms the rifle bolt is drawn back, exposing the magazine, and McAuslan's magazine had gleaming brass rounds in it. How he had managed this I still don't know, but there he was, with a loaded rifle, mounting guard at Edinburgh Castle. For a vivid moment the thought that he was going to assassinate royalty crossed my mind; then I realised, with mounting horror, that the guard's next manoeuvre was to 'ease springs', which involves working the bolt and finally pressing the trigger, which in McAuslan's case would mean scattering .303 cartridges all over the place and probably blowing someone's head off.

But nothing is too much for an R.S.M. Deftly he reached over, detached McAuslan's magazine, and conjured it out of sight. Then we were marching back to our places, and I was just breathing again when I was aware of a curious sensation at my right hip.

You know how it is – not a pain, or even a touch, but just a feeling, as though something has been taken away. I felt, rather than heard, a slight snap, and instinctively clapped my right fist to my hip. There was a movement that was not the motion of marching; and for a few seconds I knew real, paralysing terror. One of my kilt buckles, wrenched in the hurry of dressing, had given way. There was a second one, of course, but was it fastened properly? I knew, with horrifying certainty, that if I removed my fist that vast, silent crowd would be treated to the edifying sight of a Highland officer marching in his shirt-tail, while his kilt collapsed in ruins about his ankles. In that moment I really wanted to die.

I halted, turned, and shouted my orders, and then paced off to the side to take the salute. I was marching with right arm akimbo, and the military in the crowd must be wondering and whispering. I halted and turned, bringing my fist into my kidneys and clutching with my thumb; the guard came marching past, throwing on the style in their relief (McAuslan was swinging left arm and left leg together in fine abandon);

their heads snapped round in salute – which I didn't return – and they had vanished into the gateway.

I was alone, with the worst to come. I had to turn again, march to the edge of the crowd in front of the General Officer – with royalty beside him – salute, and march off again. But I couldn't salute! My saluting hand was holding up my nether garments, and if I removed it I should go down in history as the Man Whose Kilt Fell off in Front of Royalty at Edinburgh Castle.

It wouldn't do. Similarly, I could not march off without acknowledging royalty and saluting. What do you do in this case? I shall tell you. You turn smartly about, arm akimbo – it gives a Rupert of Hentzau touch, anyway – march up to the saluting base, salute left-handed, turn about, and march off through the Castle gateway, dead casual, like Caesar at Pharsalia.

In the guardroom was pandemonium. McAuslan, unseen by me, had dropped his rifle in the gateway, the R.S.M. had caught it, McAuslan had turned round and asked for it back, the R.S.M. had almost thrown him into the guardroom, and the corporal, a sensitive soul, had done a brief faint.

I waved them away. I had to go out again and take the salute of the old guard going off; I had troubles.

'Give me that kilt, McFarlane,' I said.

He goggled at me.

'Come on, man, get it off.' I had my own off by now.

'But, sir, I'm first on stag . . .'

'Well, if the Russians come you can wave your shirt-tail at them,' I snarled, more or less dragging the garment off him. I was just buckling it on when the Colonel strode in, full of joy and gladness. Royalty had thought we looked nice; the General was pleased; the American admirals had thought it was colossal; he was pleased; were we pleased? We just looked at him.

'By the way, young Dand,' he added. 'Why were you standing like a blasted ballet dancer at the finish?'

I told him. He went green, and then white, and then he sat down on a bench and began to make little moaning sounds.

Meanwhile the C.S.M. was addressing McAuslan. 'You get your kit, and when the truck comes you get on it, and go back to barracks, and stay there, oot o' sight, and if ye move wan step . . .' Then he turned to me. 'I'll get him replaced, sir. We cannae have him standing sentry, look at the condeetion of him.'

I looked, and he was in a state. Apart from his natural foulness, he was in an extremity of terror, and looking thoroughly miserable. I was about to say: 'Carry on,' when suddenly it seemed all wrong and unfair.

'No,' I said. 'Not a dam' chance. He's mounted guard, he'll do guard. Right, McAuslan? Carry on, Sergeant-Major.'

I saw the old guard – fusiliers, I think they were – off, and after that everything seemed peaceful, and none of it had ever happened. I think I slept most of the afternoon, and it wasn't until late evening that I went into the guardroom, and saw everything was in order, and it was just on sunset when I took a turn outside, and it was one of those evenings, with the black, gaunt battlements against the sky, and the lights of Edinburgh winking in the dusk below, and I found myself thinking of the generations of soldiers who had guarded this place, and the Gay Gordon, and Bonnie Dundee, and the rest of it.

I came to the gate, and there was the inheritor of the great tradition: they had given him a clean shirt, and someone had polished his boots, and he was looking less like an ill-tied sack than usual, but his face was still its customary grey, and he was standing sentry like a yokel with a pitch-fork.

He sloped arms as I came up, and in giving a butt salute managed to half-drop his rifle. I helped straighten him out, and then turned away to breathe in the evening air. And then he spoke.

''Sa'right, i'nt it?' he said.

'What's that?'

''Sa'right. Guardin' ra Castle.'

I digested this. 'Yes,' I said. 'It's all right.'

He sighed heavily. 'Ah like it fine.'

'You know what to do,' I asked him.

'Oh, aye, sir. Wan-I-take-up-a-position-at-the-main-gate. Two-I-patrol –'

'Yes, yes, I know all that. That's by the book. But you know what to do if someone tries to get past you?'

'Sure, sir. Ah'll kill the –'

'Well, yes. And turn out the guard.'

'Och, aye, sir.'

I left him standing there, and he was loving every minute of it, scruffy creature that he was. At the same time, I had nearly made a bigger fiasco of it than he, with all his natural talent, could ever have done.

At that moment I wouldn't have swapped McAuslan for the whole Household Cavalry.

McAuslan's Court-Martial

Considering his illiteracy, his foul appearance, his habit of losing his possessions, and his inability to execute all but the simplest orders, Private McAuslan was remarkably seldom in trouble. Of course, corporals and sergeants had long since discovered that there was not much point in putting him on charges; punishment cured nothing, and, as my platoon sergeant said, 'He's just wan o' nature's blunders; he cannae help bein' horrible. It's a gift.'

So when I found his name on the company orders sheet one morning shortly after his Edinburgh Castle epic, I was interested, and when I saw that the offence he was charged with was under Section 9, Para 1, Manual of Military Law, I was intrigued. For that section deals with 'disobeying, in such manner as to show a wilful defiance of authority, a lawful command given personally by his superior officer in the execution of his office'.

That didn't sound like McAuslan. Unkempt, unhygienic, and unwholesome, yes, but not disobedient. Given an order, he would generally strive manfully to obey it so far as lay within his power, which wasn't far; he might forget, or fall over himself, or get lost, or start a fire, but he tried. In drink, or roused, he was unruly, admittedly, but in that case I would have expected the charge to be one of those charmingly listed under Section 10, which begins 'When concerned in a fray . . .' and covers striking, offering violence, resisting an escort, and effecting an escape. But this was apparently plain, sober disobedience, which was unique.

With Bennet-Bruce away on a ski-ing course in Austria (how is it that Old Etonians get on glamorous courses like ski-ing and surf-riding, while the best I could ever manage was battle school and man management?) I was in command of the company, which involved presiding at company orders each morning, when the evil-doers of the previous day came up for judgment and slaughter. So I sat there, speculating on the new McAuslan mystery, while the Company Sergeant-Major formed up his little troupe on the veranda outside the office.

'Company ordures!' he roared – and with McAuslan involved, the mispronunciation couldn't have been more appropriate – 'Company ordures, shun! Laift tahn! Quick march, eft-ight-eft-ight-eft-ight eftwheeohl! Mark time!' The peaceful office was suddenly shuddering to the dint of armèd heels, an escort and the sweating McAuslan stamping away for dear life in front of my desk. 'Ahlt! Still!' bellowed the C.S.M. '14687347 Private McAuslan, J., sah!'

While the charge was read out I studied McAuslan; he was his usual dove grey colour as to the skin, and his battle dress would have disgraced a tattie-bogle. He was staring in the correct hypnotised manner over my head, standing at what he fondly believed was attention, stiffly inclined forward with his fingers crooked like a Western gun-fighter. He didn't, I noticed, look particularly worried, which was unusual, for McAuslan's normal attitude to authority was one of horrified alarm. He looked almost pugnacious this morning.

'Corporal Baxter's charge, sir,' said the C.S.M., and Corporal Baxter stood forth. He was young and moustached and very keen.

'Sah!' exclaimed he. 'At Redford, on the 14th of this month, I was engaged in detailin' men, for the forthcomin' regimental sports, for duties, in connection, with said sports. I placed the accused on a detail, and he refused to go. I warned him, and he still refused. I charged him, an' he became offensive. Sah!'

He saluted and stepped back. 'Well, McAuslan?' I said.

McAuslan swallowed noisily. 'He detailed me forra pilla-fight, sir.'

'The what?'

'Ra pilla-fight.'

It dawned. At the regimental sports one of the highlights was always the pillow-fight, in which contestants armed with pillows sat astride a greasy pole set over a huge canvas tank full of water. They swatted each other until one fell in.

'Corporal Baxter told you to enter for the pillow-fight?'

'Yessir. It wisnae that, but. It was whit he said – that Ah needed a damned good wash, an' that way Ah would get one.'

Some things need no great explanation. This one was clear in an instant. McAuslan, the insanitary soldier, on being taunted by the spruce young corporal, had suddenly rebelled; what had probably started off as a mocking joke on Baxter's part had suddenly become a formal order, and the enraged McAuslan had refused it. I could almost hear the exchanges.

But it was fairly ticklish. Young soldiers, recruits, are used to being 'detailed' for practically everything. Told to enter for sports, or read Gibbon's *Decline and Fall*, or learn the words of 'To a Mouse', they will do these things. As they get older they get a clearer idea of what is, and is not, a legitimate military order. But the margin is difficult to define. The wise n.c.o. doesn't give off-beat orders unless he is positive they will be obeyed, and Baxter was a fairly new corporal.

One thing was certain: McAuslan wasn't a new private. He might still be as backward as the rawest recruit, but he had heard the pipes at Alamein and had advanced, in his own disorderly fashion, to defeat Rommel. (God help the German who got in his way, I thought, for I'll bet his bayonet was rusty.)

And Baxter's order should not have been given to him, and he felt outraged by it. Thoughtless and zealous people like Baxter probably didn't realise that McAuslan could feel outraged, of course.

When in doubt, grasp the essential. 'You did disobey the order?' I said.

'It wisnae fair. Ah'm no' dirty.' He said it without special defiance.

'That's not the point, McAuslan,' I said. 'You disobeyed the order.'

'Aye.' He paused. 'But he had nae —— business tae talk tae me like that.'

'Look, McAuslan,' I said, 'you've been talked to that way before. We all have, it's part of the business. If you don't like it you can make a formal complaint. But you can't disobey orders, see? So I'm going to admonish you.' Privately, I was going to eat big lumps out of the officious Corporal Baxter too, but for the sake of discipline McAuslan wasn't going to know that. 'All right, Sergeant-Major.'

'Ah'm no' takin' that, sir,' said McAuslan, unexpectedly. 'Ah mean . . . Ah'm sorry, like . . . but Ah don't see why Ah should be admonished. He shouldnae hiv spoke tae me that way.' You could have heard a pin drop. For a minute he had me baffled, and then I recovered.

'You're admonished,' I said. 'For disobedience, which is a serious offence. Think yourself lucky.'

'Ah'm no' bein' admonished, sir,' he said. 'Ah want tae see the C.O.'

'Oh, don't be so bloody silly,' I said. 'You don't want anything of the sort.'

'Ah do, sir. Ah'm no' bein' called dirty.'

'You are dirty,' interposed the sergeant-major. 'Look at ye.'

'Ah'm no'!' shouted McAuslan, all sense of discipline gone.

'Quiet!' I said. 'Now, look, McAuslan. Forget it. This is just nonsense. Everyone has been called dirty, some time or other. You have, I have, probably the sergeant-major has. There's nothing personal about it. We all have.'

'No' as often as I have,' said McAuslan, martyred.

'Well, you must admit that your appearance is sometimes . . . well, a bit casual. But that has nothing to do with the charge, don't you see?'

'Ah'm no' hivin' it,' chanted McAuslan. 'Ah'm no' dirty.'

'Yes, y'are,' shouted the C.S.M. 'Be silent, ye thing!'

'Ah'm no'.'

'Shut up, McAuslan! Sergeant-major, get him out of here!'

'Ah'm no' dirty! Ah'm as clean as onybody. Ah'm as clean as Baxter . . .'

'Don't youse dare talk tae me like that,' cried the enraged Baxter.

'Ah am. Ah am so. Ah'm no' dirty . . .'

'Dammit!' I shouted. 'This is a company office, not a jungle! Get him out of here, sergeant-major!'

The C.S.M. more or less blasted McAuslan out of the room by sheer lung-power, and I heard the procession stamp away along the veranda, to a constant roar of 'Eft-ight-eft' punctuated by a dying wail of 'Ah'm no' dirty'. The nuts, the eccentrics, I thought, I get them every time. McAuslan sensitive of abuse was certainly a new one.

Five minutes later I had forgotten about it, but then the sergeant-major was back, wearing an outraged expression. McAuslan, he said, was refusing to be admonished. He was demanding to be taken before the Commanding Officer.

'He's crackers,' I said. 'Doesn't he know when he's well off?'

'He says he wants to be marched,' said the C.S.M. 'The hell wi' him. Let him go.'

'The C.O.'ll murder him,' I said. We had just got our new C.O., only a few days old, a rather precise, youngish man, decent enough, but very Sandhurst. The thought of his reaction to a disobedient McAuslan was daunting. 'What's got into him, anyway? He never minded being called dirty before.'

'Ach, it's young Baxter,' said the C.S.M. 'He's too full of himself.'

'You can see his point, mind you,' I said. 'The idea of McAuslan going into the tank in the pillow-fight isn't unreasonable. Oh, well, there it is. See that he's at C.O.'s orders at eleven.'

This is the army's procedure. If an accused man isn't satisfied with the justice he gets at the lowest level, he simply demands to be 'marched' to the next higher level, in this case the battalion commander. And so on up, if he feels like it, until he gets to the House of Lords, I suppose. I had a vision of McAuslan at Westminster, facing the Woolsack and crying: 'Ah'm no' dirty,' and their Lordships intoning their verdicts, 'Dirty, upon my honour.' Not, as I had pointed out, that his cleanliness was strictly relevant to the charge of disobedience.

McAuslan's meeting with the C.O. was brief and sensational. Watching it, I felt like one witnessing the introduction of an orang-utan to T. Petronius Arbiter; McAuslan shambled in with his escort, the C.O. shivered a little as though he didn't believe it, and if he had produced a gilded pomander and swung it under his nostrils I wouldn't have been surprised.

The evidence was called again, McAuslan's refusal to be dealt with at company level was verified, the C.O. sighed, tucked his handkerchief into his sleeve, and asked if accused had anything to say. Accused said, predictably, that he wasn't dirty. The C.O., equally predictably, said that had nothing to do with it, and that he found the case proved. He then asked, according to formula:

'Will you accept my award or go before a court-martial?' expecting the invariable acceptance. But he didn't get it. McAuslan, by this time grey with fright – the awful majesty of the C.O.'s office quite as much as the prospect of what lay ahead must have been working on him – swayed slightly at attention, coughed horribly, rolled his eyes and closed them, and whispered hoarsely:

'Ah wannae be court-martialled, sir, thank ye.'

The C.O. said, 'Good God,' and asked him to repeat himself. McAuslan did, and there was a long silence. You could see what the trouble was: the C.O. didn't want a man going for court-martial in the first week of his command; on the other hand, he was new, and felt he must play it by the book. Our old Colonel, full of sin and experience, would have sorted it out, either by terrorising McAuslan or by playing his celebrated let-me-be-your-father role and more or less charming the accused into taking seven days' confinement to barracks. But the new C.O. was uncertain and on his dignity; he made some effort to find out what was behind McAuslan's determination, but he didn't understand his man, and his austerity of manner froze McAuslan into dumb panic.

Finally the C.O. said Very well, march him out, sergeant-major, and that was McAuslan for the big time, the Bloody Assize, the works. I don't suppose he himself had more than a vague idea what a court-martial was, and he was obviously incapable of understanding the difference between the matter of his plain disobedience (which he admitted) and the matter of Baxter's alleged provocation. All he knew was that he wasn't going to be punished for his resentment at being called dirty by a young corporal with half his service.

At any other time, I believe, there might have been unofficial representations to the C.O. to clear the thing up, but everyone was too busy. Royalty was still at Holyrood, and within the week the Highland Division Games were due to take place. This had not happened on a full scale since time immemorial, for it is difficult to get all six Highland Regiments together at one time (there being an official tendency to keep the savages apart in case they start another '45 rebellion, or destroy each other, which is more likely). Any Highland Games is a spectacular show, but with a full muster of the regiments in Scotland this was expected to be something special. Apart from the normal track and field events which you get at any athletics meeting, there would be such esoteric contests as throwing the hammer, tossing the caber, Highland dancing, and piping; the tug-of-war, and the pillow-fight for which McAuslan had fastidiously refused to enter, would be the final events before the prizes were presented by one of the Royal Duchesses. Altogether it was big military, sporting, and social stuff, and McAuslan's court-martial was back-page news by comparison.

As battalion sports officer I hardly even had time to sleep; I was running myself in the quarter-mile and the relay, and I had to supervise the training of the regiment's athletes. This did not consist so much of giving them psychological pep-talks and tips on sprinting, as of keeping Wee Wullie out of the guard room, for he was anchor man and mainstay of the tug-of-war team, and he was drinking more than usual to drown his sorrows over the old Colonel's departure. We had a pretty fair team, all round; we would hold our own in piping and dancing, would probably win the relay and certainly take the high jump, for the Adjutant was a possible Olympic prospect, and we would make a respectable showing in everything else.

So it wasn't the business of making a good show in the actual competition that worried me, so much as ensuring that our entry remained sober and of sound mind, and did nothing to disgrace the regiment's fair name. With royalty present you can't be too careful, and with competitors who have knavery and mischief running thick in their blood you have to be doubly on guard. To give just one example, I uncovered the germ of a plot – just an idea, really, it hadn't got to the blue-print stage – which involved getting hold of the caber in advance and soaking it in water. A caber is several yards of tree trunk which the competitor, a man of iron muscle invariably, must throw end over end; soaked in water it becomes so heavy as to be unmanageable, and there were those in our battalion so lost to shame as to consider it a splendid idea to doctor the caber before the Argylls or the Highland Light Infantry entrants tried to throw it. It wasn't a bad scheme, at that, but the snag was how to arrange matters so that we got the use of an unsoaked caber first. They were working on this when I got wind of it and spoiled everything by threatening disciplinary action. Anyway, as I pointed out, it was too risky.

Then there was the pipe-sergeant to soothe and quieten. He was alarmed to distraction because the Adjutant 'iss participating in the godless high chump, Mr MacNeill, sir, when I want him for the foursome. Look yonder,' he cried, 'at him hurling himself over a silly bit stick when he should be at the dancing, with a one-two. He will injure himself, and I'll be left with Corporal Cattenach that has no more sense of the time than a Hawick farmer. Can you not appeal to him, sir?'

'He can win the high jump and dance in your foursome, too, pipey,' I said.

'Aye, can he, and if he strains himself, with ruptures and torn ligaments, where are we?' cried the pipey. 'Which is the more important for a Highland Games, the fine dancing or . . . or yon abomination? Any clown can loup, sir, but the dear Adjutant is a dancer in ten thousand, see the grace of him. Ach, damn,' he added petulantly, 'they have spoiled all decent sport with their bluidy athletics!'

I left him lamenting, and spent half an hour with our juvenile entry, for the Games included children's sports, and our regimental infants were toiling busily in preparation for the three-legged race, the bean bag, the bunny jump, and the under-10 eighty-yard dash. In this last we were strong, for we had the twin sons of Corporal Coupar, known locally as the Bullet-Headed Little Bandits. They were wicked, fearless, malevolent-looking little urchins of nine, infamous for their evil-doing and their language, which would have earned censure in a Tollcross pub. But they could run; years of evading the wrath of regimental cooks, their father, and those private soldiers who were sensitive to juvenile abuse had made them faster than chain lightning with a link snapped. Barring accidents, the eighty-yard dash was ours. I seized one twin as he shot by, and received a hair-curling rebuke.

'Don't use that disgusting word,' I said. 'Are you Davie or Donnie?'

'Name o' the wee man,' said he. 'Can ye no' tell? Ah'm Donnie. Ah don't look like that, surely?' And he indicated his twin with distaste. Davie retorted, unmentionably.

'David!' I beckoned him, and he came defiantly. 'Now, look, both of you. Do you want any more stories?'

The two small, ugly faces looked slightly concerned. They liked their stories.

'Right,' I said. 'Unless you cut out swearing, no more stories. You should be ashamed. What would your father say?'

Davie sniggered. 'Ye should hear him.'

I slapped him on his trouser seat. 'Don't be impertinent. And what's more, I won't let you run in the sports. Yes, I thought that would worry you. Anyway, are you going to win?'

'No kiddin',' said Donnie scornfully. 'We'll dawdle it.'

'Ye mean Ah'll dawdle it,' said Davie.

'You? You couldnae catch me in a bus.'

'Could Ah no'? You couldnae run wi' the cold.'

I rolled them on the ground briefly, which one should always do to small boys, and was preparing to go on my way when Davie picked himself up from the grass and called:

'Hey, Mr MacNeill. Is it right McAuslan's goin' tae get the jail?'

This stopped me short. 'What do you know about it?'

'Ah heard my daddy sayin' McAuslan had had it. Is that right?'

'I don't know,' I said. 'Why are you interested?'

'Och,' said Davie. 'Ah like McAuslan. He's that —— dirty.'

'Ah hate Corporal Baxter,' said Donnie viciously. 'He's a ——.'

I despaired. You might as well have tried to stop an alcoholic tippling as purify the conversation of the Bullet-Headed Little Bandits. Oddly enough, though, I felt sympathy for both their views, and in the next few days, while the athletes trained and the pipers practised, and the wooden grandstands were erected and the tents pitched and all was made ready for the Games, I found McAuslan increasingly on my mind. The Games were Friday and Saturday, and McAuslan's trial was fixed for the Friday afternoon. He looked like a dead duck, and I wondered how stiff a sentence he would get. Disobeying an order may be admonished at company level, but when it gets before a court-martial it can be a detention offence, quite easily, and McAuslan doing twenty-one days in the iron discipline of a glasshouse was a worrying thought. He wasn't exactly cut out for doing everything at the double and in spotless order.

His defending officer, the 'prisoner's friend', arrived on the Wednesday afternoon. He was a thin, nervous Cockney Jew, with a hard-worn captain's uniform and enormous horn-rimmed spectacles. His other distinguishing characteristics were a huge Adam's apple, a blue lantern jaw, a pendulous nose, and an unhappy expression.

'Name of Einstein,' he said, shaking hands limply. 'Don't make any mathematical jokes, for God's sake, I couldn't stand it. No kidding, I'm thinking of changing it to Shylock.' He laid his battered brief-case on my desk and sank into a chair, massaging his forehead. 'Honest, I've just about had it. Had to stand all the way from York. I'm bushed. Usual last-minute flap, of course. You think you've got it tough in the infantry, mate, you ought to see the Army's bloody legal department.

To give you an idea' – he removed his glasses and stared at me with great spaniel eyes – 'I still don't know the first thing about this ruddy case; not a thing! Organisation! Oh, they did give me the documents, but I seem to have left 'em somewhere. I should cocoa. As my old man said, "Any lawyer that needs a brief needs a bloody nursemaid". And he was no mug, my old man. What's the charge?'

'Disobeying an order,' I said, and he looked surprised.

'Bit of a come-down for your lot, isn't it? I mean to say, last time I was mixed up with a Highland mob it was murder, arson, and making away with Government property in the face of the enemy. Disobedience, eh? Well, it's a living. And as my old man so wisely said, bless his black heart, "Always be happy to do business with the Gentile Tribe, Frankie, you may need a free kilt some day."' His vulpine face assumed a friendly beam. 'So just fill me in, old man, would you?'

I told him the McAuslan saga, pillow-fight, new C.O., objection to being called dirty, and all, and he sat sucking his teeth and twitching.

'Well, some mothers do have them,' he observed when I had finished. 'Got a fag on you, old man?'

I lit him up and asked him how long he thought McAuslan would get.

'Get?' he said, staring at me through the smoke. 'Whaddya mean, "get"?'

'Well, he doesn't seem to have much chance –'

'Not much chance? Don't make me laugh. He's going to get acquitted, mate, don't you worry about that. All my clients get acquitted. There's more of my clients walking about free men than you've had hot dinners. "Get" forsooth! I like that.'

'I'm sorry, I –'

'What we've got to decide on,' said Einstein, waving me to silence, 'is a line of defence. Yers-ss. Let's see . . . How about steady-responsible-hard-working-soldier-victimised-by-cruel-superior? Old, but sound.'

'No, not with McAuslan . . . I don't think . . .'

'Just an idea,' he shrugged. 'Wait, I've got a good one. How about religious-fanatic-wounded-in-his-beliefs? That's a beauty. Show a court a holy man and they get the willies every time.'

'McAuslan isn't holy,' I said. 'He's probably an atheist.'

'You're not helping, you know,' said Einstein severely. 'Tell you what, is he deaf? No? It's never much good, anyway. I don't suppose he's illegitimate, either?'

'Illegitimate?'

'A bastard, you know,' he explained patiently. ''Cos if he was, and this corporal called him one, it'd be a lovely extenuating circumstance. I used that one once, out in Port Sudan. Gift from the gods. President of the court turned out to be a bastard himself. Turned a certain two years for mutinous behaviour into a straight acquittal.' He chuckled reminiscently. 'Those were the days, mate, those were the days.'

'Well, this is today,' I said with some heat, for it seemed to me Captain Einstein was approaching things in a decidedly offhand manner. 'And McAuslan . . .'

'I know, I know,' he flapped his hands at me. 'I'm just exploring, see? Getting the feel of things, looking for a line.' He meditated. 'He isn't normal and steady, he isn't religious, he isn't deaf, and he isn't a bastard. What the hell is he, a cave-man?'

'You said it, not me.'

'Oh.' He stared at me. 'Well. In that case, maybe I'd better have a little talk with him.' He slapped his pockets. 'I say, got another fag on you? I seem to have left mine . . . Ta. Yes, I'll have to reorientate a bit, I can see. To quote my old man again, "If you can't find a good line of defence, just stick to the truth." Let's go and interview the body.'

When he saw McAuslan, who was sitting on his bunk in the cells, looking foul and miserable, Einstein had a quick intake of breath, most of it cigarette smoke, and a coughing fit.

'Gawd,' he said reverently, when he had recovered. 'You don't half pick 'em, don't you? He looks like a distressed area. I can see I'm going to have to be at my talented smoothest to make *him* look good in court. Oh, well, never say die, all things are possible. I mean to say, if you've got a Church of England chaplain off on an embezzlement charge, you can do practically anything, can't you? I've done that, too. Tell you what,' he added, laying a hand on my shoulder, 'why don't you buzz off to the mess and get some drink set up while I have a word with old Private Piltdown here? See you in ten minutes.' He winked. 'And don't look so worried, old cock. Your boy is in capable hands, believe me.'

I hoped sincerely that he was right, this voluble Einstein, but I'd have been happier if he had looked just a bit less of a villain. Frankly, when it came to appearances, I'd sooner have been represented by Blackbeard Teach.

Nor did he seem terribly energetic. Having spent only ten minutes with McAuslan, he came to the mess and drank me nearly bankrupt, ate a hearty dinner, and then took seven and six off the M.O. at snooker. The following day he passed in loafing about the barracks, having a word here and there, returning frequently to the mess to hit the Glenfiddich, and generally looking like a man without a care in the world. I didn't know how legal men prepared for mortal combat, but I was pretty sure they spent more time poring over papers and hunting out surprise witnesses than swilling whisky and trying to lure people to the billiards table.

Then it was Friday morning, and I had the heats of the quarter-mile to worry about: I had modest hopes of getting into the final, and maybe picking up a point or two there. As it turned out, the thing was money for jam, thanks to

Corporal Pudden and my own cleverly psychological running. I discovered as a lad that to succeed in the quarter-mile, against any but really good runners, all you have to do is to set off at top speed from the start. This discourages the mob, who think you must be good; they tend to take it easy in consequence, and by the time they realise their mistake, when you are wheezing and reeling through the last hundred yards, it is probably too late for them to make up lost ground.

So when my heat lined up – Pudden and I were the only representatives of our regiment – and the gun barked, I went off like the clappers. As far as the back straight I was doing fine, but by three-quarters of the way round my evil living – cigarettes, marshmallows, and the like – was taking its toll, and by the time I hit the straight I was giving a fair imitation of the last survivor staggering into the garrison, weak with loss of blood. However, unknown to me, Corporal Pudden, who couldn't run particularly well, but was broad in the beam, had established himself in second place, and by judicious weaving across the track was preventing the opposition from getting past. This enabled me to get home by a comfortable margin, and Pudden, having body-checked a Seaforth who was trying to take the long way round him, just nosed out a Highland Light Infantryman for second place. So after that there was really nothing to do except put my tunic on over my strip and lounge about looking professional, watching the other heats, slapping my calves thoughtfully, and generally behaving like a man to whom both heats and finals are just formalities.

Friday morning, of course, was just the weeding out; the big stuff, finals and so on, was for next day. They were still putting up the last marquees and making a kind of royal box with red carpet when I went off to have lunch, change into my best uniform, and present myself at the opening of McAuslan's court-martial.

It was held in a big, bare room somewhere in Redford

Barracks, and such are memory's tricks that I can remember nothing more of the background than that. There was a long plain table for the members of the court, the president of which was a sad-looking Sapper colonel with bags under his eyes. There was a square, tough-looking major in the Devons, and a very pink young man with chain epaulettes on his shoulders – a cavalryman of sorts. There was also a prosecutor, tall and lean and (to me) looking full of malevolence and brains; there was Einstein, nervous and rather untidy, muttering to himself and diving in and out of his brief-case; he saw me sitting on the chairs for witnesses and spectators, and came over confidentially.

'Bit of a break gettin' an engineer for president,' he whispered. 'They're all barmy. Can't say I like the look of that major from the Bloody Eleventh, though; he'll be a martinet, no error. Dunno about the boy; that type you can never tell – might be soft-hearted, might be a sadist. Think we could risk a fag? No, better not. Bad impression.' He removed his glasses, fidgeted, and drew my attention to Prosecution. 'One of the worst, I'd say; you know, the Middle-Temple-if-it-please-your-ludship-my-pater-was-a-K.C. type. Creeps, the lot o' them.'

'How's McAuslan?' I asked.

'Clean,' said Einstein, 'thanks to the efforts of a couple of lads who've been scrubbing him half the morning. I told the brute straight, I said, 'You may be guilty, but by God, at least you're going to look innocent.' They just took him to the showers and went at him with brushes; shifted a power of dirt, they did. Hallo, curtain up.' There was a thump of marching boots outside. Einstein slid out of his seat. 'Well, into thy hands, Blind Justice, and may God defend the right, or something,' he muttered, and went back to his table.

There was a roar of commands, a stamping on the polished boards, and in came prisoner and escort, marching like crazy. McAuslan was in somebody's best tunic and tartan – certainly not his own – and for the first time in my experience his face was pink, not grey. Whoever had washed him had done a terrific job; he looked like a normal human being – well, nearly normal, for his habit of swinging leg and arm together was still apparent, and when he halted he crouched at attention rather than stood. But his hair appeared to have been stuck down with glue, and when he sat, trembling violently, in the accused's chair, he looked much as any other court-martial candidate looks – scared and lonely, but not scruffy.

There is something frighteningly simple about a court-martial. It is justice stripped to the bare essentials. Usually only prosecutor and prisoner's friend have any legal knowledge; for the rest it is common sense backed by King's Regulations and the Army Act. There is a minimum of ceremony, and for that matter a minimum of talk. But it is probably the fairest shake in the world.

The charge was read, and Einstein pleaded not guilty. The president nodded mournfully to Prosecution, who got up and began to deliver himself, outlining the case against the accused in a languid, matter-of-fact Oxford accent.

The impression he gave was that Corporal Baxter, an n.c.o. of sterling character and charming disposition, had approached McAuslan and suggested that he enter for the inter-regimental pillow-fight. McAuslan, laughing such a laugh as the pious might conceive on the lips of Satan, had refused in the most savage terms. Corporal Baxter, disappointed rather than annoyed, had pleaded with him winningly; McAuslan had repeated his refusal and added the foulest abuse. In spite of this, Corporal Baxter had persevered with forbearing firmness, but the hardened scoundrel would not be moved, and eventually, with great reluctance, Baxter had put him on a charge. Thereupon McAuslan had offered him the vilest of threats, which might well have been taken as the prelude to an assault. No assault had taken place, admittedly, but Prosecution obviously thought it had been a close thing. He then called Corporal Baxter.

Hearing it the way Prosecution had told it, I could see McAuslan already on the rockpile; there seemed no possible defence, and I was surprised to see Einstein looking bored and inattentive. I knew very little about courts.

Corporal Baxter strode masterfully in, looking slightly pale and young, with his stripes gleaming whitely, and took the oath. In more formal language he repeated what Prosecution had said.

'Let us be quite clear, Corporal,' said Prosecution suavely, when Baxter had finished. 'You ordered the accused to enter for this event, the pillow-fight. What words did you use, so well as you can recall?'

'I remember exactly, sir,' said Baxter confidently. 'I said. "You'll put your name down for the pillow-fight, McAuslan".'

'I see. And he said?'

'He said he bloody well wouldn't, sir.'

'Very good. And after you had repeated the order, and again he refused, you charged him, and he became abusive?'

'Yessir.'

'What did he say?'

Baxter hesitated. 'He called me a shilpit wee nyaff, sir.'

The president stirred. 'He called you what?'

Baxter coloured slightly. 'A shilpit wee nyaff.'

The president looked at Prosecution. 'Perhaps you can translate?'

Prosecution, hand it to him, didn't even blink. He selected a paper from his table, held it up at arm's length, and said gravely:

'Shilpit, I am informed, sir, signifies stunted, undergrown. As to "wee", that is, of course, current in English as well as in . . .' he paused for a second '. . . the Northern dialects. Nyaff, an insignificant person, a pip-squeak.'

'Remarkable,' said the president. 'Nyaff. Ny-ahff.' He tried it round his tongue. 'Expressive. Synonymous with the Norse "niddering".'

'Sir?' said Prosecution.

'Niddering,' said the president. 'A worthless person, a non-entity. Possibly a connection there. So many of these Norse pejoratives begin with "n".'

Einstein coughed slightly. 'Hebrew, too, sir. "Nebbish" means much the same thing.'

'Indeed?' The president brightened. 'I'm obliged to you. Nyaff,' he repeated with satisfaction. 'Remarkable. Do go on.'

Prosecution, looking slightly rattled, turned again to Baxter.

'And after he had called you . . . these names?'

'He called me a glaikit sumph.'

You could see Prosecution wishing he hadn't asked. The president was looking hopeful. 'Sumph,' said the president with relish. 'That's strong.' He looked inquiring, and Prosecution sighed.

'Sumph, a dullard, an uninspired person, a stick-in-the-mud. Glaikit, loose-jointed, awkward, ill-formed.' He put down his paper with resignation. 'There is more, sir, in the dialect and in ordinary speech, but I question whether . . .'

'What else did he call you?' said the president, taking control. Baxter looked sulky.

'A rotten big bastard,' he said.

'Oh.' The president looked disappointed. He shot a glance at McAuslan, as though he had hoped for better things. 'All right, then. Carry on, please.'

The major suddenly intervened. 'This was just common abuse?'

'Pretty uncommon, I should say,' observed the young cavalry-man cheerfully.

Prosecution, obviously deciding that things must be put on the right lines again, addressed Baxter:

'Common abuse or not, the point is that a definite order, clearly given and understood, was disobeyed. You are quite clear on that?'

'Yes, sir.' You could see that Baxter didn't care for courts-martial. They just exposed him to a repetition of unpleasant personalities. 'I gave him a good chance, sir, but he just kept refusin'.'

Unbelievably, McAuslan spoke. 'Ah called him a two-strippit git, as weel,' he announced.

This produced an immediate sensation in court. Prosecution rounded indignantly on the accused, the escort snarled at him to be silent, Einstein dropped his spectacles, and the president said he hadn't caught the last word properly. McAuslan, startled at the effect of his intervention, got up hurriedly, upset his chair, cursed richly, and was thrust back into his seat by a savagely whispering regimental policeman. When order had been restored, and the president had been heard to murmur, 'Git, get, geat – possibly Geat, a Goth. Wiglaf was a Geat, wasn't he?' Einstein rose for cross-examination.

'Odd kind of order, wasn't it, Corporal – to enter for a pillow-fight?'

'I was detailing men for duties connected wi' the sports,' said Baxter stiffly.

'What other events did you order people to enter?' asked Einstein.

Baxter hesitated. 'The others I ordered were for fatigues, like settin' up hurdles and helpin' wi' the tents.'

'I see. And why did you order the prisoner into the pillow-fight? Why him, particularly?'

Baxter looked sullen, and Einstein repeated his question. 'This was the only soldier you ordered to enter a specific event. Now, why him, and why the pillow-fight?'

'He was dirty, sir, and I told him he could do wi' a wash.'

'Dirty, was he? Had he been on fatigues?'

'He's always dirty,' said Baxter firmly.

'Oh, he hadn't been on fatigues? You're sure of that?'

'Well, yes, sir,' said Baxter. 'He had been on fatigues . . .'

'What fatigues?' snapped Einstein.

'Ablutions, sir.'

'So he had every right to be dirty at that time?'

'Yes, sir, but . . .'

'Never mind "but". If he was dirty then, it was only natural, considering the fatigues he had been doing, isn't that so?'

'He's always dirty, sir,' insisted Baxter. 'He's the dirtiest thing in the battalion . . .'

'Stand up, prisoner,' said Einstein. 'Now, Corporal, take a good look at him, and tell me: is he dirty?'

Baxter looked at McAuslan, balefully. 'Ye wouldnae expect him to be . . .'

'Answer my question! Is he dirty?'

'No, sir.'

'Yet you said he was *always* dirty. Well, Corporal?'

'It's the first time I've seen him clean,' said Baxter doggedly.

'Ye're a bloody liar,' said McAuslan, aggrieved.

'Ah'm no' . . .'

There were further sensations at this, culminating in a stern warning to the prisoner – I doubt if it would have been half as stern if he had employed a choice Caledonian epithet instead of Anglo-Saxon which the president knew already. Then Einstein resumed, on a different tack.

'When you gave this alleged order, Corporal . . .'

'I can't have that,' said Prosecution, rising. 'Defence's use of the word alleged is calculated to throw doubt on the witness's veracity, which is not in question.'

'Who says it's not?' demanded Einstein. 'He's admitted one mis-statement already.'

'He has done no such thing. That is deliberately to distort his evidence. I submit . . .'

'Perhaps we could rephrase the question?' suggested the president, back to his normal despondent self now that there were no further fine avenues to explore in McAuslan's vocabulary.

'Very good, sir,' said Einstein. 'Corporal, before you gave the order which you've told us you gave, did you not *suggest,* as distinct from ordering, to the accused that he enter the pillow-fight?'

'It was an order, sir,' said Baxter.

'But wasn't it given, well, jocularly. In fun, you know?'

Cunning Einstein knew quite well that if he could get even a hint of admission on this point, he had put a big nail in the prosecution's case. But not-so-cunning Baxter knew that much too.

'No, sir,' he said stoutly.

'No smile? No – well, you know – no case of, "Hey soldier, you look pretty mucky; how about getting a good wash in the pillow-fight?" Wasn't that it? And didn't the prisoner treat it as a joke, and tell you, joking in turn, to get lost? Wasn't that about it, Corporal?'

'No, sir, it was not.'

'And didn't you take offence at this, and *turn* the joke into an order?'

'No, sir, definitely not.'

'Do you know that the prisoner claims that you *did* smile, at first, and that he didn't take your order seriously until, much to his surprise, you put him on a charge?'

'I don't know that, sir.'

'You never realised that he thought you were being funny?'

'No, sir.'

'Have you ever ordered a man to go in for a pillow-fight before?'

'No, sir.'

'Ever heard of such a thing?'

'I've heard of orders being given, sir,' said Baxter boldly.

'That wasn't my question, Corporal, and you know it. Have you ever heard of a man being ordered to enter a pillow-fight?'

'No, sir.'

'So you would agree it isn't a common order?'

'No, sir.'

'Right,' said Einstein. 'Thank you, Corporal. No more questions.'

Prosecution was actually rising when Einstein bobbed up again, as though he had forgotten something.

'I'm sorry, just one more question after all. Corporal, how long have you been a corporal?'

'Three weeks, sir.'

Einstein sat down without a word.

Prosecution contented himself with re-emphasising that an order had been given and understood, and got Baxter to clarify the point about McAuslan's dirtiness: McAuslan, Baxter said, had always been dirty until the present occasion.

'When you would expect him to be looking his best?' asked Prosecution.

'Oh, yes, sir.'

'Thank you, Corporal. That's all.'

Baxter saluted and strode out, and Prosecution called Lance-Corporal Bakie, who corroborated Baxter's evidence as to McAuslan's refusal of a straightforward order. No, Bakie had not seen Baxter smile at any time, nor had McAuslan appeared to regard the order as anything but a serious one. In Bakie's view, the refusal had been pure badness on McAuslan's part, but then McAuslan was notoriously a bad bas . . . a bad soldier. Dirty? Oh yes, something shocking.

Einstein didn't even bother to cross-examine, and when Bakie stood down Prosecution announced that that was it, from his side. He seemed satisfied; he had made his point clearly, it seemed to me. Einstein, muttering and rummaging through his papers, presently rose to open the defence, and to an accompaniment of crashing furniture and stifled swearing, Private McAuslan took the stand.

Looking at him, as he stood listening in evident agitation while they explained what taking the oath meant, I decided that while he was certainly clean for once, that was about all you could say for him. He looked like Sixteen-string Jack on his way to Tyburn, keenly conscious of his position.

Einstein got up, and McAuslan clung to him mentally like a monkey to its mother. Then Einstein started questioning him, slowly and gently, and to my surprise McAuslan responded well. No, he had not taken the order seriously; he had thought Baxter was at the kidding; who ever heard of a fella bein' told tae get intae a pilla-fight? In a military career that stretched from Tobruk onwards (trust Einstein) McAuslan had never heard of such a thing. Oh, aye, Baxter had been smilin'; grinnin' a' ower his face, a' the fellas in the room had seen it.

'Have you ever refused an order, McAuslan?' said Einstein.

'S'help ma Goad, no, sir. Ye can ask Mr MacNeill.'

'You realise that if you have, and been convicted of it, that may appear during this trial? In which case, you know, you can be charged with perjury?'

McAuslan called the gods of Garscube Road to witness his innocence. I was pretty sure he hadn't ever been disobedient – dirty, idle, slovenly, drunk, you name it, McAuslan had been it, but probably he had never wilfully disobeyed a lawful command.

'But, look here, McAuslan,' said Einstein. 'You said some pretty rough things to the corporal, you know. We heard them. How about those?'

'That wis when he got nasty, and started sayin' Ah wis dirty,' said McAuslan vehemently. 'Ah'm no' havin' that. Ah'm no' dirty. He'd nae business tae say that.'

It sounded convincing, although I was certain Einstein had rehearsed him in it. Despite his original protestations to me and to the C.O., when his rage was hot against the upstart Baxter, McAuslan must know he was generally regarded as personally fit only for the dead cart. There had been times in the past when he had seemed to take a satisfaction in his squalor; he had been forcibly washed more than once.

'So, this is your case, then.' Einstein, hands on hips, stared at the floor. 'You thought the corporal was joking, and so you didn't take his order seriously. When he said you were dirty and should enter the pillow-fight to get a wash, you resented it, but you didn't think he really meant you to enter the pillow-fight?'

'That's right, sir.'

'And then he charged you, and you swore at him.'

'Aye.'

'You aren't charged with swearing at him, of course,' Einstein was casual. 'And you contend that when Corporal Baxter says you're a dirty soldier, he is not telling the truth.'

'He's not, sir. Ah'm no' dirty. Ye can ask Mr Mac . . .'

Not if you've any sense, you won't, I thought. I'd do a lot for McAuslan, but perjuring myself to the extent of saying he wasn't dirty would have been too much.

'Tell me, McAuslan,' said Einstein confidentially. 'The reason why you didn't take the order seriously was that you felt that it was silly and unreasonable, wasn't it? I mean, the corporal was really telling you, in a rather nasty way, to get washed. That right? And you knew that wasn't sensible. Oh, I know you'd been on ablutions, but his order implied that you were habitually filthy, didn't it? And you knew that wasn't right?'

Prosecution rose languidly. 'Really, I feel the witness is being led, rather. At this rate defence might as well give his evidence for him.'

There was a bit of legal snarling, and the president mumbled at them, and then Einstein resumed.

'Did you think such an order, given seriously, could reasonably apply to you?'

'No, sir. Ah didnae.'

God forgive you, McAuslan, I thought. Morally, I may be on your side, but legally you're a perjured ruffian. And Einstein, the clown, was making it worse.

'You take a pride in your appearance, McAuslan?'

'Yes, sir.'

Now I'd heard everything.

Einstein sat down, and Prosecution came slowly to his feet, stropping his claws. McAuslan turned to face him as if he were one of the Afrika Korps. Now, I thought, you poor disorderly soldier, you're for it, but somehow it didn't turn out that way. McAuslan knew his story, and he stuck to it: he hadn't disobeyed, he wasn't dirty. Prosecution put his questions suavely, sneeringly, angrily, and Einstein never made a murmur, but McAuslan just sat there with his ugly head lowered and said, 'No, sir,' or 'Ah didnae, sir'. Prosecution's cross-examination was falling flat; you can't play clever tricks with a witness who just persists in dogged denial, and eventually he gave it up. McAuslan went back to the accused's chair, and I felt that on balance he had made not a bad show – better than I'd expected, by a long way.

Then the blow fell. Einstein called Private Brown, who testified that Baxter had been leering wickedly, and had not intended the order seriously; not at first, anyway. Baxter thought he was good, Brown opined, and often took the mickey out of the fellas. So far so good; Brown stuck to his story under cross-examination, and then Prosecution drove his horse and cart through the middle of the defence's case.

'The court has been told that the accused didn't take the order seriously,' he informed Brown, 'and it has been implied that his reason for this attitude was that such an order couldn't apply to him. He contends – the defence will correct me if I'm wrong – that he is a clean soldier, and that therefore the order to enter the pillow-fight (and consequently get a bath) couldn't be taken seriously. What do you think of that?'

Einstein was up like a shot. 'Witness's opinion of evidence is not itself evidence.'

Prosecution bowed. 'All right, I'll change the question. Is McAuslan a clean soldier?'

Brown, who was well named Daft Bob, grinned. 'Ah widnae say that, sir.'

You could feel the court stiffen.

'You wouldn't?' Prosecution's voice was honeyed. 'What would you call him?'

Brown, realising that this mattered, and torn between the fear of the court and loyalty to one who was, after all, his comrade, hesitated.

'Ah don't know, sir.'

'Oh, yes, you do. Is he clean or not, smart or not?'

'He's no' very clean, sir.' A pause. 'We had to wash him once.'

'So his contention that he couldn't believe the order was serious is simply nonsense?'

'Ah . . . Ah suppose so, sir.'

Einstein did his best in re-examination, but it was no use. No honest witness from the battalion could have called McAuslan anything but dirty, and Einstein had made his cleanliness the keystone of the defence. Why he had, I couldn't guess, but he had cooked McAuslan all the way. Prosecution was looking serene when Daft Bob stood down, the court was looking solemn and stern, Einstein was looking worried.

There was a pause, and then the president asked if the defence had any further witnesses. Einstein looked blank for a minute, with his mouth open, said 'Errr' at some length, and then ended abruptly, 'Yessir. Yes, one more, sir.' He stood up, straightened his rumpled tunic, and called out:

'Regimental Sergeant-Major Mackintosh!'

If he had called General de Gaulle I'd have been less surprised. I couldn't think of a good reason for calling the R.S.M., just a few bad ones. If Einstein was hoping to get helpful evidence here, he was, as the Jocks say, away with the fairies.

The R.S.M. came in, like Astur the great Lord of Luna, with stately stride. He was in great shape, from the glittering silver of his stag's head badge to the gloriously polished black of his boots, six and a quarter feet of kilted splendour. He crashed to a halt before the president, swept him a salute, took the oath resoundingly, kissed the book – the sheer military dignity of that one action would have won Napoleon's heart – and sat down, folding the pleats of his kilt deftly beneath him. Einstein approached him like a slightly nervous ambassador before a throne.

'You are John Mackintosh, Regimental Sergeant-Major of this battalion?'

'I am, sir.'

'I see, yes.' Having established that, Einstein seemed uncertain how to proceed. 'Er . . . tell the court, please, er . . . Mr Mackintosh – have you always been with this regiment?'

'No, sir,' said the R.S.M. 'Having completed my early service in this regiment, I was for twelve years in the Brigade of Guards. The Scots Guards, to be exact.'

'Thank you,' said Einstein. 'May I ask what rank you attained – in the Guards?'

'Drill Sergeant, sir. I served in that capacity at the Pirbright depot.'

Which is to say that Mackintosh had been one of the two or three smartest and most expert parade-ground soldiers in the world. It didn't surprise me.

'And after that?'

'I was attached to the Second Commando durin' the late war, sir, before returnin' to the Scots Guards in 1943. Shortly afterwards I was transferred to this battalion.'

'As R.S.M.?'

'In my present capacity, sir; yes.'

Which rounded off his military service nicely, but hadn't done much to clear up the case of Rex v. McAuslan. Einstein was scratching himself; Prosecution was looking slightly amused.

'Tell me, Mr Mackintosh,' said Einstein. 'Having served in the Guards, as you've told us, would you say . . . well, would you disagree, if I said you were probably a leading authority on military standards and deportment?'

The R.S.M. considered this, sitting upright like a Caesar, one immaculate hose-topped leg thrust forward, hand on knee. He permitted himself a half-smile.

'I would nott disagree, sir – no. But if there is any credit in that, it belongs entirely to the Guards, and to my present regiment.'

'Well, that's very nicely put,' said Einstein. 'However, I think we'd all agree that you are an expert in that field.'

Go on, I thought, ask him what he thinks of McAuslan; let's really go out with a bang, so that we can all whimper later.

'What is your opinion,' said Einstein carefully, 'of the standard of drill and dress in this battalion?'

'It is high, sir,' said the R.S.M.

'You've seen to that?'

'Not I alone, sir. I believe I can say, with some confidence, that the battalion will bear comparison wi' any in Scotland, or wi' any regiment of the Line.'

'With the Guards?' asked Einstein mischievously.

'Hardly that, sir.' The R.S.M. gave another of his paternal half-smiles. 'Capability of smartness,' he went on impressively, 'is a pre-requis-ite of a Guardsman. This is not so in a Highland regiment, to the same extent. We do nott hand-pick for size, for example. But I would have not the slightest quaahlms, sirr, in matchin' this battalion, for turn-oot and drill, wi' any in the worrld outside the Brigade.'

'I'm sure you wouldn't,' said Einstein, pleasantly. 'I think, in fact, if I remember rightly, that this battalion recently provided a very special honour guard for a royal occasion, didn't it? Which would bear out what you've been telling us?'

'You're referring, sir, to the guard-mounting at Edinburgh Castle? Yes, the battalion provided the guard on that occasion.' The R.S.M. glanced in my direction. 'Mr MacNeill, there, was in charge of the guard-mountin'. With myself, of course.'

Then it hit me. I saw where Einstein was going, and it froze my marrow. Oh, yes, the R.S.M. and I had been there, and we weren't the only ones.

'Of course,' Einstein was continuing. 'It was a very responsible occasion, I imagine, for both of you. On such occasions, Mr Mackintosh, I imagine that really extra-special care is taken with the guard – with its appearance, turn-out, and so on?'

'Naturally so, sir.'

'The battalion will give of its very best, in fact – in drill, turn-out, and so forth?'

'Yes, sir.' There was a slight frown on the R.S.M.'s face; he was wondering why Einstein was hammering so obvious a point.

'But of course, that's a question of the men involved, isn't it? That's what it boils down to – you put your best men on to a guard like that. In front of royalty, I mean, only the best will do, won't it?'

Still frowning, the R.S.M. said, 'I think that is quite obvious, sir.'

'Good,' said Einstein happily. 'I'm glad you agree. Tell me, Mr Mackintosh: do you see anyone in this room who was a member of that guard of honour? That very special guard on which, as you've told us, only the very smartest and best in the battalion would do?'

The R.S.M. had once stopped a burst from a German mortar; I doubt if it hit him harder than the implication of what he had been saying when he digested the question, surveyed the room, and saw McAuslan – McAuslan who, although he was the central figure of the trial, hadn't been referred to since the R.S.M. entered the room, and whom Mackintosh had naturally not connected with all the questions about smartness and turn-out and the battalion's standards. But, if he had been slow before, the R.S.M. was fast enough to see now how he had been hooked. Perhaps he blinked, but that was all.

'Do you see anyone of that guard, Mr Mackintosh?' Einstein repeated gently.

'The accused,' said the R.S.M., looking at McAuslan as though he was Hamlet's father. 'I see Private McAuslan.'

There was a sharp intake of breath from one of the court; all three of them stiffened.

'The accused,' repeated Einstein slowly, 'was a member of that guard, which consists, I think, of five private soldiers apart from N.C.O.s. Five men out of a battalion of – how many?'

'Seven hundred and forty-six on parade strength, sir, thirty-two on leave, five sick, eleven on courses . . .'

'Quite, quite,' interrupted Einstein. 'We get the point.' He sighed and took off his glasses. 'So when five private soldiers were needed for the most important ceremonial occasion – a royal occasion – that your battalion has participated in since the war, I dare say, when smartness, appearance,' – he paused – 'and cleanliness are all-important – McAuslan was one of the five on parade?'

Nicely put, you had to admit it.

'Yes, sir,' said the R.S.M. slowly.

'Thank you, Mr Mackintosh, no more questions,' said Einstein, and sat down. I was too scared to look at Prosecution. Let him bound to his feet now and ask Mackintosh his opinion of McAuslan's bodily condition, and the R.S.M. was caught between perjury and ridicule. And not only he; the battalion could have been made to look a laughing-stock. But Prosecution, when I dared to look, was plainly too bewildered to think quickly enough, and Mackintosh knew better than to give him a chance. The R.S.M. rose, as though that was all, crashed his foot on the boards, gave the court a look that commanded dismissal if ever a look did, saluted, turned about, and strode majestically from the room. Prosecution made no attempt to have him stopped; either he was too shaken by the R.S.M.'s bombshell, or he simply didn't think it worth while cross-examining. At any rate he just sat there, looking slightly peeved, while the R.S.M. strode out (only Einstein and I knew he was running away, for the first time in his life). The door closed.

After that the president called for closing addresses, and Prosecution got slowly to his feet and repeated the order-was-clearly-given-and-disobeyed line; it sounded lame, but it was all he could do. Then Einstein got up and laid about him. It was fine, impassioned stuff which left the impression that McAuslan was the R.S.M.'s admired and special favourite, doted upon for his salubrious brilliance and perfect cleanliness. How could this model soldier, this paragon who had been specially selected for the guard of honour (I tried not to remember the true circumstances) be represented – as the prosecution had tried to represent him – as noisome and unseemly? Plainly, Einstein asserted, Corporal Baxter was mistaken, to say the least of it. Plainly, McAuslan was entitled to think that he was being jested with when he was told to enter the pillow-fight and get washed. His personal cleanliness, which was the crux of the whole affair, had just been demonstrated in the most convincing manner, by a highly senior warrant officer who judged by the standards of the Brigade of Guards. And so on. It would have made you weep; it really would.

The court was out for less than twenty minutes. They found McAuslan not guilty.

'Key witness at the last minute,' said Einstein to me as he shovelled his papers away. 'Never fails. And why? Let me tell you, mate. Court-martials are human, unlike judges; they like you to make their flesh creep; they want you to slip the ace down your sleeve just when all is lost. "Make 'em feel warm and clever, son, and you'll sit on the Woolsack yet," my dear old dad used to say. Mind you, that R.S.M. of yours is a bloody jewel, he really is. Perfect witness. Ah well,' he buckled his brief-case up, 'that's show business. See you in court, old man.'

It is a matter of record that Private McAuslan, on realising that he was not going to be shot, shambled straight from the court to the battalion sports office and there entered for the inter-regimental pillow-fight. He was not going to have it supposed, he explained, that he was feart. Far from it; his cleanliness having been established by process of law – Justice on this occasion not merely being blindfolded but having a bag over her head as well – he was aflame to get on that pole and belt the hell oot o' thae ither fowk from the ither mobs. He had, he observed, shown that – Baxter that he couldnae talk tae him like that; now, let him be provided with a pillow and give him some fighting room.

His entry being accepted, he went to bask in the glory which briefly surrounds all soldiers who have faced the ultimate military trial and got away with it. Not that there was much congratulation from his fellows; the battalion simply shook its head and remarked that he was as lucky as he was dirty. But the Bullet-Headed Little Bandits, Donnie and Davie, rejoiced in his delivery, and delighted in the rumour that Corporal Baxter had wept on hearing the verdict, and had vowed to nail McAuslan for insolence in entering for the pillow-fight after all.

Saturday was clear and brilliant, and the sports field was all gay dresses and uniforms; the women were wearing the 'new look' then, with ankle-strap shoes and big, bucket hats; the sun shone on green grass and white marquees and panting Highlanders in singlets; there were refreshments and small talk and the tinkle of well-bred laughter, and in the distance the beat of pipes and drums from the little arena where the dancing and piping were being judged. Royalty was there in the person of a Duchess, surrounded by a gracefully inclining crowd from which there rose a continual hum of murmured pleasantries and nervous jealousy. There were officers of rank, blazered civilians, elderly gentlemen with kilts too long and memories even longer; young officers whose accents had grown remarkably refined overnight flirted with the Edinburgh belles; there were the occasional rumbles of applause as a race finished, and much calculating as the results came in to decide which regiment was out in front; the pipe-sergeant, skipping with nervousness, was there to hustle the Adjutant, flushed from his victory in the high jump, to the dancing stage, inquiring anxiously about strains and ruptures; the various colonels affected a fine disinterest in the competitive side of things and watched the scoreboard like hawks; starters' guns cracked, debs squeaked, subalterns giggled, sergeants swore softly, hats were raised, glasses were emptied, programmes were consulted, and I weighed up the lean, sallow Cameron Highlander who had clipped two seconds off my time in the heats of the quarter, and wondered if I had an extra five yards somewhere in me for the final.

As it turned out, I hadn't. In spite of the gallant blocking tactics of Corporal Pudden, that Cameron hung at my elbow like a shadow, and in the final straight, when he drew ahead, I made my burst too soon and hadn't anything left for the last twenty yards. He could have beaten me anywhere, any time, I think, so it made no odds. A Black Watch came third.

We took the relay, however, no thanks to me, for running

fourth I inherited a lead of thirty yards which a lanky Seaforth reduced to five; he came desperately near to catching me at the finish, but at the risk of thrombosis and nervous exhaustion I managed to stay in front.

We were doing respectably enough, one way and another, for the tug-of-war team were having a field day in the heats of that event, thanks to the colossal weight of the battalion cooks, under their sergeant, and the tremendous brawn of Provost Sergeant McGarry and Wee Wullie, who was the anchor. The cook sergeant, or master gyppo, was only about five feet high, but he was about eighteen stone in weight, and his assistant cooks were full of high living and endurance. McGarry would have given a gorilla a run for its money, and Wee Wullie, the rope like a thread in his paw, was as immovable as the city hall. They pulled a wiry H.L.I. team to pieces in the first round, and walked away with the Argylls in the second, to the great satisfaction of the pipe-sergeant.

'The Campbells iss beat,' said he. 'Glory to God and to the master gyppo, see the champion size of him. He is like Donald Dinnie for strength, or A. A. Cameron that could lift a Clydesdale horse and cart. Wait you till they meet the Black Watch in the final, and some of the Colonel's good manners will disappear; he cannae abide the Black Watch. I don't mind them mysel'; it's the Argylls I cannae stomach. I'll go over to their pipey, Sergeant Macarthur, in a minute and have a wee gloat.'

The day wore on in a golden haze; I spent most of my time lolling on a grassy bank, smoking the cigarettes which I had been avoiding while in training, strolling up to the marquee for lunch, full of content that the battalion was acquitting itself well (not that the sports officer gets any credit for that, only blame if they do badly), and stopping by the children's sports in the afternoon to watch Donnie and Davie perform in the infants' foot-race. A good proportion of the crowd were here, including the Duchess and her train; children get them every time.

Fortunately the well-bred spectators were at a sufficient distance not to see the raw work that was being pulled in some of the events. I watched a tiny blonde of the Argyll and Sutherlands take the egg-and-spoon race with her egg firmly clamped down by a thumb, and in the boys' obstacle race things happened during the crawl under the tarpaulin that would have disgraced a gladiatorial combat. One unfortunate little Seaforth emerged into the light crying, with his belt knotted round his ankles – yes, there are lessons in imperial history even in a regimental children's athletic meeting.

But the infants' foot-race was a horror. I had reassured myself by careful inquiry beforehand that the wise money was riding on Davie at odds on, with Donnie evens and no one else quoted. The thing appeared to be sewn up, and the Bullet-Headed Little Bandits set a cracking pace after some excellent elbow-work at the start. They were neck and neck to within feet of the tape, and then Donnie stumbled, his brother checked instinctively, and a foxy-faced little ruffian in the Camerons shot through to take the decision literally by a head.

There was light laughter and applause from the gallery, and obscene lamentation from the defeated participants. I saw Davie's little gargoyle face distorted with grief as the stewards shooed him away, while Donnie appeared to be entering some form of official protest; he almost caught the Cameron child by the tea-tent, but fear lent the winner wings and he escaped. I reflected that it was going to take more than a mere bedtime story to console the twins for this.

I was studying the scoreboard back at the main arena when the pipe-sergeant skipped up to announce that we had come third in the piping and second in the dancing, which wass not too bad at all, at all, 'although mind you, Mr MacNeill, sir, there is chudges there that are more concerned to give the prizes to regiments wi' royal colonels-in-chief than to honest dancers. I'm no' sayin' the princess had anythin' to do wi' it, mind, but there's an H.L.I. man yonder wi' a winner's ticket an' him wi' no more grace and music than the M.O.'s dog. He iss chust a yokel.'

'Never mind,' I said, counting up. 'If we take a place in the pillow-fight and win the tug-of-war we'll finish top of this heap yet.' They were the only events left, and from all over the ground people were converging on the space in front of the stand where the pillow-fight tank stood below the royal box; the preliminary rounds were already being decided amidst shrieks of laughter and monumental splashings, and the pipey and I made our way round until we could get a view of the tank and the combatants crouched precariously on the pole two feet above the water's chilly surface.

The science of pillow-fighting lies in the balance. You sit astride the pole, legs dangling or crossed beneath it, and hammer your opponent with your pillow (which after the first few rounds is sopping wet and heavy). The trick is hitting with controlled force, for if you swing wildly and miss, your own momentum will put you in the drink.

McAuslan didn't know this, but he had a technique of his own, and it worked. Of course, being more ape than man he had an advantage, but no idea of how to exploit it. He just sat astride, ankles locked, hair plastered down, head sunk between his shoulders, face shining with bestial fear, and clung to the pole like a limpet. Let them hit him all they wanted, he didn't care; the word went round that he was paralysed with fear at the thought of contact with water, which may well have been true. At any event, he won two bouts against opponents who overbalanced in their energy, while McAuslan, without striking a blow, concentrated on staying perpendicular.

His third fight was a closer thing, for he was up against the Seaforth colonel's batman, a herculean thug who battered so hard that McAuslan fell sideways but managed to keep his feet wrapped round the pole, and hung head down above the water. The batman thrashed away at him, leaning over to get at him, and McAuslan in his desperation managed to catch the other's pillow and drag him down to destruction.

This feat received the biggest cheer of the day, while McAuslan, clinging on like some great sloth, worked his way along the pole to safety.

'That brute's prehensile,' muttered the Seaforth colonel, and our colonel, the very one who had seen McAuslan consigned to a court-martial, said happily that he wouldn't be surprised.

It would be nice to record that McAuslan continued to triumph through the final round, but it didn't happen. I was beginning to wonder if Corporal Baxter's well-meant efforts to introduce our contestant to water were not going to be frustrated after all, when he met his match. It was an epic contest, in its way, for McAuslan was pitted in the final against the Argyll's padre, a fat and sporting cleric, toughened by countless General Assemblies, and with a centre of gravity so low that he was practically immovable.

He swung a powerful pillow, but for once McAuslan, supposing no doubt that since his opponent was a man of God he would be a soft touch, came out swinging himself. They clobbered each other heartily for a few seconds, and then McAuslan's pillow slipped from his hand, and he was left defenceless. He gave a despairing cry, the crowd roared, and the padre, full of the lust of holy slaughter like Archbishop Turpin at Roncesvalles, humphed along the pole for the kill. He brandished his pillow aloft, and McAuslan, all decency gone, grappled with him; they swayed together for a moment, and then with shrieks of shipwreck and foundered mariners, they plunged into the tank.

The surface boiled and heaved for a few moments, and then the padre emerged with a fine porpoise action, and was understood to complain that McAuslan had bitten his foot. Presently the culprit broke surface, looking like Grendel's mother, to be disqualified for wrestling and ungentlemanly conduct, or whatever it is called under pillow-fighting rules. It was fair enough, I suppose, and my sympathies were with the limping padre, Argyll though he was. Any man who has had McAuslan gnawing at him under four feet of water deserves all the commiseration he can get.

After this the tug-of-war was an anti-climax, especially as we disposed of the Black Watch in two straight pulls, despite the fact that Wee Wullie had obviously taken a liquid lunch ('weel gassed,' observed the pipe-sergeant, 'stiffer than a caber') and insisted on pulling sideways instead of straight back. This seemed to alarm the Black Watch more than his own side, who were used to him, and the massive strength of McGarry and the master gyppo did the rest.

There remained only the prize-giving, presided over by the Duchess, with R.S.M. Mackintosh beside her in full fig, roaring out the names as the winners came forward. If you have seen one sports prize-giving you have seen them all; the polite clapping and murmurs of 'Ahhm, well done' from the Quality gathered behind the platform, and the cries of 'Aw-haw-hey, we're a wee boys' from the hoi-polloi out in front as their champions are rewarded; the little table with its silverware and certificates; the tousled competitors hurrying up to shake hands and receive their prizes; the cool Duchess (or whoever it is) in her picture hat, smiling and offering pleasant congratulations – it may happen elsewhere, but there is something uniquely British about it; it is one of those pointless important rituals that we could not conceivably give up, especially if it happens to be raining.

As battalion sports officer, I collected the shield along with my opposite number from the Camerons – when everything was tallied up it was discovered that our regiments had tied for first place – and the rest of the presentations went more or less according to plan: Wee Wullie did not fall down when he and the tug-of-war specialists came forward; the pipe-sergeant, I was intrigued to notice, for all his strictures on the winner of the dancing, cheered and applauded wildly when that worthy received his trophy. But what fascinated me most was to see McAuslan shamble up behind the Argyll padre to receive his runners-up award for the pillow-fight: someone should have photographed it – McAuslan getting a prize for something.

Being him, he hadn't had time to change, and only last-minute modesty had caused him to put on his tunic above his sodden gym shorts; he was, as usual, in a state of acute anxiety, and he shook hands with the Duchess like a badly wound-up clockwork toy, clutching his prize of saving certificates as if it was a reprieve.

She smiled at him as he stood dripping and shuffling, and then – I'm prepared to believe that royalty are clairvoyant – to the statutory 'Well done' she added:

'You must be dreadfully chilly; I'm sure you'll be glad to get into your nice uniform again.'

It was kindly meant of course, and it was certainly kindly received. Probably only the R.S.M. and I appreciated the full irony of it, but McAuslan blossomed like a June flower. As if a court-martial wasn't enough, here was a Duchess implying that he, McAuslan, wasnae dirty; for a moment he looked like Galahad receiving the victor's crown from a Queen of Beauty, and it wouldn't have astonished me if he had knelt and pressed the hem of her dress to his lips. But he did the Glasgow equivalent, which was to blush and say, 'Och, ta, but,' and then withdrew, trailing damp clouds of glory.

No doubt there was a moral in it somewhere; McAuslan,

the dirtiest soldier in the world, getting prizes and escaping unscathed from courts-martial and having Duchesses paying him indirect compliments: considering, I decided that the kindly providence that watches over drunks and children must be guiding McAuslan's destiny as well. I just hoped it wouldn't work too hard; the kind of luck he'd been having he'd probably end up Chief of the Imperial General Staff. Mind you, we've had nearly as bad.

And that was it, apart from one trivial incident which shortened a few life expectancies and, to me at least, was a fitting epilogue to a fairly eventful few days. The children received their prizes right at the finish, and one of the last was the award to the winner and runner-up of the infants' eighty-yard dash. The Quality were smiling indulgently as the little dears came forward, the Duchess was at her most charming, the crowd applauded loudly, and even R.S.M. Mackintosh wore a paternal expression.

And then little Donnie stepped forward to receive his second prize. The Duchess beamed on him fondly – in his little kilt, and with his normal lowering expression, he looked like a rather cute little Highland bull – shook his hand, and said:

'I think you ran very well; and you were really unlucky not to win.'

To which the gentle child, lifting up his earnest gargoyle face, replied in the accent of Maryhill Road, but with fearful clarity:

'Ach, yon Cameron —— tripped me. It was a —— swiz.'

There was a few seconds' horrified frozen silence, in which the Duchess's charming smile altered by not one fraction, and a ghastly sigh rippled through the ranks of the Quality. And then R.S.M. Mackintosh, his years of Guards' training no doubt coming to his aid, leaned forward and said in a diplomatic whisper which was audible twenty yards away:

'He is saying "Thank you very much", Your Highness. In Gaelic.'

You cannot shake a Regimental Sergeant-Major; whatever the situation, he is unconquerable.

'How very nice of him,' said the Duchess, still smiling, as Donnie trotted away. 'How awfully nice.'

You cannot shake a royal Duchess either.

McAUSLAN IN THE ROUGH

FOR

SIE, CARO, AND NICKY

SOME MORE STORIES

Bo Geesty

> See this fella, Bo Geesty? Aye, weel, him an' his mates, they wis inna Foreign Legion, inna fort, inna desert, an' the wogs wis gettin' tore in at them. An' a' the fellas inna fort got killt, but when the relief colyum arrived a' the fellas inna fort wis staundin' up at the wall, wi' their guns an' bunnets on, like they wis on guard. But they wis a' deid. The fellas in the relief colyum couldnae make it oot; they thought the place must be hauntit. So they did. It wis a smashin' picture, but.
>
> – Private McAuslan, as critic, on the film of P.C. Wren's *Beau Geste*

Fort Yarhuna lies away to the south, on the edge of the big desert. It was there, or something like it, in the days when the Sahara was still grassland; in more modern times it saw long-range patrols of Alexander the Great's mercenaries from fair Cyrene across the sandhills eastward, and it received the battered remnants of Hannibal's regiments after Zama. It was garrisoned by Roman legionaries before the Vandals swept into it from the west, or Arab riders from the Great Sand Sea brought the first camels and planted the date-palms in the little village beneath its walls; it shielded the Barbary rovers' sea-nests until a little detachment of U.S. Marines marched across the desert to plant the Stars and Stripes for the first time on foreign soil. The Caliphs ornamented its gateway, the Crusaders built the little shrine in the courtyard, the Afrika Korps stored the petrol for their panzers in its stables, the Highland Division left their inevitable 'H.D.' trademark on its walls, and Private Fletcher (I suspect) scribbled 'Kilroy was here' and 'Up the Celtic' on its main gate. That was during the Twelve Platoon occupation, circa A.D. 1946.

The reason for Fort Yarhuna's long existence is that it commands a crossing of the great caravan trails, the last oasis on the edge of nowhere. The great trains from the south, with their ivory and gold and slaves, paused here before the last lap north to Tripoli and Tunis, or before they turned eastward for Egypt; coming in the other direction, it was where the Mediterranean traders tightened their girths and sharpened their weapons against the Touareg bandits who infested the southern roads through the biggest wasteland in the world. Fort Yarhuna, in fact, has seen a lot of hard service and is a very hot station. Its importance to me is that it was my first very own independent command, and the significance of that is something which Hannibal's men, and Alexander's, to say nothing of the Romans, Vandals, Crusaders and Leathernecks, would be the first to appreciate.

Why we had to garrison it, nobody knew. The battalion was stationed on the coast, in civilisation, the war was over, and there was nothing to do except show the flag, bathe, beat retreat every Friday with the pipes and drums to impress the locals, and wait to be demobilised. But Higher Authority, in Cairo, decreed that Fort Yarhuna must be garrisoned – they may have had some vague fears of invasion from the Belgian Congo, or been unduly impressed by seeing *The Desert Song*, but more probably it was just military tidiness: Fort Yarhuna had always been manned, and it was officially in our battalion area. So, since I had been commissioned for six months and attained the giddy height of lieutenant, I was instructed to repair to Fort Yarhuna with two platoons, place it in a state of defence, occupy it for a month in the name of the King and the United Nations, close its gate at sunset, see that the courtyard was swept and free from litter, and in the event of an Arab uprising (I'm sure someone had seen

The Desert Song) defend it to the last round and the last man etc., etc.

Of course, there wasn't a chance in a million of an Arab uprising. Since the Italians had been heaved out in the war, all that the genial Bedouin wanted to do was carry on loafing in the sun, catching cholera and plodding his caravans through Yarhuna village from nowhere to yonder; the nearest thing to illegal activity was the local pastime of looting the debris of war which Montgomery's and Rommel's men had left spread over the countryside, for in those days the whole way from Egypt to Tunis was a great junkyard of burned-out tanks, wrecked trucks, abandoned gear, and lost ammunition dumps. And whatever Cairo thought, the local official opinion was that the Arabs could have it, and welcome.

I was more concerned at the possibility of a Twelve Platoon uprising. A month stuck in a desert fort would be no joy to them, after the fleshpots of the coast, and while six months had established a pretty good working relationship between me and my volatile command of Glaswegians and Aberdeenshire countrymen, I was a trifle apprehensive of being their sole authority and mentor so far away from the battalion, where you have the whole apparatus of Army, Colonel, Regimental Sergeant-Major and provost sergeant to back you up.

The Colonel, that kindly, crafty old gentleman, gave me sound advice before I set out. 'Work 'em stupid,' he said. 'Every parade – reveille, first inspection, cook-house, and company office – must be on the dot, just as though you were in the battalion. Anyone drags his feet by as much as a second – nail him. I don't care if half the detachment's on jankers. But if you let 'em slack off, or have time to be bored, they'll be sand-happy before you know it. It can happen well inside a month; ennui has undermined more outpost garrisons than plague or enemy action, take my word for it.' And he went on to tell me harrowing tales of Khyber forts and East African jungle stockades, called for another whisky, and assured me it would be great fun, really.

'To keep you occupied, you're to dig for water, *inside* the fort itself. The place hasn't been occupied for years, but there's got to be a well somewhere, the Sappers say. If one is found, it'll save the water-truck coming down every second day. You can pick up the drilling equipment at Marble Arch depot – they'll give you a driver to work it – while Keith takes the detachment down to Fort Yarhuna and settles 'em in.'

Keith was the second-lieutenant who commanded Eleven Platoon – the garrison of Yarhuna was to be a two-platoon force – so I despatched him and the command to the fort, while I went with one section to Marble Arch for the drilling gear. It was a long, dusty, two-day haul east on the coast road, but we collected the drilling-truck from the Service Corps people, were shown how the special screw attached to its rear axle could drill a ten-foot shaft six inches across in a matter of minutes, and told that all we had to do was proceed by trial and error until we struck water.

I was in haste to get back along the coast and down to Fort Yarhuna to assume command before Keith did anything rash – young subalterns are as jealous as prima donnas, and convinced of each others' fecklessness, and Keith was a mere pink-cheeked one-pipper of twenty years, whereas I had reached the grizzled maturity of twenty-one and my second star. Heaven knew what youthful folly he might commit without my riper judgement to steady him. However, we paused for a brief sight-see at Marble Arch which, as you may know, is one of the architectural curiosities of North Africa, being a massive white gateway towering some hundreds of feet out of the naked desert, a grandiose tombstone to Mussolini's vanity and brief empire.

It was probably a mistake to stop and look at it: I should have remembered that in the section with me was Private

McAuslan, the dirtiest soldier in the world, of whom I have written elsewhere. Short, be-pimpled, permanently unwashed, and slow-witted to a degree in the performance of his military duties, he was a kind of battalion landmark, like the Waterloo snuff-box. Not that he was a bad sort, in his leprous way, but he was sure disaster in any enterprise to which he set his grimy hand. As his platoon commander, I had mixed feelings about him, partly protective but mostly despairing. What made it worse was that he tried to please, which could lead to all sorts of embarrassment.

When we got out of the truck to view the arch he stood scratching himself and goggling balefully up at it, inquiring of his friend Private Fletcher:

'Whit the hell's yon thing?'

'Yon's the Marble Arch, dozey.'

'Ah thought the Marble Arch wis in London. Sure it is.'

'This is anither Marble Arch, ye dope.'

'Aw.' Pause. 'Who the hell pit it here, then? Whit fur?'

'The Eyeties did. Mussolini pit it up, just for the look o' the thing.'

McAuslan digested this, wiped his grimy nose, and like the Oriental sage meditating on human vanity, observed: 'Stupid big bastard', which in its own way is a fair echo of contemporary opinion of Il Duce as an imperialist.

The trouble was that they wanted to climb the thing, and I was soft enough to let them; mind you, I wanted to climb it myself. And Marble Arch is really big; you climb it by going into a tiny door in one of its twin columns, ascending some steps, and then setting off, in total darkness, up an endless series of iron rungs driven into the wall. They go up forever, with only occasional rests on solid ledges which you find by touch in the gloom, and when you have climbed for about ten minutes, and the tiny square of light at the top of the shaft seems as small as ever, and your muscles are creaking with the strain of clinging to the rungs, you suddenly realise that the black abyss below you is very deep indeed, and if you let go . . . Quite.

McAuslan, naturally, got lost. He strayed on to one of the ledges, apparently found another set of rungs somewhere, and roamed about in the stygian void, blaspheming horribly. His rich Parkhead oaths boomed through the echoing tunnels like the thunderings of some fearful Northern god with a glottal stop, and the ribaldries of the rest of the section, all strung out in the darkness on that frightening ladder, mocking him, turned the shaft into a deafening Tower of Babel. I was near the top, clinging with sweating fingers to the rungs, painfully aware that I couldn't go back to look for him – it would have been suicide to try to get past the other climbers in the blackness – and that if he missed his hold, or got exhausted playing Tarzan, we would finish up scraping him off the distant floor with a spoon.

'Don't panic, McAuslan,' I called down. 'Take it easy and Sergeant Telfer'll get you out.' Telfer was at the tail of the climbing procession, I knew, and could be depended on.

'Ah'm no' —— panickin'' came the despairing wail from the depths. 'Ah'm loast! Ach, the hell wi' this! —— Mussolini, big Eyetie git! Him an' his bluidy statues!' And more of the like, until Telfer found him, crouched on a ledge like a disgruntled Heidelberg man, and drove him with oaths to the top.

Once at the summit, you are on a platform between two enormous gladiatorial figures which recline along the top of the arch, supporting a vast marble slab which is the very peak of the monument. You get on to it by climbing a short iron ladder which goes through a hole in the slab, and there you are, with the wind howling past, looking down over the unfenced edge at the tiny toy trucks like beetles on the desert floor, a giddy drop below, and the huge sweep of sand stretching away to the hazy horizon, with the coast road like a string running dead straight away both sides of the arch. You must be able to see the Mediterranean as well, but curiously enough I don't remember it, just the appalling vastness of desert far beneath, and the forced cheerfulness of men pretending they are enjoying the view, and secretly wishing they were safely back at ground level.

We probably stayed longer than we wanted, keeping back from the edge or approaching it on our stomachs, because the prospect of descent was not attractive. Eventually I went first, pausing on the lower platform to instruct McAuslan to stay close above me, but not, as he valued his life, to tread on my fingers. He nodded, ape-like, and then, being McAuslan, and of an inquiring mind, asked me how the hell they had got they dirty big naked statues a' the way up here, sir. I said I hadn't the least idea, Fletcher said: 'Sky-hooks', and as we groped our way down that long, gloomy shaft, clinging like flies, a learned debate was being conducted by the unseen climbers descending above me, McAuslan informing Fletcher that he wisnae gaunae be kidded and if Fletcher knew how they got they dirty big naked statues up there, let him say so, an' no' take the mickey oot o' him, McAuslan, because he wisnae havin' it, see? We reached the bottom, exhausted and shaking slightly, and resumed our journey to Fort Yarhuna, myself digesting another Lesson for Young Officers, namely: don't let your men climb monuments, and if they do, leave McAuslan behind. Mind you, leaving McAuslan behind is a maxim that may be applied to virtually any situation.

We reached Yarhuna after another two-day ride, branching off the coast road and spending the last eight hours bumping over a desert track which got steadily worse before we rolled through Yarhuna village and up to the fort which stands on a slight rise quarter of a mile farther on.

One look at it was enough to transport you back to the Saturday afternoon cinemas of childhood, with Ronald Colman tilting his kepi rakishly, Brian Donlevy shouting 'March or die, mes enfants', and the Riffs coming howling over the sand-crests singing 'Ho!' It was a dun-coloured, sand-blasted square structure of twenty-foot walls, with firing-slits on its parapet and a large tower at one corner, from which hung the D Company colour, wherever Keith had got that from. Inside the fort proper there was a good open parade square, with barracks and offices all round the inside of the walls, their flat roofs forming a catwalk from which the parapet could be manned. It was your real Beau Gests fort and it was while my section was debussing that I heard McAuslan recalling his visit to the pictures to see Gary Cooper in Wren's classic adventure story. ('Jist like Bo Geesty, innit, Wullie? Think the wogs'll get tore in at us, eh? Hey, mebbe Darkie'll prop up wir deid bodies like that bastard o' a sergeant in the pictur'.' I'll wear gloves if I prop you up, I thought.)

Keith, full of the pride of possession, showed me round. He had done a good job in short order: the long barrack-rooms were clean if airless, all the gear and furniture had been unloaded, the empty offices and store-rooms had been swept clear of the sand that forever blew itself into little piles in the corners, and he had the Jocks busy whitewashing the more weather-worn buildings. Already it looked like home, and I remember feeling that self-sufficient joy that is one of the phenomena of independent command; plainly Keith and the Jocks felt it, too, for they had worked as they'd never have done in the battalion. I went through every room and office, from the top of the tower to the old Roman stable and the cool, musty cells beneath the gatehouse, prying and noting, whistling 'Blue heaven and you and I', and feeling a growing pleasure that this place was ours, to keep and garrison and, if necessary, defend. It was all very romantic, and yet practical and worthwhile – you can get slightly power-crazy in that sort of situation, probably out of some atavistic sense inherited from our ancestors, feeling secure and walled-in against the outside. It's a queer feeling, and I knew just enough from my service farther east to be aware that in a day or two it would change into boredom, and the answer, as the Colonel had said, was to keep busy.

So I was probably something like Captain Bligh in the first couple of days, chasing and exhorting, keeping half the detachment on full parade within the fort itself, while the other half went out on ten-mile patrols of the area, for even with a friendly population in peacetime you can't know too much about the surrounding territory. To all intents it was just empty desert with a few Bedouin camps, apart from Yarhuna village itself. This was a fair-sized place, with its oasis and palm-grove, its market and some excellent Roman ruins, and about a hundred permanent huts and little houses. It boasted a sheikh, a most dignified old gentleman whose beard was bright red at the bottom and white near his mouth, where the dye had worn off; he visited us on our second day, and we received him formally, both platoons in their tartans and with fixed bayonets, presenting arms. He took it like a grandee, and Keith and I entertained him to tea in the company office, with tinned salmon sandwiches, club cheese biscuits, Naafi cakes, a tin of Players and such other delicacies as one lays before the face of kings. The detachment cook had had fits beforehand, because he wasn't sure if Moslems ate tinned salmon; as it turned out this one did, in quantity.

He had an interpreter, a smooth young man who translated into halting English the occasional observations of our guest, who sat immovable, smiling gently beneath his embroidered black kafilyeh, his brown burnous wrapped round him, as he gazed over the square at the Jocks playing football. We were staying for a month? And then? Another regiment would arrive? It was to be a permanent garrison, in fact? That would be most satisfactory; the British presence was entirely welcome, be they Tripoli Police or military. Yes, the local inhabitants had the happiest recollections of the Eighth Army – at this point the sheikh beamed and said the only word of English in his vocabulary, which was 'Monty!' with a great gleam of teeth. We required nothing from the village? Quite so, we were self-sufficient in the fort, but he would be happy to be of assistance . . . And so on, until after more civilities and another massive round of salmon sandwiches, the sheikh took a stately leave. It was at the gate that he paused, and through his interpreter addressed a last question: we were not going to alter or remove any of the fort buildings during our stay? It was a very old place, of course, and he understood the British valued such things . . . a smile and a wave took in the carved gateway, and the little Crusaders' shrine (that surprised me, slightly, I confess). We reassured him, he bowed, I saluted, and the palaver was finished.

I'm not unduly fanciful, but it left me wondering just a little. Possibly it's a legacy of centuries of empire, but the British military are suspicious of practically everyone overseas, especially when they're polite. I summoned the platoon sergeants, and enjoined strict caution in any dealings we might have with the village. I'd done that at the start, of course, parading the whole detachment and warning them against (1) eating fruit from the market, (2) becoming involved with local women, (3) offending the dignity or religious susceptibilities of the men, and (4) drinking native spirits. The result had been half a dozen cases of mild dysentery; a frantic altercation between me, Private Fletcher (the platoon Casanova), and a hennaed harpy of doubtful repute; a brawl between McAuslan and a camelman who had allegedly stolen McAuslan's sporran; and a minor riot in Eleven Platoon barrack-room which ended with the confiscation of six bottles of arak that would have corroded a stainless steel sink. All round, just about par for the course, and easily dealt with by confinement to the fort for the offenders.

That in itself was a sobering punishment, for Yarhuna village was an enchanting place apart from its dubious fleshpots. Every day or so a little caravan would come through, straight out of the Middle Ages, with its swathed drivers and jingling bells and veiled outriders each with his Lee Enfield cradled across his knee and his crossed cartridge belts. (What the wild men of the world will do when the last Lee Enfield wears out, I can't imagine; clumsy and old-fashioned it may be, but it will go on shooting straight when all the repeaters are rusty and forgotten.) The little market was an Arabian Nights delight with its interesting Orientals and hot cooking smells and laden stalls – lovely to look at, but hellish to taste – and I have an affectionate memory of a party of Jocks, bonnets pulled down, standing silently by the oasis tank, watching the camels watering, while the drivers and riders regarded the Jocks in turn, both sides quietly observing and noting, and reflecting on the quaint appearance of the foreigners. And for one day a travelling party of what I believe were Touaregs camped beyond the village, a cluster of red tents and cooking fires, and hooded men in black burnouses, with the famous indigo veils tight across their faces and the long swords at their girdles. They made no attempt to speak to us, but a few of them rode up to watch Twelve Platoon drilling outside the gate; they just sat their camels, immovable, until the parade was over, and then turned and rode off.

'There's your real Arabis,' said Sergeant Telfer, and without my telling him he posted four extra sentries that night, one to each wall. He reported what he had done, almost apologetically; like me, he felt that we were playing at Foreign Legionnaires, rather, but still . . . Everything was quiet, the natives were friendly, the platoons were hard-worked and happy, and it was a good time to take precautions. We were in the second week of our stay, and there was just the tiniest sense of unease creeping into everyone's mind. Perhaps it was boredom, or the fact of being cooped up every night in a stronghold – for what?

Perhaps it was the desert, hot as a furnace floor during the day, a mystery of silver and shadow and silence by night; as you stood on the parapet and looked out across the empty dunes, you felt very small indeed and helpless, for you were in the presence of something that had seen it all, through countless ages, something huge beside which you were no bigger than an ant. It was a relief to come down the steps to my quarters, and hear the raucous Glasgow patter from the cheerful barrack-room across the square.

And still nothing happened – why should it, after all? – until the beginning of the third week, when we started drilling for water. We had lost the first two weeks because of some defective part in the rear-axle drilling mechanism, and a spare had taken time to obtain from Marble Arch. It was a minor inconvenience, for the water-truck came from the coast three times a week, but a well would be a good investment for the future, for the only alternative water-supply was the oasis, and one look at its tank, with camels slurping, infants paddling, horses fertilising, grandmothers washing the family's smalls, and everyone disposing prodigally of their refuse, suggested that our little blue and yellow purification pills would have had an uphill fight.

With the truck fixed, we looked for a likely spot to drill.

'We need a diviner,' I said. 'One of those chaps with a hazel stick who twitches.'

'How about McAuslan?' suggested Keith. 'He's allergic to water; all we have to do is march him up and down till he starts shuddering, and that's the spot.'

Eventually we decided just to drill at random, in various parts of the parade ground, for none of the buildings contained anything that looked remotely like the remains of a well. I tried to remember what I had ever learned of medieval castle or Roman camp lay-out – for Yarhuna's foundations were undoubtedly Roman – prayed that we wouldn't disturb any temples of Mithras or Carthaginian relics, and went to it. We drilled in several parts of the square, and hit nothing but fine dry sand and living rock. Not a trace of water. Some of the locals had loafed up to the gate to watch our operations, but they had no helpful suggestions to offer, so at retreat we closed the gates, put away the drilling-truck, and decided to have another shot next day.

And that night, for the first time, the ghost of Fort Yarhuna walked.

That, at least, was the conclusion reached by Private McAuslan, student of the occult and authority on lonely desert outposts, whose Hollywood-fed imagination could find no other explanation when the facts reached his unwashed ears, as they did next morning. What had happened was this.

On the cold watch, the one from 2 to 4 a.m., the sentry on the parapet near the tower had seen, or thought he had seen, a shadowy figure under the tower wall, just along from his sentry beat. He had challenged, received no reply, and on investigating had found – nothing. Puzzled, but putting it down to his imagination, he had resumed his watch, and just before 4 a.m. he had *felt* – he emphasised the word – someone watching him from the same place. He had turned slowly, and caught a fleeting glimpse of a form, no more, but again the parapet had been empty when he went to look. He raised no alarm at the time, because, with Highland logic, he had decided that since there was nothing there, there was nothing to raise an alarm for, but he had told Sergeant Telfer in the morning, and Telfer told me.

I saw him in my office, a tall, fair, steady lad from the Isles, called Macleod. 'You didn't get a good clear sight of anyone?' I said.

'No, sir.'

'Didn't hear anyone drop from the parapet, either into the fort or over the wall into the desert?'

'No, sir.'

'No marks to show anyone had been there?'

'No, sir.'

'Nothing missing or been disturbed, Sergeant Telfer?'

'Nothing, sir.'

'Well, then,' I said to Macleod, 'it looks like the four o'clock jump – we all know what can happen on stag; you think you see things that aren't there . . .'

'Yes, sir,' said Macleod, 'I've had that. I wouldnae swear I *saw* anything at all, sir.' He paused. 'But I felt something.'

'You mean something touched you?'

'Nat-at-at, sir. I mean I chust *felt* some-wan thair. Oh, he wass thair, right enough.'

It was sweating hot in the office, but I suddenly felt a shiver on my spine, just in the way he said it, because I knew exactly what he meant. Everyone has a sixth sense, to some degree, and most of its warnings are purely imaginary, but when a Highlander, and a Skye man at that, tells you, in a completely matter-of-fact tone, that he has 'felt' something, you do not, if you have any sense, dismiss or scoff at it as hallucination. Macleod was a good soldier, and not a nervous or sensational person; he meant exactly what he said.

'A real person – a man?' I said, and he shook his head.

'I couldnae say, sir. It wasnae wan of our laads, though; I'm sure about that.'

I didn't ask him why he was sure; he couldn't have told me.

'Well, he doesn't seem to have done any damage, whoever he was,' I said, and dismissed him. I asked Telfer, who was a crusty, tough Glaswegian with as much spiritual sensitivity as a Clyde boiler, what he thought, and he shrugged.

'Seein' things,' he said. 'He's a good lad, but he's been starin' at too much sand.'

Which was my own opinion; I'd stood guard often enough

to know what tricks the senses could play. But Macleod must have mentioned his experience among his mates, for during the morning, while I was supervising the water-drilling, there came Private Watt to say that he, too, had things to report from the previous night. While on guard above the main gate, round about midnight, he had heard odd sounds at the foot of the wall, outside the fort, and had leaned out through an embrasure, but seen nothing. (Why, as he spoke, did I remember that P.C. Wren story about a sentry in a desert fort leaning out as Watt had done, and being snared by a bolas flung by hostile hands beneath?) But Watt believed it must have been a pi-dog from the village; he wouldn't have mentioned it, but he had heard about Macleod . . .

I dismissed the thing publicly, but privately I couldn't help wondering. Watt's odd noises were nothing in themselves, but considered alongside Macleod's experience they might add up to – what? One noise, one sand-happy sentry – but sand-happy after only two weeks? And yet Fort Yarhuna was a queer place; it had got to me, a little, in a mysterious way – but then I knew I was devilled with too much imagination, and being the man in charge I was probably slightly jumpier with responsibility than anyone else.

I pushed it aside, uneasily, and could have kicked the idiot who must have mentioned the word 'ghost' some time that day. That was the word that caught the primitive thought-process of McAuslan, and led him to speculate morbidly on the fate of the graveyard garrison of Fort Zinderneuf, which had held him spellbound in the camp cinema.

'It'll be yin o' they fellas frae Bo Geesty,' he informed an admiring barrack-room. 'He's deid, but he cannae stay aff parade. Clump-clump, up an' doon the stair a' night, wi' a bullet-hole in the middle o' his heid. Ah'm tellin' ye. Hey, Macleod, did your bogle hiv a hole in his heid?'

'You'll have wan in yours, McAuslan, if ye don't shut upp,'

Macleod informed him pleasantly. 'No' that mich will come oot of it, apart from gaass.'

My batman, who told me about this exchange, added that the fellas had egged McAuslan on until he, perceiving himself mocked, had gone into sulky silence, warning them that the fate of Bo Geesty would overtake them, an' then they'd see. Aye.

And thereafter it was forgotten about – until the following morning, at about 5 a.m., when Private McLachlan, on guard above the main gate, thought he heard unauthorised movement somewhere down in the parade square and, being a practical man, challenged, and turned out the guard. There were two men fully awake in the gate-guardroom, and one of them, hurrying out in response to McLachlan's shout, distinctly saw – or thought he distinctly saw – a shadowy figure disappearing into the gloom among the buildings across the square.

'Bo Geesty!' was McAuslan's triumphant verdict, for that side of the square contained the old stables, the company office, and Keith's and my sleeping-quarters, and not a trace of anyone else was to be found. And Keith, who had been awake and reading, was positive that no one had passed by following McLachlan's challenge ('Halt-who-goes-there! C'moot, ye b— o' hell, Ah see ye!')

It was baffling, and worrying, for no clue presented itself. The obvious explanation was that we were being burgled by some Bedouin expert from the oasis – but if so, he was an uncommon good second-storeyman, who could scale a twenty-foot wall and go back the same way, unseen by sentries (except, possibly, by Macleod), and who didn't steal anything, for the most thorough check of stores and equipment revealed nothing missing. No, the burglar theory was out. So what remained?

A practical joker inside? Impossible; it just wasn't their style.

So we had the inescapable conclusion that it was a coincidence, two men imagining things on successive nights. I chose that line, irascibly examined and dismissed McLachlan and his associates with instructions *not* to hear or see mysterious figures unless they could lay hands on them, held a square-bashing parade of both platoons to remind everyone that this was a military post and not Borley Rectory, put the crew of the drilling-truck to work again on their quest for a well, and retired to my office, a disquieted subaltern. For as I had watched the water-drill biting into the sand of the square, another thought struck me – a really lunatic idea, which no one in his right mind would entertain.

Everything had been quiet in Fort Yarhuna until we started tearing great holes in the ground, and I remembered my hopes that we wouldn't disturb any historic buried ruin or Mythraic temple or ancient tomb or – anything. You see the train of thought – this was a fort that had been here probably since the days when the surrounding land had been the Garden of Eden – so the Bedouin say, anyway – and ancient places have an aura of their own, especially in the old desert. You don't disturb them lightly. So many people had been through this fort – Crusaders, barbarians, Romans, Saracens, and so on, leaving something of themselves behind forever, and if you desecrate such a place, who knows what you'll release? Don't misunderstand me, I wasn't imagining that our drilling for water had released a spirit from its tomb deep in the foundations – well, not exactly, not in as many words that I'd have cared to address to anyone, like Keith, for example. That was ludicrous, as I looked out of my office and watched the earthy soldiery grunting and laughing as they refilled yet another dead hole and the truck moved on to try again. The sentry on the gate, Telfer's voice raised in thunderous rebuke, someone singing in the cookhouse – this was a real, military world, and ghosts were just nonsense. More things in heaven and earth . . . *ex Africa semper aliquid novi*

. . . Private McAuslan's celluloid-inspired fancies . . . a couple of tired sentries . . . my own Highland susceptibility to the fey . . . I snapped 'Tach!' impatiently in the fashion of my MacDonald granny, strode out of my office and showed Private Forbes how to take penalty kicks at the goal which the football enthusiasts had erected near the gate, missed four out of six, and retired grinning amidst ironic cheers, feeling much better.

But that evening, after supper, I found myself mounting the narrow stairway to the parapet where the sentries were just going on first stag. It was gloaming, and the desert was taking on that beautiful star-lit sheen under the purple African sky that is so incredibly lovely that it is rather like a coloured postcard in bad taste. The fires and lights were twinkling away down in the village, the last fawn-orange fringe of daylight was dwindling beyond the sand-hills, the last warm wind was touching the parapet, the night stillness was falling on the fort and the shadowy dunes, and Private Brown was humming 'Ye do the hokey-cokey and ye turn aroond' as he clattered up the stairway to take his post, rifle in hand. Four sentries, one to each wall – and only my imagination could turn the silhouette of a bonneted Highlander into a helmeted Roman leaning on his hasta, or a burnoused mercenary out of Carthage, or a straight-nosed Greek dreaming of the olive groves under Delphi, or a long-haired savage from the North wrapping his cloak about him against the night air. They had all been here, and they were all long gone – perhaps. And if you smile at the perhaps, wait until you have stood on the wall of a Sahara fort at sundown, watching the shadows lengthen and the silence creep across the sand invisible in the twilight. Then smile.

I went down at last, played beggar-my-neighbour with Keith for half an hour, read an old copy of the *Tripoli Ghibli* for a little while longer, and then turned in. I didn't drop off easily; I heard the midnight stag change over, and then the two o'clock, and then I must have dozed, for the next thing I remember is waking suddenly, for no good reason, and lying there, lathered in sweat that soaked the clean towel which was our normal night attire, listening. It took a moment to identify it: a cautious scraping noise, as of a giant rat, somewhere outside. It wasn't any sound I knew, and I couldn't locate it, but one thing was certain, it hadn't any business to be going on.

I slid out and into my trousers and sandals, and stood listening. My door was open, and I went forward and listened again. There was no doubt of it; the sound was coming from the old stable, about twenty yards to my left, against the east wall. Irregular, but continuous, scrape-scrape. I glanced around; there were sentries visible in the dying moonlight on the catwalks to either side, and straight ahead on the gate-wall; plainly they were too far away to hear.

As silently as possible, but not furtively, for I didn't want the sentries to mistake me, I turned right and walked softly in front of the office, and then cut across the corner of the parade. The sentry on the catwalk overhead stiffened as he caught sight of me, but I waved to him and went on, towards the guardroom. I was sweating as I entered, and I didn't waste time.

'Get Sergeant Telfer, quietly. Tell him to come to the stable, not to make a sound. You three, come with me; you, McNab, up to the parapet, and tell the sentries on no account to fire until I give the word. Move.'

Thank God, you don't have to tell Jocks much when there's soldiering to do; within five minutes that stable was boxed as tight as a drum – four of us in front of it, in line, crouching down; two riflemen some yards behind, to back up, and two men with torches ready to snap on. The scraping sound was still going on in the stable, quite distinctly, and I thought I could hear someone gasping with exertion. I nodded to Telfer, and he and one of the Jocks crept forward to the stable door, one to each of the heavy leaves; I could see Telfer's teeth, grinning, and then I snapped – 'Now!', the doors were hauled back, the torches went on – and there they were.

Three Arabs, glaring into the torch-light, two of them with shovels, a half-dug hole in the floor – and then they came hurtling out, and I went for the knees of the nearest, and suddenly remembered trying to tackle Jack Ramsay as he came weaving through our three-quarters at Old Anniesland, and how he'd dummied me. This wasn't Ramsay, though, praise God; he came down with a yelp and a crash, and one of the Jocks completed his ruin by pinning him by the shoulders. I came up, in time to see Telfer and another Jock with a struggling Arab between them, and the third one, who hadn't even got out of the stable, being submerged by a small knot of Highlanders, one of whom was triumphantly croaking 'Bo Geesty!' No doubt of it, McAuslan had his uses when the panic was on.

We quieted the captives, after a moment or two, but there wasn't a word to be got out of them, and nothing to be deduced from their appearance except that they weren't genuine desert Buddoos, but more probably from the village or some place farther afield. Two of them were in shirts and trousers, and none of them was what you would call a stalwart savage; more like fellaheen, really. I consigned them to the guardroom, ordered a fifty per cent stand-to on the walls, and turned to examine the stable.

They had dug a shallow hole, no more, in the middle of the stable, and the reek was appalling. Camel stables are odorous at the best of times, and this one had been accommodating beasts, probably, since Scipio's day. But we had to see what they'd been after, and since a good officer shouldn't ask his men to do what he won't do himself . . . I was eyeing one of the fallen shovels reluctantly when a voice spoke at my elbow.

'Jings!' it said. 'Hi, sir, mebbe it's treasure! Burried treasure!'

I wouldn't have thought McAuslan's deductive powers that fast, myself, but he explained that there had been treasure in Bo Geesty – 'a jool, the Blue Watter, that Bo Geesty pinched aff his aunty, so he did.' From the glittering light in his eye I could see that his powers of identification would shortly lead him to the dream-stage where he was marrying Susan Hayward, so I indicated the shovel and asked him would he like to test his theory.

He began digging like a demented Nibelung, choking only occasionally as his shovel released noxious airs, exclaiming 'Aw, jeez!' before falling to again with energy. His comrades stood aside as he hurled great lumps of the ordure of centuries from the hole – even for McAuslan, I decided this was too much, and offered to have him spelled, but he wouldn't hear of it. He entertained us, in gasps as he dug, with a synopsis of the plot of *Beau Geste*, but I can't say I paid much attention, for I was getting excited. Whatever the Arabs had been after, it must be something precious – and then his shovel rang, just like the best pirate stories, on something metallic.

We had it out in another five minutes, and my mounting hopes of earth-shaking archaeological discovery died as the torches revealed a twentieth-century metal box for mortar bombs – not British, but patently modern. I sent the others out, in case it was full of live ammo., and gingerly prised back the clasps and raised the lid. It was packed to bursting with papers, wedged almost into a solid mass, because the tin had not been proof against its surroundings, and it was with some difficulty that I worked one loose – it was green, and faded, but it was undoubtedly a bank-note. And so were all the rest.

They were, according to the Tripoli police inspector who came to examine them next day, pre-war Italian notes, and totally worthless. Which was a pity, since their total face value was well over a hundred million lire; I know, because I was one of the suffering members of the court of inquiry which had to count them, rank, congealed and stinking as they were. As the officer who had found them, I was an obvious candidate for membership of that unhappy court, when we got back to the battalion; I, a Tripoli police lieutenant, a major from the Pay Corps, and a subaltern from the Green Howards, who said that if he caught some contagious disease from this job he was going to sue the War Office. We counted very conscientiously for above five minutes, and then started computing in lumps; the Pay Corps man objected, and we told him to go to hell. He protested that our default of duty would be detected by higher authority, and the Green Howard said that if higher authority was game enough to catch him out by counting this lot note by note, then higher authority was a better man than he was. We settled on a figure of 100,246,718 lire, of which we estimated that 75,413,311 were too defaced to be accepted as currency, supposing the pre-war Italian government were still around to support them.

For the rest, the court concluded that the money had been buried by unknown persons from Yarhuna village, after having possibly been looted from the Italian garrison who had occupied the fort early in the war. The money had lain untouched until water-drilling operations, conducted by Lieutenant D. MacNeill, had alarmed the villagers, who might have supposed that their treasure was being sought, they being unaware that it was now quite worthless. Hence their attempts to enter the fort nocturnally on at least three occasions to remove their hoard, on the last of which they had been detected and apprehended. It was difficult to see, the court added, that proceedings could justifiably be taken against the three captured Arabs, and their release was recommended. Just for spite we also consigned the notes themselves to the care of the provost marshal, who was the pompous ass who had convened the court in the first place, and signed the report solemnly.

'Serve him right,' grunted the Green Howard. 'Let him keep them, and press 'em between the leaves of his confidential reports. Or burn 'em, if he's got any sense. What, you're not taking one of them, are you? – don't be mad, you'll catch the plague.'

'Souvenir,' I said. 'Don't worry, the man it's going to is plague-proof.'

And when I handed it over, with a suggestion that it should be disinfected in a strong solution of carbolic, McAuslan was enraptured.

'Och, ta, sir,' he said, 'that's awfy decent of ye.'

'Not a bit; you're welcome if you want it. You dug it up. But it's worthless, mind; it won't buy anything.'

He looked shocked, as though I had suggested an indecency.

'Ah widnae spend it,' he protested. 'Ah'll tak' it hame, for a souvenir. Nice to have, like – ye know, tae mind us of bein' inna desert.' He went slightly pink. 'The fellas think Ah'm daft, but Ah liked bein' inna fort – like inna Foreign Legion, like Gairy Cooper.'

'You've been in the desert before, though. You were in the 51st, weren't you – Alamein and so on?'

'Aye, so Ah wis.' He sniffed thoughtfully, and rubbed his grimy nose. 'But the fort wis different.'

So it was, but I didn't quite share his happy memories. As a platoon commander, I was painfully aware that it was the place where Arabs had three times got past my sentries by night. One up to them, one down to us. I was slightly cheered up when – and this is fact, as reported in the local press – a week later, the warehouse where the provost marshal had deposited his noisome cache was broken into by night, and the caseful of useless lire removed. There was much speculation where it had gone.

I can guess. Those persistent desert gentlemen probably have it down in Yarhuna village to this day, and being simple men in some things, if not in breaking and entering, they doubtless still believe that it is a valuable nest-egg for their community. I don't know who garrisons Fort Yarhuna now – the Libyans, I suppose – but if there's one thing I'd bet on, it is that when the military move out again, shadowy figures will move in under the old carved gate by night, and put the loot back in a nice safe place. And who is to question their judgement? Fort Yarhuna will still be there a thousand years after the strongest banks of Europe and America have passed into ruins.

Johnnie Cope in the Morning

When I was a very young soldier, doing my recruit training in a snowbound wartime camp in Durham, there was a villainous orderly sergeant who used to get us up in the mornings. He would sneak silently into our hut at 5.30 a.m., where we were frowsting in our coarse blankets against the bitter cold of the room, suddenly snap on all the lights, and start beating the coal-bucket with the poker. At the same time two of his minions would rush from bunk to bunk screaming:

'Wake-eye! Wake-eye! I can see yer! Gerrup! Gerrup! Gerrup!'

And the orderly sergeant, a creature devoid of pity and any decent feeling, would continue his hellish metallic hammering while he shouted:

'Getcher cold feet on the warm floor! Har-har!' and sundry obscenities of his own invention. Then all three would retire, rejoicing coarsely, leaving behind them thirty-six recruits suffering from nervous prostration, to say nothing of ringing in the ears.

But it certainly woke us up, and as I did my first early morning fatigue, which consisted of dragging a six-foot wooden table-top down to the ablutions and scrubbing it with cold water, I used to contrast my own miserable lot with that of his late majesty Louis XIV of France, whose attendants used a very different technique to dig him out of his scratcher. As I recalled, a valet in velvet-soled shoes used to creep into the royal bedchamber at a fairly civilised hour, softly draw back the curtains a little way, and then whisper: 'It is my humble duty and profound honour to inform your majesty that it is eight-thirty of the clock.' That, now, is the way to break the bad news, and afterwards the body of majesty was more or less lifted out of bed by a posse of princes of the blood who washed, fed, watered and dressed him in front of the fire. No wooden tables to scrub for young Louis.

And as I wrestled with my brush in the freezing water, barking my knuckles and turning blue all over, I used to have daydreams in which that fiend of an orderly sergeant was transported back in time to old Versailles, where he would clump into the Sun-King's bedroom in tackety boots at 5.30, guffawing obscenely, thrashing the fire-irons against the fender, and bawling:

'Levez-vous donc, Jean Crapaud! Wake-eye, wake-eye! Getcher froid pieds on the chaud terre! I can see yer, you frog-eating chancer! Har-har!'

While I concede that this kind of awakening could have done Louis XIV nothing but good, and possibly averted the French Revolution, the whole point of the daydream was that the orderly sergeant would undoubtedly be flung into an oubliette in the Bastille for lèse majesté, there to rot with his red sash and copy of King's Regulations, while virtuous recruits in the twentieth century drowsed on until the late forenoon.

And while I stood mentally picturing this happy state of affairs, and sponging the icy water off the table-top with the flat of my hand, the sadistic brute would sneak into the ablutions and turn the cold hose on us, screaming:

'Two minnits to gerron rifle parade, you 'orrible shower! Har-har! Mooo-ve or I'll blitz yer!'

I wonder that we survived that recruit training, I really do.

You may suppose that that orderly sergeant's method of intimating reveille was as refined a piece of mental cruelty as even a military mind could devise, and I daresay if I hadn't later been commissioned into a Highland regiment I would agree. But in fact, there I discovered something worse, and it used to happen once a week, regularly on Friday mornings. In nightmares I can hear it still.

On the other six days of the week reveille was sounded in the conventional way at six, by a bugler on the distant square playing the famous 'Charlie, Charlie, get out of bed'. If you were a pampered brute of an officer, you used to turn over, mumbling happily, and at six-thirty your orderly would come in with a mug of tea, open the shutters, lay out your kit, and give you the news of the day while you drank, smoked, and coughed contentedly.

But on Fridays it was very different. Then the duty of sounding reveille devolved on the battalion's pipes and drums, who were bound to march round the entire barrack area, playing full blast. The trouble was, in a spirit of *schadenfreude* comparable with that of the Durham orderly sergeant's, they used to assemble in dead silence immediately outside the junior subalterns' quarters, inflate their beastly bags without so much as a warning sigh, poise their drum-sticks without the suspicion of a click, and then, at a signal from that god-forsaken demented little kelpie of a pipe-sergeant, burst thunderously into the squealing cacophony and ear-splitting drum rolls of 'Hey, Johnnie Cope, are ye waukin' yet?'

Now, 'Johnnie Cope' is one of the most magnificent sounds ever to issue from musical instruments. It is the Highlanders' war clarion, the tune that is played before battle, the wild music that is supposed to quicken the blood of the mountain man and freeze the foe in his tracks. It commemorates the day two and a half centuries ago when the broadswords came whirling out of the mist at Prestonpans to fall on Major-General John Cope's redcoats and cut them to ribbons in something under five minutes. I once watched the Seaforths go in behind it against a Japanese-held village, and saw for the first time that phenomenon which you can't really appreciate until you have seen it – the unbelievable speed with which Highland troops can accelerate a slow, almost leisurely advance into an all-out charge. And I've heard it at military funerals, after 'Lovat's Lament' or 'Flowers of the Forest', and never failed to be moved by it. Well played, it is a savage, wonderful sound, unlike any other pipe march – this, probably, because it doesn't truly belong to the Army, but to the fighting tails of the old clansmen before the government had the sense to get them into uniforms.

But whatever it does, for the Jocks or to the enemy, at the proper time and occasion, its effect at 6 a.m. on a refined and highly-strung subaltern who is dreaming of Rita Hayworth is devastating. The first time I got it, full blast at a range of six feet or so, through a thin shutter, with twenty pipers tearing their lungs out and a dozen side-drums crashing into the thunderous rhythm, I came out of bed like a galvanised ferret, blankets and all, under the impression that the Jocks had Risen, or that the MacLeods were coming to settle things with me and my kinsfolk at long last. My room-mate, a cultured youth of nervous disposition, shot bolt upright from his pillow with a wordless scream, and sat gibbering that the Yanks had dropped the Bomb, and, as usual, in the wrong place. For a few deafening moments we just absorbed it, with the furniture shuddering and the whole room in apparent danger of collapse, and then I flung open the shutters and rebuked the musicians, who were counter-marching outside.

Well, you try arguing with a pipe-band some time, and see what it gets you. And you cannot, if you are a young officer with any notions of dignity, hie yourself out in pyjamas and bandy words with a towering drum-major, and him resplendent in leopard skin and white spats, at that hour in the morning. So we had to endure it, while they regaled us with 'The White Cockade' and the 'Braes of Mar', before marching off to the strains of 'Highland Laddie', and my room-mate said it had done something to his inner ear, and he doubted if he would ever be able to stand on one leg or ride a bicycle again.

'They can't do that to us!' he bleated, holding his nose and blowing out his cheeks in an effort to restore his shattered ear-drums. 'We're officers, dammit!'

That, as I explained to him, was the point. Plainly what we had just suffered was a piece of insubordinate torture devised to remind us that we were pathetic little one-pippers and less than the dust beneath the pipe-band's wheels, but I knew that if we were wise we would just grin and bear it. A newly-joined second-lieutenant is, to some extent, fair game. Properly speaking, he has power and dominion over all warrant officers, N.C.O.s and private men, including pipe- and drum-majors, but he had better go cannily in exercising it. He certainly shouldn't start by locking horns with such a venerable and privileged institution as a Highland regimental pipe band.

'You mean we'll have to put up with that . . . that infernal caterwauling every Friday morning?' he cried, massaging his head. 'I can't take it! Heavens, man, I play the piano; I can't afford to be rendered tone-deaf. Look what happened to Beethoven. Anyway, it's . . . it's insubordination, calculated and deliberate. I'm going to complain.'

'You're not,' I said. 'You'll get no sympathy, and it'll only make things worse. Did complaining do Beethoven any good? Just stick your head under the pillow next time, and pretend it's all in the mind.'

I soothed him eventually, saw that he got lots of hot, sweet tea (this being the Army's panacea for everything except a stomach wound) and convinced him that we shouldn't say anything about it. This, we discovered, was the attitude of the other subalterns who shared our long bungalow block – which was situated at some distance from the older officers' quarters. Complain, they said, and our superiors would just laugh callously and say it did us good; anyway, for newcomers to a Highland unit to start beefing about the pipe band would probably be some kind of mortal insult. So every Friday morning, with our alarms set at five to six, we just gritted our teeth and waited with towels round our heads, and grimly endured that sudden, appalling blast of sound. Indeed, I developed my own form of retaliation, which was to rise before six, take my ground-sheet and a book out on to the patch of close-cropped weed which passed in North Africa for a lawn, and lie there apparently immersed while the pipe band rendered 'Johnnie Cope' with all the stops out a few yards away. When they marched off to wake the rest of the battalion I noticed the pipe-sergeant break ranks, and come over towards me with his pipes under his arm. He was a small, bright-eyed, elfin man whose agility as a Highland dancer was legendary; indeed, my only previous contacts with him had been at twice-weekly morning dancing parades, at which he taught us younger officers the mysteries of the Highland Fling and foursome reel, skipping among us like a new-roused fawn, crying 'one-two-three' and comparing our lumbering efforts to the soaring of golden eagles over Grampian peaks. If that was how he saw us, good luck to him.

'Good morning to you, sir,' he said, with his head cocked on one side. 'Did you enjoy our wee reveille this morning?'

'Fairly well, thanks, pipey,' I said, and closed my book. 'A bit patchy here and there, I thought. Some hesitation in the warblers –' I didn't know what a warbler was, except that it was some kind of noise you made on the pipes '– and a bum note every now and then. Otherwise, not bad.'

'Not – bad?' He went pale, and then pink, and finally said, with Highland archness: 'Would you be a piper yoursel', sir, perhaps?'

'Not a note,' I said. 'But I've heard "Johnnie Cope" played by Foden's Motor Works Brass Band.'

For a moment I thought he was going to burst, and then he began to grin, and then to laugh, shaking his head.

'By George,' said he. 'A brass band, hey? Stop you, and I'll use that on Pipe-Major Macdonald, the next time he starts bumming his chat. No' bad, no' bad. And does the ither subalterns enjoy oor serenade?'

'I doubt if they've got my ear for music, pipey. Most of them probably think that if you played "Too Long in this Condition" it would be more appropriate.'

He opened his eyes at that. 'Too Long in this Condition' is a pibroch, long and weird and full of allusions to the MacCrimmons, and not the kind of thing that ignorant subalterns are expected to know about.

'Aye-aye, weel,' he said, smiling. 'And you're Mr MacNeill, aren't you? D Company, if I remember. Ahhuh. Chust so.' He regarded me brightly, nodded, and turned away. 'Look in at the office sometime, Mr MacNeill, if you have the inclination. Chust when you're passing, you understand.'

And that small conversation was a step forward – a bigger one, really, than playing for the company football team, or getting my second pip as a full lieutenant, or even crossing the undefined line of acceptance by my own platoon – which I did quite unintentionally one night by losing my temper and slinging a mutinous Jock physically out of the canteen, in defiance of all common sense, military discipline, and officer-like conduct. For the pipey and I were friends from that morning on, and it is no small thing to be friends with a pipe-sergeant when you are trying to find your nervous feet in a Highland regiment.

He was in fact subordinate to the pipe-major and the drum-major, who were the executive heads of the band, but in his way he carried more weight than either of them. He was the musician, the authority on air and march and pibroch, the arbiter when it came to any question of quality in music or dancing. Years at his trade had left him with a curious deformity in which the facial muscles had given way on one side, so that when he blew, his cheek expanded like a balloon – an unnerving sight until you got used to it. He had enormous energy, both in movement and conversation, and was never still, buzzing about like a small tartan wasp, as when he was instructing young pipers in the finer points of their art.

'God be kind to me!' he would exclaim, leaping nervously round some perspiring youth who was going red in the face over the intricacies of 'Wha'll be King but Cherlie'. 'You're not plowing up a pluidy palloon, Wilson! You're summoning the clans for the destruction of the damned Hanovers, aren't you? Your music is charming the claymore out of the thatch and the dirk from the peat, so it is! Now, tuck it into your oxter and wake the hills with your challenge! Away you go!'

And the piper would squint, red-faced, and send his ear-splitting notes echoing off the band-room walls, very creditably, it seemed to me, and the pipey would call on the shades of the great MacCrimmon and Robin Oig to witness the defilement of their heritage.

'It's enuff to make the Celtic aura of my blood turn to effluent!' was one of his more memorable observations. 'It's a gathering of fighting men you're meant to be inspiring, boy! The noise you're makin' wouldnae collect a parcel of Caithness tinkers. You'll be swinging it, next! Uplift yourself, Wilson! Mind, it's not bobby-soxers you're tryin' to attract, it's the men of might from the ends of the mountains, with their bonnets down and their shoes kicked off for the charge. And again – give your bags a heeze and imagine you're sclimming up the Heights of Abraham with Young Simon's caterans at your back and the French in front of you, not puffing and wheezing oot some American abomination at half-time at a futball match!'

And eventually, when it had been played to his satisfaction he would beam, and cry:

'There! There's Wilson the Piper, waking the echoes in majesty before the face of kings, and the Chermans aall running away. Now, put up your pipes, and faall oot before you spoil it.'

This was his enclosed, jealously-guarded world; he had known nothing else since his boy service – except, as he said himself, 'a wee bitty war'. Pipers, unlike most military bandsmen, tend to be fighting soldiers; in one Highland unit which I visited in Borneo only a few years ago, the band claimed to have accounted for more Communist terrorists than any of the rifle companies. And in peacetime they were privileged people, with their own little family inside the regiment itself, and the pipey presided over his domain of chanters and reeds and dirks and rehearsals and dancing, and kept a bright eye cocked at the battalion generally, to make sure that tradition was observed and custom honoured, and that there was no falling off in what he would describe vaguely as 'Caledonia'. If he hadn't been such a decent wee man, he would undoubtedly have been a 'professional Highlander' of the most offensive kind.

The only time anyone ever saw the pipe-sergeant anything but thoroughly self-assured and bursting with musical confidence was once every two months or so, when he would produce a new pipe-tune of his own composition, and submit it, in a state bordering on nervous hysteria, to the Colonel, with a request that it might be included in the next beating of Retreat.

'Which one is it this time, pipey?' the Colonel would ask. '"The Mist-Covered Streets of Aberdeen" or "The 92nd's Farewell to Hogg Market, Calcutta"?'

The pipey would scowl horribly, and then hurriedly arrange his face in what he supposed was a sycophantic grin, and say:

'Ach, you're aye joshing, Colonel, sir. It's jist a wee thing that I thought of entitling "Captain Lachlan Chisholm's Fancy", in honour of our medical officer. It has a certain . . . och, a captivatin' sense of the bens and the glens and the heroes, sir – a kind of . . . eh . . . miasma, as it were – at least, I think so.'

'Does it sound like a pipe-tune?' the Colonel would ask. 'If so, by all means play it. I'm sure it will be perfectly splendid.'

And at Retreat, with the pipey in a frenzy of excitement, the band would perform, and afterwards the pipey would approach the Colonel and inquire:

'How did you like "Captain Lachlan Chisholm's Fancy", Colonel, sir?'

And the Colonel, leaning on his cromach, would say:

'Which one was that?'

'The second last, sir – before "Cock o' the North".'

'Oh, that one. But that was "Bonnie Dundee", surely? At least, it sounded like "Bonnie Dundee". Come to think of it, pipey, your last composition – what was it? – "The Unloading of the 75th at Colaba Causeway", or something – it sounded terribly like "Highland Laddie". Of course, I haven't got your musical ear . . .'

'And he can say that again, and a third time in Gaelic,' the pipey would rage in the band-room afterwards. 'God preserve us from a commanding officer that has no more music than a Border Leicester ewe! "The Unloading of the 75th", says he – dam' cheek, when fine he knows it was caalled "The Wild Green Hills of – of – of – ach, where the hell was it, now . . .'

'Gorbals Cross,' the pipe-major would suggest.

'No such thing! And, curse him, he says my composeetions sound like "Bonnie Dundee" and "Highland Laddie", as if I wass some penny-whistle street-musician hawkin' my tinny for coppers along Union Street. Stop you, and I'll fix his duff wan o' these days. I'll write a jazz tune, and get it called "Colonel J. G. F. Gordon's Delight", and have it played in aall the dance-halls! He'll be sorry then!'

And yet, there was no one in the battalion who knew the Colonel better than the pipey did, or was more expert in dealing with that tough, formidable, wise old commanding officer. The truth was that in some things, especially his love for his regiment, the wily Colonel could be surprisingly innocent, and the pipey knew just where and when to touch the hidden nerve.

As in the case of Private Crombie, which would have sent our modern Race Relations Board into screaming fits of indignation.

He was in my platoon, one of a draft which joined the battalion from the Liverpool Scottish. They were fascinating in their way – men with names like MacGregor and Cameron and MacPherson, and all with Scouse accents you could have cut with a knife. Genuine Liverpool Scots, in fact, sons and grandsons of men who had settled on Merseyside, totally Lancashire in everything but name and race. But even among them, Private Crombie stood out as something special. He was what used to be called a Negro.

Which would not have mattered in the least, but he also happened to be a piper. And when he marched into company office about three days after he joined, and asked if he could apply to join the battalion pipes and drums, I confess it came as a shock. No doubt it was all the fault of my bad upbringing, or the dreadful climate of the 1940s, but my immediate (unspoken) reaction was: we can't have him marching in the pipe-band, out in the open with everyone looking. We just can't.

I maintain that this was not what is called race prejudice, or application of the colour bar. It was, as it appeared to me, a sense of fitness. If he had been eight feet tall, or three feet short, I'd have thought the same thing – simply, that he would have looked out of place in a Highland regimental pipe-band. But that, obviously, was something that could not be said. I asked him what his qualifications were.

He had those, all right. His father had taught him the pipes – which side of his family was black and which white, if either was, I never discovered. He had some sort of proficiency certificate, too, which he laid on my desk. He was a nice lad, and painfully keen to join the band, so I did exactly what I would have done in anyone else's case, and said I would forward his application to the pipe-major; my own approval and the company commander's went without saying, because it was understood that the band, or any other specialist department, got first crack at a qualified man. He marched out, apparently well pleased, Sergeant Telfer and I looked at each other, said 'Aye' simultaneously, and awaited developments.

What happened was that the pipe-major was on weekend leave, so Crombie appeared for examination before the pipe-sergeant, who concealed whatever emotion he felt, and asked him to play.

'I swear to God, Mr MacNeill,' he told me an hour later, 'I hoped he would make a hash of it. Maybe I was wrong to think that, for the poor lad cannae help bein' a nigger, but I thought . . . well, if he's a bauchle I'll be able to turn him doon wi' a clear conscience. Weel, I'm punished for it, because I cannae. He's a good piper.' He looked me in the eye across the table, and repeated: 'He's a good piper.'

'So, what'll you do?'

'I'll have to tell the pipe-major he's fit for admeession. He's fitter than half the probationers I've got, and that's the truth. I chust wish to God he was white – or no' so black, anyway.'

Remember that this was over fifty years ago, and there have been many changes since then. Also remember that Highland regiments, being strongly national institutions, are sensitive as to their composition (hence the old music-hall joke on the lines of: '"Issacstein?" "Present, sir." "O'Flaherty?" "Present, sir." Woinarowski?" "Present, sir." Right – Cameron Highlanders present and correct, sir."')

Carefully, I asked:

'Does his colour matter?'

'You tell me, sir. What'll folk think, if they see our pipe-band some day, on Princes Street, and him as black as the ace o' spades, oot front, in a kilt and bunnet, blawin' away?'

I could pretend that I rejected this indignantly, like a properly enlightened liberal, but I didn't. I saw his point, and I'd have been a hypocrite if I'd tried to dismiss it out of hand. Anyway, there were more practical matters to consider. What would the pipe-major say? What, if it came to that – and it would – would the Colonel say?

The pipe-major, returning on Monday, was in no doubts. He wasn't having a black piper, not if the man was the greatest gift to music that God ever made. The pipey, genuinely distressed, for he was torn between his sense of fitness on the one hand, and an admiration for Crombie's ability on the other, asked the pipe-major to give the lad an audition. The pipe-major, who didn't want to be seen to be operating a colour bar, conceived that here was a way out. He listened to Crombie, told him to fall out – and then made the mistake of telling the pipe-sergeant he didn't think the boy was good enough. That did it.

'No' good enough!' The pipey literally danced in front of my table. 'Tellin' *me*, that's been pipin' – aye, and before royalty, too, Balmoral and all – since before Pipe-Major MacDonald had enough wind to belch oot his mither's milk, that my judgement is at fault! By chings, we've lived tae see the day, haven't we chust! No' good enough! I'm tellin' you, Mr MacNeill, that young Crombie iss a piper! And that's that. And fine I know MacDonald iss chust dead set against the poor loon because he's as black as my boot! And from a MacDonald, too,' he went on, in a fine indignant irrelevance, 'ass if the MacDonalds had anything to hold up their heids aboot – a shower of Argyllshire wogs is what they are! And anither –'

'Hold on, pipey,' I said. 'Pipe-Major MacDonald is just taking the line you took yourself – what's it going to look like, and what will people think?'

'Beside the point, sir! I'm no' havin' it said that I cannae tell a good piper when I hear one. That boy's good enough for the band, and so I'll tell the Colonel himself!'

And he did, in the presence of Pipe-Major MacDonald, myself (as Crombie's platoon commander), the second-in-command (as chief technical adviser), the Regimental Sergeant-Major (as leading authority on precedent and tradition), and the Adjutant (as one who wasn't going to be left out of such a splendid crisis and scandal). And the pipe-major, who had the courage of his convictions, repeated flatly that he didn't think Crombie was good enough, and also that he didn't want a black man in his band, 'for the look of the thing'. But, being a MacDonald, which is something a shade craftier than a Borgia, he added: 'But I'm perfectly happy to abide by your decision, sir.'

The Colonel, who had seen through the whole question and back again in the first two minutes, looked from the pipe-major to the pipey, twisted his greying moustache, and remarked that he took the pipe-major's point. He (the Colonel) had never seen a white man included in a troop of Zulu dancers, and he'd have thought it looked damned odd if he had.

The Adjutant, who had a happy knack of being contentious, observed that, on the other hand, he'd never heard of a white chap who *wanted* to join a troop of Zulu dancers, and would they necessarily turn him down if one (a white chap, that was) applied for membership?

The Colonel observed that he, the Colonel, wasn't a bloody Zulu, so he wasn't in a position to say.

The second-in-command remarked that the Gurkhas had pipe bands; damned good they were, too.

The Colonel looked at the R.S.M. 'Mr Mackintosh?'

This, I thought, would be interesting. In those days few

R.S.M.s had university degrees, or much education beyond elementary school, but long experience, and what you can only call depth of character, had given them considerable judicial wisdom; if I were on trial for murder, I'd as soon have R.S.M. Mackintosh on the bench as any judge in the land. He stood thoughtful for a moment, six and a quarter feet of kilted, polished splendour, and then inclined his head with massive dignity towards the Colonel.

'It seems to me, sir,' he said carefully, 'that we have a difference of expert opeenion. The pipe-sergeant holds that this soldier is a competent piper; the pipe-major considers he is nott. But, not bein' an expert mysel', I don't know what standard is required of a probationary piper?' And he looked straight at the pipe-major, who frowned.

'The boy's no' that bad,' he conceded. 'But . . . but he'll look gey queer on parade, sir.'

The second-in-command said that you couldn't put a square peg in a round hole. Not unless you forced it, anyway, in his experience.

The Adjutant said someone would be sure to make a joke about the Black Watch. Which, since we weren't the Black Watch, would be rather pointless, of course, but still . . .

The Colonel said the Adjutant could stop talking rot, and get back to the point, which was whether Crombie was or was not a fit and proper person to be admitted to the pipe band. It seemed to the Colonel that, in spite of the pipe-major's reservations about his proficiency, there was no reason why Crombie couldn't achieve a satisfactory standard . . .

The second-in-command said that many black chaps were, in point of fact, extremely musical. Chap Armstrong, for example. Not that the second-in-command was particularly partial to that kind of music.

The Adjutant opened his mouth, thought better of it, and the Colonel went on to say that it wasn't a man's fault what colour his skin was; on the other hand, it wasn't anyone's fault that a pipe band was expected to present a certain appearance. There he paused, and then the pipe-sergeant, who had held his peace until the time was ripe, said:

'Aye, right enough. Folk would laugh at us.'

The Colonel, without thinking, said stiffly: 'Oh? Who?'

'Oh . . . folk, sir,' said the pipey. 'People . . . and ither regiments . . . might . . .'

The Colonel looked at him, carefully, and you could see that the die was cast. It wasn't that the Colonel could be kidded by the pipey; he wasn't the kind of simpleton who would say 'Damn what other people and other regiments think, Crombie is going to play in the pipe band, and that's that.' But if he now made the *opposite* decision, he might be thought to be admitting that perhaps he *did* care what other people thought. It was a very nice point, in a delicately balanced question, the pipey had just made it a little more tricky for him, and both the Colonel and the pipey knew it.

'Mr Mackintosh?' said the Colonel at length, and everyone knew he was looking for confirmation. He got it.

'The pipe-major, sir, describes Crombie as nott bad,' said the R.S.M. slowly. 'The pipe-sergeant says he is good. So I take it he can qualify as a probationary piper. That bein' so – we've taken him as a soldier. Whatever work he's suited for, he should be given. If he's fit to march in a rifle company, I'm poseetive he's fit to march in the pipes and drums.' And again he looked at the pipe-major.

'Good,' said the Colonel, and because he was an honest man he added: 'I'm relieved. I'd not have cared to be the man who told Crombie the band couldn't take him. I've no doubt he knows exactly how good a piper he is.'

And Crombie played in the pipe-band – having been admitted for all the wrong reasons, no doubt. I'm perfectly certain that the Colonel, the pipe-major, and the pipe-sergeant (in his own perverse way) wished that he just wasn't there, because he *did* look odd, in that day and age, and there's no use pretending he didn't. Although, as the second-in-command remarked, some people probably thought that a pipe-band looked a pretty odd thing in the first place; some people thought it *sounded* odd, too – not as odd as those bands one saw at the cinema, though, with the chap Armstrong and fellows called Duke and Earl something-or-other. Probably not titled men at all, he suspected.

Personally, I was glad about Crombie. It wasn't just that I felt the same way as the R.S.M. (that deep and mysterious man), but that I could see that Crombie loved what he was doing, and was good at it. And when I review my memories of that pipe-band now, fifty years on, I don't think of Crombie at all, which probably proves something. Mention 'pipers' to me, and my immediate recollection is of 'Johnnie Cope', and the way they used to batter our ear-drums on a Friday at dawn.

Incidentally, that peculiar little bit of subaltern-baiting came to an abrupt end, thanks to the cunning of Lieutenant Mackenzie, in a week when I was out on detachment. It seems that the Colonel stayed late in the mess one Thursday night, his wife being away in Cairo, and yarned on with the subalterns in the ante-room until after two in the morning. And being too tired to make the two-mile drive home to the married quarters, he accepted the suggestion of Mackenzie that he stay over for the night – in a vacant room in the subalterns' quarters. So the Colonel borrowed a pair of pyjamas and burrowed in for the night, remarking cheerfully that he hoped he'd sleep as soundly as he used to do when he, too, was a one-pipper with not a care in the world.

'And he did, too – until precisely 6 a.m.,' Mackenzie informed me later. 'And then the pipey and his gang sneaked up, as usual, and took deep breaths, and started blowing the bloody roof off, right outside the old boy's kip. I've never,' Mackenzie went on contentedly, 'actually seen a hungry vulture with a fire-cracker tied to its leg. And, brother, I don't need to. He came out of that room like Krakatoa erupting, fangs bared and blood in his eye. I'd no idea the old man could shift like that. And I'll bet you've never seen an entire pipe band in full flight, either – not just retreating, but running like hell, and somebody with his foot through the big drum. If the Colonel hadn't been in bare feet, he'd have caught someone, and there'd have been murder done. Anyway, when the smoke had cleared, he was understood to say that the pipe-band could henceforth sound "Johnnie Cope" on the other side of the barracks, round Support Company, and if they ever set foot within two hundred yards of any officers' quarters again, he, personally, would reorganise them in several unusual ways. This is an edited version, of course. And that,' concluded Mackenzie smugly, 'is the pipey's eye on a plate. Thank your clever old Kenny. We'll sleep in peace on Fridays after this.'

Strangely enough, we didn't. Probably we were suffering from withdrawal symptoms, but Friday reveille, with only the distant drift of the band, found us fractious and peevish. Even my room-mate said he missed it, rather; he liked the bit where the drummers crashed out their tattoo at the beginning, it made him feel all martial, he said. We didn't actually go the length of asking the band to come back, but there was no doubt of it, Friday wasn't the same any more.

The only time I heard them beat reveille outside the subalterns' quarters again was a long time after, when we had moved back to Edinburgh, and the old Colonel had gone. It was on my last Friday in the Army, just before I was demobilised, and I like to think it was the pipey's farewell gift. It had all the old effect – I finished up against the far wall, thrashing feebly in a state of shock, while 'Johnnie Cope' came thundering in like a broadside. I had a new room-mate by this time, a stranger to the battalion, and when he could make himself heard he announced his intention – he was a large, aggressive young man – of going out and putting an immediate stop to it.

'Don't you dare,' I shouted above the din. 'Let them alone. And think yourself privileged.'

Nowadays, in my old age, I'm accustomed to waking up in the ordinary way, with a slightly fuzzy feeling, and a vague discontent, and my old broken shoulder aching, and twinges in my calves and ankles. And sometimes, if my thoughts turn that way, I can think smugly that one of the compensations nowadays is that there are no tables to scrub, or men of ill-will hitting the coal-bucket with the poker, or hounding me out into the ablutions through the snow – and then I feel sad, because never again will I hear 'Johnnie Cope' in the morning.

General Knowledge, Private Information

All my life I have been plagued by a marvellous memory for totally useless information. Probably no other human being now alive could tell you (or would want to, for that matter), all in one breath, that the woman in whose coal cellar Guy Fawkes hid his explosives was called Mrs Bright, that Casanova, Charlemagne, and Hans Andersen were all born on 2 April, and that Schopenhauer couldn't abide carters cracking whips beneath his bedroom window. And add, for good measure, the names of the Oxford batsmen who succumbed to Cobden's devastating hat-trick in the University match of 1870.

You get no marks for knowing these things, as people were always telling me at school. Other children knew the subjunctive of *moneo*, and exactly where to drop the perpendicular in Pythagoras, how to dissect an adverbial clause (I didn't even know what an adverb was, and don't push me even now), and how to do volumetric analysis. They absorbed these matters without difficulty, and poured them out on to paper at examinations, while I sat pathetically, having scrawled my name, and the number '1' in the margin, wondering if the examiners would allow me anything for knowing that the ice-cream Chico Marx sold in *A Day at the Races* was 'tutsi-fruitsi', and that there was an eighteenth-century buccaneer who became Archbishop of York, that the names of the *Bounty*'s quartermasters were Norton and Lenkletter, or that Martin Luther suffered from piles.

It wasn't even respectable general knowledge, and heaven knows I tried to forget it, along with the identities of the playing cards in Wild Bill Hickok's hand when he was shot, the colours of all the football teams in the old Third Division (Northern Section), and the phrase for 'Do you surrender?' in the language which Tarzan spoke to the apes. But it still won't go away. And an exhaustive knowledge of utter rubbish is not a social asset (ask anyone who has been trapped next to me at a party) or of more than limited use in keeping up with a television quiz show. Mr Paxman's alert, glittering-eyed young men, bristling with education, jab at their buzzers and rattle out streams of information on Sumerian architecture and Gregorian music and the love poetry of John Donne while I am heaving about in my armchair with my mouth full, knocking over tea-cups and babbling frantically: 'Wait, wait! – King's. Evil! No, no, dammit – the other thing that Shelley's nurse died of – didn't she? – No, wait – Dr Johnson – or Lazarus – or, or what's his name? – in that play – not bloody Molière! – hang on, it's coming! The . . . the other one – with the drunk grandee who thinks he's somebody's father . . .'

And by then they are on to Hindemith or equestrian statues at Sinigaglia. It is no consolation to be able to sit growling jealously that there isn't one of them who could say who it was that Captain Kidd hit over the head with a bucket, or what it was that Claude Rains dropped into a wastepaper basket in the film *Casablanca* – and then memory of a different kind takes hold, and I am back in the tense and smoky atmosphere of the Uaddan Canteen, sweating heavily on the platform with the other contestants, and not a murmur from the Jocks and Fusiliers packed breathlessly waiting in the body of the hall, with a two-pound box of Turkish Delight and the credit of the regiment to play for, as the question-master adjusts his spectacles, fixes me with a malevolent smile, and asks:

'What were the names of the five seventeenth-century statesmen whose initials made up the word "Cabal"?'

There are no such general knowledge quizzes nowadays – and

no such sublimely-inspired authorities as Private McAuslan, savant, sage, universal man, and philosopher extraordinary. For reviewing his long, unsoldierly, and generally insanitary career, I'd say that that was McAuslan's big moment, when he rose above his unseemly self and stood forth whole, a bag of chips in his hand and the divine fire of revelation in his mind.

If you doubt this, I can only tell you that I was there and saw it happen. But to explain it properly, and obtain a true perspective, I have to go back a few days earlier to the battalion concert which, along with the Colonel's liver, was the origin of the whole thing.

If you have attended a battalion concert in an overseas garrison you will know that they are, theatrically speaking, unique – and not merely because nothing works, including the curtain. The whole production is ill-conceived and badly under-rehearsed to begin with, half the cast have to be press-ganged into appearance, the standard of performance would shame a kindergarten pantomime, the piano is untuned, the lighting intermittent, C Company's tenor (who thinks he is Scotland's answer to Gigli) butchers his way through 'Ave Maria' and 'Because God made thee mine' to demented applause from the sentimental soldiery, one of the storemen does conjuring tricks with a pullthrough and pieces of four-by-two cleaning cloth, the idiot Lieutenant MacNeill, shuffling and crimson with embarrassment, does his supposedly comic monologue and dies standing up, the Adjutant, who is prompting in the wings, loses his script and puts the entire stage-crew under close arrest in a voice shrill with hysteria while the audience roars 'Encore', and everybody on the safe side of the footlights loves it. Except the Colonel.

This is because he is stuck in the middle of the front row, surrounded by all the visiting brass and their wives, and knowing that the climax to the whole terrible show, which his soldiery are waiting for like knitting-women impatient for the tumbril, will be the moment when the battalion funny-man comes on and does the court-jester bit. Our own local comedian was an evil and disreputable Glasgow keelie called McCann, the scruff of A Company, and generally regarded as that unit's answer to Private McAuslan. He came bauchling confidently on, his wits honed by years of abusing referees, policemen and tram conductors, convulsed the hoi-polloi with his grating catch-phrase ('Hullaw rerr, fellas, see's a knife, Ah wantae cut up a side street'), and set the tone by winking at the Colonel and addressing him affably as 'china'.

Thereafter, with delicately edged allusion and innuendo, he took the mickey out of his commanding officer in a performance judged with such a niceness that it stopped just a shaved inch short of outright insubordination. It really was masterly, in its way, and would have won plaudits from Will Kemp and Archie Armstrong, who would have expected to go to the Tower, if not the block, for it. And the Colonel, pipe clenched in his teeth, took it with an eager, attentive smile that promised penalties unmentionable for Private McCann if ever he was damnfool enough to get himself wheeled into the orderly room on a charge.

The last act of the evening, after McCann had bounced off to tumultuous applause (with the Colonel clapping grimly and regularly) was a complete anti-climax. It was a general knowledge test among teams from the six companies, devised by the Padre, and it laid the expected theatrical egg, with the mob streaming away to the canteen before it was finished. But the Colonel sat it out, and was heard to say in the mess afterwards that it had been the only decent event on the programme. Presumably anything looked good to him after McCann.

'The rest of it,' he observed to the Fusilier Colonel, who had been an interested (and, during McCann's turn, an inwardly delighted) guest, 'was just bloody awful. Of a piece with all modern entertainment, of course. Haven't had a decent film, even, since *Snow White*. At least these general knowledge quizzes serve some useful purpose – anything does that imparts information to the men. God knows most of 'em could do with some education, considering the drivel that's served up to them as entertainment.' And he had the crust to scowl at me – which, considering he had dragooned me into the show in the first place ('A good officer ought to take part in all his men's activities; give 'em your monologue'), was pretty cool, I thought.

The Fusilier Colonel said he doubted if the general knowledge competition we had heard that night was very educational; it had consisted, he pointed out, of questions mostly about sport.

'Nothing wrong with that,' said our Colonel. 'Shows a healthy outlook. Have another gin.'

'Thanks,' said the Fusilier Colonel. 'What I meant was, to be really useful a general knowledge quiz ought to be more broadly based, don't you think? I mean – football and racing are all very well, but general knowledge should take in, well, art, politics, literature, that sort of thing.' He took a sip of his gin and added: 'Perhaps your Jocks aren't interested, though.'

That, as they say, did it. But for McCann, and the fact that our Colonel's liver must have been undergoing one of its periodic spells of mutinous behaviour, he'd probably just have grunted agreement. As it was, he stopped short in the act of refuelling his pipe and asked the Fusilier Colonel what the devil he meant. The Fusilier Colonel said, nothing, really, but general knowledge quizzes ought to be about general knowledge. They'd had one in his battalion, and he'd been astonished at how much his chaps – quite ordinary chaps, he'd always thought – knew about all sorts of things.

Our Colonel did a brief, thoughtful quiver, looked across

the mess with that chin-up, faraway stare that his older comrades associated with the Singapore siege, and said, was that so, indeed. He finished filling his pipe, and you could see him wondering whether the Fusilier Colonel had somehow managed to enlist the entire Fellowship of All Souls in his battalion. Then he looked round, and if ever a man was taking inventory of his own unit's intellectual powers, he was doing it then. There was the Padre, with an M.A. (Aberdeen), and the M.O. with presumably some scientific knowledge – pretty well versed in fishing, anyway – and then his eye fell on me, and I knew what he was thinking. A few days before he'd heard me – out of that fund of my trivia – explaining to the Adjutant, who was wrestling futilely with a crossword, that the term 'derrick' derived from the name of an Elizabethan hangman. Eureka, he was thinking.

'Tell you what,' he said to the Fusilier Colonel. 'How'd you like to have one of these quiz competitions – between our battalions? Just for interest, eh?'

'All right,' said the Fusilier Colonel. 'A level fiver?'

'Done,' said our Colonel, promptly, and in that fine spirit of philosophic inquirers bent on the propagation of knowledge for its own sake they proceeded to hammer out the rules, conditions and penalties under which the contest would be conducted. It took them three double whiskies and about half a pint of gin, and the wheeling and dealing would have terrified Tammany Hall. But finally they agreed that the two teams, four men strong, should be drawn from all ranks of the respective battalions, that the questions should be devised independently by the area education officer, that the local Roman Catholic padre should act as umpire (our Colonel teetered apprehensively over that, and presumably concluded that the Old Religion was marginally closer to our cause – Jacobites, Glasgow Irish, and all that – than to the Fusiliers'), and that the contest should be held in a week's time on neutral ground, namely the Uaddan Canteen. And when, with expressions of mutual good will, the Fusilier Colonel and his party had left, our Colonel called for another stiff one, mopped his balding brow, refilled his pipe, and took the operation in hand. He formed the Padre and myself into an O-Group, with the Adjutant co-opted as an adviser, told the rest of the mess to shut up or go to bed, announced: 'Now, this is the form,' and paced to and fro like Napoleon before Wagram, plotting his strategy. Dividing his discourse under the usual subheadings – object, information, personnel, communications, supply, and transport – he laid it all on the line.

'These Fusiliers,' he said, smoking thoughtfully. 'Probably quite brainy. Never can tell, of course, but they put up a dam' fine show at Anzio, and Colonel Fenwick is nobody's fool. Don't be discouraged by the fact that they've had one or two of their chaps through Staff College – the kind of idiot who can write p.s.c. after his name these days is, to my mind, quite unfit for brain-work of any kind and usually has to be excused boots.' The Colonel had not been to Staff College. 'However, we can't afford to take 'em lightly. Their recruiting area is the north-east of England, which I grant you is much like the Australian outback with coal-mines added, but we can't count too much on that. There's a university thereabouts – which reminds me, Michael, we'll have to check on where this area education officer hails from. The chap who's setting the questions. Fenwick proposed him – bigod, I'll bet he's a Geordie –'

'He's a Cornishman,' said the Adjutant. 'Pen-pal, or some such name.'

'Thank God for that,' said the Colonel. 'You're sure? Right, then, we come to our own team. You, Padre, and you, young Dand, will select as your team-mates the two most informed, alert and intelligent men in the battalion. Officers or other ranks, I don't care which – but understand, I want a team who can answer the questions put to them clearly, fully, and accurately, and in a soldier-like manner. No dam' shuffling and scratching heads. When a question's asked – crack! straight in with the answer, like that.'

'Provided we know the answer,' said the Padre, and the Colonel looked at him like a dyspeptic vulture.

'This battalion,' he said flatly, 'knows all the answers. Understand? What's the shortest book in the Bible?'

'Third John,' said the Padre automatically.

'There you are, you see,' said the Colonel, shrugging in the grand manner. 'It's just a matter of alertness and concentration. And – training.' He wagged his pipe impressively. 'Some form of training is absolutely essential, to ensure that you and the rest of the team are at a highly-tuned pitch on the night of the contest. The questions are to fall under the headings of general knowledge; art and literature and music and what-not; politics; and sport. I suppose,' he went on reflectively, 'that you could read a bit . . . but don't for God's sake go swotting feverishly and upsetting yourselves. Some chaps at Wellington used to, I remember – absolutely hopeless on the day. I,' he added firmly, 'never swotted. Just stayed off alcohol for twenty-four hours in advance, went for a walk, had a bath and a good sleep, a light breakfast . . . well, here I am. So just keep your digestions regular, no late hours, and perhaps brush up a bit with . . . well, with some of those general knowledge questions in the *Sunday Post*. I don't doubt the education officer will draw heavily on those. Anyway, they'll get you into the feel of the thing. Apart from that – any suggestions?'

The Adjutant said he had a copy of *Whitaker's Almanack* in the office, if that was any use.

'Excellent,' said the Colonel. 'That's the sort of practical approach we need. Very good, Michael. No doubt there's some valuable stuff in the battalion library, too.' (I knew of nothing, personally, unless one hoped to study social criminology through the medium of *No Orchids for Miss Blandish* or *Slay-ride for Cutie.*)

'And that,' said the Colonel, ordering up four more big ones, 'is that. It's just a question of preparation, and we'll have this thing nicely wrapped up. I've every confidence, as usual –' he gave us his aquiline beam '– and I feel sure that you have, too. We'll show the Fusiliers where the brain-power lies.'

The trouble with the Colonel, you see, was that he'd been spoiled by success. Whether it was taking and holding a position in war, or thrashing all opposition at football, or looking better than anyone else on ceremonial parades, or even a question of the battalion's children topping the prize-list at the garrison school, he expected no less than total triumph. And perhaps because he so trustingly expected it, he usually got it – and a trifle over. It was a subtle kind of blackmail, in a way, and that crafty old soldier knew just how to operate it. Leadership they call it.

I've seen it manifest itself in most curious ways, as when the seven-year-old daughter of Sergeant Allison was taking a ballet examination in Edinburgh – and there, just before it began, was the Colonel, in tweeds and walking-stick, just looking in, you understand, to see that all was in order, gallantly chatting up the young instructresses in their leotards, playing the genial old buffer and missing nothing, and then giving the small and tremulous Miss Allison a wink and a growling whisper before stalking off to his car. The fact was, the man was as nervous as her parents, because she was part of his regimental family. 'He'll be there at the Last Judgement,' the M.O. once said, 'cadging a light off St Peter so that he can whisper "This is one of my Jocks coming in, by the way . . ."'

It followed that the quiz against the Fusiliers assumed an importance that it certainly didn't deserve, and I actually found myself wondering if I ought to try to read right through the

Britannica beforehand. Fortunately common sense reasserted itself, and I concentrated instead on selecting the remaining two members of the team – the Padre insisted that was my affair; he was going to be too busy praying.

Actually, it wasn't difficult. The Padre and I had agreed that in the quiz he would deal with questions on what, in a moment of pure Celtic pessimism, he irritably described as 'the infernal culture' – that is, literature, music and the arts – while I would look after the general knowledge. So we needed a political expert and a sporting one. The political expert was easy, I said: it could only be Sergeant McCaw, Clydeside Communist and walking encyclopedia on the history of capitalist oppression and the emergence of the Working Man.

The Padre was horrified. 'Ye daren't risk it! The man's a Bolshevik, and he's cost me more members than Sunday opening. He'll use the occasion for spouting red propaganda – man, Dandy, the Colonel'll go berserk!'

'He's about the only man in this battalion whose knowledge of Parliament goes beyond the label of an H.P. sauce bottle,' I said. 'It would be criminal not to pick him – he can even tell you what the Corn Laws were.'

'Is that right?' said the Padre, metaphorically pulling his shawl round his shoulders. 'I fear the worst. Stop you till he starts calling Churchill a fascist bully gorged on the blood of the masses. What about sport?'

'Forbes,' I said. 'From my platoon. He's the man.'

'Yon? He's chust a troglodyte.'

'Granted,' I said, 'but if you knew your Reasons Annexed as well as he knows his league tables, you'd be Moderator by now.' And in the face of his doubts I summoned Private Forbes – small, dark, and sinful, and the neatest inside forward you ever saw.

'Forbes,' I said. 'Who holds the record for goals scored in a first-class match?'

He didn't even blink. 'Petrie, Arbroath, got thirteen against

Aberdeen Bon-Accord in 1889. He wis playin' ootside right, an' –'

'Right,' I said. 'Who got most in a league game?'

'Joe Payne, o' Chelsea, got ten when he was playin' fur –'

'What's the highest individual score in first-class cricket?'

'Bradman, the Australian, he got 452 in a State game –'

'How many Britons have held the world heavyweight title?'

'None.' He took a breath. 'Bob – Fitzsimmons – wis – English – but – he – was – namerrican – citizen – when – he – beat – Corbett – an' – Toamy – Burns – wis – a – Canadian – but – that – disnae – count – an' –'

'Fall out, Forbes, and thank you,' I said, and looked at the Padre, who was sitting slightly stunned. 'Well?'

He sighed. 'When you consider the power of the human brain, ye feel small,' he began, and I could see that we were going to be off shortly on another fine philosophic Hebridean flight. So I left him, and went to find Sergeant McCaw and confirm his selection.

The next week was just ridiculous. You'd have thought the Jocks wouldn't even be interested in such an arcane and contemptible business as an inter-regimental general knowledge competition, but they treated it like the World Cup. Scotsmen, of course, if they feel that national prestige is in any way at stake, tend to go out of their minds; tell them there was to be a knitting bee against England and they would be on the touch-line shouting 'Purl, Wullie! See's the chain-stitch, but!' And as is the case with British regiments anywhere, they and the Fusiliers detested each other heartily. That, and the subtle influence which I'm sure the Colonel percolated through the unit by some magic of his own, was enough to make the quiz the burning topic of the hour.

I first realised this when, during a ten-minute halt on a short route march, Private Fletcher of the lantern visage and inventive mind mentioned the quiz to me, and observed artlessly, as he borrowed a light: 'Would be a' right if ye knew what the questions wis goin' tae be, wouldnit?' Once upon a time I'd have thought this just a silly remark, but I knew my Fletcher by now.

'It would,' I said. 'But if somebody was to bust into the education officer's premises at night, and start rifling his papers, that wouldn't be all right. Know what I mean?'

'Whit ye take me fur?' He was all hurt surprise. 'Ah wis just mentionin'. Passin' the time.' He paused. 'They say the odds is five tae two against us.'

'You mean there's a book being made? And we're not favourites?'

'No kiddin', sur. The word's got roond. See the Padre? He's a wandered man, that; he disnae know what time it is. Ye cannae depend on him.'

'He's an intelleck-shul, but,' observed Daft Bob Brown.

'Intellectual yer granny. Hear him the ither Sunday? On aboot the Guid Samaritan, an' the Levite passin' by on the ither side, an' whit a helluva shame it wis, tae leave some poor sowel lyin' in the road? Well seen the Padre hasnae been doon Cumberland Street lately. Ah'd dam' soon pass by on the ither side. Becos if Ah didnae, Ah ken fine whit I'd get – half a dozen Billy Boys fleein' oot a close tae banjo me.'

This naturally led to a theological discussion in which I bore no part; I'd been lured into debate on the fundamentals with my platoon before. Nor was I surprised that they held a poor opinion of the Padre's intellect – he did have a tendency to wander off into a kind of metaphysical trance in the pulpit. Skye man, of course. But I was intrigued to find that they were interesting themselves in the quiz; even Private McAuslan.

'Whit's an intelleck-shul?' he inquired.

'A clever b—', explained Fletcher, which is not such a bad definition, when you come to think of it. 'Don't you worry, dozey,' he went on. 'It disnae affect you. An intellectual's a fella that can think.'

'Ah can think,' said McAuslan, aggrieved, and the platoon took him up on it, naturally.

'What wi'?'

'Your brains are in your bum, kid.'

'Hey, sir, why don't ye hiv McAuslan in yer quiz team?'

'Aye, he's the wee boy wi' the brains.'

'Professor McAuslan, N.B.G., Y.M.C.A. and bar.'

'Right – fall in!' I said, for McAuslan's expression had turned from persecuted to murderous. He shuffled into the ranks, informing Fletcher raucously that he could think, him, he wisnae so bluidy dumb, and Fletcher wis awfy clever, wasn't he, etc., etc.

But I hadn't realised quite how gripped they were by quiz fever until I became aware, midway through the week, that I was being taken care of, solicitously, like a heavy-weight in training. I was conscious, in my leisure moments, of being watched; outside my window I heard my orderly say: 'It's a' right; he's readin' a book,' and on two other occasions he asked pointedly if he could get me anything from the library – a thing he'd never done before. My platoon behaved like Little Lord Fauntleroys, obviously determined to do nothing to disturb the equilibrium of the Great Brain; the Padre complained that he could get no work done for Jocks coming into his office to ask if he was all right, and could they get him anything. Sergeant McCaw, whose feeling for the proletariat did not prevent his being an oppressively efficient martinet with his own platoon, and consequently unpopular, reported that he had actually been brought tea in the morning; he was suspicious, and plainly apprehensive that the jacquerie were about to rise.

It reached a peak on the Thursday, when I was playing in a company football match, and was brought down by one of the opposition. Before I could move he was helping me up – 'awfy sorry, sir, ye a'right? It was an accident, honest.' And this from a half-back whose normal conduct on the field was that of a maddened clog-dancer.

By the Saturday afternoon I was convinced that if this kind of consideration didn't stop soon, I would go out of my mind. The Padre was feeling it, too – I found him in the mess, muttering nervously, dunking egg-sandwiches in his tea and trying to eat them with a cigarette in his mouth. I believe if I had said anything nice to him or asked him who wrote *The Tenant of Wildfell Hall* he would have burst into tears. The Colonel stalked in, full of fight, shot anxious glances at us, and decided that for once breezy encouragement would be out of place. The Adjutant said hopefully that he'd heard there was a touch of dysentery going round the Fusilier barracks, but on the other hand, he'd also heard that they had a full set of *The Children's Encyclopedia*, so there wasn't much in it, either way, really. You could feel the tension building up as we sat, munching scones; I was getting into a nervous state, and showed it by quoting to the Padre, 'I would it were bedtime, Hal, and all well,' and he started like a convulsed impala and cried: '*Henry the Fourth*, Part One! Or is it Part Two? No – Part One! – I think . . . Oh, dear, dear!' and sank back, rubbing his brow.

It was a relief finally to get to the Uaddan Canteen, already filled with a light fog of smoke from the troops who packed the big concert hall. The rival factions of supporters had arranged themselves on either side of the centre aisle, so that on one hand the sea of khaki was dotted with the cockades on the caps which the Fusiliers had folded and thrust through their epaulettes, and on the other by dark green tartan shoulder flashes. There were even redcaps at the back of the hall; I found myself wondering whether there had ever been a general knowledge contest in history where they had called in the police even before the start.

In the centre of the front row sat the area commander, a portly, jovial brigadier with his complexion well seasoned by sun and booze, and on either side of him the Colonels, talking across him with a smiling jocularity you could have sliced bread on. Officers of both regiments, plus a few of the usual commissioned strays, made up the first two rows, and immediately behind them on the Highland side I saw the serried ranks of Twelve Platoon, with Private McAuslan to the fore eating chips from a huge, steaming bag with cannibal-like gusto. You could almost smell them on the platform.

All this I observed through a crack in the curtains at the back of the stage, where we and our opponents were briefly assembled, smiling uneasily at each other until we were given the word to file out on to the platform. We came out to a reception reminiscent of a Nuremberg rally which has got out of hand; the Fusiliers thundered their boots on the floor, while stern Caledonia on the other side got up and roared abuse across the aisle, sparing a decibel or two for the encouragement of their team. 'There's the wee boys!' I recognised the cry of Private Fletcher, while McAuslan signified his support by standing on his chair and clapping his hands rhythmically above his head – unfortunately he was still holding his supper in one hand, not that he minded; if you're McAuslan, a few chips in your hair is nothing.

We took our places, each side ranged on hard chairs behind two long Naafi tables on either side of the stage, and the question-master, a horn-rimmed young man with a long neck and the blue Education Corps flash on his shoulder, assembled his papers importantly at a little table in between. He was joined by Father Tuohy, the Roman Catholic chaplain, known locally as the Jovial Monk, who mitted the crowd to sustained applause, told a couple of quick stories, exchanged gags with the groundlings, and generally set the scene. (If ever the Palladium needs a compère at the last minute, they can simply engage the nearest military priest; I don't know why, but there never was an R.C. padre yet who couldn't charm the toughest audience into submission.)

Tuohy then explained the rules. There would be individual questions to each man in turn, on his particular subject. If he answered correctly, he got one point and could opt for a second slightly harder question, worth two points, and if again successful, attempt a third still harder question, worth three. If he failed at any stage he kept the points he had, but the question which had stumped him went to the opposition, who scored double if they got it right. At any turn, a contestant could ask for a ten-point question, which would be a real stinker, split into five parts, with two points for each, but unless he got at least four of the parts right, he scored nothing at all. It sounded fairly tricky, with pitfalls waiting for the ambitious.

While he talked, I glanced at our opponents – three officers, one of them a stout, shrewd-looking major, and a bespectacled warrant officer who looked like a Ph.D. and probably was. I glanced along at my companions: Forbes, looking villainous and confident, was sitting up straight with his elbows squared on the board; McCaw, beside him, showed signs of strain on his sallow, tight-skinned face; next to me the Padre was humming the Mingulay boat song between his teeth, his Adam's apple giving periodic leaps, while he gazed up at the big moths fluttering round the lights. It was sweating hot.

'Right,' said Father Tuohy, smiling round genially. 'All set?' I could glimpse the sea of faces in the hall out of the corner of my eye; I wished I hadn't eaten so many scones, for I was feeling decidedly ill – why? For a mere quiz? Yes, for a mere quiz. There was a muscle fluttering in my knee, and I wanted a drink, but I knew if I picked up the tumbler in front of me I'd drop it in sheer nervousness. Right – I'd play it safe, dead safe; no rash scrambling after points; nice and easy, by ear.

'First general knowledge question to the Fusiliers,' said the question-master; he had a rather shrill Home Counties voice. 'What is a triptych?'

Well, thank God he hadn't asked me. 'Screens' flashed across my mind, but I didn't know, really. Private Fletcher evidently did, though, for in the pause following the question a grating Scottish voice from the body of the hall observed audibly:

'That's a right Catholic question, yon!'

Father Tuohy snorted with amusement, and composed himself while the Fusilier major answered – I don't know what he said, but it earned him a point, and he asked for a second question.

'With whom or what,' said the question-master, 'was Europa indiscreet – not necessarily on the firing-range?' He smirked, lop-sidedly; ah-ha, I thought, we've got an intellectual joker here.

'A bull,' said the major, and looked across at me. I knew what he was thinking; the questions, for an army quiz, were middling tough; if he flunked on the third, would I be able to answer it and net six points? Wisely, at that stage of the game, he passed, and the question-master turned to me, his glasses a-gleam. Easy, easy, I thought, just sit and listen – and then some dreadful automatic devil inside me seized on my tongue and made me say, in a nonchalant croak:

'I'd like a ten-pointer, please.'

The Padre actually gave a muted scream and shuddered away from me, the question-master sat up straight, there was a stir on the platform, a gasp from the hall, and then a bay of triumph from Twelve Platoon: 'Darkie's the wee boy! Get tore in!' Just for a moment, amidst the horrifying realisation of what I'd done, I felt proud – and then I wanted to be sick. My fiend had prompted me to put on a show, for reasons of pure bravado; if I managed to lift ten points it would be a tremendous psychological start. And if I failed? From the tail of my eye I could see the Colonel; he was clicking his lighter nervously.

'For ten points then,' said the question-master, rummaging out another sheaf of papers. 'I'm going to give you the names of five famous horses, both real and legendary. For two points each, tell me the names of their owners.' He paused impressively, and apart from the subterranean squelching in my throat, there wasn't a sound. 'Ronald. Pegasus. Bucephalus. Black Auster. And –' he gave me what looked like a gloating grin '– Incitatus.'

Silence in the hall, and then from somewhere in Twelve Platoon a voice said in horrified awe: 'Bluidy hell!' The Colonel's lighter clattered on the floor, I felt about two thousand eyes riveted on my sweating face – and relief was flooding over me like a huge wave. Take it easy, I was saying to myself; don't let your tongue betray you. By a most gorgeous fluke, you're in business. I took a deep breath, tried to keep my voice from shaking, and said:

'In the same order . . . ahm . . . yes . . . the owners . . . er, would be.' I paused, determined to get it right. 'The Seventh Earl of Cardigan, Bellerophon, Alexander the Great, Titus Herminius – in Macaulay's "Lays" – and the Roman Emperor Caligula.'

Forgive me for describing it, but in a life that has had its share of pursed lips, censorious glares, and downright abuse and condemnation, there haven't been many moments like that one. It rocked the hall, although I say it myself. The question-master, torn between admiration and resentment at seeing one of his prize questions hammered into the long grass, stuttered, and said: 'Right! Ten points – yes, ten points!', the front two rows applauded briskly, the Fusilier major shaded his face with his hand and said something to the man next him, and Twelve Platoon threw up their sweaty nightcaps with abandon. ('Gi' the ba' tae Darkie! Aw-haw-hey! Whaur's yer triptyches noo?' etc.) I lit a cigarette with trembling hands.

In my relief, I'm afraid I paid little attention to the other questions of that round – I know the Padre stopped at two, having identified the opening words of *Treasure Island* and the closing sentence of *Finnegans Wake* (trust the Army Education Corps to give James Joyce a good airing), and McCaw picked up useful yardage over Lloyd George and the peerage. It was Forbes who really stole the show – either in emulation or out of sheer confidence he demanded a ten-pointer and was asked what sports he would expect to see at The Valley, Maple Leaf Gardens, Hurlingham, Hileah and – this was a vicious one – Delphi. He just cleared his throat, said 'Way-ull', and then trotted them out:

'Fitba' – aye, soccer' (this with disdain for the effete term), 'ice hockey, ra polo, racin', in America, an' athletics – the Greeks in the auld days.'

I applauded as hard as any one – frankly, while I knew Forbes was an authority, he'd shaken me with his fifth answer. I should have realised that the *Topical Times* and *Book of Sporting Facts* researchers cast their nets wide. (The Colonel was equally astonished, I imagine, over Hurlingham; you could see him thinking it was time Forbes was made a corporal.)

We finished the first round leading 26–15, and then the contest developed into a long, gruelling duel. I don't remember all that much of it accurately, but some memories and impressions remain. I know the Padre, after a nervous start, ran amuck through the Augustan writers and various artists of the Renaissance, with a particularly fine flourish over an equestrian statue of Gattemalatta, by Donatello, which had the Jocks chanting: 'See the Padre, he's the kid!' Sergeant McCaw started no fires by attempting ten-point questions, but he was as solid as a rock on such diverse matters as the Jewish Disabilities Bill, the General Strike (I could hear the Padre mumbling snatches of prayer during this answer and trying not to catch the Colonel's eye), and the results of celebrated by-elections. He seldom failed to answer all three of his questions. Forbes was brilliant, but occasionally erratic; he shot for too many ten-pointers and came adrift as often as not, on one occasion even forgetting himself so far as to engage in a heated debate with Father Tuohy on whether gladiatorial games were or were not sport. ('Hoo the hell's a fella expected tae know whit a Roman boxin'-glove's called in Latin?') Nor, it was clear, would he have included the Emperor Commodus in his list of Great Heavyweights. I did reasonably well, but never equalled my opening effort. I tried one more ten-pointer, and crashed heavily over the Powers involved in the Pragmatic Sanction (really, I ask you), but scored a mild tactical success over the question-master by insisting that the victorious commander against the Armada was Effingham, not Drake. Father Tuohy backed me up (affecting not to hear the cry of 'Your side got beat, onywye, padre' from some unidentified student of Elizabethan history in the audience), but the question-master hated me from that moment on.

We came to the half-way stage with a comfortable lead, and our Colonel produced a cigar from his sporran and sat back. He was anticipating, and not wisely, for in the second half we began to come adrift. The Fusiliers were finding their stride; two of them were only average, but the bespectacled genius of a warrant officer and the rotund major were really good. The major twice snapped up three-point questions on which I had failed (how was I to know the names of *all* the Valkyries), and on his own account displayed a knowledge of classical music and Impressionist painting which was almost indecent. I scrambled one ten-pointer by identifying five of the occupants of the stagecoach in the film of that name, and got a life-saving eight points from another ten-pointer by naming four of the Nine Worthies (God bless my MacDonald granny for keeping *Dr Brewer's Reader's Handbook* where my infant hands could get at it), but for the rest I was content to sit on my first two questions most of the time and take no chances. Forbes did well, with some fine work on baseball and the dimensions of football pitches, and McCaw continued his sound, stone-walling game, surviving one particularly blistering attack concerned with Gladstone's Midlothian campaign, and for good measure quoting 'Keep your eye on Paisley', to the delight of the St Mirren supporters present.

The Padre was erratic. He pasted the Lake Poets all round the wicket, and caused some stir among the betting fraternity at the back of the hall by bagging two ten-pointers in succession (five trickily obscure quotations from modern poets, and a tour de force in which he identified five of the plays possibly attributable to Shakespeare outside the recognised canon. I can still hear that lilting Island voice saying slowly, 'Aye, and then there wass *The Two Noble Kins-men,* aye . . .'). But he shocked the home support by confusing George Eliot with George Sand, and actually attributed an Aytoun quotation to Burns; it began to look as though he was over-trained, or in need of the trainer's sponge. And so we came to the final round, with a bare seven-point lead, and Father Tuohy announced that the last eight questions would decide the fate of the two-pound boxes of Turkish Delight which were the winners' prizes – to say nothing of the regimental honour and the Colonels' fivers.

We were proceeding in reverse order in this half of the contest, so that the sporting questions came first, and general knowledge last. I wondered if I dare caution Forbes not to try for a ten-pointer, decided not to, and sat trembling while he did just that. I needn't have worried: it was a football question, and he rattled off the names of forgotten Cup-winning teams without difficulty. And then his opposite number tried his first ten-pointer of the night, licking his lips and shredding a cigarette in his fingers, and as he identified obscure terms from croquet, backgammon, sailing, golf, and real tennis the Fusiliers' boot-stamping rose to a crescendo. We were still holding on to our seven-point margin.

McCaw looked awful. Normally pallid, he now appeared to have been distempered grey, but he folded his arms, gulped, went for three questions, got the first two, and then stumbled horribly over the third: 'In American politics, what are the symbols of the two main parties?' He got the donkey, and then dried up. God forgive me, I toyed with the idea of doing elephant imitations, but my sporting instinct and a well-grounded fear that my trumpeting would not go undetected kept me silent. Still, he had got three points: our lead stood at ten. His opposite number blew up on his first question, and we came to the Padre's turn. His hands clamped on his knees below the table, he put up his head, sniffed apprehensively, tried to smile pleasantly at the question-master, and asked for the first of his three questions in a plaintive neigh.

'What,' said the question-master, 'are the books of the Pentateuch?'

It was, for the Padre, the easiest question he had had all night. They might as well have asked him his name. I relaxed momentarily – this was one certain point in the bag – and then to my utter horror heard him begin to babble out the books – of the Apocrypha.

We can all do it, of course – the sudden blank spot, the ridiculous confusion of names, the too-hasty reply. 'Wrong,' squeaked the question-master, and the Padre for once swore, and slapped his head, and cried 'No, no, no!' softly to himself in sheer anguish. And we sat, feeling the chill rising, as the bespectacled warrant officer snapped up the Padre's question, got two points for it, conferred briefly with the stout major, and elected for the regulation three questions, which he answered perfectly for a total of another six. Our lead had been cut to a mere two points.

It was nasty. I looked across at the stout major, and he grinned at me, drumming his fingers on the table. I grinned back, sweating. The dilemma was – should I go for the regulation three questions, which at best might give me a total of six points? If I got the six, then his only hope would be a ten-point question; if I stumbled on any of my questions, he could have a shot at them for bonus points, and with his own questions still to come he could probably win the match. Again, he might fail one of his questions, and I would have a chance at it . . .

Or should I try for ten? If I did, and got it, that was the game in the bag; if I came a cropper, he had only three points to make on his own questions for victory. I looked along at my companions; the Padre was sunk in gloom, but Forbes suddenly spread his ten fingers at me, scowling fiercely. McCaw nodded.

'Ten-pointer, please,' I said, and the Jocks chanted encouragement, while the stout major smiled and nodded and called softly: 'Good luck.'

And then it came, in all its horror. 'What were the names of the five seventeenth-century statesmen whose initials made up the word "Cabal"?'

'Ca-what?' said a voice in the audience, and was loudly shushed.

I didn't know. That I was sure of. For a dreadful moment I found myself thinking of cabalistic signs – the zodiac – and I hate to think what I looked like as I stared dumbly at the question-master. A cornered baboon, probably. Think, you fool, I found myself muttering – and out of nowhere came one gleam of certain light – whatever the C in Cabal stood for, I knew it wasn't Clarendon.

That, you'll agree, was a big help – but at least it was a start. Charles II – Dutch Wars – broom at the mast – de Ruyter climbing a steeple in childhood – *1066 and All That* – 'They'd never assassinate me, James, to put you on the throne' – Restoration drama – dirty jokes in *The Provoked Wife* – oh, God, why hadn't I paid attention in history classes? – oranges, Nell

Gwynn, Chelsea Hospital, licentious libertines – Buckingham! It must be! Nervously, I ventured: 'Buckingham?'

The question-master nodded. 'One right.'

And four to go – but three would get me a total of eight points, even if I didn't get the last name. I went for the two A's – Ask-something – no, Ash! Ashley! I gulped it out, and he nodded. The other A was as far away as ever, but a worm of memory was stirring – one of them was a Scotsman – Laurieston? Something like that, though. And then it came.

'Lauderdale?'

'Right. Two more.'

I was buffaloed. I caught the major's eye; he was no longer smiling. One more would do – just one, and I was safe.

'I'll have to count you out, I'm afraid,' said the question-master, and he began to intone 'Five-four-three –', and the Fusiliers took it up, to be shushed angrily by their Colonel. The temptation to shout 'Clarendon! And to hell with it!' was overpowering – Cla – Cl-something – oh, lord –

'Clifford!' I shrieked, all restraint gone, and the question-master snapped his fingers.

'Right. Four out of five gets you eight points. Bad luck with the fifth – it's Arlington.'

I should have got that. It's the name of a private baths in the West End of Glasgow – if you can't remember that sort of thing, what can you remember?

Now it was for the Fusilier major. We were ten points up – he could just tie the match if he went for the big one, which of course he did, smiling in a rather frozen way, I thought.

'Good luck,' I said, but he didn't need it. He identified the five Great Lakes without a tremor (pretty easy, I thought, after my abomination, but that's the quiz business for you). And as the audience roared in frustration, Father Tuohy scratched his head and said, well, that was it. The match was drawn.

And then the babble broke out in the hall, with sundry

crying for a tie-breaker to be played. Father Tuohy looked at the question-master, who spread his hands and looked at the top brass in the front row, and they looked at each other. The mob was beginning to chant 'extra time!', and Father Tuohy said, well, he didn't know; the only people who were in no doubt were the seven other contestants and me. We were all busy shaking hands in relief and getting ready to pile for the exit and something long and cold. And then the brigadier, rot him, got up and addressed the question-master as the noise subsided.

'There seems to be a feeling that we ought to try to – ah – fight it out to a decision,' he said. 'Can't you set a few more questions to each side?'

The question-master, stout fellow, said his questions were exhausted, including the ten-pointers. They had been carefully balanced, he explained earnestly, and he wouldn't like to think up questions on the spur of the moment – not fair to either side, sir, really . . .

This didn't satisfy the audience. They began to chant and stamp in rhythm, and the brigadier smiled indulgently and asked the Colonels what did they think? Both of them obviously wanted only to let well alone, with honours even, rather than risk last-minute defeat, but they didn't dare say so, and sat pretending genial indifference in an uneasy way. We stood uncertainly on the platform, and then the brigadier, with the air of a happy Solomon – my heart sank at the satisfied glitter in his eye – said, well, since there was apparently a general desire to see a decision one way or another, he had an idea which he thought might meet with universal approval.

I've nothing against brigadiers, as a class, but they do seem to feel a sense of obligation to sort out the lower orders' problems for them. High military rank does this to people, of course, and they tend to wade in, flat-footed, and interfere under the impression that they are being helpful. Also, this brigadier was obviously bursting to cut the Gordian knot and win the plaudits of all. So we on the platform resumed our seats miserably, and he seized the back of a chair and unveiled his brain-child.

'What I'd like to propose,' he said, meaning 'What I intend to dictate' – 'is that we should settle this absolutely splendid contest with one final question. It so happens that, listening to the perfectly splendid answers that we've heard – and I would like to take this opportunity of congratulating both teams on an admirable performance – a jolly good show, in fact – and I know their commanding officers must be delighted that they have so many . . . ah . . . clever . . . ah . . . knowledgeable, and . . . ah, yes, cultured intellects . . . in their battalions . . .'

The Fusilier major caught my eye, raising his brows wearily, and the Padre muttered 'Get on with it, get on with it', while the brigadier navigated back to square one.

'As I was saying, listening to this . . . ah, display of talent, I couldn't help remembering a quiz question of which I heard many years ago, which always struck me as very ingenious and interesting, and I'm sure you'll all agree when you hear it.'

I'd have been willing to lay odds against that, but the polite soldiery gave him a mild ovation, and on he went.

'My proposal is that I set this question to both sides, and whichever can answer it should be declared the winner. All right?'

Of course it was all right; he was the brigadier. Ivan the Terrible might as well have asked the serfs if it was all right.

'Well, here it is then,' went on this high-ranking buffoon, beaming at his own ingenuity. 'It's a sporting question –' my heart leaped as I saw Forbes sit forward expectantly '– but I have to confess it is a *trick* question.' He smiled impressively, keeping us waiting. 'Now, here it is – and if anyone can answer it, I'm sure you'll agree his side *deserves* to win.' There wasn't a sound in the hall as he went on, slowly and deliberately:

'In a game of association football, how is it possible for a player to score three successive goals –' he paused, and added the punch-line '– *without any other player touching the ball in between.*'

He smiled contentedly around at the stricken quiet which greeted this, said 'Now', and waited. Immediately there was a babble of voices asking him to repeat it, and while he did I glanced along at Forbes. He was frowning in disbelief, as well he might, for the thing was patently impossible. I know the rules of football as well as the next man, and it just isn't on – when a goal is scored, the *other* side have to kick off, which involves another player . . . I thought feverishly. Unless someone put through his own goal, and then took the kick-off – but even then, he had to pass to *someone* – you can't score direct from a kick-off . . . It was beyond me, and I glanced apprehensively across at the Fusiliers. But they were plainly baffled, too.

'Well, now, come along.' The brigadier was grinning with pure restrained triumph. 'Surely we have some football enthusiasts . . .'

'Ye cannae do it.' This was Forbes, outraged at what he accounted a heretical question. 'Ye're no' on.' In the heat of the moment, he forgot all respect due to rank, glaring at the brigadier, and the brigadier let it pass, contentedly, and said:

'I will concede that it is highly unlikely. I doubt if it has ever happened in a game, or ever will. But under the rules it is theoretically possible. So.'

It was one of *those* questions, like the 155 break at snooker – it never happens, but it could. Thunderous consultation was taking place in the audience, with what appeared to be a fight breaking out in Twelve Platoon – and then Forbes was claiming attention again, shaking his black-avised head in furious disbelief.

'It isnae in the rules of fitba',' he pronounced. 'It's impossible. Ye cannae . . .'

'Is that a confession of defeat from your side?' asked the brigadier, with silken cunning, and I hurriedly said 'No, no!'

and gestured Forbes to sit down. He did, glowering, and I looked anxiously again at the Fusiliers, but the stout major was shrugging his shoulders.

'Come along, come along.' The brigadier was enjoying himself thoroughly, confounding the rabble at their own game. And as the platform sat in stale-mated silence, he looked round. 'Let's throw it open to the *supporters* of both sides, shall we? Anyone – from either battalion? You can win it for your side. All right?'

They sat, glowering at him in baffled silence – all except in Twelve Platoon's seats, where some huge upheaval was going on. To my astonishment I saw McAuslan, apparently trying to wrestle free from Fletcher, mouthing inaudibly, raising a grimy hand in the press.

'No one?' the brigadier was saying genially. 'Well, now, that's – what? You wanted to say something?'

McAuslan was struggling up, ignoring Fletcher's fierce command of 'Siddoon, ye bluidy pudden! Whaddy *you* know?' He lurched past Fletcher into the aisle, his face contorted, and said in a gravelled whisper:

'Please, sur. Ah think . . . Ah think Ah know the answer, but.'

From that moment the evening took on a dream-like quality as far as I was concerned. There he was, Darwin's discovery, in his usual disreputable condition, buttons undone, hair awry, shoe-laces trailing, and – I tried not to look – his bag of chips still clutched in one hand. Suddenly he must have realised where he was and what he was doing, for he paled beneath his grime – he was out there in the open, with everyone looking, facing Authority, and this was a situation which McAuslan normally avoided as the blindworm shuns the day. The Colonel had slewed round in his seat, and was staring at him as one on whom the doom has come – well, no one likes to see McAuslan step forth as a representative of his command – and the brigadier blinked in disbelief and started back, before recovering and exclaiming: 'Excellent! Good show! Let's hear it!'

McAuslan closed his eyes and swayed, mouthing a little, as was his wont. I could only guess that a sudden blinding belief that he, McAuslan, was for once possessed of knowledge denied to lesser men had got him up on his feet, but he was visibly regretting it now. I had a momentary vision of him transformed, with golden curls around his battered brow, and satin small-clothes in place of his unspeakable khakis, standing on a little stool and being asked: 'When did you last see your father?' And then reality returned, and the brigadier was saying kindly:

'Come forward a little, and speak up, so everyone can hear.'

McAuslan did an obedient forward shamble, and then the brigadier noticed the bag of chips, McAuslan noticed him noticing, and for a fearful moment I thought he was going to proffer the greasy mess and invite the brigadier to help himself. Instead, he hurriedly stuffed the bag inside his shirt, wiped his hands almost audibly on his thighs, and croaked:

'Weel, it's like this, see.'

And we waited, breathless, for the Word.

'A fella – he's a centre-forward,' said McAuslan, and stopped, terrified. But he rallied, and went on, in a raucous whisper: 'He pits the ba' through his own goal. That's one, right?' The brigadier nodded. 'Well, then, this same fella picks up the ba' and kicks off, frae the centre. But he disnae pass, see. No' fear. He belts the ba' doon the park, and chases after it, and a dirty big full-back ca's the pins frae him –'

'Tackles him foully,' our Colonel put in hurriedly, out of ashen lips. The brigadier, intent on McAuslan's disquisition, nodded acknowledgement of the translation.

'So,' McAuslan gestured dramatically. 'Penalty! Oor boy grabs the ba' – naebody else has touched it, mind, since he kicked aff – pits it on the spot, an' lams it in. Two, right?'

'That's right!' exclaimed the brigadier. He seemed quite excited. 'And then?'

'Aye, weel, then.' McAuslan glanced round uneasily, realised yet again that all eyes were on him, swallowed horribly, scrabbled at his perspiring brow, and ploughed gamely on. 'Soon as the goal's scored – the ref. whistles for hauf-time. An' when they come oot fur the second hauf, it's oor boy's turn tae kick aff, see, 'cos the ither side kicked aff at the start o' the game. So – he does the same thing again – batters it doon the park, gets the hems pit oan him again by the dirty big full-back –

'The same full-back fouls him yet again,' translated the Colonel, his head bowed.

'That full-back wants sortin' oot,' said someone. 'Jist an animal.'

'– and there's anither penalty,' McAuslan gasped on, his eyes now closed, 'an' oor boy shouts, "Ma ba", and takes it again and belts it –'

'You've got it!' cried the brigadier. 'First-rate! Well done!' For a moment he looked as though he might grasp McAuslan's hand, but thought better of it. 'Do you know, you're the only person I've ever heard answer that question, since it was first told to me, oh, thirty-five years ago, at Eton. Where did you hear it?'

McAuslan confessed that it hadn't been at Eton, but inna boozer onna Paurly Road in Gleska; he had heard it affa fella. The brigadier was astonished. Meanwhile, around them, the audience were demanding that the answer be repeated, while those who had understood it were vociferous in complaint that it was a daft question, it couldn't happen – not in a real game.

'I told you,' said the brigadier knowingly, 'that it was *most* unlikely. A hypothetical question, purely hypothetical, which our . . . ah . . . colleague here has answered most satisfactorily.'

The assembly bayed their disapproval of this – you cannot take liberties with football where British soldiers are concerned, and they felt the brigadier's question was facetious, if not downright ridiculous. (Which it was, if you ask me.) There were those insubordinate enough to suggest, from the back of the hall, that it was the kind of question that would have appealed only to a brigadier or a McAuslan. But the brigadier's serenity was not to be disturbed; he awarded the laurel wreath, so to speak, to McAuslan, who was now quite overcome at his own temerity, and was shuffling uneasily like a baited bear in the presence of mastiffs. The brigadier then congratulated our Colonel, who was looking as though the House of Usher had fallen on him, and led the applause. There wasn't much, actually, as the mob was streaming for the exits in disgust.

On the platform I scooped up one of the boxes of Turkish Delight, and gave it to Forbes to pass on to McAuslan – after all, he had succeeded where the cream of two battalions' brains had failed, and presumably earned the Colonel a fiver. Forbes sniffed.

'Dam' funny fitba' matches they must hiv at Eton, right enough,' was all he said, but I know he presented the prize to its rightful owner, for I chanced by Twelve Platoon's barrack-room later that night, just to make sure the lights were out, and heard things. I had been marvelling at the fact that McAuslan's memory, which normally couldn't hold much beyond his own name, had somehow retained the answer to a catch-question overheard in a public house. Of all the useless, irrelevant information – and then I thought of my own vast store of mental dross, and humbly put the matter out of my mind.

At which point, appropriately, there floated out of the darkened barrack-room window a familiar voice:

'See, Fletcher, Ah'm no sae dumb. No' me. Who answered

the man's hypodermical question, hey? Wisnae you, oh no, an' wisnae Forbes, or Darkie –'

'Ach, sharrup braggin', McAuslan. It's aboot the only thing you ever kent in yer life – an' a dam' silly question, too. Here, gie's a bit o' yer Turkish Delight, ye gannet.'

'Fat chance,' observed Private McAuslan, munching with audible contentment. 'Youse hivnae got the brains tae know tae pit it in yer mooth. Youse arenae intelleck-shull.'

And every time I watch the keen young brain-workers on television effortlessly fielding questions on French literature and microbiology and Etruscan art, I think to myself, yes, all very well, but let's hear you tell us how a footballer can score three goals in a match without anyone else touching the ball in between . . .

Parfit Gentil Knight, But

The last place you would have expected to hear Private McAuslan sing was the Colonel's office; it wasn't that sort of place, and McAuslan wasn't that sort of chorister. In fact, it was news to me that he sang at all. But I knew his voice too well to mistake the keening, raucous note that drifted in through the open green shutters on the warm North African air, and the effect was such that the Colonel, who had been discussing pistol-shooting with Bennet-Bruce, the Adjutant and myself, paused in mid-sentence to listen in disbelief.

'What the devil's that?' he demanded, and having stalked to the window like a dyspeptic Aubrey Smith, exclaimed: 'Good God, it's that fellow McAuslan. Is he drunk?'

It seemed plausible. I couldn't imagine a sober McAuslan, who in addition to being the dirtiest soldier God ever made was also of a retiring disposition and terrified of authority, being so incautious as to play Blondel outside a building containing the Colonel, the R.S.M., and the provost staff. But there he was, shuffling along the back path, waking the echoes with a parody of 'The Man Who Broke the Bank at Monte Carlo'.

'Ah wis walkin' doon the Garscube Road,
Ah wis taken unawares;
They wis shoutin' honey pears,
Git up them spiral stairs!
Oh-h-h come oot, come oot,
They're sellin' fruit,
They say –'

What they said was lost in the crash of a ground-floor shutter being thrust violently open, and the voice of the provost sergeant administering a scarifying rebuke. The song stopped abruptly, and the blackened sepulchre of D Company did a hasty shamble round the corner of the building to safety.

'Blast!' said the Colonel. 'Why the blazes must McGarry be so officious? I wanted to hear the rest of it.'

There was a pause, and the Adjutant coughed diffidently. 'It goes . . . er, something like this, sir.' And he continued, in recitatif, where McAuslan had left off:

'They're selling fruit,
They say that plums is – or are – good for the gums,
And noo – now – they're selling green yins to the Fenians.'

He paused, blushing, and the Colonel regarded him with something like awe.

'Where on earth did you learn that, Michael?'

The Adjutant said he had heard his batman singing it a good deal; you could see he was slightly uneasy about admitting acquaintance with the ribaldries of the barrack-room. But the Colonel, a keen student of battalion folk-lore, was all for it.

'Extraordinary, I thought I knew all the Jocks' songs, but that's a new one on me. What's it mean – you know, what's behind it?'

Adjutants are used to answering colonels' questions on virtually anything; really, it's what they are paid for.

'Well, sir,' said Michael, 'so far as I can judge it's about this chap who is walkin' doon – er, walking, on the Garscube Road, which is actually a street in the north-west part of Glasgow, close to Maryhill Barracks, where the H.L.I. have their depot – I did my primary training there, actually –'

'I know all about Maryhill Barracks,' said the Colonel, testily. 'Get on with it.'

'Well, the chap was taken unawares, it seems, sir, by other people shouting, er, "Honey pears", you see.'

'And what in God's name are honey pears?'

'Well, actually,' the Adjutant was beginning to flounder, when Bennet-Bruce put in:

'I think it's rhyming slang, sir, like "apples and pears" for stairs. It's one of the Jocks' slogans.'

'Ah,' said the Colonel wisely. He knew, if anyone did, about those curious barbaric cries like 'Way-ull' and 'Oh-h, Sarah!' and 'Sees-tu' which are the curious currency of the Scottish soldier's speech; they come, no one usually knows whence, and as often as not vanish as inexplicably. 'Well, go on,' he told the Adjutant.

'Well, sir, they also shout "Get up the . . . the, er, them stairs." You've heard them shouting it to each other, sir, I'm sure. Not just in our battalion; it's a catch-phrase on the wireless.' Which, of course, it was, round about the end of the war.

'But the bit about the fruit?' inquired the Colonel. 'What's that about green things for Fenians?'

The Adjutant was looking buffaloed, so I helped him out.

'It isn't really easy to explain, sir. Green is the Catholic colour – Celtic, and so on – and the implication is that Fenians – Catholics – will be eager to buy, er, green yins – green ones, green groceries, and so forth. There are alternative endings to the song, like "Cherries for the hairies" –'

'What's a hairy?'

'A girl, sir, in Glasgow. Pronounced herry. And I've heard "Grapes for the Papes", too, sir.'

'Pape means a Roman Catholic,' said the Adjutant brightly, and the Colonel withered him with a look.

'I'm not entirely ignorant, Michael. It seems to me this song has decided religious overtones. Extraordinary. Is it intended to be provocative, I wonder? – I gather from the sporting news that Celtic aren't doing too well these days. However, this has nothing to do with pistol-shooting, gentlemen, fascinating though it may be. McAuslan's in your platoon, isn't he, Dand? Well, tell the brute to confine his singing to the canteen, or somewhere where I don't have to listen to it.'

Which was hardly fair, when you consider how eager he'd been to hear the rest of it, but colonels are like that. So are company commanders; Bennet-Bruce tore mild strips off me afterwards because it had been one of my Jocks who had disturbed the peace of the Colonel's sanctum. 'You'll have to do something about that chap,' he said. 'It's bad enough that he goes absent about once a month and is, at a conservative estimate, the filthiest thing that ever put on uniform. We can't have him caterwauling under H.Q. Company windows as well.'

'I didn't create McAuslan,' I protested. 'I just got him wished on me – by you, I may point out.'

'Haven't heard him singing before, at that,' said Bennet-Bruce, skilfully changing the subject. 'It's odd – I mean, he's a pretty morose specimen, isn't he? Anyway, chew him up a bit, will you?'

I didn't, of course. There's no point, with the McAuslans of this world. And I wouldn't have given his vocalising another thought if I hadn't heard him at it again, in D Company ablutions, on the following day. This time it was 'Don't fence me in', with what he supposed was an American accent. I addressed Private Forbes, who was sitting on his bed with some of the boys.

'Forbes,' I said, 'what's with McAuslan?'

'You mean, havin' a wash?'

'He's washing, you say? And singing. What's he got to be so happy about?'

Forbes and the boys grinned. 'Search me, sir,' said Forbes, and from the secret look on his face I knew something was going on. There's a curious military shorthand which exists, in a Jock's expression and tone of voice, and if you can read it, it's worth a dozen confidential reports. I wasn't expert, like the Colonel, who could limp through a barrack-room kit inspection, smiling under his brows, and tell you afterwards which men were anxious about something, and which were content, and which were plotting devilment. But I was getting to know my platoon a little.

'It's a rerr terr,' observed Daft Bob Brown.

'McAuslan hivin' a bath,' said Forbes.

'See the man wi' the padded shoulders,' said McGlinchey, and began to hum, 'Cuddle up a little closer, baby mine', at which the boys chuckled and winked at each other.

'How's Mr Grant and Mr MacKenzie gettin' oan wi' the wee brammer frae the hospital?' asked Forbes irrelevantly, and seeing my look, added hastily: 'Aw-right, sir, Ah'm no' lookin' at you! Ah'm no' lookin' at you! Jist askin'.'

'Jist askin',' said Daft Bob.

'Whay-hay-hay-ull,' murmured McGlinchey.

'No kiddin', those two ought tae be gettin' bromide in their tea,' said Forbes.

'Nae haudin' them in.'

'She's a wee stotter, though, sho she is.'

They nudged each other and avoided my eye. Right, I thought, two can play at this game, so I observed casually:

'When was our last platoon route march – two weeks ago, wasn't it? I think we ought to have another in the next day or so. The long one, down to Fort Yarhuna, where the sand is. We can camp out overnight.' I gave them my benign platoon commander's beam. 'And sweep under your bed, Forbes, it's filthy. McGlinchey, I saw rifle oil on your small pack this morning; show it scrubbed at company office by five o'clock. Right, carry on.'

This is known as panicking them; I left the barrack-room in the comforting knowledge that they were calling down curses on my head and each others' – Forbes's especially, for provoking discord with sly allusions. It was all trivial stuff, of course, but interesting in its way. What, I wondered, could McAuslan's taking a bath – a portent, admittedly – have to do with the romantic entanglements of Lieutenants Grant and MacKenzie? My platoon obviously knew, and were disposed to be merrily sly.

As to Grant and MacKenzie, there was no mystery. They were the leading contenders in the championship for Ellen Ramsey, a phenomenon who had arrived on the scene a few weeks previously. She was the daughter of the R.A.M.C. colonel who ran the local military hospital, and, in the descriptive phrase of Private Forbes, a wee brammer, or, if you prefer it, a stotter. To quote the Adjutant, she had the message for the chaps. She was about nineteen, and as beautiful as only an English girl can be, very blonde, very cool, and with a smile like a toothpaste advertisement. The sight of her skipping across the tennis court in her white shorts had moved even the second-in-command of the battalion, an aged bachelor who despised all women, to bite through the stem of his pipe; even the Colonel observed that she was a damned nice gel, unlike the usual little floozies who distract my subalterns and cause 'em to make fools of themselves. That was the unusual thing about Ellen Ramsey; she wasn't just beautiful, she was nice with it.

So thought every man in the garrison, with Grant and MacKenzie well ahead of the field, and their rivalry, in that enclosed society, was what Forbes would have called 'the talk o' the steamie', which means common gossip. There was apparently no other competition – there seldom is, where Highlanders are concerned. They have a built-in advantage in the uniform, of course, which seems to attract women like flies; even American airmen, loaded with money and Hollywood glamour, can't really compete. I think, too, there is possibly a kind of barbaric magnetism about military Scotsmen – 'it is,' as small, plump, bald and bespectacled Major Bakie of Support Company used to say, 'the wild beast in us, the primitive, feral quality of the bens and glens and things.' He presumably knew, since he was married with a large family.

In any event, Grant and MacKenzie competed hotly for the favours of Ellen Ramsey, and the community watched with mild interest.

Personally, I couldn't have cared less. I was a confirmed misogynist of about ten days' standing, as a result of my trip to Malta with the battalion football team. There, in the intervals of going frantic over the team's performance and frustrating the villainies of Lieutenant Samuels, R.N., who had tried to harness their ability to his own money-mad schemes, I had become impassioned of a pert brunette in the paymaster's department, who had given me over for a sergeant in the Pioneer Corps (a sergeant, and a pioneer at that). I had rebounded to a red-haired temptress named Gale something-or-other, who had drunk my Pimms No. 1s and eaten my dinners at Chez Jim's, and had then turned out to be engaged to a local civilian.

So I had brought my fractured heart and ego back to North Africa, a changed and bitter man. I was through with women – finished, you understand. I could view even Ellen Ramsey with a dispassionate and jaundiced eye, smiling cynically at the folly of those who danced attendance on her. She didn't interest me. Anyway, MacKenzie was two inches taller than I was, with the flaming red hair of his tribe, and an undoubted gift of charm, and Grant owned a Hudson Terraplane. So I didn't mind taking up snooker again.

But Ellen Ramsey's affairs were all a far cry from McAuslan taking a bath, or so I thought until I had occasion to visit the hospital a couple of days later to see one of my Jocks who was recovering from a broken leg. Mrs Ramsey, Ellen's mother, a chatty, fearfully-fearfully Army wife who was the hospital's unofficial almoner, invited me to stay for tea, and in the course of a nonstop recital of the difficulty of getting domestic help in North Africa and the handlessness of Arab women as hospital staff, she suddenly asked:

'By the way, I wonder if you know a soldier in your battalion – yes, he must be in your battalion, because he wears a kilt, and talks in that strange way – I can *never* understand it – yes, he's called McAllan, or McClossan – something like that?'

'Would it be McAuslan, perhaps?' I wondered.

She said, yes, it would be, such an *odd* man. That clinched it; I admitted, cautiously, that I thought I had heard the name.

'We see a great deal of him here,' she said. 'At least, Ellen does. I'm not quite sure about him – he seems rather, well – rough, you know. Oh, quite harmless, I'm sure, but he hangs about, you know what I mean, in such a silent way, and he looks – well, rather uncouth. I don't mean to be unkind, because he's always perfectly civil, when he talks, which he seldom does – not to me, at least, but of course I hardly see him. He seems very interested in Ellen, but of course all young men are – we've grown used to that.' She gave that whimsical, satisfied, fed-up smile. 'But he is rather different – well, he is rather . . .' she hunted for a word and came out with a beauty – '. . . shop-soiled, I think. Common, really.'

Uncommon, was the way I'd have described McAuslan, but for the rest I knew exactly what she meant. Having him about the premises was rather like playing host to Peking Man, until you got used to it. But her report was disturbing.

'Do you mean he annoys Ellen?' I asked.

'Oh, no – not at all. She rather likes him – and he was very good to her, really. Rather a knight-errant, in fact. You know that Ellen shops in the afternoons, down at the bazaar, for flowers and fruit and things for the patients? Well, on one of her first trips, a week or so ago, she went beyond the main market, down to the place they call the Old Suk, near the harbour –' I knew it, a rough quarter, and out of bounds to troops. 'She tried to buy something from a stall – I forget what – and the proprietor, who seems to have been one of the more beastly Arab vendors, got unpleasant, and tried to bully her into buying at an exorbitant price. She wouldn't, of course, and then some of his friends collected, and one of them tried to get her wrist-watch, and it was all very horrid and frightening, as you can imagine, because of course she doesn't speak any Arabic, and there wasn't a white person about, and they were menacing her – you know what they can be like. Of course, she was a little idiot to go there unescorted, but she didn't know, you see.'

I saw, and knowing what out-of-bounds markets in the Middle East can be like, I could guess that for a girl straight out from England it must have been a terrifying experience.

'Well, it was becoming really unpleasant, with these awful people pawing at her, and trying to snatch her shopping-bag, and laughing, and so forth, when suddenly this man McCollin –'

'McAuslan.'

'– came on the scene. He asked her if she was all right, and she told him, and he turned on the biggest Arab, and told him in no uncertain terms to take himself off.' That must have been something to hear, too. 'But the Arabs wouldn't, at first, so he suddenly rushed at one of them, and knocked him down. That seemed to bring them to their senses, for they left Ellen and McAllan alone, and he brought her back to the main shopping streets. She was badly shaken, poor child, and it was really awfully kind of him.'

One up to you, McAuslan, I thought; that's your next offence scrubbed off before you've committed it. He could have got himself very badly beaten up, or even killed, mixing it with the kind of unlicensed victuallers who inhabited the Old Suk – where he had no business to be, of course, but that was by the way.

'And since then,' Mrs Ramsey continued, 'he seems to have appointed himself Ellen's unofficial bodyguard. She finds him waiting outside the hospital gates each afternoon, and he carries her basket, and I gather makes himself extremely useful in finding the best stalls and the cheapest prices. He seems to have a way with the Arab shopkeepers, you know what I mean? And afterwards he escorts her back again, carrying her parcels. My husband has nicknamed him "Ellen's poodle", but I'm afraid he isn't what you would call house-trained. She asked him in for tea one afternoon – I gather he was extremely reluctant, and really she should have known better – and I was glad, I can tell you, that there was no one else on the verandah. It was rather embarrassing – well, I found it impossible to make out what he said, for one thing, and he seemed quite unaccustomed to afternoon tea, poor man. Yes, he is rather rough.'

'Just as well, really,' I found myself saying. 'It has its uses, doesn't it?'

'You mean – oh, rescuing Ellen. Yes,' she laughed a little doubtfully, 'I suppose so. Oh, he seems to make himself useful, so I don't mind – as long as she doesn't invite him to our next cocktail party. That would be a little too much. You will be coming, Mr MacNeill, won't you? – Saturday, at seven.'

'That's awfully kind of you,' I said, 'but I've a dreadful feeling I'm orderly officer this weekend. If I can't make it, please accept my apologies in advance.'

I wasn't going to make it, which was petty, if you like, but somehow I suddenly felt I'd had just a trifle too much of Mrs Ramsey's hospitality – house-trained though I presumably was. Poor McAuslan – he wouldn't bat an eye when confronted with half a dozen Arabi thugs, but he must have been scared stiff in the presence of the gracious Mrs Ramsey and her best bone china. I thought of that scruffy, awkward figure glowering uncertainly at the thin brown bread and mumbling incoherently over his cup, and found I was cutting at the air with my walking-stick as I walked down the hospital drive.

Poor unseemly Glasgow Galahad. He had done a very proper, brave thing – gallant, if you like – and his eventual reward had been to feel uncomfortable and humiliated in the presence of the Colonel's lady – not that she could help being what she was any more than he could. And fairly obviously he had been sore smitten by Ellen Ramsey, which no private soldier of McAuslan's social undesirability could afford to be – not even in the democratic aftermath of the Second World War. We are meant to pretend that social distinctions are a thing of the past, but as in all things it depends who are the individuals involved. Take McAuslan, and you might as well apply the conventions of the Middle Ages. You wouldn't want him hanging round your daughter, I'll tell you.

Still, I found myself disliking Mrs Ramsey's *grande dame* implications. And also regretting – as I'd often done – Private McAuslan's thick-headedness; why hadn't he just faded out gracefully, after doing his good deed? But he hadn't, and he didn't – the day after I had been at the hospital I happened to be driving down town to the Stadium, and saw Ellen Ramsey obviously coming back from her afternoon's shopping. She was sitting in one of those two-person horse-gharries, looking like the front row of the chorus, and who should be in the other seat, half-hidden under a load of parcels, but Old Man Karloff himself. He was grinning, in a bashful sort of way, and obviously as pleased as Punch – no wonder he had started taking baths and went about the place singing.

I wondered if I should do something about it. It seemed to me that McAuslan was liable to get himself hurt. But what to do? He was infringing no military rule; he wouldn't, poor soul, have understood what it was all about – neither, I think, would Ellen Ramsey. It was all so trivial and unimportant – but so are many potentially disastrous things, and they become disasters simply because, being trivial at the outset, you can't take hold of them.

Anyway, it all came to a head a few days later, in a way which, looking back, seems totally unreal. I went to Mrs Ramsey's cocktail party after all – well, it was free drink and liver on sticks, and I wasn't going to face the Saturday night cold meat in the mess with the prospect of being roped in to the second-in-command's bridge game afterwards. So I went to the hospital, where the garrison's finest were circulating and knocking back the gin; there were about thirty people on the Ramseys' verandah, making the usual deafening cocktail-party chatter, and I latched on to a glass and made heavy play among the cheese and grapes and wee biscuits with paste on them. In between I heard about adrenalin from old man Ramsey, his wife told me that she didn't know what she was going to do about the Arab hospital sweepers who were certainly pilfering from the stores not that she minded the loss so much as the fact that they would certainly contaminate the foodstuffs, the Padre from the Fusiliers wanted to know, in a round-about way, what provision was made for the spiritual nourishment of Anglicans in a Highland battalion, and the dockyard captain, plashing with gin, told me about his early training days on a windjammer. All the usual stuff, and then, having done my duty, I retired to a corner to chat up one of the nurses – you can't be a misogynist for ever.

It was then I noticed Ellen Ramsey. She was, as usual, between MacKenzie and Grant, but I noticed she kept glancing in my direction – well, poor butterfly, I thought, it was bound to happen sooner or later. And then she gave me an undoubted look, and I detached myself and went over to a quiet corner of the verandah. She slipped away from MacKenzie and Grant and came across.

'You're Dand MacNeill, aren't you?' she said, and I found

myself reflecting comfortably that two centuries earlier some fair Venetian had probably said, 'You're Giacomo Casanova, aren't you?' in just the same way. So I gave my nonchalant bow, and then she ruined the effect by saying,

'Yes, Jimmy said you were.' Jimmy was Grant, the Terraplane-driver.

'Do you mind if I ask you something?' she went on. Frankly, I didn't; faced with something that looks like the young Lana Turner, I'm as impressionable as the next man.

'I'm probably being silly, but – well, I thought I ought to ask someone. Look – you're John McAuslan's platoon commander, aren't you?'

I hadn't expected that, at any rate – it was nearly as surprising as hearing someone use McAuslan's Christian name – bad platoon commander that I was, I'd never really thought of his having one. But the surprises hadn't really started.

'I know I'm being stupid,' she said, looking embarrassed, 'but I had a rather odd experience this afternoon. No, please don't laugh. It's just – well, he's been helping me quite regularly lately, down at the market, carrying parcels and that sort of thing, you know, being generally useful . . .'

'I know, your mother told me.'

'Yes, well, then you know he helped me out with some beastly Arab – and he seemed very anxious to go on helping, and well, he *did* know his way around the market, you know . . .' She shrugged, and spilled some drink from her glass. 'Oh, damn, sorry . . . but, well, he seemed all right, although he looked pretty awful – well, he does, doesn't he? And then . . . this afternoon . . .'

'What about this afternoon?' I asked, feeling all sorts of nameless dreads.

'Well, this afternoon –' she looked me in the eye '– he proposed to me.'

For a moment I nearly laughed, and then, very quickly, I

didn't want to. She wasn't even smiling – her pretty face was perplexed and unhappy. I was relieved, and astonished, and angry, and – no other word for it – fascinated.

'Let me get it right. McAuslan proposed to you – marriage?'

'Yes, on the way home. We usually come back by horse-carriage, and it was a nice afternoon, and I thought it would be nice to drive along the front, and look at the wrecks in the bay – and on the way . . . he asked me to marry him.'

Oh, God, McAuslan, I thought. Think of the improbable, and he'll do it every time.

'I didn't really understand at first – you know he doesn't talk very much – well, he hasn't to me, at least. Just when we were in the market, and so on, and I don't understand a lot of it anyway – it's his accent. And when he started talking this afternoon, I couldn't make much of it out, and then it dawned on me . . . there wasn't any doubt of it. He was proposing.'

'You're sure?' I was trying to hold on to reality. 'What did he say, exactly?'

'Oh, gosh, I couldn't reproduce it.' She was very much a schoolgirl, really. 'But he said, 'We could get married' – merit, he called it. He said it again.'

'You're sure . . . he wasn't being funny?'

'Oh, no. No. He was dead serious. I've been proposed to before – once – not half as seriously as he did. He meant it. It never even occurred to me to treat it as a joke.' She looked uncertain, frowning. 'I couldn't have.'

'What did you say – I mean, if it's any of my business?'

'Well, when I'd got over the surprise, and realised he was being serious, I said – I said no. Look, honestly, I know this sounds terribly silly to you, and you probably think I'm an idiot, or that I think it's all a big giggle, or something, but I don't – really, I don't. I mean, if I had, I wouldn't have wanted to tell you, would I?'

'Well,' I said. 'Well – why are you . . . telling me?'

'Because I'm worried. All right, you probably think it's a great hoot, but it isn't. I said no, you see . . . and he asked me again, in that sort of dogged way, and I said, "No, look, please, it isn't on. I mean, I don't want to get married." And he asked me again, very seriously, and I said no, and tried to explain . . . and then – you won't believe this . . .'

'I'll believe anything,' I said, and meant it.

'Well, he started to cry. He just looked at me, very steadily, and then tears started to run down his cheeks. Positive tears, I mean. He didn't sob, or anything like that. He just . . . well, wept. I asked him not to, but he just stared at me, and then he climbed out of the carriage, and walked away. I didn't know what to think. And then he came back, and looked at me, and said, "It's no' bluidy fair." That's what he said. And then he said, "Good afternoon" and walked off. I mean, it's mad, isn't it?'

She stood smiling at me, with that puzzled look in her big, blue eyes, and I wondered for an instant if this was some fearful joke thought up by her and Messrs MacKenzie and Grant to take the mickey out of me. But it wasn't, and she was worried.

'Well,' I said, 'I don't know about mad – but it's certainly unexpected. I don't really know . . .'

'Look, I'm awfully sorry even mentioning it . . . I feel an awful fool . . . but . . . I mean he's really a terribly nice person – I think – but, well, it worries me. He can be pretty savage, you know – if you'd seen him with that Arab, I mean, just for a minute he was really berserk. I mean, he seemed pretty badly cut-up this afternoon – he really looked awful – more awful, I mean.' She suddenly put down her glass. 'Look, I don't think I'm a *femme fatale*, or anything, and I know it sounds like something out of *Red Letter*, but he wouldn't do anything silly, would he?'

The answer to that was yes, of course, he being McAuslan, but whatever it was, it would be some folly no one had thought of yet.

'No,' I said, 'I shouldn't think so.'

'Please, don't think I'm being stupid – well, I am, I suppose, getting all in a tizzy about nothing. Only I wanted to tell someone – and you're his platoon commander – and he said something about you once – not today – and well . . . I wouldn't want him to think that I was laughing at him, or anything like that. I mean most boys . . .' She gave a gesture that would have belted Grant and MacKenzie right in the ego '. . . you know how it is. But, he's so serious . . . he really is. It's really silly, isn't it? And I'm the genuine dumb blonde, aren't I?'

No, I thought, you're a rather nice girl; dumb, yes, in some ways, but nice with it.

'Well,' I said, 'you didn't laugh at him, so . . .'

'No,' she said, 'I didn't laugh.'

'So that's all there is to it,' I said.

'Look . . . maybe I shouldn't have said anything . . . I mean, he won't get into any kind of trouble, will he?'

'Why should he? Proposing isn't a crime.'

'No, I suppose not . . . but if Daddy knew, he'd be hopping mad. Mummy,' she added elegantly, 'would bust a gut. And I hate to think what Jimmy Grant or Kenny would do about it.'

'If either Lieutenant Grant or Lieutenant MacKenzie were ill-advised enough to try to do anything about a member of my platoon,' I said, 'you would be bringing fruit and flowers for them in the afternoons.'

'Good. Could you get me another punch, please? I feel I need it after all this confessional stuff. Look, do you think I'm barmy? It all sounds so dam' silly, doesn't it?'

Take anyone's proposal of marriage, and the chances are it will sound silly. Hollywood has overworked the truth of how people talk to the extent that reality, when you come across it, usually sounds corny. I remember a fellow in Burma being shot in the leg, and he rolled over shouting: 'They got me! The dirty rats, they got me!' Put that into fiction and people will laugh at it, but I heard it happen.

Similarly, the remarkable conversation I had just had with Ellen Ramsey. It was, as she said, damned silly, but I knew it was true, and that to McAuslan it had probably been a bit of a tragedy, and in no way funny. The thought of her and McAuslan doing the Jane Austen bit – and no doubt looking like something left out for the cleansing department while he did it – should, in theory, have been ludicrous. But she didn't think so, and neither did I. It was pathetic, and rather touching, and not for the first time I found myself uncomfortably moved by that uncertain, unhappy, vulnerable little tatterdemalion. It must have hurt him, and I wondered how he was taking it.

It wasn't just a sentimental consideration, either. I knew my McAuslan; under the bludgeonings of fate, in whatever form, his normal reaction was to go absent, and I didn't want that. He had been over the wall too often in the past, and if he did it again he could be in serious trouble. So I took the precaution of checking the guardroom list that midnight, and sure enough, his name was among those who had failed to book in by 2359 hours.

Normally, when a man does that, you expect to see him returned within a few hours, full of flit and defiance, by the gestapo. But I decided to take no chances; I rang a friend in the provost marshal's office, one of the half-human ones, and asked him to do a quick sweep with his redcaps for one McAuslan, J., that well-known wanderer, and whip him back to barracks as fast as possible.

'I don't want him going A.W.O.L., Charlie,' I explained. 'His record won't stand it. Try the Old Suk; he's probably rolling in some gutter with a skinful of arak.'

'It beats me why you want him back,' said Charlie, 'but leave it to me; my boys'll find him.'

But they didn't. Sunday noon came, without result, and McAuslan's name went up on the board as absent without leave. That was bad enough; my next fear was that he had done something really daft, like hopping an outward-bound ship, in which case his absence would become desertion. He couldn't, I asked myself, do anything worse, could he? Jilted people are capable of anything, and I began to see visions of McAuslan à la Ophelia, floating belly-up with rosemary and fennel twined in his hair. It had got to the point where I was trying to translate 'Adieu, cruel world' into Glasgow patter, when the mess phone rang.

'We got your lad,' said Charlie. 'Not in the Suk, not in Puggle Alley, not on the harbour – guess where? Out on the beach, looking at the wrecks, for God's sake. Talk about eccentrics.'

'Thanks, Charlie. How is he?'

'Tight as a coot, but past the fighting stage – now. We had a little trouble. He should be arriving at your rest home any minute. O.K.?'

I thanked him and hung up, quite unreasonably relieved. Then after a few minutes I went round to the guardroom, and Sergeant McGarry admitted me to a cell to view the remains.

Even by McAuslan standards, his condition was deplorable. He had evidently got extremely wet, and thereafter spent the night on a well-nourished compost heap, his sporran and one boot were missing, his matted hair hung over a face that looked like a grey-washed cathedral gargoyle, and he had a new black eye. He was also three-parts drunk, and swayed to and fro on the edge of his plank-bed, making awful sounds.

Becoming aware of me he tried to focus, made an effort to get up, and wisely desisted.

'Ah'm – Ah'm awfy – sorry, sir,' he said at last, articulating with difficulty.

'So am I,' I said, and he groaned.

'Ah'm gaunae – gaunae be sick,' he announced.

'Sergeant McGarry!' I shouted. 'He's going to be sick. Get a bucket, or something –'

McGarry's face appeared at the grille in the cell door, scowling horribly.

'Spew on my floor, ye beast, and I'll tear the bones from your body.'

'Ah'm no' gaunae be sick,' McAuslan decided, and McGarry vanished. Psychologists take note.

I doubted if there was much to be accomplished in the prisoner's present condition, but you have to go through the motions. He would be before the Colonel in the morning, and if by previous inquiry you can discover some extenuating circumstance, or even coach the accused in what to say – or what not to say – it all helps.

'McAuslan,' I said, 'this is the fourth time this year. You'll be for detention, you realise that? Maybe in barracks, maybe in the glasshouse. You got fourteen days last time. You don't want to go to the Hill, do you?'

No reply. He was gargling to himself, staring down at his hands in a bemused way, giving occasional small hiccups. I didn't seem to be getting through.

'McAuslan, you were absent nearly a whole day. That's serious. How are you going to explain it to the Colonel?'

He looked vacantly at me, and began to mumble, at first incoherently, but then words began to come out. I don't know what I expected – I've heard guardroom depositions that you wouldn't believe, including a confession of murder, and poured-out grievances going back in harrowing detail to infancy – but none that astonished me more than McAuslan's. And yet, it was perhaps perfectly natural – but I'd never have heard it if he hadn't been deep in drink.

'. . . no good enough,' he muttered. 'No' good enough. It's no' bluidy fair, so it's no'. Never done nuthin'.' His eyes were unnaturally bright, but didn't seem to be seeing anything.

'Ah'm – no' good enough. No' bluidy fair. Lot o' bluidy snobs. Thinkin' Ah'm jist a yahoo. Ah'm no'. Thought she wiz different, but, no' like the rest o' them bluidy snobs. See her mither, an' her sang-widges – bluidy awfy, they wiz.' He gulped resoundingly. 'Auld cow. No' good enough for her. Jist a yahoo. Sergeant Telfer says Ah'm jist a yahoo – a'body does. And her, she thinks Ah'm no' good enough. And Ah'm jist – jist . . .' He began to sob, deep in his chest, '. . . no' good enough. No' good enough.'

I just stood listening; there was nothing else to do.

'Never got made lance-corporal – an' Boyle did, an' him's scruffy as – as – as me. Wisnae fair – wisnae my fault – no' bein' good enough. Ah didnae think she mindit, though – an' Ah sortit that wog oot, doon the bazaar. Ah did. "You leave the lassie alone, ye black bastard," Ah says, "or Ah'll banjo ye. Git up tae me, son," Ah says, "ye'll git the heid oan ye." That sortit him, right enough. Aye, but Grant an' MacKenzie an' them, bet ye they couldnae 'a sortit him. But they're good enough – toffee-nosed an' talkin' posh – good enough, aye. Ah'm no' good enough – Ah'm a yahoo – no' good enough. Sno' bluidy fair, so it's no' – no' bein' good enough!'

Maybe I'm soft, but I felt my eyes stinging. I squatted down in front of him as he rocked on the bench, working his hands between his knees. Self-pitying drunks are ten a penny, but what was coming out of him wasn't just ordinary self-pity. All right, he was abysmally stupid, and by exhibiting a phenomenal degree of wooden-headedness he had got himself hurt. So what do you do – tell him to get hold of himself and not be a fool? Perhaps. But when someone has spent a young life-time getting hurt, in ways which most of us can't imagine, then when he commits a really outstanding folly, and is reduced to utter abject misery, it may be as well to go easy.

'Of course you're good enough, son,' I said, and presumably he heard, for he shook his head.

'Ah'm no' like Grant an' MacKenzie an' them. Bluidy wee snobs – her an' her sang-widges. Thinkin' Ah'm jist a yahoo – Ah'll show them – Ah'm no' jist a yahoo – mebbe Ah didnae go tae a posh school, an' talk toffee-nosed, but Ah'll dae a'right. When Ah git oot, Ah'll dae a'right – there a fella in the Garngad – wi' a haulage business – gimme a job. Ah'll be fine, nae fear. Ah'll no' be oan the burroo –' that is, unemployed. 'See Grant an' MacKenzie, but, bluidy wee toffee-noses, see them oan the burroo. Thinkin' Ah'm no' good enough. An' Ah'm no'! She disnae think Ah'm – Ah'm – good enough. Oh, Goad, Ah feel awfy! Oh, Goad, Ah'm awfy ill!'

He clutched himself and rolled around for a moment, but then steadied up, called on his Maker a few times, and observed fearfully that he was for the hammer the morn.

'Darkie'll nail me. He's a bastard, yon Darkie, so he is. He'll dae me. He's done me afore. They – they like daein' me!'

Since I *was* Darkie, this was slightly disturbing. It also suggested that McAuslan was well beyond the bounds of comprehension, so I decided to take my leave. I kicked on the door for Sergeant McGarry, and as he was opening up, I looked at McAuslan, crouched on his bench, sunk in dejection. It always comes as a shock when you see into someone's mind – it can be terribly corny, and trite, and obvious, and yet totally unexpected. It never seems quite real. It wasn't, I could agree with him, bloody fair.

'No' good enough,' he muttered again, as the door closed.

The Colonel evidently agreed with him, for next morning he heaved the book at him – twenty-eight days' cells, which was the maximum he could do in the guardroom, without being sent to the military prison at Heliopolis. Sensibly, McAuslan took it without comment, beyond a mumbled apology, and that was that. He laboured, for the ostensible good of his soul and the damage of the battalion gardens, for his daily eight hours, and McGarry locked him up at night. I kept an eye on him, to see how he was bearing up, but beyond the fact that he got filthier by the day – which was absolutely normal – there was nothing to report. No signs of unhinged personality, or anything, although with him it was always difficult to tell. Whatever had been working in him that night, he seemed to have got over it.

It must have been in the last week of his sentence, and I was in company office late in the afternoon, when the battalion post clerk brought in the mail. It was a big batch, because there had been some mix-up at the airport that had delayed things for several days; I sent for one man from each platoon to help sort it, splitting it into platoon bundles. The man from my platoon was Daft Bob Brown; he carried off a great heap of letters for his barrack-room, and as I was leaving the office I met him going down the company steps, a bundle of envelopes still in his hand.

'Where away with those?' I asked.

'Guardroom, sir. McAuslan's mail.'

I was surprised. 'He gets plenty, doesn't he?'

'No kiddin', sir. If it wisnae for him, postie wid be oot o' a job.'

'But –' I said. 'How's that? He can't read or write.'

'That's right, sir. Ah write his letters for him – me an' the fellas.'

'And read them, too – the one's he gets, I mean?'

'Aye, sure. It's a helluva job, too. Ye should see the amoont he gets – shake ye rigid.'

'Well, I'm damned.' This was intriguing. 'Who writes to him – his people?'

Daft Bob guffawed. 'No' on yer nelly. It's the birds.'

'The birds?'

'The talent, the hairies, the glamouries.' He took pity on my ignorance. 'The women.'

'Women? You mean young women? Girls? Writing to McAuslan?'

'No hauf. He's a helluva man for the lassies, yon.'

'I don't believe it,' I said. 'Now, look, hold on. Let's get it straight. You say that women write to McAuslan – and he writes to *them*? Or rather, you and the others write for him? What about, for heaven's sake?'

'Oh, Goad, the passion,' said he. 'It's like somethin' oot the *Sunday Post*, no kiddin'. "Ah-love-ye, Ah-love-ye, Ah'm-pinin'-away-fer-ye," a' the time. Me an' the boys is hairless, keepin' up wi' it.'

'Come off it, Brown,' I said. 'You're telling me that McAuslan exchanges love letters with – with hordes of women? Don't give me that – I mean, look at him. He isn't Tyrone Power, is he? What woman in her right mind –'

'Ach, they don't know ony better. Look, sir, ye know the addresses that turns up in greatcoat pockets, frae wee lassies that works in the packin' sheds in Blighty? Ye know, they pit their addresses in the pockets, so that fellas that gits the coats'll write tae them? Some fellas diz, but no' often. Weel, McAuslan collected a whole lot o' these addresses, and gits us tae write tae the women for him.'

Freud, you should be living at this hour, I thought, someone hath need of thee.

'What for?' I demanded.

'Ah dae ken. It's a good baur, though. He tells us whit tae say – Goad, ye should see it. He's gaun tae mairry them, an' tak' them tae his place on the Riviera when he gets his demob, and Goad kens whit else. There's nae haudin' 'im in. An' they believe it, too.'

'You're having me on, curse you,' I said. 'It isn't true.'

'Ah'm no', sir, honest tae Goad. Ask Forbes, or Chick, or onybody.'

'But – how long has this been going on?'

'Oh, months, sir. Och, it's jist a baur. Ah postit a couple for 'im the ither day – while he was on jankers. One tae a wumman in Fife, an' one tae Teeny Mitchell in Crosshill, an' one tae –'

'Stone me!' I exclaimed. 'The – the – trifler! I could wring his unwashed neck! You mean he's pouring out his revolting heart to all these unsuspecting females –'

'Oh, he's daein' a' that. A right Don Joo-an.'

'And I was sorry for him. No, nothing, Brown. All right, take our lousy Lothario his billet-doux, and just hint to him, gently, from me, that – oh, what's the use? Carry on.'

I went on my way to the mess, reflecting with mixed feelings on Private McAuslan, demon lover extraordinary. I gave up; life is too short, really. And as I went up the mess steps, I found running through my head the words and music of:

> Ah wis walkin' doon the Garscube Road,
> Ah wis taken unawares –

Fly Men

I had the Padre trapped and undone, helpless in my grasp; the rocks were about to fall and crush him. In fact, he was snookered, with the white jammed in behind the black on the bottom cushion, and pink masking the blue at the top end of the table. Also, he was twenty-five points behind.

Reluctant to admit defeat, as the Church of Scotland always is, he played for time. He stood there sweating and humming Crimond, a sure sign of his deep disturbance, fiddled with his cue, dropped the chalk, ran a finger behind his dog-collar, wondered irritably when the Mess Sergeant was going to announce dinner, and finally appealed for help to the M.O., who had been offering him gratuitous advice throughout the game but now, in the moment of crisis, had retired to the bar and was tying salmon-lures. (The M.O. did this habitually, carrying the tackle in his enormous pockets, and fiddling with bits of thread and feather at the slightest excuse.)

'Now Israel may say and that truly, we're stymied,' said the Padre. 'Lachlan, will you look at this situation. What's to be done?'

'Put up a prayer,' said the M.O. irreverently, with his mouth full of red worsted. He glanced at the table. 'Left-hand side, a bit of deep screw, and come off three cushions.' And then, just as the Padre had resigned himself and was preparing to attempt his own patent version of the massé shot, which in the past had necessitated heavy stitching in three different parts of the cloth, the M.O. added artlessly:

'Here, did you know that Karl Marx was related on his mother's side to the Duke of Argyll?'

'Is that so?' said the Padre, feigning interest and glad of any respite. 'I never –'

'Lay off,' I said firmly. I had been here before. When it came to gamesmanship the M.O. and Padre could make Stephen Potter look like a girl guide. I knew that the M.O.'s irrelevant interruption at a crucial stage of the game had been perfectly timed so that the Padre could delay his shot until dinner intervened, or I forgot the score, or a new war broke out, and I wasn't having it. I had been pursuing the Padre across the snooker table for weeks, and now I had him gaffed at last.

'Take your shot, you fugitive from the Iona Community,' I said. 'Play ball.' And as he sighed and stooped over the table, remarking that there was no balm in Gilead, I added some gamesmanship of my own. 'You're twenty-five behind, bishop, and dead, dead, dead.'

'The poor soul, have some respect for his cloth,' said the M.O., and it was at that moment, with the Padre poised on the lip of destruction, that the Adjutant came in to announce that we had smallpox in the battalion.

'Smallpox?'

The M.O. ran a hook into his thumb in his startled reaction, and swore luridly, the Padre's cue rattled on the floor, and I suspect I just stood and gaped. And then the Adjutant, who was normally a slightly flustered, feckless young man, given to babbling, took things in hand.

'Hunter, C Company, is in base hospital under observation. They suspect it's smallpox –'

'Suspect? Don't they know?' said the M.O., sucking his injured thumb.

'They're pretty certain. He's been vaccinated fairly recently, but apparently that's not infallible, right, doc? Okay, the Colonel's on his way in to barracks from his home, and the first thing is to get every Jock who is out of barracks back here, at once, for quarantine and new vaccination. You'll be at it all night,

Lachlan, I'm afraid. You, Dand,' he went on to me, 'get over to the M.T. sheds, take every truck you can find, as many N.C.O.s as there are in barracks – I'll get someone to round 'em up – and go down town for the Jocks. Sweep them in, wherever they are –'

'It's Saturday night,' I said. 'They'll be spread half-way to Cairo . . .'

'I know that. At a rough guess eighty per cent of the battalion must be down there. You go through every club, canteen, dance-hall and gin-mill in the in-bounds area – I want them all, you understand. No stragglers, nobody overlooked. Start at the "Blue Heaven" and send out foot patrols from there. Don't bother about the Suk, just yet. Just round them up, get them back here, tip 'em out at the gates, and back for another haul. Right – move!'

I was moving, fast, when the M.O., who was barking abuse down the phone at some unfortunate operator, turned and yelled after me:

'When were you last vaccinated?'

'Burma, '45,' I said, disappearing. The M.O.'s motto was, if it moves, stick a needle in it, and if I was going to have a hectic night combing out the Jocks from an Arab seaport which was more like a labyrinth than a town, I preferred to do it without a fresh load of his bugs coursing through my blood-stream.

'Take a wireless and op. with you,' shouted the Adjutant. 'I'll be in orderly room, taking signals.'

'Roger!' I wasted one second putting my head in at the billiard-room door and telling the barman: 'Don't let anyone move those balls – I want his heart's blood!' and then I was in flight for the M.T. sheds.

It would be nice to record that within two minutes I was humming down-town with a well-organised convoy behind me, but it never works out that way in the Army. I had to dig the M.T. sergeant out of the mess where he was playing darts, he had to start a hue and cry for drivers, some idiot had lost the key of the petrol store, the lead three-tonner wouldn't start ('C'mon, ye thrawn old bitch, cough for your feyther,' the driver was saying as he perspired at the handle), the Adjutant's promised N.C.O.s were slow to materialise – and then Regimental Sergeant-Major Mackintosh appeared, armed with his nominal rolls, and looking like an Old Testament prophet who had just been having words with the Lord and getting the worst of it. But, as usual, everything flowed into place under his Olympian influence; N.C.O.s and drivers appeared, trucks started, headlights flashed on in the velvety African dusk, the M.T. sergeant roared 'Embus!' and the R.S.M. addressed me gravely through my truck window.

'If I may advise, sir,' said he, in that grave and heavy voice which he reserved for subalterns, rather like Polonius addressing a half-witted prince, 'you might be best to stay doon the toon, supervisin' the collection of battalion personnel. I shall remain here to receive them.' He paused, thinking. 'I know you are aware, sir, that it is of the utmost importance that we bring back every wan of them. It may be difficult. There is a native population in the toon of an estimated wan hundred thousand souls –' (trust a Highland R.S.M. to say 'souls', not people) '– so our men may be haard to find. Weel, just you stick at it, Mr MacNeill, and we'll get the job done, *namanahee*.'

Looking back, I realise that the R.S.M. was a desperately anxious man that night. Of course, he was an old and experienced soldier, and I know now that he was contemplating what an epidemic of that hideous disease might do to a battalion that had survived everything the Germans and Japanese could give it. Vaccinations, as the M.O. said, are not infallible. But I didn't really understand this at the time; I suppose I was young and callous and preoccupied with the job in hand. To tell the truth, I was rather excited, and slightly apprehensive on a different account.

As a subaltern, you get used to doing pretty well anything. In my brief time I had been called on to command a troop-train, change a baby's nappies, quell a riot of Arab nationalists, manage a football team, take an inventory of buried treasure, and partner a Mother Superior at clock-golf. This was in the days when the British Army was still spread all round the globe, acting as sentry, policeman, teacher, nurse and diplomat in the wake of the Second World War, and getting no thanks for it at all. It was a varied existence, and if I'd been ordered to redecorate the Sistine Chapel or deliver a sermon in Finnish, I'd hardly have blinked an eyelid before running to the R.S.M. pleading for assistance.

But descending on an Arab city on a Saturday night to round up 800 Scottish soldiers, many of whom would doubtless be well gone in liquor and ready to prove it, was a new one. Still, that was what I got my £9 a week for, so as instructed I descended on the 'Blue Heaven', which was a cabaret-cum-canteen-cum-dance-hall just in-bounds from the prohibited Suk, or native market area. The 'Heaven' was a well-known magnet for the more discerning revellers of the battalion, inasmuch as it provided local beer, Eurasian hostesses who danced with the troops and persuaded them to buy the champagne of the house (an unspeakable concoction known as 'Desert Rose' in affectionate memory of the Eighth Army public conveniences), an energetic Arab orchestra, and two belly-dancers of grotesque proportions called Baby Boadicea and Big Aggie. If I could clear the clientele out of that on a Saturday night I would be doing well; I could despatch the foot-patrols to less raucous establishments like the Y.M.C.A. and the Church of Scotland Club to pry the patrons loose from their Horlicks and copies of *Life and Work*.

When we pulled up outside, the 'Blue Heaven' was jumping like a geyser. The Arab musicians were administering extreme unction to 'In the Mood', a glee-club of military amateurs was singing on the steps (they were bundled into the trucks before they knew it), and inside the establishment appeared to be on fire, so thick was the smoke. There seemed to be about two hundred tables, crowded with soldiers and airmen, all well-Brylcreemed and with their caps shoved under their shoulder-straps, the beer bar looked like the storming of the Bastille, and on a stage at the far end, Big Aggie, her brave vibrations each way free, as the poet says, was undulating with abandon, watched by an admiring circle of Jocks, arms folded, bonnets pulled down over their eyes, and mouths open in awe. Arbroath, you could almost hear them thinking, was never like this.

Calling the meeting to order was my immediate problem, made no easier by the fact that I was in civilian clothes. I shouted 'Quiet!' at the top of my voice, without effect, seized a pint glass tankard, and hammered it on the table. Naturally it broke, leaving me with a splintered glass knuckle-duster, at the sight of which a battered Jock sitting nearby exclaimed 'Name o' Goad!' and vanished beneath his table, advising his friends that I was a wild man and was going to claim them. For the rest, no one paid much attention, and I was left looking like a Broomielaw pub brawler in a Harris tweed jacket, which is a nice thought. Fortunately the M.T. sergeant took over, hammering a chair on the floor and roaring until the general din had subsided, Big Aggie stopped gyrating, and the Arab answer to Glenn Miller died away in an unmusical squawk.

'All right,' I said loudly, divesting myself of my broken glass. 'All Highlanders are to return to barracks at once. There are trucks outside. Fusiliers and other British troops, return to your own units as quickly as possible. Don't ask questions, don't waste time, don't wait to finish your drinks. Move – now.'

This elicited the usual loyal response from the troops – a mutinous baying punctuated by cries of 'Why don't you get a job?' and 'Awa' hame, yer tea's oot.' I knew enough not to stand waiting, but to get out and leave it to the M.T. sergeant and his minions to clear the place, which they did in ten minutes flat. As the crowd streamed out, snarling, puzzled, resentful or resigned, but at least obedient, I was buttonholed near the door by a small, perspiring Italian, who proved to be the proprietor, demanding to know why I was summarily closing his establishment, depriving himself and his numerous family of their livelihood, and assuring me that anyone who alleged he sold kif (which is hashish) to young soldiers was a liar. Nor did he water his beer, or run a bawdy-house, the hostesses being all cousins of his wife's on leave from their convent, and it was a vile calumny if anyone said his cigarettes were smuggled in from Tangier. Would I honour him by having a drink in his office?

I quieted him and went outside. It looked like the beach at Dunkirk, with Jocks piling into the trucks, drunks being lifted over the tailboards, the M.T. sergeant despatching the first of the foot patrols for stragglers, a fight or two breaking out here and there, and a Highland corporal arguing with two red-capped military policemen over the custody of a marvellously inebriated private who was lying prostrate on the bonnet of the M.P.'s jeep singing 'Hand me down my walking cane' in a Glasgow accent. All in all, it was fairly normal, and no different probably from the usual chucking-out time at the 'Blue Heaven'; most of them were going quietly, and I discovered why when a warrant-officer of the Fusiliers approached me and asked if it was right there had been a smallpox outbreak.

Since the murder was out, I told him yes, and to get his men home as fast as he could – and then a dreaded and remembered voice addressed me plaintively from the back of the first of our battalion trucks, which was fully loaded and ready to leave.

'Hi, Mr MacNeill! Hi! Sir! Here a minute. Ah'm no' hivin' this! You let me oot this truck, Michie, or Ah'll melt ye, so I wull!'

This was all I needed. I sighed and went over.

'What is it, McAuslan? Stand still and stop thrashing about. What's the matter?'

He emerged from the press of close-packed bodies, and clung to the tailboard, Old Pithecanthropus Erectus in person, even more grimy and dishevelled than usual by reason of his Saturday-night potations, and full of indignation.

'Here a bluidy liberty, sir,' said he. At a rough guess, he was about six pints ahead. 'Ah'm no' standin' fur it! Sharrup, Michie! Sir, they say Ah'm bein' took back tae barracks because Ah've got the poax.'

'You've what?' I couldn't believe I'd heard aright.

'The poax. Ah hivnae got the poax. Dam' sure I hivnae. Ah'm no' like that. That's a bluidy awfu' thing tae say. Ah hivnae –'

'Oh, shut up!' I said, reasoning with him, and trying not to laugh. Trust McAuslan to get it wrong. 'No one's saying you've got the . . . the pox, you silly oaf –'

'They are but! It's that Michie started it, an' Fletcher an' a', saying Ah've got the poax an'll hiv tae go tae the hospital, an' get pit on the V.D. list –'

Sober, McAuslan might or might not defend his personal reputation; flown with wine he invariably did, and in forceful terms. Knowing my man, I sought to reassure him.

'You've got it wrong, McAuslan. They're just kidding you. It's a smallpox scare – *small*pox, see, which is a different thing altogether – and much more serious. But you haven't got it, I'm quite sure.' (It was tricky, considering McAuslan's permanently insanitary condition, guaranteeing that he hadn't got something or other – and then the chill thought struck me that he might yet catch it; we all might.)

'Anyway, everyone's got to go back to camp and into quarantine,' I concluded. 'And get vaccinated again. That's all there is to it.'

'Aw.' He digested this, the primitive features registering what passed with him for thought. 'Zat right? Smallpox – no' the poax? Cos Ah hivnae got the poax. Ah hivnae. See, Michie, ye bluidy liar.' Virtuously he went on, proclaiming his purity: 'Ah been tae the M.O.'s lectures, and seen thae fillums aboot catchin' the clap an' that. An' Ah'm no' like that, sir, sure ye know Ah'm no'. An' Ah hivnae got the poax –'

'Aye, ye have,' said an anonymous voice from the depths of the truck. 'Ye've got everything, you. Ye're manky, McAuslan. Ye've got the bluidy plague. We'll a' catch it aff yez . . .'

I cut off McAuslan's impassioned denials, explained to him again that his associates were simply making game of him, told the rest of them to shut up, assured him that I personally had every confidence in his physical and spiritual hygiene, and was turning away when, just as the truck was revving up, a snatch of conversation from its cargo reached my ears over the Jocks' chatter.

'Hey, Toamie, ye hear aboot Karl Marx?'

'Who's he?'

'Groucho's brither.'

'Away, he's no'.'

'He's a bluidy Russian.'

'How wid you know? Onywye, Karl Marx's feyther was a charge hand in a pub at Tollcross . . .'

The truck rolled away, no doubt with lofty debate about Karl Marx's parentage continuing (and Private McAuslan still loudly boasting his freedom from infection), and I pondered for a minute, as I watched the other trucks rumble past with their cargoes for quarantine, how these odd catch-phrases and slogans flew about Scottish battalions. Totally irrelevant, all of them. Only an hour earlier I had heard the M.O. mention Karl Marx, by way of persiflage, and now the Jocks had caught wind of it, and the great revolutionary's name would become part of their jargon for a space, a byword; there would be Karl

Marx jokes, and he would be scribbled on walls, and fitted into marching-songs, and then he would vanish as suddenly from their culture, leaving a mystery, like Kilroy and Chad, for etymologists and philologists to theorise over – supposing they ever heard of it.

It took the best part of five hours to clear the town, with the trucks thundering to and fro, foot patrols beating up the bars and cafés and every conceivable haunt that might contain a Serviceman, Highland or otherwise, and a loud-speaker jeep touring the streets brassily ordering everyone back to barracks. The townsfolk themselves, who were used to the eccentricities of the British military, paid no attention; they lounged at the doorways of the Italian bars, or squatted on the street corners, or hurried past, like sheathed black shadows, in the direction of the Suk. I wondered if any of our fellows had strayed down there – it had only recently been placed out of bounds, as a result of nationalist agitation, culminating in a few outbreaks of rioting which had been dispersed by the local police, with the military standing by with fixed bayonets and empty magazines. Its only conceivable attraction at night-time (apart from the doubtful thrill of wandering in a genuine Arab city which hadn't changed much from the days of Dragut Reis and Kheyr-ed-Din Barbarossa) was the native bordellos, which were not widely patronised. Apart from the fact that we were a youngish battalion, and young soldiers in those days were far less addicted to brothel-creeping than their anxious elders supposed, it was recognised that the Suk could be a highly dangerous place. Besides, like McAuslan, they had been to the M.O.'s lectures.

By two o'clock the operation was virtually complete. I learned then over the signal set from battalion that the R.S.M. had accounted for all but about half a dozen Jocks, and it was likely that the last foot-patrols would bring them in. From my point of view it had been a tedious rather than a troublesome business –

indeed, the only real bother had occurred at the Salvation Army Reading Room, of all places, where one of our more studious privates, a graduate of St Andrews, had resented his ejection at the hands of one of Sergeant McGarry's provost corporals. As far as I could gather from a distraught Miss Partridge, the formidable spinster who ran the place, the root of the trouble had been the corporal's attitude towards reading in general, and this had somehow been taken by our private as a slight upon Goethe, whose works he had been studying. I wasn't clear how matters had developed, but expressions like 'philistine' and 'hun-loving bastard' had been bandied, and then the furniture had started to fly in earnest, the place being half-wrecked before the champion of German literature had been hauled off to the regimental sin-bin.

'It was a disgraceful scene,' said Miss Partridge, 'but really – what did we fight the war for? If one cannot carry the works of a distinguished author on one's shelves, foreigner though he be, without this sort of thing happening . . . well, it reminds one of the worst excesses of the Brownshirts.'

I told her I doubted if freedom of publication had really been at issue, since I questioned whether the corporal's literary taste and prejudice rose much above the *Beano* and the Rangers football programme notes, but she said she would speak to the Padre about it.

I soothed her with apologies and promises that the battalion would clean up and make good any damage, advised her to go to the hospital for vaccination, and walked wearily back to the 'Blue Heaven' and my temporary H.Q., which was the back of a 15-cwt truck containing my signal set.

The M.T. sergeant, who was holding the fort with about half a dozen Jocks, reported that the last foot-patrols had come in, bringing with them five Jocks who had been discovered in various holes and corners; he had despatched them to the battalion. I raised the Adjutant on the set, told him that seemed to be the lot, and could we now come home to bed.

He said 'Hold on', there was muttered consultation audible through the crackling of the set, and then he came through again.

'Something's come up,' he said. 'We got your last five Jocks, but there are still two unaccounted for.' More crackling. 'Fagan and Hamilton – both C Company.'

'Well, God knows where they are,' I said. 'We've been everywhere except the bottom of the bay. And the Suk, of course.'

'Yes,' he said, and there was a heavy pause. Then he went on: 'Listen, Dand, it doesn't look too good. We've been checking around in the last hour, and those two are definite contacts – I mean they were in Hunter's company in the last forty-eight hours. Dand – you hearing me O.K.? They're contacts – we've got to get them back.'

'I'm hearing you,' I said. 'Any suggestions where we should look?'

'Yes,' he said, and through the static I could hear him taking a big breath. I knew then it was going to be bad news.

'Listen carefully,' the crackling voice went on. 'We think they're both A.W.O.L. In fact, we know Fagan is – he hasn't been seen since the day before last, when he was with Hunter in the Uaddan bar. Hamilton's been gone since noon yesterday – but he's a pal of Fagan's, so they may be together. And you know what Fagan's like.'

I did; everyone did. A bad man from way back, with a crime sheet from here to Fort George. Not the same kind of bad man as Wee Wullie, whose peacetime service was one long drunken brawl but who was worth a hundred when the shot started flying, or the egregious Phimister of Support Company, who had gone absent almost weekly since his enlistment but had passed up the chance to escape from the Japanese at Singapore to let another man go in his place. Fagan was a real Ishmael, a slovenly, brutish, dishonest menace, a deserter in peace and war, whose conscription had been hailed with relief by the police of Glasgow's Marine Division. Since then he had been the regimental Public Enemy No. 1, and his periodic absences had been almost welcome.

But this time he might be carrying smallpox with him. I clamped the sweaty ear-piece to my head and listened.

'We've been digging around,' went on the Adjutant. 'We think he's in the Suk, and that he's maybe trying a home run.'

'You mean, all the way to Blighty?'

'Yes. He's been borrowing money.' The Adjutant's voice was beginning to crack with the strain of talking through the static. 'Deserters have found ships before; the Colonel thinks Fagan's maybe on the same lark. We've got to stop him.'

That went without saying. A smallpox carrier bound for Britain – the thought was enough to freeze the blood.

'But the Suk –' I was beginning.

'I know – but we think we know where he *might* be. You know the Astoria? Well, the rumour is it's the local equivalent of the Pioneer and Finlayson Green. You know what I mean.* It's just a chance, but it's all we've got. So it's worth trying, at any rate.'

'You've been doing overtime on the intelligence work, haven't you?' I said, admiringly. 'But look, Mike, isn't this a job for the redcaps?'

'No, it's not!' I started violently as the Colonel's voice rasped out of the earphones – the old villain had been listening in.

* The Pioneer was a legendary hotel in Bombay during the last war where, it was said, deserters from the forces in India could find a clandestine passage back to Britain, being smuggled out on homeward-bound ships. Finlayson Green is a pleasant, tree-shaded sward near the Singapore waterfront; it used to be said that if a deserter loitered there long enough, furtive little Chinese would appear and offer to arrange his passage to Australia.

'Official intervention in the Suk is *out* of the question in the present delicate state of affairs.' He meant the trouble there had been with the nationalists, and he was probably right. But then came what was, for him, the real reason. 'And I'm not turning the damned military police out for one of our people. MacNeill? Are you listening, MacNeill?'

'Yes, sir. I'm listening, sir. Sir.'

'Right. Anyway, we don't know for certain that he's in this blasted brothel or whatever it is. But it's my guess, knowing the fellow's record, that he *is* deserting, and that that's where he'll be. If he's not, we've lost nothing by looking. If he is, I want him back. Got that?'

I said I had got it, and the Adjutant came on again.

'You've still got Keil –' (this was the M.T. sergeant) '– and some chaps? Good. Don't take more than four. Just a quick tool in, through the Astoria like a dose of salts, and out again – right? Nothing to it.'

This is the kind of hearty instruction that turns subalterns' hair grey before their time. My guess was he'd be calling me 'old boy' in a minute.

'And don't, for God's sake, cause a diplomatic incident, old boy,' he went on. 'Just a quick tool in, all right –'

'Yes, and out again,' I said. 'I know. Mike, this is bloody dicey –'

'Piece of cake, laddie. Oh, one other thing – he may be armed.' I made egg-laying noises as he added almost apologetically: 'Seems he had a German Luger in his kitbag – you know what the Jocks are like for souvenirs – well, it's gone.'

'Oh, great,' I said. 'Sure he hasn't got an open razor and a set of brass knuckles as well?'

'Knowing Fagan, he quite probably has. Look, take it easy. There's a fair chance he isn't even there – in which case we'll have to get the redcaps –' It was probably imagination, but I thought I heard a Colonel-like snarl in the background. 'Now, in you go. Good luck. Anything else?'

I tried to think of something crushing, but couldn't.

'Did you know,' I said, 'that Karl Marx's ancestors emigrated to Russia from Inverary?' I listened to his anxious gabble of inquiry for a minute, and switched off.

So, there we were. A possibly armed potential deserter perhaps holed-up in a dive in a sensitive native quarter. The diversions the Army can think up for its junior officers are nobody's business. It's like a mixture of running an asylum and being a trigger-man for Al Capone.

I called up Keil and his worthies, and we conferred by the tailboard. The street was very quiet now – it was almost 3 a.m. – but there was a good moon, which would be handy in the unlit Suk.

'Anyone know the Astoria?' I asked, and after an embarrassed pause one of the Jocks reluctantly admitted that he did.

'Right, you're with me. And you two, and you, Sergeant Keil.' I told them quickly what the operation was, and I'd have sworn that they looked pleased as they listened. Anything for a tear, as they say in Glasgow. They looked handy men – but suddenly I wished they were my own platoon Jocks – the massive Wee Wullie, the saturnine Fletcher and the wicked Forbes – yes, even the great unwashed McAuslan, who could, in his own words, 'take a lend o' anybody – and his big brother'. Not, when I thought about it, that we were likely to run into violent trouble – I hoped.

The Suk began at the old city wall, only a hundred yards from the 'Blue Heaven', and once through the massive stone gateway you were in another world. Twisting, unpaved streets, black and shuttered houses jammed crazily against each other, with occasionally a light filtering through an ornately-latticed window or from a dimly-lit doorway; shadowy figures standing back under overhangs or moving in the dark alleys on either side – it was just like Pepe le Moko's Casbah, complete with romantic Middle Eastern night sounds, like:

'Whaur ye goin', Jock? Looking for bonnie lassie, yes? Come on in – hey, mac, where's your kilt?' And chants anent Auntie Mary and her canary. If you doubt this, you should know that the Arab is possibly the best imitator of the Scottish accent in either hemisphere, and loves to air his knowledge of the patois. So far from making a silent, unseen foray into the Suk, we were followed with interest by commentators on either side, and invitations from blessed damozels leaning out of the second-storey windows. I plodded grimly on, while the Jocks replied in kind, and presently we finished up in front of the neighbourhood's three-star caravanserai, a substantial building in mouldering stucco with 'Astoria' across the top of its peeling porch, a well-closed front door, piles of garbage out in front, and an admiring crowd watching us from either end of the street. There were lights in some of the windows, showing through dirty curtains, and the whole place looked as attractive as a disused gypsy caravan.

I confess I wondered what course of action to take. By rights I should have sent a man to guard the back door, but such was the town planning of the Suk that this would probably have entailed a walk of half a mile and then getting lost. I looked at the massive front door. Humphrey Bogart, who must have been in this situation dozens of times, would just have sidled in, somehow, shot a couple of hoods, seized a smouldering-eyed beauty by the wrist to make her drop her dagger, laughed mirthlessly, browbeaten Sydney Greenstreet, and then taken Fagan in an arm-lock and bundled him out to a waiting taxi. However, there were no taxis in the Suk, so I just knocked on the door. It seemed the obvious thing to do.

If no one had answered, frankly I'd have been at a loss, but presently the door opened, a vague female shape appeared in a very tight blue dress, a slim hand holding an unlit cigarette emerged from the shadows, and a husky voice said:

''Allo, dolleeng – gotta light?'

I hadn't, as it happened, so I just said: 'Good evening', and as near as a toucher added: 'I wonder, do you happen to have a Mr Fagan staying in the hotel?' But fortunately, just as she was saying: 'C'mon een, Jock – breeng you' friends', Sergeant Keil, a highly practical man, decided to take a hand. Where he came from, you didn't loiter outside a potentially hostile front door, in case the occupants dropped a sewing-machine on you from an upper window. He was past me and into the dingy hallway before I could carry the courtesies any further. The female shape squealed and disappeared, the three Jocks surged in after Keil, more or less bearing me with them, and my education in ferreting out deserters began from that moment.

What you actually do is go up the stairs three at a time, flinging open every door you come to, and waking the dead with your shouting. If the inmates show resentment, you pass on, leaving the door open, whereupon they come out to express their indignation, and your associates, following some distance behind, can identify them and see they're not the men you're after. There were, in fact, four rooms on each of the Astoria's three floors, and I wouldn't have believed you could get so many Arabs, lascars, Negroes and their assorted ladies into twelve apartments without everyone suffocating. Within sixty seconds of Keil's eruption through the front door, there was a milling mass of multi-coloured humanity, in various stages of undress from full jellabah and boots to complete nudity, on the first two landings. I was struggling upwards past a grossly overweight lady who, I think, was Italian, and shrieking to wake the dead – and one of the deserters, Private Hamilton, was emerging from a doorway on the third floor, his mouth wide with fright, and then doubling back towards his room.

Keil got him by the ankle, they thrashed about in the doorway, and one of the other Jocks hauled Hamilton upright and jammed him against the wall. He was naked except for a pair of khaki slacks, and his first words were those of the Glasgow keelie trapped and helpless:

'Don't hit me, mister!'

'Where's Fagan?' snapped Keil, just as I got free of Madame Butterfly and about eleven small brown children who were darting about the stairway like tadpoles, and came pounding up to the top floor. Behind and below me it sounded like the sinking of the *Titanic*; there were pursuing feet, but as I reached the landing the largest of Keil's Jocks slipped past me on to the top step, effectively barring the way up.

'Where's Fagan?' Keil was shouting again, and as his fist drew back the cornered Hamilton said:

'Eh? Eh?' and jerked his head towards the closed doorway next to his own. Keil threw himself at it, but it was too stout for him. He thumped the panels, shouting:

'Fagan! Ye've had it! Come oot!'

I glanced down over the rickety banister. In the dim light of the stairwell two rings of faces, one at each landing, were staring up – every colour from white to jet black, mouths open, frightened, bewildered, angry, and, above all, vocal. My Italian woman seemed to be dying on a permanent Top C, a large brown man with woolly silver hair was shouting and shaking his fist, and the rest of them were just generally joining in. I began to feel decidedly uncomfortable – not that they looked terribly dangerous, but it seemed to me our unorthodox entry into the Hotel Astoria was going to cause some stir in the neighbourhood generally, with possible ensuing diplomatic complications. But curiously, my chief emotion was a feeling rather like shame – at having roused and terrified so many ordinary citizens, and created bedlam in their hotel. It seemed a bit much – and then I remembered Fagan was a deserter possibly carrying smallpox.

Keil and another Jock were trying to burst in the door, still without success. Hamilton, released now, was standing pale and petrified; he was a gangly, freckled youth with a weak face and sandy hair.

'Hamilton,' I said. 'Fagan's in there – anyone with him?'

He licked his lips. 'A bint.'

I motioned Keil away from the door, put my head to the panels and called: 'Fagan!' No reply. I tried again, and this time there was the clatter of something being over-turned, and a female squeal, instantly hushed.

'Fagan,' I called again. 'This is Lieutenant MacNeill, of D Company. Come on out and give yourself up.'

This time there was silence, and while I stood listening Keil darted into the doorway of Hamilton's room, and came back to report that from the window he could see there was a roof adjoining the back of the building – a possible means of escape from Fagan's room.

'Fagan,' I tried again. 'Listen to me. You can't get away – we've got men all round the hotel. Now, listen. One of your friends, Hunter, is in hospital with smallpox. You were with him two days ago – that means you may be carrying it. You've got to get vaccinated, quickly – or you may get it yourself and spread it all over. D'you understand, Fagan? This is serious, man!'

There was a thin, wailing sound from inside, and a man's voice cursing, more clattering and rustling. I banged on the door, and suddenly his voice sounded:

'Gerraway or I'll blow yer —— head aff!'

'Oh, don't be a damned fool! You've had it, man! You've only been absent two days – what are you worrying about? But if you resist arrest, and try to get away when you're a smallpox carrier, you'll go inside forever. For God's sake man –' and it sounded terribly melodramatic, but it was true '– you can't go spreading a deadly disease about among innocent people. Come on – open the door! Fagan! D'you hear?'

There followed a couple of minutes' silence from the room – more than compensated for by the Pilgrim's Chorus on the stairs – and then I thought I heard sounds of movement again.

'Fagan?'

Feet sounded on the other side of the door, and his voice came through the panels:

'MacNeill?'

'Yes.'

A pause, and then: 'Hunter's got smallpox?'

'That's right.'

'Is that —— true?'

'Yes.'

'D'ye swear that?'

At first I wasn't sure what he'd said; it was an unexpected question. But it was no time for quibbles. I said yes.

There was the sound of a key turning, and then the door opened. Like Hamilton, he was wearing only khaki slacks, a big, sallow, narrow-featured man with thick hair on his chest and shoulders. His hands were empty.

I motioned him out, and glanced into the room. There was no light, but the moon showed that the window had been thrown up, a jacket was lying over the sill, and crouched down beside the bed, on one knee, was an Arab girl – maybe not Arab, probably half-caste, wearing only a white petticoat. I had an impression of long black hair and big eyes staring fearfully; she looked about fifteen.

'Where's the Luger?' I said to Fagan, and he just stared at me. I reflected that it had probably been tossed far out of the window before he opened the door.

'All right,' I said to Keil. 'Take them down and back to the truck.'

'Wai' a minute,' Fagan said. He looked at me. 'This sma'-pox. Ah've been —in' vaccinated.' He jerked his head towards the doorway; the girl was inside still, making tiny whimpering sounds. 'She hisnae. Ye'll get her —in' vaccinated.'

I daresay it shouldn't have startled me, but it did. Likewise Sergeant Keil, and with an N.C.O.'s suspicious mind he demanded:

'Whit the hell you on, Fagan?'

Fagan stared at him, and said deliberately: 'Ah'll be lookin' for you one o' these days, china.' Then he turned back to me. 'Ye'll see she gets vaccinated?'

I didn't suppose that the local native authorities would even think of trying to vaccinate the population of the Suk; twenty to thirty thousand is a lot of people, especially when they don't much hold with Western medicine. Fagan wanted to make sure for her.

'I'll see she gets it,' I said.

He kept staring at me a moment. 'Right?' he said.

'Right,' I said.

He went downstairs without another word.

Our strategic withdrawal from the top floor of the Hotel Astoria was a fairly fraught business; for a while I didn't think we were going to make it. Keil, with Fagan and Hamilton escorted by two of the Jocks, made it easily enough, simply by snarling menacingly as he descended and offering to murder anyone who got in his way. But my own exit was complicated by the fact that I'd promised to take Fagan's bint along; she screamed and wept and tried to hide under the bed until the remaining Jock lost his temper, slapped her soundly, and took her over his shoulder in a fireman's lift. We set off down, myself leading, and by this time the manager had appeared at the head of the excited multitude on the lower landings. At least, I imagine he was the manager – he was a six-foot

Soudani-looking gentleman, with tribal cuts across his cheeks, a tarboosh on his head, and a British Army greatcoat. He was also carrying a club, and he affected to believe that, apart from disturbing the peace of his hostelry and forcing entry, I was intent on kidnapping one of his guests for immoral purposes. 'Scotch bastard!' was the chorus of his complaint, in which the assembly joined with a will. Fortunately two native constables arrived, a discussion ensued, and when I could get a word in – and that word was 'smallpox' – the more or less European element gave one great wail and fled. We inched our way out, the manager demanding to know who was going to pay for Messrs Fagan and Hamilton's penthouse accommodation, so I gave him ten lire, at which he beamed alarmingly and asked me to stay the night with his sister. Honestly, I reflected as we hurried back to the truck, I'd have been better working hard at school and getting into university instead of letting the Army get its hooks on me.

We dropped the girl off at the hospital, and really the most painful part of the whole night was watching the poor soul's hysterical submission to the vaccination administered by a medical orderly. For some reason I felt I owed it to Fagan to see the job actually done – I hadn't worked it out, but I had a feeling that if it hadn't been for her, he'd have been over the rooftops and far away by now. Anyway, the nurses took charge of her, I made my last call over the set to the battalion, learned that Hamilton and Fagan were in safe hands and every Jock was now accounted for, and that I could go to bed. It was after four, and the dark blue sky was bright orange at its eastern edge when I dismissed the truck at the barrack gates.

There were lights on in the H.Q. building and one or two of the barrack-blocks, but I was too bone-weary to go across. All I wanted was a long cold beer and bed, so I went to the deserted mess, got a bottle from the ice-box, and drank it in the empty, musty billiard-room. The balls on the table lay as we had left them; I stood smoking and studying them tiredly and finally rolled them into the pockets – the Padre's infernal luck would have got him out of the snooker, anyway; it always did. Heaven knows how they put in their time at theological faculties, I thought, as I slumped into an armchair, and the next thing I knew the Adjutant was shaking me awake, the sun was streaming in through the shutters, and the waiters were clattering crockery in the dining-room across the hall.

The Adjutant was as offensively bright as an advertisement for liver salts, throwing open shutters and singing to himself.

'Eggs and b. coming up in a moment,' he cried. 'Good old egg and b. Haven't you been to bed, you foolish subaltern? Drowning your sorrows in drink,' he went on, picking up my fallen beer-glass from the floor, 'or just sleeping off the great anti-climax.'

'Wrap up,' I growled. 'What anti-climax?'

'Didn't someone tell you – oh, probably not, we didn't hear until an hour ago, while you were sunk here in your hoggish state of alcoholism. Ramsey phoned from base hospital – Hunter hasn't got smallpox. Nothing like it. Septic prickly heat, apparently, and not very extensive at that, but it seems some young doctor panicked and sent the balloon up, ringing the alarum bells and crying 'Blow, wind, come wrack' – and since by one of those damnable coincidences all the senior staff were out of town, well . . . we had a great smallpox drama for nothing.'

He giggled, idiotically if you ask me (but then, an effervescent Adjutant was the last thing I needed in the early morning), and went on:

'The M.O. went berserk, of course, when he heard – he'd been at it all night, up to his knees in lymph and lancets, using miles of sticking-plaster, and the entire battalion has got sore arms for nothing. Dammit,' he added, 'I believe I'm starting to itch myself.'

'And serves you right!' I snarled. 'While I've been tangling with armed deserters, earning a reputation as a white slaver, and getting mobbed by angry wogs – oh, and Miss Partridge is raising hell because the Jocks bust up her reading-room. I hope you enjoy dealing with her.'

'Well, at least we've got Fagan in the coop,' said he. 'The Colonel's very pleased about that – thinks you handled it admirably. Come on, eggs and b., toast, coffee and all good things –'

'Oh, you go and get raffled, Michael Adjutant,' I said. 'I'm going to bed.'

And that should have been the end of it, but there was a curious appendix. When I got up, after lunch, my orderly loafed in, on the pretext of cleaning up the room, but actually to convey the latest scandal and get my reaction. He pottered about handlessly, as usual, knocking my personal effects around, and after several irrelevant comments about the weather, observed:

'You're a right fly man, you.'

I said 'Eh?' intelligently, and he added: 'They say Fagan's doin' his nut in the cooler. Haw!'

I didn't get the drift of this, so I told him to stop destroying the furniture and explain.

'Fagan's up tae high doh,' said he, from which I gathered that Fagan was extremely annoyed and disturbed. 'He says – or the boys say – you spun him a tale aboot Hunter hivin' smallpox, and Hunter didnae hiv smallpox at a'. An' Fagan's sayin' yer a bluidy leear – Ah mean, that you kidded him into givin' hisself up. That's whit the boys say – right fly man, you.'

'Hold on!' I protested. 'This is drivel! I thought Hunter *did* have smallpox – everyone did. Heavens above, d'you think I'd have been tearing through the Suk like a man demented, looking for one piddling little deserter – well, two, if you count Hamilton – if we hadn't thought there was a risk of epidemic?

Come away, McClusky! We didn't realise it wasn't smallpox until – when? About seven this morning, I suppose.'

'That a fact?' he said. 'No kiddin'.' And until you have heard a Glaswegian use these expressions you don't know anything about scepticism and amused disbelief. 'Aye, weel.' He continued to potter, grinning secretly to himself. 'That's whit the boys are sayin' – that ye kidded Fagan intae the cooler. No' bad. Serve 'im right. Naebody likes him. But he's in a hell of a sweat about it – says he's gaunae claim ye when he gets the chance.'

'Fagan,' I said, 'can think what he likes. I couldn't care less. But I did *not* lie to him to get him to give himself up. You can tell him that, if you like, and add that he isn't worth it, anyway, and –'

'Okay, okay, sir,' he said. 'Ah'm just sayin' whit the boys are sayin'. Keep the heid – sir? Sno' ma fault. Right?' He shook his head, still grinning, as he stirred the contents of my wardrobe thoughtfully. 'Right fly man ye are, though, so ye are.'

The trouble was, he said it admiringly. Obviously the garbled tale would be all over the battalion about how the Macchiavellian MacNeill had conned Fagan into giving himself up by lies and false pretences. And I was still young enough to resent that fact – I didn't want to be thought of as a 'fly man', whatever status that might confer in the Jocks' curious scale of ethics.

I told the Colonel about it when I went over to the mess, where he was lingering over his after-lunch whisky with the Adjutant, and he just roared with laughter, like the wicked old man he was. Then he regarded me from beneath his bushy brows, and remarked:

'I don't know how long it took me – about twenty years, I'd say – yes, it would be in Ahmedabad, probably about '33 or '34 – before the Jocks started to call me a "fly man". Quite mistakenly, I assure you. You've managed it in about six months –

very good going indeed.' He gave me his quizzical grin. 'You probably *are* a fly man, young Dand. Shouldn't be surprised if the Jocks are right.'

'Well, sir, they're dead wrong if they think I spun Fagan –'

'Of course they are. In this instance. Don't take it to heart, boy. This isn't the Fifth Form at St Dominics; it's a battalion of Scottish Highlanders – heavens, I'm telling *you*! You *are* one. They value all sorts of things – the usual military virtues and so on – but most of all, they tend to respect what the uncharitable would call craft. Like the Italians in that, I suppose. If they choose to think you're a fly man, just be thankful – however unearned you may feel the reputation is. You'll be surprised how useful it is.' He smiled under his moustache. 'If your night's frolicking in the Suk has taught you that, all the better. You can't learn too much.'

'That reminds me,' said the Adjutant. 'I learned something last night – nothing of consequence, really, but it was quite new to me. Did you know, sir,' he said to the Colonel, 'that Karl Marx's grandmother was a Campbell?'

The Colonel raised an eyebrow. 'No,' he said, with mild interest, 'I didn't know that.' He thought about it a moment, and sniffed. 'Mind you, I can't say I'm in the least surprised.'

McAuslan in the Rough

My tough granny – the Presbyterian MacDonald one, not the pagan one from Islay – taught me about golf when I was very young. Her instruction was entirely different from that imparted by my father, who was a scratch player, gold medallist and all, with a swing like de Vicenzo; he showed me how to make shots, and place my feet, and keep calm in the face of an eighteen-inch putt on a downhill green with the wind in my face and the match hanging on it. But my granny taught me something much more mysterious.

Her attitude to the game was much like her attitude to religion; you achieved grace by sticking exactly to the letter of the law, by never giving up, and by occasional prayer. You replaced your divots, you carried your own clubs, and you treated your opponent as if he was a Campbell, and an armed one at that. I can see her now, advanced in years, with her white hair clustered under her black bonnet, and the wind whipping the long skirt round her ankles, lashing her drives into the gale; if they landed on the fairway she said 'Aye', and if they finished in the rough she said 'Tach!' Nothing more. And however unplayable her lie, she would hammer away with her niblick until that ball was out of trouble, and half Perthshire with it. If it took her fifteen strokes, no matter; she would tot them up grimly when the putts were down, remark, 'This and better may do, this and waur will never do,' and stride off to the next tee, gripping her driver like a battle-axe.

As an opponent she was terrifying, not only because she played well, but because she made you aware that this was a personal duel in which she intended to grind you into the turf without pity; if she was six up at the seventeenth she would still attack that last hole as if life depended on it. At first I hated playing with her, but gradually I learned to meet her with something of her own spirit, and if I could never achieve the killer instinct which she possessed, at least I discovered satisfaction in winning, and did so without embarrassment.

As a partner she was beyond price. Strangely enough, when we played as a team, we developed a comradeship closer than I ever felt for any other player; we once even held our own with my father and uncle, who together could have given a little trouble to any golfers anywhere. Even conceding a stroke a hole they were immeasurably better than an aged woman and an erratic small boy, but she was their mother and let them know it; the very way she swung her brassie was a wordless reminder of the second commandment, and by their indulgence, her iron will, and enormous luck, we came all square to the eighteenth tee.

Counting our stroke, we were both reasonably close to the green in two, and my granny, crouching like a bombazine vulture with her mashie-niblick, put our ball about ten feet from the pin. My father, after thinking and clicking his tongue, took his number three and from a nasty lie played a beautiful rolling run-up to within a foot of the hole – a real old Fife professional's shot.

I looked at the putt and trembled. 'Dand,' said my grandmother. 'Never up, never in.'

So I gulped, prayed, and went straight for the back of the cup. I hit it, too, the ball jumped, teetered, and went in. My father and uncle applauded, granny said 'Aye', and my uncle stooped to his ball, remarking, 'Halved hole and match, eh?'

'No such thing,' said granny, looking like the Three Fates. 'Take your putt.'

Nowadays, of course, putts within six inches or so are frequently conceded, as being unmissable. Not with my grandmother; she would have stood over Arnold Palmer if he had been on the lip of the hole. So my uncle sighed, smiled, took his putter, played – and missed. His putter went into the nearest bunker, my father walked to the edge of the green, humming to himself, and my grandmother sniffed and told me curtly to pick up my bag and mind where I was putting my feet on the green.

As we walked back to the clubhouse, she grimly silent as usual, myself exulting, while the post-mortem of father and uncle floated out of the dusk behind us, she made one of her rare observations.

'A game,' she said, 'is not lost till it's won. Especially with your Uncle Hugh. He is –' and here her face assumed the stern resignation of a materfamilias who has learned that one of the family has fled to Australia pursued by creditors, '– a *trifling* man. Are your feet wet? Aye, well, they won't stay dry long if you drag them through the grass like that.'

And never a word did she say about my brilliant putt, but back in the clubhouse she had the professional show her all the three irons he had, chose one, beat him down from seventeen and six to eleven shillings, handed it to me, and told my father to pay for it. 'The boy needs a three iron,' she said. And to me: 'Mind you take care of it.' I have taken care of it.

But all this was long ago, and has nothing much to do with the story of Private McAuslan, that well-known military disaster, golfing personality and caddy extraordinary. Except for the fact that I suppose something of that great old lady's personality stayed with me, and exerted its influence whenever I took a golf club in hand. Not that this was often; as I grew through adolescence I developed a passion for cricket, a love-hate relationship with Rugby, and some devotion to soccer, so that golf faded into the background. Anyway, for all my early training,

I wasn't much good, a scratching, turf-cutting 24-handicapper whose drives either went two hundred yards dead straight or whined off at right angles into the wilderness. I was full of what you might call golfing lore and know-how, but in practice I was an erratic slasher, a blasphemer in bunkers, and prone to give up round about the twelfth hole and go looking for beer in the clubhouse.

In the army there was less time than ever for golf, but it chanced that when our Highland battalion was posted back to Scotland from North Africa shortly after the war we were stationed on the very edge of one of those murderous east coast courses where the greens are small and fast, the wind is a howling menace, and the rough is such that you either play straight or you don't play at all. This, of course, is where golf was born, where the early giants made it an art before the Americans turned it into a science, and whence John Paterson strode forth in his blacksmith's apron to partner the future King James II in the first international against England. (That was a right crafty piece of gamesmanship on James's part, too, but it won the match, so there you are.)

In any event, the local committee made us free of their links, and the battalion had something of a golfing revival. This was encouraged by our new Colonel, a stiffish, Sandhurst sort of man who had decided views on what was sport and what was not. Our old Colonel had been a law unto himself: boxing, snooker, billiards-fives, and working himself into hysterics at battalion football matches had been his mark, but the new man saw sport through the pages of *Country Life*. Well, I mean, he rode horses, shot grouse, and belonged to some ritzy yacht club on the Forth where they drank pink gin and wore handkerchiefs in their sleeves. To a battalion whose notions of games began and ended with a football, this was something rich and strange. But since he approved of golf, and liked to see his officers taking advantage of the local club's hospitality, those of us who could play did so, and a fairly bad showing we made. Subalterns like myself plowtered our way round and rejoiced when we broke 90; two of our older majors set a record in lost balls for a single round (23, including five found and lost again); the Regimental Sergeant-Major played a very correct, military game in which the ball seldom left the fairway but never travelled very far either; and the M.O. and Padre set off with one set of clubs and the former's hip flask – their round ended with the Padre searching for wild flowers and the M.O. lying in the bracken at the long fourteenth singing 'Kishmul's Galley'. It was golf of a kind, if you like, and only the Adjutant took it at all seriously.

This was probably because he possessed a pair of pre-war plus fours and a full set of clubs, which enabled him to put on tremendous side. Bunkered, which he usually was, he would affect immense concern over whether he should use a seven or eight iron – would the wind carry his chip far enough? should he apply top spin?

'What do you think, Pirie?' he would ask his partner, who was the officers' mess barman but in private life had been assistant pro. at a course in Nairn and was the only real golfer in the battalion. 'Should I take the seven or the eight?'

'For a' the guid ye are wi' either o' them ye micht as weel tak' a bluidy bulldozer,' Pirie would say. Upon which he would be sternly reprimanded for insubordination, the Adjutant would seize his blaster, and after a dozen unsuccessful slashes would snatch up the ball in rage and hurl it frenziedly into the whins.

'It's a' one,' Pirie would observe. 'Ye'd have three-putted anyway.'

'I can't understand it,' I once heard the Adjutant say in the mess bar, in that plaintive, self-examining tone which is the hallmark of the truly bum golfer. 'I've tried the overlap grip, I've tried the forefinger down the shaft; I've stood up from the ball and I've crouched over it; I've used several stances, with my feet together, my feet apart, and my knees bent – everything! But the putts simply won't go down. Pirie here will confirm me. I don't understand it at all. What do you think, Pirie?'

'Ye cannae bluidy well putt,' said the unfeeling Pirie. 'That's a' there is to it.'

Mess barmen, it need hardly be added, are privileged people, and anyway the Adjutant and Pirie had once stood back to back in an ambush on the Chocolate Staircase, and had an understanding of their own. It was something which the new Colonel would not have fully appreciated, for he had not served with the regiment since before the war, and was as big a stickler for military discipline as long service on the staff could make him. He did not understand the changes which six years of war had wrought, most especially in a Highland regiment, which is a curious organisation in the first place.

It looks terribly military, and indeed it is, but under the surface a Highland unit has curious currents which are extremely irregular. There is a sort of unspoken yet recognised democracy which may have its roots in clanship, or in the Scottish mercenary tradition, and which can play the devil with rank and authority unless it is properly understood. The new Colonel obviously was unaware of this, or he would not have suddenly ordained, one fine bright morning, that whenever an officer played golf he should have a soldier to caddy for him.

In feudal theory, even in military theory, this was all very well. In the egalitarian atmosphere of a Highland battalion, circa 1947, it was simply not on; our old Colonel wouldn't even have thought of it. Quite apart from the fact that every man in the unit, in that Socialist age, knew his rights and was well aware that caddying wasn't covered by the Army Act – well, you can try getting a veteran of Alamein and Anzio to carry golf clubs for a pink-cheeked one-pipper, but when that veteran has not only learned his political science at Govan Cross but is also a member of an independent and prideful race, you may encounter difficulties. However, the Colonel's edict had gone forth, and after it had been greeted in the mess with well-bred whistles and exclamations of 'I *say*!' and 'Name o' the wee man!', I was left, as battalion sports officer, to arrange the impressment of suitable caddies.

'The man's mad,' I told the Adjutant. 'There'll be a mutiny.'

'Oh, I don't know,' he said. 'You could try picking on the simple-minded ones.'

'The only simple-minded ones in this outfit are in our own mess,' I said. 'Can you imagine Wee Wullie's reaction, for example, if he's told to caddy for some of our young hopefuls? He'll run amuck.' Wee Wullie was a giant of uncontrolled passions and immense brawn whose answer to any vexing problem was usually a swung fist. 'And the rest of them are liable to write to their M.P.s. You don't know the half of it in Headquarter Company; out where the rest of us live it's like a Jacobin literary society.'

'Use tact,' advised the Adjutant, 'and if that fails, try blackmail. But whatever you do, for God's sake don't provoke a disciplinary crisis.'

In other words, perform the impossible, and the only normal way to do that was to enlist the Regimental Sergeant-Major, the splendid Mr Mackintosh. But I hesitated to do this; like a scientist on the brink of some shattering experiment, I was fearful of releasing powers beyond my control. So after deep thought I decided to confine my activities to my own platoon, whom I knew, and made a subtle approach to the saturnine Private Fletcher, who was the nearest thing to a shop steward then in uniform. We were soon chatting away on that agreeable officer-man basis which is founded on mutual respect and makes the British Army what it is.

'Fletcher,' I said casually, 'there are a limited number of

openings for Jocks to caddy for the officers when they play golf. It's light work, in congenial surroundings, and those who are fortunate enough to be selected will receive certain privileges, etc., etc. Now those loafers up in Support Company would give their right arms for the chance, but what I say is, what's the use of my being sports officer if I can't swing a few good things for my own chaps, so –'

'Aye, sir,' said Fletcher. 'Whit's the pey?'

'The pay?'

'Uh-huh. The pey. Whit's the rate for the job?'

This took me aback. It hadn't occurred to me to suggest paying Jocks to caddy, and I was willing to bet it hadn't occurred to the Colonel either. Fall in the loyal privates, touching their forelocks by numbers, would be his idea. But I now saw a way through this embarrassing problem; after all, I did have a sports fund at my disposal, and a quarter-master who could cook a book to a turn.

'Well, now,' I said, 'we ought to be able to fix that easily enough. Suppose we say about a shilling an hour . . .' The fund ought to be able to stand that, under 'miscellaneous'.

'Aw, jeez, come aff it, sir,' said Fletcher respectfully. '*Two* bob an hour, an' overtime in the evenin's. Double time Setterdays an' Sundays, an' a hardship bonus for whoever has tae carry the Adjutant's bag. Yon's a bluidy disgrace, no kiddin'; the man's no fit tae play on the street. Ye'll no' get anyone in his right mind tae caddy for him; it'll have tae be yin o' the yahoos.' He fumbled in his pocket. 'I've got a wee list here, sir, o' fellas that would do, wi' the rates I was mentionin' just now. Wan or two o' them have played golf theirsel's, so they mebbe ought tae get two an' six an hour – it'll be kinda professional advice, ye see. But we'll no' press it.'

I looked dumbly at him for a moment. 'You knew about this? But, dammit, the Adjutant only mentioned it half an hour ago . . .'

He looked at me pityingly as I took his list. Of course, I ought to have known better. All this stuff about Highlanders' second sight is nonsense; it's just first-class espionage, that's all.

'Well,' I said, studying the list, 'I don't know about this. I'm sure it's all very irregular . . .'

'So's the employment o' military personnel ootwith military duties,' said Fletcher smugly. 'Think if somebody frae the *Daily Worker* wis tae get word that wee shilpit Toamy frae the Q.M. store – him wi' the bad feet – wis humphin' the Adjutant's golf-sticks a' ower the place. They might even get a picture of him greetin' –'

'Quite, quite,' I said. 'Point taken. All right, two bob an hour, but I want respectable men, understand?'

'Right, sir.' Fletcher hesitated. 'Would there be a wee allowance, mebbe, for wear an' tear on the fellas' civvy clothes? They cannae dae the job in uniform, and it's no fair tae expect a fella tae spile his glamour pants and long jaicket sclimmin' intae bunkers –'

'They can draw white football shirts and long khaki drills from the sports store,' I said. 'Now go away, you crimson thief, and see that nobody who isn't on this list ever hears that there's payment involved, otherwise we'll have a queue forming up. I want this thing to work nice and smoothly.'

And of course it did. Fletcher had picked eight men, including himself, of sober habit and decent appearance, and the sight of them in their white shirts and khaki slacks, toting their burdens round the links, did the Colonel's heart good to see. It all looked very military and right, and he wasn't to know that they were being subsidised out of battalion funds. In fact, I had quietly informed the Adjutant that if those officers who played golf made an unofficial contribution to the sports kitty, it would be welcome, and the result was that we actually showed a profit.

The Jocks who caddied were all for it. They made money,

they missed occasional parades, and they enjoyed such privileges as watching the Adjutant have hysterics while standing thigh-deep in a stream, or hearing the Padre addressing heaven from the midst of a bramble patch. It was all good clean fun, and would no doubt have stayed that way if the new Colonel, zealous for his battalion's prestige, hadn't got ambitious.

He didn't play golf himself, but he took pride in his unit's activities, and it chanced that on one of his strolls across the course he saw Pirie the barman playing against the better of our elderly majors. The major must have been at his best, and Pirie's game was immaculate as usual, so the Colonel, following them over the last three holes, got a totally false impression of the standard of golf under his command. This, he decided, was pretty classy stuff, and it seems that he mentioned this to his friend who commanded the Royals, who inhabited that part of the country. Colonels are forever boasting to each other in this reckless way, whereby their underlings often suffer most exquisitely.

Anyway, the Colonel of the Royals said he had some pretty fair golfers in his mess, and how about a game? Our Colonel, in his ignorance, accepted the challenge. I privately believe that he had some wild notion that because we had caddies in nice white shirts we would have a built-in advantage, but in any event he placed a bet with the Royals' C.O. and then came home to tell the Adjutant the glad news. We were to field ten players in a foursomes match against the Royals, and we were to win.

Now, you may think an inter-regimental golf match is fairly trivial stuff, but when a new and autocratic Colonel is involved, puffed up with regimental conceit, and when the opposition is the Royals, it is a most serious matter. For one thing, the Royals are unbearable. They are tremendously old, and stuffed with tradition and social graces, and adopt a patronising attitude to the rest of the army in general, and other Scottish units in particular. Furthermore, they can play golf – or they could then – and of this the Adjutant was painfully aware.

However, like the good soldier he was, he set about marshalling his forces, which consisted of making sure that he personally partnered Pirie.

'We know each other's game, you see,' he told me. 'We blend, as it were.'

'You mean he'll carry you round on his back,' I said. 'You don't fool me, brother. You see that partnering Pirie is the one chance you've got of being in a winning pair.'

'Look,' he said. 'I've got to work with the Colonel; I see him every day, don't I? I've got to salvage something from what is sure to be a pretty beastly wreck. Now, how about the second pair? The Padre and the M.O., eh? They always play together.'

'They'll be good for a laugh, anyway,' I said. 'Unless the Royals go easy on them out of respect for the clerical cloth, or the M.O. can get his opponents drunk, they don't stand a prayer.'

'Then there's young Macmillan – he's not bad,' said the Adjutant hopefully. 'I saw him hole a putt the other day. You could partner him yourself.'

'Not a chance,' I said. 'The best he's ever gone round in is 128, with a following wind. Furthermore he giggles. I want to succumb with dignity; either I partner the R.S.M. or you can get yourself another boy.'

'Old man Mackintosh, eh?' said the Adjutant. 'Well, he's a steady player, isn't he? Can't think I've ever seen him in the rough.'

'That's why I want him,' I said. 'I want to play a few of my shots from a decent lie.'

'You've got a rotten, defeatist attitude,' said the Adjutant severely.

'I'm a rotten, defeatist golfer,' I said. 'So are you, and so are the rest of us, bar Pirie.'

'Ah, yes, Pirie,' said the Adjutant, smirking. 'He and I should do not too badly, I think. If I can remember not to overswing; and I think I'll get the pro. to shave my driver just a teeny fraction – for balance, you know – and get in a bit of practice with my eight iron . . .'

'Come back to earth, Sarazen,' I said. 'You've still got two couples to find.'

We finally settled on our two elderly majors, Second-Lieutenant Macmillan, and Regimental Quartermaster Bogle, a stout and imposing warrant officer who had been known to play a few rounds with the pipe-sergeant. No one knew how they scored, but Bogle used to say off-handedly that his game had rusted a wee bitty since he won the Eastern District Boys' Title many years ago – heaven help us, it must have been when Old Tom Morris was in small clothes – and the pipey would nod sagely and say:

'Aye, aye, Quarters, a wee thing over par the day, just a wee thing, aye. But no' bad, no' bad at all.'

Personally I thought this was lying propaganda, but I couldn't prove it.

'It is,' admitted the Adjutant, 'a pretty lousy team. Oh, well, at least our caddies will look good.'

But there he was dead wrong. He was not to know it, but lurking in the background was the ever-present menace of Private McAuslan, now preparing to take a hand in the fate of the battalion golf team.

He was far from my mind on the afternoon of the great match, as the R.S.M. and I stood waiting outside the clubhouse to tee off. Presently my own batman, the tow-headed McClusky, who was caddying for me, arrived on the scene, and shambling behind him was the Parliamentary Road's own contribution to the pollution problem, McAuslan himself.

'What's he doing here?' I demanded, shaken.

'He's come tae caddy,' explained McClusky. 'See, there's only eight caddies on the list, an' ten o' ye playin', so Fletcher picked anither two. Him an' Daft Bob Broon.'

'Why him?' I hissed, aware that our visitors from the Royals were casting interested glances towards McAuslan, whose grey-white shirt was open to the waist, revealing what was either his skin or an old vest, you couldn't tell which. His hair was tangled and his mouth hung open; altogether he looked as though he'd just completed a bell-ringing stint at Notre Dame.

'Fletcher said it would be a'right.'

'I'll talk to Master Fletcher in due course,' I said. 'But you ought to have known better, at least. Well, you can darn your own socks after this, my lad.' I turned to McAuslan. 'You,' I hissed, 'button your shirt and try to look half-decent.'

'Ah cannae, sir, but.' He pawed unhappily at his insanitary frontage. 'The buttons his came aff.'

I'd been a fool to mention it, of course. I wondered momentarily if there was time to dismiss him and get a replacement, but the first foursome was already on the tee. 'Well, tuck the damned thing in at least, and get hold of yourself. You're caddying for the Regimental Sergeant-Major.'

I don't know which of them was hit hardest by this news; probably no two men in the battalion were as eager to shun each other's company. McAuslan went in fear and horror of the majestic Mackintosh; the R.S.M., on the other hand, who had been brought up in the Guards, regarded McAuslan as a living insult to the profession of arms, and preferred to ignore his existence. Now they were in enforced partnership, so to speak. I left them to renew old acquaintance, and went to watch the first shots being exchanged on the tee.

Pirie and the Adjutant were our openers, and when Pirie hit his drive out of sight you could see the Adjutant smirking approval in a way which invited the onlookers to believe that he, too, was cast in the same grand mould. Poor sap, he didn't seem to realise that he would shortly be scooping great lumps out of the fairway while Pirie gritted his teeth and their opponents looked embarrassed. Not that the Royals looked as though pity was their long suit; it is part of their regimental tradition to look as much like army officers as possible – the type who are to be seen in advertisements for lime juice, or whisky, or some splendid out-of-doors tobacco. They were brown, leathery, moustached upper-crust Anglo-Scots, whose well-worn wind-cheaters and waterproof trousers could have come only from Forsyth's or Rowan's; their wooden clubs had little covers on their heads, their brogues had fine metal spikes, and they called each other Murdoch and Doug. Nowadays they broke stocks or manage export concerns, and no doubt they still play golf extremely well.

Our second pair were Damon and Pythias, the two elderly majors, who took the tee with arthritic moans. Rivals for the same girl when they had been stationed at Kasr-el-Nil before the war, they disliked each other to the point of inseparability, and lived in a state of feud. If they could manage to totter round the eighteen holes they would at least put up a show, which was more than I expected from our third couple, the Padre and the M.O.

They were a sight to see. The M.O., eating pills and wearing gym shoes, was accompanied by a caddy festooned with impedimenta – an umbrella, binoculars, flask, sandwich case and the like. Golf, to the M.O., was not to be taken lightly. The Padre, apart from his denim trousers, was resplendent in a jersey embroidered for him by the market mammies of some St Andrew's Kirk in West Africa, a souvenir of his missionary days. A dazzling yellow, it had his name in scarlet on the front – 'Rev. McLeod', it said – while on the back, in many colours, was the Church of Scotland emblem of the burning bush, with 'Nec tamen consumebatur' underneath. The Padre wouldn't have parted with it for worlds; he had worn it under his battledress on D-Day, and intended to be buried in it.

The M.O., breathing heavily, drove off, which consisted of swinging like a Senlac axe-man, overbalancing, and putting up a ball which, had he been playing cricket, would have been easily caught at square leg.

'"Gregory, remember thy swashing blow,"' quoted the Padre. 'Man, but there's power there, if it could be harnessed. Don't you worry, Lachlan, I'll see to it', and he wandered off towards the ball to play the second shot after his opponents had driven off – which they did, very long and very straight.

Second-Lieutenant Macmillan and R.Q.M.S. Bogle were next, Macmillan scraping his drive just over the brow of the hill fifty yards in front of the tee. Then the MacNeill-Mackintosh combo took the stage, and as we walked on to the tee with the Colonels and attendant minions watching from the clubhouse verandah, I could hear the R.S.M.'s muttered instructions to the shuffling McAuslan: '. . . those are the wooden clubs with the wooden heads; the irons have metal heads. All are numbered accordin' to their purpose. When I require a parteecular club I shall call oot the number, and you will hand it to me, smertly and with care. Is that clear?'

God help you, you optimistic sergeant-major, I thought, and invited him to tee off – whoever fell flat on his face in front of the assembled gallery, it wasn't going to be me. He put a respectable drive over the hill, our opponents drove immaculately, and we were off, four golfers, three caddies, and McAuslan shambling behind, watching the R.S.M. fearfully, like a captured slave behind a chariot.

Looking back, I can't say I enjoyed that match. For one thing, I was all too conscious of what was happening in the foursomes ahead of us, and over the first nine at least it wasn't good. From time to time they would come into view, little disheartening tableaux: the M.O. kneeling under a bush, swearing and wrestling with the cap of his flask; R.Q.M.S. Bogle trying to hit a ball which was concealed by his enormous belly, while Macmillan giggled nervously; our elderly majors beating the thick rough with their clubs and reviling each other; the Adjutant's plaintive bleat drifting over the dunes: 'I'm awfully sorry, Pirie, I can't imagine what's happened to my mid-irons today; either it's the balance of the clubs or I'm over-swinging. What do you think, Pirie, am I over-swinging?' And so on, while the wind blew gently over the sunlit course, ruffling the bent grass, and the distant sea glittered from its little choppy wavelets; it was a brisk, beautiful backdrop totally out of keeping with the condition of the tortured souls trudging over the links, recharging all their worst emotions and basest instincts in the pursuit of little white balls. It makes you think about civilisation, it really does.

I refer to the emotions of our own side, of course. The Royals, for all I know, were enjoying it. My own personal opponents seemed to be, at any rate. They were of the type I have already described, trim, confident men called Hamilton and Dalgliesh – or it may have been Melville and Runcieman, I can't be sure. They played a confident, rather showy game, with big, erratic drives and carefully-considered chips and putts – which, oddly enough, didn't give them much edge on us. Mackintosh was a steady, useful player, and I'd been worse; we weren't discontented to reach the turn one down.

I had arranged for the pipe-sergeant to station himself at the ninth green, to give progress reports on the other games, and he was bursting with news.

'Sir, sir, the Adjutant and Pirie iss in the lead! They're wan hole up, sir, an' Pirie playin' like God's anointed. The Adjutant iss a shambles, poor soul, and him such a charmin' dancer, but Pirie is carryin' the day. His drives iss like thunderbolts, and his putts is droppin' from wherever. Oh, the elegance of it, and the poor Adjutant broke his driver at the eighth an' him near greetin'. But they're wan up, sir.'

'How about the others?'

'The majors is square, but failin' rapidly. I doot Major Fleming'll be to carry home; the endurance is not in him. Bogle an' the boy – Mr Macmillan, that is – are two doon, an' lucky at that, for Bogle's guts is a fearful handicap. They hinder his swing, ye see, and he's vexed. But he's game, for a' that, an' wan o' the Royals he's playin' against has ricked his back, so there's hope yet.'

Ahead in one game, square in one, behind in two; it could have been worse. 'How about the Padre and the M.O.?'

The pipe-sergeant coughed delicately. 'Seven doon, sir, and how they contrived to save two holes, God alone knows. It's deplorable, sir; the M.O. has been nippin' ahint a bush after every hole for a sook at his flask, and iss as gassed as a Ne'erday tinker. The poor Padre has gone awa' into one o' they wee broon things –'

'Into what?'

'Into a dwalm, sir, a revaree, like a trance, ye ken. He wanders, and keeks intae bunkers, and whistles in the Gaelic. There's nae sense in either o' them, sir; they're lost to ye.' He said it much as a Marshal of France might have reported the defeat of an army to Napoleon, sad but stern. 'And yerself, sir? One doon? What iss that to such men as yerself and the Major, see the splendid bearin' of him! Cheer up, sir, a MacNeill never cried barley; ye had your own boat in the Flood.'

'That was the MacLeans, pipey,' I said sadly. The Colonel, I was thinking, wasn't going to like this; by the same process of logic, he wasn't going to like his sports officer. Well, if Pirie kept his winning streak, and the two old majors lasted the distance – it was just possible that the R.S.M. and I might achieve something, who knew? But the outlook wasn't good, and I drove off at the tenth in no high spirits.

And it was at this point that Private McAuslan began to impose his personality on the game. Knowing about McAuslan, you might think that an odd way of putting it – interfere with something, yes; wreck, frustrate or besmirch – all these things he could do. But even with his talent for disaster, he had never been what you could call a controlling influence – until the R.S.M., playing our second shot at the tenth, for once hooked, and landed us deep in tiger country.

We thrashed about in the jungle, searching, but there wasn't a hope, and with the local five-minute rule in operation we had to forfeit the hole. Personally, if it had been our opponents, I'd have suggested they drop a new ball and forfeit a stroke, but there it was. We were two down, and the R.S.M. for once looked troubled.

'I'm extremely sorry aboot that, sir,' he confided to me. 'Slack play. No excuse. I'm extremely sorry.'

I hastened to reassure him, for I guessed that perhaps to the R.S.M. this match was even more important than to the rest of us. When your life is a well-ordered, immaculate success, as his was, any failure begins to look important. Perfection was his norm; being two down was not perfection, and losing a ball was inexcusable.

Meanwhile, I was aware of voices behind us, and one of them was McAuslan's. He had been quiet on the outward half, between terror of the R.S.M. and his own inability to distinguish one club from another – for he was illiterate, a rare but not unknown thing in the Army of those days. Perhaps his awe of Mackintosh had diminished slightly – the serf who sees his overlord grunting in a bunker gets a new slant on their relationship, I suppose. Anyway, the fearful novelty of his situation having worn off, he was beginning to take an interest, and McAuslan taking an interest was wont to be garrulous.

'Hey, Chick,' I heard him say, addressing my caddy. 'Whit we no' finishing this hole fur?'

'We've loast it,' said McClusky. 'We loast wir ba'.'

'So whit? Hiv we no' got anither yin?'

'Aye, we've got anither yin, but if ye lose a ba' ye lose the hole. It's the rules.'

A pause. Then: 'Ah, —— the rules. It's no' fair. Sure it's no fair, huh, Chick?'

'Aw, Goad,' said McClusky, 'Ah'm tellin' ye, it's the rule, ye dope. Same's at fitba'.'

'Weel, Ah think it's daft,' said McAuslan. 'Look, at fitba', if a man kicks the ba' oot the park –'

'All right, McAuslan, pipe down,' I said. I knew that one of the few abstract ideas ever to settle in that neanderthal mind was a respect for justice – his sense of what was 'no' fair' had once landed him in a court-martial – but this was no time for an address by McAuslan, Q.C. 'Just keep quiet, and watch the ball. If you'd done it last time we might not have lost the hole.' Which wasn't strictly fair, but I was punished for it.

'Quaiet, please,' said one of our opponents. 'No tocking on the tee, if you don't mind.' And he added. 'Thenk-you.'

The crust of it was, he hadn't even teed up. Suddenly I realised what had been wrong with this game so far – I'd had half my mind on the other matches, half on my own play: I hadn't really noticed our opponents. And that's no good. Ask Dr Grace or Casey Stengel or my Highland granny – you've *got* to notice the opposition, and abominate them. That totally unnecessary 'Quaiet, please' had made it easy.

Our opponents drove off, respectably, and Mackintosh, subconsciously trying to redeem his lost ball, tried a big one, instead of his usual cautious tee-shot. It soared away splendidly, but with slice written all over it; it was going to land well among the whins.

'Keep your eye on it!' I shouted, and McAuslan, full of zeal, bauchled masterfully across the tee, dragging his bag, his eyes staring fixedly into the blue, roaring:

'Ah see it! Ah've spotted the b—! Don't worry, sir! Ah see –'

Unfortunately it was one of those high plateau tees, with a steep drop to whins and rough grass at the start of the fairway. McAuslan, blind to everything except the soaring ball, marched into the void and descended with a hideous clatter of clubs and body, to which presently he added flowers of invective picked up on the Ibrox terracing. He crawled out of the bushes, blaspheming bitterly, until he realised the R.S.M.'s cold eye was on him; then he rose and limped after the ball.

The opponent who had rebuked me – I think of him as Melville – chuckled.

'Thet's a remarkable individual,' he said to me. 'Wherever did you get him?' A fair enough question, from anyone meeting McAuslan for the first time, but with just a hint of patronage, perhaps. 'You ott to keep an aye on him, before he hurts himself,' went on Melville jocularly. 'Aye don't think he's doing anything for your partner's peace of mind, eether.'

It might have been just loud enough for Mackintosh to hear; I may have been wrong, but I think I know gamesmanship when I hear it. Coming on top of the 'Quaiet, please', it just settled my hate nicely; from that moment the tension was on, and I squared up to that second shot in the deep rough, determined to hit the green if it killed me. Four shots later we were in a bunker, conceding a hole that was hopelessly lost. Three down and seven to play.

Not a nice position, and McAuslan didn't help things. Perhaps his fall had rattled him, or more probably his brief sally into the limelight had made him more than normally self-conscious. He accidentally trod in the tee-box at the twelfth, and had to have his foot freed by force (the fact that Melville muttered something about 'accident-prone' did nothing for my temper). Then he upended the R.S.M.'s bag, and we had to wait while he retrieved the clubs, scrabbling like a great beast with his shirt coming out. I forced myself to be calm, and managed a fairish drive to the edge of the short twelfth green; Mackintosh chipped on well, and we halved in three.

The thirteenth was one of those weird holes by which games of golf are won and lost. Our position was fairly hopeless – three down and six – and possibly because of that we played it like champions. The R.S.M. drove straight, and for once he was long; I took my old whippy brassie with its wooden shaft, drove from my mind the nameless fear that McAuslan would have an apoplectic fit or shoot me in the back while I was in the act of swinging, and by great good luck hit one of those perfect shots away downhill. It flew, it bounced, it ran, trickling between the bunkers to lie nicely just a yard on to the green.

Melville and Co. were in dire straits. They took three and were still short of the green, and I was counting the hole won when Melville took out his number seven iron and hit the bonniest chip I ever hope to see; of course it was lucky, landing a yard short of the flag with lots of back spin, and then running straight as a die into the cup, but that's golf. They were down in four, we were on in two, and Mackintosh had a fifteen-yard putt.

He strode ponderously on to the green, looked at the ball as though to ask its name, rank and number, and held out his hand for his putter. McAuslan rummaged fearfully, and then announced tremulously:

'It's no' here, sir.'

And it wasn't. Sulphurous question and whimpering answer finally narrowed the thing down to the point where we realised it must have fallen out when McAuslan, Daedalus-like, had tried to defy gravity at the eleventh tee. He was driven, with oaths and threats, to fetch it, and we waited in the sunlight, Melville and his friend saying nothing pointedly, until presently McAuslan hove in view again, looking like the last survivor of

Fort Zinderneuf staggering home, dying of thirst. But he had the club.

'Ah'm awfu' sorry, sir. It must hiv fell oot.' He wiped his sweating grey nose audibly, and the R.S.M. took the putter without a word, addressed the ball briefly, and sent it across the huge waste of green dead true, undeviating, running like a pup to its dinner, plopping with a beautiful mellow sound into the tin.

(It's a strange thing, but when I think back to that heroic, colossal putt – or to any other moment in that game, for that matter – I see in my imagination the R.S.M., not clothed in the mufti which I know he must have been wearing, but resplendent in full regimentals, white spats, kilt, dress tunic and broadsword, with a feather bonnet on top. I *know* he wasn't wearing them, but he should have been.)

And as we cried our admiration, I thought to myself, we're only two down now. And five holes to go. And I heard again that old golfing maxim: 'Two up and five never won a match.' Well, it might come true, given luck.

It certainly began to look like it, for while our drives and approaches were level at the fourteenth, the R.S.M. played one of his canny chips while our opponents barely found the green. Their putt was feebly short, and mine teetered round the hole, took a long look in, and finally went down. One up and four.

The fifteenth was a nightmare hole, a par-three where you played straight out to sea, hoping to find a tiny green perched above the beach, with only a ribbon of fairway through the jungle. This was where Mackintosh's cautious driving was beyond price; I trundled on a lamentable run-up that missed the guarding bunker by a whisker, and then Melville, panicking, put his approach over the green and, presumably, into the North Sea. All square with three to play.

For the first time I was enjoying myself; I felt we had them on the run, whereupon my Presbyterian soul revolted and slapped me on the wrists, urging me to be calm. So I drove cautiously and straight, the R.S.M. put us within pitching distance, and my chip just stayed on the back of the green. Melville played the like into a bunker, they took three to get pin-high, and the R.S.M.'s putt left me nothing to do but hole a twelve-incher. For the first time we were in front. And only two holes remained.

The seventeenth was the first half of a terribly long haul to the clubhouse. It and the eighteenth were par fives, where our opponents' longer hitting ought to tell. But Melville's partner duffed his drive, and while we broke no records in getting to the edge of the green in five, he and his partner undertook a shocking safari into the rough on both sides, and were still off the green in six. I was trembling slightly as I chipped on, and more by luck than judgement I left it within a foot of the cup. Unless they sank their approach, which was unthinkable, we had the match won. I glanced at the R.S.M. His face was wooden, as usual, but as we waited for their shot his fingers were drumming on the shaft of his putter.

Melville's partner, hand it to him, was ready to die game. 'This goes in,' he said, shaping up to his ball, which was on the wrong side of a bunker, fifteen yards from the flag. 'Pin out, please.'

And Private McAuslan, the nearest caddy, ambled across the green to remove the flag.

I should have known, of course; I should have taken thought. But I'd forgotten McAuslan in the excitement of the game; vaguely I had been aware of his presence, when he sniffed, or grunted, or dropped the clubs, or muttered, 'Aw, jeez, whit a brammer' when we hit a good shot, or 'Ah, ——', when our opponents did. But he hadn't broken his leg, or gone absent, or caught beri-beri, or done anything really McAuslan-like. Now he tramped across to the flag, his paw outstretched, and I felt my premonition of disaster too late.

He claimed afterwards it was a wasp, but as the Adjutant said, it must have been a bot-fly, or maybe a vulture: no sane wasp would have gone near him, in his condition. Whatever it was, he suddenly leaped, swatting and cursing, he stumbled, and his great, flat, ugly, doom-laden foot came down on our ball, squashing it into the turf.

I think I actually screamed. Because the law is the law, and if your caddy touches your ball in play, let alone tries to stamp the damned thing through to Australia, you forfeit the hole. Even Melville, I'll swear, had compassion in his eyes.

'Dem bed luck,' he said to me. 'Aym offly sorry, but thet puts us all square again.'

McAuslan, meanwhile, was gouging our ball out of the green, as a hungry boar might root for truffles. Presently, from the exclamations around, he gathered that somehow he had erred; when he understood that he had cost us the hole, and probably the game, his distress was pitiful to see and disgusting to hear. But what could you say to him? It had all been said before, anyway, to no avail. Poor unwashed blundering soul, it was just the way he was made.

So certain victory had been taken from us, and now all was to play for at the last hole, where the pipe-sergeant was skipping with excitement on the tee. On hearing how we stood he sent a runner post-haste to Aix with the news, and then delivered himself.

Unbelievably, of the other four games we had won two and lost two, and but for the M.O.'s drunken folly we might even have been ahead 3–1. Pirie and the Adjutant had won, two and one ('and oh, the style of yon Pirie, sir! Whaur's yer Wullie Turnesa noo, eh?'). The two elderly majors, against all the odds, had triumphed at the eighteenth by one hole; it appeared that the corpulent Major Fleming, about to give up the struggle at the fifteenth, had been roused by his partner's taunt that the girl in Kasr-el-Nil had said that she couldn't abide fat men, and had told him (the partner) that she could never love a man as overweight as Fleming, who would certainly be dead of a stroke before he was forty. Inflamed, Fleming had carried all before him, and even with the Padre and M.O. going down to cataclysmic defeat, 9 and 7, the overall prospects had looked not bad. Macmillan and Bogle had fought back to level terms ('and auld Bogle wi' his guts in a sling and pechin' sore, sore') and at the sixteenth one of their opponents, whom the pipey had earlier reported as suffering from muscle strain, had wrenched his shoulder.

He had been about to give up and concede the game, when the Padre, happening by from the scene of his own rout, had suggested that our M.O., who had taken his flask for a sleep in the rough, be summoned to examine the sufferer. They roused the M.O. from beneath a bush, and after focusing unsteadily on the affected part he had announced: 'In my professional opinion this man cannot be moved without imperilling his life. Call an ambulance.' Alarmed, they had asked him what the Royal was suffering from, and he had replied: 'Alcoholic poisoning', and then collapsed himself into a bunker. So indignant had the injured Royal – a senior and extremely stiffish company commander – been that he had insisted on carrying on, and Bogle and Macmillan had lost, two down.

So it was up to the R.S.M. and me to win or lose the whole shooting-match, and as I looked at the huge eighteenth, with its broad fairway just made for the big driving of our opponents, I almost gave up hope. The worst of it was, if it hadn't been for that grubby moron's great flat feet we would have been walking home now, with the thing in the bag; he was mumping dolefully somewhere in the background. I knew I was silly, feeling so upset over a mere game, but what would you? One does.

I watched Melville drive off, and he must have been feeling the pressure, for he hooked shockingly into a clump of firs. Now's your chance, I thought joyfully, and taking a fine easy swing I topped my drive a good twenty yards down the fairway. Shattered, I watched the R.S.M. prepare to play the second; he had said not a word during the McAuslan débâcle, but for once there was the beginning of a worried frown on the great brow, and with cause, for he sliced his shot away to the high outcrop of rock which ran between the fairway and the sea. The ball pinged among the crags, and then vanished on to the crest, far out in badman's territory. To make it worse, Melville's partner hit a colossal spoon from the trees, leaving them only a longish iron to the green.

This was plainly the end, I thought, as I set off up the bluff in search of the ball, with McClusky trailing behind. We tramped what seemed miles over the springy turf, and found the ball, nicely cocked up on a tuft with the ground falling away sharply ahead to the wide fairway, and three hundred yards off the green, hemmed in by broad deep bunkers. It was a lovely lie, downhill and wide open save for a clump of boulders about two hundred yards off on the right edge of the fairway; there was a following wind, the sea was sparkling, the sun was warm, and everything was an invitation to beat that ball to kingdom come and beyond. Anyway, there was nothing to lose, so I unshipped the old brassie, took a broad stance, waggled the clubhead, did everything wrong, lifted my heel, raised my head, turned my body, and lashed away for dear life. And so help me I leaned upon that ball, and I smote it, so that it rose like a dove in the Scriptures, whining away with an upward trajectory beyond the ken of man, and flew screaming down the wind.

I've never hit one like it, and I never will again. It was the Big One, the ultimate, and no gallery thundering with applause could have acknowledged it more appropriately than my own ruptured squawk of astonishment and McClusky's reverent cry of: 'Jayzus!' For one fearful moment I thought it was going to develop a late slice, but it whanged into the clump of rocks, kicked magnificently to a huge height as it skidded on, fell within thirty yards of the green, and rolled gently out of sight somewhere beside the right-hand bunker.

We hurried down to join the others on the fairway, where Melville was unlimbering his three iron. He hit a reasonable shot, but was well short; his partner's seven was way too high, and plumped into the short rough just off the green to left. My spirits soared; we were in business again with a stroke in hand, assuming the R.S.M. had a reasonable lie, which seemed probable. We made for the right-hand bunker; I thought I must be just short of it – and then my heart sank. We were in it; right in.

Foul trolls from the dark ages had dug that bunker. It was just off the green, a deep, dark hideous pit fringed by gorse, with roots straggling under its lips, and little flat stones among the powdery sand. My great, gorgeous brassie shot had just reached it, so that the ball was nestling beside a root, with just room for a man to swing, and eight feet of bank baring its teeth five yards in front of him. I've seen bunkers, and bad lies in them, but this was the nadir.

We looked, appalled, and then that great man the R.S.M. climbed down into the depths. McAuslan, hovering on the bunker's edge, clubs at the high port, dropped everything as usual, but the R.S.M. simply snapped: 'Number nine'; even he looked like one on whom the doom has come. He waited, hand out, eyes fixed on the barely-visible tip of the flag, while McAuslan rummaged among the irons on the grass, and handed one down to him. The R.S.M. took the club, and addressed the ball.

It was hopeless, of course; Nicklaus might have got out in one, but I doubt it. The R.S.M. was just going through the motions; he addressed the ball, swung down, and then I saw his club falter in mid-descent, an oath such as I had never heard sprang to his lips, but he was too late to stop. The club descended in a shower of sand, the ball shot across the bunker with frightful speed, hit a root, leaped like a salmon, curved just over the lip of the bunker, bounced, hung, and trickled away down the steep face of the bank on to the green. For a minute I thought it was going in, but it stopped on the very lip of the hole while the sounds of joy and grief from the people wildly rose.

For a moment I could only stare, amazed. I was aware that Melville was chipping on a yard short, and that his partner was holing the putt; they were down in six. I had a tiny putt, two inches at most, for a five and victory, and for the first time in that game the shade of my grandmother asserted herself, reminding me of Uncle Hugh, and chickens unwisely counted. 'Never up, never in,' I thought, and crouched over the ball; I tapped it firmly in, and that was the ball game.

The Royals were extremely nice about it; splendid losers they were, and there was much good-natured congratulation on the green itself, from our immediate opponents and the other players as well. I detached myself and looked for the R.S.M., but he was not in sight; I went over to the scene of his great shot, and there he was, still standing in the bunker, like a great tweed statue, staring at the club in his hand. And before him, Caliban to Prospero, McAuslan crouched clutching the bag.

'McAuslan,' the R.S.M. was saying. 'You gave me this club.'

'Aye – eh, aye, sir.' He was snuffling horribly.

'What club did I require you to give me?'

'Ra number nine, sir.'

'And what club did you give me?'

McAuslan, hypnotised, whimpered: 'Oh, Goad, Ah dunno, sir.'

'This, McAuslan,' said the R.S.M. gravely, 'is nott a number nine. It is, in fact, a number two. What is called a driving iron. It is not suitable for bunker shots.'

'Zat a fact, sir?'

The R.S.M. took a deep breath and let it out again. He was looking distinctly fatigued.

'Return this club to the bag,' he said, 'put the bag in my quarters, go to the sergeants' mess – the back door – and tell the barman on *my* instructions to supply you with one pint of beer. That's all for now – right, move!'

McAuslan hurled himself away, stricken dumb by fear and disbelief. As he clambered out of the bunker the R.S.M. added:

'Thank you for bein' my caddy, McAuslan.'

If McAuslan heard him, I'm sure he didn't believe what he heard.

The R.S.M. climbed out heavily, and gave me his slight smile. 'Thank you, sir, for a most enjoyable partnership; a very satisfactory concluding putt, if I may say so.'

'Major,' I said – my emotion and admiration were such that I had slipped into the old ranker's form of address – 'any infant could have holed it. But that bunker shot – man, that was incredible!'

'Incredible indeed, sir. Did you see what I played it wi'? A number two iron – a flat-faced club, sir! Dear me, dear me. By rights I should be in there yet – and I would have been thanking McAuslan for that, I can tell you!'

'Well, thank goodness he did give you the wrong club. You couldn't have played a finer shot, with a nine or anything else.'

'Indeed I couldn't. Indeed I couldn't.' He shook his head. 'By George, Mr MacNeill, we had the luck with us today.'

'Hand of providence,' I said lightly.

'No, sir,' said the R.S.M. firmly. 'Let us give credit where it is due. It was the hand of Private McAuslan.'

His Majesty Says Good-Day

Nowadays, if ever my thoughts stray back across the years to Private McAuslan, I can feel a strange expression stealing across my face. I know, without glancing in the mirror, that I'm beginning to look like a large and truculent Uriah Heep, cringing but defiant, as though uncertain whether to grovel or hit out blindly. It's a conditioned reflex, born from the countless times I've stood at the elbows of outraged colonels and company commanders, making placatory noises and muttering balefully that I'm sure the accused won't do it again, given a second chance. (He did, though, every time.)

This is the penalty you pay for commanding the dumbest and dirtiest soldier in the world: on the one hand you have to chastise and oppress him for the good of his soul, and on the other you have to plead his cause and defend him, almost to the point of defiance, from the wrath of higher authority. The devil's advocating I did for that man would have earned a standing ovation from Lincoln's Inn; I can't count the passionate appeals or the shameless distortions of King's Regulations that I have advanced to excuse his tardiness, stupidity, dirt, negligence, and occasionally drunkenness and absence without leave. Not, admittedly, with great success. I would only add that if any young lawyer wants practice in defending deservedly lost causes, let him assume responsibility for McAuslan for one calendar month. After that, he'll have nothing to learn.

I suppose, recalling the time I sweated through his court-martial for disobedience, or the occasion when he fell prone in an intoxicated condition, wearing only his shirt and one army boot, before an officer of general rank, that his last clash with military authority was trivial by comparison. I only remember it because it was the last, and took place, appropriately, on the day before he and I were demobilised. (There was a kind of awful kismet about the fact that he was with me to the end.) Yet, paltry though it was, it was essentially McAuslan, in that it demonstrated yet again his carelessness, negligence, and indiscipline, and at the same time his fine adherence to principle.

I had just taken my final company orders in the office, and was sitting reflecting solemnly that tomorrow I would be a soldier no more, and from that my grasshopper mind started musing on how certain other military men must have felt when their tickets finally came through. Not the great martial names; not the Wellingtons and Napoleons and Turennes, but some of those others who, like me, had been what Shakespeare called warriors for the working day – the conscripts, the volunteers, the civilians who followed the drum and went to war in their time, and afterwards, with luck, picked up their discharges and back money and went home. Not soldiers at all, really, and quite undistinguished militarily – people like Socrates and Ben Jonson, Lincoln and Cobbett, Bunyan and Edgar Allen Poe, Gibbon and Cervantes, Chaucer and John Knox and Daniel Boone and Thomas Cromwell. (McAuslan was trouble enough, but I'd hate to take responsibility for a platoon consisting of that lot.)

And yet, I found it comforting to think that they too, like McAuslan and me – and perhaps you – had once stood nervously on first parade in ill-fitting kit, with their new boots hurting, feeling lost and a long way from home, and had done ablutions fatigue, and queued for the canteen and cookhouse, and worried over the state of their equipment, and stood guard on cold, wet nights, and been upbraided (and doubtless upbraided others in their turn) as idle bodies and dozy men, and thought longingly of their discharge, and generally shared that astonishing experience which, for some reason, men seem to prize so highly. Having been a soldier. It doesn't matter what happens to them afterwards, or how low or high they go, they never forget that ageless company they once belonged to. And if you think that there is not a special link between McAuslan and Socrates and Chaucer and Abe Lincoln, you are dead wrong.

I had just got to the point in my reverie where I was assuring the assembled Athenians that McAuslan's habitual uncleanliness had probably rendered him immune to poison, when I heard the voice of the man himself raised raucously in the company store across the way. Not that that was unusual, but the form of words was novel.

'That's mines,' he was protesting. 'That's ma private property. Sno' yours. Smines. An' Ah'm bluidy well keepin' it, see? Ah've peyed for it!'

'What d'ye mean, paid for it? When did you ever pay for anything, McAuslan?'

I recognised the voice of young Sergeant Baxter – the same Baxter who, as an over-zealous corporal, had recently been responsible for McAuslan's court-martial. That McAuslan had escaped untarnished had merely confirmed the evil relations between them. Privately, I didn't care for Baxter; he was too officious, but he knew his stuff and was keen, and when Sergeant Telfer had returned to civilian life – as a hotel porter, and the hotel was lucky, in my opinion – it would have been unfair to deny Baxter his third tape. But he was woefully short of experience still, as his next words showed.

'And get your heels together when you talk tae me, McAuslan!' His voice was shrill. 'An' you address me as "sergeant"!'

'That'll be right!' roared McAuslan. 'Ah can jist see me. Ye're no' comin' the acid wi' me, *Sergeant* – Ah want it back, and I want it noo!'

'Well, ye're no' gettin' it, so fall oot!' snapped Baxter, and I decided to intervene before they fell to brawling.

'What's all the noise, sergeant?' I said, as I went into the store, and Baxter came rapidly to attention. He was pink with outrage, a pleasing contrast to the pastel grey of McAuslan's contorted features. The greatest walking disaster to befall the British Army since Ancient Pistol was modishly clad in a suit of outsize denims in which he appeared to have been scraping the Paris sewers, but his fists were clenched and he was obviously on the brink of unlawful assault of a superior.

'It's this – this man, sir!' said Baxter unnecessarily. 'He's trying to lay claim to Army property!'

That was new; McAuslan's normal behaviour with War Department equipment was to lose or defile it as quickly as possible. As it transpired, in this case he had done both.

'It's ma bay'net, sir!' He looked to me in dishevelled appeal. 'This bas –, *Sarn't* Baxter – he'll no gie it back tae me. An' it's mines! Ah've peyed for it!'

And sure enough, Baxter was holding a sheathed bayonet, one of the old sword type with the locking-ring that went on the short Lee Enfield, since superseded by other marks, although there were still a number of them about.

'Haud yer tongue, McAuslan,' said Baxter, and to me: 'He's due for demobilisation tomorrow, sir, and I was seein' that he handed in all his kit properly – it's in a disgraceful state, sir, there's all kinds o' things missin', an' nae foresight on his rifle, an' the barrel red rotten wi' rust, too –'

'Hold on a shake,' I said, puzzled. 'I didn't know you were due out tomorrow, McAuslan.' I had been acting company commander for the past three weeks, and had lost track of my platoon's domestic affairs. 'What's your number?'

'14687347PrivateMcAuslansah!'

'Your demob number,' I said patiently.

'Oh. Hey. Aye. Eh – 57, sir.'

It was the same as mine, which was curious. 'But you've been in the Army longer than I have – you were in the desert in '42. How come you weren't demobbed long ago?'

He pawed uncertainly with his hooves, ran a hand through his Gorgon locks – something that I hoped was a piece of old string fell out – and said uneasily:

'Weel, see, sir, it's like this. When Ah j'ined up, Ah got back-squadded a few times – ye know? An' –'

'Back-squadded?' scoffed Baxter. 'I would think so. It took them two years tae learn you to slope arms.'

'Ah got ma bluidy knees broon, onywye!' McAuslan rounded on him. 'More'n you ever did! Niver saw an angry German, you –'

'That'll do, McAuslan,' I said. 'Go on.'

He muttered and looked at the floor. 'An' Ah did a bit o' time, too – the glass-hoose at Stirlin'.' Memory stirred his shuffled features into vengeful patterns. 'There was this rotten big sarn't inna Black Watch, right pig he wis, an' he had a down on me, an' he sortit me oot, and got me the jail. Oh, he was a right swine o' a man, so he wis –'

'Yes, I see,' I said. 'And you're going out tomorrow?' Champagne at the War Office tonight, I thought. 'And what's all this about a bayonet?'

'It's mines,' he said doggedly, glowering at the weapon in Baxter's hand. 'But Ah lost it, a while back, an' they made me pey for it – stopped it oot ma money, they did.' He blinked piteously at me, like a widow evicted. 'They gie'd me anither bayonet – that's it ower there, wi the rest o' ma kit.' He pointed to a mouldering heap lying on the floor on a torn ground-sheet; there was what looked like a large rusty nail among the debris, and I recognised it as one of the new pig-sticker bayonets.

'How the hell did it get in that condition?' I demanded.

'Ah dunno.' He wiped his nose audibly. 'Ah think it must hae been the damp.'

He met my speechless glare, and wilted. 'Ah'm sorry, sir, like. Ah'll maybe gie it a wee clean.' And he began rooting through his military effects, like a baboon poking among twigs.

'Come out of that!' I exclaimed hastily. 'Leave it alone; the less it's – disturbed, the better. Now, what about this other bayonet?' I indicated the weapon in Baxter's hand.

'Well, sir, it's mines, like Ah'm sayin'. See, Ah lost it, two year ago, in the Tripoli barracks, an' had tae pey for it but Ah found it again the ither day, when Ah wis sortin' oot ma kit for tae hand in tae the quartermaster. There it wis, wrapped up in a pair o' ma auld drawers at the bottom o' ma kitbag.' He beamed through his grime, while I made the appalling deduction that the lower strata of his kitbag had lain undisturbed for two long years, old drawers and heaven knew what besides. I was just glad I hadn't been there when he finally opened it all up; it must have been like excavating a catacomb.

'But, see, sir,' he went on earnestly. 'Ah've handed in the pig-sticker they issued me wi' when Ah lost ma auld bayonet. An' Ah peyed for that auld bayonet. So noo that Ah've found it again, it belangs tae me. Sure that's right, sir?'

This sounded like logic. I looked at Baxter.

'He's got a point,' I said.

'But, sir!' Baxter protested. 'It's still Army issue. He – he cannae *buy* War Department weapons. I'm sure of that. I never heard of such a thing, sir.'

Neither had I – but that's my McAuslan. If you've never heard of it – not so fast. He's probably done it.

'Well, since he has paid for it,' I said, 'at least he's entitled to his money back.'

'Ah'm no' wantin' ma money back,' proclaimed McAuslan. 'Ah want ma bay'net. Ah paid for that bay'net. Smines. Sno' yours –'

'Shut up,' said Baxter indignantly. 'Ye're no' gettin' it.'

'Aw, sure Ah am, sir? He'd niver've known it wis there, even, if he hadnae come pokin' his nose in when Ah wis sortin' oot ma things.' You're a better man than I am, Baxter, I thought. 'He's got nae right tae try tae tak' it off me. Onywye, two o' the boys that wis in ma platoon in the desert got keepin' their side-arms, when they wis invalided oot in '42. Major MacRobert let them; he wis oor company commander then.'

Trust Big Mac. His company hadn't been a company to him; it had been a fighting tail.

'But you can get it credited to you, in money,' I said.

'Ah want the bay'net, sir. Ah had it a long time. Ah wis awfy sorry when I lost it.' He scratched himself unhappily. 'Ah had yon bay'net since Ah j'ined up at Maryhill. Had it in a' sorts o' places. Inna desert, too. Sure an' Ah did.'

All sorts of places, I knew, covered Tobruk, Alamein, and Cameron Ridge. I remembered the kukri, carefully oiled and polished, that lay at the bottom of my own trunk.

'I think we could let him keep it,' I said after a moment, 'and just forget about it, Sergeant Baxter.'

'Well, sir,' he began doubtfully, but even he wasn't looking quite so adamant. 'It's a dangerous weapon, sir – I don't know if it's legal . . . the police . . .'

'We needn't worry about that,' I said. What Baxter meant was that to allow cold steel into the hands of a Glasgow man is tantamount to running guns to the Apaches, but I couldn't see McAuslan flourishing his bayonet in gang warfare. He wasn't the type – and uncharitably I reflected that the gangs were probably pretty choosy who they admitted, anyway.

Baxter held it out to him, and McAuslan took it, dropped it, cursed, scrabbled it up, wiped his nose, cleared his throat thunderously, and said, 'Ta.'

'Carry on, McAuslan,' I said, and just to remind him that it wasn't Christmas I added: 'And now you've got it, you can clean the dam' thing.'

He shambled off – and perhaps it was association of ideas,

but when I went back to my billet the first thing I did was to get my broadsword out of the cupboard and look it over. I'd never used it, of course, although it had come close to drawing blood – mine – on one occasion. Back in North Africa, the old Colonel had been inflamed by something he had read in a book about Rob Roy; it had said, he told us, that in the old days many Highlanders had worn their broadswords on their backs, with the hilt at the right shoulder, so that they could whip them out more quickly than from the hip. We would do this on ceremonial occasions, and the English regiments would go green with envy. So he had us out behind the mess, practising, and how the Adjutant didn't decapitate himself remains a mystery. Even the Colonel had to admit, reluctantly, that to have all his officers minus their right ears would present an unbalanced appearance, so the idea was shelved.

Anyway, even if I hadn't drawn it since, there it was – the claymore, the great sword. You're an odd kind of Highlander if you can slip your hand inside that beautiful basket-hilt without thinking of Quebec and Waterloo and Killiecrankie and Culloden and feeling the urge to kick off your shoes. I'd have to turn it over to the pipe-sergeant, now that I was leaving.

Naturally, I had mixed feelings about that, too. Perhaps I'd been looking forward for so long to being a civilian again that now it came as an anti-climax. When I'd been called up as a conscript during the war it had been a great adventure; I'd been an eager eighteen, brought up on war movies and Stout-hearted Stories for Boys, I'd wanted to get into it, my friends were going into uniform, the Germans and Japanese patently needed sorting out, and I genuinely wanted to fight for my country. Soldiering was also obviously preferable to swotting in a university (which had turned me down, anyway).

And I suppose I had known, at the back of my mind, that when it was all over I would want to look back and say I'd been in it. (No doubts about survival, you notice.) As Dr Johnson pointed out, a man who hasn't soldiered envies the man who has. Illogical, no doubt – immoral, even, by today's standards – but understandable. My own guess is that old Sam privately regretted not being out in the '45 himself, if only for the free beer and conversation.

But if my initial boyish enthusiasm had never quite rubbed off – although I'll confess there was one night outside Meiktila, with the Japanese White Tigers fooling about round our observation post, when it had worn fairly thin – it had been modified. You could not serve in the British wartime army without being infected by 'ticket' mania – in other words, the anticipation of your eventual discharge. I'd dreamed about it from Derby to Deolali, from freezing parades in Durham to sweltering route-marches in Bengal; on the lower decks of troopers, with the hammock of Grandarse Green slung perilously two inches above me and five hundred bodies snoring close-packed around us; on night stags in Burma when the 'up-you' beasts croaked in the jungle and the moon-shadows hypnotised you as they crept towards your rifle-pit; in steamy Northern Naafis, where you hunched miserably over your mug of tea and spam sandwich with damp serge chafing your neck; in the white-washed stuffiness of my subaltern's billet in Libya, when I lay awake wondering why my platoon seemed to find me an object of derision and dislike – in any of these places, if you had offered me my ticket I'd have snapped your hand off. (But I wouldn't have missed it, not any of it.)

However, dreaming of your ticket is one thing; picking it up is another. Four years is a long time, when it covers the span from boyhood to manhood; you get used to the Army, and provided you'd come through in one piece, and your loved ones likewise, you could look back and say it hadn't been a bad war. That may sound terrible – when I think of those slow-motion moments south of the Irrawady, and the Japanese corpse smell, and our own dead wrapped in blood-stained blankets, it sounds downright obscene – but it's what my generation thought, and perhaps still does. Not, mark you, that we'd want to do it again, and the idea of our children doing it is simply unthinkable.

At any rate, in the last few months before my demobilisation I had pondered on getting out, and at one time had come close to staying in. That had been the old Colonel's fault. Shortly before his own retirement he had loafed into my office one day, ostensibly to inspect some barrack-room repairs, but in fact to do his Ancient Mariner act. He had cornered me, discoursed at length on the joys of a soldier's life, reviewed my own service so far, and hinted that, while permanent commissions were not easy to come by, a word or two in the right place . . . It was not put anything like as bluntly as that, and took about half an hour, while he sat, puffing at his lovat pipe, dusting tobacco fragments off his kilt, one leg crossed over the other, and wrapping his message up elegantly in reminiscence of service life, from Japanese prison camp to guard duty at Balmoral. And he convinced me, hands down; even years later, when I was an encyclopedia salesman in Canada, I never heard a sales pitch to equal it.

'Whatever they say about this blasted bomb,' he said finally, 'we're going to need soldiers, if only to walk over the ruins. And we're the best there are, you know. And when the Empire goes, as it certainly will –' this was an old Colonel talking, in 1947 '– someone's going to have to leave it tidy, so that it will take the native politicians that much longer to mess it up again.' He rubbed his long nose, and did his bushy-browed Aubrey Smith grin. 'It'll all be done for nothing, of course, in the long run; always has been. Ask the Romans. But it's still got to be done – was that your quarter-master, Blind Sixty, who passed the door just now? Wasn't wearing his hat – whenever that man goes about without his bonnet on, there's a crisis at hand. Someone been stealing four-by-two, probably. Anyway, young Dand, don't you ever have tea for visitors in your office? In my young day, D Company hospitality was a byword . . .'

And when finally he had gone, he'd left me full of fine thoughts, in which I soldiered on and became Colonel of the Regiment myself, some day, maybe a general, even, with five rows of gongs, and an honourable record, and a paragraph in *Who's Who.* I tried to convince myself that he hadn't given exactly the same pep-talk to every subaltern in the battalion, but concluded that he probably had. Anyway, I applied for the appropriate signing-on forms, swithered over them, filled them in, kept them three weeks in my desk – and finally tore them up.

It wasn't just that the Colonel himself had gone by then (the new man was all right, in his precise, formal way, but not my kind of C.O., really), that the Adjutant had announced, with Bertie Woosterish cries, that he was going to take his demobilisation and make a pile in the City, bowler-hat and all, or that new subalterns were coming in and the atmosphere was changing, with the last happy-go-lucky vestiges of war-time soldiering going out and the somehow more austere sense of peace coming in. It was simply a realisation that (as Socrates and the boys no doubt said themselves) I wasn't a professional soldier.

I wondered, contemplating that broadsword on the last afternoon, how many Highland Scots really were. To fight briefly in a good cause, or for money, or for fun – these are reasons in the Highland tradition, but dedication to a lifetime of soldiering was something else.

I shoved the sword back in its scabbard, and took it across to the pipe-band office – responding, on the way, with a rude gesture to Lieutenant MacKenzie's cry of 'There goes the D'Artagnan of D Company; his father was the finest swordsman in France.' The pipey was perched behind his desk, looking as usual like a parrot bent on mischief; I don't remember saying goodbye to him, but I recollect that somewhere in the store-room behind him someone was singing 'Macgregor's Gathering' in a nasal Gaelic tenor:

> Glenstray and Glen Lyon no longer are ours
> We're landless! – landless! – landless Gregora!

And the pipey, wagging his head, remarked:

'That's the Macgregors for ye; aye greetin' about something.'

And I felt really sad, then, at the thought of leaving it all – but cheered myself up with the thought that tomorrow I'd be a free agent again, not subject to discipline or bugle-calls or King's Regulations (which was pathetic, when you think of the disciplines and calls and regulations of a civilian working life). I wouldn't have to feel responsible any more, for anyone but myself – certainly not for thirty-six hard-bitten, volatile and contrary Scotsmen who for their part could not wait to kiss the army goodbye. I would miss them, but there were definite compensations. Wee Wullie, for one, could put the entire military police force in hospital, Private Fletcher could start a Jocks' Trade Union, the whole platoon could mutiny and take to the hills, and I, the footloose civilian, could say it was nothing to do with me.

Biggest bonus of all, I could no longer be called to account for the vagaries of 14687347, Private McAuslan, J. He, henceforth, could get tight, or go absent, or set fire to his billet, or fall in the Clyde, or assault the Lord Provost, or lose the atomic bomb (he'd scored four out of six on those, so far) and no one could turn a reproachful eye on me. After tomorrow, he was on his own.

Tomorrow, as it turned out, was a long day. I had a premonition that it was going to be when the truck came to pick me up at first light to catch the morning train out of Edinburgh; there, snuggled up by the tailboard, and looking like the last man off the beach at Dunkirk, was the original Calamity Jock himself. By his hideous snuffling, and the fact that he appeared to be in the terminal stages of pneumonia, I deduced that he had spent his last night in the Army celebrating; he was so hung over you could have pegged him on a line. He gave me a ghastly, red-rimmed grin as I threw my valise over the tailboard, and croaked:

'Hullaw, rerr, sir.'

'Morning, McAuslan. How are you?'

'Smashin', sir.' He coughed retchingly, plucked a mangled cigarette end from the corner of his mouth, and wheezed: 'Goad, Ah'll hiv tae give these up. Hey, but, we're gettin' oor tickets the day, aren't we, sir?'

'That's right,' I said, and beat a hasty retreat to the front cab. I had no desire to encourage conversation with a McAuslan who would become increasingly garrulous as he emerged from his excesses of the night before. There was a long train journey to the demobilisation centre at York, and while I was nominally in charge of the party – there were four other Jocks in the back with McAuslan – the farther I could stay away from him the better I'd like it. If you think my non-fraternising policy deplorable, I can only reply that you haven't seen McAuslan drying out. For that matter, you wouldn't seek his company if he was stone-cold sober.

The truck rolled off, and I imagine we had gone all of thirty yards before he fell over the tailboard. It transpired that he thought he had forgotten his kitbag, had risen in alarm, and toppled shrieking into the void. He was crawling out of a deep puddle like some monster emerging from Jurassic swamps, vituperating horribly, when we picked him up and bundled him into the truck again, his companions handling him gingerly.

'Tak' yer hands aff ma body!' was all the thanks they got.

'Look at the state ye've got me in! Me in ma best battle-dress, too! Lookarit! Covered in glaur!'

If anything, I'd have said immersion in the puddle had cleaned it slightly; his best battle-dress, so-called, would have evoked cries of revulsion along Skid Row. He subsided in the truck, grunting and mumping and pawing the water from the greasy line of medal ribbons tacked above his left breast-pocket, from which the button was inevitably missing. As I retrieved a sodden packet of Woodbines from the puddle where he had dropped it, I had a sudden thought.

'McAuslan,' I said, 'have you got your travel warrant and paybooks?' One thing I didn't need was McAuslan without the documents necessary to speed him smoothly out of my life.

He suspended his toilet to rummage, breathing heavily, and produced from the recesses of his clothing two tattered lumps of paper, like very old manuscripts that have lain neglected in a damp tomb; they proved to be his Army paybooks, parts 1 and 2. But no travel warrant; he goggled dirtily when I demanded where it was, wiped his nose, and said he didnae know aboot that, but. So we had to wait, and I stamped impatiently and consulted my watch, while one of the Jocks ran back to company office, and by sheer luck returned with the warrant, which McAuslan had neglected to draw from the clerk.

'Keep it, Sempill,' I told the Jock. 'Don't let it, or him, out of your sight. You,' I snarled at McAuslan, 'sit still, or so help me I'll turn you over to the redcaps for . . . for conduct prejudicial to good order and military discipline, and you'll never get out of the Army, see?'

'Yessir. Right sir. No' kiddin', sir.' The threat obviously got through to him. He was poking at the contents of his Woodbine packet; a few dripping little cylinders rapidly disintegrating into mush in his palm. 'See ma bluidy fags.'

'Oh, Lord,' I said, 'take these.' And I thrust my cigarette packet into his hand, and ran to the cab. We broke the speed limit all the way up Leith Walk, and arrived at Waverley Station in the nick of time to catch the train. McAuslan was last aboard, roaring in panic as he retrieved his kitbag, which had somehow slipped half-down between train and platform as we moved off. From my carriage window I saw bag and man being dragged to safety by his mates; imagine King Kong on the Empire State Building, wearing a balmoral bonnet and being enveloped in rising clouds of steam, and you have the picture.

I can't say I enjoyed that journey. Travel in British trains in the immediate post-war period was slow, uncomfortable, and involved frequent clanking halts in the middle of nowhere. It seemed inevitable that McAuslan would take it into his head to descend at one of these, and rootle under the wheels, or take off into the wilds of Berwickshire, or pull the communication cord. I stood nervously in the corridor all the way to Newcastle, being trampled and shoved and leaned on – you didn't expect to get a seat in those days – and waiting for the noises of alarm and excursion to break out farther down the train, where he and his associates were. But he was reserving his energies, apparently, for when we got over the border.

Once we reached England, he began to exhibit his best form; his hangover had presumably receded. During the halt at Newcastle he lost his bonnet in the men's lavatory and started an altercation in the refreshment room where, he alleged, they were trying to short-change him over the price of a pie and a cup of tea. (Since he could barely count beyond five, I wasn't prepared to take his word for it.) At Durham he tried to climb, smoking and coughing thunderously, into a nonsmoker, whence he was ejected by an indignant dowager. He called her a cheeky auld bizzum and she threatened to complain to his commanding officer. (I was in the adjacent corridor, averting my gaze and trying to look inconspicuous.) At Darlington, where I allowed him one pint of beer at his earnest request, I was silly enough to take my eye off him, and when the guard's whistle blew he was nowhere to be seen. Fortunately the train did one of those hesitant starts, clanking a few yards and stopping, and our frantic search eventually discovered him on another platform, wrestling with one of those little football machines, all encased in glass, in which two teams of tiny metal men kick at a ball in response to little levers which you work on the outside. Beautifully ugly little Victorian creations, which seem to have vanished now. McAuslan, full of animation, was yanking the handle and roaring: 'Come away the Rangairs! Itsa goal! Aw, Wullie Waddell, he's the wee boy!'

We pried him loose, ignoring his cries that he was entitled to his penny back, and just managed to get him into the guard's van.

At York, which we reached in the afternoon, we parted. The Jocks were taken off by a warrant officer, and I went to the officers' mess, relieved in the knowledge that McAuslan would spend his last two hours in the Army under competent military control.

'See yez at the kittin'-oot centre,' said he as we went our separate ways, and I confess to a momentary hope that we might miss each other; for all the attachment that had grown up between us in our chequered acquaintance, I'd had, on the whole, just about enough.

It's one of the tricks of memory that all I can remember of my actual demobilisation is playing table billiards in the mess while waiting for the formalities to begin; of the process which turned me from a trusty friend of King George into a civilian I can recall nothing, beyond signing something, and being given a small booklet which was my actual discharge, and informed me that I was entitled to keep the permanent title of lieutenant, to wear my uniform for one more month, if I wanted to, and to consider myself a Reservist Class A. They thanked me, politely, and told me that if I followed the signs in the corridor I would arrive at the kitting-out centre, where I would be issued with civilian clothes, the gift of the Government.

It was a huge place, like an aircraft hangar, with row upon row of counters, and suits hanging on racks, and great square cardboard boxes. There were armies of little men helping the newly-fledged civilians to make their choice, and great throngs of figures in various stages of khaki undress wandering about, rather bewildered, feeling the material as though they didn't quite believe it was there. I remember a stout captain in the Loyals, in his vest and service dress trousers, doubtfully examining a civilian shirt and saying that he didn't care for stripes, actually, and a grizzled little corporal of Sherwood Foresters comparing a thick grey Army issue sock in one hand, and a dark blue civilian one in the other; his bare feet were thrust into black civilian shoes.

I took two shirts – any shirts – and collars, and a brass stud from the tray provided, and walked round to where the suits were. They were mostly brown and blue, and a long line of men in their underclothes were struggling into trousers, and adjusting braces, and queuing up for the long mirrors, in front of which they stood looking rather embarrassed, turning this way and that and patting their stomachs, while the rest of us waited our turn. The only thing in common was the close-cropped Army hair-style; for the rest there were pale-looking men who had spent their service in stores and offices, and bronzed mahogany muscle-men from the Far East and the North African garrisons – the man in front of me, bronzed and bare to the waist, had a crude blue-and-red tattoo on his arm, showing a knife impaling a skull, with underneath 'Death Before Disonour' (one spelling mistake for a Hogg Market tattooist wasn't bad). Underneath his right shoulder, when he turned, was the white star-shape of a bullet wound, and I speculated on whether it was the Jap 300 rifle that had done it, and where – anywhere between Silchar Track and the Pegu

Yomas, probably. Behind me was a stout and impatient ex-warrant officer, holding in his belly under the unaccustomed brown worsted trousers, and muttering: 'Bloody army, bloody organisation, can't even get rid of us decently. Have you seen the quality of this rubbish? I wouldn't give it for a blanket to our dog.'

The strange thing was, where you would have expected cheerful chatter and laughter, from men who had travelled hopefully for so long, and were now arriving, there was very little noise at all; indeed, they seemed quietly irritable, as though the bleak utility of the new civilian clothing was symbolic, and they didn't much like the look of it. Was this what civvy street was going to be like?

On a long table to one side lay the battle-dress jackets of those waiting to try their new suits; I wish I had a picture of it. There were the shoulder flashes – Buffs, Green Howards, Durhams, Ox and Bucks, Devons, K.O.Y.L.I., North Staffords, King's Own, the yellow lion of the Scottish Division, the shoulder flash of the Sappers, the red and blue of the Artillery, the Welsh black pigtail flash, and my own green and yellow strip of tartan; the blancoed stripes and the cloth officers' pips; the little red service chevrons, the Tate and Lyle badge of a regimental sergeant-major; the glittering crown and stripes of a colour-sergeant. And the ribbons – the well-known 'Spam' of 1939–45, the yellowish rectangle of North Africa, the tricolour of France and Germany, the green-striped ribbon of the Italian campaign, the watered colours of the Atlantic Star, and the red-yellow-blue of Burma. And the badges in the caps – the Britannia of the Royal Norfolks, who alone can take a lady into barracks; the back-to-back of the Gloucesters, the red hackle of the Black Watch, the St Andrew's Cross of the Camerons ('two crossed bars o' quarter-master's soap wi' auld Wimberley keekin' ower the top,' as the pipey used to say); the Maltese Cross of the Border Regiment, the flag-carrying lamb of the

Queen's, the brown cockade of Ulster, and the white horse of Hanover. A lot of service, a lot of time; a lot of long hot and cold marches to battles whose echoes had died away, and the owners, who had spent so many years earning the little badges, were now devoting all their minds to trouser-creases and shoulder-padding.

Most of them at least had some idea of what they ought to look like, from their dim recollections of prewar days; I didn't. As I pulled up my reddish-brown herring-bone trousers – they seemed ridiculously loose and flappy – I realised that I had never worn a formal suit in my life. At school it had been blazer and flannels, and my kilt on Sundays. I tried the waistcoat and jacket and decided I looked like a Victorian commercial traveller. Still, it would do; I gave way to the ex-W.O. behind me, who bustled up to the mirror and exclaimed, 'God sake, more like a bleedin' kitbag with string round the middle than a bloody suit. There's room for the whole bleedin' Pioneer Corps in the crotch o' this lot.'

I recovered my battle-dress jacket and kilt and went to try on a hat. They were trilbys, brown and blue, each with a tiny coloured feather peeping pathetically over the band. A stout, moustachioed Irish sergeant laid aside his rakish bonnet with its coffee-coloured plume, and placed a grey pork-pie on his cropped skull. He gulped at his reflection, and turned to me:

'Jayzus, will you look at that! The bloody silly things they expect a man to put on his head.'

He must have thought exactly the same thing about his cockaded bonnet, once – but over the years he had grown into it, so to speak, his whiskers and personality had expanded with it, and now the civilian headgear looked ludicrous. He twitched it off and wandered off moodily in search of something else.

I tried on a hat; it felt and looked foolish and – what was the word? – trivial. Like the Ulsterman, I'd got used to the extravagance of military fashion. Why, in succession over the years I'd worn the rakishly-tilted forage cap, the tin hat, the old solar topee, the magnificent broad-brimmed bush hat of the Fourteenth Army (which isn't just a hat, really, but a sort of portable umbrella-cum-hotel, with a razor-blade tucked into the band), the white-trimmed cap of the Indian Army cadet, the Highland tam-o'-shanter, and the red-and-white diced glengarry with its fluttering tails. Surprising, in the austere atmosphere of a modern war. And now, this insignificant thing with its tiny brim, perched foolishly above my ears. It didn't even make me look like a gangster.

I stuffed it hurriedly into the big cardboard box I'd been given, adding it to the pile I'd collected. Shirts, shoes, socks, a quietish brown tie – I noticed that everyone else was doing the same thing. Nobody was going to venture out in his civvy duds – they would wear their uniforms at least until they got home, and gradually transform themselves into civilians. (Remember how on building sites, even well into the 1950s, you would see workmen putting on old, worn battle-dress jackets after their day's work, or faded blue R.A.F. tunics? Others, like me, hung them away in cupboards to keep the moths happy, and tried them on twenty years after, puffing hopelessly as we tried to make them meet across middle-aged spread.)

I had resumed my uniform, and was tying up my box with string, when a voice floated over from behind a long rack of blue suits.

'Name o' Goad,' it was saying. 'Hi, Mac, this a' ye've got? Nae glamour pants? Nae long jaickets? An' no' a pair o' two-toned shoes in the place! Ye expect me to go oot wearin' one o' these b'iler suits?'

I should have hurried away, but the sight of McAuslan playing Beau Brummel was too good to miss. I peeped cautiously round the end of the rack, and felt like Cortez when with eagle eyes he gazed on the Pacific.

McAuslan was surveying himself in a mirror, striking what he imagined to be a pose appropriate to a man about town; either that or he was trying to keep his trousers up with no hands. He was crouching slightly forward, arms back, like a swimmer preparing for a racing dive. On the back of his head was a brown pork-pie hat, in tasteful contrast to the dark blue serge trousers which were clinging, by surface tension, presumably, to his withers, and depending baggily to his calves – he still had his army boots on, I noticed – and the final flamboyant touch was provided by the identity discs on a dirty string which he still wore over a new civilian shirt and collar.

'Bluidy awfu',' he remarked at last, to a weary-looking counterman. 'Nae drape at a'. Youse fellas arenae in touch. The bottom o' the breeks ought tae hang casual-like, ower the boots. See this lot – ma feet's just stickin' oot the end like a pair o' candles oot o' jeely-jars.'

'Who the hell d'you think you are?' said the counterman. 'Ray Milland?'

'Watch it,' said McAuslan warningly, and waggled his feet to turn so that he could get a different view. This achieved the sought-after casual break of the trousers over the instep, inasmuch as the whole lot fell around his ankles, and he cursed and staggered about.

'You'll pay for that lot, if you damage them!' cried the counterman. 'For God's sake, how can you try them on without braces? Here, let's sort you out.' And between them they hauled up the trousers, adjusted the braces, and considered the result.

'Hellish,' was McAuslan's verdict. 'The cut's diabolical. See – ma flies is doon at ma bluidy knees.'

'Monsieur hasn't really got the figure, has he?' said the counterman, a humorist in his way. 'You don't happen to have a third buttock, or something, do you?'

'None o' yer lip,' said McAuslan, outraged. 'Ah didnae dae six years sojerin' just tae get pit oot in the street lookin' like Charlie Chaplin. Fair does – could Ah go jiggin' at the Barrowland or Green's Playhoose in the like o' these?'

'Depends whether they go in for fancy dress,' said the counterman, and McAuslan, turning in wrath, caught sight of me watching in stricken fascination. His gargoyle face lit up, and he cried:

'Hi, Mr MacNeill! Jist the man! Gie's a hand tae get sortit oot here, sir, wull ye? This fella's got nae idea.'

Well, heaven knew I wasn't short of practice in rendering the subject fit for public scrutiny; after two years of 'sortin' oot' McAuslan I could have valeted Gollum. I helped to adjust his trousers, approved the fit of his jacket, joined in deploring the fact that it had 'nae vents up the back; they're a' the rage wi' the wide boys', and assisted in the selection of a tie. This took a good twenty minutes, while I marvelled that the man who had been notoriously the scruffiest walking wreck in the ranks of the Western Allies should be so fastidious in his choice of neckwear.

'Nae style,' he sniffed, and wiped his nose. 'But it'll hiv tae do till I get doon the Barras.' (The Barrows is a market in down-town Glasgow where you can buy anything.) 'It's no bad, but.' And he pawed with grubby fingers at the muted grey tie which the counterman and I had suggested. 'Whit d'ye think, sir?'

'Not bad at all,' I said, and meant it. In a way, it was quite eery; there was McAuslan's dirty face, frowning earnestly from under the brim of a neat trilby, with the rest of him most respectably concealed in a blue serge suit which, considering that he was built along the lines of an orang-utan, fitted him surprisingly well. If you'd held him still, and scrubbed his face and hands hard with surgical spirit, he'd have looked quite good. Not that *Esquire* would have been bidding for his services, but he was certainly passable. I guessed that five minutes would be all he'd need to turn his new apparel into something fit for scaring birds, but just at the moment he looked more presentable than I'll swear he'd ever been in his life before.

He seemed to think so, too, for after shambling about a bit in front of the mirror, peering malevolently, he expressed himself satisfied – just.

'Ah'll tak' it,' he remarked, with the resigned air of a Regency buck overcome with ennui. 'But the shoulders isnae padded worth a tosser.'

I'd thought he would want to stride forth in his new finery, but he insisted on packing it all into the box, and resuming his befouled and buttonless battle-dress tunic, his stained kilt, puttees, and boots, which restored him to the dishevelled and insanitary condition I knew so well.

'Nae doot aboot it, uniform's more smarter,' he observed, adjusting his bonnet to the authentic coal-heaver slant over the brows. I caught sight of myself, watching him in the mirror, and was startled to see that I was smiling almost wistfully.

'Right,' said he, 'we're aff. Be seein' ye, china,' he added to the counterman, and we made our way out into the open air, carrying our new clothes in their fine cardboard boxes. In addition I had my ashplant and a small suitcase; McAuslan humphed along with his kitbag over his shoulder.

My train, a local to Carlisle, was due to leave in about an hour; McAuslan – after I had consulted time-tables on his behalf and checked his warrant – would have to catch a later train going through to Glasgow. I don't remember how we got to the station, but I know it was a beautiful golden August evening, and the streets were busy and the pavements crowded with people making their way home. There was time to kill, so I said to him:

'I didn't get any lunch, did you?'

'Couple o' wads'n a pie.'

'Fancy a cup of tea?'

'Aye, no' hauf. Jist dae wi' a mug o' chah. Thanks very much, sir.'

We made our way towards a café beside the station, and I said,

'You don't call me "sir" any more, you know. We're civilians now.'

This seemed to surprise him. He thought about it, and said:

'That's right, innit? Aye, we're oot.' He shook his head. ''Magine that. It's gaunae be . . . kinda funny, innit? Bein' in civvy street. Wonder whit it's gaunae be like, eh?'

'We'll find out,' I said. 'Let's get in the queue.' The café, short-staffed as most places were in the post-war, operated on the self-service principle, with two perspiring waitresses dispensing tea and buns at a counter. 'No, hold on,' I said. 'You bag a table and I'll get the teas.' And while McAuslan gathered up our kit, I moved quickly to the end of the queue, just getting there before a bullet-headed private in the King's Liverpool.

'Bleedin' soldiers in skirts,' he muttered taking his place behind me, and as I turned to stare at him I realised I'd seen him in the demob centre earlier; sure enough, he too was carrying a cardboard box. Our eyes met, and he gave me a defiant stare.

'Awright, wack,' he said truculently. 'Doan't think you can throw those aboot any longer.' And he indicated my pips. 'Ah doan't give a —— for officers, me; niver did, see?'

There was no answer to it, now; I didn't have the Army Act behind me any longer, and any embittered ex-soldier could give me all the lip he liked. So I fell back on personality, and tried to stare him down, like a Sabatini hero quelling the canaille with a single imperious glance. It didn't work, of course; he just grinned insolently back, enjoying himself, and jeered:

'Go on, then, *leff*-tenant. What you gonna do aboot it?'

I had no idea, fortunately, or I might have done something rash. And at that moment McAuslan was at my elbow, smoothing over the incident diplomatically.

'Bugger off, scouse,' he said, 'or Ah'll breathe on ye.'

'You'll what?' scoffed the Liverpool man, and McAuslan came in, jaw out-thrust.

'Hold it!' I said, and got between them. 'Ease off, McAuslan. If our friend here wants to get cheeky with a fellow-civilian, he's entitled to. And if the fellow-civilian decides to belt the hell out of him,' I went on, turning to the scouse, 'that's all right, too, isn't it? You can't throw these pips at me either, son. All right?'

It startled him – it startled me, for that matter, but it worked. He muttered abuse, and I turned my back on him, and McAuslan hovered, offering, in a liberal way, to put the boot in, and gradually their discussion tailed off in dirty looks, as these things will. I collected our teas, and we got a table by the window, McAuslan still simmering indignantly.

'Pit the heid on him, nae bother,' he muttered, as we sat down. 'Bluidy liberty, talkin' tae you like that.'

'It's a free country,' I said. 'Forget it.'

'Aye, but –' he frowned earnestly. 'Ye see whit it is; he knows you cannae peg him any longer, an' he's jist takin' advantage. That's whit he wis doin', the ——'

'Cheers,' I said, smiling. 'Drink your tea.' McAuslan might not be a fast thinker, but when he grasped the implications of a situation he liked to explain them to feebler minds. To change the subject I asked:

'What are you going to do when you get home?'

He took an audible sip of tea and looked judicious. 'Aye, weel, Ah'll tak' a look roon', see whit's daein'. Ye know. Ah'm no' hurryin' mysel'. Gaunae take it easy for a bit.'

'You live with your aunt, don't you?' I remembered that the

platoon roll had given 'Mrs J. M. Cairns, aunt' as his next-of-kin; also, irrelevantly, that his religion was Presbyterian and his boots size 8.

''At's right. She's got a hoose in Ronald Street. Ah don't know, but; I might get a place mysel'.'

'How about a job?'

'Aye.' He looked doubtful. 'Ah wis on the burroo afore the war' – that is, drawing unemployment pay – 'but Ah done some pipe-scrapin' up at Port Dundas, an' Ah wis wi' an asphalter for a bit. No' bad pey, but Ah didnae like workin' wi' tar. Gets in yer hair an' yer claes somethin' hellish.' His face brightened. 'But Ah'm no' worryin' for a bit. Ah'll tak' my time. There's this fella I know in the Garngad; Ah could get a job wi' him, if the money's right.' He gave an expansive gesture which knocked over his tea-cup; with a blistering oath he pawed at it, and overturned my cup as well. In the ensuing confusion I hurriedly went for two fresh cups, leaving him apologising luridly and mopping up with his bonnet.

'Awfy sorry aboot that,' he said when I returned, 'makin' a mess a' ower the place. Clumsy – that's whit the R.S.M. used to say. 'Ye're handless, McAuslan.' Put the fear o' death in me, he did.'

'Well, he won't do that any more,' I said.

'Naw. That's right.' He took a gulp of tea, and sighed. 'He was a good man, but, that Mackintosh. He was gae decent tae me.' And he looked across at me. 'So wis you. So wis Sarn't Telfer, an' Captain Bennet-Bruce . . .'

'This is worse than Naafi tea, isn't it?' I said, and he agreed, remarking that he could have produced better himself, through the digestive process. Then suddenly he asked,

'Whit ye gaunae do in civvy street yersel', sir?'

'Newspapers,' I said. 'I'm going to be a reporter.'

'Zattafact?' He beamed. 'Here, that'll be rerr. Goin' tae the fitba' matches – free?'

'Probably.'

'An' – an', interviewin' fillum stars?' he went on, his imagination taking wing.

'Well, I shouldn't think –'

'– an' gettin' the goods on the bad bastards in the corporation, like Alan Ladd in the pictures! Here, that's a gran' joab! Ah could jist be daein' wi' that.' You could see him envisaging himself perched on the corner of an editor's desk, with his hat tilted back, addressing Veronica Lake as 'baby'.

'Aye, but,' he added, and fell silent, and I knew what he was thinking. He had come into the Army illiterate, and in spite of the Education Sergeant's perseverance, he was going out not much better. He frowned at his cup. 'Ah doubt Ah wouldnae be up tae it, though.' He drank again. 'Ah'll jist see whit's daein'.'

I looked across at him, scruffy and hunched over his cup, and had a sudden picture of thirty years on, and saw him as one of these seedy wee Glasgow men one encounters coming out of pubs – the threadbare coat, the dirty white scarf knotted to conceal the absence of collar (and sometimes of shirt), the broken shoes, the thin greying hair defiantly brushed, and still with a gamin jauntiness in the way they shuffle along, looking this way and that with their bright, beaten eyes. And I had a thought that choked me – of the heat and dust and thunder of Alamein, and the flower of the finest military machine ever to come out of the Continent being broken and scattered, and chased out of Africa, and I felt a terrible anger at – at I don't know what. The world, or the system, or something. My hand was shaking, I know, as I put down my cup.

It subsided after a moment or two, while I carefully drank my tea, into an uncomfortable feeling that was half annoyance and half embarrassment. I can't define it, even now. I suppose it sprang from all I knew about McAuslan, and all the trouble and alarm and impatience and fury he had caused me, and the responsibility I'd carried for him. But in the past I'd always known what to do about it; we had been bound rigidly inside the Army framework. Now that was all over, but the feelings were still there, without the means to cope with them – or with him. I was worried about him – God knew he hadn't been fit, most of the time, to go about unattended in uniform; what he would be like in civilian life, with no one to watch him, and berate and bully him and pick up the can for him, I couldn't imagine. Strictly speaking, it was none of my business; it was almost impertinent to think that it was. But responsibility doesn't just end – or if it does, the feeling of it doesn't.

'Here,' I said, 'I'll have to shift myself if I'm to catch that train.' I shoved a threepenny bit under my cup and started to collect my things, knowing that I couldn't just go off and leave it as it was. Without really thinking, while we both got up and made the preliminary noises of farewell, I pulled out my pen and a scrap of paper, and scribbled my home address. It was just a gesture; I had no connections, I couldn't offer any constructive help, and I knew it. But it seemed the least I could do.

'That's my home, and phone number,' I said, with a momentary qualm at the thought of what McAuslan might do to the internal economy of the G.P.O. if he tried to make a telephone call. 'If there's anything I can do . . . you know, any time, if you think I can help, or . . . I mean, you need any . . . I mean, have any problems . . .' I was making a right hash of it, I realised. 'Anyway, that's where I am.'

'Oh, ta,' he said. 'Very nice of ye.' And he took the paper, handling it reverently, as he always did when confronted with the mysteries. But there was an odd expression on his rumpled face as he looked at it, a trace of that slow, dawning self-assertion that I remembered before his court-martial, a slight tilt of his head as he looked at me, a stiffening of the Palaeolithic frame.

'Thanks very much,' he said. 'But yez don't need tae worry aboot me. Not at a'. Ah'll be fine; nae bother.' It wasn't anything like a snub, just a self-respecting reminder of what I'd said myself earlier; that we were both civilians now. I could have kicked myself for my clumsiness, and tried to shrug off my embarrassment.

'You know,' I said, 'it would be nice to . . . to keep in touch.'

God, I thought, what am I saying? Keep in touch with McAuslan; the mind boggled.

'Och, sure,' he said, jauntily. 'We'll be around.'

We were outside the café by this time; the station entrance was just along the way.

'Well,' I said, and held out my hand. 'Good luck, McAuslan.' And why I added it, I don't know, but I said: 'Thanks for everything.' It was not a statement that could be defended on any logical ground, but I meant it.

'Och,' he said, 's'been nice knowin' ye. Orrabest, sir.'

We shook, and picked up our parcels.

'Aye, weel,' he said, 'Ah'll jist tak' a dauner roon the toon afore my train goes.'

'Mind you don't miss it.'

'Nae fears,' he said, and with a nod set off down the pavement towards a pedestrian crossing, cardboard box in one hand, kitbag on the other shoulder – bauchling jauntily along, with one hose-top already wrinkling down to his ankle, his scruffy kilt swinging. I watched him go, slightly sad, but – I must confess it honestly – with considerable relief. I knew he wouldn't get in touch – even if he wanted to, the mechanics of the thing would defeat him. I just hoped the world would be kind to him, the sturdy, handless misfit, with his bonnet cocked at a pathetically jaunty angle, and the other hose-top now descending to join the first.

He turned on to the crossing, and I moved off to the station entrance, and just as I reached it there was a hideous shriek of brakes from behind me, a woman screamed in alarm, someone shouted, and I looked round to see a lorry half-slewed round on the crossing, and under its near front wheel a cardboard box, squashed flat. For an instant my heart died, and then to my relief I saw him, skipping like a startled sloth from under the very bonnet, his kitbag falling to the pavement, where its top burst, scattering the contents among the pedestrians.

There were oaths and cries, mainly from McAuslan, standing raging in the gutter, while a red-faced driver leaned from the lorry's cab, hurling abuse at him. Phrases like 'bloody daft jay-walker, where the 'ell d'you think you're goin'?' and 'You in yer bluidy van, ye near kilt me!' floated on the summer evening air. Then the driver was descending from his cab, McAuslan was stooping to gather the gruesome litter that had fallen from his bag, and at the same time was directing a flood of colourful invective over his shoulder.

'Ah wis oan the crossin', ye daft midden!'

'Nowhere bloody near it! Niver even looked! Just come slap across t'road!'

'Away, you, an' bile yer can!'

'Think you own t'bloody street, then?'

On the pavements, people had stopped. So had the traffic, with the lorry blocking one side of the road, and horns were honking. A small crowd was gathering, as McAuslan, still exchanging personalities with the driver, scooped up his effects and stuffed them into his bag. A policeman was approaching – no, there were two policemen, and a bus conductor, who by his gestures appeared to be prepared to offer evidence.

I watched, fascinated. My first instinct was to go to the scene of the upheaval, naturally, but then I checked. No one was hurt, there was nothing to it; the disorderly idiot had just managed to put his foot in it again, and there was no useful purpose to be served by interfering. I watched the gendarmes arrive with official calm, while the lorry driver, full of virtuous outrage, stated his case, and McAuslan, protesting vehemently, pointed to the squashed ruins of the box beneath the wheel.

'Ma new suit! Ma new civvy shoes! Look at yon! Hoo the hell am Ah gaunae be able to wear them noo? Him an' his bluidy van . . .' With his bonnet gone, his hose-tops down, his face contorted with misery and rage, and his tunic and kilt looking as though they were joining in the general depression, he was a woeful sight to see. 'Ah'm no' hivin' this! Yon man's a road-hog! He near did for me, so he did!'

One of the policemen was ushering him back across the pavement; the other was directing the driver to get his van in to the side. One of the small throng watching stepped forward and picked up McAuslan's kitbag, unfortunately by the wrong end, and the contents came cascading out again. And I froze as I saw, among the litter of unwashed laundry and oil-smeared clothing, the unmistakable brassy glitter of rounds of .303 ammunition, tinkling away across the pavement.

'Oh, no!' I exclaimed aloud, as the second policeman stooped and picked up one of the rounds in one hand – and the old sword bayonet in the other – looked at them, and then at McAuslan, and then drew himself up purposefully.

I didn't waste time wondering how he'd got live ammunition in his luggage; souvenirs, maybe – he was idiot enough. It wouldn't have surprised me if that kitbag had also contained several live grenades and a two-inch mortar. Sufficient that he had got himself into dire trouble, and the Law were taking out their notebooks, while the protesting author of the scene was backed against the wall, roaring:

'Keep the heid! Whit aboot yon lorry-driver then? Ah'm no' hivin' it! The man's a menace . . .'

The lorry-driver had come back to watch, and doubtless contribute his quota, the small crowd were looking on astonished, amused, intrigued. The second policeman was holding out a handful of live rounds, speaking sternly, and the ape-like, hounded wretch in the middle was protesting violently and obviously wishing he could burrow under the wall.

I had taken a half-pace forward, and stopped. What did I think I was going to do, anyway? Conditioned by years of sorting things out for McAuslan, standing between him and authority, taking responsibility for him, I had been about to intervene. And then the wonderful realisation flashed across my mind. It wasn't my place to, any longer. Three hours ago it would have been my bounden duty – and now? Legally speaking, I was no longer responsible for McAuslan's random wanderings in front of lorries, for his offering insulting language, for his being illegally in possession of Army property, to wit, live ammunition, or for his resistance to arrest which would probably follow. I had no longer any right to interfere. He was his own man, now, and it would be sheer patronising officiousness to pretend otherwise. I was (as his own attitude had reminded me) a mere civilian, with no authority over him. 'It's nothing to do with me,' I actually said aloud, and a passerby looked curiously at me. And dammit, while I might feel a sentimental concern for him, responsibility was something else. Besides, I knew from bitter experience what getting involved with McAuslan was like; there was no future in it. He was free, white (well, greyish) and twenty-one, let him fight his own battles for a change, and – and I had a train to catch in three minutes.

So I swore, and shook my head for the thousandth time, turned to a military policeman in the station entrance and said: 'Would you mind keeping an eye on my things for a moment, corporal?' And then I pulled down my bonnet, took a firm grip on my ashplant, said 'Oh, hell' with deep weariness, and like a man reshouldering an enormous burden, but with a strange lightness of heart, strode off purposefully towards the group on the other side of the road.

THE SHEIKH AND THE DUSTBIN

The Servant Problem

One of the things I never learned from my tough grandmother (the golfing Calvinist, not the Hebridean saga-woman) was how to deal with domestic help, and this although she was an authority, having been both servant and mistress in her time. As a girl, straight from the heather, she had been engaged as kitchenmaid at one of those great Highland shooting lodges to which London society used to repair a century ago, and being a Glencoe MacDonald of critical temper and iron will, she had taken one cold Presbyterian look at the establishment with its effete southern guests and large inefficient staff and decided, like Napoleon contemplating the map of Europe, that this would never do. Within six weeks she had become senior housemaid, by the end of the season she was linen-mistress, and before her twentieth birthday she was head housekeeper and absolute ruler of the place, admired and dreaded by guests and staff alike. I can only guess what she was like as a teenage châtelaine, but since in old age she reminded you of a mobile Mount Rushmore, handsome, imposing, and with a heart of stone, it is a safe bet that living in that lodge must have been like being a galley slave in a luxury liner. Knowing her zeal for order and reform, I suspect that her aim would be that of an enlightened prison governor – not to break the spirit of the inmates altogether, but to see that they went back into the world better and wiser human beings.

Whatever effect she had on those sophisticated ladies and worldly gentlemen – and I'm sure she taught them that there were higher things in life than grouse-shooting and flirtation – they can have been in no doubt that the Highland servant, whether lowly menial or autocratic housekeeper, was very different from the southern domestic. My grandmother was not alone in her generation in simply not knowing what servility meant; indeed, mere civility was no commonplace, as witness the famous John Brown, whose devotion to Queen Victoria was matched only by his rudeness. My grandmother, who gave respect only when she felt it was due, which wasn't often, used to recall (without a glimmer of a smile) an event from her early years in service when the lodge's head cook, another stern Caledonian, noted for her prowess at whist drives, was called in by her employers to take part in a bridge game, there being a shortage of players among the guests. As luck had it, the cook partnered a Prince of the blood, who took mild exception to her bidding, whereon the cook rose in her wrath before the Quality assembled, and hurled down her cards, exclaiming: 'Away, ye crabbit auld Prooshan, and play by yersel'!' Nor was she dismissed; a Prince may be a Prince, but a Highland cook who knows the secrets of venison and cold salmon is something else.

It may be significant, too, that grandmother's only joke was based on the English master–Highland servant relationship. It described how a chimpanzee escaped from the circus and was found dead in a ditch by two ghillies employed at the local castle, then occupied by a London shooting-party. The ghillies had never seen a chimpanzee before, and didn't know what to make of it. At last the elder said: 'It's ower hairy for a MacPherson, no' broad enough in the chest for a Fraser, and too long in the lip for a Cameron – away you up to the big hoose, Erchie, and see if ony o' the gentry's missing.'

[I told that joke in the mess once, with mixed success: the Padre worked it, with Gaelic subtlety, into a sermon, but the second-in-command looked puzzled and asked: 'And was anyone from the big house missing? No? Oh . . . bit of a mystery then, what?']

However, you will note that there are two butts of the joke – the foreign gentry and the ignorant ghillies – which says something about grandmother's outlook on life. Her censure knew no class boundaries; dukes and dustmen alike (and grandsons) had to be kept in their place, and she was the woman to do it, even when she was very old. My heart bled for her own maidservants when, as a small boy, I used to visit her home, that still, immaculate domain with its softly-chiming clock, redolent of beeswax and lavender, all swept and polished to perfection. I lived on tiptoe there, giving ornaments a wide berth, wondering at her bookshelves where Cruden's *Concordance* and Bunyan's *Holy War* lay beside long outdated fashion magazines from Paris, pushing in my chair to the exact inch when I received the almost imperceptible nod of dismissal from the stately, white-haired figure at the end of the table, straight and stiff as her own ebony walking-cane; dreading the cold eye and sharp, quiet voice, even when they were addressed to her maids and not to me. How they endured her, I'll never know; perhaps they knew what I sensed as an infant: like her or not, you could be *sure* of her, and that is a quality that can count far beyond mere kindness.

Anyway, with that background I ought to have mastered the servant problem, but I never have, not from either side. On the occasions when I have had to serve, I have been a disaster, whether shirking my fagging duties at school, or burning toast, dropping plates, and letting the cookhouse boiler go out as a mess orderly and assistant scullion at Bellahouston Camp, Glasgow. Nor am I one of nature's aristocrats, born to be ministered to and accepting it as my due; anything but. I hate being waited on; servants rattle me. I find their attentions embarrassing, and they know it, damn them. There was a butler once, about seven feet tall, with a bald head and frock coat, who received me at a front door; he looked me up and down and said: 'Good morning, sir. Would you care to wash . . . at all?' I can't describe what he put into that pause before the two final words, but it implied that I was filthy beyond his powers of description. Nor am I deceived by the wine-waiter unctuously proffering his bottle for my inspection: this bum wouldn't know it from turpentine, is what he's thinking.

Such an advanced state of doulophobia is bad enough in civilian life; for an army officer it is serious, since he has to have a body-servant, or orderly, or batman, call it what you will, whether he likes it or not. This did not trouble me when I first encountered it as a cadet in India; we had native bearers who brought our morning tea, cleaned our kit and rooms, laid out our uniforms, dressed us on ceremonial occasions, and generally nannied us through a fourteen-hour day of such intensive activity that we couldn't have survived without them; there was even a *nappy-wallah* who shaved you as you sat bleary-eyed on the edge of your cot – and never have I had a chin so smooth. It seemed perfectly natural fifty years ago; it would not have seemed natural from a white servant – and before anyone from the race relations industry leaps in triumphantly with his labels, I should remark that the Indian cadets were of the same opinion (as often as not, so-called race prejudice is mere class distinction) and were, on the whole, less considerate masters than we were. My own bearer was called Timbooswami, son and grandson and great-grandson of bearers – and proud father of an Indian Army officer. So much for the wicked old British Raj.

My troubles began when I joined my Highland battalion in North Africa and had to have a batman from the ranks of my own platoon. No doubt I had been spoiled in India, but the contrast was dramatic. Where I had been accustomed to waking to the soft murmur of '*Chota hazri*, sahib', and having a *pialla* of perfectly-brewed tea and a sliced mango on my bedside table, there was now a crash of hob-nailed boots and a raucous cry of 'Erzi tea! Some o' it's spillt, an' there's nae sugar. Aye, an' the rain's oan again.' Not the same, somehow. And where once there had been a fresh-laundered shirt on a hanger, there was now a freckled Glaswegian holding up last night's garment in distaste and exclaiming: 'Whit in Goad's name ye been daein' in this? Look at the state o' it. Were ye fu', or whit? Aye, weel, it'll hiv tae dae – yer ither yins arenae back frae the *dhobi*. Unless he's refused them. Aye. Weel, ye gettin' up, or are ye gaunae lie there a' day . . . sur?'

That was Coulter. I got rid of him inside three days, and appealed to Telfer, my platoon sergeant, for a replacement. And I hate to record it, for I like to think well of Telfer, who was a splendid soldier, but he then did one of the most diabolic things any sergeant could do to his new, green, and trusting platoon commander. Without batting an eye, and with full knowledge of what he was doing, this veteran of Alamein and Anzio glanced at his platoon roll, frowned, and said: 'What about McAuslan?'

Innocent that I was, those doom-laden words meant nothing to me. I didn't know, then, that McAuslan was the dirtiest soldier in the world, a byword from Maryhill Barracks to the bazaars of Port Said for his foulness, stupidity, incompetence, illiteracy, and general unfitness for the service, an ill-made disaster whom Falstaff wouldn't have looked at, much less marched with through Coventry. This was the Tartan Caliban who had to be forcibly washed by his fellows and locked in cupboards during inspections, whom Telfer was wishing on me as batman. In fairness I can see that a sergeant might go to desperate lengths to keep McAuslan off parade and out of public view, but it was still a terrible thing to do to a subaltern not yet come of age.

I had seen McAuslan, of course – at least I had been aware

of a sort of uniformed yeti that lurked at the far end of the barrack-room or vanished round corners like a startled sloth at the approach of authority, which he dreaded; I had even heard his cry, a raucous snarl of complaint and justification, for beneath his unkempt exterior there was a proud and independent spirit, sensitive of abuse. He had fought in North Africa, mostly against the Germans, but with the Military Police on occasion; his crime-sheet was rich in offences of neglect and omission, but rarely of intentional mischief, for McAuslan had this virtue: he tried. In a way he was something of a platoon mascot; the other Jocks took a perverse pride in his awfulness, and wouldn't have parted with him.

Of all this I was happily ignorant at the time, and it gave me quite a start when I got my first view of him, crouched to attention in my doorway, eyeing me like a wary gargoyle preparing to wrestle; he always stood to attention like that, I was to discover; it was a gift, like his habit of swinging left arm and left leg in unison when marching. He appeared to be short in stature, but since he was never fully erect one couldn't be sure; his face was primitive and pimpled, partly obscured by hair hanging over an unwashed brow, his denims would have disgraced an Alexandrine beggar (and possibly had), but the crowning touch was the filthy napkin draped carelessly over one forearm – I believe now that he was trying to convince me that he had once been a waiter, and knew his business.

'14687347Pr'iteMcAuslansah!' he announced. 'Ah'm yer new batman, Sarn't Telfer sez. Whit'll Ah clean first?'

The smart answer to that would have been 'Yourself, and do it somewhere else', but I was a very new second-lieutenant.

'Ah brung ma cleanin' kit,' he went on, fishing a repulsive hold-all from inside his shirt. 'Oh, aye, it's a' here,' and he shook out on to the table a collection of noisome rags and old iron in which I recognised a battered Brasso tin, several bits of wire gauze and dried-up blanco, a toothbrush without bristles, and a stump of candle. (That last item shook me; was it possible, I wondered, that he performed his toilet by this illumination alone? It would have explained a lot.) It all looked as though it had been dredged from the Sweetwater Canal.

He made a sudden shambling pounce and snatched two rusted objects from the mess with a glad cry. 'Aw, there th'are! Goad, an' me lookin' a' ower the shop! Ah thought Ah'd loast them!' He beamed, wiping them vigorously on his shirt, adding a touch of colour.

'What are they?' I asked, not really wanting to know.

'Ma fork an' spoon! They musta got in there that time I wis givin' ma mess-tins a wee polish – ye hiv tae scoor them, sur, ye see, or ye get gingivitis an' a' yer teeth fa' oot, the M.O. sez.' He peered fondly at the rusting horrors, like an archaeologist with burial fragments. 'Here, that's great! It's been a dam' nuisance bein' wi'oot them at meal-times,' he added, conjuring up a picture so frightful that I closed my eyes. When I opened them again he was still there, frowning at my service dress, which was hanging outside the wardrobe.

'That's yer good kit,' he said, in the grim reflective tone in which Sir Henry Morgan might have said: 'That's Panama.' He took a purposeful shuffle towards it, and I sprang to bar his way.

'It's all right, McAuslan – it's fine, it's all clean and ready. I shan't need it until five-thirty, for Retreat.' I sought for some task that should keep him at a safe distance from my belongings. 'Look, why don't you sweep the floor – out in the passage? The sand keeps blowing in . . . and the windows haven't been washed for weeks; you could do them – from the outside,' I added hastily. 'And let's see . . . what else?' But he was shaking his matted head, all insanitary reproach.

'Ah'm tae clean yer kit,' he insisted. 'Sarn't Telfer sez. Ah've tae polish yer buttons an' yer buits an' yer Sam Broon an' yer stag's heid badge, an' brush yer tunic, an' press the pleats o' yer kilt, an' bell yer flashes wi' rolled-up newspaper, an' wash an' dry yer sporran, and see the *dhobi* starches an' irons yer shirts, an' melt the bastard if he disnae dae it right, an' mak' yer bed . . .' He had assumed the aspect of a dishevelled Priest of the Ape People chanting a prehistoric ritual, eyes shut and swaying slightly, '. . . an' lay oot yer gear, an' blanco yer' webbin', an' bring yer gunfire in ra mornin', and collect yer fag ration, an' fetch ye tea an' wee cakes frae the Naafi for yer elevenses unless ye fancy a doughnut, an' take ma turn as mess waiter oan guest nights, an' . . .'

'Stop!' I cried, and he gargled to a halt and stood lowering and expectant. It was that last bit about being a mess waiter that had hit home – I had a nightmare vision of him, in his unspeakable denims, sidling up to the Brigadier's wife with a tray of canapés and inquiring hoarsely, 'Hey, missus, ye want a sangwidge? Ach, go on, pit anither in yer bag fur efter . . .'

'We can discuss it tomorrow,' I said firmly. 'My kit's all ready for Retreat, and I'm on the range until five, so you can fall out until then. Right?'

It isn't easy to read expressions on a face that looks like an artist's impression of Early Man, but I seemed to detect disappointment in the way he blinked and drew his forearm audibly across his nose. 'Can Ah no' help ye oan wi' yer gear?' he suggested, and I snatched my bonnet from beneath his descending paw in the nick of time and hastily buckled on my belt and holster. 'Thanks all the same, McAuslan,' I said, withdrawing before he decided my collar needed adjustment – and he looked so deprived, somehow, that like a soft-hearted fool I added: 'You can comb the sporran if you like . . . you better wash your hands first, perhaps, and be sure to hang it straight. Right, carry on.'

They say no good deed ever goes unpunished, but I could not foresee that in combing the big white horse-hair sporran he would drop it on the floor, tramp on it, decide that it needed rewashing, and then try to dry it over the cookhouse stove while the master-gyppo's back was turned. They got the blaze under control, and probably only the gourmets noticed that the evening meal tasted of burned horse-hair. Meanwhile McAuslan, escaping undetected through the smoke, galloped back to my billet and tried to repair the charred remnant of my sporran by scraping it with my *sgian dubh*, snapping the blade in the process; he next tried daubing the stubble with white blanco, and dripped it on my best black shoes, which he then rendered permanently two-tone by scrubbing the spots with his sleeve. Warming to his work, he attempted to steal a sporran from Second-Lieutenant Keith next door, was detected and pursued by Keith's batman, and defended his plunder by breaking my ashplant over the other's head. After which they called the provost staff, and the Jeeves of 12 Platoon was removed struggling to the cells, protesting blasphemously that they couldnae dae this tae him, he hadnae finished gettin' Mr MacNeill ready fur tae go on Retreat.

All this I learned when I got back from the range. I didn't attend Retreat – well, you look conspicuous in mottled grey brogues and a bald, smoking sporran – and was awarded two days' orderly officer in consequence; it was small comfort that McAuslan got seven days' jankers for brawling and conduct prejudicial. I summoned him straight after his sentence, intending to announce his dismissal from my personal service in blistering terms; he lurched into my office (even in his best tunic and tartan he looked like a fugitive from Culloden who had been hiding in a peat-bog) and before I could vent my rage on him he cleared his throat thunderously and asked:

'Can Ah say a word, sur?'

Expecting apology and contrition, I invited him to go ahead, and having closed his eyes, swayed, and gulped – symptoms, I was to learn, of embarrassment – he regarded me with a sort of nervous compassion.

'Ah'm sorry, sur, but Ah'm givin' notice. Ah mean, Ah'm resignin' frae bein' yer batman. Ah'm packin' it in, sur, if ye don't mind.' He blinked, wondering how I would receive this bombshell, and my face must have been a study, for he added hastily: 'Ah'm sorry, like, but ma mind's made up.'

'Is it, by God?' I said. 'Well, get this straight, McAuslan! You're not *resigning*, my son, not by a dam' sight, because –'

'Oh, but Ah am, sur. Beggin' yer pardon. Ah want ye tae understand,' he continued earnestly, 'that it's nuthin' personal. Ye're a gentleman, sur. But the fact is, if Ah'm lookin' efter you, Ah hivnae time tae look efter mysel' – an' Ah've got a lot o' bother, I can tell ye. Look at the day, frinstance – Ah wis rushed, an' here Ah'm oan jankers – och, it's no' your fault, it's that wee nyaff o' a batman that works fur Mr Keith. Nae co-operation –'

'McAuslan,' I said, breathing hard. 'Go away. Go quickly, before I forget myself. Get your infernal carcase on jankers, and tell the Provost Sergeant he can kill you, and I'll cover up for him –'

'Awright! Awright, sur! Ah'm gaun!' He beat a shambling retreat, looking puzzled and slightly hurt. 'Keep the heid, sur.' He saluted with crestfallen dignity. 'Ah wis just gaun tae say, ye'll be needin' anither batman, an' ye could dae worse than Chick McGilvray; he's Celtic-daft an' a bit casual, but – awright, sur, Ah'm gaun! Ah'm gaun!'

You know, when our sister regiment, the Black Watch, was first raised centuries ago, it was unique in that every *private soldier* had his own batman – and in next to no time that great fighting regiment had mutinied. It was now clear to me why: several hundred batmen in the McAuslan mould had simply proved too great a strain.

On the principle that any recommendation of his must be accursed, I did not approach McGilvray. Instead I spoke sternly to Sergeant Telfer – who had the grace to admit that eagerness to get shot of McAuslan had warped his judgment – and told him I would engage replacements on a trial basis. There was no shortage of volunteers, for a batman's life is a cushy billet, with perks and time off, but none of them was any real improvement on Coulter, although all were grace itself compared to the Dark Destroyer who had succeeded him.

There was Fletcher, Glasgow spiv, dead shot, and platoon dandy, who kept my kit immaculate – and wore it himself in his sorties after female talent. Next there was Forbes, nicknamed Heinie after Himmler; he was small, dark, and evil, a superb footballer who performed his duties with ruthless efficiency, but whose explosive temper bred friction with the other batmen. After him came Brown, alias Daft Bob, an amiable dreamer who supported Partick Thistle (that's a tautology, really) and was always five minutes late; he was also given to taking afternoon naps on my bed with his boots on. And there was Riach, who came from Uist and belonged to that strict religious sect, the Wee Frees; he had a prejudice against working on the Sabbath, and only did it under protest. (I once asked him how, during active service in the Far East, he had brought himself to kill Japanese on Sunday, and he ground his teeth in a grim, distant way and said that was all right, it was a work of necessity and mercy.)

I parted from each trialist in turn, without rancour. Perhaps I was hard to please – no, I was impossible to please, partly because I disliked being waited on and feeling my privacy invaded, but also because it was dawning on me that Scots (as I should have learned from my grandmother) are not natural servants; they have too much inborn conceit of themselves for the job, and either tyrannise their employers, like my grandmother and Coulter (although I'm sure her technique was that of the rapier, where his was the bludgeon), or regard them as victims to be plundered in a patronising way. Of course there are exceptions; Hudson of *Upstairs, Downstairs* does exist, but you have to be exceptional yourself to employ him (I never thought the Bellamy family were *quite* up to him, and I doubt if he did either).

Anyway, there were no Hudsons in 12 Platoon, and I wondered how it was that the other young officers got by – MacKenzie, heir to a baronetcy, had an easy, owner-serf relationship with his orderly, and the rest of the subalterns seemed to take personal attendance for granted, without noticing it. That is the secret, of course: you have to be of the fine clay that isn't even aware of servants, but regards them as robots or talking animals who just happen to be around, lubricating you unobtrusively through life. The moment you become sensitive to their mere presence, never mind their thoughts, you stamp yourself as a neurotic peasant, like me, unfit to be looked after. So I concluded – and it never occurred to me that I was someone's grandson, and possibly seeking an unobtainable ideal.

Finally, in despair, I offered the job to McAuslan's nominee, McGilvray, a grinning, tow-headed Glaswegian who confessed that he hadn't volunteered because he didn't think he was cut out for it – that was a change, anyway. Mind you, he was right, but he wasn't alone in that, and he was a cheery, willing vandal who, beyond a tendency to knock the furniture about and gossip non-stop, had only one serious defect: I had to darn his socks. This after I had noticed him limping slightly, made him take off his plimsolls, and discovered two gaping holes repaired by whipping the edges together into fearsome ridges.

'No wonder you get blisters, you Parkhead disaster,' I rebuked him. 'Did no one ever teach you to darn? Right, get me some wool and a needle and pay attention . . .'

Darning socks was a vital art in those days; if you couldn't darn you couldn't march – unless you were one of those eccentrics who dispensed with socks and filled their boots with tallow, and I wasn't having him doing that, not within fifty yards of my perfumed bower. But my tuition was wasted; he

under the little gold pagoda where L— bought his lot and J— had his hat shot off and the ground was dark and wet with blood – while all *that* was happening, a world and a lifetime away, *this* was here: the quiet room, just as it had always been, just as it is now. The porcupine-quill inkstand that the old man brought home from East Africa, the copy of *Just William* with its torn spine, the bail you broke with your fast ball against Transitus (it must have been cheap wood), the ink-stain low down on the wallpaper that you made (quite deliberately) when you were eight . . . Nothing changed, except you. Never call yourself unlucky again.

I couldn't sleep in bed that night. I did something I hadn't done since Burma, except on a few night exercises: I went out into the garden with a blanket and rolled up under a bush. God knows why. It wasn't affectation – I took good care that no one knew – nor was it sheer necessity, nor mere silliness in the exuberance of homecoming. At the time I felt it was a sort of gesture of thanksgiving, and only much later did I realise it was probably a reluctance to 'come home' to a life that I knew there could be no return to, now. Anyway, I didn't sleep a bloody wink.

After just a few days at home (which was in Northern England) I took off for Scotland. My excuse was that I had to make the visits I had promised, but the truth was I was restless and impatient. Three years of adventure – because there's no other word for that kaleidoscope of travel and warfare and excitement and change in strange lands among weird exotic peoples – had done its work, and once the elation of just being home, so long dreamed of, had passed, there was the anti-climax, the desire to be off and doing again. It was no big psychological deal of the kind you see in movies; I wasn't battle-happy, or 'mentally scarred', or hung up with guilt, nor did patrols of miniature Japanese brew up under my bed (as happened to one of my section whenever we came out of the line: we used to tell him to take his kukhri to them, and when he had done so to his satisfaction, swearing and carving the air, we all went back to sleep again, him included). It was just that my life was now outside that home of boyhood, and I would never settle there again. Of course no word of this was said, but I'm sure my parents knew. Parents usually do.

I was nearly two weeks in Scotland, staying at small hotels and making my afternoon calls on families who had been forewarned of my coming; it was a succession of front-rooms and drawing-rooms, with the best tea-service and sandwiches and such extravagance of scones and home-made cakes as rationing allowed (I had to remind myself to go easy on the sugar, or I would have cleaned them out), while I was cross-examined about Drew or Angus or Gordon, and photographs of the poor perishers were trotted out which would have curled their toes under, and quiet aunts listened rapt in the background, and younger brothers and sisters regarded me with giggling awe. They were such nice folk, kind, proper, hanging on every word about their sons, tired after the war, touchingly glad that I had come to see them. It was fascinating, too, to compare the parents with the young men I knew, to discover that the dashing and ribald Lieutenant Grant was the son of a family so douce that they said grace even before afternoon tea; that the parents of the urbane Captain D—, who had put him through Merchiston and Oxford, lived in a tiny top-floor flat in Colinton; and that Second-Lieutenant Hunter, a pimply youth with protruding teeth, had a sister who was a dead ringer for Linda Darnell (and whose R.A.F. fiancé stuck to her like glue all through tea).

But the most interesting calls were the last two. The first was to a blackened tenement in Glasgow's East End, where McGilvray's widowed mother lived with his invalid great-uncle, on the third floor above a mouldering close with peeling walls, urchins screaming on the stairs, and the green tramcars clanging by. Inside, the flat was bright and neat and cosy, with gleaming brass, a kettle singing on the open black-leaded grate, an old-fashioned alcove bed, and such a tea on the table as I had not seen yet, with gingerbread and Lyle's golden syrup. Mrs McGilvray was a quick, anxious wee Glasgow body, scurrying with the tea-pot while Uncle chuckled and made sly jokes at her; he was a small wheezy comedian with a waxed moustache and a merry eye, dressed in his best blue serge with a flower in his buttonhole and a gold watch-chain across his portly middle; he half-rose to greet me, leaning on a stick and gasping cheerfully, called me 'l'tenant', informed me that he had been in the H.L.I. in the first war, and wha' shot the cheese, hey? (This is a famous joke against my regiment.) When he had subsided, wiping his eye and chuckling 'Ma Goad, ma Goad', Mrs McGilvray questioned me nervously across the tea-cups: was Charlie well? Was Charlie behaving himself? Was Charlie giving me any bother? Was Charlie saving his pay or squandering it on drink, cards, and loose women? (This was actually a series of questions artfully disguised, but that was their purport.) Was Charlie attending Church? Was he taking care? Were his pals nice boys?

'In Goad's name, wumman,' cried Uncle, 'let the man get his tea! Yattety-yattety-yattety! Charlie's fine! Thur naethin' wrang wi' him. Sure that's right, L'tenant?'

'He's fine,' I said, 'he's a great lad.'

'There y'are! Whit am Ah aye tellin' ye? The boy's fine!'

'Aye, well,' said Mrs McGilvray, looking down at her cup. 'I aye worry aboot him.'

'Ach, women!' cried Uncle, winking at me. 'Aye on aboot their weans. See yersel' anither potato scone, L'tenant. Ma Goad, ma Goad.'

'Does he . . .' Mrs McGilvray hesitated, 'does he . . . do his work well? I mean . . . looking after you, Mr MacNeill?'

'Oh, indeed he does. I think I'm very lucky.'

'Ah'd sooner hae a cairter lookin' efter me!' wheezed Uncle. 'Heh-heh! Aye, or a caur conductor! Ma Goad, ma Goad.'

'Wheesht, Uncle! Whit'll Mr MacNeill think?'

'He'll think yer an auld blether, gaun on aboot Cherlie! The boy's no' a bairn ony langer, sure'n he's no'. He's a grown man.' He glinted at me. 'Sure that's right? Here . . . will ye tak' a wee dram, L'tenant? Ach, wheesht, wumman – can Ah no' gie the man a right drink, then? His tongue'll be hingin' oot!' At his insistence she produced a decanter, shaking her head, apologising, while he cried to gie the man a decent dram, no' just dirty his gless. He beamed on me.

'Here's tae us! Ninety-Twa, no' deid yet!'

'Whisky at tea-time – whit'll Mr MacNeill think o' ye?' wondered his niece, half-smiling.

'He'll no' think the worse o' me for gie'n him a wee dram tae the Ninety-Twa,' said Uncle comfortably. He raised his glass again. 'An' tae the Bantam's, hey, L'tenant? Aye, them's the wee boys! Ma Goad, ma Goad . . .'

Mrs McGilvray saw me to the door when I left, Uncle crying after me no' tae shoot ony cheeses gaun doon the stair. When I had thanked her she said:

'I wonder . . . Charlie doesnae write very often. D'you think . . . ?'

'He'll write every week,' I assured her. 'He's a great lad, Mrs McGilvray. You're very lucky.'

'Well,' she said, clasping her hands, 'he's always been right enough. I'm sure you'll look after him.' We shook hands and she pecked me quickly on the cheek. 'Take care, laddie.'

Uncle's hoarse chuckle sounded from the inner room. 'Come ben, wumman! Whit'll the neebors say, you hingin' aboot the stairheid wi' sojers!'

She gave me a despairing look and retreated, and I went down the stairs, stepping over the children and reflecting that I was certainly not going to be able to change my batman now.

The final visit was to MacKenzie's people, who lived in a fifteenth-century castle-cum-mansion in Perthshire, a striking piece of Gothic luxury in beautiful parkland with a drive a mile long through banks of cultivated heather; it contained its own salmon river, a fortune in standing timber, and a battalion of retainers who exercised dogs, strolled about with shotguns, and manicured the rhododendrons. Sir Gavin MacKenzie was his son thirty years on, tall, commanding, and with a handshake like a mangle; the red had apparently seeped from his hair into his cheeks, but that was the only difference. In manner he was cordial and abrupt, a genuine John Buchan Scottish aristo – which is to say that he was more English than any Englishman could ever hope to be. If you doubt that, just consider such typical 'Englishmen' as Harold Macmillan, David Niven, Alec Douglas-Home, Jack Buchanan, Stewart Granger, and Charles II.

This was the only visit on which I actually stayed on the premises overnight. We dined at a long candle-lit table in a large and clammy hall with age-blackened panelling covered with crossed broadswords, targes, and flintlocks, with silent servitors emerging occasionally from the gloom to refuel us. At one end sat Sir Gavin in a dinner jacket and appalling MacKenzie tartan trews cut on the diagonal; at the other, Lady MacKenzie, an intense woman with a staccato delivery who chain-smoked throughout the meal. From time to time she and her husband addressed each other in the manner of people who have met only recently; it was hard to believe that they knew each other well enough to be have begotten not only their son but a daughter, seated opposite me, a plain, lumpy sixteen-year-old with the magnificent MacKenzie hair, flaming red and hanging to her waist. The only other diner was a pale, elderly man with an eye-glass whose name I didn't catch – in fact, looking back, I'm not sure he was there at all, since he never spoke and no one addressed him. He drank most of a bottle of Laphroaig during the meal, and took it with him when the ladies withdrew, leaving old man MacKenzie and me to riot over the port.

Coming on the evening of the day I had spent with the McGilvrays, it was an odd contrast. Lady MacKenzie had chattered non-stop about her son, but without asking any questions, and his sister had not, I think, referred to him at all, but since she had the finishing-school habit of talking very quickly to her armpit it was difficult to be sure. Sir Gavin had spoken only of the Labour Government. Now, when we were alone, he demanded to know why, in my opinion, Kenny had not joined the Scots Guards, in which he, Sir Gavin, had held an exalted position. Why had he chosen a Highland regiment? It was extraordinary, when he could have been in the Brigade; Sir Gavin couldn't understand it.

I said, trying not to smile, that it was possible some people might prefer a Highland regiment, and Sir Gavin said, yes, he knew *that*, but it wasn't the point. Why young Kenneth? It seemed very odd to him, when the family had always been in the Brigade, and he could have kept an eye on the boy – 'I mean, I don't know your Colonel – what's his name? No, don't know him. Good man, is he?'

'They don't come any better,' I said. It seemed fairly obvious to me why young Kenneth, a firebrand and a maverick, had chosen not to be in father's regiment, but that could not be said. Sir Gavin looked glum, and said he didn't know anything *about* Highland regiments – fine reputation, of course, but he didn't know how they *were*, d'you see what I mean? With the Guards, you knew where you were. Life for a young officer was cut and dried . . . Highland regiment, he wasn't so sure. Suddenly he asked:

'Is he a *good* officer?'

'Kenny? Yes. His Jocks like him.'

'His what?'

'His Jocks – his men.'

'Oh.' He frowned. 'What about your Colonel?'

'I'm sure he thinks Kenny's a good officer.' Indeed, Sir Gavin didn't know about Highland regiments, where the opinion of the men is the ultimate test, and every colonel knows it. Sir Gavin chewed his cigar and then said:

'You were a ranker, weren't you? Very well – in Burma, would you have . . . accepted Kenneth as your platoon commander?'

I mentally compared Kenny with the brisk young man who'd once challenged me to a spelling bee and caught me out over 'inadmissible', and who'd died in a bunker entrance the next day. A good subaltern, but no better than MacKenzie.

'Yes,' I said. 'Kenny would have done.'

'You think so?' he said, and suddenly I realised he was worried about his son. In the Guards, he could have served *with* him in spirit, so to speak – but he didn't know how Highland regiments *were*, he'd said. Did the boy fit into that almost alien background? Was he a good officer? Like Mrs McGilvray, he aye worried about him, if for a different reason. So it seemed sensible to start talking about Kenny, describing how he got on in the regiment, how he and his platoon sergeant, McCaw, the Communist Clydesider, formed a disciplinary alliance that was a battalion byword, recalling incidents in which Kenny had figured, our own companionship, things like that, no doubt babbling a bit, while Sir Gavin listened, and kept the decanter going, now and then asking a question, finally sitting in silence for a while, and then saying:

'Well, I'm glad he's all right. Thank you.'

It was two in the morning when we finally rose, port-bloated and drowsy – he must have been partially kettled, for he insisted on a frame of snooker with accompanying brandies before we parted for the night. 'John'll look after you,' he said, hiccoughing courteously, and I was aware of a dim sober figure at the foot of the massive staircase, waiting to conduct me to my room – which brings me back, after this digression of homecoming, to where I was in the first place.

John was a footman, the only one I have ever encountered outside the pages of Georgette Heyer and Wodehouse, and he would have fitted into them perfectly, along with the rest of the MacKenzie menage. No doubt I was a trifle woozy with tiredness and Croft's Old Original, but I have no impression that I had to stir so much as a finger in order to get into bed. His shadow flitted about me, my clothes vanished, towel and soap and warm water swam into my ken, followed by pyjamas and a cup of some bland liquid, and then I was between the sheets and all was dark contentment. When I woke two hours later there was a tray at the bedside with various mineral waters, biscuits, and a glass of milk, all under a dim night-light. I think the milk had been spiked, for the first two hours after waking next morning passed in a beatific haze; I seem to remember curtains being drawn and a cup of tea appearing, and then I was borne up gently into a sitting position and presently subsided, shaven, while a voice murmured that my bath had been drawn – not filled or running, you understand, but drawn. At that point he vanished, and when I emerged from the bathroom, more or less awake, there was a breakfast tray on the window table, with porridge and Arbroath smokies and ham and eggs and such morning rolls as God's Own Prophet eats only in Glasgow bakeries; the *Scotsman* and the *Bulletin* lay beside it (not that I was fit for more than the Scottykin comic strip), my clothes were laid out, pressed, brushed, and beautiful, my shoes a-gleam, and even my cap badge and sporran chains had been polished.

This, it slowly dawned on me, was living, and it took an immense effort to decline the MacKenzies' invitation to stay on, but I suspected that after a few days of John's attention I would have forgotten how to tie my shoe-laces and wave bye-bye. As I travelled south again, and later on the flight to Cairo, I had day-dreams in which the press-gang had been reintroduced, and John had been crimped into my personal service; it would give me a new outlook on life, and I would rise effortlessly to general rank and a knighthood, possibly even C.I.G.S., for nothing less was conceivable with that mysterious retainer sorting me out; I would have to live up to the ambience he created. At that point the dreaming stopped, as I realised that I simply wasn't made for that kind of destiny, or for the ministrations of people like John.

This was driven home with a vengeance in Benghazi, of all unlikely places, where I had to spend three days between flights on the way back to the battalion. I had just entered the room allotted me in the transit camp when there was a clump of martial feet on the verandah, and into the doorway wheeled a gigantic German prisoner-of-war. From the crown of his blond shaving-brush skull to his massive ammunition boots and rolled socks must have been a cool six and a half feet; in between he wore only tiny khaki shorts and a shirt which appeared to have been starched with concrete. He crashed to attention, stared at the wall, and shouted:

'Saar, Ai em yewer betmen. Mai nem is Hans. Pliz permit thet Ai unpeck yewer kit.'

My immediate reaction was: how the hell did we ever beat this lot? For what I was looking at was one of Frederick William's Prussian giants, the picture of a Panzer Grenadier, the perfect military automaton. He was, I learned later, captured Afrika Korps, waiting to be repatriated and meanwhile employed to attend transients like myself. When I had recovered and told him to carry on, he stamped again, ducked his head sharply, and went at my valise like a great clockwork doll, unpacking and stowing with a precision that was not quite human; it was a relief to see that there wasn't a knob on the side of his neck.

It was my first encounter with the German military, and I didn't mind if it was the last. In his heel-clicking way he was as perfect a servant as John had been, for while John had worked his miracles without actually being there, apparently, and never obtruding his personality, Hans succeeded by having no personality at all. It was like having a machine about the place, bringing tea by numbers; you could almost hear the whirr and click with every action. In fact, he was a robot-genie, with the gift of sudden shattering appearance; he would be out on the verandah, standing at ease, and if I so much as coughed he would be quivering in the doorway shouting 'Saar!', ready to fetch me a box of matches or march on Moscow. I began to understand Frederick the Great and Hitler; given a couple of million Hanses at your beck and call, the temptation to say 'Occupy Europe at once!' must be overpowering.

I say he had no personality, but I'm not so sure. In three days he never betrayed emotion, or even moved a facial muscle except to speak; if he had a thought beyond the next duty to be performed, you would never have known it. But on the last night, I had gone up to the mess in khaki drill, having left my kilt hanging by its waist-loops on the cupboard door. Coming back, I glanced in at my window, and there was Hans standing looking at the kilt with an expression I hadn't seen before. It was a thoughtful, intense stare, with a lot of memory behind it; he moved forward and felt the material, traced his thumb-nail along one of the yellow threads, and then stepped back, contemplating it with his cropped head on one side. I may be wrong, but I believe that if ever a man was thinking, 'Next time, you sons-of-bitches', he was. I made a noise approaching the doorway, and when I went in he was turning down the bed, impassive as ever.

But whatever secret thoughts he may have had in his Teutonic depths, Hans, as a servant, was too much for me – just as the disembodied John had been. As I observed earlier, you have to be a Junker, or its social equivalent (with all that that implies) to be able to bear having the Johns and Hanses dance attendance on you; if you are just a gentleman for the working day, you must stick to your own kind.

I reached the battalion the following evening, asked the jeep driver to drop off my kit at my billet, and walked over to 12 Platoon barrack-room. They were there, loafing about, lying on their cots, exchanging the patter, some cleaning their kit, others preparing to go out on the town: the dapper Fletcher was combing his hair at a mirror, fox-trotting on the spot; Forbes, in singlet and shorts, was juggling a tennis ball on his instep; Riach was writing a letter (to the Wee Frees' Grand Inquisitor, probably); Daft Bob Brown was sitting on his bed singing 'Ah've got spurrs that jingle-jangle-jingle, so they doo-oo!' and at the far end Private McAuslan, clad à la mode in balmoral bonnet and a towel with which he had evidently been sweeping a chimney, was balanced precariously on his bed-end, swiping furiously at moths with his rifle-sling; from his hoarse vituperations I gather he blamed their intrusion on Sergeant Telfer, the Army Council, and the Labour Government of Mr Attlee. He and Sir Gavin MacKenzie should have got together.

One of the corporals saw me in the doorway and started to call the room to attention, but I flagged him down, and the platoon registered my appearance after their fashion.

'Aw-haw-hey, Wullie! The man's back!'

'See, Ah told ye he hadnae gone absent.'

'Hiv a good leave, sur?'

'Way-ull! Back tae the Airmy again!'

'Whit did ye bring us frae Rothesay, sur?'

'Aye, it'll be hell in the trenches the morn!' and so on with their keelie grins and weird slogans, and very reassuring it was. I responded in kind by bidding them a courteous good evening, looked forward to meeting them on rifle parade at eight and kit inspection at ten, and acknowledged their cries of protest and lamentation. McGilvray came forward with my Sam Browne in one hand and a polishing rag in the other.

'Yer leave a'right, sur? Aw, smashin'. Ah'm jist givin' yer belt a wee buff – Captain McAlpine asked tae borrow it while ye were away, an' ye know whit he's like – Ah think he's been hingin' oot a windae in it; a' scuffed tae hellangone! But the rest o' yer service dress is a' ready; Ah bulled it up when Ah heard ye wis back the night.'

Well, I thought to myself, you're not John or Hans, thank God, but you'll do. They can keep the professionals – and they can certainly keep McAuslan, and the farther away the better – and we'll get by very nicely.

He was looking at me inquiringly, and I realised I had been letting my thoughts stray.

'Oh . . . thanks, McGilvray. I saw your mother and great-uncle; they're fine. Come and finish the belt in my room and I'll tell you about them.' I was turning away when a thought struck me, and I paused, hesitating: I could sense that stern shade with her black ebony cane frowning down in disapproval from some immaculate, dusted paradise, but I couldn't help that. 'Oh, yes, and you'd better bring your socks with you.'

Sorry, Granny MacDonald, I thought, but a man's got to do what a man's got to do.

Captain Errol

Whenever I see television newsreels of police or troops facing mobs of rioting demonstrators, standing fast under a hail of rocks, bottles, and petrol bombs, my mind goes back forty years to India, when I was understudying John Gielgud and first heard the pregnant phrase 'Aid to the civil power'. And from that my thoughts inevitably travel on to Captain Errol, and the Brigadier's pet hawks, and the great rabble of chanting Arab rioters advancing down the Kantara causeway towards the thin khaki line of 12 Platoon, and my own voice sounding unnaturally loud and hoarse: 'Right, Sarn't Telfer – fix bayonets.'

Aid to the civil power, you see, is what the British Army used to give when called on to deal with disorder, tumult, and breach of the peace which the police could no longer control. The native constabulary of our former Italian colony being what they were – prone to panic if a drunken *bazaar-wallah* broke a window – aid to the civil power often amounted to no more than sending Wee Wullie out with a pick handle to shout 'Imshi!'; on the other hand, when real political mayhem broke loose, and a raging horde of fellaheen several thousand strong appeared bent on setting the town ablaze and massacring the European population, sterner measures were called for, and unhappy subalterns found themselves faced with the kind of decision which Home Secretaries and Cabinets agonise over for hours, the difference being that the subaltern had thirty seconds, with luck, in which to consider the safety of his men, the defenceless town at his back, and the likelihood that if he gave the order to fire and some agitator caught a bullet, he, the subaltern, would go down in history as the Butcher of Puggle Bazaar, or wherever it happened to be.

That, as I say, was in the imperial twilight of fifty years ago, long before the days of walkie-talkies, C.S. gas, riot shields, water cannon, and similar modern defences of the public weal – not that they seem to make riot control any easier nowadays, especially when the cameras are present. We didn't have to worry about television, and our options for dealing with infuriated rioters were limited: do nothing and get murdered, fire over their heads, or let fly in earnest. There are easier decisions, believe me, for a youth not old enough to vote.

The Army recognised this, and was at pains to instruct its fledgling officers in the techniques of containing civil commotion, so far as it knew how, which wasn't far, even in India, with three centuries of experience to draw on. Those were the postwar months before independence, when demonstrators were chanting: 'Jai Hind!' and 'Pakistan zindabad!', and the Indian police were laying about them with *lathis* (you really don't know what police brutality is until you've seen a *lathi* charge going in), while the troops stood by and their officers hoped to God they wouldn't have to intervene. Quetta and Amritsar were ugly memories of what happened when someone opened fire at the wrong time.

Bangalore, where I was completing my officers' training course, was one of the quiet spots, which may have been why the authorities took the eccentric view that instruction in riot control could be imparted through the medium of the theatre. If that sounds unlikely, well, that's the Army for you. Some genius (and it wasn't Richard Brinsley Sheridan) had written a play about aid to the civil power, showing the right and wrong ways of coping with unrest; it was to be enacted at the garrison theatre, and I found myself dragooned into taking part.

That's what comes of understudying Gielgud, which is what I like to think I had been doing, although he didn't know it. In the last relaxed weeks of our officers' training, a few of us cadets had been taking part in a production of *The Harbour Called Mulberry* for India Radio, with Cadet MacNeill as the Prussian general riveting the audience with his impersonation of Conrad Veidt; it was natural that when Gielgud's touring company arrived in town with a double bill of *Hamlet* and *Blithe Spirit*, and some of his cast went down with Bangalore Belly, our amateur group should be asked to provide replacements in case they needed a couple of extra spear-carriers. I was fool enough to volunteer, and while we were never required even to change into costume, let alone go on stage, we convinced ourselves that we were, technically, understudying the lead players – I mean to say, Bangalore Belly can go through unacclimatised systems like wildfire, and in our backstage dreams we could imagine being out there tearing the Soliloquy to shreds while Gielgud was carted off to the sick-bay. He wasn't, as it happened, but no doubt he would have been reassured if he'd known that we were ready to step in.

That by the way; the upshot was that, having drawn attention to ourselves, my associates and I were prime targets when it came to choosing the cast for the aid-to-the-civil-power play, a knavish piece of work entitled *Nowall and Chancit*. I played Colonel Nowall, an elderly and incompetent garrison commander, which meant that I had to wear a white wig and whiskers and make like a doddering Aubrey Smith in front of a military audience whose behaviour would have disgraced the Circus Maximus. The script was abysmal, my moustache kept coming loose, the prop telephone didn't ring on cue, one of the cast who took acting seriously dried up and fainted, and in the last act I had to order my troops to open fire on a rioting crowd played by a platoon of Indian sepoys in loin-cloths who giggled throughout and went right over the top when shot with blank cartridges. The entire theatre was dense with cordite smoke, there seemed to be about seven hundred people on stage, and when I stood knee-deep in hysterical corpses and spoke my deathless closing line: 'Well, that's that!' it stopped the show. I have not trod the boards since, and it can stay that way.

My excuse for that reminiscence is that it describes the only instruction we ever got in dealing with civil disorder. Considering that we were destined, as young second-lieutenants, to lead troops in various parts of the Far and Middle East when empires were breaking up and independence movements were in full spate, with accompanying bloodshed, it was barely adequate. Not that any amount of training, including my months as an infantry section leader in Burma, could have prepared me for the Palestine troubles of '46, when Arab and Jew were at each other's throats with the British caught in the middle, as usual; the Irgun and Stern Gang were waging their campaign of terror (or freedom-fighting, depending on your point of view), raid, ambush, murder, and explosion were commonplace, the Argyll and Sutherlands had barbed wire strung across the *inside* corridors of their Jerusalem barracks, and you took your revolver into the shower. It was a nerve-racked, bloody business which you learned as you went along; commanding the Cairo-Jerusalem night train and conducting a security stake-out at the Armistice Day service on the Mount of Olives added years to my education in a matter of days, and by the time I was posted back to my Highland battalion far away along the North African coast I felt I knew something about lending aid to the civil power. Of course, I didn't know the half of it – but then, I hadn't met Captain Errol.

That wasn't his real name, but it was what the Jocks called him because of his resemblance to Flynn, the well-known actor and bon viveur. And it wasn't just that he was six feet two, lightly moustached, and strikingly handsome; he had the same casual, self-assured swagger of the man who is well content with himself and doesn't give a darn whether anyone knows it or not; when you have two strings of ribbons, starting with the M.C. and M.M. and including the Croix de Guerre and a couple of exotic Balkan gongs at the end, you don't need to put on side. Which was just as well, for Errol had evidently been born with a double helping of self-esteem, advertised in the amused half-smile and lifted eyebrow with which he surveyed the world in general – and me in particular on the day he joined the battalion.

I was bringing my platoon in from a ten-mile route march, which they had done in the cracking time of two and a half hours, and was calling them to march to attention for the last fifty yards to the main gate, exhorting McAuslan for the umpteenth time to get his pack off his backside and up to his shoulders, and pretending not to hear Private Fletcher's *sotto voce* explanation that McAuslan couldn't march upright because he was expecting, and might, indeed, go into labour shortly. Sergeant Telfer barked them to silence and quickened the step, and I turned aside to watch them swing past – it was a moment I took care never to miss, for the pride of it warms me still: my platoon going by, forty hard young Jocks in battle order, rifles sloped and bonnets pulled down, slightly dusty but hardly even breaking sweat as Telfer wheeled them under the archway with its faded golden standard. Eat your heart out, Bonaparte.

It was as I was turning to follow that I became aware of an elegant figure seated in a horse-ghari which had just drawn up at the gate. He was a Highlander, but his red tartan and white cockade were not of our regiment; then I noticed the three pips and threw him a salute, which he acknowledged with a nonchalant forefinger and a remarkable request spoken in the airy affected drawl which in Glasgow is called 'Kelvinsaid'.

'Hullo, laddie,' said he. 'Your platoon? You might get a couple of them to give me a hand with my kit, will you?'

It was said so affably that the effrontery of it didn't dawn for a second – you don't ask a perfect stranger to detach two of his marching men to be your porters, not without preamble or introduction. I stared at the man, taking in the splendid bearing, the medal ribbons, and the pleasant expectant smile while he put a fresh cigarette in his holder.

'Eh? I beg your pardon,' I said stiffly, 'but they're on parade at the moment.' For some reason I didn't add 'sir'.

It didn't faze him a bit. 'Oh, that's a shame. Still, not to panic. We ought to be able to manage between us. All right, Abdul,' he addressed the Arab coachman, 'let's get the cargo on the dock.'

He swung lightly down from the ghari – not the easiest thing to do, with decorum, in a kilt – and it was typical of the man that I found myself with a valise in one hand and a set of golf-clubs in the other before I realised that he was evidently expecting me to tote his damned dunnage for him. My platoon had vanished from sight, fortunately, but Sergeant Telfer had stopped and was staring back, goggle-eyed. Before I could speak the newcomer was addressing me again:

'Got fifty lire, old man? 'Fraid all I have is Egyptian ackers, and the Fairy Coachman won't look at them. See him right, will you, and we'll settle up anon. Okay?'

That, as they say, did it. 'Laddie' I could just about absorb (since he must have been all of twenty-seven and therefore practically senile), and even his outrageous assumption that my private and personal platoon were his to flunkify, and that I would caddy for him and pay his blasted transport bills – but not that careless 'Okay?' and the easy, patronising air which was all the worse for being so infernally amiable. Captain or no captain, I put his clubs and valise carefully back in the ghari and spoke, with masterly restraint:

'I'm afraid I haven't fifty lire on me, sir, but if you care to climb back in, the ghari can take you to the Paymaster's Office in HQ Company; they'll change your ackers and see to your kit.' And just to round off the civilities I added: 'My name's

MacNeill, by the way, and I'm a platoon commander, not a bloody dragoman.'

Which was insubordination, but if you'd seen that sardonic eyebrow and God-like profile you'd have said it too. Again, it didn't faze him; he actually chuckled.

'I stand rebuked. MacNeill, eh?' He glanced at my campaign ribbon. 'What were you in Burma?'

'Other rank.'

'Well, obviously, since you're only a second-lieutenant now. What kind of other rank?'

'Well . . . sniper-scout, Black Cat Division. Later on I was a section leader. Why . . . sir?'

'Black Cats, eh? God Almighty's Own. Were you at Imphal?'

'Not in the Boxes. Irrawaddy Crossing, Meiktila, Sittang Bend –'

'And you haven't got a measly fifty lire for a poor broken-down old soldier? Well, the hell with you, young MacNeill,' said this astonishing fellow, and seated himself in the ghari again. 'I'd heap coals of fire on you by offering you a lift, but your platoon are probably waiting for you to stop their motor. Bash on, MacNeill, before they seize up! Officers' mess, Abdul!' And he drove off with an airy wave.

'Hadn't you better report to H.Q.?' I called after him, but he was through the gate by then, leaving me nonplussed but not a little relieved; giving lip to captains wasn't my usual line, but he hadn't turned regimental, fortunately.

'Whit the hell was yon?' demanded Sergeant Telfer, who had been an entranced spectator.

'You tell me,' I said. 'Ballater Bertie, by the look of him.' For he had, indeed, the air of those who command the guard at Ballater Station, conducting Royalty with drawn broadsword and white spats. And yet he'd been wearing an M.M. ribbon, which signified service in the ranks. I remarked on this to Telfer, who sniffed as only a Glaswegian can, and observed that whoever the newcomer might be, he was a heid-case – which means an eccentric.

That was the battalion's opinion, formed before Captain Errol had been with us twenty-four hours. He had driven straight to the mess, which was empty of customers at that time of day, smooth-talked the mess sergeant into paying the ghari out of bar receipts, made free with the Tallisker unofficially reserved for the Medical Officer, parked himself unerringly in the second-in-command's favourite chair, and whiled away the golden afternoon with the *Scottish Field*. Discovered and gently rebuked by the Adjutant for not reporting his arrival in the proper form, he had laughed apologetically and asked what time dinner was, and before the Adjutant, an earnest young Englishman, could wax properly indignant he had found himself, by some inexplicable process, buying Errol a gin and tonic.

'I can't fathom it,' he told me, with the pained expression he usually reserved for descriptions of his putting. 'One minute I was tearing small strips off the chap, and the next you know I was saying 'What's yours?' and filling him in on the social scene. Extraordinary.'

Having found myself within an ace of bell-hopping for Captain Errol by the same mysterious magic, I sympathised. Who was he, anyway, I asked, and the Adjutant frowned.

'Dunno, exactly. Nor why we've got him. He's been up in Palestine lately, and just from something the Colonel said I have the impression he's been in some sort of turmoil – Errol, I mean. That type always is,' said the Adjutant, like a dowager discussing a fallen woman. 'Wouldn't be surprised if he was an I-man.'

'I' is Intelligence, and the general feeling in line regiments is that you can keep it; I-men are disturbing influences best confined to the higher echelons, where they can pursue their clandestine careers and leave honest soldiers in peace. Attached to a battalion, they can be unsettling.

And Captain Errol was all of that. As he had begun, with the Adjutant and me, so he went on, causing ripples on our placid regimental surface which eventually turned into larger waves. One of the former, for example, occurred on his first night in the mess when, within half an hour of their first acquaintance, he addressed the Colonel as 'skipper'. It caused a brief silence which Errol himself didn't seem to notice; officially, you see, there are no ranks in the mess, but junior officers (of whom captains are only the most senior) normally call the head man 'sir', especially when he is such a redoubtable bald eagle as our Colonel was. 'Skipper' was close to the edge of impertinence – but it was said so easily and naturally that he got away with it. In fact, I think the Colonel rather liked it.

That, it soon became plain, was Errol's secret. Like his notorious namesake, he had great charm and immense style; partly it was his appearance, which was commanding, and his war record – the family of Highland regiments is a tight little news network, and many of the older men had heard of him as a fighting soldier – but most of it was just personality. He was casual, cocky, even insolent, but with a gift of disarmament, and even those who found his conceit and familiarity irritating (as the older men did) seemed almost flattered when he gave them his attention – I've seen the Senior Major, a grizzled veteran with the disposition of a liverish rhino, grinning sourly as Errol teased him. When he was snubbed, he didn't seem to notice; the eyebrow would give an amused flicker, no more.

The youngest subalterns thought him a hell of a fellow, of course, not least because he had no side with them; rank meant nothing to Errol, up or down. The Jocks, being canny judges, were rather wary of him, while taking advantage of his informality so far as they thought it safe; their word for him was 'gallus', that curious Scots adjective which means a mixture of reckless, extrovert, and indifferent. On balance, he was not over-popular with Jocks or officers, especially among the elders, but even they held him in a certain grudging respect. None of which seemed to matter to Errol in the least.

I heard various verdicts on him in the first couple of weeks.

'I think he's a Bad News Type,' said the Adjutant judicially, 'but there's no doubt he's a character.'

'Insufferable young pup,' was the Senior Major's verdict. 'Why the devil must he use that blasted cigarette holder, like a damned actor?' When it was pointed out that most of us used them, to keep the sweat off our cigarettes, the Major remarked unreasonably: 'Not the way he does. Damned affectation.'

'I like him,' said plump and genial Major Bakie. 'He can be dashed funny when he wants. Breath of fresh air. My wife likes him, too.'

'Captain Errol,' observed the Padre, who was the most charitable of men, 'is a very interesting chentleman. What d'ye say, Lachlan?'

'Like enough,' said the M.O. 'I wouldnae let him near my malt, my money, or my maidservant.'

'See him, he's sand-happy. No' a' there,' I heard Private McAuslan informing his comrades. 'See when he wis Captain o' the Week, an' had tae inspect ma rifle on guard? He looks doon the barrel, and says: 'I seem to see through a glass darkly.' Whit kind o' patter's that, Fletcher? Mind you, he didnae pit me on a charge, an' me wi' a live round up the spout. Darkie woulda nailed me tae the wall.' (So I would, McAuslan.)

'Errol? A chanty-wrastler,' said Fletcher – which, from that crafty young soldier, was interesting. A chanty-wrastler is a poseur, and unreliable.

'Too dam' sure of himself by half,' was the judgment of the second-in-command. 'We can do without his sort.'

The Colonel rubbed tobacco between his palms in his thoughtful way, and said nothing.

Personally, I'd met plenty I liked better, but it seemed to me there was a deeper prejudice against Errol than he deserved, bouncy tigger though he was. Some of it might be explained by his service record which, it emerged, was sensational, and not all on the credit side. According to the Adjutant's researches, he had been commissioned in the Territorials in '39, and had escaped mysteriously from St Valéry, where the rest of his unit had gone into the P.O.W. bag ('there were a few heads wagged about that, apparently'). Later he had fought with distinction in the Far East, acquiring a Military Cross ('a real one, not one of your up-with-the-rations jobs') with the Chindits.

'And then,' said the Adjutant impressively, 'he got himself cashiered. Yes, busted – all the way down. It seems he was in charge of a train-load of wounded, somewhere in Bengal, and there was some foul-up and they were shunted into a siding. Some of the chaps were in a bad way, and Errol raised hell with the local R.T.O., who got stroppy with him, and Errol hauled out his revolver and shot the inkpot off the R.T.O.'s desk, and threatened to put the next one between his eyes. Well, you can't do that, can you? So it was a court-martial, and march out Private Errol.'

'But he's a captain now,' I said. 'How on earth –?'

'*Chubbarao*, and listen to this,' said the Adjutant. 'He finished up late in the war with those special service johnnies who were turned loose in the Balkans – you know, helping the partisans, blowing up bridges and things and slaughtering Huns with cheese-wire by night. Big cloak-and-dagger stuff, and he did hell of a well at it, and Tito kissed him on both cheeks and said he'd never seen the like –'

'So that's where he got the M.M.'

'And the Balkan gongs, and the upshot of it was that he was re-commissioned. It happens, now and then. And of late he's been undercover in Palestine.' The Adjutant scratched his fair head. 'Something odd there – rumours about terrorist suspects being knocked about pretty badly, and one hanging himself in his cell. Nasty business. Anyway, friend Errol was shipped out, p.d.q., and now we're landed with him. Oh, and another thing – he's to be Intelligence Officer, as if we needed one. Didn't I say he was the type?' The Adjutant sniffed. 'Well, at least it should keep him out of everyone's hair.'

The disclosures of Errol's irregular past were not altogether surprising, and they helped to explain his *alakeefik* attitude and brass neck. Plainly he was capable of anything, and having hit both the heights and the depths was not to be judged as ordinary mortals are.

His duties as I-man were vague, and kept him out of the main stream of battalion life, which may have been as well, for as a soldier he was a contradictory mixture. In some things he was expert: a splendid shot, superb athlete, and organised to the hilt in the field. On parade, saving his immaculate turn-out, he was a disaster: when he was Captain of the Week and had to mount the guard, I suffered agonies at his elbow in my capacity as orderly officer, whispering commands and telling him what to do next while he turned the ceremony into a shambles. Admittedly, since McAuslan was in the guard, we were handicapped from the start, but I believe Errol could have reduced the Household Cavalry to chaos – and been utterly indifferent about it. Doing well or doing badly, it was all one to him; he walked off that guard-mounting humming and swinging his walking-stick, debonair as be-damned, and advising the outraged Regimental Sergeant-Major that the drill needed tightening up a bit. (He actually addressed him as 'Major', which is one of the things that are never done. An R.S.M. is 'Mr So-and-so'.)

Being casual in all things, he was naturally accident-prone, but even that did nothing to deflate him, since the victim was invariably someone else. He wrecked the Hudson Terraplane belonging to Lieutenant Grant, and walked away without a scratch; Grant escaped with a broken wrist, but there was no restoring the car which had been its owner's pride.

He was equally lethal on blue water. Our garrison town boasted a magnificent Mediterranean bay, strewn with wrecks from the war, and sailing small boats was a popular pastime among the local smart set; Errol took to it in a big way, and from all accounts it was like having a demented Blackbeard loose about the waterfront. I gather there is a sailing etiquette about giving way and not getting athwart other people's hawses, of which he was entirely oblivious; the result was a series of bumps, scrapes, collisions, and furious protests from outraged voyagers, culminating in a regatta event in which he dismasted one competitor, caused another to capsize, and added insult to injury by winning handsomely. That he was promptly disqualified did not lower the angle of his jaunty cigarette-holder by a degree when he turned up at the prize-giving, bronzed and dashing, to applaud the garrison beauty, Ellen Ramsey, when she received the Ladies' Cup. She it was who christened him the Sea Hog – and was his dinner companion for many nights thereafter, to the chagrin of Lieutenant MacKenzie who, until Errol's arrival, had been the fair Ellen's favoured beau.

None of which did much for Errol's popularity. Nor, strangely enough, did an odd episode which I thought was rather to his credit. The command boxing tournament took place, and as sports officer I had to organise our regimental gladiators – which meant calling for volunteers, telling them to knock off booze and smoking, letting them attend to their own sparring and training in the M.T. shed, and seeing that they were sober and (initially) upright on opening night. If that seems perfunctory, I was not a boxer myself, and had no illusions about being Yussel Jacobs when it came to management. Let them get into the ring and lay about them, while I crouched behind their corner, crying encouragement and restraining the seconds from joining in.

The tournament lasted three nights, and in winning his semi-final our heavyweight star, Private McGuigan, the Gorbals

Goliath, broke a finger. Personally I think he did it on purpose to avoid meeting the other finalist, one Captain Stock, a terrible creature of blood and iron who had flattened all his opponents with unimagined ferocity; he was a relic of the Stone Age who had found his way into the Army Physical Training Corps, this Stock, and I wouldn't have gone near him with a whip, a gun, and a chair. Primitive wasn't the word; he made McAuslan and Wee Wullie look like Romantic poets.

Left to find a substitute willing to offer himself for sacrifice at the hands of this Behemoth, I got no takers at all, and then someone said he had heard that Errol used to box a bit, and must be about the right weight. There was enthusiastic support for this suggestion, especially from the older officers, so I sought the man out in his room, where he was reclining with a cool drink at his elbow, shooting moths with an air pistol – and hitting them, too.

'What makes you think I could take Stock, if you'll pardon the expression?' he wondered, when I put it to him. 'Or doesn't that matter, as long as we're represented?'

'Someone in the mess said you used to be pretty useful . . .'

'Did they now? That's handsome of them.' He grinned at me sardonically. 'Who proposed me – Cattenach?' This was the second-in-command, Errol's principal critic. 'Never mind. It's not on, Dand, thanks all the same. I haven't boxed for ages. Too much like work.'

'There's no one else in the battalion,' I said subtly.

'Stop waving the regimental colours at me.' He picked off a large moth on the wing, bringing down a shower of plaster. 'Anyway, I'm an interloper. Let Cattenach take him on if he's so damned keen; God knows he's big enough. No, you'll just have to tell 'em I've retired.'

So I reported failure, and there was disappointment, although no one was daft enough to suggest that Errol was scared. The Adjutant, who was a romantic, speculated that he had probably killed a man in the ring – his fiancée's brother, for choice – and vowed never to box again; he would have joined the Foreign Legion, insisted the Adjutant, if it hadn't been for the war. Others joined in these fine flights, and no one noticed the Colonel sauntering out of the mess, but later that evening he told me casually that I could pencil in Errol for the final; he had been persuaded, said the Colonel, filling his pipe in a contented way. Knowing his fanaticism where the battalion's credit was concerned, I wondered what pressure he had applied, and concluded that he probably hadn't needed any, just his gentle, fatherly insistence which I knew of old. He could have talked a salmon out of its pool, the same Colonel – and of course the possibility that his man might get half-killed wouldn't even cross his mind.

It crossed mine when I saw Errol and Stock face to muzzle in the ring; so might Adonis have looked in the presence of a silverback gorilla. Stock stood half a head taller, two stone heavier, and about a foot thicker, especially round the brow. He came out at the bell like a Panzer tank – and Errol moved round him as though on rollers, weaving and feinting until he'd sized him up, and then began systematically left-handing him to death. It was Carpentier to the town drunk; Stock clubbed and rushed and never got near him until the second round, when he had the ill-judgment to land a kidney-punch. Errol came out of the clinch looking white and wicked, and thereafter took Stock apart with clinical savagery. The referee stopped it in the third, with Stock bloodied and out on his feet; Errol hadn't a hair out of place, and I doubt if he'd been touched more than half a dozen times.

But as I said, he got no credit from that fight. It had been so one-sided that all the sympathy was for the battered Stock, and there was even a feeling that Errol had been over-brutal to a man who wasn't in his class as a boxer. Which was unfair, since he had been reluctant to fight in the first place – my guess is that he knew exactly how good he was, and that Stock would be no contest. But if he compared the polite clapping as he left the ring with the thunder of applause for his groggy but gamely smiling opponent, it didn't seem to worry him; he strolled back to the changing-room cool and unruffled as ever.

It was immediately after this that he finally fell from grace altogether, and the mixed feelings of the mess hardened into positive dislike. Two things happened to show him at his worst; neither was earth-shattering in itself, but in each case he displayed such a cynical indifference that even his friends could find no excuses.

In the first instance, he stole another man's girl – and it wasn't a case of cutting out someone like MacKenzie, the battalion Lothario, with Ellen Ramsey, whose admirers were legion (including even the unlikely Private McAuslan, whose wooing I have described elsewhere). Boy met, dated, and parted from girl with bewildering speed in post-war garrisons, and no harm done; Errol himself must have been involved with half the nurses, A.T.S., Wrens, and civilian females, and no one thought twice, except to note jealously that while the rest of us had to pursue, he seemed to draw them like a magnet.

But the case of Sister Jean was different. She was a flashing-eyed Irish redhead, decorative even by the high standard of the hospital staff, and her attachment to a U.S. pilot at the bomber base was the real thing, what the Adjutant called Poignant Passion, engagement ring, wedding date fixed, and all – until Errol moved in on the lady. I was on detachment at Fort Yarhuna during the crisis, but according to MacKenzie it had started with casual cheek-to-cheek stuff on the dance-floor at the Uaddan Club, progressing to dates, picnics, and sailing-trips on Errol's dinghy while the American was absent on his country's service, dropping sandbags on the desert (I quote MacKenzie). In brief, Jean had been beglamoured, her fiancé had objected, a lovers' quarrel had ensued with high words flying in Irish and American, the ring had been returned, the pilot had got himself posted to Italy in dudgeon, and the hapless patients in Sister Jean's ward were learning what life was like under the Empress Theodora.

'Talk about hell hath no fury,' said MacKenzie. 'She's lobbing out enemas like a mad thing. You see, not only is her romance with Tex kaput, *bus*, washed up; on top of that, the unspeakable Errol has given her the gate and is pushing around the new Ensa bint – who is a piece of all right, I have to admit. What women see in him,' he added irritably, 'I'm shot if I know. The man's a tick, a suede-shoe artist, a Semiramis Hotel creeper of the lowest type.'

'Didn't anyone try to steer him away from Jean?' I asked, thinking of the Colonel, who when it came to intervening in his junior officers' love lives could have given Lady Bracknell a head start. 'Why didn't you tackle him yourself?'

'Come off it. Remember what happened to Stock? Actually, Ellen Ramsey did get stuck into him at one stage . . . gosh, she's a honey, that girl,' said MacKenzie, smiling dreamily. 'I think I'll take her grouse-shooting when we go home. You know, dazzle her with Perthshire . . . Eh? Oh, well, she tore strips off Errol, and he just laughed and said: 'Why, darling, I didn't know you cared,' and swanned off, cool as be-damned, to take Jean swimming. And now, having wrecked her future, and Tex's, he goes around blithe as a bird, as though nothing had happened. Yes – a total tick, slice him where you will.'

A fair assessment, on the face of it, and the temperature dropped noticeably in the mess when Errol was present, not that he seemed aware of it. Otherwise the incident was closed; for one thing, there were far more urgent matters to think about just then. Political trouble was beginning to brew in our former Italian colony, with noisy nationalist demonstrations, stoning of police posts by Arab gangs, and the prospect that we would be called out to support the civil administration.

If there's going to be active service, the last thing you need is discord in the mess.

Even so, Errol's next gaffe came close to blowing the lid off with his bête noire, Cattenach, the second-in-command; it was the nearest thing I ever saw to a brawl between brother-officers, and all because of Errol's bloody-minded disregard for other people's feelings. He had set off early one morning to shoot on the salt flats outside the town, and came breezing in just as we were finishing breakfast, calling for black coffee and telling Bennet-Bruce that his shotgun (which Errol had borrowed, typically) was throwing left. Bennet-Bruce asked if he'd had any luck.

'Nothing to write to the *Field* about,' said Errol, buttering toast. 'In fact, sweet dam'-all, except for a couple of kites near the Armoury. Weird-looking things.'

Cattenach lowered his paper. 'Did you say near the Armoury? Where are these birds?'

'Where I left them, of course; somewhere around the Armoury wall. They weren't worth keeping.'

Cattenach looked thoughtful, but went back to his paper, and it wasn't until lunchtime that he returned to the subject. He brought his drink across from the bar and stopped in front of Errol's chair, waiting until he had finished telling his latest story and had become aware that Cattenach was regarding him stonily. The second-in-command was a lean, craggy, normally taciturn man with a rat-trap mouth that made him look like one of the less amiable Norman barons.

'You may be interested to know,' he said curtly, 'that the "kites" you shot this morning were the Brigadier's pet hawks.'

There was a startled silence, in which the Padre said: 'Oh, cracky good gracious!', and Errol cocked an incredulous eyebrow. 'What are you talking about – hawks? Since when do hawks stooge around loose, like crows!'

'They were tame hawks – something unique, I believe,' said

Cattenach, enjoying himself in his own grim fashion. 'A gift to the Brigadier from King Idris, after the desert campaign. Quite irreplaceable, of course, as well as being priceless. And you shot them. Congratulations.'

Well, you and I or any normal person would at this point have lowered the head in the hands, giving little whimpering cries punctuated by stricken oaths and appeals for advice. Not Errol, though; he just downed his drink and observed lightly:

'Well, why didn't he keep them on a leash? I thought it was usual to put hoods over their heads.'

We stared at the man, and someone protested: 'Oh, come off it, Errol!', while Cattenach went crimson and began to inflate.

'Is that all you've got to say?' he demanded, and Errol regarded him with maddening calm.

'What d'you expect me to say? I'm sorry, of course.' If he was he certainly didn't sound it. 'I'll send the old boy a note of apology.' He gave Cattenach a nod that was almost dismissive. 'Okay?'

'Just . . . that?' growled Cattenach, ready to burst.

'I can't very well do anything else,' said Errol, and picked up a magazine. 'Unless you expect me to rend my garments.' To do him justice, I believe that if anyone else had brought him the glad news, he'd have shown more concern, but he wasn't giving Cattenach that satisfaction – just his cool half-smile, and the second-in-command had to struggle to keep a grip on himself in the face of that dumb insolence. He took a breath, and then said with deliberation:

'The trouble with you, and what makes you such an unpleasant regimental liability, is that while most of us couldn't care more, you just couldn't care less.'

No one had ever heard Cattenach, who was normally a quiet soul, talk with such controlled contempt – and in the mess, of all places. A little flush appeared on Errol's cheek, and he rose from his chair, but only to look Cattenach in the eye and say:

'You know, that's extremely well put. I think I'll enter it in the mess book.'

That was when I thought Cattenach was going to hit him – or try to, because Errol, for all his composure, was balanced like a cat. Suddenly it was very ugly, the Padre was making anxious noises, and the Adjutant was starting forward, and then Cattenach turned abruptly on his heel and stalked out. There was a toe-curling silence – and of course I had to open my big mouth, heaven knows why, unless I thought it was time to raise the conversation to a higher plane.

'Why can't you bloody well wrap up, just for once?' I demanded, and was told by the Adjutant to shut up. 'I think you've said enough, too,' he told Errol. 'Right – who's for lunch?'

'I am, for one,' said Errol, unabashed. 'Drama always gives me an appetite,' and he sauntered off to the dining-room, leaving us looking at each other, the Padre muttering about the pride of Lucifer, and the M.O., after a final inhalation of the Tallisker, voicing the general thought.

'Yon's a bad man,' he said. 'Mercy is not in him.'

That was a fact, I thought. Not only had he shown a callous disregard for the feelings of the Brigadier, bereaved of his precious pets, he had strained the egalitarian conventions of the mess to the limit in his behaviour to Cattenach – who, mind you, had been making a meal of his own dislike for Errol. It was all enough to make one say 'Tach!', as my grandmother used to exclaim in irritation, and lunch was taken in general ill-temper – except for Errol, who ate a tranquil salad and lingered over his coffee.

And then such trivia ceased to matter, for at 2.15 came the sudden alarm call from the Police Commissioner to say that the unrest which had been simmering in the native quarter had suddenly burst into violence: a mob of Arab malcontents and *bazaar-wallahs* were rioting in the Suk, pillaging shops and fire-raising; one of the leading nationalist agitators, Marbruk es-Salah, was haranguing a huge gathering near the Yassid Market, and it looked only a matter of time before they would be spilling out of the Old City and rampaging towards the European suburbs. Aid to the civil power was a matter of urgency – which meant that at 2.45 the two three-ton trucks bearing the armed might of 12 Platoon pulled up on the great dusty square east of the Kantara Bridge, and I reviewed the force with which I was expected to plug that particular outlet from the native quarter.

In theory, the plan for containing unrest was simple. The Old City, an impossible warren of tall crumbling buildings and hundreds of crooked streets and narrow alleys, spread out like a huge fan from the waterfront; beyond the semi-circular edge of the fan lay the European suburbs of the Italian colonial era, girdling the squalid Old City from sea to sea in a luxurious crescent of apartment buildings, bungalows, shops, restaurants, and broad streets – a looter's paradise for the teeming thousands of the Old City's inhabitants, if they ever invaded in force. To make sure they didn't, the 24 infantry platoons of our battalion and the Fusiliers were supposed to block every outlet from the Old City to the New Town, and since these were innumerable, careful disposition of forces was vital.

Kantara was an easy one, since here there was an enormous ditch hemming the native town like a moat, and the only way across was the ancient bridge (which is what Kantara means) which we were guarding. It was a structure of massive stones which had been there before the Caesars, twenty feet broad between low parapets, and perhaps twice as long. From where I stood on the open ground at its eastern end, I could look across the bridge at a peaceful enough scene: a wide market-place in which interesting Orientals were going about their business of loafing, wailing, squatting in the dust, or snoozing in the shadows of the great rickety tenements and ruined walls of the Old City. Behind me were the broad, palm-lined boulevards of the modern resort area, with dazzling white apartments and pleasant gardens, a couple of hotels and restaurants, and beyond them the hospital and the beach club. It looked like something out of a travel brochure, with a faint drift of Glenn Miller on the afternoon air – and then you turned back to face the ancient stronghold of the Barbary Corsairs, a huge festering slum crouched like a malignant genie above the peaceful European suburb, and felt thankful for the separating moat-ditch with only that single dusty causeway across it.

'Nae bother,' said Sergeant Telfer. Like me, he was thinking that thirty Jocks with fifty rounds apiece could have held that bridge against ten times the native population – provided they were empowered to shoot, that is. Which, if it came to the point, would be up to me. But we both knew that was highly unlikely; by all accounts the trouble was at the western end of the Old City, where most of our troops were concentrated. Kantara was very much the soft option, which was presumably why one platoon had been deemed enough. They hadn't thought it worth while giving us a radio, even.

Since it was all quiet, I didn't form the platoon up, but showed them where, in the event of trouble, they would take up extended line, facing the bridge and about fifty yards from it, out of range of any possible missiles from beyond the ditch. Then they sat in the shade of the trucks, smoking and gossiping, while I prowled about, watching the market for any signs of disturbance, vaguely aware of the discussion on current affairs taking place behind me.

'Hi, Corporal Mackie, whit are the wogs gettin' het up aboot, then?'

'Independence.' Mackie had been a civil servant, and was the platoon intellectual. 'Self-government by their own political leaders. They don't like being under Allied occupation.'

'Fair enough, me neither. Whit's stoppin' them?'

'You are, McAuslan. You're the heir to the pre-war Italian government. So do your shirt up and try to look like it.'

'Me? Fat chance! The wogs can hiv it for me, sure'n they can, Fletcher? It's no' my parish. Hi, corporal, whit wey does the government no' let the wogs have it?'

'Because they'd make a bluidy mess o' it, dozy.' This was Fletcher, who was a sort of Churchillian Communist. 'They're no' fit tae run a mennodge. Look behind ye – that's civilisation. Then look ower there at that midden o' a toon; that's whit the wogs would make o' it. See?'

So much for Ibn Khaldun and the architects of the Alhambra. Some similar thought must have stirred McAuslan's strange mental processes, for he came out with a nugget which, frankly, I wouldn't have thought he knew.

'Haud on a minnit, Fletcher – it was wogs built the Pyramids, wisn't it? That's whit the Padre says. Aye, weel, there ye are. They cannae be that dumb.'

'Those werenae wogs, ya mug! Those were Ancient Egyptians.'

'An Egyptian's a wog! Sure'n he is. So don't gi' me the acid, Fletcher. Anyway, if Ah wis a wog, Ah wid dam' soon get things sortit oot aboot indamapendence. If Ah wis a wog –'

'That's a helluva insult tae wogs, right enough. Ah can just see ye! Hey, fellas, meet Abu ben McAuslan, the Red Shadow. Ye fancy havin' a harem, McAuslan? Aboot twenty belly-dancers like Big Aggie frae the Blue Heaven?' And Fletcher began to hum snake-charmer music, while his comrades speculated coarsely on McAuslan, Caliph of the Faithful, and I looked through the heat haze at the Old City, and thought about cool pints in the dim quiet of the mess ante-room.

It came, as it so often does, with daunting speed. There was a distant muttering from the direction of the Old City, like a wind getting up, and the market-place beyond the bridge was suddenly empty and still in the late afternoon sun. Then the muttering changed to a rising rumble of hurrying feet and harsh voices growing louder. I shouted to Telfer to fall in, and from the mouth of a street beyond the market-place a native police jeep came racing over the bridge. It didn't stop; I had a glimpse of a brown face, scared and staring, under a peaked cap, and then the jeep was gone in a cloud of dust, heading up into the New Town. So much for the civil power. The platoon were fanning out in open order, each man with his rifle and a canvas bandolier at his waist; they stood easy, and Telfer turned to me for orders. I was gazing across the bridge, watching Crisis arrive in a frightsome form, and realising with sudden dread that there was no one on God's green earth to deal with it, except me.

It's quite a moment. You're taking it easy, on a sunny afternoon, listening to the Jocks chaffing – and then out of the alleys two hundred yards away figures are hurrying, hundreds of them, converging into a great milling mob, yelling in unison, waving their fists, starting to move towards you. A menace beats off them that you can feel, dark glaring faces, sticks brandished, robes waving and feet churning up the dust in clouds before them, the rhythmic chanting sounding like a barbaric war-song – and you fight down the panic and turn to look at the khaki line strung out either side of you, the young faces set under the slanted bonnets, the rifles at their sides, standing at ease – waiting for you. If you say the word, they'll shoot that advancing mob flat, and go on shooting, because that's what they're trained to do, for thirty bob a week – and if that doesn't stop the opposition, they'll stand and fight it out on the spot as long as they can, because that's part of the conscript's bargain, too. But it's entirely up to you – and there's no colonel or company commander to instruct or advise. And it doesn't matter if you've led a section in warfare, where there is no rule save survival; this is different, for these are not the enemy – by God, I thought, you could have fooled me; I may know it, but I'll bet they don't – they are civilians, and you must not shoot unless you have to, and only you can decide that, so make up your mind, Dand, and don't dawdle: you're getting nine quid a week, after all, so the least you can do is show some initiative.

'Charge magazines, Sar'nt Telfer! Corporals, watch those cut-offs! Mackie – if McAuslan gets one up the spout I'll blitz you! Here – I'll do it!' I grabbed McAuslan's rifle, jammed down the top round, closed the cut-off, rammed home the bolt, clicked the trigger, and thumbed on the safety-catch while he squawked indignantly that he could dae it, he wisnae stupid, him. I shoved his rifle into his hand and looked across the bridge again.

The rattle of the charging magazines had checked them for barely an instant; now they were coming on again, a solid mass of humanity choking the square, half-hidden by the dust they were raising. Out front there was a big thug in a white burnous and red tarboosh who turned to face the mob, chanting some slogan, before turning to lead them on, punching his arms into the air. There were banners waving in the front rank – and I knew this was no random gang of looters, but an organised horde bent on striking where they knew the forces of order were weakest – I had thirty Jocks between them and that peaceful suburb with its hotels and pleasant homes and hospital. Over their heads I could see smoke on the far side of the market . . .

'Fix bayonets, Sarn't Telfer!' I shouted, and on his command the long sword-blades zeeped out of the scabbards, the locking-rings clicked, and the hands cut away to the sides. 'Present!' and the thirty rifles with their glittering points went forward.

That stopped them, dead. The big thug threw up his arms, and they halted, yelling louder than ever and shaking fists and clubs, but they were still fifty yards from the bridge. They eddied to and fro, milling about, while the big burnous exhorted them, waving his arms – and I moved along the line, forcing myself to talk as quietly as the book says you must, saying the proper things in the proper order.

'Easy does it, children. Wait for it. If they start to come on, you stand fast, understand? Nobody moves – except Fletcher, Macrae, Duncan, and Souness. You four, when I say 'Load!' will put one round up the spout – but don't fire! Not till I tell you.' They had rehearsed it all before, the quartet of marksmen had been designated, but it all had to be repeated. 'If I say 'Over their heads, fire!', you all take aim, but only those four will fire on the word. Got it? Right, wait for it . . . easy does it . . . take Blackie's name, Sarn't Telfer, his bayonet's filthy . . . wait for it . . .'

It's amazing how you can reassure yourself, by reassuring other people. I felt suddenly elated, and fought down the evil hope that we might have to fire in earnest – oh, that's an emotion that comes all too easily – and walked along the front of the line, looking at the faces – young and tight-lipped, all staring past me at the crowd, one or two sweating, a few Adam's apples moving, but not much. The chanting suddenly rose to a great yell, and the crowd was advancing again, but slowly this time, a few feet at a time, stopping, then coming on, the big burnous gesticulating to his followers, and then turning to stare in my direction. You bastard, I thought – you know what it's all about! We can fire over your head till we're blue in the face, but it won't stop you – you'll keep coming, calling our bluff, daring us to let fly. Right, son, if anyone gets it, you will . . .

They were coming steadily now, but still slowly; I judged their distance from the bridge and shouted: 'Four men – load! Remainder, stand fast! Wait for it . . .'

A stone came flying from the crowd, falling well short, but

followed by a shower of missiles kicking up the dust ahead of us. I walked five slow paces out in front of the platoon – believe it or not, that can make a mob hesitate – and waited; when the first stone reached me, I would give the order to fire over their heads. If they still kept coming, I would take a rifle and shoot the big burnous, personally, wounding if possible – and if that didn't do it, I would order the four marksmen to take out four rioters. Then, if they charged us, I would order rapid fire into the crowd . . .

By today's standards, you may think that atrocious. Well, think away. My job was to save that helpless suburb from the certain death and destruction that mob would wreak if they broke through. So retreat was impossible on that head, never mind that soldiers cannot run from a riot and if I ordered them to retire I'd never be able to look in a mirror again. But above all these good reasons was the fact that if I let that horde of yelling maniacs reach us, some of my Jocks would die – knifed or clubbed or trampled lifeless, and I hadn't been entrusted with thirty young Scottish lives in order to throw them away. That was the real clincher, and why I would loose up to three hundred rounds rapid into our attackers if I had to. It gets terribly simple when you're looking it in the face.

The shouting rose to a mad crescendo, they were a bare thirty yards from the bridge, the burnous was leaping like a dervish, you could sense the rush coming, and without looking round I shouted:

'Four men – over their heads . . . fire!'

It crashed out like one report. One of the flag-poles jerked crazily – Fletcher playing Davy Crockett – and the crowd reared back like a horse at a hedge. For a splendid moment I thought they were going to scatter, but they didn't: the big burnous was playing a stormer, grabbing those nearest, rallying them, urging them forward with voice and gesture. My heart sank as I took Telfer's rifle, for I was going to have to nail that one, unarmed civilian that he was, and I found myself remembering my awful closing line: 'Well, that's that' from that ghastly play in Bangalore . . .

'Having fun, Dand?' said a voice at my elbow, and there was Errol beside me, cupping his hands as he lit a cigarette. Thank God, reinforcements at the last minute – and then I saw the solitary jeep parked by the trucks. Nobody else. He drew on his cigarette, surveying the crowd.

'What'll you do?' he asked conversationally – no suggestion of assuming command, you notice; what would *I* do.

'Shoot that big beggar in the leg!'

'You might miss,' he said, 'and sure as fate we'd find a dead nun on the ground afterwards. Or a four-year-old orphan.' He gave me his lazy grin. 'I think we can do better than that.'

'What the hell are you on, Errol?' I demanded, in some agitation. 'Look, they're going to –'

'Not to panic. I'd say we've got about thirty seconds.' He swung round. 'You, you, and you – run to my jeep! Get the drum of signal wire, the cutters, the mortar box, and double back here – now! Move!'

'Are you taking command?'

'God, you're regimental. I'll bet you were a pig of a lancejack. Here, have a fag – go on, you clot, the wogs are watching, wondering what the hell we're up to.'

The lean brown face with its trim Colman moustache was smiling calmly under the cocked bonnet; his hand was rock-steady as he held out the cigarette-case – it was one of those hammered silver jobs you got in Indian bazaars, engraved with a map and erratic spelling. And he was right: the yelling had died down, and they were watching us and wondering . . .

Three Jocks came running, two with the heavy drum of wire between them on its axle, the third (McAuslan, who else?) labouring with the big metal mortar box, roaring to them tae haud on, he couldnae manage the bluidy thing, damn it tae hell . . .

'Listen, Dand,' said Errol. 'Run like hell to the bridge, unrolling the wire. When you get there, cut it. Open the mortar box – it's empty – stick the end of the wire inside, close the lid. Got it? Then scatter like billy-be-damned. Move!'

Frankly, I didn't get it. He must be doolaly. But if the Army teaches you anything, it's to act on the word, no questions asked – which is how great victories are won (and great disasters caused).

'Come on!' I yelled, and went for the bridge like a stung whippet, followed by the burdened trio, McAuslan galloping in the rear demanding to know whit the hell was gaun on. Well, I didn't know, for one – all I had room for was the appalling knowledge that I was running straight towards several hundred angry *bazaar-wallahs* who were bent on pillage and slaughter. Fortunately, there isn't time to think in fifty yards, or to notice anything except that the ragged ranks ahead seemed to be stricken immobile, if not silent: the big burnous, out in front, was stock-still and staring, while his followers raged behind him, presumably echoing McAuslan's plea for enlightenment. I had a picture of yelling, hostile black faces as I skidded to a standstill at the mouth of the bridge; the two Jocks with the wire were about ten yards behind, closing fast as they unreeled the long shining thread behind them; staggering with them, his contorted face mouthing horribly over the mortar box clasped in his arms, was Old Insanitary himself. He won by a short head, sprawling headlong and depositing the box at my feet.

'The cutters!' I snapped, as he grovelled, blaspheming, in the dust. 'The cutters, McAuslan!'

'Whit cutters?' he cried, crouching like Quasimodo in the pillory, and then his eyes fell on the menacing but still irresolute mob a scant thirty yards away. 'Mither o' Goad! Wull ye look at yon? The cutters – Ah've goat them! Here th'are, sur – Ah've goat them!' He pawed at his waist – and the big wire cutters, which he had thrust into the top of his shorts for convenient carriage, slid out of view. And it is stark truth: one handle emerged from one leg of his shorts, the second handle from the other.

I'm not sure what I said, but I'll bet only dogs could hear it. Fortunately MacLeod, one of the wire-carriers, was a lad of resource and rare self-sacrifice; he hurled himself at McAuslan, thrust his hand down the back of his shorts, and yanked viciously. There was an anguished wail and a fearsome rending of khaki, the cutters were dragged free, and as I grabbed them in one hand and the wire in the other, McAuslan's recriminations seemed to fill the afternoon. He was, it appeared, near ruined, an' see his bluidy troosers; there wis nae need for it, MacLood, an' ye'll pey for them an' chance it, handless teuchter that ye are . . .

For some reason that I'll never understand, it steadied me. I clipped the wire, and as I unsnapped the mortar box catches it dawned on me what Errol was up to, the lunatic – and it seemed only sensible to lift the lid slowly, push in the wire, fumble artistically in the interior before closing the lid as though it were made of porcelain, and spare two seconds for a calculating look at the bewildered mob beyond the bridge. To my horror, they were advancing – I looked back at the platoon, fifty yards off, and sure enough Errol was kneeling at the other end of the wire, which was attached to a metal container – a petrol jerry-can, as it turned out. He had one hand poised as though to work a plunger; with the other he waved an urgent signal.

'Get out of it!' I yelled, and as MacLeod and his mate scattered and ran I seized McAuslan by the nape of his unwashed neck, running him protesting from the bridge before throwing him and myself headlong.

It worked. You had only to put yourself in the shoes of

Burnous and Co. to see that it was bound to. We weren't wiring things up for the good of their health, they must have reasoned: that sinister mortar box lying on the bridge must be packed with death and destruction. When I had rolled over and got the sand out of my eyes they were in full retreat across the market square, a great disordered rabble intent on getting as far as possible from that unknown menace. In a few seconds an army of rioters had been turned into a rout – and the man responsible was sitting at his ease on the jerry-can, giving me an airy wave of his cigarette-holder as I trudged back to the platoon.

'You mad son-of-a-bitch!' I said, with deep respect, and he touched his bonnet in acknowledgement.

'Psychology, laddie. Not nearly as messy as shooting poor wee wogs, you bloodthirsty subaltern, you. That would never have done – not on top of the Brigadier's hawks. Not all in one day. Cattenach would have had kittenachs.' He chuckled and stood up, smoothing his immaculate khaki drill, and shaded his eyes to look at the distant remnant of the riot milling disconsolately on the far side of the market-place.

'Aye, weel, they'll no' be back the day,' he said, imitating a Glasgow wifey. 'So. Where will they go next, eh? Tell me that, MacNeill of Barra – or of Great Western Road, W.2. Where . . . will . . . they . . . go?'

'Home?' I suggested.

'Don't you believe it, cock. Marbruk wasn't with 'em – he'll still be holding forth to the main body down at Yassid. Oh, if we'd lost the bridge he'd have been over sharp enough, with about twenty thousand angry wogs at his back. But now . . . I wonder.'

I was still digesting the outrageous bluff he'd pulled. I indicated the jerry-can and the string of wire running to the bridge. 'Do you usually carry that kind of junk in your jeep?' I asked, and he patted me on the shoulder, as with a half-wit.

'I'm the Intelligence Officer, remember? All-wise, all-knowing, all full of bull. Oh, look – soldiers!' Half a dozen Fusilier trucks were speeding down the New Town boulevard towards us, and Errol shook his head in admiration as he climbed into his jeep.

'Locking the stable door,' said he, and winked at me. 'I'd better go and see which one they've left open. Buy you a drink at Renucci's, nine o'clock, okay?' He waved and revved off with a horrific grinding of metal, changing gears with his foot, which takes lots of practice.

When I showed the Fusilier Company Commander the mortar box with its fake wire he didn't believe it at first, and then congratulated me warmly; when I told him it had been Errol's idea he grunted and said, 'Oh, him', which I thought both ungrammatical and ungrateful, and told me I was to withdraw my platoon to the hospital. So I passed the remainder of that fateful day chatting up the nursing staff, drinking tea, and listening with interest to Private McAuslan telling Fletcher that it was a bluidy good job that bomb hadnae gone off on the bridge, because me an' Darkie an' MacLood an' Dysart would hiv' got blew up, sure'n we would.

'It wisnae a bomb, ye bap-heid! He wis kiddin' the wogs. There wis nothin' tae it.'

'Are you tellin' me, Fletcher? Ah wis there! Ah cairrit the bluidy thing! Help ma Goad, if Ah'd known! That man Errol's a menace, so he is; he coulda goat us a' killed, me 'an Darkie an' MacLood an' Dysart . . .' You can fool some of the people all of the time.

It was only when the alert was over, and I had sent the platoon back to barracks with Telfer and foregathered at Renucci's for the promised drink with Errol, that I learned what had been happening elsewhere. It had been high drama, and the clientele of Renucci's bar and grill were full of it. After our episode at the bridge, things had fallen out as Errol had foreseen: Marbruk es-Salah, after whipping up his followers at Yassid Market, had launched them at dusk through the old Suk slave-market in an attempt to invade the business area of the New Town, two miles away from Kantara. Part of the Suk had been burned and the rest pillaged, and the enormous crowd would undoubtedly have broken out with a vengeance if they had not suddenly lost their leader.

'Nobody seems to know exactly what happened,' a stout civilian was telling the bar, 'except that Marbruk was obviously making for the weakest point in the security cordon – you won't credit it, but there wasn't even a constable guarding the Suk Gate. God knows what would have happened if they'd got beyond it; sheer devastation and half the New Town up in smoke, I expect. Anyway, that's when Marbruk got shot –'

'But you said there were no troops there,' someone protested.

'Nor were there. It seems he was shot *inside* the Suk. What with the uproar and the fact that it was dark, even his immediate henchmen didn't realise it at first, and when they did – sheer pandemonium. But they'd lost all sense of direction, thank God – otherwise we wouldn't be standing here, I daresay.'

'Who on earth did it? Did the police get him?'

'You're joking, old boy! In the Suk, during a riot, at night? I should think our gallant native constabulary are too busy drinking the assassin's health.'

'I heard they got Marbruk's body out . . .'

I lost the rest of it in the noise, and at that moment Errol slipped on to the stool next to me and asked what I was drinking.

'Antiquary – hang on, I want to hear this.'

'Evening, Carlo.' Errol rapped the bar. 'Antiquary and Glenfiddich and two waters, at your good pleasure.' He seemed in fine fettle, glancing bright-eyed over the crowd. 'What's to do?'

'Marbruk's dead.'

'You don't say? That's a turn-up.' He whistled softly, fitting a cigarette into his holder. 'How'd it happen?'

I indicated the stout civilian, who was continuing.

'. . . probably one of his political rivals. You know what they're like – pack of jackals. With Marbruk gone, there'll be a fine scramble among his lieutenants.'

'It wasn't one of the gang with him,' said a police captain. 'Burgess saw the body and talked to informers. Shot twice, head and heart, almost certainly with a rifle, from a roof-top.'

'Good God! A sniper? Doesn't sound like a *bazaar-wallah*!'

'Whoever it was, here's to him,' said the stout civilian. 'He probably saved the town in the nick of time.'

Our whisky arrived and Errol studied the pale liquid with satisfaction. 'First today. *Slàinte mhath.*' He sipped contentedly. 'Yes, that's the good material. Had dinner?'

'Too late for me, thanks. I'll have a sandwich in the mess. I've got a report to write.'

'How Horatius kept the bridge?' He grinned sardonically. 'You can leave me out of it.'

'Don't be soft! It was your idea that did it!'

'They won't like it any better for that. Oh, well, please yourself.'

'Look, if it wasn't a rival wog, who was it?' someone was exclaiming. 'It can't have been police or military, without authority – I mean to say, it's simple murder.'

'And just Marbruk – the king-pin. A political rival would have tried to knock out that right-hand man of his, Gamal Whatsit, wouldn't he?'

'Well, perhaps . . . or it may just have been a personal feud . . .'

Errol was lounging back on his stool, studying the menu on the bar, but I had the impression he was listening, not reading. I noticed that like me he was still in K.D., belt, and revolver, and less spruce than usual: there was a smudge of oil on his shirt and one sleeve was dirty. He looked tired but otherwise at peace with the world.

'When you've finished inspecting me, MacNeill,' he said, still scanning the menu, 'how about getting them in again?'

'Sorry. Two more, Carlo.'

'Anyway, it was a damned fine shot,' said the police captain. 'Two damned fine shots – and as you say, just in time, from our point of view.'

'You won't break a leg looking for the murderer, eh?'

'Oh, there'll have to be an inquiry, of course . . .'

'I'll bet there will,' Errol murmured, and laughed softly – and something in the sound chilled my spine as I put my glass to my lips. Sometimes a sudden, impossible thought hits you, and in the moment it takes to swallow a sip of whisky you know, beyond doubt, that it's not only possible, but true. It fitted all too well . . . 'killing Huns with cheese-wire by night' . . . the expertise with small arms . . . the rumours of anti-terrorist brutalities in Palestine . . . the scientific destruction of a boxing opponent . . . the cold-blooded nerve of his bluff at Kantara Bridge . . . all that I knew of the man's character . . .

'Steak, I think,' said Errol, closing the menu. 'About a ton of Châteaubriand garni – that's parsley on top, to you – preceded by delicious tomato soup. Sure I can't tempt you? What's up laddie, you look ruptured?' The whimsical glance, the raised eyebrow, and just for an instant the smile froze on the handsome face. He glanced past me at the debating group, and then the smile was back, the half-mocking regard that was almost a challenge. 'The cop's right, don't you agree? A damned good shot. You used to be a sniper – what d'you think?'

'Someone knew his business.'

He studied me, and nodded. 'Just as well, wasn't it? So . . . as our stout friend would say – here's to him.' He raised his glass. 'Okay?'

'*Slàinte*', I said, automatically. There was no point in saying anything else.

We drank, and Errol turned on his stool to the dining-room arch immediately behind him. A little Italian head-waiter, full of consequence, was bowing to a couple in evening dress and checking his booking-board.

'Table for one, please,' said Errol, and the little man bared his teeth in a professional smile.

'Certainly, sir, this way –' His face suddenly fell, and he straightened up. 'I regret, sir – for dinner we have to insist on the neck-tie.'

'You don't mean it? What, after a day like this? Oh, come off it!'

'I am sorry, sir.' The head-waiter was taking in Errol's informal, not to say untidy, appearance. 'It is our rule.'

'All right, lend me a tie, then,' said Errol cheerfully.

'I am sorry, sir.' The waiter was on his dignity. 'We have no ties.'

Errol sat slowly upright on his stool, giving him a long, thoughtful look, and then to my horror laid a hand on his revolver-butt. The head-waiter squeaked and jumped, I had a vision of inkpots being shot off desks – and then Errol's hand moved from the butt up the thin pistol lanyard looped round his neck, and smoothly tightened its slip-knot into a tie.

'Table for one?' he asked sweetly, and the head-waiter hesitated, swallowed, muttered: 'This way, sir,' and scurried into the dining-room. Errol slid off his stool, glass in hand, and gave me a wink.

'Blind 'em with flannel, laddie. It works every time.' He finished his drink without haste, and set his glass on the bar. 'Well . . . almost every time.' He gave his casual nod and sauntered into the dining-room.

The investigation of Marbruk es-Salah's murder came to nothing.

There was no more nationalist unrest until long after our departure, when a republic was established which turned into a troublesome dictatorship – so troublesome that forty years later the American air force raided it in reprisal for terrorist attacks, bombing our old barracks. This saddened me, because I had been happy there, and it seemed wasteful, somehow, after all the trouble we'd had just preserving that pleasant city from riot and arson and pillage. I'm not blaming the Americans; they were doing what they thought best – just as we had done. Just as Errol had done.

I lost sight of him when I was demobilised; he was still with the battalion then, going his careless way, raising hackles and causing trouble. Many years later, a wire-photo landed on my newspaper desk, and there he was among a group of Congo mercenaries; the moustache had gone and the hairline had receded, but there was no mistaking the cigarette holder and the relaxed, confident carriage; even with middle-aged spread beneath his flak-jacket, he still had style. Yes, I thought, that's where you would end up. You see, there's no place for people like Errol in a normal, peace-time world; they just don't belong. Their time lay between the years 1939 and 1945 – and even then they sometimes didn't fit in too comfortably. But I wonder if we'd have won the war without them.

The Constipation of O'Brien

Apart from the three afternoons devoted to games (which in our battalion meant football, no matter what the time of year) the most popular event of 12 Platoon's working week was undoubtedly the Education Period. Not that they were especially thirsty for academic improvement, but the period came last on Friday afternoon, at the end of the week's soldiering, and following immediately after a bathing parade which consisted of lolling on the warm sand of a gloriously golden North African beach, idly watching the creamy little waves washing in from the blue Mediterranean – the kind of thing millionaires would have paid through the nose for, but which in those balmy post-war years the British Army provided free. And there was no Hotel Ptomaine just over the skyline in those days, crammed with reddened tourists, bad drains, and abominable canned music; just a thousand miles of nothing stretching literally to Timbuctoo on the one hand, and Homer's sunlit sea on the other, apparently unsailed since Ulysses went down over the horizon to distant Djerba.

It was, consequently, a fairly torpid audience that I used to find awaiting me in the platoon lecture room afterwards, all 36 of them jammed into the two back rows, snoozing gently against the whitewashed walls, whence Sergeant Telfer would summon them to git tae the front and wake yer bluidy selves up. When they had obeyed, blinking and reluctant, I would announce:

'Right. Education Period. Pay attention, smoke if you want to. Now, what we're going on with this afternoon is . . . '

The formula never varied; it was as settled and comforting as a prayer. Whether the subject was British Way and Purpose (whatever that was, something to do with why we'd fought the war, as if anybody cared), or Care of the Feet, or How-to-get-civilian-employment-when-you-are-demobilised (a particularly useful lecture that, since it was delivered by a subaltern who'd never held a steady job in his life to a platoon who'd spent most of their time on the dole), or any of the numerous subjects prescribed by the Army Bureau of Current Affairs, it was invariably introduced as 'what we are going on with'. Why, I don't know; it probably dated from Marlborough's time, and it has been the signal for successive legions of young British soldiers to settle themselves contentedly on their benches and sleep with their eyes open, dreaming about Rita Hayworth (or Florrie Ford or Nell Gwynn, depending on the era) while their platoon commander gasses earnestly at them.

There is a whole generation of elderly men in these islands today who, if you whisper 'what we are going on with' in their ears, will immediately relax, with an expression of feigned interest in their glassy eyes, gently munching their lips as a prelude to dropping off. That's what army education does for you. The only way I ever discovered of reclaiming my platoon's attention during a lecture was to drop in a reference to football or women; once, to settle a bet with the Adjutant, I read them a very long passage from Hobbes' *Leviathan*, and when they were drowsing nicely I suddenly began a sentence with the words 'Gypsy Rose Lee' – the effect was electric: 36 nodding heads snapped up as though jerked by wires, quivering like ardent gundogs, and 72 eyes gleamed with animation. From a lecturing point of view it posed me a difficult problem of smooth continuity, but it won me my bet.

Two subjects only were barred at education periods – religion and politics. In fact, they could be mentioned provided they weren't, in the Army's mysterious phrase, discussed 'as such' – a distinction which went for nothing when Lieutenant MacKenzie, product of Fettes and the grouse-moors, and politically somewhere to the right of Louis XIV, got embroiled during a lecture (on Useful Hobbies, of all things) with his platoon sergeant, one McCaw, who in civilian life was a Communist Party official on Clydeside. Exchanges like: 'If ye'll pardon me for sayin' so, comrade – Ah mean, sir' and 'I'll pardon nothing of the sort, my good man – I mean, sergeant – the General Strikers should have been put up against a wall and shot, and don't dam' well argue', are not conducive to good order and military discipline. Especially when the platoon sit egging on their betters with cries of: 'Kenny's the wee boy! Kenny's tellin' 'im!' and 'Get tore in, McCaw! Go on yersel'!'

So politics we avoided, gratefully; for one thing, the Jocks knew far more about it than we did. Religion was even trickier, with that fundamentalist-atheist, Catholic-Protestant mixture – I recall one ill-advised debate on 'Does God Exist?' which would have had the Council of Trent thumbing feverishly through their references, and ended with a broken window. And of course religion in the Scottish mind – or the Glasgow mind, anyway – is inextricably bound up with sport, to such an extent that I have seen an amiable dispute on the offside rule progress, by easy stages, through Rangers and Celtic, to a stand-up fight over the fate of some ancient martyr called the Blessèd John Ogilvie, in which Private Forbes butted a Catholic comrade under the chin. I wouldn't have thought either of them cared that much, but there you are.

Thereafter I confined the education periods to personal monologues on Interesting Superstitions, How Local Government Works, and What Should We Do with Germany Now? That last elicited some interesting suggestions, until they discovered that I wasn't advocating mass bombing or deportation, but social and political restructuring, as laid down in the Army pamphlet. After that they just dozed off again in the warm North

African afternoon, salty and soporific from their swimming, until the cook-house call sounded for tea.

And then one day the Colonel, finding mischief as colonels will, discovered that his clerk at company headquarters couldn't orient a map. This is a simple technical matter of laying a map out so that its north corresponds with magnetic north; normally you do it with an army compass. Apparently the clerk couldn't use a compass, which didn't surprise me – I knew there was at least one member of my platoon who didn't know north from south, and God help the man who tried to teach him. But the Colonel was shocked; he sent out word that every man in the battalion must become a proficient map-reader henceforth, so on the next education period my lecture-room had 18 maps and compasses laid out on the big table, one to every two men, working together. This is a very sound idea; it halves the chance of total ignorance, theoretically anyway.

Looking over my platoon, I wasn't so sure. Most of them were bright boys, but there in the front rank stood the legendary Private McAuslan, the dirtiest soldier in the world, illiteracy and uncleanliness incarnate, glaring with keen displeasure at the compass in his grimy hand.

'Whit the hell's this, then? Darkie no' gaun tae give us a speech the day? Ah thought we were jist meant tae *listen* tae edumacation. Sure that's right, Fletcher?'

'Sharrup,' said Private Fletcher. 'Yer gaun tae learn tae read a map.'

'But Ah cannae read. Darkie knows Ah cannae read. Sure he knows Ah've been tae the Edu-macation Sergeant for a course, an' the daft bugger couldnae learn me anythin'. He's a clueless nyaff, yon,' added McAuslan, in disgust at the Education Sergeant's shortcomings. 'Couldnae teach ye the right time, him.'

'Readin' a map's no' like readin' a book, dozy. It's jist a matter o' lookin' at the map an' seein' where ye are.'

McAuslan digested this, slowly, strange expressions following each other across his primitive features. Finally:

'Ah know where Ah am. Ah'm here.' He dismissed the map with a sniff that sounded like a sink unblocking. 'An' Ah don't need this bluidy thing tae tell me, either.'

At this point, fortunately, Sergeant Telfer called them to attention, and I got off to a smooth start by telling them that what we were going on with this afternoon was map-reading and, more specifically, map-orientation.

'It's quite easy,' I said, with lunatic optimism, aware of McAuslan's fixed stare; it was rather like being watched by a small puzzled gorilla with pimples. 'We just have to turn the map round so that it points north. Right?' I decided, in an unwise moment, to conduct a simple test, just to make sure that everyone knew what the points of the compass were – McAuslan. I was pretty certain, didn't know them from Adam, but there might be others in the platoon who shared his ignorance.

'Suppose that's north,' I said, indicating the wall behind me, 'where is south-west?'

Indulgently, the platoon pointed as one man to the correct far corner of the room – with the usual single exception. McAuslan was pointing to the ceiling. By heaven, I thought, ex McAuslano semper aliquid novi. How had he worked that one out?

'Haud on, sur,' he said, and I realised that his raised hand had been designed simply to catch my attention. 'Ah mean, 'scuse me.' He breathed heavily. 'Wid ye mind repeatin' that?'

'It's all right, McAuslan,' I said hurriedly. 'I'm just establishing that if that's north, then that's south, and that's east, over there, and that's west. See?'

'But you said –'

'Now, the points of the compass are divided into 360 degrees, which means that between each of the four main points there are –'

My frantic burst to escape from him didn't work; his hand was up again, and he was frowning like a judge who has just heard a witness use an obscenity.

'Degrees?' he said suspiciously.

'That's right, McAuslan,' I beamed. 'Degrees; 360 of them –'

'Like onna thermometer?'

I fought back a vision of myself lying in a fever, with McAuslan kneeling by my bed in a nurse's wimple, trying to take my temperature with an army compass. 'Not exactly,' I said, and strove to think of a simple explanation. By God, it would have to be simple. 'Let's see,' I said, improvising madly, 'the degrees on a thermometer go up and down, but the degrees on a compass go round in a circle.'

Well, I know I'm a rotten teacher, but with McAuslan it was hard to know where to begin, honestly. And there were 35 other men in the platoon to think of, who knew what I was talking about, badly and all as I might be doing it. While McAuslan was reflecting on degrees which rotated, as against those which leaped perversely up and down, I hastened on to a practical demonstration of the army compass, showing how it must be applied to the eye so that one could see the reflected numbers moving past. Within two minutes the platoon had mastered the art, and were turning their maps in a soldier-like manner to point north, with the compasses pointing neatly along the magnetic north line.

'That's it,' I said. 'Now they're oriented, and if we take them outside, and orient them again, we can establish our own position on the maps, and then compare features on the maps with the things we actually see in front of us. Let's – yes, McAuslan?'

He was glowering at me in accusation. 'Sur,' he demanded. 'These maps pointin' north?'

I admitted it, uneasily.

'But you,' he remonstrated, 'said *that* wis north.' And he

pointed to the wall behind me. 'That's no' the way the maps is pointin'. Oh, no. They're pointin' ower there, an' –'

It was entirely my fault, of course, for using an arbitrary illustration. 'I'm sorry, McAuslan,' I said. 'Before, what I meant was, *supposing* that wall *was* north; it isn't, really, but I was just trying to show . . . to find out . . . if everybody knew the points of the compass . . .'

He regarded me more in unwashed sorrow than anger. 'Ye got it wrong,' he said, tolerantly. 'That wall's no' north at a'. That's north, where the maps is pointin', where the fellas has turned them, see, ower there, an' –'

'That's right!' I cried. 'And we found out north by looking into our compasses, and turning them, and watching the numbers, the degrees, and – oh, God, everyone outside, Sergeant Telfer, and we'll do it again!'

I wouldn't have you think that I was callously abandoning McAuslan in his ignorance. After the lesson was over, and the rest of the platoon had shown that they could orient and take bearings competently, I took him aside for some special tuition. Sergent Telfer, while I was busy with the others, had shown him how to hold the compass to his eye, as a preliminary to taking a bearing, and McAuslan, having snivelled over it and complained that the bluidy thing widnae haud still, had attempted to level it out, and torn the metal cover off – a feat roughly equivalent to biting a rifle in two.

So when the others had gone I strove to impart to him the rudiments of map-reading, beginning with the fact that the sun rose in the east – yes, invariably, I said, because after half an hour of McAuslan's company you began to doubt even the verities. There it was, going down in the west, and up there was north. That, I eventually drove home, was where the compass needle always pointed, provided you stayed well away from heavy metal objects.

'"Samazin"', was his verdict, when I had finished; he regarded the compass with some of the satisfaction Galileo might have shown in identifying a new heavenly body. 'A'ways the same way. It's a great thing, right enough.'

'You can test it out when we go on a night exercise next week,' I said. 'We'll find the North Star, and you'll see that the needle always points to it. Okay, fall out, and tell the Cook-Sergeant I said you could get a late tea.'

It was more, I reflected virtuously, than I would get myself; the officers' mess waiters would have removed the last curled-up sandwiches long ago. However, I was compensated by the glow of satisfaction at having taught McAuslan something – it didn't happen often, heaven knows, and when it did you felt like a don whose favourite student has got a starred first. I was so chuff with myself that I even boasted mildly about my triumph at dinner.

'Don't believe it,' said the Colonel. 'Fellow doesn't know right from left. Never did.'

'That's a different thing, sir,' I said. 'A compass doesn't tell you that. But it does point north, and McAuslan knows it – now.'

'You're not claiming McAuslan can *read* a compass?' said MacKenzie. 'I won't have that.'

'No,' I said, 'but he can look at a needle. Which is as much as most of your platoon can do. I'll bet. I don't see anybody in A Company giving Copernicus a run for his money, if it comes to that.' For I was naturally defensive about McAuslan; the trouble was, everyone in the mess knew it.

'I'll grant you he can look at a needle,' said the Adjutant, 'but knowing McAuslan's capacity for lousing things up, I'm willing to bet that any compass that has been in his hands for two minutes will probably point south, strike twelve, and sound the alarm.'

'You'd think McAuslan was the only dumb brick in this battalion,' I said warmly. 'When I think of some of the troglodytes I see shambling about headquarters – to say nothing of MacKenzie's shower of first-class minds in A Company, who have to be taught a drill for getting into bed –'

'My platoon,' said MacKenzie, continuing the debate on the high level which I had set, 'can map-read a ruddy sight better than yours can.'

'Your platoon,' I said, 'have difficulty reading the *Beano*, because the words are too long, and don't have the syllables split up with hyphens, like *Chicks Own*.'

'Like to bet?' snapped MacKenzie, and of course that did it. I was preparing to take him up on it when the Colonel, having heard the magic word 'bet', said he was glad to see this spirit of healthy competition, because it augured well for the series of night exercises he was planning; having given orders that his battalion should become experts in map and compass work, he was all afire to test the results.

'We'll do the paratrooper stunt,' said he, stuffing tobacco into his eager pipe. 'You know, chaps taken out in closed trucks dropped in pairs at intervals, so that they haven't the foggiest where they are. Each pair has a map, a compass, and a box of matches, and they find their way home again. Test of skill and initiative; first-class, absolutely. Give platoon commanders –' he prodded his pipe-stem at MacKenzie and me '– like Kenny and Dand a chance to prove their points, eh?'

MacKenzie and I looked at each other, mentally computing what the harvest might be if our platoons were dropped by night in desert country and had to find their way back. I didn't fancy it, myself; night exercises are tricky at the best of times, but conducted on the edge of the Sahara, with people like McAuslan staggering about in circles unaided, they could be suicidal.

'Of course,' said the Colonel, reading our thoughts, 'we'd stick close to the coast, among the villages; don't want anyone striking out for the Congo by accident, do we?'

'Well, sir,' I began cautiously, trying not to think of McAuslan let loose in an unsuspecting Arab village in the dark,•'I'm not sure –'

'I am,' said the Adjutant happily. 'Your man McAuslan will never make it, for one. Dammit, he can get lost in the canteen. Drop him from a closed truck and he's liable to turn up twenty miles out to sea.'

'Not he,' said MacKenzie, derisively. 'He can't stand water, which is why Dand's chaps have to wash him from time to time.'

Which was true, but I was too busy thinking to resent it.

'You did say, sir,' I addressed the Colonel, 'that the idea would be to drop people in pairs?'

'No so fast,' said MacKenzie. 'I get it – you'll see to it that McAuslan is teamed up with some map-reading genius who'll find his way home for him. No soap, Dandy; you send him out with an ordinary member of your platoon, or there's no bet.'

'What is the bet?' said the second-in-command, emerging from behind his decanter.

'That McAuslan, dropped from a closed truck at night, with an average Jock from Dand's platoon as his sidekick, won't find his way back to a given point within a reasonable time. Hang it all,' he added, for despite being a MacKenzie and red-haired, he was a reasonable youth, 'it isn't really a bet at all, it's a stone-cold cert. I'll go easy with you, you silly MacNeill,' he went on to me. 'I'll make it a straight hundred lire – or a slap-up dinner at the club. Well?'

I was nailed to the wall, of course; I'd talked myself into it. I rescued the port before the M.O. could get his hands on it, poured an inspirating glass, and thought, while they watched me.

'Stop looking so damned MacNeillish,' grinned MacKenzie. 'Put up or climb down.'

'This would be a full-scale company exercise – three platoons, all ranks, dropped in pairs?' I looked at the Colonel, and he nodded. 'Usual form,' he said, which was all I wanted to know. MacKenzie leaped in, all suspicion.

'You can't partner McAuslan yourself, mind. It's got to be an average Jock –'

'Don't worry,' I said. 'I'll send him out with Wee Wullie.'

The Adjutant looked surprised. 'That's handicapping yourself a bit, isn't it? Wee Wullie's not exactly your brightest star. I mean, I concede that if you sent McAuslan out with Captain Cook, they'd both probably finish up at the bottom of a well, but . . .'

Wee Wullie, I should explain, was my platoon incorrigible, a rugged giant of extraordinary strength and evil temper, given to alcoholic excesses on a heroic scale which frequently involved him with the military police and provost staff. He would have been posted or locked up for ever long ago, for his crime sheet was encyclopaedic, but Wee Wullie had a fighting record from the war that counter-balanced his misdemeanours, and the Colonel, who had known him from way back, was as sentimentally protective as a mother-hen. He was eyeing me thoughtfully as the Adjutant spoke; like me, the Colonel knew that Wee Wullie had once performed an incredible solo march in the Western Desert in '42, carrying a German prisoner most of the way. But his feat had been distinguished for its sheer endurance, not for his sense of direction; he wasn't, I was ready to admit, the ideal choice to pilot such a walking disaster as McAuslan through desert country in the dark. But the Colonel had said that the exercise would take the 'usual form'; I knew exactly what that meant, and MacKenzie either didn't or had forgotten.

'Wee Wullie's the man I want dropped with McAuslan,' I said. 'You can't complain that he's an above-average Jock for skill and intelligence. All right, Kenny, you're on for a hundred lire.'

'Me too,' said the Adjutant, with that innocent, sporting look that English gentlemen assume when they know they've got the opposition cornered. 'I was in on this to start with; my jibes and taunts got MacNeill all steamed up, and I want my whack at his money.'

'Wagering is sinful and an abomination,' sighed the Padre. 'Will ye be wanting odds, Dand?'

I absorbed as much of the anti-McAuslan money as I felt my £9 a week salary could afford – the Colonel for once hung back on a bet, which was comforting – and went away to think, avoiding the second-in-command, who had surfaced again from his port, and wanted to ask me if *Chicks' Own* wasn't that comic paper of his youth in which the animals wore clothes – there was some damned tiger in short pants, as he recalled . . . I made my excuses and slipped out to the verandah. I'd been a mug; McAuslan couldn't find his way out of a paper bag, and would undoubtedly get lost on an unprecedented, nay monumental, scale. It wasn't losing the lire I minded – well, not all that much, anyway – it was the credit of the thing. Subalterns are proud of their platoons, and I was obsessively proud of mine, McAuslan included. Unwashed, ugly, useless, accident-prone, illiterate, and altogether fit to be first stoker at Gehenna he might be, but he was one of my Jocks – and he'd been good enough to go in at Alamein and beyond. And he tried – he tried *me*, but that wasn't the point.

Could he conceivably chart a course across several miles of unknown country by night? No, he couldn't. Neither, probably, could Wee Wullie – but the Colonel had said 'usual form', and therein lay the one gleam of hope.

The kind of exercise the Colonel envisaged, you see, isn't merely a test of map-reading skill. What happens is that a whole company, officers, N.C.O.s, Jocks and all, are loaded into trucks after dark, the tarpaulins are pulled down, and the trucks are driven away perhaps six or seven miles. The occupants are dropped in pairs, with maps, etc., at intervals of perhaps five minutes each, on an arc of a huge semi-circle whose centre is the home base to which they must find their way before dawn. But that's only the half of it. In between them and home another company is dropped, whose duty it is to prevent the first company getting through.

You can guess the results. I've played this particularly brutal game half a dozen times, in England, India, Palestine and elsewhere, and it invariably finished up as a series of fearful brawls in the dark. I recall one nightmare at Bangalore where I was teamed up with an enthusiastic Sikh cadet who believed that the best way of outwitting our fellow-students was to stalk them through the gloom and hit them with an entrenching-tool handle. And a similar exercise near Nazareth which ended as a pitched battle between Coldstream Guardsmen and the R.A.F. Regiment, with myself as an unfortunate umpire in between, firing Verey flares and futilely blowing my whistle.

In fact it has this virtue, that it is probably the best training for real warfare – night fighting, at any rate – that you can possibly get. There are those, like my Sikh, who treat it simply as an excuse for a good turn-up, which is really to miss the point. At their best, night exercises teach the young soldier that darkness, which he has learned to fear from childhood, is really a friend; that patience, and waiting, and lying doggo for hours if necessary, pay off far better than boldness and initiative. I wasn't exactly a cat-eyed Mohican myself, but by the time the Burma campaign was over I had learned that in the dark he who stays still stays longest. Twenty years later, when I woke up at home one chilly night, and thought I heard mysterious noises downstairs, I was delighted to find that I could still glide out into the gloom without a sound or even a creaking board, every nerve alert, totally self-possessed and controlled, right up to the moment when I missed by footing on the stairs and crashed roaring into the hall and broke my toe. But you know what I mean.

However, knowing what my company was like, I had a pretty fair idea that any night exercise was liable to end in mayhem, which was why I wanted to team McAuslan with Wee Wullie. Skilled map-readers and night guides they might not be, but any opposition who tried to bar their progress would be well advised to take a couple of Rugby League teams along; McAuslan could, in his own phrase, 'handle himsel'', but Wee Wullie, giving of his best, was about as manageable as a rogue elephant in steel-toed boots. He could, at least, preserve McAuslan from capture in the early stages of the exercise; meanwhile the rest of the platoon and I would be combing the African night for them, and would shepherd them safely in to base.

It was at least feasible, provided the eccentric pair, the idiot misfit and the Cowcaddens Caveman, didn't go badly astray, or break a leg, or start an Arab uprising, before we found them. That would be the dicey part, calling for some clever stalking and enormous luck; my hopes were not raised by their performance on the brief night lesson which I conducted for the platoon on the regimental football pitch on the eve of the exercise itself, to give them a refresher course on using the stars and night map-reading. Wee Wullie arrived on the parade about two-thirds drunk (his normal condition, I realised with sudden misgivings, on any night after the canteen closed) and with a piece of rusty barbed wire tangled round his right ankle; he had evidently picked it up by accident somewhere, without noticing, which gives you a notion of what Wee Wullie was like. He stood there, swaying gigantically in the gloom, like Talus the Man of Brass with a bonnet on top, breathing heavily and reeking like a spirit vault. McAuslan I identified in the dark by his hideous sniffing, and when they and the rest of the platoon had settled down, and all were craning obediently up at the beautiful starlit black sky, I started in.

'That's the North Star, there – easily identifiable because it never moves, and the two end stars of the Plough, just there, always point directly at it. Well, not exactly directly, but as near as dammit. You've got the Plough, McAuslan? That thing there, like a bloody great ladle – that's roughly how it'll be pointing tomorrow night, and since you'll be in the desert south of here, the North Star is roughly in the direction you want to make for. Okay?' I sought for some familiar allusion that might fix it in what passed for his memory. 'That's north, see – in that direction. That's where Glasgow is, near enough. Right? Just remember, Glasgow's the direction you're heading if you go north.'

It was risky, of course; I didn't want the night exercise to finish with McAuslan on Argyle Street, but that was a chance one had to take.

'Aye, right, sir. Ah've got it covered.' Seen in dim profile, peering up into the heavens, he looked like some prehistoric moon-worshipper. ''At's a North Star, there – Ah'll find it the morra nicht, nae bother – cannae miss; it's right ower the Naafi.'

'Oh, my God. You won't be standing here tomorrow night; you won't be able to see the Naafi. You'll be out in the desert; you'll have to find it from the Plough, don't you see?'

'Aw.' He thought about this. 'Lotta stars, in't there? See, there's the Constipation of O'Brien.'

For a giddy moment I thought I had misheard him. Faintly I asked:

'What did you say?'

'The Constipation of O'Brien. See, up there –' he placed one sloth-like paw on my shoulder and pointed with the other. ''Ere it's. Thon's O'Brien – ye can see the star that's his heid, and they's his airms, an' his legs, an' they three wee stars is his belt, an' they ither stars is his –'

'Dear God,' I said, 'the Constellation of Orion. How the –

yes, yes, that's it, McAuslan! That's splendid! Well done! But how on earth did you know that?'

'Och, the Padre showed me them, in a book he's got. Efter you wis tellin' me aboot the compass aye p'intin' north, an' said we wis gaunae look at the stars, Ah thought Ah micht as weel get genned up aforehand. So Ah asked the Padre.' For a fleeting moment I wondered, why the Padre; was there in McAuslan's unfathomed mind a connection between religion and the astral bodies, between the cosmos and . . . ? 'Ah seen the book lyin' on his desk wan day when Ah had tae clean oot his office when Ah wis on jankers,' he went on, shattering my speculation. 'So Ah asked him yesterday, an' he showed me a' aboot O'Brien, an' Gasser an' Bollocks, the Heavenly Twins, an' –'

To say that I was astonished is to say nothing; I was gratified, deeply. McAuslan taking so much interest as to conduct his own personal researches was something new, and highly encouraging. I congratulated him again on his zeal, and felt so uplifted that I expanded perhaps rather incautiously in answering a question from one of the other Jocks on the difference between True and Magnetic North. (One north, I felt, was probably as many as McAuslan could cope with, and I had skirted the subject previously.) I know that in answering the Jock I exceeded my remit by remarking that Columbus, on his great voyage, had been much disturbed to see that the compass needle gradually ceased to point directly to the North Star as he sailed west; this brought a horrified squawk from McAuslan, clamouring for an explanation of this heresy, and I would probably have been on that football pitch until 4 a.m., explaining with a sleeping platoon around me, but fortunately at this point Wee Wullie was resoundingly ill, and in the ensuing confusion I dismissed the parade. McAuslan, incidentally, lost the way back to his barrack-block, which was a full two hundred yards away – possibly he was still intent on studying the Constellation of Orion and its internal disorders – and Wee Wullie had to be carried to bed. Not good omens, however you looked at them.

There were even worse ones in store on the day of the exercise itself; the Colonel, with his genius for complicating things in the interests of keeping his soldiery up to the mark, and satisfying his insatiable regimental ego, had devised an additional wrinkle in the exercise. The place that we eager map-readers were going to have to find in the dark was the Yarhuna Road bridge, which lay about two miles south of the town, on the edge of the desert; on the bridge itself the defending company was to leave a red storm lantern, and anyone who got within sight of it undetected would be adjudged to have found his way home successfully. But that wasn t enough for the Colonel; to add to the sport, and prove how good we were, he had told the Artillery Commander who was providing the defending company that we would engage to stalk the lantern and extinguish it, all unseen and mysterious.

'He's been reading too many romantic novels about the 'Forty-five,' I told the Adjutant. 'That bridge'll be crawling with Gunners; you won't be able to get a mouse through.'

'Come, come,' he said, 'where's your Highland craft and cunning? All you have to do is sneak through the gloom like Rob Roy, taking care not to stand on twigs and milk-bottles, gliding stealthily past the drowsing sentinels –'

'Are you taking part?' I demanded coldly.

'Not a prayer,' he said. 'I'll be in bed, dreaming about the goodies I'm going to buy with your hundred lire after McAuslan finds the source of the Nile. Have fun.'

That reminded me that the real object of the exercise was simply to get McAuslan within sight of the lamp, which with good luck and management and Wee Wullie clobbering the opposition, might just be possible. Refinements like stalking the lamp over the last couple of hundred yards could take their chance – it might be fun to try it, though, and with that in mind I arranged that my own map-reading partner should be Lance-Corporal Macrae: he had been a professional ghillie and stalker in peace-time, adept at getting American tycoons and fat maharajahs within blasting distance of stags. Given sufficient time and darkness he could lift an eagle chick from its mother without her noticing, and as we rumbled out in the closed truck that midnight I explained to him that if he could exercise his talents by extinguishing the lamp undetected, it would probably earn him a weekend pass from a gratified Colonel.

'The rest of you,' I told the close-packed mass of bodies in the darkened truck, 'concentrate on getting within sight of the red light. If you get that far without being picked up by the Gunners, you'll have scored. Okay? After that, you can have a go at stalking the lamp, but that's just the icing on the cake. I don't suppose there'll be much chance of getting past the last guards near the bridge – it's pretty bare country, but have a try. But the main thing is to get within sight of it, so when you're dropped, in a few minutes' time, get a good bearing on the North Star, and start using your maps . . .'

'That's it, Wullie,' McAuslan's voice sounded hoarsely out of the steaming press. 'Gottae get a bearin'. See where north is. That's whit jiggered Columbus; didnae ken whaur he wis gaun, see, 'cos his compass wisnae p'intin' –'

'And remember,' I said finally, 'our password is 'Din', and the password of the Artillery company who're trying to stop us is 'Gin'. So if anyone challenges you with 'Gin', just get the hell out of it, quickly. If they get hold of you – use your own initiative.'

They gave happy growls in the dark, and McAuslan was heard to observe that he wid melt onybuddy that said 'Gin' tae him. At this point the truck halted, and I peered under the tarpaulin at the silent African night; just a thin moon, fortunately, but enough to show the silent dunes and scrub, empty and desolate.

'First two out,' I said, and two of the Jocks dropped over the tailboard. 'I think we're somewhere west of the Yarhuna Road. Good luck.'

We drove on, stopping every five minutes to drop another pair. Macrae and I were going to be last out, and I held Wee Wullie and McAuslan back as penultimate pair. Wee Wullie, who had cunningly been kept on fatigues that evening as long as decency allowed, to prevent him drinking the canteen dry in advance, had only had time for about eight pints before taps, so he was relatively sober and consequently morose. To McAuslan's repeated inquires about whether he had the map, and the compass, and the matches, and could take a bearin', 'cos if we don't we'll be away for ile, he responded with irritable grunts; when the time came for him to drop, he went over the tailboard like a silent mammoth, swinging down one-handed from the overhead stanchion to land noiselessly in the sand, while McAuslan fell over me, muttering:

'Sure ye got the matches, big yin? Ah cannae see a bluidy thing – whaur's the tailboard, but? Och, ta, sur – there we are. Staun' frae under, big yin, Ah'm gaunae jump!'

He took a shambling dive over the tailboard, and the sound of rending cloth and an appalling oath split the night. As the truck jerked forward and their two dim figures receded into the gloom it appeared that McAuslan, his denim trousers in rags about his ankles, was grovelling at Wee Wullie's feet, complaining that his bluidy breeks wis tore; the trooser-erse, he lamented, wis oot o' them. I didn't hear any more, but with any luck McAuslan's semi-nudity would delay their exploration of the wilderness in which they had been left, and Macrae and I would have a chance to double back and find them.

It wasn't easy. The truck, on its last leg, doubled and turned bewilderingly – I wondered if MacKenzie had got at the driver

– and Macrae and I were finally deposited on an utterly flat stretch of desert track with not a landmark in sight. A look at the stars confirmed that we were south-east of the Yarhuna Road bridge, and we ploughed confidently for home, but with no high hopes that our course would intersect that of the McAuslan-Wullie partnership, presumably labouring somewhere to westward.

We got our first definite fix after about twenty minutes, on a small Arab village called Qufra which I remembered from a route march. We were a good six miles from the Yarhuna Road bridge, but what was worse, Qufra had a Gunner patrol in it – we'd probably have walked into them, but a dulcet Liverpool voice drifting over the sand warned us in time. I hadn't expected them to be this far out; you don't usually reckon on meeting opposition until you're fairly close to home, where they can narrow the angle on you. We skirted the village, plodding through bad, shifting sand, and made another mile before we had to duck into a wadi to avoid more Gunners, camped out having a smoke near a palm grove.

It had been fairly placid thus far, and quite pleasant walking through the warm African night, admiring the moon shadows on the dunes, and pausing whenever a village or other landmark came in sight, to check our position on the map. But now the moon went down, leaving only the star-sheen, and ground black with shadows in visibility of about twenty yards. We went cautiously now, keeping apart, and presently received intimation that the exercise was warming up: sounds of tumult and combat came drifting out of the dark ahead, cries of 'Din!' and 'Gin, you bastard!', accompanied by a steady pounding which reminded me of balmy evenings on Chowringhee, Calcutta, when we used to take the air outside Jimmy's Kitchen and the Nip Inn, listening to the rhythmic thumping from the bushes on the darkened Maidan, where the Cameronians and Royal Marines were relieving the American Air Force of their wallets.

The battle ahead gradually faded into the distance, and we scouted forward to a low wall skirting what seemed to be an ancient Moslem temple. I thought I remembered it from the map, but it would have been too risky to strike a match, so we crouched in silence, listening and waiting.

That was a mistake. It gave me time to think, and my imagination being what it is, the sight of that gaunt, eerie little ruin began to work on me. A slight wind had got up, rustling the weeds in the enclosure and sighing dolefully in the broken dome; it was suddenly chill and quiet, and the dark was closing in, bringing uncomfortable thoughts of deserted churchyards, with yawning graves, Black Masses, unholy conjurings, and satanic rites. It's fearful what a mixture of Highland atavism and Presbyterian upbringing can do at two in the morning; before I knew it I was muttering Forbidden Words like 'Tripsaricopsem', and wondering perversely if the formula for raising Auld Horny in a kirkyard would charm up Mahound in a Moslem cemetery. Let's see, you mutter the Lord's Prayer backwards, and presently the Devil appears round the church in the form of a toad . . . inevitably I found the words going through my brain: 'Amen ever and ever for glory the . . .'

A sudden hideous keening wail sounded from behind the ruin, Macrae dived beneath the cover of the wall, my hair bristled up on my scalp, and I stared horrified as the Devil suddenly came surging round the corner of the temple. For a dreadful moment I thought I'd unleashed the Powers of Darkness just by thinking about them, and then I realised that if this truly was His Infernal Majesty, he wasn't in the form of a toad; furthermore he was clad mostly in a pair of drawers, cellular, soldiers for the use of, and moving at a hell of a clip with three Artillerymen after him roaring 'Gin!' By way of answer he was crying 'Mither o' Goad!', which seemed out of character, and something in the way he attempted to leap the wall and failed, bringing down a hail of rock on Macrae and me, provided a positive identification.

'McAuslan!' I shouted, and then the Gunners came pounding over the top, with cries of triumph, and the night got interesting. I rolled down a sandy slope, locked in the arms of one of them, with McAuslan clutching at my leg and apparently trying to bite it. We snarled 'Din!' and 'Gin!' and 'Aw, jeez, they tore ma bluidy shirt aff, an' me wi' nae breeks!' respectively, and I escaped possible gangrene only by shouting: 'It's me, McAuslan! Worry him, boy!' We punched and wrestled blasphemously in the dark, McAuslan observing bitterly that he wis aboot sick o' this, and whaur wis Wullie wi' the bluidy compass, and then more Gunners came on the scene, and it would have gone hard with us if the night had not also produced Wee Wullie, in the nick of time. I had a Gunner sitting on my chest, demanding my name and number, and had just played my last desperate card, which was to threaten him with court-martial for assaulting a superior, when something like a rushing mighty wind swept away my oppressor, and presently Macrae and I were sitting on the temple wall, panting and licking our wounds, and listening to the appalling noise of our platoon giant dealing with about a dozen frantic Artillerymen, and evidently enjoying it.

We left him to it, and when we had found McAuslan crawling about on all fours in the gloom alternately snuffling piteously because he had lost a boot in the mêlée and mumbling to himself that the North Star pointed to Glasgow, we took stock. Our maps and compasses had gone, trodden into the field of battle where Wee Wullie could be distantly heard singing 'One-Eyed Riley' with a ring of his slain presumably around him.

'He's an awfy man, yon,' said McAuslan in an awed whisper. 'Like a wild beast, so he is. Cannae read a map for toffee, but – an' Ah kept tellin' 'im, Ah did. "Yer erse is oot the windy, big yin," Ah sez, but he had a flask o' rum in his pocket, an' there wis nae pittin' sense intae 'im, an' –'

'Just as well,' I said. 'Now, listen, McAuslan. We haven't far to go – a mile or so at most. All you have to do is keep quiet, and let Macrae and me find the way. Right? Quiet, you understand, and stick like a limpet or so help me I'll brain you. If we strike trouble, leave it to us; I want you to get within sight of that red light, that's all – never mind about stalking it or doing anything clever. Just stand up and yell for the nearest officer, see?'

'Aw,' he said, doubtfully, 'but Ah thought –'

'Don't think! You're not paid to think! Just do as you're told.'

'Awright, sur. Awright. But Ah'm no wandered, me. Ah ken the password, Ah can see the North Star, right enough, an' aw, see there, there's ra Constipation o' O'Brien again, jist like in ra Padre's book, an' –'

'Come on!' I snapped, and we set off into the night, two desperate men and the amateur astronomer in his cellular drawers, ambling behind with his eyes glued to the North Star, blaspheming as he fell over things.

I was beginning to think we'd make it when we struck the Yarhuna Road, but some clever Gunner officer outguessed us; naturally we didn't follow the road itself, but kept to the scrubby country a couple of hundred yards off on one side, and that's where the crafty brute had planted his ambush. They came out of the ground like phantoms, chanting 'Gin!', and we could do nothing but scatter and run, McAuslan gallumphing unevenly away into the gloom in his one boot, clutching his underpants in desperation and crying that it was a bluidy liberty. He had a stalwart Gunner in close pursuit, and was plainly done for; in the meantime, Macrae was nabbed, and I only escaped by selling a dummy to an assailant who must have been a Rugby player, because he bought it by sheer instinct. I ran my hardest for about a quarter of a mile, lay up in a dry ditch until the pursuit had tailed away, and then stole ahead.

It was easier now; apart from being on my own, I found I was moving into populated country, with people blundering through the night in all directions, occasionally muttering 'Din' and 'Gin' hopefully. It took just a little time and patience to get me to the top of a dune where I could look down on the road bridge, with its guttering red lamp. There were a few sentries staked out at a sporting distance from the bridge, and off to one side what looked like a group of umpires with a flashlight, and beyond them a couple of three-ton trucks with troops round them – captured map-readers who had surrendered their identity discs and been brought in. Another truck was coming down the road, headlights on, to pull up beside the first two and disgorge its disgruntled cargo. McAuslan, I reflected, would probably be among them.

However, so far as I could judge, fewer than half the company had been caught; the night must be full of skulkers like me, some of them lurking as I was within sight of the lamp. There wasn't much cover, but there were tongues of shadow right up to the bridge itself; if one could just take time, and crawl the furlong or so undetected . . . I cursed the luck that had put Macrae into the bag; if anyone could have got there, he could. Still, I could have a go; there was no disgrace in failing at this stage.

It took me about an hour, quite enjoyable in its way, to work my way down to within a stone's throw of the lamp. It was flat-on-your-belly stuff, an inch at a time, listening to the darkness, and twice some mysterious radar stopped me just in time while a shadow ahead resolved itself into a prone Gunner, waiting motionless for unwary stalkers. Each time I had to retreat painfully slowly and take a new tack, with my clothes full of itching sand and my stomach feeling as though it had been through a bramble bush. Then I struck what looked like a good line along a fold of dead ground, worming forward until I was close in to the bridge, snug in a patch of inky shadow, with the lamp not twenty yards ahead, just asking for it. Talk about your Chingachgook, thinks I, and was bracing myself to dive the last few yards when a voice out of the night offered me a cigarette. It was a Gunner captain, sitting still as a post within a yard of me; he had been watching my progress, he said, for several minutes.

'I'd have challenged, but you seemed to be having such fun. Gin, by the way.'

'Din,' I said, rolling over on my back and accepting his cigarette, 'you rotten sadist. MacNeill, Lieutenant, D Company, and you're not getting my I.D. discs, either; I got within sight of your kindly light.'

'Most of your chaps did, but everyone who tried to stalk the lamp has been nailed. Bound to be,' he went on smugly. 'I think we've got it pretty well sewn up. In fact, I'd say it's about time we called it a night, wouldn't you? Getting on for dawn, and I'm damned cold – can't see any of your latecomers doing any better . . . hullo, who's that?'

He was looking towards the bridge; in the dim glow of the red lamp a figure could be faintly seen, shambling uncertainly and pawing in a disoriented manner, like a baboon with a hangover. I stared with a wild surmise – I knew that Lon Chaney silhouette, even to the draggling outline of its cellular drawers . . .

'Hey, you!' cried the Gunner Captain, and the figure started, lurched, and stumbled; there was a clatter and a mouth-filling guttural oath – and the lamp was out, plunging the bridge into blackness. There were yells of astonishment, someone blew a whistle, the Gunner Captain swore horribly and started shouting for his sergeant, people ran around in the dark, and for about two minutes chaos reigned. Personally I just lay there and smoked, waiting for enlightenment.

It came when someone brought a torch and they focused it on the figure which lay snuffling and swearing beside the wreckage of the lamp, bewailing the fact that he had got ile a' ower his drawers, an' them his only clean pair. He sat blinking and aggrieved in the spotlight while the Gunners regarded him with dismay, demanding to know who he was and where he had come from.

'Good Lord!' said one, 'he's still got his tags on!' And sure enough, he still had his identity discs round his unwashed neck. Which meant he hadn't been picked up by the defenders – somehow he had avoided capture, and here he was in undisputed possession of the lamp which he had undoubtedly extinguished, glaring in baleful distress at his inquisitors and wiping his nose fretfully.

'Who the hell are you?' demanded the Gunner Captain in wrath. 'And why the hell are you half-naked?'

I realised there were unplumbed mysteries here, and they must be played for all they were worth.

'He's McAuslan. One of my Jocks,' I said, with just a hint of complacency. 'Yes, as I hoped, he's bagged the lamp. He's pretty good at this sort of thing, of course.' Good might not be the appropriate word, but it would do. 'Well done, McAuslan. Yes, you see, he likes to wear as little as possible when he's stalking; in fact he usually does it entirely stark. He's –'

'Ah wis jist gaun ower the bridge for a –' McAuslan was beginning, but fortunately the rest was lost in Gunner upbraidings and demands for explanation. I hustled him to his feet, whispering sharply to him to keep his lip buttoned, for I knew the half had not been told unto me, and whatever it was I didn't want the Gunners to hear it. They weren't in the mood.

'How the blazes did he get through?' demanded the Captain. 'Dammit, our posts were as tight as a tick – he couldn't have!' Aggrievedly he added: 'Nobody saw him!'

'That,' I pointed out, perhaps tactlessly, 'is the object of the exercise. You confirm he's still got his tags, and he put out the lamp? Fine; let's go, McAuslan.'

We left them recriminating, and I got him in the lee of a truck. 'Right,' I said. 'Talk.'

'Ah wis jist gaun ower the bridge for . . . tae do . . . Ah mean . . .' he began miserably, holding his drawers up. 'Ah mean, Ah wantit fur tae relieve mysel'. Ah wis fair burstin', honest, so Ah wis,' he continued earnestly. 'No kiddin', sur, Ah didnae mean tae break their lamp, straight up, but yon man roared at me, an' Ah jist couldnae help it. An' Ah wis burstin' –'

'That's all right, McAuslan; it doesn't matter. How in God's name did you manage to get in at all? The last thing I saw you were out yonder, with a Gunner breathing down your neck. Didn't he catch you?'

'Aw, him.' He made a dismissive gesture, unwisely with the hand holding his pants up, and grabbed them just in time. 'Big animal he wis. He got haud o' me, an' sat on ma heid, but Ah wis too fly fur 'im. Ye see, when he says 'Gin' tae me, Ah says "Gin" back tae him. 'Whit's that?' says he. 'Gin', says Ah. 'Ah'm on your side, Jimmy.' An' the silly big soad let me up, an' Ah clattered 'im wan an' left 'im haudin' himsel'. He wis a right mug, yon,' added McAuslan, with some satisfaction.

'Well I'm damned!' I said reverently. Talk about peasant cunning. 'But how on earth did you get in – I mean, not only within sight of the lamp, but actually up to it? That was . . . well, marvellous – they had sentries everywhere!'

'Ah, weel, ye see,' he said, hitching up his underwear and assuming a professorial pose, 'it wis like this. When Ah got awa' frae the mug – 'Gin', says he, wid ye believe it? – Ah took a look fur ra North Star, but Ah couldnae see the bluidy thing. It must hiv gone oot, or somethin'. Onywye, Ah wis aboot fed up wi' the map-readin' lark – Ah mean, Ah could've done it nae bother, efter a' ye'd tellt me, but Wee Wullie had loast ra map, an' ra compass – och, he's a right big eedjit, yon,' said McAuslan with feeling. 'Nae sense, an' him half-fleein' wi' rum. He's an awfy man in drink, so he is. An' he's nae use wi' a map, onywye. He wis wandered. He wandered *me,* Ah don't mind tellin' ye,' he added indignantly. 'So when Ah got awa' frae the mug, Ah hid in a ditch fur a wee while, an' along comes a truck. It stoaped, so Ah crawled underneath, so's they widnae see me. They wis Gunners, an' soon they brought along some o' oor boys that they'd nabbed, an' pit them in ra truck, an' startit up. An' Ah wis fed up trampin' through the sand, so Ah jist catched hold o' the pipes unner ra truck, an' got me feet roon' them, an' they brung me in. An' when they stoapt by the brig Ah jist let go an' cam' oot, an' Ah wis burstin' somethin' hellish, so Ah went fur –'

'Stop, stop,' I said, trying to take it in. By his own account he had travelled about a mile clinging to the bottom of a three-ton truck, with a desert road speeding by a couple of feet beneath his ill-covered rump. I shuddered, and looked at him with awe. Initiative, I was thinking, determination, endurance . . . map-reading and compass work not so hot, admittedly, but maps aren't everything.

'Ah'm sorry aboot the lamp, though, sur . . . it was a accident, Ah didnae see the thing, an' when he shoutit Ah jist breenged intae it, an' . . . Ah suppose,' he added, wrinkling his urchin face dolefully, 'that it'll mean anither stoppage oot ma' pey, an' Ah'm still payin' fur the tea urn Ah dropped on cookhoose fatigue, an' MacPherson's glasses, an' . . .'

'No,' I said emphatically, 'it won't be stopped out of your pay. Or if it is, you'll easily be able to pay for it out of the three hundred lire you've earned tonight. Never mind why.' I looked at him, backed up defensively against the truck, clutching his revolting drawers, knuckling his grubby nose. 'Son, you're great. Just don't tell anyone how you got through to the lamp, understand? They didn't spot you, so they're not entitled to know. Right – hop into the truck and we'll get you back to barracks, and you can change out of your evening clothes. Well done, McAuslan.'

'Och, ta very much, sur. That's awfy good o' ye,' said McAuslan – but he said it with a strained, worried look which puzzled me until he added, pleadingly: 'Afore Ah get intae ra truck . . . Ah'm still burstin', no kiddin' . . .'

For the record, MacKenzie and the Adjutant and the Padre paid up like gentlemen – suspicious gentlemen, but I didn't enlighten them. I turned the money over to McAuslan, enjoining him to put it straight into saving certificates for himself and Wee Wullie. They didn't, I'm afraid. Instead they went on a magnificent toot the following Saturday, which concluded with Wee Wullie staggering back to barracks with McAuslan on his back finding his way, he alleged, by the stars. I might have taken more satisfaction in the success of his navigation if I hadn't been the orderly officer who met them at the gate.

The Sheikh and the Dustbin

When I was a young soldier, and had not yet acquired the tobacco vice (which began with scrounging cigarettes at route-march halts when everyone else lit up and I felt left out) I used to win cross-country races. This surprised me, for while I had been athletic enough at school I had never been fleet of foot; in the infants' egg-and-spoon race, and later in the hundred yards, I would come labouring in well behind the leaders, and as a Rugby full-back I learned to be in the right place beforehand because I knew that no amount of running would get me there in time if I wasn't. So it was a revelation, when the Army hounded us out in the rain to run miles across soggy Derbyshire in P.T. kit, to discover that I could keep up a steady stride and finish comfortably ahead of the mud-splattered mob, winning 7*s*. 6*d*. in saving certificates and having the Company Sergeant-Major (who was seventeen stone, all fat, and smoked like a chimney) wheeze enthusiastically: 'Aye, happen lad'll mek a Brigade rooner! Good at all sport, are yeh, MacNeill? Play football, roogby, cricket, do yeh? Aye, right, yeh'll be left inner in't coompany 'ockey team this art'noon, an' report to't gym fer boxin' trainin' on Moonday. Welter-weight, are yeh – mebbe middle-weight, we'll see. Done any swimmin', 'ave yeh? 'Ow about 'igh joomp . . . ?' That's the military mind, you see; if you're good at one thing, you're good at everything.

It didn't take long to convince him that I'd never held a hockey stick in my life and was a wildly unscientific boxer, but being a resourceful old warrant officer he made good use of my running ability, in a rather unusual way – and did much to advance my military education. For during those weeks of basic training I was detailed several times to escort prisoners to the military jail, the idea being that if during the journey by rail and road a prisoner somehow won free of the Redcap to whom he was handcuffed, I would run him down – what I was to do when I caught him was taken for granted. It never came to that; all our malefactors went quietly to the great grim converted factory at Sowerby Bridge which was the North Country's most feared and fearsome glasshouse and remains in my memory as one of the most horrible places I have ever seen. If my cross-country talents did nothing else, they won me a first-hand look at an old-style military nick which convinced me that, come what might, I was going to be a good little soldier.

The bleak walls and yards with their high wire-meshed gates, the lean, skull-faced guards screaming high-pitched, the crop-headed inmates doubling frantically wherever they went, our prisoner having to strip naked at high speed in the cold reception cell under the glaring eye of what looked like a homicidal maniac in khaki – all these were daunting enough, but what chilled my marrow was the sight of a single, everyday domestic object standing outside a doorway: an ordinary dust-bin. Only this one had been burnished until it gleamed, literally, like silver; you could have shaved at it without difficulty. The mere thought of how it had got that way told me more about Sowerby Bridge than I wanted to know; think about it next time you put out the rubbish.

I don't suppose that military prisons are quite as stark as that in this enlightened age (where did they go, those gaunt, shrieking fanatics of staff men? Do they sit, in gentle senility and woolly slippers, watching *Coronation Street*?) but in their time they were places of dreadful repute – Stirling, and Aldershot (whose glazed roof is supposed to have inspired the name 'glasshouse'); Heliopolis, outside Cairo, where prisoners were forced to run up and down the infamous 'Hill', and Trimulghari, in India, home of the soul-destroying well drill in which wells had to be filled and emptied again and again and again. Perhaps rumour made them out worse than they were, but having been inside Sowerby Bridge, I doubt it. Reactionary old soldiers speculate wistfully on their reintroduction for modern criminals and football hooligans, forgetting that you can no more bring them back than you can bring back the world they belonged to; like conscription, they are just part of military history – for which the football hooligans can be thankful.

However, this is not a treatise on glasshouses, and if I have reflected on them it is only because they are part of the train of thought that begins whenever I remember Suleiman ibn Aziz, Lord of the Grey Mountain, who had no connection with them personally. But he was a military prisoner, and belongs in the same compartment of my memory as Sowerby Bridge, and barred windows, and Lovelace's poem to Lucasta, and 'jankers', and McAuslan and Wee Wullie labouring on the rockpile, and the time I myself spent in cells as a ranker (the sound of that metal-shod door slamming is one you don't forget in a hurry, when you've been on the wrong side of it), and all my varied thoughts and recollections about what the Army used to call 'close tack'. Detention, in other words, and if it has two symbols for me, one is that gleaming dustbin and the other is old Suleiman.

He was quite the unlikeliest, and certainly the most distinguished prisoner ever to occupy a cell in our North African barracks. I won't say he was the most eccentric, because those bare stone chambers at the back of the guardroom were occasionally tenanted by the likes of McAuslan and Wee Wullie, but he was more trouble than all the battalion's delinquents put together – something, fortunately, which happened only on Hogmanay, when it was standing-room only in the cells and Sergeant McGarry's provost staff were hard pressed to accommodate all the revellers.

They were busy enough during the rest of the year, too, but not because our Jocks were rowdier than any other soldiers; if our cells were well used it was because the Colonel, unlike some commanders, refused to use the glasshouse as a dumping-ground for incorrigibles. To him, a man in Heliopolis was a dead loss to the regiment, and a failure, and he would move heaven and earth to keep our worst offenders out of the Big House – especially if they had been good men at war. Wee Wullie's record of violence and drunkenness should have put him on the Hill for years – but Wullie had played the soldier when it counted, in the Western Desert, and the regiment had a long memory. As it did for the remarkable Phimister, a genuine hero of Japanese captivity who must thereafter be forgiven for spending more time on the run from the Redcaps than he did on parade. It wasn't easy, and the Colonel had to do some inspired string-pulling on occasion, but no one doubted it was worth it. A Highland regiment is a family, and settles its own differences within itself – if that sounds trite, it's true. So when Phimister went walkabouts yet again and was picked up trying to board a tramp steamer in Tunis, or Wullie overturned a police jeep and battled with its occupants, or McAuslan went absent and tried to pawn a two-inch mortar in the bazaar (so help me, it's a fact), there was no thought of shipping them to the glasshouse; they did their time in our own cells under the iron hand of McGarry, digging and carrying in sweltering heat, deprived of tobacco and alcohol, and safely locked in at night. It was genuine hard labour, they hated it, it kept them out of trouble, and as McGarry used to say:

'They come tae nae herm wi' me. What? They were never so weel aff in their lives! Wullie's sober an' McAuslan's clean, an' that's mair than ye can say when they're on the ootside. I don't gi'e them any bother – an' by God they don't gi'e me any.'

Looking at McGarry, you might have feared the worst from that last remark. All provost staff tend to resemble galley oversees, and he was rather like an outsize Ernest Brognine playing Ivan the Mad Torturer, but the appearance was deceptive. Despite barrack-room gossip, McGarry never laid hands on a man unless he was hit first, in which case he hit back – once. (The exception was Wee Wullie, who had to be hit several times.) For the rest, McGarry got by on presence and personality; the mere sight of that huge figure at the top of the guardroom steps, thumbs hooked in the top of his kilt as he coldly surveyed the scene, was the most potent disciplinary force in the battalion.

It was into this strange guardroom world that Suleiman ibn Aziz came unexpectedly on a summer night. I was orderly officer, and had just finished the routine inspection of prisoners to make sure they were still breathing and not trying to tunnel their way out. There were two in residence: McAuslan starting fourteen days after his brief career as a mortar salesman, and Phimister as usual. I was signing the book when I noticed that one of the four vacant cells was open – and within there was an undoubted rug on the floor, a table, chair, chest-of-drawers, jug and wash-basin, and in place of the usual plank and blanket there was a pukka bed, with sheets and pillows. I thought I must be seeing things.

'Who in the world is that for?' I asked. 'Don't tell me you've got the Brigadier in close tack!'

'Nae idea, sir,' said McGarry. 'I just got word tae have a cell ready, an' then the Adjutant himsel' turns up tae see tae the furniture. It's no' a regular client, anyway.'

'Somebody from outside? He must be pretty special. But why us?'

'Strongest jyle in the province, this,' said McGarry, not without satisfaction. 'God kens what kind o' sodgers Mussolini built this barracks for, but he wasnae takin' ony chances wi' his defaulters. These walls is six feet thick. There's tae be a special sentry on the door, too.'

This was unprecedented – as was the appearance of the Colonel, Adjutant, and second-in-command at the main gate just after Last Post, when a staff car arrived bearing the Provost Marshal and a small figure in a black burnous and silver-trimmed *kafilyeh* handcuffed to a Redcap escort. He stood sullenly while the Colonel and the Provost Marshal conferred briefly, and then he was uncuffed and brought up the guard-room steps for delivery to McGarry; I had only a glimpse of a lean, lined swarthy face with an enormous beak of a nose and a white tuft of beard, and two bright angry eyes glaring under the *kafilyeh* hood. They hustled him inside, and the Adjutant, who had been hovering like an agitated hen, beckoned me to follow to his office, where the Colonel was sounding off at the Provost Marshal:

'. . . and you can tell G.H.Q. that I don't take kindly to having my barracks turned into a transit camp for itinerant bedouin. What did you say the beggar's name was?'

'Suleiman ibn Aziz, sir,' said the P.M. 'Known in Algeria as the Lord of the Grey Mountain, apparently.' He hesitated, looking apologetic. 'In Morocco they call him the Black Hand of God. So I'm told, sir.'

'Never heard of him,' said the Colonel. 'How long are we supposed to keep him?'

'Just a week or two, I hope – until the French come to collect him. I know it's a nuisance, sir, but there's really nothing to worry about; he's over seventy.'

'I'm not in the least worried,' snapped the Colonel, who didn't like the P.M. at the best of times. 'Nor am I a damned innkeeper. Why's he so important, anyway?'

'Well, sir,' said the P.M., looking impressive, 'I'm sure you've heard of Abd-el Krim . . . ?' The Adjutant's head came up at that famous name; like me, he knew his P. C. Wren. The Colonel frowned.

'Krim? The chief who led the Riff Rebellion in Algeria, back in the twenties? Gave the French Foreign Legion a hell of a dance, didn't he? Yes, I've heard of him . . .'

'The Red Shadow!' said the Adjutant brightly, and the Colonel gave him a withering look.

'Thank you, Michael, you can play a selection from *The Desert Song* later.' He turned back to the P.M. 'I thought Krim surrendered to the French 20 years ago – what's this bird got to do with him?'

'Absolutely right, sir, Krim did surrender,' said the P.M. 'But Suleiman didn't. He'd been Krim's right-hand man from the start of the Riff revolt, near the turn of the century, commanded his cavalry – he was the man who drove the Legion out of Taza in '24, overran their forts, beat up their columns, played hell all over. Real *Beau Geste* stuff,' he was going on enthusiastically, until the Colonel raised a bleak eye from scraping his pipe. 'Yes, well . . . he had something like 20,000 Riffs behind him then, but when the French really went to town in '26 Krim packed in with most of 'em, and Suleiman was left with just a handful. Swore he'd never give up, took to the Moroccan mountains, and has been hammering away for twenty years, off and on – raiding, ambushing, causing no end of trouble. The French captured him twice, but he escaped both times.' The P.M. paused. 'The second time was from Devil's Island.'

There was silence, and the Colonel stopped scraping for a moment. Then he asked: 'Where did you learn all this?'

'Intelligence bumf, sir – it's all in the dossier there. Just came in this afternoon. Suleiman was picked up only two days ago, you see, by one of our long-range groups south of Yarhuna, acting on information from the French in Oran –'

'What the devil was he doing over here? We're more than a thousand miles from Morocco!'

The P.M. looked perplexed. 'Well, it's rather odd, actually. When he escaped from Devil's Island it was early in the war, about '41. He managed to get back across the Atlantic, God knows how – he was nearly seventy then, and he'd had a pretty rough time in captivity, I believe. Anyway, he reached Morocco, got a few followers, and started pasting the French again, until our desert war was at its height in '42, when for some reason he came east and pitched in against Rommel.' The P.M. spread his hands in wonder. 'Why, no one knows . . . unless he regarded the Germans as allies of the Vichy Government. When the war ended the French were still after him, and for the past year or so he's been hiding out down south, quite alone. There was no one with him in the village where our people found him.'

'And the French still want him? At this time of day?' The Colonel blew through his pipe. 'What do they intend to do with him, d'you know?'

The P.M. hesitated. 'Send him back to Devil's Island . . . so Cairo tell me, anyway. It seems the French regard him as a dangerous public enemy –'

'In his seventies? Without followers? After he's been on our side in the war?'

'It's up to the French, sir. We're just co-operating.' The P.M. shifted in his chair, avoiding the Colonel's eye. 'I ought to mention – there's a note in the dossier – that Cairo regards this as a top security matter.'

'Indeed?' The Colonel's tone was chilly. 'Then why don't they put him in Heliopolis, instead of my guardroom?'

The P.M. looked embarrassed. 'Well, we're convenient here, of course – next to French territory. If they took him to Cairo, it would be bound to get talked about – might get into the papers, even.' He glanced round as though expecting to find reporters crouched behind his chair. 'You see, sir, the French want to keep it hush-hush – security, I imagine – and Cairo agrees. So the transfer, when it's made, is to be discreet. Without publicity.' He smiled uneasily. 'I'm sure that's understood.'

The Colonel blew smoke, considering him, and just from the

angle of his pipe I knew he was in one of his rare cold rages, though I wasn't sure why. The P.M. knew it, too, and fidgeted. Finally the Colonel said:

'We'll look after your prisoner, Provost Marshal. And if we don't come up to G.H.Q. Cairo's expectation as turnkeys, I suggest they do the job themselves. Convey that, would you? Anything else?'

The P.M., who wasn't used to mere Colonels who raised two fingers to Cairo, got quite flustered, but all he could think of to add was that Suleiman ibn Aziz spoke Arabic and Spanish but only a little French, so if we needed an interpreter . . .

'Thank you, my Adjutant speaks fluent French,' said the Colonel, and the Adjutant, who had spent a hiking holiday in the Pyrenees before the war, tried to look like an accomplished linguist. The P.M. said that was splendid, and made his escape, and we waited while the Colonel smoked grimly and stared at the wall. The second-in-command remarked that this chap Suleiman sounded like an interesting chap. Enterprising, too.

'Imagine escaping from Devil's Island, at the age of 70!' The Adjutant shook his head in admiration. 'Poor old blighter!'

'You can probably save your sympathy,' said the Colonel abruptly. 'From what I've heard of the Riffs' treatment of prisoners I doubt if our guest is Saladin, exactly.' He gave a couple of impatient puffs and laid down his pipe. 'Still, I'm damned if we'll be any harsher than we must. You're orderly officer, MacNeill? See McGarry has him properly bedded down and I'll talk to him in the morning – you *do* speak French, don't you, Michael? God knows you've said so often enough.'

The Adjutant said hastily that he'd always managed to make himself understood – of course, he couldn't guarantee that an Arab would understand the Languedoc accent . . . why, in Perpignan they spoke French with a *Glasgow* accent, would you believe it, mong jew and tray bong, quite extraordinary . . . Listening to him babble, I resolved not to miss his interview with Suleiman next day. When the others had gone he began a frantic rummage for his French dictionary, muttering vaguely bon soir, mam'selle, voulez-vous avez un aperitif avec moi, bloody hell, some blighter's knocked it, and generally getting distraught.

'Never mind your aunt's plume,' I said. 'What's the old man so steamed up about?'

'I'll just have to speak very slowly, that's all.' He rumpled his fair hair, sighing. 'Eh? The Colonel? Well, he doesn't like having his guardroom turned into a political prison – especially not for the Frogs. You know how he loves *them*: "Brutes let us down in '14, and again in '40 –"'

'I know that, but what's wrong with having to look after an old buddoo for a week or two?'

'It's politics, clot. The Frogs want to fix this old brigand's duff, and no doubt our politicians want to keep de Gaulle happy, so the word goes to Cairo to co-operate, and we lift him and hand him over – but quietly, without fuss, so it doesn't get in the papers. See?'

'What if it does?'

'God, you're innocent. Look, the old bugger's past it, the Frogs are just being bloody-minded, we're co-operating like loyal allies – but d'you think Cairo wants to be *seen* helping to give him a free ticket back to Devil's Island? So we get the job, 'cos we're out here far beyond the notice of journalists and radicals – anti-colonialists and so on – who'd make a martyr of the old boy if they heard about it. Are you receiving me?'

'Well . . . sort of . . . but he's a rebel, isn't he?'

'Certainly, fathead, and ten years ago no one would have given a hoot about handing him over. But it's different now. Don't you read the papers? The old enemies are the new patriots. Gandhi's a saint these days . . . so why shouldn't this old villain be a hero? After all, he always has been, to some people – fighting for his independence, by his way of it. Suppose his name was William Wallace – or Hereward the Wake? See what I mean?'

It was new stuff to me, in 1947. Yes, I was an innocent.

'So that's why the Colonel gets wild,' said the Adjutant. 'Being used as a stooge, because Cairo hasn't got the guts to pass this Suleiman on openly – or to tell the Frogs to take a running jump. Which is what the Colonel would do – partly because he can't stand 'em, but also because he's got a soft spot for the Suleimans of this world. God knows he fought them long enough, on the Frontier, and knows what a shower they are, but still . . . he respects 'em . . . and this one's over the hill, anyway. That's why he's hopping mad at Cairo for giving him a dirty job, but it's a lawful command, and he's a soldier. So, incidentally, are you,' added the Adjutant severely, 'and you ought to have been in the guardroom hours ago, examining padlocks. I don't suppose *you* speak French? No, you ruddy wouldn't . . .'

All was well in the guardroom, and through the grille in his cell door I could see the prisoner on the bed, still wrapped in his burnous, snoring vigorously.

'By, but that's an angry yin!' said Sergeant McGarry. 'Hear him snarl when I asked if he wantit anything? I offered tae get him some chuck, but I micht as weel ha'e been talkin' tae mysel'. Who is he, sir?'

I was telling him, when the gargoyle features of Private McAuslan appeared at the grille of the neighbouring cell, a sight that made me feel I should have brought some nuts to throw through the bars.

'Hullaw rerr, sur,' said he, companionable as always. 'Who's ra auld wog next door? See him, Ah cannae get tae sleep fur him snorin'. Gaun like a biler, sure'n he is.'

'He's a reporter frae the *Tripoli Ghibli*, come tae interview ye an' write yer life story,' said McGarry, and suddenly snarled: 'Sharrap an' gedoon on yer cot, ye animal, or I'll flype ye!'

McAuslan disappeared as by magic. I finished telling McGarry what I knew about his prisoner, and he shook his head as we stood looking through the grille.

'Black Hand o' God, eh? He's no verra handy noo, puir auld cratur. Mind you, he'll have been a hard man in his time.'

That was surely true, I thought. In the dim light I could make out the hawk profile and the white stubble on the cropped skull where the *kafilyeh* had fallen away; he looked very frail and old now. The Lord of the Grey Mountain, who had led the great Riff *harkas* against the French invaders and fought the legendary Foreign Legion to a standstill, the drawn sword of Abd-el Krim, the last of the desert rebels . . . It was inevitable that I should find myself thinking of the glossy romance that had been shown at the garrison cinema not long ago, with its hordes of robed riders thundering over the California sandhills while Dennis Morgan sang the new words which, in the spirit of war-time, had been set to the stirring music of Romberg's Riff Song:

Show them that surrender isn't all!
There's no barricade or prison wall
Can keep a free man enslaved . . .

It was pathetically ironic, looking in at the little old man who had been the anonymous inspiration for that verse, and had spent a lifetime fighting for the reality of its brave message, even taking part in the greater cause against Germany. The film fiction had ended in a blaze of glory; the tragic fact was asleep in a British Army cell, waiting to be shipped away to a felon's death in exile, the scourge of the desert keeping McAuslan awake with his snoring.

His interview with the Colonel next day was a literal frost, for during fifteen minutes' laboured interrogation by the Adjutant he spoke only once, and that was to say 'Non!' Seen in daylight he was a gaunt leathery ancient with a malevolent eye in a vulpine face whose only redeeming feature was that splendid hooked nose, but he carried himself with a defiant pride that was impressive. Seated in his cell, refusing even to notice his visitors, he might have been just a sullen little ruffian, but he wasn't; there was a force in the spare small body and a dignity in the lifted head; whether he understood the Adjutant's questions about his welfare (which sounded like a parody of *French without Tears*, with such atrocities as 'Etait votre lit tendre . . . suffisant douce, I mean', which I construed as an inquiry about the comfort of his bed) it was hard to say, since he just stared stonily ahead while the Adjutant got pinker and louder. That he was getting through became apparent only with the last question, when the Colonel, who had been getting restive, interrupted.

'Ask him, if we give him the freedom of the barracks, will he give his word of honour not to try to escape?'

This was the Colonel sounding out his man, and it brought the first reaction. Suleiman stiffened, stared angrily at the Colonel, and fairly spat out 'Non!' before standing up abruptly and turning on his heel to stalk across to the window, thus indicating that the palaver was finished.

'Well, he can give a straight answer when he wants,' said the Colonel. 'He doesn't lie at the first opportunity, either. Keep his cell locked at night, McGarry, with a sentry posted, but during the day he can sit on the verandah or in the little garden if he likes. The more he's in open view, the easier he'll be to watch. And he's not to be stared at – see that that's understood by all ranks, Michael. Very well, carry on.'

So we did, and in the following days the small black-robed figure became a familiar sight, seated under an arch of the guardroom verandah or in the little rock-garden at the side, the armed sentry at a tactful distance and McGarry as usual at the head of the steps. According to him Suleiman never uttered a word or showed any emotion except silent hatred of everything around him; at first he had even refused to sit outside, and only after McGarry had taken out the chair two or three times, leaving the cell door open, had he finally ventured forth, slowly, making a long survey of the parade square before seating himself. He would stay there, quite motionless, his hands folded before him, until it was time to go to his cell to pray, or the orderly brought his meals, which were prepared at an Arab eating-house down the road. He never seemed to see or hear the sights and sounds of the parade-ground; there was something not canny about the stillness of the small, frail figure, his face shaded from the sun by the silver-trimmed *kafilyeh*, as though he were under a spell of immobility, waiting with a furious patience for it to be lifted.

The Provost Marshal must have got word of the freedom he was being given, for he called to protest to the Colonel about such a focus of nationalist unrest being in full view from the gate where local natives were forever passing by. What the Colonel replied is not recorded, but the P.M. came out crimson and sweating, to the general satisfaction.

For there was no doubt of it, in spite of his hostile silence and cold refusal even to notice us, a sort of protective admiration was growing in the battalion for the ugly little Bedouin warlord. Everyone knew his story by now, and what was in store for him, and sympathy was openly expressed for 'the wee wog', while the French were reviled for their persecution, and our own High Command for being art and part in it.

'Whit wye does the Colonel no' jist turn his back an' let him scarper?' was how Private Fletcher put it. 'So whit if he used tae pit the hems oan the Frogs? A helluva lot we owe them, an' chance it. Onywye, they say the wee fellah got tore in oan oor side in the war – is that right, sur? Becuz if it is, then it's a bluidy shame! We should be gi'in' him a medal, never mind sendin' him back tae Duvvil's Island!'

'Sooner him than me,' said Daft Bob Brown. 'Ever see that fillum, *King o' the Damned*? That wis aboot Duvvil's Island – scare the bluidy blue lights oot o' ye, so it wud.'

'We should gi'e him a pound oot the till an' say "On yer way, Cherlie",' said Fletcher emphatically. 'That's whit Ah'd dae.'

You and the Colonel both, Fletcher, I thought. Scottish soldiers have a callous streak a mile wide, compensated by a band of pure marshmallow, and either is liable to surface unexpectedly, but if there is one thing they admire it is a fighting man, and it doesn't matter whether he's friend or foe, fellow or alien. Suleiman ibn Aziz was a wog – but he was a brave wog, who had gone his mile, and now he was old and done and alone and they were full of fury on his behalf. Barrack-room sentimentality, if you like, which overlooked the fact that he had been a fully-paid-up monster in his time; that didn't matter, he wis a good wee fellah, so he wis.

Their regard showed itself in a quite astonishing way. It was a regimental tradition for Jocks entering or leaving barracks to salute the guardroom, a relic of the days when the colours were housed there. Now – and how it began we never discovered – they started to extend the time of their salutes to cover the small figure in the burnous seated in the garden; I even saw a sergeant give his marching platoon 'Eyes left!' well in advance so that Suleiman was included, and the Regimental Sergeant-Major, who happened to be passing (and missed nothing) didn't bat an eyelid. Highland soldiers are a very strange law unto themselves.

I doubt whether Suleiman noticed, or was aware of the general sympathy. His own obvious hostility discouraged any approaches, and the only ones he got came from his fellow-prisoner McAuslan. The great janker-wallah was never one to deny his conversation to anybody unlucky enough to be within earshot, and since his defaulters' duties included sweeping the verandah and weeding the garden, Suleiman was a captive audience, so to speak; the fact that he didn't understand a word and paid not the slightest heed meant nothing to a blether of McAuslan's persistence. He held forth like the never-wearied rook while he shambled about the flower-bed destroying things and besmirching himself, and the Lord of the Grey Mountain sat through it like a robed idol, his unwinking gaze fastened on the distance. It was a pity he didn't speak Glasweigian, really, because McAuslan's small-talk was designed to comfort and advise; I paused once on a guardroom visit to listen to his monologue floating in through the barred window:

'. . . mind you, auld yin, there's this tae be said for bein' in the nick, ye get yer room an' board, an' at your time o' life the Frogs arenae gaun tae pit ye tae breakin' rocks, sure'n they're no'? O' course, Ah dae ken whit it's like in a French cooler, but ach! they'll no' be hard on ye. An' ye never know, mebbe ye'll get a chance tae go ower the wa' again. They tell me ye've been ay-woll twice a'ready, is that right? Frae Duvvil's Island? Jings, that's sumpn! Aye, but – mah advice tae ye is, don't try it while ye're here, for any favour, becuz that big bastard McGarry's got eyes in his erse, an' ye widnae get by the gate. Naw, jist you wait till ra Frogs come for ye, an' bide yer time an' scram when their back's turned – they're no' organised at a', ra Frogs. Weel, ye ken that yersel'. Here, but! it's a shame ye couldnae tak' Phimister wi' ye – him that wis in the cell next door tae me, the glaikit-lookin' fella. He's no' sae glaikit, Ah'm tellin' ye! Goad kens how many times he's bust oot o' close tack – he wid hiv ye oan a fast camel tae Wogland afore ra Frogs knew whit time it wis! Jeez, whit a man! Aye, but ye'll no' be as nippy as ye were . . . ach, but mebbe it'll no' be sae bad, auld boy! Whitever Duvvil's Island's like, it cannae be worse'n gettin' liftit by the Marine Division in Gleska, no' kiddin'. See them? Buncha animals, so they are. Did Ah no' tell ye aboot the time Ah got done, after the Cup Final? It wis like this, see . . .'

To this stream of Govan consciousness Suleiman remained totally deaf, as he did to all the sounds around him – until the seventh day, when the pipe band held a practice behind the transport sheds in preparation for next day's Retreat: at the first distant keening note his head turned sharply, and after a moment he got up and walked to the edge of the garden, evidently trying to catch a glimpse of the pipers. For a full half hour he stood, his hawk face turned towards the sound, and only when it ended did he walk slowly back to the guardroom, apparently deep in thought. There he suddenly rounded on McGarry, growling: 'L'Adjutant! Monsieur l'Adjutant!'. The Adjutant was summoned forthwith, and presently came to the mess with momentous news: Suleiman ibn Aziz had demanded curtly that he be allowed to witness the band's next performance.

I have written elsewhere of the Arab's delight in the sound of bagpipes, and how they would flock to listen whenever the band appeared in public. But Suleiman's interest was so unexpected and out of keeping with his grim aloofness that there was something like delight in the mess, and there was a big turn-out next day when the Adjutant conducted him to join the Colonel before H.Q. Company, where a chair had been provided for him. He went straight to it, ignoring the Colonel's greeting, and sat erect and impassive as the band swung on in full fig, the drums thundering and the pipes going full blast in 'Johnnie Cope'; they marched and counter-marched, the tartans swinging and the Drum-Major, resplendent in leopard-skin, flourishing his silver staff, through 'Highland Laddie', 'White Cockade', and 'Scotland the Brave', and he watched with never a flicker on his lined face or a movement of the fingers clasping his burnous about him. When they turned inwards for their routine of strathspey and reel he lifted his head to the quickening rhythm, and when they made their final advance to 'Cock o' the North' he leaned forward a little, but what he was making of it you couldn't tell. When the Drum-Major came forward to ask permission to march off, the Colonel turned to him with a smile and gesture of invitation, but he didn't move, and the Colonel returned the salute alone. The band marched away, and the Adjutant asked if he'd enjoyed it; Suleiman didn't reply, but sat forward, his eyes intent on the band as they passed out of sight.

'Oh, well, we did our best,' muttered the Adjutant. 'Don't suppose we could expect him to clap and stamp. At least he didn't walk out –'

Suleiman suddenly stood up. For a moment he continued to stare across the parade ground, then he turned to the Colonel, and for the first time there was a look on his face that wasn't baleful: his eyes were bright and staring fiercely, but they were sad, too, and he looked very old and tired. He spoke in a harsh, husky croak:

'La musique darray maklen! C'est la musique, ça!'

It was the first time he'd ever offered anything like conversation – whatever it meant. 'What did he say?' the Colonel demanded. 'Music of what?'

The Adjutant asked him to repeat it, but Suleiman just turned away, and when he was asked again he shook his head angrily and wouldn't answer. So the Adjutant took him back to the guardroom while the rest of us argued about what it was he'd said; he seemed to have been identifying the music, but no one could tell what 'darray maklen' meant. The first word might be 'arrêt', meaning anything from 'stop' to 'detention', but the Adjutant's dictionary contained no word remotely like 'maklen', and it wasn't until the end of dinner that the Colonel, who had been repeating the phrase and looking more like an irritated vulture by the minute, suddenly slapped the table.

'Good God! That's it, of course! Morocco! It fits absolutely. Well, I'll be damned!' He beamed round in triumph. 'The music of Harry Maclean! That's what he was saying! Talk about a voice from the past. Oh, the poor old chap! The music of Harry Maclean . . .'

'Who's Harry Maclean?' asked the Adjutant.

'Kaid Maclean . . . oh, long before your time. Came from Argyll, somewhere. One of the great Scotch mercenaries . . . packed in his commission in the '70s and went off to train the Sultan of Morocco's army, led 'em against all sorts of rebels – of whom our guest in the guardroom would certainly be one: Maclean was still active when the Riffs broke loose. Amazing chap, used to dress as a tribesman (long before Lawrence), got to places no European had ever seen. Oh, yes, Suleiman would know him, all right – may have fought with *and* against him. And he remembers the music of Harry Maclean . . . you see, Maclean was a famous piper, always carried his bags with him. I heard him play at Gib., about 1920, when I was a subaltern – piped like a MacCrimmon! He was an old man then, of course – big, splendid-looking cove with a great snowy beard, looked more like a sheikh than the real thing!'* The Colonel laughed, shaking his head at the memory, and then his smile faded, and after a moment he said: 'And we've got one of his old enemies in the guardroom. An enemy who remembers his music.'

There was quiet round the table. Then the second-in-command,

* Sir Harry Aubrey de Vere Maclean (1848–1920), joined the Army in 1869, fought against Fenian raiders in Canada, and in 1877 entered the service of Sultan Mulai Hassan of Morocco as army instructor. In an adventurous career lasting more than thirty years 'Kaid Maclean' became something of a North African legend: he was the trusted adviser of the Sultan and his successor, campaigned against rebel tribes, survived court intrigues, journeyed throughout Morocco and visited the forbidden city of Tafilelt, and was once kidnapped (at the second attempt) and held to ransom by insurgents. Although unswervingly loyal to his employer, he was recognised as an unofficial British agent, and was created K.C.M.G. when he attended King Edward VII's coronation as one of the Moroccan delegation. Maclean was a genial, popular leader although, as his biographer remarks, 'being of powerful physique he was able to deal summarily with insubordinate individuals'. He was an enthusiastic piper who also played the piano, guitar, and accordion. (See the *Dictionary of National Biography*.)

who seldom said much, surprised everyone by remarking: 'We ought to do something about that.'

'Like what?' asked the Colonel quickly.

'Well . . . I'm not sure. But if this fellow Suleiman did know Maclean, it would be interesting to get him talking, wouldn't it? Not that he's shown himself sociable, but after today . . . well, you never know.'

'Oh, I see.' The Colonel sounded almost disappointed. 'Yes, I suppose it would.'

'Have him into the mess, perhaps,' said the Senior Major. 'Dinner, something like that?'

'He wouldn't come,' said Bennet-Bruce.

'No harm in asking,' said the second-in-command.

'That's what you think,' said the Adjutant bitterly. 'Every time I speak to him he just glares and turns his back – I'm beginning to think I've got B.O.'

'Then don't ask him,' said the Senior Major. 'Just bring him along, and once he's here, chances are we can thaw him out.'

'Ye daurnae offer him drink!' protested the M.O.

'Of course not – but we can lay on Arab grub, make him feel at home . . . well, it would be a gesture,' said the second-in-command. 'Show him that we . . . well, you know . . . I don't suppose he'll get many invitations, after he leaves here.' He glanced at the Colonel, who was sitting lost in his own thoughts. 'I move we ask him to the mess. What d'you think, sir?'

The Colonel came back to earth. 'Certainly. Why not? Have him in tomorrow – make it a mess night.' He pushed back his chair and went out, followed by the seniors.

'Sentimental old bird, the skipper,' said Errol.

'How d'you mean?' said MacKenzie.

'Well, he's been on the wee wog's side all along – who hasn't? Now this Harry Maclean thing . . . it just makes having to turn Suleiman over to the French that much harder, doesn't it?'

'You're a perceptive chiel,' nodded the Padre.

'It doesn't make much odds,' said the Adjutant gloomily. 'It's rotten whichever way you look at it.' He glanced across at Errol who was flicking peanut shells at the Waterloo snuff-box. 'What would you do . . . if it was you?'

'If I were the Colonel – and felt as sorry for old Abou ben Adem as he does?' Errol gave his lazy smile. 'I certainly wouldn't connive at his escape – which is the thought at the back of everyone's mind, only we're too feart to say so. I might write to G.H.Q., citing his war service and decrepitude, and respectfully submitting that the French be told to fall out –'

'He's already done that,' said the Adjutant. 'Got a rocket for not minding his own business.'

'Well, *shabash* the Colonel sahib! But that's all, folks. He's done his best – so all we can do is give Suleiman the hollow apology of a dinner to show our hearts are in the right place, and wish him *bon voyage* to Devil's Island.'

'That's a lousy way to put it!' snapped MacKenzie.

'Only if you feel guilty, Kenny,' said Errol. 'I don't. He's a tough old bandit, down on his luck . . . and a damned bad man. No, I'd hand him over, with some regret, as the Colonel will. But unlike the Colonel I won't vex myself wondering what Harry Maclean would have done.'

'That's a bit mystical,' protested the Adjutant.

'Is it? You're not Scotch, Mike. The Colonel is – so he gets daft thoughts about . . . oh, after the battle . . . kinship of old enemies . . . doing right by the shades. Damned nonsense, but it can play hell with a Highlander in the wee sma' hoors, especially if he's got a drink in him. Read between the lines of *The Golden Bough* sometime.' Errol stifled a yawn and got up. 'It was written by a teuchter, incidentally.'

'Interesting,' said the Padre. 'Well, what *would* Harry Maclean do about Suleiman?'

Errol paused at the door. 'Shoot the little bugger, I should think. He probably spent half his life trying.'

Acting on the Senior Major's advice, the Adjutant didn't invite Suleiman formally, but simply conducted him to the mess, where we had assembled in the dining-room. The table was blazing with our two centuries' worth of silver, much of it loot – Nana Sahib's spoons, the dragon candlesticks from the Opium Wars, the inlaid Ashanti shield (now a fruit-bowl), the silver-gilt punchbowl presented by Patton in Normandy, the snuff-box made from the hoof of the Scots Greys' drumhorse, the porcelain samovar given to a forgotten mercenary who had helped to stop the Turks at Vienna and whose grandson had brought it to the regiment. It was priceless and breathtaking; Suleiman could not doubt that he was being treated as a guest of honour. The Pipe-Sergeant had even bullied the Colonel into letting him compose a special air, 'The Music of Suleiman ibn Aziz' – it was impossible to stop the pipey creating new works of genius, all of which sounded like 'Bonnie Dundee' or 'Flowers of the Forest', depending on the tempo; it remained to be seen which had been plagiarised when the pipey strode forth to regale us after dinner.

Poor soul, he never got the chance. Suleiman took one look at the gleaming table, the thirty expectant tartan figures, the pipers ranged against the wall, the Colonel welcoming him to his seat – and straightway stormed out, raging and cursing in Arabic. Why, I'm still not sure; he must have known it was kindly meant, and we could only assume that he regarded all Franks as poison and any overture from them as an insult. The mess reaction was that it was a pity, but if that was how he felt, too bad. Strangely enough, it didn't diminish the sympathy for him, and it was a reluctant Adjutant who had to tell him next day (Sunday) that the French were coming earlier than expected, and he would be leaving the following Thursday. Either because he was taken aback, or was still in a passion over the dinner fiasco, Suleiman let fly a torrent of abuse in *lingua franca*, shook his fist in the Adjutant's face, and rounded things off by spitting violently on the floor.

Which was distressing, and hardly reasonable since he'd known he was going sooner or later, but the explanation emerged three nights after. On Monday he was still in a villainous temper, but McGarry thought he looked unusually tired, too, and he wouldn't leave his cell to sit on the verandah. On Tuesday he kept his bed, sleeping most of the day. In the small hours of Wednesday morning he broke out.

He must have been working at the single bar of his cell window since his arrival, presumably calculating that he would have it loose by the end of the second week. The advance of the French arrival had upset his plans, and he had spent two and a half nights digging feverishly at the concrete sill – with what tool, and how he had not been detected, we never discovered. Only a chance look through the grille by the sentry discovered the bar askew, and thirty seconds later the guard were doubling out of barracks in the forlorn hope of catching a fugitive who had the choice of melting into the alleys of the city not far off, or vanishing into the Sahara which stretched for two thousand miles from our southern wall.

It was sheer blind luck that they came on him hobbling painfully along a dry ditch on the desert road; being reluctant to lay hands on an old man who was plainly on his last legs, they called on him to stop, but he just kept going, panting and stumbling, until they headed him off, when he turned at bay, lashing out, and after a furious clawing struggle he had to be carried bodily back to the guardroom, literally foaming at the mouth. Taken to a new cell, he collapsed on the floor, too exhausted to resist an examination by the M.O. which revealed what was already obvious – that he was an unusually hardy old man, and dead beat. Even so, an extra sentry was posted under his window.

There was no point in reporting the incident to the Provost Marshal, and for the last twenty-four hours before the French were due he was just confined to his cell, sitting hunched up on his cot, ignoring his food; having made his bid and failed he seemed resigned, with all the spirit drained out of him.

Then, late in the afternoon, he began to sing – or rather to chant, a high wailing cry not unlike the *muezzin*'s prayer call, but with a defiant note in it – the kind of thing which prompts the Highlander to remark: 'Sing me a Gaelic song, granny, and sing it through your nose.' It reminded me of something else, but I wasn't sure what until the Padre, who happened to be in our company office, cocked an ear to the distant keening sound and quoted:

'"The old wives will cry the coronach, and there will be a great clapping of hands, for I am one of the greatest chiefs of the Highlands."'

'I never knew that,' said Bennet-Bruce. 'I always thought you were a clergyman from Skye.'

'Pearls before swine,' said the Padre. 'I'm telling you what old Simon Fraser said before they took the head off him on Tower Green.' He listened, eyes half-closed. 'I wonder if our old buddoo isn't saying the same thing.'

'Why should he? No one's going to cut his head off.'

'Perhaps not,' said the Padre. 'But if that's not a coronach then I never heard one.'

Whatever it was, it didn't exactly set the feet tapping; the high wavering cry raised the hairs on my neck – and not on mine alone. The Colonel left his office early to get out of earshot, and the Adjutant, kept at his desk, was noticeably not his usual Bertie Woosterish self: he tore my head off over some routine inquiry, slammed his window shut, and gave vent to his feelings.

'Gosh, I'll be glad to get shot of him! Nothing but trouble! We didn't *ask* to be landed with him, we've tried to make things as easy for him as we can, tried to be decent – and the little bastard spits in our eye, gets the Colonel in the doghouse with Cairo, treats *me* like dirt, tries to bust out –'

'Well, you can't blame him for that, Mike.'

'– and generally gets right on the battalion's collective wick! Of course I don't blame him.' The Adjutant stared gloomily out of the window. 'That's the trouble. I'm all *for* him. We all are – and he doesn't even know it. He thinks we're as big a shower as the French and G.H.Q. He hates our guts.' He brooded at me in a pink, bothered way. 'Why shouldn't he? And why the hell should we worry if he does? You think I need a laxative, don't you?'

'I think you need some tea,' I said. But I thought he was right: Suleiman, somehow, had got in among us, and it would have been nice to think that he knew we were on his side – for all the good *that* would do him. A selfish, childish wish, probably, but understandable.

Because I wanted to be there when he left, I had arranged to be orderly officer next day, and after dinner I went to tell McGarry that the French probably wouldn't take him before noon. McGarry promised to have him ready; the few belongings that had come with him were in an unopened bundle in the office safe, and the man himself was asleep.

'Nae wonder, after the fight he pit up. No' the size o' a fish supper, but it took four o' them tae carry him in, an' him beatin' the bejeezus oot o' them. Say that for him,' McGarry nodded admiringly. 'He's game.'

Just how game we discovered next morning when the orderly took breakfast into the cell, and Suleiman came at him from behind the door like a wildcat, knocked him flying, ducked past McGarry, and was heading for the wide blue yonder when he went full tilt over McAuslan, who was scrubbing the floor. In the ensuing mêlée which involved two sentries (with McAuslan wallowing in suds imploring all concerned to keep the heid) Suleiman managed to grab a bayonet, and murder would have been done if McGarry had not weighed in, clasping both of Suleiman's skinny wrists in one enormous paw and swinging him off his feet with the other. Even then the little sheikh had fought like a madman, struggling and kicking and trying to bite until, to the amazement of McAuslan:

'. . . a' the fight seemed tae go oot o' him, an' he lets oot sich a helluva cry, an' ye know whit? He jist pit his heid on big McGarry's chest, like a wean wi' his mither, an' grat. No, he wisnae bubblin' – no' that kinda greetin', jist shakin' an' haudin' on like there wisnae a kick left in him. An' big McGarry pit him on his feet, an' says: 'Come on, auld yin', an' pits him back in the cell – an' then turns on me, fur Goad's sake, an' starts bawlin' tae get the flair scrubbit an' dae Ah think Ah'm peyed tae staun' aboot wi' no' twa pun' o' me hingin' straight! Ye'd think it wis me had been tryin' tae murder hauf the Airmy an' go absent, no' the wee wog!'

All this I learned when I checked the guardroom at nine – the facts from McGarry, the colour from Our Correspondent on Jankers. Suleiman had stayed quiet in his cell.

The French arrived at eleven in the Provost Marshal's car and an escorting jeep: a major and captain in sky-blue kepis, a *sous-officier* in the navy tunic and red breeches of the Légion Etrangère, two privates with carbines, and a Moorish interpreter. The officers and the P.M. were escorted to the mess for hospitality while the rankers stayed with their vehicles; the *sous-officier*, a moustachioed stalwart with a gold chevron and no neck, paced up and down exchanging appraising glances with McGarry on the guardroom verandah.

There seemed to be more casual activity than usual in the vicinity that morning: several platoons were drilling on the square, various Jocks had found an excuse for moving to and from the nearer buildings, and others were being unobtrusive in the middle distance; nothing like a crowd, just a modest gathering, not large enough to excite the displeasure of R.S.M. Macintosh as he made his magisterial way across the parade, pausing to survey the platoons who presently stopped drilling and stood easy, but did not dismiss. It was all very orderly, but in no way official; they were waiting to see Suleiman ibn Aziz go, without being too obvious about it. The windows and verandahs of the farther barrack-blocks had their share of spectators, and the Padre and M.O. were coming through the main gate and mounting the guardroom steps, returning the magnificent salute of the *sous-officier* – he was a slightly puzzled *sous-officier*, judging by the way he was studying the square: why so many Ecossaises about, he might well have been wondering. Was this how les Dames d'Enfer kept discipline, by example? What would Milor' Wellington have said? He shook his head and resumed pacing, and the Ecossaises regarded him bleakly from under their bonnet-brims.

'Now's the time for the English to attack,' observed the M.O.

'Right enough, Lachlan,' agreed the Padre. 'The Auld Alliance is looking gey fragile.' He consulted his watch. 'Band practice shortly, I think – there, what did I say?'

From behind the band office came the warm-up notes of a piper, and then the slow measured strains of 'Lovat's Lament', the loveliest and most stately of slow marches. The Padre nodded approval.

'Aye, that's pipey. Not bad, for a man that never set foot on Skye.'

'Who's idea's this?' I asked. 'The Colonel's?'

'Why don't you ask him?' said the M.O. 'Here he is, wi' the Comédie Francaise.'

The Colonel and Adjutant were emerging from the tamarisk grove that screened the mess, with the French officers and the P.M. The R.S.M. let out a splendid Guards-trained scream of 'Attain-shah!' and there was an echoing crash of heels on the square. The Padre chuckled.

'Canny Macintosh! You notice he didn't say "Parade-shun!" Because there is no parade, of course. A nice distinction.'

I followed the Colonel's party into the guardroom, the *sous-officier* and the Moorish interpreter bringing up the rear. Suleiman, with McGarry standing by, was sitting beside the table, very composed, the lean brown face impassive under the silver-edged *kafilyeh* – it was hard to believe that this frail, quiet little man had twice tried to break out, fighting like a wild beast and trying to stab a sentry with his own bayonet. He didn't get up, and the French Major smiled and turned to the Colonel.

'I am pleased he has caused you no inconvenience, sir.' He spoke English with barely a trace of accent.

'None whatever,' said the Colonel. 'All ready, Sarn't McGarry? Very well, sir.'

The Major nodded to the *sous-officier,* who strode across and snapped an order. Suleiman didn't stir, and the *sous-officier* repeated it in an explosive bark that was startling in its unexpected violence. But not as startling as what followed. McGarry stiffened to his full height and rasped:

'You don't talk tae the man like that, son!'

The *sous-officier* didn't speak the language, but he knew cold menace when he heard it, and gave back as though he'd been hit – which, in my opinion, he nearly had been. The others stared, all except the Colonel, who had tactfully turned aside to listen to something that the Adjutant wasn't saying. There was an embarrassed pause, and then Suleiman glanced up at McGarry and, with the smallest of deprecating gestures, rose to his feet. He turned his back on the *sous-officier,* looked McGarry full in the face, and made the quick graceful heart-lips-brow salutation of the *salaam*.

For once McGarry was taken flat aback, and then he did the only thing he could do – stamped his heel and nodded. Suleiman turned away and calmly surveyed the waiting officers; he looked for a moment at the Colonel and then said something in Arabic to the interpreter, who passed it on in French to the Major, indicating the bundle of coarse cloth on the table which contained Suleiman's belongings. The Major looked surprised, shrugged, and turned to the Colonel.

'It seems there is something he wishes to leave with you.'

He gave an order to the *sous-officier*, and we waited expectantly while the bundle was unwrapped. Outside the pipey could still be heard running through his repertoire; he was on to the marches now, with a kettle-drum rattling accompaniment, but you couldn't tell whether Suleiman was hearing it or not. He was standing absolutely still, his hands clasped before him, looking straight ahead at the Colonel, but he must have been watching out of the corner of his eye, for as the *sous-officier* began to take out the bundle's contents – a packet of papers, a bunch of keys, a couple of enamelled boxes, a few rather fine-looking ornaments which were probably gold and silver, one or two strands of jewellery – he gave another grunt in Arabic and thrust out his hand, palm up. The *sous-officier* was holding a packet about a foot long, wrapped in red muslin; he passed it to the interpreter, who handed it nervously to Suleiman.

You could have heard a pin drop while the little man flicked a hand to indicate that the rest of his goods should be parcelled up again, and then stood looking down at the red packet, turning it in his hands, clasping it as though reluctant to let it go. Then his head came up and he walked across to the Colonel and held it out to him with both hands. The Colonel took it, and as he did so Suleiman suddenly clasped both his hands over the Colonel's on the package, holding the grip hard and staring fiercely into the Colonel's face. Then he let go, inclined his head gravely, and stepped back. The Colonel said 'Thank you', and Suleiman ibn Aziz walked out of the guardroom.

On the verandah he paused for a moment, looking at the Jocks in the square who were waiting to see him go. The unseen Pipe-Sergeant and the kettle-drums were waking the echoes, and I heard the Padre murmur to the M.O.:

'That'll be "The Music of Suleiman ibn Aziz", I daresay – it sounds just like "The Black Bear" to me, but then I haven't the pipey's imagination.'

Suleiman ibn Aziz went down the steps and into the waiting car, the French officers exchanged salutes with the Colonel and climbed in, the legionnaires piled into the jeep, the *sous-officier* exchanged a last stare with McGarry, the sentry on the gate presented arms as the vehicles drove through, and the Jocks on the square began to drift away.

The Colonel was holding the red muslin package. 'Right, let's have a look at it,' he said, and led the way back into the guardroom, for he knew McGarry would be as curious as the rest of us. We all stood round as he unwrapped the cloth, and when the contents lay on the table nobody spoke for quite some time. We just looked at it and let the thought sink in.

It was an Arab dagger, and not a rich or ornamental one. The sheath was cracked and discoloured, and while the blade was classically curved and shone like silver, it was pitted with age, the brass cross-hilt was scarred, the pommel had lost its inlay, and the haft was bound with wire in two places. You wouldn't have given two ackers for it on a bazaar stall – unless you had laid it across your finger and noted the perfect balance, or lowered its edge on to a piece of paper and watched it slice through of its own weight.

The Colonel fingered his moustache, gave a little cough, said 'Well,' and was silent. He picked the dagger up again, weighed it in his hand, and said at last: 'Not the most valuable of his possessions, I daresay. But certainly the most precious.'

'He must have had it a long time,' said the Adjutant. In a wondering tone he added: 'He gave it to us.'

The Colonel pushed the blade home. 'Right. Get it cleaned up and sterilised – God knows who it's been in. It can go with the mess silver.' He caught the Adjutant's doubtful frown. 'Well, why shouldn't it? If some cavalry regiment can use Napoleon's brother's chamber-pot as a punchbowl, I see no reason why you shouldn't cut your cheese with a knife that's been through the Riff Rebellion.'

'Absolutely, sir!' agreed the Adjutant hastily. 'I'll see the mess sergeant looks after it right away.' Then he looked worried. 'I say, though – we ought to have given old Suleiman some cash for it – you know, bad luck not to pay for a knife. Cuts friendship, my aunt used to say.'

The Colonel paused in the doorway. 'I'm afraid his luck can't get much worse, Michael.' He frowned, considering. 'And I'm not sure that we were ever friends, exactly. Put it with the silver anyway.'

McAuslan, Lance-Corporal

To hear him talk, usually at the top of his raucous voice, you might have thought that Private McAuslan was a violent man, but he wasn't, really, except under extreme provocation. Being unclean, dim, handless, illiterate, and ugly, he attracted a good deal of abuse from comrades as well as superiors, but while he didn't take it gladly his response seldom went beyond verbal truculence. Any day you might hear his warning roar of 'Watch it, china!' floating from the windows of 12 Platoon barrack-room, followed by furious threats to melt, claim, sort out, or banjo his critic, but there it would end, as a rule; his associates knew just how far it was safe to rib him, and that there were some subjects best left alone. His intelligence, for example: he was used to being called dumb, dozy, clueless, and not the full hod of bricks, and that was all right, being the small change of military conversation; only if the ridicule went too far, or became too penetrating, was physical eruption liable to follow, as young Corporal Crawford learned to his cost.

He was a weapons instructor who, during a lecture, was unwise enough to make fun of McAuslan's inability to see through a well-known optical illusion. Bren gun magazines are kidney-shaped; lay them side by side and one looks larger than the other because its convex edge is longer than the concave edge of the magazine beside it; change them over, and the one which looked smaller now appears to be the bigger . . . a simple trick which causes much hilarity among five-year-olds.

Whether McAuslan had reached that stage, intellectually, was debatable, but he wasn't amused. I wasn't present, but according to my informant, Private Forbes, Crawford had been squatting over the magazines on the floor, switching them round and jeering at McAuslan's failure to see that they were identical, and McAuslan, having glowered at them in genuine baffled fury, had suddenly kicked Crawford full in the solar plexus, lifting him several feet and laying him out cold. Which had earned McAuslan fourteen days in the cooler, as well as demonstrating that there are few things more dangerous than presenting a primitive mind with an insoluble problem, never mind mocking it. Good teachers know this; bad ones, like Crawford, are appalled when they learn it the hard way.

The only other time I knew McAuslan moved to calculated assault (occasional canteen disturbances don't count, in Scottish regiments) was when he attacked an Arab vendor who had been threatening Ellen Ramsey on a shopping expedition, but that had been simple gallantry. Any normal – or in McAuslan's case, sub-normal – man would have been glad to play knight-errant to the fair Ellen, although in justice to the lad I believe he would have been just as forward in the defence of Gagool the Crone. For there was a champion inside McAuslan's ill-made frame, and a strong sense of fair play – his concept of what was, in his own words, 'no' fair', got him court-martialled once. But, as I say, he wasn't normally given to hitting people, and when I heard that he and Private Chisholm were in cells for fighting in (and incidentally wrecking) the battalion's modest library, I was moved to do some preliminary investigating before their inevitable appearance in front of the Colonel.

For one thing, the locale was unusual, and for another, Chisholm was a civil, sober, and well-bred lad, the product of an Edinburgh public school, and a most unlikely antagonist for McAuslan, if only because each probably had difficulty understanding what the other was saying, a common prerequisite to disagreement. I visited them in the guardroom, starting with Chisholm as the more likely to provide a coherent explanation.

He didn't, as it turned out. Indeed, he was reticent to the point of embarrassment, and would say only that there had been a private difference of opinion, which since he was sporting a splendid black eye was an obvious understatement. I warned him that the Colonel would require rather more detail, and passed on to intrude on Private Grief in person; he was sitting on his cell floor, bruised and foul, moodily pulling threads from a blanket and looking like a disgruntled cave-dweller.

'Chisholm made a pretty good job of you,' I observed, breaking the ice tactfully.

'Chisholm's a ——', he said, with unusual venom, and then rose and crouched apologetically to attention. 'Ah beg yer pardon, sur; Ah shouldnae hiv said that. Awfy sorry. Aye, but he should've knowed better, so he should. Ah mean, he's no' a yahoo, is he? Chisholm, he's meant tae be eddimacated, fella that's been tae a posh school, an' that –'

'All right, McAuslan,' I said patiently. 'What happened?'

He scowled, with an indignant snuffle. 'He insultit me.'

'Insulted you?' It seemed unlikely, if not impossible. 'How?'

'Aye, weel, ye see. It wis because o' because. That's whit startit it.'

Not for the first time with him, I found myself doubting my senses. 'I'm sorry, you'll have to say that again. It was because of what?'

'Because. Whit he said aboot because.'

'I'm not with you, McAuslan. Why do you keep saying because?'

'Because that's whit it wis aboot. Because.'

I felt that if I asked 'Who's on first?' he would reply 'No, he's on third,' like Abbot and Costello, so I tried a new line.

'Shut up, McAuslan. Now, we'll start again. Why were you in the battalion library?'

'Tae listen tae because.'

'So help me God, if you use that word again I'll forget myself. *What* were you listening *to*?'

'Ah'm tellin' ye, sur! Because!' His simian brow was bedewed with sweat, and he was plucking lumps from the blanket as he strove to enlighten me. 'Ah wis listenin' tae because! Onna gramyphone. Ye know, Because Goad made thee mine Ah'll cherish thee, but. Itsa song onna record onna gramyphone. Ye must hae heard it, sur!' He regarded me in desperate appeal. 'Because?'

It dawned. In the library the Padre maintained a portable gramophone and a selection of records for the battalion's music-lovers, of whom the battered wretch before me was apparently one – and that was enough to beggar belief, but that's McAuslan for you.

'I see,' I said. 'I'm sorry, McAuslan, I didn't understand. I must be slow today. You went to the library to listen to a record of the song entitled "Because", and –'

'Onna gramyphone.'

'As you say, on the gramophone. Then what happened?'

'Aye, weel, like Ah'm sayin', Ah'm listenin' tae ra record – here it's a smashin' record, but! Ye know it, sur? Yon man Tawber – he's a Hun, but jeez, whit a voice!' His pimpled countenance took on a look of holy rapture. 'He minds me a bit o' Jackie O'Connell that used tae be in C Company, ye mind him? Irish boy, sang like a lintie, "Ah'm on'y a Wanderin' Vagabond" an' "Bless this Hoose" an' –'

'Hold it, McAuslan! You were listening to "Because", sung by Richard Tauber. Fine. Then what happened?'

'Aye, weel, sur, like Ah tellt ye, Ah'm listenin' tae ra record, an' wee Tawber's givin' it lalldy, when Chisholm comes in an' starts pickin' oot some o' the ither records that's there – there's some right bummers, Ah'm tellin' ye, bluidy screechin' Eyeties, ye widnae credit it – an' efter a bit he sez: "Ye gaunae play that record a' night, then?" "Take yer time, pal," Ah sez, "Ah'm listenin' tae ra music here." So he stauns aroon' an' then sez: "Ye've played it hauf a dozen times a'ready. Hoo aboot givin' some ither buddy a chance?" "Look, mac," sez Ah, "just haud on an' ye'll get the gramyphone when Ah'm finished, see? Whit ye in such a hurry to play, onywye?" "Ah've got some *music* here," sez he, nasty-like, "jazz classics an' chamber music, for your information." "Jazz classics?' sez Ah. "There's no such thing, an' Ah can mak' better chamber music in a latrine bucket." "Ah suppose ye think that cheap syrup ye're playin' is music?" sez he. "Cheap syrup?" sez Ah – an' that wis when Ah stuck one oan him.'

As Wanger used to say, no doubt. Well, it was fascinating, all right, and revealed a side to McAuslan which I had never dreamed of. And yet why not? Breasts didn't come any more savage than his, and if Tauber soothed it, splendid. But that wasn't really the point.

'In other words, you were hogging the gramphone, and he objected, and you belted him. You're just a hooligan, aren't you?'

'Oh, haud on, sur, it wasnae that, but!' he protested. 'Ah'd hiv let him hiv the gramyphone if he hadnae been so sniffy, the toffy-nosed Embro git! But Ah wisnae havin' him sayin' that aboot the greatest song ever wrote! No' on yer life!' His unwashed face quivered with outrage. '"Cheap syrup", sez he! That wis why Ah clocked him, an' then he clocked me, an' we got tore in, an' then the Gestapo came an' beltit the both o' us an' pit us in the tank.' He snorted and sat down abruptly, plainly much moved. 'The cheek o' him! No, Ah wisnae havin' that, no' aboot "Because".' He gave a rasping sigh, scratching himself in a way that determined me to have a shower presently. 'Think mebbe Sarn't McGarry'd gi'e us a cuppa chah, sur?'

'Try asking him and see what you get,' I suggested, and he

shuddered. He and the Provost Sergeant were old acquaintances. 'But, look here, McAuslan, you can't clock people just because they don't like "Because".' Now I was doing it. 'People are entitled to express their opinions – I mean, it's a nice song, but –'

'Itsa greatest music onybody ever made up.' He said it with a grim intensity that quite startled me. 'It's marvellous. Nuthin' like it. No' even in Church.'

'That's your opinion, but the fact that Chisholm doesn't share it is no reason to start a brawl and break up the library. Or for getting a man with a clean sheet into trouble, you horrible article. Not that he isn't to blame, too. Anyway, whatever the Colonel gives you – and I hope it's plenty – the first thing you and Chisholm do when you get out is apologise to the Padre, pay for the damage, and put in seven nights fatigue at the Church. Got that?'

'Yessur, rightsur! But Chisholm shouldnae hiv insultit –'

'Shut up about Chisholm! Anyway, what the hell's so special about "Because"?' I asked out of irritated curiosity, and was given the brooding, reproachful stare of the great anthropoid at zoo spectators; he even stopped scratching.

'It's bluidy great,' he said solemnly. 'Wonderfullest song ever wrote. 'Atsa fac', sur.'

He really meant it, and I knew McAuslan well enough to be aware that when he believed something, it was engraved on marble, or whatever his brain was made of. And while musical obsession was something new, well, different strains work their magic on different ears, and if he was enthralled by 'Because', I wasn't going to argue – on his recent showing, it wouldn't have been safe. I left his cell thinking there were many things that I knew not, and the deeps of McAuslan's mind was the first of them. Why 'Because'? Was I missing something? I whistled the tune absently, and paused, repeating the words under my breath.

Because you come to me
With naught save lo-ove . . .

'Beg pardon, sir?' said Sergeant McGarry anxiously, and I left hurriedly, still pondering why that ordinary (even syrupy, as Chisholm had said) little tune should stir such passion in my platoon's answer to Karloff. Tauber sang it beautifully, to be sure, but hardly well enough to justify battery. Having nothing better to do, I turned off to the library, which was empty at that time of night and still bore signs of the evening's discord; 'Because' was still on the gramophone, so I cranked the handle and let her rip, and Tauber hadn't unleashed more than a couple of sobs before there was a cry of alarm from the inner office and the Padre shot out, pale-faced and hiding his spectacles; he stopped with a gasp of relief and subsided on a chair.

'Thank God it's yourself – for a minute I thought it was yon Gorbals troglodyte back again. Has McGarry bound him with fetters of brass, I hope?'

'Sorry I startled you, bishop. Just doing some research on Tauber.'

The Padre cocked a critical ear. 'Ah, the Chernan lieder. Chust so. Fine voices, but they aye sound to me as though they've got something trapped. I'm an Orpheus Choir man myself, and a wee bit of Brahms, but I've no taste. "Because", eh? I once knew a tenor who sang it in the Gaelic . . . mind you, he was from Tiree . . .'

'Wonder why it appeals to McAuslan?'

'Who can say?' The Padre prepared to go into a Hebridean philosophic trance. 'Barrack-room sentiment? Childhood memory? Maybe his mother sang him to sleep wi' it.' He shivered. 'Can ye picture such a woman? Mrs Medusa McAuslan. Aye, well, I could have seen her son far enough this night, the ruffian. And yet,' he gave a reflective sigh, 'there's consolation in it, too. Better that he and Chisholm should thrash each other over music than over cards or drink or the Rangers and the Celtic. D'ye not think so, Dand?'

One who didn't was the Colonel. He gave them three days in close tack, with stoppage of pay for damages. The platoon, when the cause of the brawl became known, waxed hilarious over McAuslan's Orphean tendencies, but when I heard that Private Fletcher had serenaded beneath his cell window with a ribald version of 'Because', I thought it time to warn them that they were playing with dynamite, and added that if in future McAuslan was provoked to violence by musical humour, the joker could expect no mercy, d'you get that, Fletcher? I probably needn't have bothered, for soon after his release the episode was forgotten in a new sensation from which McAuslan emerged, briefly, as something of a celebrity.

I have described the great Inter-Regimental Quiz elsewhere. What happened was that, to settle a bet between our colonels, a team from the neighbouring Fusiliers was matched against one from our battalion in a general knowledge competition, held in the presence of the Brigadier, garrison society, and a baying mob of supporters from both regiments. After a gruelling struggle in which I, for one, was drained of my great store of trivia, and the Padre was reduced to the point where he couldn't tell the Pentateuch from the Apocrypha, the contest ended in a tie, at which stage the Brigadier, who was the biggest idiot ever to wear red tabs, said the thing should be settled by one sudden-death question which he would put to both sides and, if they couldn't answer, to their supporters. Naturally we all cried sycophantic agreement, and the Brigadier, bursting with self-satisfaction, propounded the most fatuous hypothetical trick-question you ever heard: how can one player score three goals at football without anyone else touching the ball in between?

We didn't know, of course, and suggested politely that the

thing was impossible. Not so, said the Brigadier smugly; it was unlikely, granted, but theoretically possible – and that was the great moment when McAuslan, eating chips in the audience, rose from his seat like a fly-blown prophet and gave the right answer.* It seemed he had once heard it in a Glasgow pub; what that says about the Brigadier's intellectual circle you must judge for yourselves. Anyway, the Brigadier was delighted, and congratulated McAuslan, who won a box of Turkish Delight for his pains.

A harmless incident, apparently, but pregnant with disaster. For the Brigadier, gratified that his ridiculous question had broken the deadlock, remarked to our Colonel in the mess afterwards that he'd been impressed by that odd-looking bird who'd come up with the answer. What was his name again? McAuslan, eh? Not the kind, from his appearance. whom you'd expect to be able to solve a knotty problem like that – why, the Brigadier had been stumping people with it for years. Well, it just went to show, you couldn't judge a sausage by its . . . by its . . . oh, dammit, he'd forget his own name next . . . yes, by its skin, that was it.

'Kind of chap I used to watch out for in my battalion days,' mused the Brigadier. 'Chaps with potential often look a bit . . . well, strange. Wingate, for instance.' I had a brief dreadful vision of McAuslan leading the Chindits, and then the Brigadier dispelled it with one of the most shocking suggestions ever made.

'This chap McAuslan,' he asked the Colonel, 'ever thought of making him an N.C.O.?'

The Colonel admitted later that he hadn't been so shaken by a question since the Japanese interrogated him on the Moulmein railway – and at least he'd been able to tell them to go to hell. With the Brigadier – whom he'd been heard to describe as an ass

* Which is long and complex, and may be found in *McAuslan in the Rough*.

who ought to be put in charge of a company store and excused boots – he decided to employ controlled sarcasm.

'Interesting idea, sir,' he said smoothly. 'Of course, we've thought long and hard about McAuslan. Haven't we, MacNeill? We don't overlook men of his calibre, not in this battalion. But as you know, sir, there are some men who simply won't accept promotion. Pity, but what can one do? Waiter, another round here.' Perfectly true, and totally misleading – there *are* men who won't take promotion, but McAuslan was the last who was likely to get the chance.

The Brigadier frowned and said exceptional men should be persuaded; it was the Army's duty to make them realise their full potential. The Colonel smiled – I guessed he was on the point of suggesting innocently that the Brigadier should take McAuslan into Brigade H.Q., possibly in Intelligence, but fortunately someone came up at that moment and the subject was changed.

'That's what they put in command of brigades nowadays,' observed the Colonel, when the Brigadier had gone. 'Well, thank God they kept him in Cairo during the war. Waiter, bring me another – and you can stop smirking, young Dand, and concentrate on keeping that blot McAuslan out of the public eye in future.'

That was easier said than done at the best of times, and now a combination of circumstances arose to make it impossible. First, Bennet-Bruce went off on yet another of those luxurious courses that seem to come the way of military Old Etonians – if it wasn't Advanced French at Antibes it was water-skiing at Djerba – and our company came under the temporary command of that debonair and dangerous exquisite, Captain Errol. Secondly, the rest of the battalion, Colonel, H.Q., Support Company and all, went off on a seven-day exercise in the big desert, leaving only D Company to rattle about in the deserted barracks; officially we were maintaining a military presence, but in fact we were cleaning and decorating the transport sheds for the big occasion of the regimental year, Waterloo Night, which would be celebrated with dance and revelry on the evening of the battalion's return. Thirdly, Private McAuslan went with a fatigue party to collect extra furniture for the dance from the Brigade quartermaster.

All innocent events in themselves; it was their coincidence that made them lethal.

The Brigadier, returning from what must have been an unusually excellent lunch, happened by just as the fatigue party were loading their truck, and recognised McAuslan (as who wouldn't) among them. Feeling paternal, he summoned the toiler and asked him what was all this nonsense about refusing promotion, eh? What McAuslan said is not recorded; no interpreter was present, and he was presumably in his usual state of stricken incoherence before High Authority. The Brigadier shook his head kindly and spoke of ambition and advancement; he may even have told McAuslan there was a baton in his knapsack (it was his good luck he couldn't see inside McAuslan's knapsack, not after lunch). Finally, he said why didn't McAuslan change his mind and accept a lance-corporal's stripe as the first step to higher things. I assume that at this point McAuslan made some noise which was taken for assent, for the Brigadier cried capital, capital, he would see to it, and 'Carry on, Corporal!'

Most great military blunders stem from the good intentions of some high-ranking buffoon, but in fairness it has to be said that the Brigadier was seeing McAuslan at his best – awestruck dumb, naked save for identity discs and khaki shorts which gave no real idea of how revolting he looked in uniform, and engaged in the only work of which he was capable; to wit, carrying heavy and unbreakable objects across level ground under supervision. Even so, one good look at that neanderthal profile should have warned even a staff officer;

perhaps he was short-sighted, and the lunch had been quite exceptional.

Strictly speaking it isn't a Brigadier's business to interfere in minor promotions, and if when he phoned the barracks he'd got the Colonel or Bennet-Bruce they would have thanked him for his recommendation and then forgotten about it. But in their absence he got Errol, who could have given lessons in mischief to Loki, and when the Brigadier said that a tape should be stuck on McAuslan's arm forthwith, our temporary commander said he would be delighted to comply; he'd often thought McAuslan was due for a boost upstairs, and he would take the liberty of congratulating the Brigadier for having spotted talent from his Olympian height, or words to that effect. Knowing Errol's line of oil, I imagine the Brigadier may have wondered if he shouldn't have put McAuslan straight up to sergeant.

So there it was: the appointment of 14687347 McAuslan, J., to lance-corporal (acting, unpaid) went on company orders that afternoon, and my reaction, on returning from a hard day in the transport shed and suffering a minor apoplexy when I heard the news, was to inquire of Errol if he had gone doolaly, and if not, what was he playing at?

'Respecting the wishes of my superiors,' he said languidly, with his feet on the desk. 'Have some tea.'

'Are you kidding? Look – hasn't anyone told you about McAuslan? The brute's illiterate, his crime sheet's as long as a toilet roll, he's had to be forcibly washed God knows how often, he doesn't know left from right, can't tell the time of day, and is, at a conservative estimate, the dirtiest and dumbest bad bargain His Majesty's made since Agincourt!'

'You paint a pretty picture,' he said. 'Care to argue with the Brigadier, Mr MacNeill?'

'Care to explain to the Colonel, Captain Errol? He'll have your guts for garters.'

'I'm just the slave of duty. When Brigadiers say unto me, go – I've gone already.'

'Look,' I said, 'it isn't on. For one thing, my Jocks won't wear it. Can you see them taking orders from that . . . that walking tattie-bogle? They'll mutiny.'

'I doubt it,' he said. 'Anyway, he's been promoted. What d'you want me to do – bust him straight back? Without a reason?'

'I've just given you about seventeen!'

'For not promoting him, yes. Not for busting him. There's a difference. The deed's been done, he's got his stripe, and he's entitled to his chance.' He raised a mocking eyebrow. 'You ought to appreciate that – you've been a lance-jack yourself, and see where it got you.'

'You're a bastard, you know that?'

'So they tell me,' said Errol complacently. 'Come on, let's have a drink and I'll play you fifty up before dinner.'

It was only when my initial outrage at the Brigadier's folly (and Errol's malicious acquiescence) had subsided that the enormity of the thing really sank in. McAuslan simply couldn't begin to be a lance-corporal. You just had to picture the sequence of events when he shambled out, looking as though he'd just been cut down from the Tyburn gibbet, with a new stripe on his sleeve: the Jocks would collapse in mirth, McAuslan would give an order, it would not be taken seriously, and he would charge someone with disobedience – assuming he knew how. Then what? How could I, with a straight face, punish an honest soldier for ignoring an order given by a deadbeat whose military unfitness was a battalion byword? It might even be argued that McAuslan, whose imperative vocabulary consisted mainly of 'Sharrup!' and 'Bugger off!' was incapable of giving a lawful command. Suddenly the Nuremberg trial took on a whole new aspect, and I had to fight down a vision of the Tartan Caliban sitting in the dock scratching himself while the Nazi war criminals scrambled to keep away from him. More immediate pictures presented themselves: McAuslan, whose mere touch brought rust, inspecting rifles . . . McAuslan reprimanding someone for slovenliness . . . McAuslan calling the roll when he couldn't even read. It was all a nightmare, impossible.

The effect on discipline would be disastrous. It was also, incidentally, most unfair to the man himself. Lance-corporal (which is an appointment, without even the dignity of a rank) is the most thankless number you can draw in the Army, a dogsbody's job with responsibilities but no real power, as I knew from experience of which Errol had reminded me, although he probably didn't know that I'd been a lance-jack no fewer than four times and been busted back to private on three of them – for losing, on different occasions, a tea-urn, a member of my section, and a guardroom.* I had painful memories of trying to take charge, at the age of nineteen, of ten men all older and longer served than I was, of being the butt both of superiors and subordinates, and of the shame of those three reductions to the ranks. The fourth promotion, in Burma, was different; then it was life or death, with no time for doubts or indecisions, and I had kept my stripe. But it's no fun, having that one tape (look what it did to Hitler) and for McAuslan, with all his natural handicaps, I could see it being traumatic.

I was dead wrong. Whoever suffered from that promotion, it wasn't him. He took to that stripe like a Finnish sailor to schnapps; you'd have thought he'd been born with it. With the help of a new suit of khaki drill (issued, I later discovered,

* The tea-urn is presumably still lying somewhere near the summit of Scafell Pike. The man who went missing from my section, on a night exercise in Norfolk, turned up the following day, drunk. The guardroom was an enormous bell-tent which was removed from over my sleeping head by Royal Scots Fusiliers and Cameronians celebrating Hogmanay at Deolali, India.

on the orders of the unpredictable Errol) he managed to look semi-human for his first few hours in authority, and in that time he became, in his own mind at least, a lance-corporal. He didn't look, act, or sound like one, but he plainly *felt* like one, God help us. The presence of that newly-blancoed white chevron on his ill-fitting sleeve seemed to fill him with aggressive confidence, and he lumbered around like a badly-wrapped mummy bellowing irrelevant orders at anything that moved. And like many a dim-wit before and since he got by on the sheer force of his own ignorance and the tolerance of those around him. Greeted with derision by his section, he didn't seem to notice; having reduced the elementary business of marching them to the transport sheds to a shambolic rout, he simply blared abuse – and they got there, eventually; after all, they knew the way. With no idea of how to organise a work-gang, he just repeated, with coarse embellishments, the orders of the full corporal in overall charge, and since no one paid any attention, no harm was done. He thought he was doing fine.

He wouldn't have survived ten minutes of normal military duty, but supervising men as they heave planks and trestles around is simple stuff, and with the battalion away there was a relaxed and informal atmosphere undisturbed by parades, bugle calls, sergeant-majors, and the usual disciplinary apparatus with which he couldn't have begun to cope.

To our shame, Sergeant Telfer and I kept out of the way. Our unspoken excuse was that we had to oversee the hanging above the bandstand of the Waterloo Picture, a gigantic oil painting (by Lady Butler, I think) which normally hung in the mess but was publicly displayed on this annual occasion. It showed the great moment which was the regiment's pride, when our predecessors, having taken everything the French could throw at them, had caught hold of the stirrup leathers of the advancing Scots Greys and launched themselves against the overwhelming strength of Napoleon's army in what posterity calls the Stirrup Charge; there has never been anything like it in war, and the Emperor himself is said to have stared in disbelief at 'those Amazons' and 'the terrible grey horses'. We hung it just so, in its massive gilt frame, and as we worked we could hear, from the far end of the great echoing shed, sounds of the New Order being imposed on Three Section: McAuslan's raucous bellows of 'Moo-ove yersels, ye idle bums, or Ah'll blitz ye!' and 'Ah heard that, Fletcher! Whit d'ye think this is on mah sleeve – Scotch mist?' responded to with derisive obscenities. Obviously the section thought him a great hoot.

I knew that wouldn't last long. Being ordered about by McAuslan might be an amusing novelty for a few hours, especially when the orders were superfluous, but they'd get fed up fast enough when the orders mattered and had to be obeyed, and the total unfitness of the thing came home to them. We had an example of this when Telfer put Three Section to tidying up the outside approaches to the sheds and I suggested that the stone borders of the paths could do with a lick of whitewash. Before Telfer could translate this into an order, Lance-Corporal Grendel, who had been lurking attentively, sprang into executive action.

'Whitewash, sur! Right, sur, right away!' He lurched forward, tripping on his untied laces, full of martial zeal. 'Youse men – Forbes, Fletcher, Leishman! Get yersels doon ra Q.M. store! Get ra whitewash'n'brushes! C'moan, c'moan, c'moan, Ah'm no talkin' tae mysel'! Moo-ove, ye shower, or Ah'll be havin' ye!'

The sheer volume and violence of it was paralysing. For a moment they stared in disbelief; then, as it dawned that the joke was no longer a joke, and the Despised Unwashed was become the Voice of Authority, Fletcher's jaw tightened angrily and I caught his eye just in time.

'Right, off you go,' I said. 'Three cans should do, and six brushes. Carry on, you three.' They went, Fletcher casting a baleful glance at McAuslan who, ill-dressed in a little brief and insanitary authority, pursued them with invective. It was like listening to a Guards Drill Sergeant finally cracking up.

'Ye hear that, ye middens? Three drums'n'six brushes, an' don't be a' bluidy day aboot it! Ah'm watchin' ye, Fletcher! Ah've got your number, boy! Double, ye horrible heap, ye! Keep the eye doon, Forbes, or yer feet won't touch! Moo-ove yer idle body, Leishman, Ah can see ye –'

'Take it easy, Corporal,' I said, 'they're going.' He wheeled round obediently, falling over himself and scrambling to disorderly attention, and I was about to advise him to moderate his word of command when I caught the glazed fanatical gleam in his eye and realised that the brute was drunk with power; the heady wine of authority was coursing through his system, and he was ready to decimate whole armies. It was quite frightening, in a bizarre way: McAuslan as Captain Bligh. A new and alarming prospect opened up – mutiny, for if this personality change was permanent it could only be a matter of time before Fletcher or some other indignant soul planted the tyrant one and qualified for a court-martial. Already I could hear the Colonel's incredulous question: 'You say Fletcher assaulted a superior? Who, for heaven's sake?' and my hollow reply: 'Lance-Corporal McAuslan, sir . . .' No. Something would have to be done, and speedily, whether the Brigadier and Errol liked it or not.

I was still debating the possibility of sending McAuslan on leave, or hiring Arab thugs to kidnap him, when we finished work for the day. Three Section, I was relieved to see, fell in of their own accord and marched back to the barrack-block paying no heed to Mad Lejeaune of the Legion, who lumbered in their wake, bawling the step – not only out of time with the squad, but with himself, too. His new uniform was fit only for the incinerator by this time, and his stripe was starting to come loose, which I hoped was an omen.

And then in a moment it was all out of my hands and forgotten about. Errol was just coming off the phone when I entered the company office, and before I could begin an impassioned plea for McAuslan's reduction to the ranks on whatever pretext, he was issuing orders.

'You know Bin'yassar Convent, don't you? The Mother Superior's been on the line to Brigade – it seems a big caravan of desert buddoo have shown up at the oasis, and she doesn't like the look of them. You'll take Eleven Platoon, battle order, three days' rations, they'll wear their tartans, and I'm giving you a piper. Get out there right away, sit down in the convent, and show the flag – you know the drill. It's almost sure to be a false alarm, but we've got to keep the old girl happy. Right, move!'

It was a routine operation I had performed before, which was presumably why I'd been picked this time. The convent was about thirty miles away, on the very edge of the big desert, a relic of the days when the Crusaders patrolled the caravan trails. From time immemorial it had been occupied by the Sisters of some Order or other, and since it was in our protected zone we were occasionally called on to ferry supplies, make road repairs, and stand guard against possible emergencies. The North Sahara is one of the last lawless places on earth, or was then, and its inhabitants spend much of their time moving around; they may be anything from the gentlest of nomad herdsmen to Hoggar slavers and Targui gun-runners, and when they suddenly materialise on your doorstep it is as well to take precautions. The Mother Superior wasn't a nervous woman, but as she explained in broken English when the platoon and I arrived that evening, some of her nuns were, and would we please play our music to reassure them and warn off these desert intruders.

Looking south from the high convent wall I couldn't blame the nuns; there must have been two or three hundred black or red tents pitched round the palms of the oasis a mile away, with camel and horse herds as well as the usual goats. A reek of bitter smoke and other interesting African aromas drifted across the low sandhills, with the murmur of a great multitude. Through my binoculars I could make out groups of armed riders swathed in black, but whether they were wearing the veils which would have identified them as Touareg I couldn't be sure. It was unlikely, so close to the coast. In fact, it all looked a good deal more romantic and sinister than it was; I doubted if tribesmen had laid a finger on Bin'yassar Convent in seven centuries, and the greatest danger from the present incursion was the cholera with which they would undoubtedly contaminate the local wells.

However, there was the drill to go through, starting with the piper playing on the wall at sunset to let the Bedouin know we were in residence, and a parade outside next morning, with kilts and fixed bayonets. Highlanders are the most conspicuous troops there are, which was why we got this sort of job; the wildest of wild men in North Africa (or anywhere else for that matter) can recognise 'Cock o' the North' when they hear it, and know they are in touch with the Army – it's not a threat or even a warning so much as a signal, and unless they are really looking for trouble it has only one practical effect: they come closer to gaze silently on these strange northern barbarians in their weird green skirts and funny hats, and to listen to the eerie thrilling sound which fascinates the native ear from Casablanca to the South Seas. (Maybe we *are* one of the Lost Tribes; I wouldn't be surprised.)

So during our stay there was a permanent semi-circle, thousands strong, a few hundred yards from the walls, staring in dead silence at the kilted sentries and waiting for the piper to start up again. They were entirely peaceful, but I suppose our presence may have spared the nuns some pilfering and annoyance. That was all there was to it, except that I had to spend every spare hour in attendance on the ancient Mother Superior, who was a clock-golf freak and counted all time lost when she wasn't beating the daylights out of visitors with her putter. Constant practice had sharpened her game to the point where she could have given Greg Norman a stroke a hole, and after two days of watching her sink fifteen-footers I didn't care if I never saw a golf ball again. (You were called on to do some peculiar things in the old British Army, but I can't recall many stranger than following that bird-like little old woman in her white robe and wimple as she hopped round the clock-golf layout, rattling her putts across the baked earth with invariable accuracy and chirping triumphantly in Italian. Beaten seven and five in a Garden of Allah in the Sahara Desert. I wonder if it's still there.)

On the third morning the oasis was deserted; the buddoo had vanished back into the big desert. The Catholic members of Eleven Platoon went to an early Mass while the Protestants stood about outside with arms folded, sniffing; I thanked the Mother Superior for her marathon putting lesson; the entire convent staff stood on the walls waving as we left, apparently convinced that we alone had saved them from sack and pillage – and only as we drove back into town did I recall that other minor crisis I had left behind in barracks three days ago. Had the iron discipline of Lance-Corporal McAuslan provoked a mutiny yet? Had he perhaps failed in some duty and been reduced to the ranks – the battalion would have been back home for two days now (I had missed the Waterloo Ball the previous night) and I couldn't believe that the Colonel would lose much time in returning him to private life, so to speak. Yet with McAuslan, you never knew; he might have got himself recommended for a commission by now, or deserted.

I was not kept in suspense. Almost the first thing I saw as our lead truck turned into the barrack gate was the familiar unkempt figure crouching in the little rock-garden outside the guardroom, apparently foraging for bugs under stones. He had all the appearance of a defaulter on fatigues, which suggested that he was a private again, but with the sleeve of his denims in its usual mouldering state it was hard to tell whether there was still a stripe there or not. I got out, told the trucks to carry on to the barrack-block, and addressed him.

'What happened to you?'

He rose, shedding loose soil and debris, and gave me cordial greeting. 'Aw, hullaw rerr, surr. Ye got back. The Fenian wimmen a'right, then?'

I assured him that the convent was safe, and repeated my question, and he wiped his nose audibly with a hand covered in compost; it didn't make him a whit dirtier than he already was.

'Ah got stripped,' he announced, and heaved a sigh of deep resignation. 'Bustit.'

'Oh dear, that's a shame,' I lied. 'How did it happen?'

'Aye, weel, ye see.' He frowned, meditating, and passed a hand through his tangled hair, dislodging a well-built earthworm. 'It wis because o' MacGonagal.'

For a wild moment I thought he meant the poet. You see why: from taking up the cudgels in one branch of the arts, music, it would be a short step to brawling on the slopes of Parnassus – and then I remembered there was a MacGonagal in Three Section, a pugnacious Glaswegian recently posted to us from the Highland Light Infantry.

'He got impident, an' Ah belted him.' That settled which MacGonagal it was, anyway. 'It was just last night, efter the Waterloo Ball, when we were clearin' up on the bandstand, pittin' the furniture away, an' that –'

'Don't tell me the band had been playing "Because" and MacGonagal didn't like it.'

'Ach, no.' He made a contemptuous gesture, scattering loam broadcast. 'They widnae hiv the gumption tae play onything that good. Naw, MacGonagal just startit makin' remarks, an' Ah wisnae havin' it –'

'McAuslan,' I said patiently. 'You were still a lance-corporal, weren't you? Yes, so if MacGonagal was insolent to you, the proper course was to book him, not belt him. Right?'

'Ye don't understand, sur. It wisnae me he was cheeky to. Ah couldnae book him.' He clawed at his midriff in perplexity, and there was a sound of damp cotton tearing. 'It was just that he startit makin' insultin' remarks, about the pictur'. Ye know, the big pictur' o' oor fellas haudin' ontae the cavalry's stirrups an' chargin' alang wi' them an' gettin' tore intae ra Frogs. Aye, ra Stirrup Charge. Here, it's a smashin' paintin', yon, so it is!' He beamed in admiration through his grime. 'Ought tae be onna calendars an' whusky bottles, so it should.'

I decided I wasn't hearing aright. McAuslan the music critic I had been prepared to accept – just. But McAuslan stirred to violence because of aspersions cast on a Victorian painting . . . no. Where would it end? He'd be battering people over Henry Moore and Stravinsky before you knew it.

'What,' I asked with bated breath, 'did MacGonagal say about the painting, McAuslan?'

'He said it wis bluidy rubbish,' replied McAuslan indignantly. 'Ah didnae mind that, but. Fella's entitled tae his opinion, like ye said. But then he sez: "Whit's it meant tae be aboot, onywye?" So Ah tellt him. Ah sez: "That's oor fellas – oor regiment, no' the bluidy H.L.I. – haudin' ontae the cavalry's stirrups an' chargin' alang wi' them an' gettin' tore intae ra Frogs. Winnin' ra Battle o' Waterloo, MacGonagal," Ah sez, "pittin' the hems on Napoleon, see?" "Zatafact?" sez he – ye know, sarcastic-like. "Weel, Ah'll tell ye sumpn, McAuslan," sez he. "Ah don't think your bluidy regiment wis chargin' wi' the cavalry at a'. Ah think they were tryin' tae haud them back."'

'Dammed cheek!' I exclaimed.

'That's whit Ah said!' cried McAuslan, vindicated. 'Ah sez:

"Look, MacGonagal, no bluidy fugitive frae the Hairy-Legged Irish is gaun tae say that aboot *this* regiment! Ye bluidy leear, you tak' that back or Ah'm claimin' ye!" "Ach, away an' shoot a few more cheeses," sez he, an' gives me the V-sign. So that wis when Ah pit the heid on him.'

So it hadn't been a case of wounded artistic sensibilities, but of regimental honour, which was rather different.

'An' he beltit me back, an' we got tore in.' His voice took on a plaintive chant which was familiar. 'An' then the Gestapo came, an' beltit the both o' us, and pit us in the cooler –'

'Yes, I understand,' I said. 'Well, he had provoked you, but you shouldn't have hit him, just the same.' An intriguing thought struck me. 'You came up before the Colonel this morning, I suppose – what did he say when he heard why you'd been fighting?'

'Och, he wis awfy decent, but. He's a great man, yon,' said McAuslan affectionately. 'When we wiz marched in, an' the R.S.M. cries: "Here Lance-Corporal McAuslan an' Private MacGonagal been gettin' wired intae each ither' – or sumpn like that, onywye – ra Colonel tak's one look at me an' sez: "Ah don't believe it." Funny, him sayin' that, sur; Ah mean, Ah've been marched in before.' He shook his matted head, puzzled, and I didn't like to tell him it was the lance-corporal's stripe the Colonel hadn't been able to believe.

'Aye, weel, he heard the evidence frae ra Gestapo, an' we didnae hiv nuthin' tae say, so he gives MacGonagal seven days and shoots him oot. Then he sez tae me: "Ah sympathise wi' yer reaction, Corporal, but Ah'm afraid ye cannae continue as an N.C.O. Ah'll hiv tae reduce ye tae the ranks, an' gi' ye one day's C.B." But he smiled, quite joco. An' that wis it.'

Trust the Colonel to find a painless way of busting him. It had been bound to happen eventually, and it couldn't have been done more tactfully – mind you, the excuse had been made in heaven. I surveyed him, grubby and dishevelled but apparently content, and since we were conversing so amiably, for once, I ventured a sensitive question.

'Tell me, McAuslan . . . something that's been puzzling me. That tune, "Because". Where did you first hear it, d'you remember? And why do you like it so much? Does it just appeal to you, or is there some special reason?'

'Och, Ah can tell ye that, sur.' He scratched happily. 'First time Ah ever heard "Because" wis in the auld Happy Days cabaret in Port Said, back in '42. Ye know the Happy Days, sur – in behind Simon Arts?* No? Aye, weel, that's where Ah heard it. Greatest tune that ever wis. So it is. Efter that, Ah used tae get ma mate Wullie Ferguson tae play it on his mooth-organ, when we wis inna desert, inna war.'

'Fifty-first Div? Eighth Army?'

'That's right, sur. Wullie played it awfy bonny, but.'

'What happened to him?'

'Wullie? He bought his lot just efter Alamein. Land-mine.' He shook his head. 'He wis a good mucker, just the same, Wullie.'

So that was it. Only it wasn't, apparently, for he went on:

'But whit Ah like best aboot "Because" is that it minds me o' the auld Happy Days. Aw, we had some rerr terrs in that place, Ah'm tellin' ye!' He scrubbed his nose with his sleeve, beaming with reminiscence. 'Aye, wi' the wog band playin' "Because". See, there wis this big belly-dancer, an' it wis her signature tune, an' she did her stuff tae it. Goad, but Ah fancied that wumman! Never got near her, mind. None o' us did. But the tune stuck in ma heid. Fatima, her name wis.' He gave a rasping sigh. 'Ma Goad, see her an' her tambourine!'

Well, there are worse reasons for being a music-lover, I

* A famous department store on the Port Said waterfront, correctly spelled Simon Arzt but known to servicemen as 'Simon Arts'.

suppose. He sighed again and spat, surveying the guardroom rockery with sloth-like reluctance.

'Aye, weel, this'll no' pay the rent. Mind if Ah cairry on, sur? Ah've tae finish weedin' this lot or big McGarry'll kill me, swine that he is.' He scooped up a pawful of mud. 'It wid scunner ye, no kiddin'. Stoor an' muck an' wee crawly beasties! See them, Ah hate them! Ach!'

'Carry on, McAuslan,' I said, and as I turned away I added, not quite insincerely: 'Anyway, I'm sorry you lost your stripe.'

'Ach, Ah'm no' bothered,' said he, clawing at the soil. 'It's better bein' back wi' the boys, Fletcher 'n' Forbes an' them. Ah didnae like havin' tae boss them aboot. Ye know sumpn, sur?' He paused, squatting, weighing a handful of ordure in a philosophic way. 'Ye hiv tae be a right pig tae get promotion. Aye, an' it turns ye intae a worser pig, the higher up ye get, Ah'm sure o' that. Weel, ye ken that yersel'.' Grunt, grunt, I thought. 'So Ah'm no' carin' aboot getting bustit. Ah wisnae much o' a lance-jack onywye. Ah did everythin' wrang.'

'Oh, I don't think you did too badly,' I consoled him. 'At least you never lost a guardroom.'

'Loast a guardroom?' said McAuslan incredulously. 'How the hell could Ah? Ah mean, Ah know Ah'm dumb, but it would tak' a right bluidy eejit tae dae that!'

'You're probably right,' I said humbly. 'Carry on, McAuslan.'

The Gordon Women

There is a story they tell in Breadalbane:

Gordon of Achruach was at feud with Campbell of Kentallan, who hired certain Gregora, landless men, who took the Gordon unawares while he was hunting in the Mamore. And they cut off his head and put it in a bag to show the Campbell that the work was done. That was the way of it.

And as they fared for Kentallan the Gregora came by the Gordon's door at Achruach, and went in, and the Gordon's wife (little knowing she was a widow) bade them to table, as the custom is, and went out for the Athol brose. And while she was gone the Gregora winked at one another, and set the Gordon's head on a dish, with an apple in the mouth, to see what the good wife would make of it. That is the Gregora for you, hell mend the black pack of them.

And the good wife came in, and saw her man's head bloody on the board, but kept her countenance and said never a word, only smiled on the Gregora and bade them good cheer. The Gregora wondered at this. Has she not seen it? was in the mind of each of them. Still looked she never on the head, but said a word to her ghillie and sent him forth. And smiling on the Gregora, she told them a tale, never looking at the head, and held them spellbound, for she was great at the stories, and very fair besides. The Gregora wondered, has she not seen it yet? This is not canny, was in their minds, and they said they must be for the road, but she held them there by her tale and her presence, and so they bided whether they would or no. That was the way of it.

And still she spoke and looked not on the head, until the ghillie returned with her men of Achruach, who came in swift and sudden and stood behind the Gregora seated, one to one, and each Gordon with his dirk at a dirty Gregora neck. And she told on till the tale was done – aye, she was great at the stories – and then said she: 'I see my man is come home, and has but an apple to eat. Give him to drink also, wine red and warm.' And at her word they slew the Gregora where they sat, and the red blood ran. That was the way of it.

And the ghillie said: 'Oh, mistress, how did you keep your countenance this long while in the presence of yon fell thing, and beguile these stark men?' And she answered: 'The day I cannot keep my countenance, and hold men in their place and work my will on them, that is a day you will never see.'

That was the way of it. That was a woman of the Gordons for you.

Wade's House stands on the rocky side of a lovely little green cleft in the hills, with a deep brown burn gurgling under its white walls. In summer it is half-hidden among the rowans and silver birches and tall bracken, and you can pass by on the main highway two hundred yards below and never know it is there, which may be why General Wade made it his headquarters when he was building those roads which tamed the Scottish North two and a half centuries ago. It was the edge of beyond in his day, the last outpost before the hostile wilderness which Wade himself described as 'a land as far away as Africa', the home of the last savages in Europe, the Highland clans. From his little valley he could look up at Ben Dorain, the first spur of the great Grampian range towering away north-east to the mists; only a few miles ahead of him was the mouth of the Killing Place, Glencoe, under the shadow of the most menacing mountain in Britain, the Buchaille Etive; how harsh and dangerous to his English ears must have sounded the names of those wild tracts beyond the hills – Rannoch, Badenoch, Lochaber, and they weren't the half of it.

But, good for Wade, he succeeded where the Romans had failed. He pushed his roads through the heart of the Highlands and along the chain of government outposts on the loch sides, Fort William, Fort Augustus, and Fort George, letting in the law and the red soldiers who between them finally put the hems (and the breeks) on the wild men of the north. It all came to an end at Culloden – and a right mess that was, thanks to the MacDonalds and Lord George Murray and (to give the swine his due) the Duke of Cumberland, who had learned the vital lesson that if you can stop Scotland scoring in the first ten minutes, you stand an excellent chance, because they tend to lose interest. After that there was nothing for Ronald and Donald to do, once they had emerged cursing from the heather, but join the Highland regiments cunningly established by the government as a safety valve through which the clansmen could vent their exuberance on the enemies of the Crown for a change – which is how I came to return to Wade's House two centuries later.

I had known it from childhood, because after the general finished his roads and went home it had reverted to my uncle's family (a small, aggressive colony of Gordons who had come down from the north in the remote past to establish themselves among the local Stewarts, Camerons, Campbells, Black Mount MacDonalds, and those perpetual pests, the MacGregors), and when he married my aunt they farmed from Wade's House and kept the nearby hotel, an impressive tourist lodge catering for fishers, guns, and a strange new breed, the skiers, who in those pre-war days were just beginning to hurl themselves down the slopes of Ben Lawers. My uncle was a tall, courtly gentleman, a former county cricketer who dreamed that his nephew (with the advantage of English summers to practise in) would some day confound the Australians who were carrying all before them in that era of Bradman and O'Reilly. In my holidays he would have me out on the hotel tennis court, heaving up my juvenile leg-spinners until my wrist creaked, and once I twisted so hard that I achieved a googly and he lost it against the dark conifers and was trapped dead as mutton leg before.

He took me off in triumph to the still-room and filled me with orange juice, and showed me off to a vaguely-remembered group of large, tweedy, moustached men who spoke with the accents of Morningside and Kelvinside and the Home Counties; I think of them whenever I see a whisky advertisement in the

New Yorker. They belonged to a world of which I was barely conscious then, of plus-fours and brass-capped shotgun shells, fishing flies and glossy magazines on low oak tables, stuttering motor cars with running-boards, and pipes smoking fragrantly; they had a sound and a smell and a presence that died in September, 1939.

There was another world outside the hotel, and its centre was Wade's House, from which my aunt used to send me out with the dinner-pails for the farm-men on the hill; I would trudge up through the heather and wait to take back the empty containers, watching the shy, silent men with their lean brown faces and wishing I could understand them. They were distant and wary of the small boy in his school jersey, and on the rare occasions when they spoke their voices were odd and high-pitched. I wondered if I seemed as strange to them; when one of them once asked me my name and I told him, he looked at me with a queer smile as though wondering: how did that happen? I was reminded of them years later, in Saskatchewan, when I saw Blackfeet straight off the reservation; they had the same quiet durability and strange shifting quality; you had an uncomfortable feeling that you had better watch them. When they came to the hotel in the evening, it was to the big public bar at the back, a thousand miles from the tweed and leather lounge of the motorists at the front, and I noticed with admiration the ease with which my uncle and aunt moved between the two worlds, at home in either.

To my childish mind, one world was safe and the other wild. In Wade's House I had discovered a book by a man called Neil Munro about these very hills; it was full of dangers and onfalls and swords in the night, and as I snuggled down in bed it was comforting to know that the walls were feet thick, for I could picture the edge of the rocky burn beneath my deep-embrasured window, and Col of the Tricks was standing there under the silent trees, with his bonnet drawn down, smiling to himself and turning his dirk in his hand, and his face was the face of the men on the hill.

It wasn't all imagination. Once I woke to the sound of stealthy footsteps and whispers under my window, and when I reported this sensation to my aunt in the morning she smiled in mock wonder and teased me by humming 'Watch the wall, my darling, while the gentlemen go by', which I neither understood nor connected with the big salmon wrapped in ferns in the stone larder or the fact that Jeannie the maid was scrubbing scales from the back door step. On other occasions there would be a couple of hares or a brace of birds hanging under the rowans; in my infant innocence I assumed that a friend had left them – which was true, in a way. Once, in the season of the year, a great haunch of venison turned up mysteriously in the garage, and my uncle became as fretful as his genial, easygoing nature would allow.

'Oh, dear, I wish Jock wouldn't do it,' he sighed. 'Or Archie, or whoever it is this time. It's embarrassing.'

'A switch for the laird from the laird's man,' said my aunt cryptically. 'It's probably the Dipper. Jock and Archie are busy on Lochnabee these days, according to Jeannie.'

'Not again!' groaned my uncle. 'Do they know how long they can get, if the gadgers catch them?'

'Probably, dear, but the gadgers never do. Don't worry about them.'

'I don't worry about *them*. I worry about meeting the Admiral or old Buchanan and having them tell me that another stag's vanished without trace, or that there isn't a fish left in Loch Tulla, and who on earth can have done it? It puts me in a very difficult position.'

'No, it doesn't,' said my aunt. 'The position's perfectly easy – you don't know.'

'I can guess. If it isn't Jock, it's Archie, or the Dipper, or Roy

Ban, or Wee Joe, or any one of a dozen. It wouldn't be so bad if I didn't employ half of them.'

'What's a gadger, Aunt Alison?' I asked, and was told gently to run along and play with my ball, none the wiser.

Over the years I began to understand. Agriculture and legitimate field sports were the principal local industries, but poaching and illicit distilling ran them a close second, it being well known that a switch from the braeside, a fish from the burn, and a stag from the hill were the right of every Highlander, and that if he chose to manufacture his own drink it was nobody else's business. The surrounding estates, which catered for visiting sportsmen, employed armies of keepers and watchers who waged a constant war against the local poachers – this was before the big gangs from far afield came to despoil the glens systematically – and the Excisemen or 'gadgers' (so called from the word gauger) combed the woods and corries in search of unlawful stills. Sometimes they even had to take to the water: my aunt had referred to Lochnabee, where the enterprising peasantry operated their little distillery in a small boat anchored in the middle of that gloomy tarn, the principle being that if the Law appeared on the shore, and capture was certain, you heaved the whole caboodle over the side, got out the rods to pose as innocent fishers, and defied the gadgers to prosecute when all the evidence was at the bottom of the loch. A shocking waste of equipment, but better than being nailed in some mountain hut or woodland fastness where hurried concealment of your Heath Robinson equipment was impossible.

My uncle was right: his position *was* difficult. He was by way of being what in England would be called the squire, because although his farm and hotel were small concerns compared to the great estates around, he and his had been there as long as Ben Lui, while the estates were new and commercial. He knew half his people were out with guns and nets and snares by night, lifting what wasn't theirs, and distilling the good news in secret, but what was he to do – clype on his own folk? He couldn't have proved anything, anyway. Tell them to stop it? Tell the fish to keep out of water. At the same time, he was on good terms with his neighbours, like the Admiral and other landlords, and being a gentleman and sensible of his conflicting loyalties, it troubled him. My Aunt Alison, not having been born with his social scruples, and having a wicked sense of humour, found it all rather funny, and suffered no pangs when goodwill offerings appeared mysteriously on the step. She knew they were not bribes, but tribute.

My uncle died early in the war, but where another childless widow might have sold up, Aunt Alison continued to run farm and hotel as though it were a matter of course for a woman past middle age, thereby confirming the suspicion that she had been the real manager all along; and she was accepted in that strong masculine world without question. She had been a great beauty, one of your tall northern blondes with eyes like sapphires, and even when she was white-haired she continued to flutter the hearts of such susceptible local bachelors as the Admiral and Robin Elphinstone, much to her amusement; she treated them as she treated everyone, with that frank easiness and direct good humour that you often find in northern women; it stops short of being hard, but there is a tough streak of realism in it, and a touch of mischief – Stevenson caught it exactly with Miss Grant, the Lord Advocate's daughter, in *Catriona*. Aunt Alison had the same gift of tongues: educated Edinburgh in the drawing-room for her guests, pure Perthshire on the hillside when Dougal neglected the sheep-dipping, but with the same calm, pleasant delivery.

I had not seen her for three years when military duty took me north from Edinburgh not long after the battalion came home from North Africa. A truck-load of ammunition had to be taken from Redford Barracks to Fort William, and since an officer had to be in charge of that dangerous cargo I was told to take a 15-cwt, a driver, and two men as escort, and set off forthwith. The trip would take me past my aunt's door, so I got the Colonel's leave to stay over a couple of nights. As escort I chose Lance-Corporal Macrae and Private McAuslan – and if it strains belief that I should want to take McAuslan anywhere, I can plead good reason. He had just emerged, acquitted and crowing, from a court-martial for disobedience to a newly-promoted and officious young corporal, and, knowing my men, I didn't want them falling foul of each other again in my absence. Macrae I took because he'd been a ghillie and stalker in that part of the country, and I thought he would enjoy it. Kind-hearted subaltern, you see; if I'd known what was brewing in Darkest Perthshire I'd have chosen more carefully.

Part of our load had to be dropped off at Dunkeld – why they needed land-mines there I can't imagine – so from Ballinluig we took the northern road which carries you along the Tummel and the Garry into the wilds of Badenoch by way of Killiecrankie Pass. We stopped at the marker stone where Bonnie Dundee was killed, and surveyed the grim heights from which his claymores had descended like a thunderbolt to drive Mackay's Government regiments into the river in five furious minutes.

> Like a tempest down the ridges
> Swept the hurricane of steel

in Aytoun's splendid onomatopoeic lines – or as McAuslan put it, scowling sternly round the battlefield: 'That sortit the buggers! Here, izzat ra Bonnie Dundee in ra song, sur? He musta been a helluva boy! Five minutes, no kiddin'? He wisnae messin' aboot, wis he?' He shook his unkempt head in admiration, and I hadn't the heart to tell him that, as a staunch Protestant, he'd probably have found himself being routed along with Mackay.

It was fine scenery as we went west to Fort William, and when we had shed the last of our cargo it was a pleasantly eerie journey down through the Weeping Glen of my tough grandmother's folk, where it's always raining and even the sheep wear their shawls over their heads. We halted short of King's House for a cigarette, and McAuslan waxed indignant at my description of the Glencoe Massacre; it had been, in his opinion, weel ower the score, even fur ra bluidy Campbells – mind you, knowin' that big swine Sarn't Campbell in A Company he wisnae a bit surprised. We drove on south, and it was a beautiful summer evening when we pulled up on the gravel drive before my aunt's hotel. They were doing heavy business, by the number of cars out in front, and the big entrance hall was full of tweeds and twin-sets having afternoon tea; I exchanged glad cries of greeting with several members of the hotel staff and was informed that herself was in the office with the Admiral.

'He's still about, is he?'

'As ever, the wee pest!' said Jimmy the Porter. 'Still the lord o' creation, five foot o' wind wi' a hanky in his cuff! She's far too soft with him, and I don't give a dam if he *has* got a party of twelve for dinner! Away you in, Dand, and maybe he'll have the grace to make himself scarce.'

I escaped the mountainous hug of Bridie the linen-mistress, dried myself off, and entered the long passage to my aunt's office-sitting-room, whence came the sound of an Admiral in full voice, minatory and plaintive:

'. . . I just don't understand you, Alison, I really don't! You're a landowner yourself, but you take it far too lightly, in my opinion. Far too lightly. I'm sorry, but . . .'

'Well, we don't all strut about the place as though we had dominion over palm and pine.' She sounded more amused than impatient. 'Since when has the Excise been your business, anyway?'

'It's the business of all right-thinking people,' snapped the

Admiral. 'Of whom I had always thought you were one, Alison –'

'Ach, don't be so damned pompous, Jacky!' She was laughing at him. 'You're just being officious. And vindictive, let me tell you. I don't know which is worse.'

'I happen,' said the Admiral, 'to be a magistrate . . .' and at that point I coughed loudly, knocked, and went in. The Admiral, who resembled an ocean-going tug in a R.Y.S. blazer, was planted indignantly before the fireplace; my aunt, seated in silver-haired elegance behind her desk and looking as usual like an elderly but mischievous Norse goddess, whooped at the sight of me. 'My, will you look at the bonny sojer!' After exclamations and embraces she demanded if the Admiral remembered me, and he shook hands, beaming, crying of course, of course, the young spin-bowler, eh? I had known him from my infancy, and liked him, for he was a decent, hearty wee man, if given to self-importance. We exchanged pleasantries while my aunt watched, smiling, and then he said, well, he must be pushing along, frowned pleadingly at her and said *do* give serious thought to what I've been saying, won't you, my dear, and stumped off.

'Trouble?' I wondered. She gave her sharp, pleasant laugh, shaking her head.

'Just an attack of responsibility. Poor Jacky, he has hopes of being Lord-Lieutenant, and can't sleep for the glorious prospect. He can be a right wee pest, at that.'

'Jimmy the Porter's very word. How pestilential?'

'Och, he's heard that the Dipper has an illicit still going, so he's worked himself into a fine indignation. As if it mattered. Heavens, the Dipper's being making malt since grouse grew feathers, and who's the worse for it?' She laughed again, and frowned. 'Aye, the trouble is, I hear they're on to him – two Excisemen are up from Glasgow, and that's a sure sign. So Admiral Jacky gets all blown up with civic duty and bustles about saying it's a scandal and the law must be upheld. The wee twirp,' she added warmly. 'The truth is he has a grudge because the Dipper and the other McLarens poach him blind, and he can't catch them at it.'

'He's got a point,' I said.

'Devil a bit he has! They poach *me*, and do I ken the difference? What's a bird or a fish more or less – or a beast, either? The man's just chawed at the Dipper, and wants his own back.'

I could have pointed out that they didn't poach her more than enough to keep the game alert, no doubt because the Dipper was her faithful slave, having been in my uncle's outfit (and lost an eye) in Flanders. He was the oldest and idlest of the ne'er-do-well McLarens, and performed odd jobs about the district to supplement his income from poaching and moonshining. A long grey man of deep guile and so little scruple that he lured game birds with whisky-sodden grain and shot them while they were reeling drunk. I asked if she knew where his illicit still was.

'I take good care not to. It's no business of mine. Jacky had the cheek to ask me that very question, so I advised him to look between Cruachan and Crianlarich' – a distance of over twenty miles – 'and he flew up into the trees. Well, good luck to him and the gadgers if they take the hill after the Dipper.' But she looked anxious all the same; then she was smiling again. 'So I'm to put you and your ruffians up for two nights? Well, there's no room at the inn, so you can have the house to yourselves, and see they keep their tackety boots off the furniture. They'll be teetotal – I don't think. Cook'll give them their meals here. As for you, my lad, you'll dine in state with your old aunt and try not to disgrace her. Robin Elphinstone's coming.' She winked and patted her coiffure. 'That's sure to infuriate Jacky.'

She came out with me to the truck, and won my three Jocks with the obvious pleasure she took in meeting them; it was interesting to watch their different reactions to her smiling handshake. From Brooks, the driver, an Englishman, it was a hesitant: 'Pleased to meet you, mum'; Macrae the hillman drew himself up to his lean dark height and inclined his head formally, saying: 'Mem'; McAuslan, beaming expansively, greeted her with 'Aw, hullaw rerr, missus! Hoo's it gaun?' As usual he looked as though he'd just been exhumed by Burke and Hare, but Aunt Alison didn't seem to notice; she laughed and talked for a few minutes, reminded me not to be late, and then we drove the quarter mile up the road to Wade's House in its little tree-lined valley.

It was good to be back, under the low beamed ceilings, to look round at the massive white walls hung with brasses and old prints, smell the faint drift of fir-wood, and hear the burn chuckling by. We settled in, McAuslan observing that it wis fair champion, and my aunt was an awfy nice wumman; he hoped we werenae pittin' her tae bother. I reassured him, and presently we strolled back to the hotel in the warm August dusk. I turned the three of them over to the cook and the kind of dinner soldiers dream about, and walked through to the dining-room, which was filled with hotel guests and local worthies. Those were the days of rationing and the five-shilling maximum charge, which in a Highland hotel with resources denied the city was just an invitation to gluttony. To my surprise there were a number of dinner jackets and evening dresses making a gallant protest against post-war austerity; the little Admiral, presiding (as foretold by Jimmy the Porter) over a table of twelve, even had miniature decorations on his mess jacket. He kept frowning in the direction of my aunt's private table in an alcove near the door, the object of his dark glances being Robin Elphinstone, a burly gentleman farmer of the district; if my aunt noticed she gave no sign, but surveyed the long crowded room contentedly, remarking that at her age the greatest pleasure in life was just gaping at folk. Elphinstone, no hand at the social graces, said: 'Oh, come off it, Alison, you're not that old!' with such evident sincerity that she went into fits of laughter, which attracted another indignant glare from the jealous Admiral.

'Can't stand that chap Elphinstone,' he told me later, when I ran into him in the hall and was commanded peremptorily to join him for a drink. 'He's uncouth. And we see far too much of him hereabouts.' He gestured impatiently, spilling gin. 'Your aunt is so generous, of course – wonderful woman! Gracious, delightful – couldn't say an unkind word if she wanted to.' That's all you know, Nelson, I thought. 'I do wish, though, that she'd take a firmer line with people like that. Ought to be put in his place. Not the right type at all. Do you know,' he fixed me with his glittering poached eye, 'a few years ago he lost some stock to a golden eagle up on the Conanish, and – you'll hardly credit it – there was a rumour that the bounder actually shot it! A golden eagle, my God! Imagine it!' He leaned heavily on his gin for support. 'That shows you the kind of bounder he is. Well, I ask you, is a brute like that a fit dinner companion for . . . for . . . well, for anyone, I mean to say? Have another. No, I insist . . .'

He went on to say that if the ghastly Elphinstone were so rash as to repeat the offence, and it could be brought home to him, he, the Admiral, would have no hesitation in bringing a prosecution. 'And it wouldn't be the only one, either,' he added with grim satisfaction. 'Did your aunt tell you? That old scoundrel McLaren is at his tricks again – yes, an illicit still! Would you credit it?' I said it boggled the imagination. 'It isn't enough that he and his cronies strip the country bare of game, they have to try to poison it, too, with their vile potheen, or whatever it is. Well, it's not good enough. He's going to be laid by the heels this time. Stamp it out. Someone's got to take a stand.'

He was having difficulty doing that very thing by the time his chauffeur helped him into his limousine, and I walked round to the back of the hotel where the public bar was getting out. My three Jocks were emerging with the crowd of farm-workers and ghillies, Brooks and Macrae gratifyingly sober and McAuslan happy but not obnoxious. I knew this because he was still wearing both boots; in a more advanced stage of inebriation he would have removed them and tied them round his neck (why, I never discovered); when he discarded them altogether it was a sure sign that he was approaching the paralytic. As I waited for them I caught sight of the Dipper, in his battered tweed hat and long shabby overcoat, slipping away by himself. He saw me, and gave me his slow smile and a lift of the hand before disappearing into the quiet night.

I found myself wondering about him as I lay in bed in Wade's House, listening to the burn and the sigh of the night wind in the leaves. He would know, of course, that the forces of law and order were mustering to close in, but it would not occur to him to lie low. They never had, his kind; if anything, he would go his unlawful ways harder than ever, out of pure devilment and defiance, and when the grip came he would meet it with all the craft and cunning that was in him. It would be on ground of his choosing, too, rock and heather and brown water – good luck to the Admiral and his gadgers, as my aunt had said. Yet he was no longer young, the same Dipper – he must be near seventy by now, and the legs and lungs would be failing. If it came to trouble on the hill, well . . . it would be a far cry from Loch Awe, as the saying is.

I slept sound, and half-woke only once, sometime near dawn, fancying I had heard a step on the gravel and a door closing softly. For a moment I wondered if I'd been dreaming a memory from childhood, and then I remembered that my three stalwarts were bunking down on the ground floor, and that the hotel maids were more than average pretty.

It was after nine when we got up, and to save the kitchen staff the trouble of finding a late breakfast we caught a few trout from the burn (something I hadn't done since boyhood), grilled them on hot stones, and had them in the open with tea and digestive biscuits – there are some meals so far beyond Escoffier that they belong in another world. Elphinstone had invited me to play golf at Dalmally, and since Brooks was a golfer I took him along down to the hotel; the other two were content to spend the day loafing. McAuslan had already fallen in the burn twice, and been prevented in the nick of time from eating rowan berries – like many city-dwellers discovering countryside for the first time, he was going around open-mouthed, exclaiming at the size of the heather spiders and generally communing with nature. I told Macrae to keep an eye on him, and left them at the house, with the truck parked under the trees.

It was one of those beautiful tranquil days, until we got to the hotel, where the peace had been shattered at breakfast-time by the arrival of an Admiral with blood in his eye, to quote Jimmy the Porter. For some days, apparently, a troop of stags had been observed on the lower slopes of Ben Vornach, on his land; this morning they were nowhere to be seen, having evidently been scared into the high forest, but the Admiral's head keeper had heard a shot in the night, and on venturing forth at dawn had discovered blood on the rocks, and signs of tracks carefully covered. In a word, poachers, and the Admiral's land was now being beaten, under the supervision of its owner gone berserk, in search of the carcase and clues to the miscreants.

'It's now or never, of course,' said Elphinstone, from whom I had the details in the hall. 'They wouldn't get a beast that size off the hill before first light, so it'll be snug under a ledge until they can bring it near a road and pick it up with a car. Jacky's boys will have to find it today or tomorrow at latest.' He shook his head. 'Sooner them than me, on Ben Vornach.'

'Do they know who did it?' I asked, and he looked at me slantendicular.

'Jacky thinks he does. If he heard someone had shot an

elephant when there was an "r" in the month he'd put it down to the McLarens. He's probably right, but he'll have to catch them with it. There'll be no sleep for any man of his this fine night, I'll wager.'

The Admiral's troubles didn't come singly; first it was the Dipper's illicit still, and now poachers on his own domain.

'Aye, there's a coincidence for you,' said Elphinstone. 'And don't think he hasn't noticed.'

'And why should he come bawling aboot it here, to the hotel, will you tell me?' demanded Jimmy the Porter indignantly. 'Spoiling herself's breakfast on her, as if his dam' beasts were any concern of hers! Did I not hear him at it? "This is what comes of apathy among those who should ken better," cries he, and her at her boiled eggs and the *Oban Times*. "A fine thing, when the lower orders take advantage of indifference and slack management by their betters. It's a positive encouragement to crime!' Lower orders, and be damned to him! And heckling at her, as though his bluidy stag was in her larder!'

'What did she say to him?' I asked.

'Offered him a cup o' coffee and warned him aboot apoplexy,' said Jimmy. 'She's far too easy on him. I've told her. Aye, and I told him, too. "Have ye no manners, that ye'll break in on a lady at her meat, stopping her ears wi' your drivel?" says I. "How dare you, my man?" says he. "I'll report you to your mistress!" "Ye can report me to MacCallum More and his great-grandmither," says I, "but you'll leave herself alone in her own hoose. I'm the porter," says I, "and I'll have no disturbance in this hotel, not if it was the Duke himsel"!' He went off, grindin' his teeth, vowin' vengeance on half the country.' Jimmy snorted, straightening his uniform coat. 'The impudence of the man!'

'What's apathy, Mr Robertson?' asked the junior porter.

'A disease of the spirit, boy. Apathy, says he! He'll find enough of it among his own folk by the time they've finished beatin' the bracken for his precious deer. And then he'll be off colloguin' wi' the gadgers aboot the Dipper's still. Oh, there'll be a fine crying of "Cruachan" hereabouts today!'

I asked Elphinstone if there was anything we could do, and Jimmy the Porter exclaimed in outrage.

'Do for the Admiral, d'you mean? You'll be off to your gowf, young Dand, and let the silly sailor take care of himself!'

It seemed reasonable, so Brooks and I piled into Elphinstone's ancient Argyle and were driven the few miles to Dalmally, which is one of the great undiscovered golf courses of the world. We played a leisurely threesome with one set of clubs, driving with care, for golf balls were like gold dust in those days and Dalmally's rough was like Assam after the monsoon. It was late afternoon before we set off for home, and nightfall by the time Elphinstone left us at the foot of the gravel drive winding up to Wade's House. The house, when we reached it, was in darkness, but there was light enough to reveal one disturbing absence. Our 15-cwt truck was missing.

'What the blazes?' I said. 'Macrae knows better than to take it without permission.' But Macrae wasn't there, nor McAuslan, and there was no message or explanation in the house. I was demanding of the empty night where they and the truck had got to when Brooks reminded me of something even more startling: neither of them knew how to drive.

I left him at the house in case they turned up, and set off in some alarm for the hotel – whoever had taken the truck had removed Army property for which I was responsible, and a right damfool I was going to look if it wasn't recovered forthwith. I had a half-hope it might be on the gravel sweep before the hotel, but it wasn't; the Admiral's limousine was, though, and a couple of farm lorries, which was unprecedented in a spot reserved for visitors' cars; there was also a plain black saloon with a man in a diced cap at the wheel – police. Plainly great things were happening, and I sought enlightenment from Jimmy the Porter, who was at the reception desk with the local police sergeant.

'Who else would it be but the Admiral?' snapped Jimmy. 'He's ben in herself's office wi' the gadgers and Inspector MacKendrick, planning his bluidy campaign, like Napoleon he is. No, they haven't found the stag, so he's turning his fury on the Dipper, wi' the bile spilling out of him.' He dropped his voice. 'The gadgers think they have their eye on the still, is that not the case, Rory?' He glanced at the portly Sergeant, who was looking stern and official and trying to pretend he wasn't taking sidelong keeks through the open door of the drawing-room, where the dinner guests were having coffee – it probably wasn't often that he got this close to the High Life.

'The gadgers' information is aaltogether confidential,' he said importantly. 'Classified, and canna' be divulged.'

'Classified your erse and parsley,' said Jimmy vulgarly. 'Who d'ye think ye are, the Flyin' Squad? If it's all that confidential, why are you turnin' my hotel into a damned circus? We havnae got the Dipper's still – or maybe you think Bridie the linen-mistress is his confederate, aye, his gangster's moll! Polis!'

'I've got something else for you, Rory,' I said, and told him about the missing 15-cwt. Jimmy whistled and muttered 'Dalmighty!' and the Sergeant produced his notebook and said this was very serious and the Inspector must be informed instanter. He set off majestically for my aunt's office, and I learned from Jimmy that neither McAuslan nor Macrae had been seen since the public bar closed in the afternoon. I asked him to send out scouts, discreetly, and followed the Sergeant.

The office was like an ops room on D-Day; Operation Dipper was in full swing. The Admiral, duffel-coated and binoculared, had an Ordnance Survey map spread out on the desk, and was poring over it making little barking noises; with him were the Inspector and two solid-looking men in dark coats who must be the gadgers from Glasgow, and the Admiral's stalker and a uniformed constable stood uncomfortably in the background. Unconcerned at all this official activity, Aunt Alison was seated in stately calm in her armchair; she was in evening dress, smoking a cigarette in a long holder, and knitting – a triple combination I have not seen elsewhere. She winked imperceptibly at me and grimaced towards the desk, where the Admiral was issuing his signals to the fleet, and loving it.

'... and your party will take position on the north shore of the loch, Inspector, is that clear?' So the Dipper's still was afloat this time. 'My party will be to the south. That should make it airtight. Lights on at my whistle, but not a moment before. Got that? You have the warrant, and will effect the arrest – and you gentlemen will make the confiscation! Capital! Right!' You could see he hadn't enjoyed himself so much since Jutland, rubbing his hands and looking like a triumphant toy bulldog. 'Well, Sergeant, what is it, what is it? Come along, come along, man!'

The Sergeant told him, and the Admiral glared, bewildered. 'What? A truck? What truck, man? Whose truck? Your truck? Is this true, Dand? Stolen?'

'Takken awaay wi'oot the consent o' the owner,' the Sergeant corrected him. 'By pairson or pairsons unknown ...'

'Yes, yes, yes! An Army truck? What has that ...' He gave a sudden cry of 'Ha!' and leaped vertically. 'A truck! My God – the deer! That's it – those infernal poachers have stolen it, to move the stag!' He thumped the desk with his fist, something I thought they did only in novels. 'That's it, Inspector! Look here!' He pounced on the map. 'There are only two ways to Ben Vornach for a vehicle ... the Kildurn road, there ... and the dead-end from the lodge, d'you see? They must be blocked at once!'

He wasn't slow, I'll say that for him – but then you can't afford to be, if your job has been warping aircraft carriers through the Magellan Strait. I hadn't linked the truck's disappearance with the poachers, but it made sense: every local vehicle must be known and accounted for, and here was the perfect one dropped in their lap. Thank God the non-driving Macrae and McAuslan were in the clear . . . I wouldn't be, if the Colonel got to hear about it.

My aunt counted her stitches, put down her knitting, and rose. 'I think all this excitement calls for a little refreshment,' she said, smiling at the Sergeant and gadgers. They looked hopeful, and with a glance at the Admiral and Inspector, deep in their map, she went out.

Meanwhile dissension seemed to be breaking out in the High Command. The Inspector, a young, slow-spoken man with a fledgling moustache, was plainly doubtful about undertaking two separate operations with limited resources; one or the other should be postponed, or 'I can chust see us faalin' between two stools, sir. Aye, I can that.' The Admiral wouldn't hear of it: didn't the Inspector realise, for heaven's sake, that the stag would be halfway to Glasgow by morning? As for delaying the Dipper raid, it was unthinkable; give the scoundrel another twenty-four hours and he'd have his still dismantled or moved or presented to a museum, dammit! The Inspector, sweating visibly, spoke of 'a waant of personnel', and was told not to be so damned defeatist, it was simply a matter of intelligent planning. They argued back and forth, the Admiral's voice and temperature rising with each objection, until he pointed out sternly that *he* was chairman of the Watch Committee, and before that majestic title the Inspector finally gave way, red and resentful.

'We must divide our forces!' snapped the Admiral, bursting with initiative. 'Inspector, I leave it to you to post men on those two roads to intercept the thieves. I shall proceed to Lochnabee, as planned. Certainly I shall need additional men. Sergeant, you will see to it.' That took care of that, apparently. 'If communication is necessary we shall send messengers here, to the hotel, which is our base . . . with Mrs Gordon's permission, of course,' he added with a placatory smirk to Aunt Alison, who was ushering in two maids bearing loaded trays.

'How exciting,' she said. 'Are we being commandeered?'

Good heavens, no, cried the Admiral, simply a matter of convenience, central point, lines of communication. 'And I'm sure, gentlemen,' he added impressively, 'that I speak for us all when I say how grateful we are to Mrs Gordon for . . . ah, for so kindly allowing us to use her premises, and so graciously –'

'Och, stop behaving like Rommel, Jacky,' said my aunt. 'I didn't allow anything. You just breenged in as usual. Tea or coffee, Inspector? Or a little of the creature? And don't tell me you're on duty . . . I won't have that.' She patted his arm conspiratorially. 'Help yourselves, gentlemen. There are the sausage rolls, Rory . . . Janet, a glass for the Admiral, and those sandwiches . . .'

'I say, this is awfully kind of you, Alison,' protested the Admiral, 'but I'm afraid we really don't have time –'

'You wouldn't send men out on the hill at night without something in them?' Aunt Alison reproved him. 'Not from this house! No water for the Admiral, Janet . . . Those are smoked salmon, Jacky – your favourite. Now, are our friends from Glasgow being attended to? That's a grouse pâté – you won't get that in Craigs or the Ca'doro. Sit you down, constable, and put your feet under the table . . . Rory, is that the single malt? Good lad, don't let the sausage rolls defeat you . . .'

She moved about the room, recommending and directing, seeing that plates and glasses were refilled, and even the Admiral had to admit it was a sound basis for the labours ahead. The police and gadgers obviously agreed, from the way they were engulfing the delicacies; I noticed that Janet removed an empty Glenlivet bottle when she went out for a fresh tray of sandwiches, and the Admiral allowed my aunt to prevail on him to try the pâté, and then really, Alison, we must be moving . . . well, just a spot of the ten-year-old, then . . . capital . . . not too much . . .

'It's a lot better for you than gin,' smiled Aunt Alison, pouring. 'There, we'll make a Highlandman of you yet. Not that we haven't tried . . . how many years has it been?'

'Lord, I hate to think! Let's see . . . I bought Achnafroich in '32 . . . or was it '31 . . . yes, March, '31, but I'd been coming up for years before that, you remember . . .' He sipped and reminisced, with my aunt smiling encouragement, and when he looked at his watch she remarked that he seemed to be in a most ungallant hurry to be off, which kept him protesting through another glass of the ten-year-old.

All told I'd say that collation occupied half an hour, by which time the troops were pink and contented. Finally the Admiral called a halt, thanked Aunt Alison on behalf of them all, and dispatched them to the vehicles. As they trooped out he turned to her, looking contrite.

'I say, Alison, I do apologise again. We've put you to enormous trouble – shocking imposition, I mean, intruding on you like this . . . but I'm sure you understand that I . . . well, I mean . . .'

'You wanted to give me a chance to line up with the landed gentry, didn't you?' she teased him. 'Well, it was nice of you, and I'm touched. Now, off you go, and I hope you kill a lot of Germans.'

'Oh, really, Alison! I do wish you'd be serious! It's no laughing matter – and I'm sorry, but I must ask again . . . we're going to be short-handed, so will you please allow me to take your people along? We need every –'

'I've told you, you're at liberty to approach any employee of mine, and if he wants to go, well and good.' She sat down and picked up her knitting. 'But it's up to them; I can't order them.'

'My dear, if you'll forgive me, that's nonsense. One word from you –'

'Well, I won't say it, and that's flat.' She gave him her gentlest blue-eyed smile, like the Rock of Gibraltar, and he let out a whoof of despair and impatience, said he *did* wish she'd be reasonable for once, it would make things so much easier, and stumped reproachfully out, returning immediately to thank her again for the drinks and canapés, and finally departing. Even with the door closed we could hear him trumpeting orders in the hall.

'Now you ken how the French Revolution started,' said Aunt Alison. 'Confound those McLarens!' She threw down her knitting and said something ugly in Gaelic. 'And confound Jacky for a meddling wee ass! Could he not let the Dipper alone?' She lit a cigarette and got up, tapping her foot. 'That boy Macrae of yours. Where did you say he was from?'

'Macrae?' I was startled. 'Aberfeldy. He used to be ghillie thereabouts.'

'Macrae! God save us.' She gave her sharp laugh. 'There's a name for a Highland midnight. And you're sure he's not about?'

'Not since this afternoon. Auntie dear,' I said, 'what's happening?'

'That remains to be seen,' she said. 'Dand, I want you to go to Lochnabee with Jacky.'

'What? I can't get mixed up in that sort of thing! I'm a soldier! Besides, I'm shot if I'll help nab the Dipper –'

'I'm not asking you to. Just do as you're told.' Immediately I was six years old again. 'Stay with Jacky and see what happens. Off you go, double quick. Now.'

When Aunt Alison says 'now' in that quiet way, she means yesterday. I went, and found the Admiral marshalling his squadrons in line ahead on the gravel. The police car and farm lorries were roaring off in pursuit of poachers, leaving the Admiral's limousine, the gadgers' car, and an antediluvian shooting-brake packed with the Admiral's shock-troops, three or four ghillies from his own estate. He hailed me with enthusiasm. 'Ha! In for the kill, eh? Good show! Off we go, Cameron!' We sped into the night, the Sergeant breathing heavily beside me in the back seat, the car redolent of the hotel's malt, and all the way to Lochnabee the Admiral, up front, told me what a wonderful woman Aunt Alison was, but headstrong, did I know what he meant? Pity, because she had such brains and character, and could have been such a helpful influence on the restless Jacquerie if only she would take her responsibilities more seriously . . . charming, though. Pity she hadn't been out in Wei-hai-wei when he was a young lieutenant . . . yes, wonderful . . . I looked at the back of his reddened neck, the ageing pocket Dreadnought suffused with gin, and thought of my late uncle, tall, dark, handsome Alastair of the lazy smile . . . it would have made you weep, it really would.

Lochnabee is a hill loch on the high tops, cold and black as a witch's breath, and lonely, with not a tree or a bush for miles. The last place you would choose for making funny whisky unless you were a crazy old brock like the Dipper. It was a bare two hundred yards wide, and the only road was a rough track up which we bumped and rattled in the dark – if the Dipper didn't know we were coming he must be stone deaf. We stopped a half-mile from the loch in surroundings straight from Macbeth, Act One, and the stalker scouted ahead and presently came back with the word: there was a boat on the loch.

'That's him!' cried the Admiral. 'Right! Pay attention! Right! Sergeant, Dand, stay with me! Cameron, keep the engine running! The rest of you know your positions! Move quietly' – this with his car back-firing like a Bofors – 'spread out, and wait until I bring up the car! Then I shall give the signal, and on with the lights! Got that? Remember, our man will make for the shore, so be on the look-out! He may put up a fight! Right . . . !'

It was a farce from start to finish. We waited by the car, the Admiral stumping up and down muttering 'Right!' and striking matches to look at his watch; when he shouted 'Right!' for the last time we drove the final half-mile at top speed on side-lights which is no joke halfway up a Scottish mountain, and came to a shuddering halt with the loch glinting palely in front of our bonnet. The Admiral leaped out, blowing a whistle, the headlights were switched on full, and the powerful torches of the gadgers blinked on from the other shore. Sure enough, there was a boat in the middle of the loch, with three men in it, and one of them was shouting:

'What the hell d'you think you're doing, scaring the fush? Get away, you with your pluidy motor car, and put out those pluidy lights!'

'He's bluffing!' roared the Admiral. 'Sergeant, do your duty!'

The Sergeant lumbered forward and fell in the loch. The Admiral swore on a high note, the sounds of altercation between the boat and the watchers on the far shore floated across to us, and the Sergeant emerged like some great sea-beast and shouted: 'In the King's name!' It may have been an oath or an announcement of majesty, but it got a great horse-laugh from the boat, and at that moment the car's headlights went out.

'Switch them on again, Cameron, godammit!' cried the Admiral. 'Sergeant! Where are you?' Drowning, by the sound of it, for in that sudden blackness he had evidently taken the wrong direction, and was wallowing in the shallows. 'Come out of that, you fool! Cameron, will you put on those blasted lights?' I could hear the driver cursing as he scrabbled at the dashboard, and for no apparent reason the Admiral blew his whistle again. He was stumping about in the dark, and presently there was a sharp musical sound as of metal meeting bone. 'God damn the thing! Sergeant, what the hell are you doing? Where are you, man?'

'I'm here, sir, and I'm drookit!' cried the Sergeant, but they're made of fine stuff, these Perthshire policemen, for after a few hippo-like squelches in the gloom he bawled:

'McLaren, do you hear me? The jig is up! You are surroonded on aall sides! Chust you bring in your boat this minute and surrender! We have a warrant! Do you hear me, McLaren?'

'Away you, Rory, and polish your pluidy handcuffs!' came the answer. 'Have you nothing petter to do than spoil sport, you and that merchant skipper wi' the pot belly?'

'Damn him!' cried the Admiral, enraged. 'Damn his insolence! Give yourselves up, you scoundrels, or it will the worse for you!'

'Ach, go and torpedo yourself!' laughed the voice. 'You should be in your bed, you silly sailor!'

'Now, you listen to me, McLaren!' shouted the Sergeant. 'You chust give up this nonsense like a good laad, and maybe when it comes to the charges we'll be going easy on you –'

'We'll do nothing of the dam' sort!' bellowed the Admiral. It struck me that perhaps he and the Sergeant had worked out the routine of Hard Man and Soft Man used by clever interrogators, but if they had it was wasted effort. The response from the boat was an indelicate noise, and in his fury the Admiral shouted, most unreasonably: 'Sergeant! Arrest that man!'

Knowing Rory's devotion to duty I half-expected him to strike out for the middle of the loch with his handcuffs in his teeth, but at that moment the headlights came on again, and in their glare the boating trio were seen to be on their feet, manhandling a large contraption which looked like an oil drum with metal curlicues and other interesting attachments. The Admiral let out a neighing scream.

'It's the still! Don't let them jettison it! Get a boat, Sergeant! It's no use, you villains, we've seen it! Sergeant, you're a witness! Oh, my God, it's gone!'

There was an almighty splash, the boat rocked, and a small

wave rippled across the face of the loch. The Admiral actually shook his fist, the Sergeant strode into the shallows and cried: 'I arrest you, Aeneas McLaren, alias the Dipper, for illicit distillin', you godless hound of hell, you!' The headlights blinked, dimmed, and went out again, and I climbed into the back of the car for a quiet cigarette. These big co-ordinated police operations are too much for mere military nerves.

What they would have done if the Dipper and his companions had chosen to stay where they were, I can't imagine. Stood around the loch until they grew moss, probably. But the Dipper was considerate; he and his friends rowed slowly in, singing some Gaelic boat song, and when Rory laid hands on him and said that anything you say will be taken doon and may be used in evidence against you, and haud your tongue, Dipper McLaren, and the Admiral announced triumphantly that he could expect a jail sentence without the option, the Dipper smiled on them tolerantly and asked: 'And what for, skipper? Fushin'?'

'You know damned well what for!' cried the Admiral. 'For illicit distilling! What was that you threw over the side, hey?'

'Bait,' said the Dipper, and laughed softly with the whole length of his lean body. The Admiral laughed, too, on an unpleasant note, and said he would sing a different tune when they'd dragged the loch, but I noticed the gadgers weren't smiling as they surveyed that black surface, and Rory was oddly hesitant about clapping the darbies on the prisoners, as the Admiral demanded.

'We know where to put our hands on them, sir, when required,' he said, scowling on the Dipper, and although the Admiral got quite purple about it, he couldn't get Rory to go beyond charging the trio, and finally letting them go – for, as the Sergeant fairly pointed out, we simply didn't have room in the vehicles to carry them back. The Dipper listened with amiable attention, touched his hat to the Admiral, flung his old coat about his shoulders like a musketeer, and with his two friends simply wandered off into the darkness.

It seemed a bit of an anti-climax, but although the Admiral was baulked of the satisfaction of bringing back his captives in chains behind his chariot, so to speak, he was grimly cheerful on the way home. They knew where the still was, and when it had been dredged up it would be a case of Barlinnie for three, and no nonsense. And if the Inspector had done his part with comparable efficiency, the Admiral added, that would be one gang of poachers less to trouble the countryside. Not a bad night's work, young Dand; we've earned our nightcap, what?

Any thought of nightcaps vanished from my mind as we drove over the gravel to the hotel. For there, parked outside, was my 15-cwt truck, with the Inspector and a constable standing guard.

The Admiral was out of the car like a salmon going up the Falls of Falloch, demanding information, and the Inspector gave it with disgruntled satisfaction. No, they hadn't found the deer; no, they hadn't caught the poachers. Of course, had he been given aa-dequate perr-sonnel –

'Then where the devil did you find the truck?' blared the Admiral. 'And how the devil did you get in that condition?' For both officers were plastered with mud to the waist, as though they had strayed into a peat-cutting – which, it transpired, they had: obviously it wasn't the Perthshire constabulary's night for keeping dry. The Inspector explained with what dignity he could.

He had established road-blocks as instructed, and was driving back towards the hotel with the constable when they had spotted the truck coming towards them along the Tyndrum road – the one we had taken *en route* to Lochnabee. 'You hadnae seen it – no, you would be busy up at the loch, no doubt.' The Inspector's sniff was eloquent. The truck had pulled up sharply at sight of the police car, and four men had taken to the heather, but although the officers had pursued them vigorously they had escaped in the darkness.

'Blast!' exploded the Admiral. 'But didn't you get a look at them, dammit? Can you identify them, man? You must have –'

'I haff said it wass dark, and we wass undermanned!' retorted the Inspector. 'Mind you, wan o' them sounded like a Glasgow man, for we heard him roaring in the night, and he had an accent.' He glanced at me. 'He micht have been wearing a sojer's tunic.'

'Half the demobilised men in the country wear soldiers' tunics!' snapped the Admiral. 'What a shambles! The whole thing has been bungled to the hilt!' He glared at the unfortunate Inspector. 'Well, you haven't covered yourself with glory, have you? I send you out, with precise instructions . . .'

I was no longer listening. I knew only one man in the neighbourhood who wore khaki and roared in a Glasgow accent when pursued – but it couldn't be him, surely? McAuslan, stagpoacher? Impossible; he wouldn't have known how, for one thing . . . and then I remembered Aunt Alison's words: 'Macrae! There's a name for a Highland midnight . . .' Macrae the stalker; he would know how. But that wasn't credible, either . . . we'd only been in the district twenty-four hours; they couldn't have taken to crime (and highly technical crime, too) in that time. Not McAuslan, anyway – and yet every instinct told me that, however bizarre the explanation, he was out there in the heather somewhere, doing his disorderly impression of Rob Roy, and unless immediate steps were taken he would undoubtedly blunder into the arms of the Law, and . . . It didn't bear thinking about – McAuslan, court-martialled for killing the King's deer (well, the Admiral's, anyway). What could I do?

Fortunately the Admiral and Inspector were too busy upbraiding and making excuses to notice me, and when the Admiral finally made for the hotel, muttering savagely about incompetent bumpkins and the decay of discipline, I followed, a prey to nameless fears. He surged up the steps like an icebreaker, and was heading for my aunt's office when Robin Elphinstone came out of the passage, started violently at the sight of us, and half-retreated into the passage again, looking furtive.

'Elphinstone!' cried the Admiral, scoring a bull for identification. 'What the blazes are you doing here?'

The aggressive tone seemed to strike fire in Elphinstone. He was normally a bluff, confident character, but emerging from the passage he had reacted like Peter Lorre caught in the act, twitching and glancing sideways. Now he recovered, drew himself up, eyed the Admiral with loathing, and demanded:

'Why shouldn't I be here? This hotel isn't your flagship, is it? Who the dickens d'you think you are – Captain Bligh?' He snorted and shot his cuffs rather defensively, I thought. 'If you must know, I've been having coffee with Mrs Gordon,' he added, and the Admiral ground his teeth.

'Your trousers are wet!' he said accusingly.

'So are yours,' retorted Elphinstone. 'What would you like to do – form a club?' He gave a pleased snort, wished me goodnight, and went off, but not without another wary glance back as he reached the door.

'Damned impertinence!' fumed the Admiral. 'Mark my words, that fellow wants watching. Did you see him just now – looked as though he'd had his hand in the till? What's he been up to, eh? Outsider!'

Aunt Alison was knitting placidly and listening to the wireless in the warm comfort of her room. 'Home from the wars!' she said, smiling, exclaimed at the wet state of our feet, rang for coffee and sandwiches, placed us before the fire, dispensed whisky, and listened with soothing attention while the Admiral poured out his troubles from the hearthrug, starting with the insolence and evil cunning of the Dipper ('which won't save him, I'm glad to say, once the evidence is recovered') and ending with a scathing denunciation of the luckless Inspector. He didn't refer to our encounter with Elphinstone, but I noticed his glance strayed to the muddy tracks on the carpet, as though he were trying to deduce how long his detested rival had spent on the premises.

'My, it's the exciting night you've had of it!' said Aunt Alison admiringly, and sighed. 'And the poor old Dipper's nabbed at last. Well, I won't pretend I'm not sorry for the old devil.'

'Old devil is right. But your sympathy, my dear, is far too precious to be wasted on him,' chided the Admiral. 'The fellow's been a menace for years. Well, now he's going to pay for it – and so,' he concluded grimly, 'are those infernal poachers.'

'Didn't you tell me they'd got away?'

'Thanks to that yokel policeman, yes. But the truck didn't,' said the Admiral triumphantly. 'And if the fingerprints on its steering-wheel belong to anyone named McLaren . . . well, I'd say that was conclusive, wouldn't you?'

I'd been listening with one ear, preoccupied as I was with visions of McAuslan roaming the Highland night while I sat powerless to rescue or prevent him, but at the suggestion that my truck would be Exhibit A in a poaching trial I was all attention. So was my aunt, only she seemed amused.

'Conclusive of what? Only about who was driving the truck, and took it away. But that,' she reminded him, 'is Dand's concern, Jacky. Not yours.'

'Not mine?' The Admiral went into his halibut impersonation. 'But . . . but, goodgoddlemighty, they were using it to poach my stag! They were –'

'Were they? What stag? You haven't even found it yet.' She rose, holding the decanter. 'And until you do, you'll be ill-advised to cry "Poacher!" just because you've got a bee in your bonnet about the McLarens. More toddy?'

The Admiral gargled, going puce. 'A bee? In my bonnet?

You know as well as I do they've got my stag cached out there –'

'You're blethering,' she said pleasantly, filling his glass. 'I know no such thing, and neither do you. Fingerprints, indeed! You've been seeing too many Thin Man pictures. Well, nobody's been murdered –'

'Alison!'

'– and all that's happened is that Dand's truck has been taken without his permission – and now he's got it back . . .'

'Alison, I –'

'. . . And the last thing he wants is a lot of handless bobbies crawling over it with magnifying glasses. Even if every McLaren in Scotland had his pug-marks on it, what could they be charged with except taking it away without the owner's consent? And I don't suppose you've considered the trouble and embarrassment that would cause my nephew with his superiors? Well . . .' She gave him her level, blue-eyed look. '. . . I wouldn't think much of that, I can tell you.'

She wasn't alone there: I could think of one Colonel who would hit the roof. And the Admiral, to do him justice, took the point, although it was nothing to him compared to the prospect of incurring her displeasure. That was what took him amidships, and his indignation vanished like May mist; he blinked at her in a distraught, devoted way, and admitted he hadn't thought about that side of it . . . last thing he'd want to do . . . and no doubt she was right, there was no positive proof . . . yet. But what could he say to the police? If they had reason to believe the truck had been used for criminal purposes, he didn't quite see how he . . .

'Och, use your wits, Jacky! Tell them Dand's satisfied, and doesn't wish to press matters. Bully them, man, if you have to! Goodness me, the Inspector wants to be a superintendent some day – he's not going to cross the leading man in the district, is he?'

The leading man looked doubtful. 'Well, I suppose . . . if you say so . . . it'll look a bit odd, though, after all the fuss . . .'

'Havers!' laughed Aunt Alison. 'I can just see McKendrick raising objections. A word from you and he'll be jumping through hoops and saluting.' She smiled warmly on him and sweetened the pill still further. 'You can come and tell me about it at dinner, and we'll talk it all over, the two of us.'

The Admiral cheered up considerably at this, and when he took his leave after a final toddy it was with expressions of good will all round. As the door closed Aunt Alison gave a long, delicate sigh and subsided into her chair, reaching for a cigarette.

'My God, and they talk about Sarah Bernhardt! If I'd had to be ladylike a minute longer I'd have burst!' She inhaled deeply, raising a hand to still my clamour. 'Not now, Dand. I know you're full of desperate news, but it can wait. Now . . . stiffen your drink, because I have a wee surprise for you, and I want you to sit there, keep calm, and hold your peace till it's over.'

She rose, and opened the door to the little box-room off the study. 'Come out of that,' she said, and before my disbelieving eyes Lance-Corporal Macrae sidled warily into the room, and behind him, like an anxious tomb-robber emerging from a pyramid, shambled Private McAuslan.

I don't know what I'd have said if I hadn't been bidden to silence; nothing, probably. Unexpectedness apart, they were a sight to numb the senses: Macrae was wild and dishevelled, but McAuslan looked as though he had been in the ground for centuries. Filthy I had seen him, but never like this; he had broken all previous records. Mud and slime of every shade and texture seemed to cover him, his hair was matted with it, through the beauty-pack on his face he was regarding me in terror, and then he quivered to attention as my aunt addressed them.

'You two men,' and she looked and sounded like a Valkyrie

at the end of her tether, 'will haud your wheesht, now and hereafter. Do you see? Mr MacNeill will have something to say to you later, but just now you'll go out by the back way, like mice, and up to the house without being seen. Is that clear?' She raised a finger. 'And Macrae – if ever you put your neb into West Perthshire again I'll have you hung by the heels. *Aighe-va.*'

I counted five when they had gone and, restraining myself with difficulty, asked for an explanation. Aunt Alison gave me a look.

'Are you sure you want to know?'

I pointed out that since *they* obviously knew, I ought to, if only for discipline's sake, and she sat, resting her brow on her fingertips, and finally said: 'I could greet. Dand, next time you come to see me, just bring a couple of nice wee city criminals, will you? Not reivers like Macrae. Mind you . . . if he's looking for a job when he leaves the Army . . . ach, never mind. Well, bide and listen, if your nerves can stand it.'

It seemed that on the first evening Macrae and McAuslan, refreshing themselves in the public bar, had made friends with the lads of the village, including the notorious McLarens, the Dipper's crew. They and Macrae had discovered mutual interests, and in no time he was abreast of local affairs, such as the pressing danger to the Dipper's illicit still from the Admiral and the gadgers. A raid was imminent, and what was needed, said the Dipper, was some diversion to keep the Admiral busy while the still was moved to a new hideaway – shooting a stag, for example. A task for a skilled night hunter . . . aye, but it would be worth his while. Oh, Macrae was a bit of a stalker, was he? And then they would be needing transport for the carcase the next night . . . what, Macrae knew where a truck was to be had? Here, Erchie, come you and listen to this . . .

I could contain myself no longer. 'Aunt Alison, are you telling me Macrae was bribed to poach a stag before he'd been here five minutes? I can't believe it! How do you know this, anyway?' I regarded her in sudden terror. 'Have you known all along?'

'Will you hold your peace? And don't jump to unflattering conclusions,' she said with some asperity. 'I've been telling you that since you could toddle. I knew nothing at all until this evening. But I'm not a gommeril, and like everyone else I knew the McLarens would try *some* ploy to set Jacky running in circles. And when he came yelping to me this morning that a stag had been shot, I thought, aye, that's their red herring. There was no point saying anything to Jacky, with the steam rising from him; besides, it was no business of mine. But when you came to the hotel in the evening, and said your truck was missing, and two of your lads nowhere to be found – then, it was my business.'

'When the Admiral was here, planning his raid? You never said anything. You went to arrange a snack for his men.'

She gave me a pitying look. 'Aye, didn't I just? I also went to get Rab, my grieve, because he's one that knows every mortal thing that goes on hereabouts. I don't pry as a rule, but I knew this was an emergency, and I grilled the whole black tale out of him, with the promise that if he held back he'd be on the dole tomorrow. Now, may I continue?'

Rab, under pressure, had described what my aunt had just told me – how Macrae had conspired with the McLarens, contributing some refinements of his own to their diversionary plan. The upshot was that he had gone out that first night with Erchie McLaren's rifle and a flask of rabbit's blood which he had smeared artistically on a rock on Ben Vornach; he had faked signs that a stag had been carried off through the heather, fired a shot, and so home to bed. (And I'd thought he was out wenching.)

'You mean there wasn't any dead stag? But then . . . why did they take the truck tonight, if there was no carcase to shift?'

'I guessed that before Rab got the length of telling me,' said

Aunt Alison complacently. 'They needed it to shift the Dipper's still. That was the whole point – to make Jacky think the truck was being used to carry off a carcase that didn't exist, when in fact they were getting the still away from Lochnabee.'

'But they *didn't* get it away! The Dipper had to jettison it! I saw him!'

Aunt Alison shrugged. 'Aye, well, the best-laid schemes . . . Jacky took their bait – but he went to Lochnabee as well, and no doubt got there ahead of them, and spoiled their plan. But that's by the way. All I knew, and cared about, when Rab had told his tale, was that *your* truck was about to be used for bootlegging or moonshining or whatever you call it. With one of your men, Macrae, red-hand in the mischief – and yon other poor bedraggled idiot as well, probably. What's his name? McAuslan? He hasnae the look of a gangster.'

'He's not. I shouldn't think he knew what the hell was happening. I don't think I do.'

'Well, thank your stars I did. It was plain that with Jacky bound for Lochnabee they were in great danger of getting caught, and I had to prevent that, for your sake – I don't ken what the Army does to officers whose men are lifted for moving illicit stills (or for trying to) but I'm sure it's something embarrassing. So,' she continued serenely, 'I phoned Robin Elphinstone and told him to take his car and scour the road about Lochnabee, and find those clowns of yours before the police did, and get them safe away. And to give him time to do that, I kept Jacky and his minions busy here with grouse pâté and Glenlivet. I thought it went down rather well,' said this amazing woman complacently, 'and I wasn't bad myself.'

It's remarkable, about family. You think you know them, but you don't. Here was this good, respected widow lady of advancing years, who had guided my infant steps, heard my prayers at night, and read to me from the *Billy and Bunny Book,* sitting there looking like the matriarch of some soap-opera family of

Texas tycoons, and apparently concealing the combined talents of the Scarlet Pimpernel and a Mafia godmother. I didn't know where to begin.

'You could try saying thank you, and bring me a glass of sherry,' she reproved me. 'Well, Robin didn't like it, much, but he's biddable. He took his car and waited in a quarry near the Lochnabee turn-off until your truck came by, going like fury. He saw the police car head them off, and your two boys and the McLarens taking to the heather, and being a good man on the hill himself he waited until the police had given up, and then went after your lads, leaving the McLarens to take care of themselves.' She took a wistful sip of sherry. 'It's a fact, men have all the fun. Well, he found them: the poor McAuslan cratur was up to his neck in a myrtle bog, bawling like a bull, but he got them to his car and brought them here – which wasn't so clever, but Robin has his limitations. He sneaked them in by the back, and they had barely been in here long enough to foul the carpet when we heard Jacky waking the echoes at the front door. I whipped them straight into the box-room and told Robin to make himself scarce.'

'No wonder he looked panic-stricken! Aunt Alison, he could have got the jail! So could you, I dare say . . . don't ask me for what – obstructing justice or something –'

'Ach, stop blethering, boy. What did I do but telephone a friend asking him to give two soldiers a lift?'

Legally, she may have been right: I doubt if there are laws against obtaining information from an employee with threats of dismissal, dragooning a neighbour into rescuing stray soldiers from bogs, playing Lady Bountiful to keep Excisemen from their duty, or beguiling choleric naval men with fair words and malt whisky while their mud-spattered quarry lies hidden in the next room. But they do call for an unusual ability to think on your feet, to say nothing of imperturbability, man management, and sheer cold nerve. And as I watched her now, taking a vanity mirror from her bag, turning her head critically, and adjusting a silver curl, I said as much. She was amused.

'Dear me,' she said, 'have you forgotten, when you were wee, I told you about the woman of Achruach and the Gregora? Well,' she gave a last glance at her mirror, smoothing an eyebrow, 'I may use reading glasses and gasp a bit on the stairs, but the day I cannot keep my countenance, and work my will on the likes of Robin Elphinstone and Admiral Jacky – that, nephew, is a day you will never see.'

They were feigning sleep when I got back to Wade's House, Macrae in silence, McAuslan with irregular staccato grunts which he probably imagined sounded like rhythmic breathing. I didn't rouse them, partly because I was too tired to listen to the lies of one and the pathetic excuses of the other, but chiefly because my sadistic streak was showing and I was only too pleased to let them stew in their guilty fear until morning. Even then I ignored them, telling Brooks that we would do without breakfast and get on the road at once; I had no wish to linger in a locality whose inhabitants had proved themselves about as safe as damp gun-cotton.

When we were safely south of Balquhidder I told Brooks to pull over on a quiet stretch, and went round to order the criminal element out of the back for a man-to-man chat by the roadside. Macrae, haggard but presentable, stared stolidly to his front; McAuslan was in his normal parade order, filthy, abject, crouched to attention with animal fear in every ragged line of him, and sneezing fit to rattle the windows in Crieff. Forcing myself to look more closely, I saw that he had shed most of the muck he had been wearing last night, and that he was wringing wet; a small pool was forming around his sodden boots.

'What the devil have you been doing?' I demanded.

'Please, sur,' he croaked, and sneezed again, thunderously. 'Oh, name o' Goad! Please, sur,' he repeated, through hideous snuffles, 'Corporal Macrae threw me inna burn, sur. Las' night, sur, when we wis comin' hame.'

I fought down an impulse to deal leniently with Macrae. 'Why did you do that, Corporal?'

'Tae get him clean, sir. He was manky. Ye saw him at the hotel, sir, covered wi' glaur. I wisnae lettin' him in your auntie's hoose in that state.'

'Well, that was very thoughtful of you. And by the looks of you, McAuslan, you slept in your wet uniform. Why?'

'Becos . . . aarraashaw! Aw, jeez, beg pard'n, sur! Jist a wee tickle in ma nose. Aye, weel, ye see, Ah kept ma claes on fur tae keep me warm.'

'Ah, of course. Well, we don't want them to get creased, do we, so why don't you get back in the truck – and strip the disgusting things off, you blithering clot, you! Dry your horrible self, if you know how, and wrap your useless carcase in a blanket before you get pneumonia, although why I should worry about that I'm shot if I know! Move!'

A normal enough preliminary to a meeting of minds with McAuslan. When he had vanished, sneezing and hawking, over the tailboard, I turned back to Macrae.

'Right, Corporal. Tell me about last night.'

He licked his lips, looking past me. 'Did your auntie . . . Mrs Gordon, I mean . . . not tell you?'

'She told me. Now you tell me.'

It was like getting blood from a stone. After some evasion, he admitted faking the stag-shooting. Why had he done it? Och, well, the McLarens were good lads, and it was a bit o' sport. No, he'd had no money from them. (I believed this.) Yes, he had let them take the truck in my absence, and gone with them; aye, he knew it was a grave offence, but he was deep in the business by then, and couldnae let them down;

they were good lads. Forbye, he didnae think I would ever know. Yes, he knew that conspiring with illicit distillers was a criminal matter, and that he and McAuslan might have landed in jail. Didn't he realise what a dirty trick it was to involve a meat-brain like McAuslan in the first place? At this he looked uncomfortable, and shrugged, with a sheepish little laugh – and that was when I caught the smell on his breath.

'Half a sec,' I said. 'Where did you get a drink at this time of day?'

'Drink, sir? Me, sir?'

I went straight to the truck and climbed in, ignoring the débutante squeal of McAuslan caught *en déshabillé*. Sure enough, in the well of the truck beneath the floor, safe from the prying eyes of policemen, were a dozen bottles – no labels, of course, but all filled with the water of life, clear as glass. I wetted my palm and tasted, and it was the good material, smooth and strong and full of wonder. Not more than a hundred proof, probably. I knew old soldiers who would have killed for it.

'Well, well . . . so the Dipper paid you in advance, did he?' I said. 'Generously, too – twelve bottles for nothing.'

Macrae, at the tailboard, was silent, presumably resigned to confiscation, but McAuslan, clutching his blanket about him like the oldest squaw on the reservation, was startled into contradiction.

'Wisnae fur nuthin', sure'n it wisnae.' He sounded quite indignant. 'Sure'n we shiftit his bluidy still for him.'

Like my aunt, I too can sometimes keep my countenance.

'Och, sure,' I said, 'but that's no great work.'

'Wis it no', but?' said McAuslan, and emitted another crashing sneeze. When he had finished towelling his nose with his blanket he resumed: 'See that still, sur? It wis bluidy heavy, Ah'm tellin' ye. We'd a helluva job gettin' it oot o' the boat an' into ra truck, an' –'

'What time was this?'

'Jist efter dark. Is that no' right, Macrae? Aye, soon's it wis dark, that Erchie McLaren an' anither yin came up tae the hoose, an' we a' got inna truck, an' drove up tae that loch where the Dipper has his boat . . .' He paused, apprehension clouding his primitive features as it dawned on him that he was Telling All. He gulped, gasped, closed his eyes, shuddered, was convulsed by another monumental sneeze, muttered 'Mither o' Goad, Ah've jist aboot had it!', shot an appealing look at the saturnine Macrae, and then gave me a furtive, fawning grin which I think on the whole was the most repulsive expression I've ever seen on a human face.

'Eh . . . eh . . . Ah'm awfy sorry, sur,' he said. 'Ah've forgot the rest.'

'No, you haven't, McAuslan. But you don't have to worry,' I reassured him. 'It's all right. You can tell me. Because if you don't, I'll kill you.'

He digested this, stricken, and decided there was nothing else for it. 'Aye, weel, like Ah wis sayin'. We got up tae the loch, an' the Dipper an' his boys, an' the fower of us, we got his bluidy contraption oot the boat – here, it was a right plumber's nightmare, sur, so it wis! An' that's whit they mak' ra whisky in! Ye widnae credit it. Onywye,' he went on, wiping his face with his blanket in an oratorical gesture, 'we wis staggerin' aboot wi' the thing in the watter, an' no' kiddin', sur, Ah wis aboot ruptured, an' the Dipper wis next tae me, an' he lets oot a helluva roar. "Whit's up?" sez Ah. "It's ma ee!" sez he, "it's fell oot. It's in ra watter!" Ah couldnae figure 'im oot. "Yer ee?" sez Ah. "Whit ye talkin' aboot, Dipper!" "Ma gless ee!" cries he, an' starts floonderin' in ra watter, an' efter a bit he cam' up wi' it, and slipped it back in. Tell ye the truth,' said McAuslan, 'Ah wis a bit disgustit. But we got the still on the truck, an' Ah sez tae the Dipper, "Hoo did ye lose yer ee, auld yin?" "Got it shot oot in France in sixteen", sez he. "Away!"

sez Ah. "Wis you in the Airmy?" "Wis Ah no'," sez he. "See your man MacNeill, his uncle wis ma officer. Brung me back in aff the wire efter ma ee got shot oot. Ah widnae be makin' malt the day, if it hadnae been for him."'

Actually, that was news to me. McAuslan paused to beam on me. 'He musta been a'right, your uncle, eh?'

'Yes, he was,' I said. 'Go on.'

'Aye, weel, we'd jist got the tailboard up when here's a caur comin' up the hill road tae the loch – we couldnae see it, but we heard the engine. "Claymore!" bawls the Dipper. "Here the King's Navy an' the bluidy gadgers! Oot o' this, Erchie, or we're lost men!" An' him an' his two fellas tumbled in the boat an' starts rowin', an' we got inna truck, but we couldnae tak' the road, wi' the caur comin', so Erchie jist went straight doon the side o' the hill. Inna dark, helpmaGoad! Whit a helluva ride it wis! We wis bashin' ower rocks an' breengin' through bracken, an' ma innards comin' oot ma ears, an' Erchie McLaren's roarin': "Thy will be done, oh Lord! Keep a grip o' the still, lads!" Hoo we got ontae the main road, guid kens, an' then we drove for miles –'

'Where to? Where did you take the still?' He looked blank. 'Do you know, Macrae?'

He shook his head. 'Nae idea, sir – honest. It was as black as the Earl o' Hell's breeks. Somewhere off the Tyndrum road, in a dry cave in a corrie.'

'So what was it the Dipper dropped in the loch in front of the gadgers?'

He tried in vain to keep a straight face. 'An old stove and a lot o' bed springs.'

The classic selling of the dummy, in fact. Well, good luck, Admiral, I thought. You'll drag the loch for that still, and never find it – but you'll always believe it's there, somewhere at the bottom of Lochnabee. While the Dipper sits in his dry cave, distilling away to his heart's content and quietly enjoying what, to the Highlander, is the perfect victory: the one the enemy doesn't know about.

It occurred to me that Aunt Alison's delaying tactic on behalf of my errant soldiery had also given the Dipper time to get his still safely away. Not that she could have foreseen that, of course. Interesting, though . . .

'Aye, but here, sur, ye hivnae heard the hauf o' it!' McAuslan, girding his sodden blanket about him, was eager to resume his role as saga-man. 'See efter that, but? Onna way hame we ran intae ra durty polis, an' had tae scram oot o' ra truck an' run fur it, an' Ah near drooned in a bog, an' got a' covered in –'

'Thank you, McAuslan, I know all about that.'

'– an' that man Elphinstone dragged me oot by the hair o' the heid – an' where the hell were you, Macrae?' he demanded at a sudden tangent, glaring balefully at his superior. 'Fat lot o' help you wis, an' chance it! Lookin' efter Number Wan ye wis, an' me uptae ma neck in the –'

'All right, McAuslan, that'll do . . .'

'Aye, weel, sur, Ah'm jist sayin'. Nae thanks tae Macrae Ah got oot . . . an' then the man Elphinstone got us tae his caur, an' took us tae yer auntie at ra hotel, an' –'

'McAuslan!'

'– beg pard'n sur, Missus Gordon, Ah shoulda said. Awfy sorry. An' she sez: "Jeez, will ye look at the state o' ye!", or sumpn like that, an' then the man Elphinstone cries: "Here somebuddy comin'!", an' she had us through yon door afore ye could say knife – sure'n she did, Macrae? Here, sur, wis it yon wee nyaff o' an Admiral? See the bluidy Navy, Ah hate them, so Ah do –'

'Shut up!' I shouted, and he fell silent, with the pained surprise of a Cicero cut off in full peroration by the Consuls, although I doubt if the great orator ever scrubbed his nose with his toga, or asked can Ah pit ma soaks on noo, sur, ma feet's fair freezin'?

'Wait till they're dry, idiot!' I snarled. 'Socks, forsooth! Hasn't it sunk into your concrete skull yet that you committed a crime last night? That you could have wound up in Barlinnie?'

He blinked, scratching himself while he digested this, and made a deep guttural noise of concern. 'Zattafac', sur? Here, aye, Ah s'pose that's right. Ah'm awfy sorry, sur, Ah didnae think aboot that.' He towelled his matted head in a contrite way, and then brightened. 'Aye, but it wis a'right, ye see. Your auntie – beg par'n, Missus Gordon, Ah should say – she took care o' us, nae bother. Organised, so she wis. Had us through that door sae fast wir feet didnae touch.' His gargoyle face creased in complacent approval. 'Ah think she's smashin', Ah do. Awfy nice. Awfy clever . . .'

I gave up – not for the first time. As I climbed out of the truck I realised that Macrae was regarding me warily; I knew what was going on in that practical mind, but I'd already weighed this against that and decided, reluctantly, that there was only one thing for it.

'Right, Macrae,' I said. 'In you get.'

He hesitated with his hand on the tailboard. 'Eh . . . what aboot the whisky, sir?'

'What whisky?' I said. 'Get in, and be quiet. And think yourself lucky.'

'. . . never panicked. Kept the heid. Just says, "In there, the pair o' ye, an' no' a cheep oot o' ye'.' McAuslan was still extolling Aunt Alison's presence of mind. 'Ah think she's marvellous, so Ah do. She's a great buddy . . . Ah mean, wumman . . . Ah mean, leddy.' He regarded me over the tailboard, shaking his grimy head in solemn respect, and bestowed the Glaswegian's ultimate accolade. 'She's a'right, but.'

Or as they say in Breadalbane: that is a woman of the Gordons for you.

Ye mind Jie Dee, Fletcher?

Twenty years ago Scotland's footballers were in the World Cup finals in Argentina. That bald statement gives not the remotest idea of the emotional convulsion which the event produced north of the Tweed; whenever Scottish prestige is at stake in any major international contest (war and soccer especially) the population tends to go into an inner frenzy of apprehension and wild hope, and those stern Caledonian virtues of sound judgment and common sense have to struggle for survival. Whatever the odds, however unlikely victory may be, the fever takes hold: dreams of glory and memories of past heroes and triumphs mingle with anxious speculation, and if outward opinion of the country's chances is often muted and even disparaging, don't let that fool you – under the surface all the old passions are on the boil again, the savage joy of impending conflict, the charging up of confidence, the growing, shining conviction that this time – this time, at long last! – it is all going to come true. Now and then it does, as witness Bannockburn 1314, Wembley 1928, Lisbon 1967, and Muirfield Village 1987. (The fact that other nations were also on the winning side on that last occasion is, to Scots, irrelevant. Whose game is it, anyway?)

But few things rouse Scottish emotions so much as football – another game which they regard as their personal property. England, the mother of sport, laid down with typical Anglo-Saxon tidiness the laws which imposed form and order on the old wild celebration in which two sides battled over a ball; they invented the game, but the Scots gave it the style which made it the most popular team sport on earth. More than a century ago they cast a calculating eye on football as it was played south of the Border, saw its possibilities, and transformed the charging, kick-and-rush recreation into a thing of science and even beauty; not for them to chase pell-mell after the ball with the reckless exuberance of the hunting field; they actually *passed* it to each other, ran into open space for the return, moved in ever-changing formations, perfected control with foot and head, and turned to advantage the short, wiry stature and lightning nimbleness which three generations of slum-dwelling had bred into a people who had once been the biggest in Europe. Like Pygmalion, they fell hopelessly in love with their creation, and have been faithful ever since.

For sixty years it was a blissful honeymoon, up to the Second World War. The Scottish professionals held undisputed mastery, and only England, with its tenfold superiority in sporting manpower, could hope to match if not to overtake them; Ireland and Wales provided interesting practice, and the rest of the world didn't count. Soccer was only spreading then; young enthusiasts like Nikita Khrushchev were learning the art of the sliding tackle in the Donbass, and a goalkeeper named Albert Camus was cherishing the dream (later realised) of playing for his country, but it was still a British game, and its high priests served their novitiates at Ibrox, Tynecastle, and Parkhead.

It all changed after 1945. England began to beat Scotland more often than not. Moscow Dynamo came to Glasgow and held the mighty Rangers to a draw, Austria became the first foreign side to win on Scottish soil, quicksilver South Americans dazzled the traditionalists with a style of play that ignored the old sacred forms, and when Hungary took England apart at Wembley with clinical efficiency, Britain was no longer football's Olympus, and Scotland was a second-rate power. But the Scottish temperament being what it is, the dream remained, kept alive by national sides who were occasionally brilliant, more frequently awful to the point of embarrassment, and chronically inconsistent.

This is a characteristic which has bedevilled the Scots (and not only in sport) since Macbeth was a boy. At their best they are matchless; at their worst they defy description, and you never know which extreme you are going to see. Given pygmies for opponents, they are liable to get slaughtered; faced by giants, they will run rings round them – and then snatch defeat from the jaws of victory by some last-minute folly. England, on the other hand, are steady and predictable; only they could have restored British prestige by winning the World Cup in 1966 with sound if uninspired football and bulldog determination. Scotland, who hadn't even been able to qualify, promptly suffered a rush of blood to the head and thumped them next time out, and the nation lived in a tartan euphoria – until the next disaster.

To supporters as proud and passionate as the Scots this is frustrating to the point of trauma. They bear their burden of tradition with a fierce nostalgia, knowing that their players are still the equal of any, but sensing too, in their heart of hearts, that Scotland will never win the World Cup (except in imagination every four years). But irrational hope springs eternal, fuelled by occasional wins against England, and such heady triumphs as that of 1967, when a Celtic team who were arguably the best club side ever to come out of Britain, brought back the European Cup from Portugal, and for six weeks afterwards the British Embassy staff in Lisbon were terrified to open cupboards in case little drunk men in tartan scarves fell out, demanding the fare back to Glasgow.

That victory, and an appearance in the World Cup finals of 1974 from which, by a quirk of the system, they were eliminated without actually losing a game, sustained Scotland until 1978, when they qualified for the finals yet again.

And that was when the madness took hold, and a conviction arose as never before that this would be Scotland's year at last. A new manager, Alistair Macleod, somehow convinced his eager countrymen that the Scottish team, a workmanlike enough collection, were world-beaters; Scottish fans, describing themselves as 'Ally's Army', sang excruciating victory songs beforehand and gloated that England had failed to qualify for Argentina; the presence of two insignificant sides, Peru and Iran, in Scotland's preliminary group seemed to augur a triumphal progress to the final stages, and even the fact that the fourth team in the group, Holland, were probably the best side in the world at that time, could not damp Caledonian ardour. It was in the bag, the World Cup was as good as back in Glasgow, here's tae us, wha's like us, we're the wee boys, etc., etc. . . . Never were the Fates so tempted.

Well, Scotland were clobbered 1–3 by the despised Peruvians, scrambled a draw with Iran (Iran!), and to crown all, had a player sent home for taking 'an innocuous but illegal stimulant'. There had been nothing like it since Flodden, and the anguished cries of rage and grief from the faithful were heartbreaking. Scots exultant are unbearable, but when disappointed and betrayed their recriminations are worthy of the Old Testament. I didn't see or hear it, for I was far from Scotland at the time, but I could imagine all too well what was being said – and by one voice in particular, a voice I had not heard in thirty years, but which I didn't doubt would be upraised in denunciation and wild lament, just as I remembered it from the parade grounds and barrack-rooms of North Africa. I just had to close my eyes and there it was, drifting raucously across the ether, the plainsong of ex-Private McAuslan, J., reviewing the World Cup scene and reflecting on what might have been, but was not . . .

See ra Sco'ish team in ra Argenteena? Jeez an' name o' Goad!

Ah never seen such a bunch o' bums since ra chorus at ra Metropole done ra can-can. No kiddin', they couldnae beat *me*! See the state they were in? Whaur were yer inside forwards feedin' ra centre, whaur were yer wing-hauves haudin' doon ra midfield, whaur were yer wingers crossin' ra ba', whaur were yer Tommy Walkers an' Jimmy Delaneys bangin' it in? It's a goal! Aw-haw-hey! Come away ra wee boys! Scotland furrever! HA! Fat chance onybody got tae shout *that* in ra Argenteena, but. Play fitba'? Them? They couldnae play a bluidy barrel organ if Ally Macleod was tae wind it up for them. Mind you, Ah'm no' sayin' he would make a helluva good job o' that, either. Dearie me! Come home, Macleod, yer fan club's waitin'. Pathetic, so it is.

Hey, see me, but. Ah'm staun'in' in ra Mull o' Kintyre Vaults on ra Garscube Road wi' Fletcher, watchin' it onna telly. Ah couldnae believe it, so Ah couldnae. They're playin' ra wogs – ye know, Irran. It was efter they got beat aff the dagoes – aye, Perroo, tae rhyme wi' burroo, an' that's whit the hauf o' them should be on, aye, includin' that yin that got sent hame wi' his bladder full o' diabolic aspirin or whitever it was. But whit a shambles, Ah ask ye! The Irran wogs is gaun through them like they wisnae there, an' Hartford an' wee Erchie Gemmell an' Macari an' a' the rest o' them's rinnin' aboot like chickens wi' nae heids, an' Ah says, 'Fletcher, Ah don't believe whit Ah'm seein' – it's no' happenin', it cannae be happenin', sure'n it cannae, Fletcher?'

'Can it no'?' says he. 'Ah'm no' watchin'. Ony time Ah want tae look at a tragedy Ah can go an' see "Macbeth".'

'Macbeth?' says Ah. 'Wis he yon big fella used tae play centre hauf fur Airdrie? Ach, he wisnae worth a tosser, him, great big feet clumphin' a' ower ra penalty box. Aw, jeez, will ye look at Rough? That's a' we needit, a goalkeeper frae ra Partick Thistle! Mind you, the boy's no' a bad goalie – that's the thing aboot ra Thistle, a'ways had a good goalie, ye mind Ledgerwood,

Fletcher? That wis a goalie an' a hauf – GET RID OF IT, BUCHAN! IT'S NO' YOUR BA', YOU DIDNAE PEY FOR IT!! Oh, so helpma Goad! Aw, jeez! Aw, dearie me! If auld Jimmy Delaney, auld Jie Dee, could just be oot on that park fur five minutes! Or Walker, or Last-minute Reilly, or wee Billy Steel, or McGrory, or onybuddy that hisnae two left feet! Goad, if Ah could jist be oot there masel'!'

'You!' says Fletcher. 'You couldnae get oot yer own way. Mind that own goal against A Company?'

'Aw, fur Pete's sake, Fletcher, come affit!' Ah says. 'Ye still gaun oan aboot that? Ah nivver even seen ra ba' comin', hoo wis Ah tae know McGuffie wis gaun tae dae a back pass – the eejit! – it wisnae ma fault, Ah wis markin' the winger, Ah wis –'

'It's that gommeril Macleod!' says Fletcher, glowerin' at ra telly. 'He'll haftae go! The man's no' up tae it. Trust the Esseffay tae pick a teuchter as Scotland's manager. A Macleod, no kiddin'. The Macleods is a' away wi' the fairies, everybuddy kens that. Ye know they've even got a fairy banner?'

'Zattafac'?'

'Aye, they fly it on their castle at clan gatherin's, an' Ally Macleod mustae been wearin' it draped ower his heid a' the way tae Argenteena frae Gartnavel, or he'd have seen whit a pile o' rubbish his team wis. Shootin's too good fur him –'

'Haud oan,' Ah says. 'Jist haud oan, Fletcher. Keep the heid. Cool it. Tak' it easy. DON'T PANIC!! Macleod, ye say? Weel, Ah'll tell ye sumpn, Fletcher. Ah've been watchin' while thae bums has been gettin' crucified by Perroo, an' noo by the bluidy Assyrians or whitever they are – GAUN YERSEL, JORDAN! BREENGE AT HIM! IT'S WIDE OPEN! HIT THE THING, FUR GOAD'S SAKE! Aw, ye widnae credit it! Jie Dee widda had that past ra keeper in his sleep! Honest tae Goad, they want tae wrap the ba' up in a parcel an' post it tae ra wog goalie, it'll get there sooner! Onyway, Fletcher, whit Ah'm sayin' –

Ah've been watchin', an' ye know, Ah hivnae seen *Macleod* make a single bad pass, or miss a single tackle, or balloon ra ba' ower the bar, or fa' on his erse, or dae ony o' the things thae wandered bums in blue jersies has been daein'. It's no' Macleod that's oot there playin' like he'd been ten year in the Eastern Necropolis. Leave Macleod alone, the man's daein' his best. Sich as it is. Goad preserve us frae his worst. He'll be keepin' that fur ra game against Holland.

'Whit's that ye say? Ach, whiddy ye mean, he should have watched Perroo beforehand, an' he didnae get dossiers on a' their players, an' he didnae show oor boys fillums o' the Perroovians? So whit! Naebuddy showed us fillums o' A Company, did they? Awright, awright, we got beat aff A Company! Ah know, Ah wis there, wisn't Ah? That's no' the point at a'. D'ye hear whit Ah'm sayin', Fletcher? Will ye listen? The point Ah'm makin', if Ah can get a word in edgewise – the point Ah'm makin's this: naebuddy done me a dossier on that dirty big animal that A Company had playin' at ootside right, an' kicked me stupit afore hauf-time. Ah didnae *need* a dossier, or fillums o' the beast, did Ah? No' bluidy likely. Ah just went oot there an' kicked *him* stupit in the second hauf. So the point Ah'm makin' – will ye sharrup? The point Ah'm makin', is that if ye cannae come up against a side, an' tak' them as ye find them, an' beat them at their own game, then you're no' much o' a fitba' team. Ye neednae blame it on the manager, even if he isnae fit tae be a lollipop man at the Gobi Desert Secondary School. Whaur's the Gobi Desert? Hoo the hell dae Ah know? Whitsat gottae dae wi it, that's a red herrin', Fletcher – COME OOT, ROUGH, FUR THE LOVE O' GOAD!! THE WOG'S GAUNAE SCORE! AW, LOVELY, ALAN! Aw, did ye see that? Whit a save! Oh, jeez, Ah thought fur a horrible minute . . . Ye're awright, Alan! Even if ye do take fits. Oh, gie's anither pint, Ah'm needin' it! An' a wee hauf, miss – KICK IT UP RA PARK, YE GREAT MARYHILL MUG, YE!! Aw, Goad, aw, dearie me . . .

'Awright, they're rubbish. Awright, they're hellish. Awright, they're no' fit tae play for the Normal School Reserves. So whit? They've been rubbish afore, an' they'll be rubbish again. But Ah've seen them when they wis good. Ah mind them at Wembley an' Hampden an' Lisbon an' a' sorts o' places when they made the park seem like it wis a magic carpet, and John White wi' the ba' like it wis tied tae his boots, an' Tommy Gemmell bangin' them in frae thirty yards, an' big George Young guardin' ra box like a polis, an' Denis Law flickin' it in wi' the back o' his heid, an' Slim Jim Baxter sittin' on the ba' – *sittin'* oan it, but, inside his own eighteen-yard line, waitin' fur the English tae try tae tak' it aff him! The cheek o' the man! Goad, they could dae wi' Baxter oot there the night. Jist fur five minutes. Or auld Jie Dee. Ye mind Jie Dee, Fletcher, wi' his baldy heid?

'Weel, they're daein' their best, Ah suppose. Okay, so it's no' much o' a best. They're no' very good – the noo. Ah've seen them good. Awright, awright, they're bluidy terrible the night. But – CENTRE IT, GEMMELL!! CROSS IT, YE BAMPOT, THEY'RE LINED UP WAITIN' LIKE IT WIS A BUS STOP! Aw, wid ye believe it? AFFSIDE? Hoo the hell could yon be affside? There's mair wogs in that goal area than there is in Egypt! Who's that referee, Fletcher? Whaur's he from? Does he speak English, even? He'll be a Yugoslavakian, by the looks o' him. Or a cannibal. AWAY TAE LIZARS AN' GET YER EYES TESTED, YA BIG POULTICE! Referees? Aw, Ah've had it . . .

'Whit wis Ah sayin'? Aye! Ah wis sayin' they're terrible. Aye, but, see you, Fletcher. Mind when Jordan hit ra post, an' Dalgleish pit one jist past, an' Masson scraped ra cross-bar? Suppose they'd gone in – suppose they'd been six inches the ither way – suppose they'd been three goals instead o' three misses – you'd no' hiv been bawlin'; "Bring back hangin"! Macleod's got tae die!' Aw, no! Ye'd hiv been takin' the width o' the Maryhill Road, gassed tae hellangone, singin' "Ally is ra greatest, Ally fur king, Ally fur Pope!", an' ye widnae hiv bothered yer backside if the ootfield play wis rubbish, an' the defence lookin' like a Sunday School treat in the rain, an' big Jordan performin' like he wis between the shafts o' a coal-cairt. No fears. As long as the ba' went in the wog net, or the dago net, ye widnae care hoo it got there! There's a' you ken aboot fitba', you . . .'

'Look, McAuslan,' says he. 'It didnae go in the wog net! Did it? It didnae go in the dago net! Did it? No, it didnae! *That*'s whit Ah'm complainin' aboot!'

'. . . an' ye widnae hiv cared if the whole Scots team wis mainlinin' on sulphuric acid or sherbet, ye'd hiv been screechin': "Scotland can beat ra world an' ooter space! Aw-haw-hey! We're the wee boys! We're the champs!"'

'Look, McAuslan!' cries he. 'They got *beat*! B-E-E-T! An' Ah'm scunnered! Disgustit! Ye hear me?'

'Aye, Ah hear ye. Ah know. Pathetic, so it is. But whit's the point o' belly-achin' at the boys? Ah've nae time fur that. See yon yahoos, ca' themselves supporters, mobbin' the team bus, bawlin': "Macleod is rubbish! Awa' hame, Forsyth, yer tea's oot! We want wur money back! Scotland are rubbish!" See them? Ah widnae gi'e them the time o' day. Did *they* qualify fur ra World Cup finals? No' on yer nellie! Did *they* beat ra Czechs an' ra Welsh? They did not! Did they ever dae onything but staun on ra terracin' makin' pigs o' themselves when Scotland wis winnin', and yellin' dog's abuse when they got beat? So whit entitles them . . . SEE THE WINGER, MACARI! HE'S OOT THERE LIKE RA UNKNOWN SOJER, NAEBUDDY KENS HE'S THERE! Aw, jeez, aw Goad – ye bampot, Macari, ye pudden, are ye related tae that Irranian sweeper, ye're aye gi'in' the ba' tae him! As Ah wis sayin' . . . Ach, whit the hell, itsa waste o' time. Ah've had it. Up tae here. Switch that damned telly aff, barman, or let's hiv Bill an' Ben the Floorpot Men, at least they've got mair intelligence than whit we've been watchin'

. . . Ah jist wish . . . Ah jist wish . . . Ach, whit's the use? Jie Dee disnae play here any more. Neither does Toamy Walker. Hughie Gallacher's deid, an' Ma Ba' Peter isnae aroond (thank Goad, he wis a' they needed in Cordova, anither Partick Thistle comedian – but he wis magic on his day, mind). Aye, they're a' gone. Jimmy Logie's sellin' papers oan Piccadilly, Erchie Macaulay's a traffic warden, an' Baxter's got a pub in ra Govan Road. It's no' the same . . .

'Here, but . . . that boy Souness isnae bad. An' there must be ither young fellas comin' on. When's the next World Cup, Fletcher? 1982? Dear Goad, we goat tae go through a' this again? Ah cannae stand it, so Ah cannae. But Ah'll hiftae. It's like politics an' dry rot; ye cannae get away frae them, an' there's nae cure. An' noo we're gaun tae hiv tae sit through the game against Holland – can ye picture it, Fletcher? We'll get murdered! Murdered! It'll be aboot six-nil, Ah'll no' be able tae watch . . . Mind you, Ah know the Dutch are good, but they're just eleven men, efter a'. Ye nivver know, fitba's a funny game. Aye, no' that funny. Still, Scotland cannae be worse than they were tonight . . . weel, no' much worse. Ah hope. Tell ye whit, though. Ah'll tak' them tae beat England at Wembley next year. Mebbe.

'Ye mind Jie Dee? Aw, Goad . . .'

It seems only just to record that Scotland, unpredictable as ever, played like champions against Holland and beat them convincingly – but not by a big enough margin to qualify for the final stages. Still, I have no doubt that the memory of that victory was enough to sustain McAuslan through the next World Cup, and the next, and so on for ever after.

Extraduction

> The Highland battalion in this book never existed, inasmuch as the people in the stories are fictitious . . . and the incidents have been made up from a wide variety of sources, including my imagination . . .

I wrote those words in 1970 as part of the preface to the first collection of stories about Private McAuslan and Lieutenant MacNeill, entitled *The General Danced at Dawn*. They seemed true at the time, and again four years later when I repeated them in the sequel, *McAuslan in the Rough*. Now, reading them over so long after, I'm not so sure. This closing chapter may explain why.

For thirty years after leaving the Army I had no contact with my old regiment. Of course I followed their fortunes, at first in newspapers and cinema newsreels, and later on television; just the sight of that stag's head badge or the sound of a certain pipe tune, and I would be on the edge of my seat with the hairs rising on the nape of my neck. I rejoiced the first time they escaped amalgamation (a wicked and unnecessary exercise which has since put an end to them), and felt that strange mixture of exultation and anxiety whenever I heard of them on active service in some corner of the world – Malaya, Korea, Africa, Cyprus, and, now that the frontiers have dwindled, in Ulster (which looks like an even nastier version of Palestine from where I'm sitting. Flak-jackets and camouflage blouses instead of kilt and K.D., and a most unwieldy-looking rifle in place of the lovely Lee Enfield – but I notice they still persist in wearing their bonnets pulled down like coal-heavers' caps, and the faces underneath might have come straight from my old platoon. I watch them on T.V., doing that dirty, thankless job on the graffitied streets of Belfast, and just pray that they're as quick and hard and canny as the men I knew. I needn't worry, of course. They are. But I worry, just the same.)

That was as close as I came to the regiment in three decades, although very occasionally I might run into a former comrade, now civilian – and that was a disturbing experience, because they had got so ridiculously old; why, the youngest of them was bald and middle-aged and overweight. Extraordinary, when I had hardly changed at all. Well, perhaps an inch or two on the waist and a few grey hairs . . . and then I would glance in the mirror, and compare the reflection of the dyspeptic old man glowering out at me with the fading photo of that jaunty, innocent, childlike subaltern who was here just the other day, surely? What really put the tin hat on it was when I read some years ago that the regiment's commanding officer was retiring – and recognised his name as that of a young second-lieutenant who had reported his arrival to me when I was a company second-in-command. That's when you realise that those clear bright memories, of faces you knew and voices you heard only a moment ago . . . are history. It wasn't a moment ago; it's further away in time than the Second World War was from the Boer War. And that's when you begin to wonder how well your memory has served you.

It was almost exactly thirty years to the day after I left the Army that I found myself in London *en route* for Yugoslavia, where I was to work on a film. Thirty years away from the regiment, in which time I had married, had children, emigrated, come back, worked my way from junior reporter to (briefly) the editor's chair of a great newspaper, retired from journalism, and written several books. The latest one had just come out, and before catching my plane I was to attend a signing session at Hatchards of Piccadilly.

Signing sessions are ordeals. In theory, you stand in the bookshop, and the eager public, advised beforehand that you will be there in person (wow!), flock in to buy autographed copies. In practice, you can stand all day grinning inanely behind a pile of your latest brainchild, and the only approach you get is from an old lady who thinks you're a shop assistant and wants to buy *The Beverly Hills Diet.* (This happens to all authors except the real blockbusters, and celebrities of sport and show business.)

Hatchards, fortunately, is different; being at the heart of the most literate metropolis on earth it is heaven-made for signing sessions – if you can't sell your book there, it's time to climb back on your truck. So it was with some relief that I arrived to find a modest queue forming to have their copies signed, and I was inscribing away gratefully and only wishing that my name was a more manageable length, like Ben Jonson or Nat Gould, when I became aware that the next customer in line was presenting for signature not my new novel but two battered copies of *The General Danced at Dawn* and *McAuslan in the Rough*. He was a tall, erect, very elderly gentleman in immaculate tweeds and cap, leaning on a ram's horn walking-stick and looking at me like a grimly amused Aubrey Smith. I must have gaped at him for a good five seconds before I recognised him as the Colonel whom I had described in those two books (and have described again in this one). I hadn't even heard of him since 1947, and suddenly there he was, large as life, looking nothing like the 80 that he must have been.

'Stick your John Hancock on those, will you?' he growled amiably. 'No, carry on – we'll say hullo later, when you've dealt with the rest of your public. You've put on weight,' he added as I scribbled obediently – and I won't swear I wasn't doing it with my heels together, muttering 'Yes, sir, of course, sir,' for he was every bit as imposing and formidable, even in mufti and long retirement, as he'd been in North Africa. Now he was taking up the books with a drawled 'Obliged t'you', and limping stiffly away to seat himself at the side of the shop, filling his pipe and watching me from under shaggy eyebrows with what looked like sardonic satisfaction.

I went on signing like a man in an anxious dream. It's strange – when you write a book and put a real person into it, you don't seriously consider the possibility that he'll actually *read* it – at least, I hadn't, idiot that I'd been. And now he was sitting not ten feet away, the same leathery grizzled ramrod with the piercing eye and aquiline profile, and obviously he'd read the damned things, and couldn't have failed to recognise himself . . . oh, my God, what had I said about him? With dismay I recalled that I'd described him as 'tall and bald and moustached and looking like a vulture'. Feeling sick, I shot a sidelong glance at him – well, it was true. He still did, and a fat consolation that was. Wait, though, I'd been pretty fair about his character, hadn't I? Let's see . . . I'd said he was wise, and just, and experienced and tough (but considerate), and respected . . . oh, lord, had I said 'wise' or 'crafty'? In growing panic I scribbled on, and realised that the lady whose book I'd just signed was looking at it, and then at me, with a glassy expression.

'Thank you so much. I do hope you enjoy it,' I said, beaming professionally. She gave an uneasy smile and held out the book.

'I think there's some mistake, isn't there?' she faltered.

I couldn't see one. 'With all good wishes, George MacDonald Vulture', was what I'd written, and then sanity returned and I wrenched it from her, babbling apologies, and signed a fresh copy. She hurried away, glancing back nervously, and I went on signing, trying to take a grip and telling myself that he couldn't have taken offence, or he wouldn't be here, would he?

Well, of course he hadn't. I knew that – I'd always known it, or I'd never have set typewriter to paper in the first place about him and the regiment and McAuslan and the Adjutant and Wee Wullie and the Dancing General and all the rest of them. I had done it out of affection and pride, and to preserve memories that I loved. Not strict fact, of course, but by no means fiction, either – many true incidents and characters, as well as adaptations and shapings and amalgams and inventions and disguises, but always doing my best to keep the background detail as accurate as I could, and to be faithful to the spirit of that time and those people. And because newspaper training teaches you that truth is either the whole truth or nothing, it had had to be described as fiction. Hence that preface.

Once or twice, over the years, I had regretted the blanket quality of that disclaimer – as, for example, when readers and reviewers obviously regarded as complete invention some story in the books which was 90 per cent stark truth. But there was nothing to be done about it – until that day, after the signing session, when the Colonel and I finally got together, with effusion on my side and paternal tolerance on his, and repaired to the deserted bar of a West End hotel, where we hit the Glenfiddich together, and as we talked it gradually came to me that the disclaiming preface I had written for the first two books wouldn't do for a third one, if I ever wrote it – which I have now done. I can't reword it, because there is no satisfactory way of defining the misty margins where truth and fiction mingle. The best thing is to report as accurately as I can what he said that afternoon.

We talked and laughed and reminisced, and to my boundless delight he leafed through the books, commenting and quoting with that ironic little grin that I remembered so well; he seemed genuinely pleased with them, and what with happiness and the single malt I forgot all about the plane I was supposed to be catching, and just sat there content, studying the lined brown face and hooded bright eyes, and listening to the clipped Edwardian drawl of three generations ago. At last he said:

'I've only one bone to pick with you, young fella.' He flipped open *The General Danced at Dawn* and nailed the preface with a gnarled forefinger. 'Yes, there it is. What the devil d'you mean by saying "The Highland battalion in this book never existed"?' He sat back, pipe clamped between his teeth, and fixed me with a frosty grey eye. 'You know perfectly well it existed. You were in it, weren't you? I commanded the dam' thing, I ought to know –'

'Yes, sir, I know – but I can't pretend that *all* the things in the stories actually happened . . . not in our battalion, anyway –'

'And here again,' he went on, ignoring me. 'This next phrase, or clause, or whatever you call it: "inasmuch as the people in the stories are fictitious". That's rot. In fact, I'm not sure it isn't libellous rot. Am I a fiction?' He sat upright, regarding me sternly over his pipe, looking extremely factual. 'Are you? Can you look me in the eye and tell me that McAuslan never existed? I'm dam' sure you can't – because he did.'

'Yes, but that wasn't his real name –'

'Of course it wasn't. His real name was Mac—.' He grinned triumphantly. 'Wasn't it?'

'Oh, my God,' I said. 'Yes, it was. D'you know, sir, you're the only person who's ever identified him –'

'You surprise me. I'd have thought that anyone who'd ever seen the brute closer than half a mile would have recognised him in the book at once.'

'Mind you,' I said, 'he's slightly composite. I mean, the character in the book is 90 per cent Mac—, but there's a bit of another chap in him as well.'

'Quite so. Private J—, of C Company. Sandy-haired chap, with a slight squint, shirt-tail kept coming out.'

I stared at the man in disbelief. 'How on earth did you know that?'

'Your trouble,' said the Colonel patiently, 'is that you think no one else in the battalion ever noticed anything. It was perfectly obvious – whenever you had McAuslan doing something that wasn't characteristic of Mac—, I thought: "He's got that wrong. That's not like Mac— at all. Who is it?" And then I remembered J—, and realised that you'd tacked a little of him into the character. Sometimes you changed people over altogether. Take the second-in-command . . . the man you've made the second-in-command was actually in our first battalion, and you never met him till we got back to Edinburgh, isn't that so?' He smiled at me knowingly, and took a smug sip of Glenfiddich.

'Yes, his real name was R—. That's the fellow. You're an unscrupulous young devil, aren't you?' He leafed over a few pages. 'Ah, yes, Wee Wullie – why did you call him that? You couldn't hope to disguise the real man. Not from anyone who knew him.'

'Law of libel – and a bit of delicacy,' I explained. 'After all, he's a pretty rough diamond, as I've described him.'

'Well, so he was, wasn't he? And he comes out pretty well, in your story.' He studied his glass for a long moment. 'No more heroic than he really was in fact, though. You'll have to tell the true story some day, you know.'

'I know,' I said. 'I will.'

'See that you do.' He picked up the book again, chuckled, frowned, and laid it down. 'Anyway, you shouldn't have said the battalion didn't exist, or that the people were fictitious, or given the impression that the stories were made up –'

'Well, they're a mixture – a lot of fact and a bit of fiction. The trouble is, the bits people think are fictitious –'

'Are usually the truest bits of the lot. I know. The Palestine train, and the football team in Malta, eh? And the haunted fort, and the one-hundred-and-twenty-eightsome reel?'

'Well, there's a bit of exaggeration here and there – and I *have* said that I've used my imagination –'

'As if you ever had any! Mark you – you've certainly used it in one direction.' He made a performance of filling his pipe, grumbling to himself and looking across the room. 'You've been far too dam' kind to that old Colonel,' he said gruffly.

It was my turn to study my glass. 'Not half as kind as he was to me,' I said.

We finished the bottle, and in an alcoholic haze I glanced at my watch and realised I had a bare forty minutes to get to Heathrow for my flight to Zagreb.

'Yugoslavia?' said the Colonel. 'What the devil are you going there for? Ghastly place – nothing but mountains and Bolshevik bandits.'

I explained that I was going out to write a film script – or part of a script. Another writer had done the original, but there had been cast changes and various alterations were wanted, including a new ending.

'Most films are tripe,' said the Colonel firmly. '*Bambi* wasn't bad, though. What's this one about?'

'Our special service people in the war . . . blowing up a bridge to stop a German advance. Partisans and all that.'

'Sounds all right,' admitted the Colonel. 'Who's making it – our people or the Yanks?'

'They're American producers, I believe.'

'Well, for God's sake don't let them have our chaps going about shouting "*On* the double!" and "Left face!" and saluting with their hats off. Damned nonsense!'

I dropped him off near his home in Chelsea, and the last I ever saw of him was the tall spare figure in tweeds leaning on his stick and throwing me a salute which I returned (without a hat on) as the taxi sped away. For the next year or two we exchanged Christmas cards, and now and then I heard odd scraps of gossip about him. He'd been on holiday in the Middle East, in a country where some crisis had blown up all of a sudden, and British nationals had had to be evacuated quickly – he'd taken charge, quite unofficially, of the evacuation, and everyone had got out safely. Another time, he'd visited our battalion in Northern Ireland, going out with a street patrol at night, just to get the feel of things, an octogenarian in a flak-jacket.

And then one morning I got a phone call to say that he had died, in Erskine Hospital above the Clyde, where old Scottish soldiers go. And because he was, as fairly as I could depict him, the Colonel of these stories, I inscribe this book to his memory, with gratitude and affection, and no qualms whatever about identification:

Lieutenant-Colonel R. G. (Reggie) Lees
2nd Battalion, Gordon Highlanders

'Ninety-twa, no' deid yet'